Burnt Bodies in the Abandoned Air Shaft

Huyan Yun

Translated by Guo Zhaowei

Published by New Generation Publishing in 2025
Originally published in Simplified Chinese by New Star Press Co., Ltd in 2020

Contents © Huyan Yun 2025
The right of the above author to be identified as the author of this work has been asserted in accordance with the Copyright, Designs and Patents Act 1988. British Library Cataloguing in Publication Data available.

Print ISBN 978-1-918291-93-3
Set in Times.

 New Generation Publishing

www.newgeneration-publishing.com

Huyan Yun, a famous detective and crime novelist, is known as "the revolutionary of the Chinese crime novel." His representative works include the *Reasoning Leading to Truth* series.

Guo Zhaowei, a translator whose love for a good mystery is as sharp as her language skills! Based in the UK, she holds a Merit-earning Master's degree in Management from Scotland's prestigious University of St Andrews. When she's not untangling complex concepts, you'll likely find her happily lost in the twisty pages of a detective novel. Her passion for intriguing puzzles and suspenseful storytelling shines through in her translation work, most notably in bringing Tess Gerritsen's thrilling novel *Body Double* to Chinese readers – a project that perfectly combines her skills with her love for the genre.

Prologue

1

The harmonica beeped only once!

In the dark.

It sounded suddenly, and ended abruptly, so suddenly that it was unexpected and heartbreaking.

Li Zhiyong was stunned for a moment, the handlebar in his hand was not stable, and the road was slippery due to the pattering autumn rain, so he fell off the bicycle. Fortunately, his calf supported the ground, so he did not fall with the car.

He raised his head. It was ten o'clock in the evening, the sky was not as dark as expected, but shone an obscure dark gray. Under the streetlights, countless shreds of rain fluttered indiscriminately with icy chill.

When he got on the saddle again, he suddenly found that he really didn't have the strength to pedal the uphill road in front of him. This road is not very steep, but it is very long. As usual, he would rather take a detour rather than go here, but not tonight, because there is someone waiting for him at the Moon Garden at the end of the road.

He simply pushed the bike forward slowly. This black Yongjiu bicycle was bought when he was in college. After work, he still rides it every day. It is strong and durable. There were many people who persuaded him that this kind of steel-framed bicycle was outdated long ago, and any new aluminum alloy bicycle was lighter than it, but he was reluctant to change and cherished it like an old friend. It was only at this moment that he felt that with his slightly fat body and the heavy body of his "old friend", it was as if a bear was carrying a boulder up the mountain.

The black rubber wheels rolled over the wet ground, sticking to some strips of color and sequins—presumably discarded by fans after the recent Winner concerts at the sculpture park two blocks away. The small shops on both sides of the road: Fuhua Beef, Jiashitang Pharmacy, Yilaike Clothing

Store, and Xijiao Electronic Market, as if they were mourning him, turned off the lights one by one with each step he made. Li Zhiyong was confused by this strange way of turning off the lights. He stopped, looked around. There was not a single creature on the street. He raised his double chin, and the white marble crescent sculpture on the high platform of Moon Garden was not far away.

Suddenly!

The harmonica sounded again, this time in a rapid and repeated series of syllables, tossing and turning, hoarse and sticky, as if a man who was eager to confide could never speak again in a violent sob. For some unknown reasons, the dark night trembled painfully with the sound of the harmonica, convulsing again and again, layers of gloom, shrinking step by step, and was a little unpredictable...

It seems to be the prelude to a very familiar pop song, but he just can't remember which song it was.

Then everything fell silent again.

Standing there for a long, long time. Until it is confirmed that the harmonica will not make a sound again, until the repeated syllables echoing in the eardrum disappear completely, until the rain rusts the corners of the streets and alleys, until the whole world does not have a trace of the sad aftertaste, Li Zhiyong seemed to have been lifted from a spell. He loosened his numb calf, pushed his bicycle, and slowly came to the gate of Moon Garden.

Moon Garden is a small park, no bigger than a football field, but due to the terrain—just at the top of this uphill road—it has become a "landmark" in the area. The whole park is a hill surrounded by stone walls. The gate of the park is a stone arch, which opens to the north. Inside the arch, a row of wide steps leads directly to the top of the hill. At the commanding height at the end of the steps lies a curved white marble crescent. The profile of a bearded man is engraved on it, which means "Father of Moon". It's just that the expression of this feature is really weird. His eyebrows are raised high, his bushy beard is flamboyant like an octopus tentacle, and the corners of his raised mouth are smiling very strangely. In the night, he looks like an old tomb guard with vitiligo.

Li Zhiyong propped up his bicycle and walked up the steps. After reaching the top, perhaps because he was too tired, he panted and held on to the "Father of Moon". The white marble material was covered by the rain of late autumn, and the coldness pierced his palm, so he quickly let go of his hand, rubbing the sleeve on the other side, he looked up to find the person who had made an appointment to wait here.

Here is the top of Moon Garden, a circular plaza covered with marble.

In the center is a semi-submersible fountain. The stainless steel cover emits a faint blue light in the night. An arc granite wall is arched on the south side of the plaza. It is embedded with a relief of FRP imitation copper. Li Zhiyong crossed the square and walked along the relief wall, but no one was found. Just when he was habitually tugging at his thick nose every time he was confused, he suddenly found that the person he was looking for was sitting blankly on a dark green bench outside the square, holding a harmonica. The rain cast a silver light around him.

"Xiangming!" Li Zhiyong walked over to him while shouting his name.

2

Lin Xiangming was probably thinking about something, and when he heard, his body trembled for a while, then he raised his head and looked at Li Zhiyong with a long gaze, so much so that Li Zhiyong muttered, "It's me, why? No? acknoledged? "

Lin Xiangming stood up from the bench and shaked hands with him.

"Aren't you going to find a place to hide from the rain?" Li Zhiyong said with a frown. After looking around, he found that the entire Moon Garden didn't even have a pavilion. It was his own proposal to meet here in advance, and he didn't take the rain into consideration. factors, and suddenly felt a little embarrassed.

"The rain is not heavy." Lin Xiangming said with a smile.

"Let's go, let's go, there is a Qingta community in the south of the park, and there is a small restaurant, don't look at the appearance, the food is very delicious, I invite you to have a meal there – don't tell me you had dinner. As you accompany with me!" Li Zhiyong said as he walked down the steps. They walked out of the park, Li Zhiyong pushed his bike to Qingta Community.

Lin Xiangming followed him.

The two walked for a while, not speaking at first except for the rhythmic clack of the bicycle's chain over the sprockets. This atmosphere made Li Zhiyong a little nervous, and when he was not careful, his ankle bone was knocked by a pedal.

"Ouch!" he cried out in pain.

"Are you okay?" Lin Xiangming asked.

"It's okay!" Although he was knocked, Li Zhiyong was very happy that the silence between them was broken. "You played the harmonica just now?"

Lin Xiangming made a "yeah" sound.

"It seems to be a prelude to a song..." Li Zhiyong muttered, as if hoping that Lin Xiangming would give him an answer, but Lin Xiangming said nothing.

Li Zhiyong couldn't help but glance at him, his handsome face was expressionless.

This man is such a mystery.

Li Zhiyong remembered that the "Serial Murder Case in the Western Suburbs" was halfway through. When there were more and more victims and the detection of the case could not be done, Xu Ruilong, deputy director of the Municipal Public Security Bureau, called Du Jianping, the leader of the task force: "I know a third-year student from the Chinese Police University here, majoring in criminal psychology and behavioral science, and I will send you over to help." Du Jianping was so overwhelmed by the case that he was so tired that shingles recurred. The instructions made him a little impatient: "I'm here with enough troubles – it's as messy as you can imagine, don't send an intern to me!"

"What intern!" Xu Ruilong corrected bluntly, "It's support!"

On the first day of the "support", he went directly to the case analysis meeting. Lin Xiangming's first impression on all the members of the task force was particularly good. Although the young man was handsome like a girl, he was very humble. He had already opened his laptop, but when he saw the policemen sitting around the long table, they all spread out blue notepad, he immediately put away the computer, and took out a pen and paper from the satchel. He didn't take a sip of water during the entire meeting, and he didn't show the slightest disgust at the smoke from a dozen old smoking guns in the room—even though he never smoked. He listened carefully to everyone's speech, rustling something on the paper with the pen in his hand almost constantly, but he didn't speak until the end of the meeting. Du Jianping almost forgot about him, and just before the meeting ended, he remembered that there was another one sent by the deputy director: "Xiao Lin, do you have any ideas?"

Lin Xiangming shook his head.

"Say something, the case analysis meeting is for everyone to speak up!" Du Jianping laughed, "You are the 'support' sent from above, so you have to give us support."

There was laughter in the conference room.

"I'm new here and have no experience. All you guys are my teachers. I'll follow everyone to learn more and understand more." Lin Xiangming said with a smile.

After the meeting, Du Jianping sighed with several criminal policemen: "That Xiaolin is very sensible, you should take him with you." Then he said to Li Zhiyong half-jokingly: "You should learn from Xiaolin, you see that people are so much younger than you, but he is not frizzy, but disciplined and discerning."

Li Zhiyong said nothing, "I'm afraid you're wrong this time."

Ten years ago, Li Zhiyong was twenty-eight years old. He had been in the front line of criminal investigation for six years. He had endured all kinds of hardships. The object that the leaders focus on training has never caught the eye of Du Jianping, and even gave him the nickname "Bear". This was not because of how big his arms are, but because of two reasons: First, he never washes his face or combs his hair, so he always looks gray and messy. Usually, his head is always looking at the road; second, he has a quirky temper. He is usually sullen and doesn't like to talk much, but when he discusses the case, he is stubborn. He also dared to contradict to his boss. Combining these two characteristics, even Li Zhiyong himself did not reject the nickname "Bear". Anyway, no one in the police force doesn't have a nickname. Compared with some male police officers who are nicknamed "Sister-in-law", his nickname was much better.

However, Li Zhiyong is a rough and subtle person. He likes to use his brain when handling cases. He occasionally reads "Sherlock Holmes" and deliberately exercises his observation ability on weekdays. For example, at this case analysis meeting, he found that the silent Xiao Lin seemed to be "not frizzy and well behaved", but he was actually a very assertive person.

A case analysis meeting refers to a meeting convened by relevant police officers convened by the main leader leading the investigation around a serious case. At this kind of meeting, regardless of police rank, position, or age, as long as they have opinions related to the case, they must know everything and say everything. Because the criminal investigation work itself is to restore the truth with evidence and reasoning. No one has the absolute truth before the case is solved. Therefore, they must adhere to freedom of speech and democracy, and brainstorm ideas. Therefore, it is common for quarrels to arise over whether a certain piece of evidence is reliable or whether a certain inference is reasonable, and it is common for people to argue at the meeting, but no one will bother after the meeting... Nevertheless, during the meeting, everyone will still nod at each speaker involuntarily. This kind of nod does not necessarily represent approval and support, but more of a kind of respect and habit.

But Lin Xiangming did not. Li Zhiyong found that during the whole meeting, he really listened very attentively, but rarely nodded to the speaker's speech – the only time he said a paragraph to himself, and it was just a very thoughtless one.

"The forensic doctors in the criminal technology team have already concluded that the criminals' crime patterns are the same, that is, at the moment when the victim uses the key to open the security door and the door, he unexpectedly smashes the back of the victim's head with an iron hammer. After the victims fainted, they were carried into the room to rape and murder. But everyone seemed to ignore a problem, that is, the crime time—"

Du Jianping interrupted him and said, "As we said just now, most crimes are committed after ten o'clock in the evening, and he often attacks women who live alone late at night."

"The time of the crime I'm talking about refers to the time from when the criminal appears behind the victim to when he takes out the weapon to commit the crime." Li Zhiyong said, flipping the slides on the projector to the ones he wanted to demonstrate, "Let's see, hese three crime scenes all took place in this old-fashioned slab building below six floors, one on the third floor and two on the fourth floor. I have investigated on the spot. These slab buildings are all brick and concrete structures. That kind of sensor light with very high sensitivity, then when the victim returns home around ten o'clock, walks up the steps step by step, and arrives at the door of his room, the sensor light must be on, right?"

The team members were all nodding their heads, their eyes were all blank, and they didn't understand what he was trying to say.

Only Lin Xiangming's eyes lit up.

Li Zhiyong saw it, but pretended not to see it: "Since the sensor light is on, the corridor should be very bright. In this case, when the criminal launched an attack, why did the victim not even have the instinct to resist?" He picked up the autopsy report, pointed to the line on it and said, "Look, the autopsy report clearly states that the victim's first wound was located on the occiput, the scalp was lacerated in star shape, and there were circular contusions around it, gradually lightening from the periphery to the center, with a hollow skull fracture and radial fractures... but none of the three victims had any resistance injuries on their hands, arms or shoulders, not a single one! Why?"

"Perhaps the incident happened so suddenly that they were frightened and instantly lost their reaction to resist?" Du Jianping guessed.

"If it is the first victim, such a guess is reasonable. The problem is that when the first victim appeared, we immediately issued a warning to the residents through the neighborhood committees of various streets and communities. The second victim received a door-to-door reminder from the director of the neighborhood committee because she lived alone. As for the third victim, let alone... Then, why are they still not alert at all?" Li Zhiyong turned the slides back again. At the crime scene, "Let's take a look at the corridor where the crime happened. There are many stairs in this old building, and the space at the corner of the stairs is either piled with jars or bicycles. If there can let no one to hide. Even the criminal started a sudden attack, whether it is rushing up from the lower layer or rushing down from the upper layer, the victim has a time slot that can be used to resist, and this is the 'criminal time' that I just said was ignored by everyone."

A criminal policeman suggested: "The sensor light has a time limit. What if the criminal takes off his shoes, wears socks and goes up and down the steps when the sensor light goes out, and attacks the victim?"

"Not to mention the security door and door of this old building, due to the deformation of the door frame, there is a loud noise when opening and closing, which is enough to 'wake up' the sensor light, not to mention when we open the door, if the corridor suddenly turns black, They will habitually stomp their feet to turn on the lights again to ensure that the key can be inserted into the keyhole. Of course, the most important thing is that the shoe prints left by the suspects in the corridor extracted by the comrades of the criminal technique are consistent, there is no possibility of taking off his shoes and wearing socks to attack." Li Zhiyong said.

A criminal member next to him added: "These shoe prints prove that most of the criminal followed the victims upstairs from outside the building door, and then committed the crime. In addition, we observed that the criminals' footprints upstairs were approaching the victim. These footprints didn't suddenly become sharper or narrower, nor did he leave more marks, or the stride became longer, which means that he didn't rush up to attack the victim, but walked upstairs normally—"

"This also shows once again that the victim is likely to have met the criminal, and the criminal is an acquaintance who reassures her, so she relaxed her vigilance." Li Zhiyong said.

At this moment, Li Zhiyong saw Lin Xiangming nodded lightly.

He didn't know why, but this nod made Li Zhiyong feel a little surprise in his heart.

"At ten o'clock in the evening, in the corridor illuminated by the sensor lights, the criminal approached the victim, the victim saw it but was not alert, because he was an acquaintance who could make the victims feel at ease... This may be the reason why the victim was killed. These victims enjoy possibility of testifying." Du Jianping muttered a few words to himself, looking up at Li Zhiyong, "According to your inference, has there been any change in the direction of the investigation?"

Li Zhiyong said: "I think the murderer is likely to have some unknown intimate relationship with these victims, such as relatives, lovers, old class-mates, etc. Therefore, if the investigation is carried out from the common acquaintances of the three victims , I believe it will be discovered soon!"

At this moment, Li Zhiyong suddenly noticed a hint of disappointment on Lin Xiangming's face.

"Could it be, that I say something wrong?" His heart was cold for a moment, and after returning to his seat, he drank a full cup of hot tea and did not warm up, so when Du Jianping asked him to "learn from Xiaolin" after the meeting, the first thought that popped into his mind was: "I will just ask him, where did I go wrong?"

The "Western Suburbs Serial Murder Case" that happened in September 2008 left an extremely heavy mark in the history of Chinese criminal inves-tigation with its terrifying and bloody facts, cruel and cunning criminal methods, and extremely difficult detection.

There were a total of four "Western Suburb Serial Murder Cases". If the locations of these four cases were connected in series on the city map, it would be found to be an irregular rectangle clustered in the northwest direction, and the first starting point of this irregular rectangle , was the fourth floor of a residential building in Chengyuli Community. The victim's name was Yang Hua, twenty-eight years old, an employee of a stock exchange in this city, who was a woman living alone, plump but not too beautiful. She was supposed to go to work on the day the case was dis-covered, but she never came. A colleague called her on her cell phone, but no one answered. Because the work of the stock exchange is too busy, the managers wanted to quickly find someone to fill the seat instead of looking for Yang Hua, and several colleagues later proved that "(Yang Hua) used to like to go to nightclubs after get off work and drink a lot. After that, she happened to sleep anywhere, and it's common for her to miss work the next day." So no one thought that she might have an accident. In the subsequent investigation by the police, it was found that the only reason why Yang Hua was often absent from work without being fired was that she had an improper relationship with Sun, the director of the stock exchange, and the first person to find out that Yang Hua was killed was , was also the fat director Sun with almost transparent skin.

After get off work that day, Director Sun wanted to have a tryst with Yang Hua, but there was still no answer to her cell phone, so he went directly to the door. The moment he took out the key at the door, he suddenly found that the security door was false, and the wooden door inside was not locked. An ominous premonition struck him instantly. Of course, he was not worried that something had happened to Yang Hua, but worried that his wife might have found out that he was cheating, and set up an ambush inside, ready to wait for the rabbit and catch the current one, so he Instead of going in, he turned around and went downstairs.

Of course, Director Sun would not have thought that he was seen by a friend of Yang Hua's when he hurried out of the building. This friend was also an employee of the stock exchange. She was worried that she was ill, so she came to visit after get off work and bought some fruit and milk, which happened to meet Director Sun. However, Director Sun was guilty of doing immoral things and buried his head in the collar of his trench coat. The light in the community was dark, and he did not notice that a colleague was approaching, and Yang Hua's friend always knew about his relationship with Yang Hua. This kind of thing can't be said, and she was embarrassed to say hello to the leader and pass by.

After Yang Hua's friend went upstairs, she found that the two doors were unlocked, and went straight into the house. The dark room was dead silent, and the lights were not turned on. She smelled a stench coming from her face, and a strange thought, "Why don't you put the meat in the refrigerator?" came to her mind, and then touched the switch on the wall, and turn on the light. The small living room of the old-fashioned plank building was only big enough for a refrigerator and a dining table. She called Yang Hua's name and walked into the master bedroom. The light in the master bedroom was not turned on, and she could roughly make out a naked woman lying on the bed. This friend was a little embarrassed, and wondered if Yang Hua and Director Sun had just finished and hadn't put on her clothes. When she was about to exit the master bedroom, she realized that the strong stench came from the woman lying on the bed. She was so frightened that was completely paralyzed. She didn't even dare to step forward to see if Yang Hua was dead or alive, and rolled out of the house, stumbled out of the building, and called the police.

According to the record of the 110 call recording, the first sentence she called to the police was: "My friend has an accident and seemed to have been killed. Come here quickly!"

The investigation of the crime scene showed that Yang Hua was killed between 10:30 and 11:00 the night before, and a large amount of alcohol was detected in her blood. Witnesses confirmed that she was at a house near her home that night and drank a lot of alcohol in the bar. She was staggered when she left. When she went upstairs to go home and took out the key to unlock the house, she was suddenly hit from the diagonal rear! The wound on the occipital area indicated that the murder weapon should be an iron hammer. The forensic doctor who conducted the autopsy said that Yang Hua died almost instantly because of the force of the blow. After that, the murderer took Yang Hua into the room and raped or directly said it was a corpse rape. After finishing, he left calmly, leaving only the two doors.

To the shock of the police, the murderer did not leave any evidence of his identity at the scene: because he wore gloves during the crime, his fingerprints could not be found; because the first hammer caused the death of the victim, there was no fight, no blood, hair, skin or clothes buttons were left behind; since he wore a condom during the rape, and the condom was taken away from the scene after the incident, of course, his semen could not be extracted from the victim's body. What's especially terrifying is that the genital of Yang Hua's body and the nearby bed sheets had been burned, which should be burned with some kind of portable high-temperature spray gun. Later, when the police realized the truth, they couldn't help being horrified. The murderer did this completely rationally: he would never let his pubic hair be extracted by the police, and he would not leave any of it!

Although Yang Hua's mobile phone, wallet, and necklace were taken away by the murderer, Du Jianping, the district criminal investigation team leader in charge of investigating the case, was keenly aware that this was just a trick used by the murderer to mislead the police, leading the criminal motive to robbery. The experienced Du Jianping did not believe that the deceased died of love murder from the very beginning—for example, Director Sun, who was witnessed to go in and out of the scene, was the first to rule him out as a criminal suspect— —Because numerous past cases have shown that crime scenes of love murder often present the dual contradictions of hatred and "love" for the deceased, such as stabbing a lot of knives, but carefully covering up the private parts of the deceased, but never smashing to death with a hammer , raped the corpse, burned the genitals, and then let the corpse be naked and left – this is an out-and-out rape and murder case for the purpose of venting animal desires.

And such crimes are rarely "one-hammer trading".

After asking for instructions from his superiors and getting approval, Du Jianping decisively issued three orders: the first was to set up a special task force, and he personally served as the team leader to investigate the case; the second was to hold a press conference to disclose part of the case to the media, and asking them to assist in issuing warnings to remind the general public to pay attention to safety; the third was to notify the people's armed forces and security departments in the five streets around Chengyuli and 72 communities to take proactive precautions. For those women who live alone, the neighborhood committee has to do "two things"—meeting them, and face-to-face reminders. When individual leaders were worried that the second and third orders would cause public tension, he directly threw a foul language: "There are people already dead, what are you fucking afraid of!"

Although Du Jianping realized that the most urgent task was to build a high enough firewall before the murderer commits next crime, he was still a step behind in hurrying. Just three days after Yang Hua was killed, the second case happened. The crime took place in a remote residential building on Chunliu Street. The victim, surnamed Wu, was only 23 years old this year. After listening to the Winner concert at the Sculpture Park, she was hit on the back of the head with a hammer when she returned late. She was not dead at the time, so after dragging her into the house and raping her, the murderer smashed her face with a hammer several times, making her bloody and brain-filled.

Of course, the murderer still did not leave any clues that might provide personal information, such as fingerprints, bloodstains, hair, etc., and Xiao Wu's genital was also burned.

Facing Xiao Wu's tragic death, the criminal police felt extremely heavy in their hearts. Although they faced various crimes for many years, sometimes standing in front of corpses and pools of blood would inevitably become numb, but the murderer's brutality and almost provocative way of handling the crime scene still angered every police officer involved in the case, whether criminal investigation or criminal technician, worked overtime day and night: looking for trace evidence left at the crime scene, investigating suspicious persons one by one, digging through every clue, and using big data to analyze According to the personal characteristics of the criminals, the city bureau also dispatched additional staff to the task force. And the murderer seemed to realize that the big net that rounded him up was slowly tightening, and suddenly fell dormant. For a whole month, no new cases occurred.

At that time, Du Jianping gave Li Zhiyong the task of investigating the family and social relations of the two victims together with Gao Xiaoyan, a household registration policewoman from the Chunliu Police Station. Not long after Gao Xiaoyan started working, she was a short-haired, thin, and smart girl with an ordinary appearance. She laughed like a string of wind chimes. She and Li Zhiyong are also suitable to work together. One is familiar with everyone and can find out a lot of "insiders" while joking; the other is reticent, but is serious of recording, and he is good at thinking and analysis. After being busy for nearly a month, although they didn't even catch the shadow of the murderer, they became very good friends.

"I said!" One evening, when Gao Xiaoyan and Li Zhiyong were eating ramen at a roadside stall, she suddenly said, "Why not wash your face, shave your beard, and change your clothes? And your hairy head is neither shaved nor washed, even the hens don't lay eggs in such a messy nest as your hair!"

Li Zhiyong was a little embarrassed: "I'm just too busy..."

"Come on! Who's not busy?" Gao Xiaoyan sneered, "You're not too busy, you're too lazy! Just like you, if any girl likes you, it will only be bad for her lifetime!"

Li Zhiyong touched the tip of his thick nose: "So, I never expected anyone to like me..."

"Look at you!" Gao Xiaoyan threw the chopsticks into the bowl of noodles, "Clean up yourself before go out with me tomorrow, or I won't lose my face with you!"

They've been together for almost a month, why did she only remember to remind him to pay attention to the image problem? Li Zhiyong was a little confused, but he still said "okay".

After dinner, of course they went home. Li Zhiyong had already walked to the door of his house. He was about to go upstairs, but he turned around and went to the barber shop in the community. He sat down and said to the little brother who cut his hair, "Shave it short for me."

The little brother only glanced at his hair, but didn't dare to touch it with his fingers, his face was embarrassed: "You...let's wash it first."

"OK!" Li Zhiyong agreed. After washing, he sat down on the chair in front of the barber mirror again. While cutting his hair, the barber persuaded him to keep an inch of hair, "This style won't getting dirty too quickly, and it's easy to wash." Li Zhiyong agreed, so after cutting his hair, Li Zhiyong in the mirror looked like a silly man who visited his mother-in-law's house for the first time. He thought happily: "What else can Gao Xiaoyan say to me tomorrow?"

However, Gao Xiaoyan would never again point to his appearance, and she became the third victim of the Western Suburbs serial murder case.

In fact, Gao Xiaoyan could have avoided this disaster completely. If she and Li Zhiyong went home directly after parting, nothing would happen, but according to her colleague's recollection, she suddenly returned to the police station after eight o'clock that night, and others asked her what she was doing. She said that she has been busy cooperating with the task force in investigating the case recently, and she had no time to deal with several files of those who have been released from prison, so she came to work overtime. When she left the office after overtime, the time to sign out in the communication room was 11:10 pm.

Gao Xiaoyan's house is not far away, so the next trajectory of her countdown life can basically be estimated: after she left the police station, she rode a bicycle to the downstairs of her house in ten minutes at most. With the blow of the iron hammer, she fell into a coma, but when the brave and strong girl was dragged into the room by the murderer, she suddenly woke up, fought with him, and was killed. And her struggle only shattered a glass fish tank placed on the high and low cabinets in the living room, which seemed to have no meaning to the police's detection work...

At Gao Xiaoyan's memorial service, Li Zhiyong burst into tears, and the other policemen also wept. For the police, all those who died in order to maintain people's happiness and social stability are comrades-in-arms, they are just like brothers and sisters. The death of Gao Xiaoyan made the whole detection work cast an unprecedented frustration and embarrassment. All the members of the task force, including Du Jianping, were downcast, and even the phrase "revenge for comrades" shouted at the memorial service was powerless. Yes, the pursuit and anti-chasing of police and criminals can be compared to hunting, but what is going on this time? Before even finding the shadow of the jackal, the hunter sacrificed, but he sacrificed not because he tracked the jackal, but because he became the prey of the jackal...

Therefore, after the memorial service, the words of a criminal policeman were blown into the ears of every mourner by the cold wind of late autumn. These words were considered vulgar and savage and had far-reaching implications, although it was not clear which flowers he was referring to. The girl who died with a young age, or referred to the criminal investigation work that was exhausted and at a loss, or referred to the subtle feelings of Li Zhiyong and Gao Xiaoyan, a young man and a woman, anyway, this is what he said——

"Fuck, it's over before it even begins."

4

Lin Xiangming flashed and observed carefully for a long time before reaching out and touching the surface of the light bulb, twisting it, and then jumping off the broken stool.

Li Zhiyong stood up and looked at him with a bit of confusion: "what are you looking for?"

"Look to see if anyone has screwed this light bulb recently." Lin Xiangming said, "I agree with your reasoning why the victim did not have any vigilant reasoning before he was attacked, but I think it is not rigorous enough. If the victim's floor or even the room was found before, then the murderer loosened the light bulb and hid in a dark place, waiting for the victim to launch a surprise attack after she returning at night, then the victim would indeed be caught off guard. The murderer would screw the light bulb on, then when the police investigate here, they will mistakenly believe that the light sensor has always been effective, ignoring that the murderer may have left marks on the hiding place in the corridor or left fingerprints on the light bulb – however, it seems that he did not screw it. Which means that the conclusion of your reasoning is still valid, the murderer is indeed the one who can completely relax Wu and Gao Xiaoyan."

After participating in the first case analysis meeting, although Du Jianping asked the police officers of the task force to "lead" Lin Xiangming, Lin Xiangming was maverick and quietly took the crime scene of the three cases and the surroundings. After a careful investigation, he spent the night looking at the scene investigation reports, forensic autopsy reports, witness notes and related photos of each case, and then revisited the crime scene. This time he encountered Li Zhiyong with unshaved beards, who was sitting in front of Gao Xiaoyan's house, Li Zhiyong ignored him, took a broken stool from the corridor, and stepped on it to find the light bulb.

After listening to Lin Xiangming's words, Li Zhiyong's almost numb nerves suddenly relaxed a little, but the pain in his heart still tortured him completely weak: "It's all my fault, if I could take her home that night, she wouldn't be... ..."

Lin Xiangming had already prepared to go downstairs, but turned back.

He looked at Li Zhiyong and asked, "You killed Gao Xiaoyan?"

Li Zhiyong was confused: "No..."

"Then do your business." Lin Xiangming said.

For some reason, Li Zhiyong suddenly felt a little power in his body, or Lin Xiangming's own strong magnetic field attracted him and he had to follow him downstairs... This young police academy student is handsome and melancholy, his whole body looks like the eve of a storm Like the moon in the sky, always shrouded in a mysterious and hazy halo, Li Zhiyong firmly believed that he has some kind of supernatural ability: he can see through everything in the dark, comprehend everything, and understand everything that is covered, obscured or buried, and the darker they were, the more thorough they were... He may be powerless to change them, but he can let all those who wake up after the fact see the source of misery.

Many people can't get an unpredictable prophet of fate once in their life-time of cultivation, but Lin Xiangming was born with no obstacles.

"By the way, at the last case analysis meeting, you didn't seem to agree with the investigation direction I suggested at the end?" Li Zhiyong asked loudly on purpose, hiding his guilty conscience. He believed he was really wrong, he just wanted to know why.

Lin Xiangming was silent for a moment before saying: "The most important thing that Gao Xiaoyan and you are investigating together is the interpersonal network of the first two victims, especially whether there is any intersection. If Gao Xiaoyan and them have common relatives, friends or acquaintances , with her outspoken personality, how could she not tell you a word?"

Li Zhiyong suddenly realized!

What shocked him even more was still behind.

That was at another case analysis meeting the next day. The theme of the meeting was to complete the psychological portrait of the criminal suspect (criminal personality profile) based on the evidence and clues currently available. This is Lin Xiangming's major, but Du Jianping only regarded him as an "intern" and let him listen in as usual. In addition, he arranged for an old criminal policeman named Chai Yongjin from the task force to do the dissection.

Chai Yongjin was a talktive person. He was smoking a cigarette while flipping a few pages of paper with psychological portraits written on it. He talked for a while and paused for a while. He believed that criminal sus-pects should have the following characteristics: Under the age of 20, strong and burly, with a serious tendency to violence, most likely to have received reeducation through labor for rape or fight, so he had relatively strong anti-investigation capabilities. What Chai Yongjin was particularly proud of is that he emphasized in an unquestionable tone: the criminal suspect was a floating person without a fixed occupation and lived in the basement for a long time. So they should continue to expand the scope on the basis of the investigation. "To intensify the unannounced visits and surveillance in urban villages in the southern Western Suburbs, and if necessary, all the people living there will be screened."

The criminal policemen who sat around the long table in the confer-ence room nodded and recorded. After finishing his words, Du Jianping arranged some tasks: first, to select the information on the young sexually violent criminals released in the past two years one by one; second, to send some police forces, including Li Zhiyong, to the urban villages in the southern Western Suburbs to conduct investigations. After finishing the arrangement, he asked Lin Xiangming as usual, "Xiao Lin, do you have any comments? If not, we will—"

Before the word "dismissed" was uttered, Lin Xiangming asked, "Officer Chai, can you tell me what the basis for the criminal portrait you made just now?"

The tone was as gentle as ever, but not as serious as ever.

Li Zhiyong, who had closed the notebook, couldn't help but raised his head and looked at Lin Xiangming.

Including Du Jianping, the detectives in the room were stunned, as if it was the first time that this elegant young man had another face.

Chai Yongjin involuntarily put out the cigarette he had just smoked in the ashtray and looked at Du Jianping. Du Jianping's eyes were a little dodged, which made Chai realize that he had to answer Lin Xiangming's question seriously, so he stiffened and said, "Well, that's it, we use a high-voltage electrostatic adsorption device, in the victim's room and corridor. The footprints of the suspects have been extracted. Well, you need to know that as long as you demarcate the area of the indentation and find the heavy pressure point, then, measure the longitudinal length of the spherical indentation of the forefoot or the maximum longitudinal diameter of the indentation of the heel, and multiply the measured length in centimeters by five to get an approximate age—"

"This can be faked. Besides, there is a big gap between the physical age of modern people and their actual age. It is not uncommon for a twenty-year-old to have a fifty-year-old physical fitness and a fifty-year-old person to have a twenty-year-old physical fitness." Lin Xiangming said, "You think the suspect is under twenty years old, and people of this age have a very limited maturity of mental development. Past cases have proved that no matter how experienced murderers are, they will have behavioral characteristics such as nervousness and panic when commit crimes before they are twenty years old, but the evidence collected at the three crime scenes shows that the criminal's methods are quite sophisticated and his mind is very mature. Especially when approaching the victim, he showed no 'criminal borderline characteristics', like his stride did not shorten or change in the slightest...so I don't think it would be wise to limit him to under twenty."

Chai Yongjin was shocked.

Lin Xiangming stretched out his right hand and made a "please continue" gesture with his palm tilted upwards.

Chai Yongjin was obviously nervous, he took out a cigarette package from his pocket, took out a cigarette and stuffed it back, repeating this action mechanically: "About his figure, that, it's like, his method of murder is to use a hammer to smashing the back of victim's head, generally speaking, such violent criminals are not skinny..."

"Officer Chai, there is an important formula in behavioral science to delineate the physical characteristics of serial killers, referred to as the 'AB mutual evidence formula': A. The time of a case burst is proportional to the criminal's posture; B. On the basis of the establishment of the A formula, the criminal's body is proportional to the victim's body. That is to say, in the process of committing a crime, the shorter the time from the criminal's attack to the knocking down of the victim, the thinner the criminal's body is; The criminal's body is relatively strong, and on this basis, the thinner the victim's body is, the thinner the criminal's body is, and if the victim's body is relatively strong, then the criminal's body must be stronger."

Li Zhiyong understood it all at once, and couldn't help but say, "The short duration of the case indicates that the criminal took a sneak attack, which also proves that the criminal underestimated his own physical strength and physical fitness, and he was afraid that he would not be able to kill the victim all at once. So it has to be a strike from behind or a surprise attack."

Lin Xiangming glanced at him and nodded lightly: "Contrary to what is shown in the movie, very few victims are subdued by brutal and violent criminals all at once. Even a rapist like Tyson, women will also rise up to resist for survivng. The murderer we are currently trying to arrest, no matter what kind of women hw was dealing with, will always take a surprise attack from behind, and strive to hit them, not giving the victims any chance to resist, which just shows that he's not very strong."

Chai Yongjin was completely discouraged and could not speak for a long time. Du Jianping felt a little overwhelmed: "Go on, Officer Chai, Lin is helping you improve your work!"

"I also think that this criminal is really experienced and has some anti-investigation experience, so I figured that he might have passed through and received labor education." After Chai Yongjin muttered a few words, he suddenly raised his voice, "But I dare to say that it is a sure thing that the suspect is a floating person with no fixed occupation and lives in the basement for a long time."

Lin Xiangming looked at him and said nothing.

"The criminal identification report must have been read by Officer Lin. The suspect's footprints extracted at the crime scene proved that he was wearing a pair of very cheap and worn-out 'Yangfan' sneakers. A small amount of mold was detected at the place, and this mold mainly exists in the basement or semi-basement." Chai Yongjin said, "At the same time, although the location where he committed the crime is concentrated in the Western Suburbs, it is relatively scattered, especially when the second murder occurred. That night, the joint defense team bumped into him. During the pursuit, because he was not familiar with the road conditions, he did not choose the more direct escape route that the nearby residents were familiar with. These all showed that he is not a local person, and then connected to those molds, I think it is very likely that he is a floating person without a fixed occupation, which is the so-called 'blind flow'."

What Chai Yongjin said happened on the night of the second murder. During the patrol, a joint defense team found a suspicious person on a street corner about 500 meters away from Wu's house. Because the light was too dark and his collar was erected very high, they couldn't see him clearly. When he was told to stop for inspection, he ran away. The defense team froze for a while before chasing him, and suddenly opened the distance. This man was a little panicked. In a street center park with lush green plants, he could enter the park with lush green plants as long as he dashed straight and he would get out of the intersection of the pursuers. But he turned right instead, got into an alley, and escaped... Afterwards, the torture technicians identified his footprints and the mold in the shoe prints, proving that this person is the correct one. It's the serial killer. The failure of the hunt made Du Jianping annoyed, and there was nothing more frustrating than the cooked duck he got flying again. For this reason, he called Fang Zhifeng, the nearly fifty-year-old director of the Public Security Office of Chunliu Street, and scolded him in the face. Fang Zhifeng had bitter face and said that he was going to quit this unfortunate errand that never went down day and night. Du Jianping had to appease him again, so as not to let the discouraged joint defense team completely dismiss...

After listening to Chai Yongjin's words, and thinking about the failure to hunt down the serial killer, everyone in the conference room felt that his analysis was impeccable, so they all turned their attention to Lin Xiangming, as if to say, "This time you have nothing to say. Right?" Lin Xiangming stood up, flipped through a few slides, and a large oval green space appeared on the white projection screen.

"Officer Chai, do you know here?" Lin Xiangming asked.

Chai Yongjin just glanced at it and said, "Of course, isn't this the lawn in front of Central Street Park?"

Li Zhiyong raised his head sharply!

Lin Xiangming looked at Chai Yongjin and said slowly, "Officer Chai, have you checked here in person?"

Old Chai blinked his eyes for a long time, then shook his head.

"Has anyone surveyed the way the perpetrator escaped from the joint defense team after the second murder?"

After Wu was killed, the task force carried out a very detailed investigation around the crime scene. The perpetrator's escape route to escape from the defense team was also visited, but later the task force unanimously determined that the perpetrator's choice of path when escaping was random – to put it bluntly, "running randomly". There was no value for further investigation, and no more manpower and energy were spent. As for the green space on the slide, most of the police officers had passed by and had not seen it...

Facing the dismayed look at each other in the conference room, Lin Xiangming's face showed a look of disappointment.

At this moment, Li Zhiyong raised his hand.

Lin Xiangming smiled: "Okay, then let Officer Li tell Officer Chai what this oval green space is."

"That's not a lawn," Li Zhiyong said. "It's just an oval-shaped open space covered with green gauze."

Recently, the city was making a series of image propaganda films. To this end, it was necessary to dress up the city that had been breaking ground and building buildings for several years and forming a super-large construction site. At least in the aerial photography, it must appear more green. It can't be looked like alopecia areata everywhere. But at that time, the cultivation of soilless turf had not been popularized, and the price of plastic turf was relatively expensive, so the sanitation department covered all the places with exposed loess more than 100 square meters with green gauze, which won't looked like that bad in aerial photography.

There was a commotion in the conference room, and the detectives were talking in low voices, buzzing for a long time, but the lock on their brows was still not stretched. Du Jianping tapped the table with his finger to signal everyone to be quiet, and then asked Lin Xiangming, "Lin, I don't quite understand, 'is this a real lawn', does it have anything to do with our case?"

"Of course." Lin Xiangming said calmly, "I have already checked on the spot, and the mesh width of this green gauze is usually between four and six centimeters, which is exactly the width of the toe of a pair of ordinary sneakers or leather shoes. Therefore, the murderer didn't run into the street park, not because he didn't know it was a good place to hide, but because he didn't want to trip over the toes of his shoes when he was crossing the green gauze – he isn't 'unfamiliar with the local road conditions', but really familiar with the local road conditions. Therefore, even escaping in a panic, he did not make a wrong choice. I can even be sure: he is local in Chengyuli and Chunliu Street."

"Maybe—" Chai Yongjin gritted his back molars and said, "maybe he saw the green gauze on the ground instead of lawn?"

Lin Xiangming turned around, looked at the photo on the projection screen, and sighed: "You can't tell that this photo was taken during the day as a fake lawn, not to mention it was late at night..."

After the case analysis meeting, Li Zhiyong and Lin Xiangming went downstairs together and stood in the simple yard of the criminal police team. Through the withered branches and leaves of a large locust tree, they could see the frosty gray night sky in the late autumn.

"You are just broken the statements today. "Li Zhiyong said, "You have refuted Lao Chai's conclusions, but you have not come up with new conclusions."

Lin Xiangming was silent for a moment, then said slowly: "The case is too complicated, there are too many contradictions and doubts, I still can't make an accurate profile of the suspect."

Not knowing whether he was afraid of the cold or irritable, Li Zhiyong put his hands in his trousers pockets and stomped his feet a few times. The dry leaves were smashed, making a clicking sound: "The case has not progressed at all. If he hibernates like a winter bear, we won't be able to catch him again... We can't let Gao Xiaoyan sacrifice in vain."

"No police officer sacrificed in vain." Lin Xiangming said, "Never."

5

Lin Xiangming's words were like a miraculous prophecy. No one thought that it was Gao Xiaoyan's sacrifice that opened a major breakthrough for the whole case.

Every year, China Police Officers University sent some students with excellent academic performance to various police stations, sub-bureaus and criminal police teams to "assist work". Unlike internships, this kind of "assistance work" was not the traditional sense of a master leading an apprentice, but an equal complement. Police officers who have worked for many years pass on valuable practical experience to the fledgling and high-spirited police academy students, and the police academy students, relying on their understanding and mastery of the world's advanced criminal investigation technology, help the front-line public security personnel to realize the "professional and meticulous" police work to digitization, and informatization".

One of them was Lin Xiangming's classmate from different departments of the same school. She heard that Lin Xiangming was busy with the "serial murder case in the Western Suburbs", so she offered to assist the criminal technology department of the district bureau, which was approved by the school. Because of her beautiful appearance, it caused a sensation on the first day she first arrived at the branch. The young men who were married or unmarried all pretended to pass by the door of the Criminal Technology Office unintentionally, just to look at her, but this also made everyone misunderstand, that is, this girl named Liu Simiao is very likely just a "vase" that is not useful.

It turned out they were dead wrong.

Liu Simiao, who has become the academic leader of China's criminal forensics science many years later, has shown meticulousness and excellence in the professional field since her college days. The first ray of light toward the iron-like darkness.

The entire process of criminals committing crimes was not a single, static, solidified behavior, but a complex, dynamic, and unstable chain-like system. Taking a case of robbery and murder as an example, there must be a series of behaviors such as breaking in, fighting and killing the victim, searching for property, destroying physical evidence that may reveal personal information and then leaving. In this process, most of the most valuable physical evidence was left by the victims and criminals, especially those experienced criminals, who have already put on gloves and kicked the door before committing the crime. Only shoe prints would be left, while no fingerprints would be left when rummaging through boxes. Then, it was only possible to find the criminal's hair, blood and other DNA information in the fingers and nails of the victim.

It was a pity that almost all the three victims of the "Western Suburb Serial Murder Case" were knocked down by the murderer with a hammer from behind at once, lost the ability to resist, then they were raped and killed, only Gao Xiaoyan once had an extremely short sobriety, and fought with the murderer. A fish tank was broken during the fight, so in the eyes of most criminal investigators and forensic technicians, in this case, the "interaction" between the victims and the criminal was also zero.

Liu Simiao didn't think so.

Criminal forensics work, like thousands of jobs in the world, was also "details determine success or failure". If forensic technicians ignored some inconspicuous evidence, which may lead to criminals getting away from justice. Liu Simiao attached high attention to the detailed evidences which detailed to an unimaginable level. For example, after intervening in the detection of the "Western Suburb Serial Murder Case", she insisted that the shattered glass fish tank must be restored, "because this is the only physical evidence of the interaction between the victim and the murderer."

Glass fragments, like fibrous material, are one of the most common trace evidences found at crime scenes. Since the glass fragments are likely to have traces or substances such as fingerprints, bloodstains, fibers, etc., they must be extra careful when extracting them. It's not like many domestic dramas that take a broom and pack together into the dustpan and "bring it back to the laboratory" . That's bullshit. Large pieces of glass should be taken directly by wearing medical rubber gloves and touching the broken surface of the glass, while small pieces of glass or slag such as a broken fish tank should be directly clamped with non-metallic tweezers. The criminal technicians responsible for investigating the scene of Gao Xiaoyan's murder did strictly implement the above-mentioned principles of evidence extraction, and in the subsequent inspection, no fingerprints or bloodstains of the criminal suspect were extracted from the glass fragments. At this time, Liu Simiao suddenly proposed to restore the fish tank, which made everyone feel a little incredible. Some people even sarcastically said in front of her: "A piece of shredded paper without words, can it still be spelled without words?" Liu Simiao just pretend she didn't hear it, she stayed up all day and night in the laboratory, and came out holding a basically restored rectangular glass fish tank that was pasted with transparent tape in a crisscross pattern.

"Are you really recovered?" An old criminal technican in the branch was a little surprised, "How about it, did you find any new evidence on this fish tank?"

Liu Simiao shook his head.

The old criminal sighed: "I knew it was a waste of time."

"Not necessarily." Liu Simiao pointed to a red plastic tray on the table.

The old torturer walked over and bent down to take a look. There were two very small pieces of glass inside, colorless and transparent. The only difference from the broken glass in the fish tank was that it had a curvature so slight that it was impossible to detect it unless you looked closely.

"This is..." The old criminsl technican straightened up and looked at Liu Simiao with a puzzled expression.

Liu Simiao said calmly, "Although these two pieces of glass are mixed with the broken glass in that place, they do not belong to the fish tank."

Liu Simiao's discovery made the task force both excited and confused.

The excitement is that after further identification, the two pieces of glass with curvature should be fragments of glasses, and Gao Xiaoyan does not wear glasses, and she lives alone and does not have any glasses at home, which means that the two fragments are the murderer's who was in the fight with Gao. The confusion is that what can be done to identify this, besides adding the word "short-sighted" to the characteristics of the murderer, is there anything else that will help solve the case?

At this time, another figure who played a decisive role in the detection of the case appeared.

After learning that Liu Simiao found two pieces of glasses outside the restored glass fish tank, Li Zhiyong was the most excited, but like other detectives, when his excitement wore off, he was also at a loss. What is the use of this evidence. He went to ask Lin Xiangming, Lin Xiangming thought for a moment and said, "I haven't figured it out yet..." At this moment, a pleasant music sounded in his pocket, Lin Xiangming took out the black Motorola V3 mobile phone, only looked at the caller's name on the screen, a smile formed on the corners of his mouth. After answering the call, he said a few "OK", and then said to Li Zhiyong, "Come on, let's go see a friend with me, maybe he can give us some hints. .."

It was evening, and the lights were on. The two of them rode their bicycles all the way west, and the road covered with fallen leaves had a strange smell of pine. After crossing the overpass at the Xicui intersection, they pushed their bikes into a small north-south street. On the left of the small street is the International College of the Municipal Medical University. Most of the students here are like people from South Asian countries, and on the right is a row of stores, like Weiduomei, The video store, Chi Kee Chuan Bar and Laogu BBQ are connected in series, and there are also several small restaurants selling wild vegetable buns, malatang and donkey meat. The light steamed as if it were melting. The high-powered speakers at the door of the video store played Michael Jackson's rock and roll, but the roar of the barbecue restaurant drowned out the rock music. To the north is an elementary school. Several elementary school students who had just finished their after-school classes were walking out in groups of three or five. The hawker who was waiting outside the school gate selling candied haws and stationery saw it, and hurriedly peddled to attratce the students.

Lin Xiangming and Li Zhiyong parked their bicycles at the entrance of the Laogu BBQ restaurant, and the guys in black overalls with yellow fringe hurriedly opened the door and greeted them inside. They walked in, and the laughter, the clamor, the clinking of wine glasses, the shouts to the waiter one after another, stirred together like a pot of boiling porridge.

The waiters shuttled between the yellow wooden tables and chairs, serving various colored skewers on iron plates to the diners. The inside of the store was smoky and chaotic, and everyone's faces were double-imaged. Lin Xiangming walked straight forward, took a seat in a place where one person was already sitting, greeted Li Zhiyong to sit down opposite him, and then introduced him to the boy with the baby face occupying the seat: "This is Huyan Yun, my good friend."

At the age of 20, Huyan Yun was the same age as Lin Xiangming, but he looked far from Lin Xiangming's calm and mature. The corners of his mouth and eyes were slightly upturned, more like a arrogant and childish young child. It's just his pair of small eyes that shine brightly, as if they can penetrate everyone's internal organs.

Li Zhiyong was stared at by him, and he felt uncomfortable all over, and clenched his fists to him twice.

Lin Xiangming introduced Li Zhiyong again, Huyan Yun nodded to him, then poured a cup of hot water for Lin Xiangming, put it in his hand and said, "It's cold outside, drink some hot water first." He took out a printed matter of fifty or sixty pages, the size of Sanlian Life Weekly, and began to introduce the magazines he had run with a few classmates in the university, "This is a sample issue, it's freshly released, I'll bring it to you first." He happily said to Lin Xiangming, and then he flipped through the pages, from the publication of words, editorial guidelines, call for papers to column setting, and gave Lin Xiangming a detailed introduction one by one, although the hair on his head was like a mess as if he had just woken up, but his mouth was full of grand blueprints, and he was so excited... Huyan Yun's first impression of Li Zhiyong was terrible: arrogant and unrealistic, so that when the two met again ten years later, what came to Li Zhiyong's mind was still his appearance as a junior, but at this moment, Li Zhiyong didn't look at the monk's face and looked at the Buddha's face. Since he was Lin Xiangming's friend, he couldn't embarrass him face to face, he could only sneer secretly, complaining about Lin Xiangming in his heart. Why did he introduce such a guy to himself, and he didn't know what "hint" he can tell.

Lin Xiangming was calm, and while pouring a glass of water for Li Zhiyong with simle, he ordered the food and drink, and listened to Huyan Yun, and nothing was delayed. It wasn't until Huyan Yun finished speaking that Lin Xiangming gently exhorted a few words: "At the beginning, don't spread too much, rush too hard, and think too simply." Huyan Yun poured himself a full glass of beer, grunting to his stomach and said, "Don't worry, I don't want to give anyone any big reason, I just can't stand their cynicism." Lin Xiangming nodded: "Some people revel, some people watch the night, and the various departments just doing their jobs."

From Li Zhiyong's point of view, the two of them said different things, and they didn't agree at all, but they didn't get bored with each other because they didn't talk opportunistically. For some reason, the topic suddenly turned to "Serial Murder Cases in the Western Suburbs". Lin Xiangming talked about Liu Simiao's discovery of the spectacle fragments in detail. Although the noise in the store was louder and louder, Lin Xiangming didn't raise his voice, and Huyan Yun didn't frown at the noise, he listened carefully. Li Zhiyong only redarded him as a student liked listening to criminal investigation stories like all college students. But when he heard Lin Xiangming talk about some secrets held by the police he wanted to stop them, but he held back and lowered his head eating edamame and drinking beer.

After Lin Xiangming finished speaking, the grilled skewers and stir-fried vegetables were brought up. Huyan Yun grabbed a skewer of grilled yellow croaker and began to eat. Lin Xiangming served three bowls of fried rice with eggs, and put a bowl in front of them, and then took a bowl and ate it slowly with a white porcelain spoon.

Sitting face to face, Li Zhiyong could see that although Huyan Yun's mouth was chewing, his eyes were very calm, like a Go player sitting in a Japanese-style tea room playing chess with others, concentrating on thinking about something, just twisting his fingers with not black and white piece but bamboo sticks. After eating two skewers of grilled small yellow croaker in succession, he took out two from the plastic tissue bag on the table, wiped his mouth, and said to Lin Xiangming, "This murderer should be a fan of mystery novels."

Li Zhiyong was taken aback, and before Lin Xiangming could speak, he shouted, "What? How did you know?"

Huyan Yun ignored him and continued to say to Lin Xiangming, "Assuming that the broken fish tank and glasses were caused by Gao Xiaoyan's struggle with the murderer, then what Liu Simiao recovered from the broken glass pieces in that place should be more than just a fish tank. , there should be at least one complete spectacle lens, but no, what does that mean?"

"It shows that the murderer used to look for and pick up the broken spectacle lenses very seriously when cleaning up the scene." Lin Xiangming said.

"Yes! So I am more inclined: the murderer's glasses were indeed broken by fighting with Gao Xiaoyan, and the fish tank was deliberately broken by the murderer later." Huyan Yun said, "The murderer originally wanted to pick up all the glasses fragments on the ground, but because his glasses were broken, he couldn't see the ground clearly, and he wasn't sure that he could find and pick up all the pieces. In order to cover up a tree, he had to plant a forest, so he broke the fish tank, let the shards of spectacles be mixed with the shards of glass in the fish tank so the police will ignore the shards of glasses."

Li Zhiyong couldn't help but patted the table: "Yes! Yes! Yes! That's what happened!"

Lin Xiangming also nodded: "So, why did the murderer do this?"

"Because the shards of glasses may reveal his personal information, right?" Li Zhiyong couldn't help but interject.

Huyan Yun glanced at him with a smile.

"I'll ask Liu Simiao to carefully measure and inspect the two pieces of glasses." Lin Xiangming just took out his phone, but Huyan Yun stopped him: "Xiangming, wait, there is an easier way to find the murderer. I said, he is a fan of mystery novels."

"Yes, you haven't explained how you came to this conclusion." Li Zhiyong said.

Huyan Yun said: "The method the murderer took to cover up physical evidence is from a famous Japanese reasoning comic, but it is relatively niche in China, so few of your policemen must know about it. Since he can imitate the practice of small comics, then it is not an absurd guess that he might be a fan of reasoning or even a fan of mystery novels ."

"That's it!" Li Zhiyong suddenly realized, "But you said that there is an easier way to find him..."

Huyan Yun showed an expression of "I said so clearly, how could you still don't understand", and picked up a bunch of grilled yellow croaker and said, "Judging from the murderer's clothes and living environment, his family is not rich, so he doesn't know how to shop online, and there are very few brick-and-mortar bookstores in the Western Suburbs... Let Dangdang.com and Zhuoyue.com assist the police in their investigation to see how many people living in the Western Suburbs have purchased that set of comics online, and then check them one by one..."

6

Lin Xiangming walked outside the noisy barbecue restaurant and made several consecutive calls, asking the task force to immediately contact the headquarters of Dangdang.com and Zhuoyue.com to call up the orders and subscribers names for the Japanese reasoning comics purchased online... When he turned around, he found that Huyan Yun came out with Li Zhiyong supported.

After listening to Huyan Yun's reasoning just now, Li Zhiyong had a premonition that the real murderer was about to be arrested. Not only did he not rush to the front line to capture the murderer, but he was completely powerless and fell into a certain state of paralysis. He drank cup after cup, and then simply blew on the bottle. When Lin Xiangming came out to call, he emptied five wine bottles. Huyan Yun saw the pain in his heart and didn't stop him. As a result, he drank too much and his legs were all stumbled, and as soon as they walked out of the door of the restaurant, he squatted on the side of the road and vomited. Lin Xiangming hurried over to pat him on the back, and asked the guy at the door to receive a cup of hot water.

"I don't know why he drunk so much..." Huyan Yun muttered, afraid that Lin Xiangming would blame him.

"His partner sacrificed." Lin Xiangming whispered, "In the process of solving this case."

Li Zhiyong almost vomited and sat on the ground. Lin Xiangming wiped his mouth with a tissue and brought him hot water. He took the paper cup with his hands trembling, and he spilled a little before it reached his mouth. Lin Xiangming stretched out his hand to help him hold the paper cup, which was like feeding him a drink.

After drinking the hot water, Li Zhiyong drooped his head, rested his arms on the ground, and said nothing for a long, long time, and began to mumble something. Lin Xiangming couldn't hear clearly, but when he got closer, he heard what he said: "She didn't die in vain, she didn't die in vain..."

Lin Xiangming felt that the ground was too cold, and was afraid that he would get sick after sitting for a long time. He wanted to help him up, but he not only didn't want to move, but also pushed Lin Xiangming a few times. Huyan Yun stopped a taxi and stopped in front of Li Zhiyong. Lin Xiangming pushed him into the back row, and sat beside him himself.

Huyan Yun sat in the front passenger seat and asked where Li Zhiyong's family lived. Li Zhiyong vaguely said a place name, and the driver looked back and said, "Don't vomit in my car!" Lin Xiangming immediately said, "Drive!" The tone was so severe that the driver hurriedly started the car. .

The world become quiet.

Looking out from the moving car window, the sky above the city was like a slowly flowing black river. The cold of late autumn was making the river slowly solidify and freeze. Those branches, wires and street lamps shivering in the wind went past the view like abandoned children, they are frozen in the center of the river, helpless, with no future.

Perhaps because he was afraid of the silence in the car, the taxi driver turned on the stereo, and an old song rang out. It was Zhong Zhentao singing in a hoarse voice:

In the wind in the wind, in the cold wind in my heart, I lost my dream,
It disappeared before it passed,
There's a lot of heartache right now...

In the distance, a light suddenly extinguished in the residential building, like eyes that lie down and never sleep, appearing lonely, sad and melancholy. At this moment, Li Zhiyong, who was nestled in the corner of the rear seat, suddenly muttered. At first, he couldn't hear what he was saying, but gradually he heard that it was a long series of babble: "I'm tired, so tired, I want to do it myself but I've already out of energy... I'm so busy but don't know what to do... I washed my face, cut my head, and shaved my beard, I'm neat, I won't embarrass you..." At the end, the sound of the song continued : "All the emptiness, and coldness, blowing the wind in dreams..."

During the whole process, Huyan Yun did not look back, and Lin Xiangming did not say a word.

Li Zhiyong's home was in an old building from the 1960s. His father died early, and there was only his mother in the family who had gray hair in her fifties. Seeing Lin Xiangming and Huyan Yun bring her drunken son back, she kept saying thank you to them. They put Li Zhiyong on the bed first, then closed the door of his room. His mother went to the kitchen and poured two glasses of water for them to drink. Huyan Yun said that he was not thirsty. Lin Xiangming took the glass and drank water while looking at the photo frames placed on the cabinet. The lighting in the small living room was dim. After looking for a long time, he suddenly pointed to a photo frame and asked: "has uncle ever been a policeman?"

In the photo in the frame, a stout man in an olive 83-style police uniform was tickling a fat boy in a red scarf.

"Right, both the father and the son are destined to be the police." The old lady sighed, "The old one made me worried, so does the young one."

"What happened to uncle?" Lin Xiangming asked bluntly.

"In 1996, the city's police were mobilized, and they worked hard for more than three months. Just after finishing the work, there were several cases of child abduction in the Western Suburbs. Originally, his father was supposed to take a leave of absence, but he was stubborn, and as soon as I persuaded him, he would get mad at me and asked me not take part on his affairs, just like I was the bad guy he wanted to catch. He investigated day and night, and didn't eat or drink, when he managed to catch the bad guy with great difficulty. He got angry during the interrogation, and had a heart attack. It was delayed in being sent to the hospital... It's destiny." The old lady sighed again, "I worried about Zhiyong every day when he goes to work. Every time he came back late, I was imagining bad things in my mind. Fortunately you sending him back tonight, or I—"

Before he could finish speaking, Lin Xiangming's cell phone rang. As soon as he picked it up and answered it, his expression became solemn. Before he hung up the phone, the old lady said, "You might have work, so hurry up and do your work. Be careful."

Lin Xiangming said goodbye to her and walked out the door with Huyan Yun.

After going out of the building, Lin Xiangming said to Huyan Yun, "Go back to school, I need to go back to work."

"Caught the criminal?" Huyan Yun was a little surprised, "So fast?"

Lin Xiangming shook his head: "No, that serial killer committed the crime again." Huyan Yun volunteered: "Do you need me to help you?"

"It's okay to talk about it in a detective novel, but it has to be a foreign detective novel." Lin Xiangming smiled, suddenly remembered something again, and warned again, "Your magazines, don't cover so much at first, it won't be that easy as you think..."

"Oh, come on, you are nagging more than my mother!" Huyan Yun pushed his shoulders and walked forward, "You broke the thief in the mountains, I broke the thief in my heart, the easy things are left to you, so don't chatter! "

7

The sacrifice of Fang Zhifeng, director of the Public Security Office of Chunliu Street, not only brought an end to the "serial murder case in the Western Suburbs", but also exposed the vicious murderer to the police's sight.

Fang Zhifeng was 48 years old. He was originally a security officer in a municipal cement company. He was discharged early because of hepatitis.

It happened that Chunliu Sub-district responded to the call of superiors and realized the youth and professionalization of grass-roots cadres. The old director voluntarily retired and recommended Fang Zhifeng to take over.

Fang Zhifeng had been ill for many years, his body was thin, and his face was always sallow. After taking up the post of Director of the Public Security Office, he did his best. He not only established a well-trained joint defense team, but also formulated a security patrol route according to the specific conditions of the community. And teachers from China Police Officers University were also invited to carry out law popularization and safety precaution education for residents, which greatly improved the public security situation in the community and was praised by the district government. If it weren't for the second "Western Suburb Serial Murder Case" that happened in Chunliu Street, the district would have awarded him the title of "Community Advanced Worker".

This case put a lot of pressure on him, aside from the suspect who escaped the pursuit of the joint defense team, he was scolded by Du Jianping, some residents also ridiculed him for doing everything about community security was a "paper-paste project", which made him feel disheartened and offered his resignation to the street leaders several times: "I've been busy running for more than half a year, thank you for my hard work, why don't I go home and take care of my daughter? !"

Fang Zhifeng divorced his wife very early and he raised his daughter Fang Mei alone. Fang Mei was seventeen years old and in high school. Perhaps she was frightened by her parents' quarrel when she was a child. This sick-looking girl was taciturn and was always covered in gray from head to toe, as if she was living in the shadows, which made Fang Zhifeng very worried.

Hard to withstand his repeated applications, the street leaders agreed to let him retire as soon as the case was solved. Fang Zhifeng muttered reluctantly, "I always feel that someone is watching our house lately...as the director of the public security office, I won't make anything happen to my family."

It was not until after the incident that people realized how ominous his words were.

About when Li Zhiyong was sitting and vomitting at the door of Laogu BBQ restaurant, 110 received a panic call from an old lady, saying that a neighbor had died, the host was killed, and his daughter locked herself up. In the room, I refused to open the door no matter how I called it... In view of the recent series of serial homicides in the Western Suburbs, the Municipal Bureau had opened an internal dedicated line. Any unexpected situation suspected to be related to this case will be notified immediately to the task force. A group of police from the task force were sitting in the office specially set up by the district criminal police team, eating in Lihua fast food, while assigned the task of investigating suspicious orders at the headquarters of Dangdang.com and Zhuoyue.com, when they heard the news and crime address that they had been transferred from 110, Chai Yongjin stopped in the air with a chopstick with a piece of braised octopus in between: "Isn't that Director Fang's home?" Du Jianping was still a little confused: "Which Director?" Chai replied: "Is there any other Director Chai? "

Du Jianping's head hummed, and he threw the lunch box on the table, jumped up, and ran downstairs, with a few young criminal policemen following behind, almost unable to follow him.

The results of the on-site investigation and forensic examination are as follows: The crime scene is located in Room 302, No. 4, Building 3, No. 4 Community, Chunliu Street. The deceased was the owner of the house, Fang Zhifeng. The death scene was located in front of the TV cabinet in the living room. The body was prone to the north and feet to the south. The clothes on his body were torn in several places. A clear fingerprint was extracted from a torn button, and it was still on the floor. The sneaker shoe prints that are interlaced and mixed with Fang Zhifeng's shoe prints are extracted. The sofa, dining table and chairs in the living room were either moved or overturned, and a large number of cutlery and glassware were broken, indicating that fierce fighting had taken place here. The skull of the deceased was broken down by multiple arc-shaped steps, collapsed and broken, which were obviously the result of blunt weapon smashing. No murder weapon was found at or near the scene. The door locks at the crime scene showed no signs of being picked, and the windows were all closed from the inside with no signs of damage.

When the police arrived, Fang Zhifeng's daughter Fang Mei still locked herself in the bedroom and refused to open the door, so the police had to break in. Fang Mei was alone in the room, disheveled and in a trance, cowering in the corner with tears on her face, trembling all over. Upon examination, her left shoulder was injured by a hammer. The police asked her several questions in a row, but she remained silent. In view of the possibility of post-traumatic stress, the police did not ask any further questions, and took her to the hospital by car.

According to the old lady who reported the case, at about 9:30 that night, she was watching the TV series "The Gate of the Mansion" when she suddenly heard roaring and beating from the room opposite the door, as well as big noise of furniture kicked down and utensils broken. She was very puzzled, because she the old neighbors for many years. The house was inhabited by Fang Zhifeng, the director of the street security office, and his daughter. The father and daughter never quarreled. Soon everything quieted down. The old lady opened the door, looked through the security door for a long time, and found that the two doors of the house were left open and not closed tightly. Although the lights were turned on in the house, there was no sound at all. She called a few times, "Fang", no one answered, and she called "Xiao Mei" a few times, but no one answered, so she couldn't help but get scared and pulled his son who was playing computer games out of his chair, "You accompany with me to check them." ,then the murder was discovered.

Two other important facts were quickly learned by the police in the ensuing investigation.

One was that the director of the public security office in the district specially convened each street to hold an emergency meeting that night, proposing to actively cooperate with the police, starting from the four aspects of public opinion propaganda, mobilizing the masses, strengthening joint defense, and visiting households, and increasing the deterrent response to "serial killings in the Western Suburbs.", and made the criminal "can't escape when he comit a crime again, and he will be caught when he appear again." The meeting ended at nine o'clock, and it took 30 minutes to ride a bicycle from the district government to Fang Zhifeng's house in Chunliu Street.

The other one was provided by an old man who rode a fitness bike at the outdoor gym in the No. 4 Community of Chunliu Street. He said that between 9:30 and 10:00, he saw a young man rushing out of the fourth door of Building No. 3, with a wide face and square chin, triangular eyes, a fierce look, and a shaggy moustache. "If you see him again, I must recognize him."

Based on the above circumstances, the preliminary conclusion of the police on Fang Zhifeng's murder was that the criminal of the "Western Suburb Serial Murder Case" broke into Fang Zhifeng's house that night, attacked Fang Mei who was at home alone and attempted to sexually assault her, just when Fang Zhifeng went home from get off work and fought to the death with the criminal, and was unfortunately killed. The father traded his life for time, Fang Mei took the opportunity to hide in her bedroom and locked the door. The criminal was afraid that the sound of the fighting would cause the public to call the police, so he hurriedly fled the crime scene.

However, Du Jianping also noticed a very critical problem: this time the criminal's criminal pattern was significantly different from the previous cases. He did not "kill with one blow" from behind the moment the target opened the door, but attacked after entering the room. More importantly, neither the security door nor the interior doors and windows were damaged, which is enough to show that this time it was Fang Mei who took the initiative to "open the door for the criminal".

"Fang Mei is likely to know the criminal." Du Jianping came to a conclusion, and immediately dispatched Chai Yongjin and others to the hospital, "No matter what the condition of Fang Mei is, she must tell the truth immediately! Every second of delay is reserved for the criminal!"

But before Chai Yongjin left, a sudden news made the task force pinpoint the real culprit in advance.

After receiving the police's notice of assistance in the investigation, the relevant departments of Dangdang.com and Zhuoyue.com actively cooperated and transferred all orders for the Japanese reasoning comics in the Western Suburbs. It is said that this set of comics was really niche. Only three sets were sold in the Western Suburbs in the past year: one set was bought by the district library; one set was bought by a well-known domestic cartoonist, the cartoonist was a girl with severe autism; The buyer of the last set, the order showed a person named Zhou Liping, and this person's home address was located in Dongqing Street, which was just across the street from Chunliu Street.

After the task force contacted the street police station, they learned something that made them even more excited: Zhou Liping was seventeen years old this year, and he was a classmate in the same high school as Fang Mei. His family situation was rather special. His parents divorced when he was in elementary school, and then they formed a family separetly, and no one wanted to take care of him. In the end, his aunt adopted him, but instead of living with his aunt's family, he lived in the semi-basement of the same building. This person was withdrawn and eccentric. He was once punished by the school for molesting a girl. It was especially worth noting that the ID photo brought up by the street police station showed that his appearance was exactly in line with the "wide face, square chin, triangular eyes, and a narrow chin, and furry moustache" features!

Du Jianping led a team of criminal policemen and kicked open the door of the semi-basement where Zhou Liping lived, and found the room was dark and quiet. For a moment, they thought that Zhou Liping had fled in fear of the crime. When they took flashlight on the dilapidated single bed, all the detectives couldn't help but shuddered. Zhou Liping slept upright on the bed with the quilt like a zombie, and Du Jianping had never seen such a terrifying character in his ten years as a police officer. Even ordinary people would be frightened when someone smashed their door in the middle of the night, but after this person committed numerous crimes, he could sleep peacefully, ignoring the arrest of the police as nothing!

Therefore, when Chai Yongjin and the others rushed forward bravely, roaring, scolding, tearing Zhou Liping out of bed and cuffing him, Du Jianping suddenly had a very funny feeling in his heart.

Zhou Liping didn't resist, not even make a sound with the pain when his arm was twisted backwards, he just frowned.

Du Jianping found the light switch on the wall beside the door and turned it on with a click. After the incandescent lamp above his head buzzed twice, it lit up the room with a bang. The house was small, about 11 or 12 square meters, and it was dirty everywhere: socks with a hole in the big toe were thrown under the single bed, the zipper of the simple green rice-shaped wardrobe was wide open, and the clothes inside were piled up. Like an overflowing garbage basket, an old-fashioned Lenovo 586 computer was placed on a gray computer table. The edges and seams of the keyboard and mouse were plastered, and various CDs were stacked next to each other, except "Three Kingdoms Heroes" and "Civilization II" and adults movies of various Japanese AV actresses... The room exuded a choking stench unique to adolescent boys, and the large blackened wall around the radiator, it was disgusting as if to visualize this stench. On the top of the north wall was a row of glass windows. Through the dirty glass, they could see the drainage grates like prison bars. There was a row of shoes on the windowsill. Connected into a dark green lump...

"Do you know why we arrested you? Do you know what you did? Where is the murder weapon? Are there any accomplices?" Facing this series of torrential interrogations from the police, Zhou Liping remained silent, sitting on the ground wearing a vest and pants, with a look of being manipulated by others, with an indifferent expression on his wide face covered with acne, and his cold eyes as if to freeze every problem and never thaw it. The search for Zhou Liping's room was both regretful and rewarding. Unfortunately, the key evidence of the hammer that killed four people was not found; the reward was to find a pair of sneakers under the bed. With the naked eye, it could be seen that the pattern and wear of the soles were the same as those of the criminal on the floor of Fang Zhifeng's house. The shoe prints left were exactly the same, and there were even a few glass balls embedded in them! More importantly, the fingerprints that the appraisers took from Zhou Liping's hand were immediately sent to the

Criminal Technology Appraisal Center of the sub-bureau. After computer comparison, they came to the conclusion that they were the same as the fingerprints extracted from the torn button on Fang Zhifeng's clothes!

When Chai Yongjin rushed to the hospital, told Fang Mei about the situation, and encouraged her to "don't be afraid of revenge, tell us the truth", Fang Mei raised her uninjured hand, covered her face and cried for a long time, tears streaming from her fingers before admitting that Zhou Liping and himself were classmates and liked to exchange and read some comics. On the night of the crime, when Zhou Liping came to his house to get back a set of Japanese reasoning comics he lent her, he suddenly hit her in the back of the head with a hammer, Zhou Liping rushed to rape her viciously, just as her father came back from the outside, while fighting with Zhou Liping, he told her to go back to the inner room and lock the door. After she rushed into the back room and locked the door, she was too frightened to move, until there was no sound in the living room, she still curled up in a ball, holding her breath, like a live fetus curled up in the womb of a mother who died in childbirth.

The case finally solved!

The criminal policemen who had been fighting day and night for nearly two months for the "Western Suburb Serial Murder Case" were so excited that they hugged each other, and some even cried with joy. Li Zhiyong learned the news after sobering up was the next morning. He did not cheer like other police officers, nor did he feel depressed and sad because he failed to catch Zhou Liping with his own hands. He just kept smoking stick by stick. In the evening, a colleague who came back from the cafeteria saw that the corridor was empty, and he was nowhere to be seen. On the ground were a pile of cigarette butts shaped like tombs by his feet...

8

Can't tell whether the rain was getting bigger or smaller. Before entering the small restaurant, Li Zhiyong looked up at the light bulb on the lintel. The pale yellow light illuminated some chaotic rain threads, dancing indiscriminately. It is surprising that they are so slender and thorough, as if each one had its own life and even destiny, so they were so sensitive and uneasy.

This small restaurant opened in the Qingta community, the front and the inside were not big, and only four tables can be placed in total. The yawning proprietress knew Li Zhiyong, and first asked them what they wanted to eat, and then muttered, "There's nothing left in the back kitchen. If you don't have any taboos, I'll pick up a few to cook for you!" After speaking, he opened a blue curtain next to the counter and walked into the kitchen.

Li Zhiyong picked up a white porcelain teapot with a mouth on the table and poured a cup of hot water for Lin Xiangming: "Go back to school tomorrow?"

"Yeah." Lin Xiangming picked up the cup and took a sip.

Li Zhiyong suddenly felt that he had a lot to say to him, but he didn't know where to start. The distant warmth that always existed in Lin Xiangming's body made people feel friendly but not affectionate. Maybe he and Huyan Yun were an exception? Anyway, since working together for more than half a month, Li Zhiyong became more and more familiar with him, and at the same time became more and more unfamiliar, so unfamiliar that every time he spoke, he had to weigh it up before he dared to speak.

Perhaps realizing the source of such silence in the restaurant, Lin Xiangming broke apart the disposable chopsticks, scratched the wooden thorns on it, and asked, "I heard that the entire task force is on the list of meritorious awards, only you were removed from the list?"

"Yeah, because I beat Zhou Liping too hard. According to the discipline, I was supposed to be fired from the police force. Du told the superior and gave me a balance of merits and demerits." Li Zhiyong took out a pack of cigarettes from his trousers pocket, and touched the lighter for a long time without finding it, "But I don't regret, I just want to beat him, beat him to death!"

Lin Xiangming asked lightly, "In order to force him to tell where the murder weapon is?"

"That's all excuses, I just fucking want to beat him!" Li Zhiyong said while slamming the disposable chopsticks hard. After breaking them, he thought that this should be broken, and angrily threw them on the table, "He killed so many people? Shouldn't he be beaten?!" When he said this, he glared at Lin Xiangming defiantly, but in front of Lin Xiangming's calm expression, he gradually restrained his vicious gaze and turned his head away. .He looked at the unkempt but split-eyed self reflected on the glass window, and after a long time he let out a long sigh of relief, and a large piece of invisible white frog appeared on the glass window, covering the wild beast-like face. .

There was a clanging sound of cooking spatulas in the kitchen behind the blue curtain. Li Zhiyong took a sip of hot water and asked Lin Xiangming in a low voice: "I heard that you reported to your superiors and insisted that Zhou Liping was not the real culprit of the 'Serial Murder Case in the Western Suburbs'. Is that true?"

Lin Xiangming nodded: "Yes."

"Why? Why you do that?" The anger that was finally suppressed surged up again, "Just because hey didn't find the hammer, you're going to let a murderer with four lives go unpunished? Don't look at him as a minor, with four lives which were enough to keep him locked up for a lifetime!"

"Maybe you didn't read my report." Lin Xiangming said calmly, "I didn't deny that he killed Fang Zhifeng, but the other three dead: Yang Hua, Wu and Gao Xiaoyan, I don't think he killed him. There are many reasons. In addition to the fact that the murder weapon was not found, the most important thing is that in the incident of Fang Mei's attack, the criminal methods and behavior patterns of the perpetrators were fundamentally different from those in the previous cases—"

"Why didn't I see any difference?" Li Zhiyong interrupted him, "It's just this time it not happened in the corridor, but knocked on the door and entered the house and then smashed the victim's head!"

"As far as you said, there is already a huge difference. According to the reasoning you made at the case analysis meeting, the victims of the first three cases all knew the murderer, but they were not too familiar. Letting go of their vigilance is still far from reaching the point they open the door and invite the criminal to enter the room – this is precisely the premise set by the murderer when choosing a victim. If you understand behavioral science and criminal psychology, you will understand that serial Murderers follow extremely strict standards for the selection of victims. This is not because they are used to eating salty tofu and can't eat sweet bean curd, but based on the need for self-protection and concealment. One point can be proved that the first two cases , why you and Gao Xiaoyan have been investigating and visiting for so long, and you can't find a suspect who is related to both victims, because when the murderer chooses the victim, he and the victim have absolute premise of not being able to establish any bond , this is his invisibility cloak and protective umbrella. He can't even break a single hole, otherwise he will be exposed and arrested. For Zhou Liping, Fang Mei is a classmate in the same class they borrowed books from each other. Before going to Fang Mei's house that night, Zhou Liping called her landline to ask her if she was there. After entering the house, he didn't wear gloves when 'comitting the crime', and he didn't make any disguise or make up when he escaped, even if there was no reasoning from Huyan Yun, the police will easily lock him in the subsequent investigation, which is not like a murderer who has killed three people in a row! Besides, after he was arrested, the police did not find that he had any relationship with the first three victims."

"As far as I know, for a serial killer, when the police or the external environment put too much pressure on him, it may cause his behavior to change like a genetic mutation." Li Zhiyong said dissatisfiedly, "Before Zhou Liping Before was arrested, the police, the public security joint defense and the masses had already woven an endless net to hunt him down, and they were constantly closing in on him. He couldn't be satisfied, so he had to start with acquaintances who were completely unguarded by him, anyway, he could kill the victim in the end, not afraid of being exposed—"

Suddenly, he froze.

He realized the huge hole in the sentence.

"Yes!" Lin Xiangming said quietly, "The question is, since Fang Zhifeng has already been killed, why didn't Zhou Liping kick open the thin door and kill Fang Mei?"

Li Zhiyong was speechless for a long time. At this moment, the proprietress brought a plate of garlic oats and two bowls of rice on their table, turned and went back to the kitchen. The two of them stretched out their chopsticks and ate slowly. They didn't speak for a while. Finally, Li Zhiyong spoke first: "You just mentioned Huyan Yun's reasoning, isn't it just because Liu Simiao was restoring the broken glass fish tank, when the spectacle fragments were discovered, Huyan Yun made a reasoning based on the spectacle fragments, which helped us quickly catch Zhou Liping after the incident? Although he did not say a word after the arrest, but according to his classmates, the day after Xiaoyan was killed, the scum really did not wear glasses. Because he couldn't read the writing on the blackboard in class, he asked his classmates to borrow notes to copy. The classmates asked him where the glasses were, he said they were broken. Is this reasoning worthless to you?"

"I do not deny that reasoning is a kind of truth reduction based on science and logic, but this reduction must rely on the confirmation of evidence, otherwise no matter how wonderful it is, it is only the greatest possibility of the truth – 99% close to the truth does not mean the truth." Lin Xiang Ming said, "Huyan Yun did deduce that the real murderer may be someone who likes to read inference comics, but there are many people who like to read inference comics, and because Zhou Liping likes to read inference comics, he cannot be regarded as the real murderer. This evidence is not sufficient. For the same determination as the murderer, there is only probability but no inevitability. Yes, we caught Zhou Liping through Huyan Yun's reasoning, but how is the result of the 'reverse push' that requires evidence next? We didn't find any evidence that he was related to the previous three cases, and all the evidence we could find were 'suspected connections': Zhou Liping's shoe size and gait were highly similar to the footprints left by the suspect, but we did not find the same pair of shoes; the wound was suspected to be caused by the same weapon, but the hammer was not found; The joint defense team members who chased the suspect on the night of the second murder felt that Li Zhiyong's body was very similar to the pursued person, but it was only very similar—"

"Isn't so many 'suspected' enough?"

"Not enough!" Lin Xiangming said mildly but decisively, "All the unjust, false and wrongful convictions throughout the ages were due to the fact that 'suspected' is regarded as 'fact'."

Li Zhiyong's face turned red, and it took him a long time to slap his chopsticks on his rice bowl, and sneered, "I think you're just trying to clean up Zhou Liping because of the fact that Chai's mental portrait is right and you can't keep your face down!"

In fact, the task force and the entire police force all thought so. According to Chai Yongjin's criminal personality profile, the real murderer should be a man "under 20 years old, strong and burly, with serious violent tendencies, likely to have undergone reeducation through labor for rape or fight, living in the basement for a long time, no fixed occupation", except for "floating personnel", the rest have the same characteristics as Zhou Liping. "Simply divine"! Recalling Lin Xiangming's doubts and objections to this psychological portrait, even Du Jianping couldn't help but pat Chai Yongjin on the shoulder and said, "In the end, we have to rely on the old guys who have done real swords and real guns to solve the case. The boys with professional knowledge are still a little more tender, they have read a lot of books, and they have not experienced much, they are not reliable." After learning that Lin Xiangming reported to his superiors and disagreed that Zhou Liping was the real culprit of the "Western Suburb Serial Murder Case", many criminal police officers were sneering and saying sarcastic words in front of and behind his backs. When Lin Xiangming left the task force, no one said to send him a gift. It was Li Zhiyong who stood on the window sill watching him walk out of the yard full of dead branches and leaves and left alone, feeling a little sad, so he made a special call to ask him to meet tonight.

Hearing what Li Zhiyong said just now, Lin Xiangming was neither surprised nor angry, but there was a hint of unnoticeable sadness in his eyes.

Li Zhiyong had some regrets. Although he had not been together for too long, he had already established a complex relationship with Lin

Xiangming that he had never had before: as soon as he admired him at a young age,but had the courage even Mount Tai collapses in front of him without changing his mind. He was calm, mature and restrained, deeply impressed by his extraordinary personal charm, and vaguely afraid of him, unable to see through his hidden palace, unable to guess his unpredictable scheming...Maybe there was also a little jealousy of him – not only because he was a high-caliber student at the China Police Officers University, but also because his insight into people's hearts and world affairs far exceeds that of the older himself... Li Zhiyong knew that he that sentence can't hurt Lin Xiangming, it can only hurt the friendship between them, maybe far from friendship. This kind of friendship will end with the end of the working relationship. Now because of this sarcasm, their friendship might die prematurely. So, the mixed emotions and guilt turned into a rude shout – "Madam, more beers!"

Unconsciously, he drank too much.

When they left the small restaurant, the rain had stopped, and only the cold water vapor was floating in the air. Lin Xiangming pushed the bicycle, Li Zhiyong held the seat, and staggered beside him... A gust of cold wind blew, and the bare treetops on the street invariably issued a whistle that sounded like a cry, and a few last fallen leaves turned into powder in the rotation, and the black linoleum covering the chemical barrel used for roasting sweet potatoes on the corner of the street stuck out its tongue, as if laughing, but the laugh was particularly ferocious.

The two walked all the way for a long time without speaking. Suddenly, a "leisure massage parlor" with red light bulbs lit with gauze curtains on the side of the road made a squeak of inferior sliding doors being forcibly pulled open, and then a woman in tights and black stockings appeared at the door. Made an enchanting voice: "Guys, come in for a massage?"

"Go away!" Li Zhiyong scolded.

"Fxxk you!" The woman immediately turned her face, and was about to say something even worse, when Lin Xiangming flashed the temporary work permit given to him by the city bureau, and the woman's face turned ashen with fright and kept say "sorry". She turned back to the store, closed the door with a clatter, and the curtains were pulled to turn off the lights, without saying a word. Immediately afterwards, several other massage parlors on this small street also swiped off their lights like candles in the wind.

The street fell into a dead silence like ruins.

They continued to walk forward, and unknowingly circled back to the place where they met – the gate of Wangyue Park.

Looking up at the strange and inexplicable white marble sculpture "Father of the Moon" on the high platform, for some reason, Li Zhiyong suddenly lost his temper.

"I don't understand, I just don't fucking understand. Don't we become police officers to wipe out all the bad guys? But why do you have to protect Zhou Liping?!"

"All living beings are suffering, sin is easy to characterize, but people are not easy to characterize." Lin Xiangming said calmly, "Zhou Liping is not a bad person, he just went a wrong way and did wrong things... Life is a journey of stumbling in the darkness. Some people go astray because of coincidences, some people go astray because of helplessness, and some people deliberately go astray because of strange motives. A fork in the road is not necessarily the wrong way, and the person who did the wrong thing is not necessarily a bad person. ... Besides, the worst in the world are not the worst looking people."

"Then what? "

Lin Xiangming thought for a while, and said slowly, "It's the kind of idea of 'to wipe out all the bad guys at all costs'."

Li Zhiyong's eyes turned blood red: "Isn't the goal of our efforts to create an era in which even the bad guys can't survive?"

Lin Xiangming looked into his eyes and said word by word, "Is it really a good era when a bad person can't survive?"

A word, like a basin of ice water poured over his head, made Li Zhiyong tremble: What was Lin Xiangming talking about? How can I not understand? He felt that Lin Xiangming's words were extremely absurd and ridiculous, but they had a certain sharpness to the point, just like the sudden sound of a harmonica before the meeting tonight, which was enough to make him toss and turn every night when he couldn't sleep...

Just when he wanted to ask Lin Xiangming for more reasons, Lin Xiangming stretched out his hand to say goodbye to him: "It's too late, go home early and have a rest, or your mother will worry about you again, we will have opppoortunities in the future and meet together."

Li Zhiyong suddenly became sad, stretched out a hand, shook hands with Lin Xiangming, and suddenly asked unwillingly: "Xiangming... Why do I always feel like you know the truth of the 'Serial Murder Case in the Western Suburbs' , but you just don't want to say it?"

Lin Xiangming was stunned for a moment, then pondered for a moment, then suddenly looked at the steps leading to the top of Wangyue Park and asked Li Zhiyong, "How can a person take the fifteen steps in one step?"

Li Zhiyong looked at the long, ascending steps. It had just rained. Under the illumination of the mushroom umbrella-shaped park lights, each step was shimmering irregularly because of the potholes and water.

After thinking about it for a long time, he couldn't think of an answer, so he shook his head, but Lin Xiangming just smiled and turned away.

Watching Lin Xiangming's back gradually fade away and disappear into the vast darkness, Li Zhiyong felt that no matter how he felt about Lin Xiangming, about Zhou Liping, about the "Western Suburb Serial Murder Case", and about the fifteen steps in front of him, he was always confused in his heart. This confusion was so strong, just like he was standing on the Deratization Hill ten years later.

Chapter 1

1

If the entire provincial capital was compared to a giant lying on its back, then the subway running through the city's east-west line was the giant's spine, and the Deratization Hill subway station was like the cecum that remainws useless after the degenerate tail of a primate.

Regarding the Deratization Hill subway station, a large number of terrifying and bizarre legends can be retrieved on the Internet. These legends were true and false. So that there must have some introduction instead of the readers will fall into the fog, and not distinguishing between reality and illusion, and mistaking the sins of the world for the poisoning of evil spirits.

The subway that ran through the city was built in the 1970s. It was one of the earliest subway lines built and opened in China. It had undertaken the important task of transporting citizens to work for more than 40 years. The subway started from Cherry Street Station in the west and ended at Sihaitong Station in the east – but Cherry Street Station was only the starting point for operating the subway, in other words, it was the starting point for ordinary passengers, but it was by no means the starting point of the subway itself. The internal number of the Cheery street station was the second station, and it was conceivable that there must be one before the second. This was also the case: further west from Cherry Street Station, there was a little-known station that had never been put into operation, that was, the No. 1 station, Deratization Hill Station.

In the 1960s and 1970s, due to historical reasons, major units in the city built relatively independent "compounds" around the core office area, including collective dormitories, canteens, schools and even cinemas, as well as the subway system. The 'compounds' was located in the area of Deratization Hill. Therefore, before 2008, Deratization Hill Station was the daily commuting station for subway workers, their families and students who went to school nearby. Although outsiders can't take the subway, they could go down to the ticket gate and peep inwards, so it had become a wonderland for urban adventure lovers. Everything about it was covered up, but what coverd it was not an airtight iron plate, but a layer of looming gauze, which was not allowed to be opened, but people might as well take a closer look through the gauze... So, about its there are various texts, photos and even videos that can be easily retrieved on the Internet. Some of them are true, and more are made up speculations, which made it a derivation of all kinds of nonsense in this city.

One of the most famous was the legend of the "ghost station". It was said that when the subway was being built, there was a fire here and two workers were burned to death. As a result, when it was completed and opened to traffic, the car could not go out from the Deratization Hill Station, so the "master" had to be invited. After walking around for a while, the master said that the ghosts here were too angry, and he couldn't help remove them. It might as well seal this station for ghosts to linger so that they won't get out to harm others. Then the subway start from the "Number Two" Cherry Street Station.

This legend was so widespread and influential that many writers of suspense novels had written it into their own books, claiming it to be true, but ignoring two basic facts: First, the incident two people were burn did happen, but the cause of the accident was a power outage caused by a power system failure. It was not the subway workers but two rescuers who burned to death. The departure point of the train had never been Deratization Hill Station, nor Cherry Street Station, but the Xijiao Depot. All subway trains here had daily parking, train inspection and overhaul repairs, and the routes were throughout east-west.

In addition, there was also the legend of the "last ghost subway". It was said that after the last train to Cherry Street Station leaves from Sihaitong Station, there would be a train behind it. This train had no passengers except the driver. And although it stopped at each station stops, the lights were not turned on throughout the whole process, like a black giant python all the way to the west, and would arrive at the Deratization Hill Station before 23:00, its function was to "transport the ghosts". Because many graves were dug up when the subway was built, the ghosts in the tombs were very angry, there was no sunlight inside the subway, the cold air was very heavy, so when the subway was closed for trial operation, they came out day and night to make trouble, which scared many subway company employees to death. In the end, the subway company invited the monks who were enlightened, and they did rituals for many days to appease them, and reached an agreement with them to drive an empty train before mid-night (23:00) every night to send them back to their original tombs for rest at the site where the tombs located. If they couldn't remember where the tomb was, then they would all go to the Deratization Hill Station to rest...

The legend that Deratization Hill Station is a shelter station was also ridiculous, not to mention the last train of the subway to Cherry Street Station, the departure time from Sihaitong Station was 23:40 on a daily basis, and 00:20 on Fridays past midnight, and considering the time when this subway line was closed for trial operation – on May 1, 1972, at that time, who dared to do something like the "monk's tricks"? And the last train to tansport the ghosts? However, it was said that after the last subway train, there would be another train, but it was true that it is only to pick up the subway employees after they getting off work, and the lights of the train were on and bright as day.

When looking into the causes of these legends, it was impossible not to consider the strange-sounding name of "Deratization Hill". Some boring literati who did not do rigorous research and just grabbed readers' attention based on some materials, said that this place was a random grave in the Qing Dynasty, specially burying those who suffered from plague, hence the name "Deratization Hill" . In the early years of the Republic of China, the Japanese opened a mental hospital here, where many Chinese patients died unexplainably and tragically. Till this day, in the middle of the night on Deratization Hill, their resentful spirits can still be heard screaming which was terrifying...

These groundless legends can be called a simmering with random additions after chopping up historical facts and putting them into a pot.

The origin of the name "Deratization Hill" can be traced back to Dou Yunhua, a great scholar in the Qing Dynasty. Dou Yunhua was born in the 52nd year of Qianlong's reign. He was smart and eager to learn since he was a child. Later, he became a student of Yao Nai, a generation of Wen-zong of the Tongcheng School. And he used to singing and drinking with Fang Dongshu, Yao Ying and Mei Zengliang. Although he went to Beijing several times to take the exam, he failed even in the field of Jianke, which was a disappointment. In his later years, he returned to his hometown, and took Yao Nai's sentence, and built the "Care about nothing Academy" on a wild ridge in Xishan Mountain, he taught students and writing books until the death of him in 2nd year in Xianfeng. Before Dou Yunhuan was alive, he liked to spread the precious collection of the academy's books on the ridge when on sunny days. Some students were worried that these books would be stolen by the villagers. Dou Yunhuan laughed and said, "Reading is to save people, why should we worried about the books? "This sentence was passed on to later generations, and people named this mountain "Books Drying Mountain", which shared the same pronunciation with "Deratization Hill" in Chinese.

It would be funny to say that Books Drying Mountain was a burial mound that specifically buries plague patients. In the Qing Dynasty, there was never a tombstone erected on the mountain, especially after Dou Yun-wat's death, this place became a holy place admired by students at home, how could there be tombs everywhere? In the early years of the Republic of China, there was indeed a nursing home in Lingshang, but it was a charity organization built by private merchants to raise funds for the adoption of widows and lonely people. Later, when the Anti-Japanese War broke out, this place was devastated by the war. The former academy really responded to the word "Nothing" of the "Care about nothing academy", and only the ruins were left standing here. In case of makeing people here feel sad, later the name changed to "Deratization Hill" – Deratization in Chinese was another name for squirrels among the people.

To sum up, all the terrifying legends about the Deratization Hill were mostly absurd. However, for people: those who was trouble-teller must be the troublemaker—peoplewere like this, so was the land. If there was a place where "strange tales" happened frequently and "stories people won't talk" was often mentioned, it can only mean that it had its own vampire physique, either it had produced evil spirits, or it would produce evil spirits, and it must be one of the two. ——Deratization Hill was undoubtedly the latter. This was also the fundamental reason why all kinds of spooky and terrible rumors spread like wildfire after the strange case that this book was about to tell happened.

2

On a December morning after the "Deratization Hill Case" was solved, the author of this book asked his old friend Huyan Yun to go to Deratization Hill, and asked him to tell me about the occurrence and cracking of this thrilling and strange case. When he heard my request, he didn't immediately agree, just said that it's been a long time we haven't meet each other, then have a walk on the hill.

We met at Cherry Street subway station. He still had a young baby face. He was in his thirties, but looked like he was only in his early twenties. He was wearing a Korean-style short black down jacket with a white cashmere scarf, and a pair of dark blue tight-fitting trousers, the clothing made him looked energetic and capable, and his eyes were as clear as before, but there was a faint sadness lingering between his eyebrows. I think, maybe he hasn't come out of the strange case more than a month ago.

Getting out of exit A of the subway and wait for the bus at the entrance of the Xijiao Municipal Engineering Company. It didn't take long for the bus to arrive. We sat next to each other in the double seat in the back, and as the car started, I saw out of the right window pass a khaki hillside with a grey water tower shaped like an upside-down pestle on a mound of dirt. The view here was completely different from the scenery in the city, made me feel that the Deratization Hill case had a completely different temperament compared with the cases I learned about Huyan Yun solved before. It was a kind of temperament unique to the urban-rural junction: cruel, rough, wild, dirty, like a half-human monster, above the waist was the ferocious countryside, below the waist was the monster city, grotesque and hideous.

The bus passed slowly on Yinlu Street, each stop was very short. The street was fairly clean and tidy. On both sides, there were still civilized buildings such as China Mobile Business Hall, Insurance Company, Jinjiang Inn, and Wumart Supermarket, but when we approached Qingshikou East Lane, the road suddenly narrowed like trousers, and there were many gaps in the road, fewer buildings but more bungalows. The large square windows were common here, the iron fence outside the window was stained with rust, and all kinds of weeds that can't be named grew in the gaps between the bricks...

"Get off." The car stopped, and Huyan Yun suddenly pulled me.

"We haven't arrived yet," I said. "The next stop will be Deratization Hill."

"Get off!" He swiped the bus card involuntarily, and I had to get out of the bus after him.

The place where we stood was right at the head of a stone bridge with white marble railings. Under the bridge was the wide aqueduct of Wuding River. The river running through the east and west ,and was dry, only gray-black frozen soil and some ice ballasts shining in the sun. At the western-most part of the canal, where was the top of the mountain, there was a blue-gray building with regular holes in all directions. Huyan Yun told me that it was the Qingshikou Hydropower Station built in 1964. After crossing the road, we walked westward along the north bank of the aqueduct, all the way up the steep slope, paved with uneven igneous rock or granite, and in particularly steep places there would be one or two stepped strip-stones. Stepping on it felt like the whole hillside was shaking. On our right hand side were the low brick houses that climb up the steep slopes, row upon row, the roofs were covered with black linoleum, and the mouthwash with the fragrance of spearmint slowly creeps down the ditch, a few people in red hoops were surrounding the door of a house, talking to a woman in purple long johns who was shivering from the cold. Beside the woman stands a little girl nibbling old corn, her cheeks and her padded jacket was as rough as red.

"The place in Deratization Hill can be regarded as the remnant of the Xishan Mountains to the south. If you look at the mountains, there is a clear downward trend in the Xishan Mountains." Huyan Yun pointed to the gently curving hillside in the distance and said, "After the completion of "Care about nothing academy", Dou Yunhuan was filled with emotion and wrote an essay to inscribe it, but the essay did not mention the academy, but spoke of the beauty of the Western Mountains."

It was a pity that a black dog locked in the aluminum alloy fence suddenly barked angrily at us, causing all dogs on the mountain to bark like scolding, without the quaintness of hundreds of years ago. Huyan Yun was very disappointed. We walked while chatting, and unknowingly we reached the top of the mountain and stood beside a white sign that read "everyone is responsible for forest fire prevention", and I was a little out of breath. This was a flat concrete field, surrounded by bare jujube trees and locust trees with bird cages, orioles, larks, starlings, etc., the birds were jumping and chirping, a few old people were sitting around a stone table playing poker quietly.

After a while, we continued to walk forward. There were several tall high-voltage line towers that look like a miniature version of the Eiffel Tower on the mountains, the towers connected with each other and crowded which stoppped our way upward. So we turned to the north and walked on a downhill cement road. Before walking a few steps, an east-west alley with a width of less than ten meters appeared in front of us. Perhaps because the school building on the south blocked the sunlight, the alley was abnormal. It was deserted, and there was no one at this moment. On both sides of the alley were long lead-grey walls about two meters high, the south wall was the Deratization Hill Middle School, and the north wall was—

Huyan Yun saw my question, nodded and said, "The inside is the Deratization Hill Station."

There was not a gloomy wind that usually appeared at this moment in suspense novels, but I felt my scalp was numb, and what's even worse, Huyan Yun added in a prank: "You might have read the news, the criminal was walking down this concrete road and drove to the back hill, success-fully avoiding the surveillance device."

Immediately before my eyes, a scene appeared, two scenes intertwined in the same background to be precise: a black INSPIRE driving slowly and silently through the alley, under the cover of night and driving down the mountain, leaving four bodies and a mysterious fire inside the fence for-ever; another scene was still in this alley, in the darker night, a dozen police cars, fire trucks and ambulances crowded together, and the flickering lights illuminated the night sky like an uncertain fright. People in black police uniforms, orange fire uniforms and white coats were busy and shuttled ner-vously, as if they were twisted together. The other end of the lead was the huge city with a population of 20 million at the bottom of the mountain. At the time, the sleeping city was completely unaware of the incident and the sensation it would cause, until the next morning, when people were wiping their sleepy eyes on the subway and browsing the news on their phones, they showed the same expressions of fear and surprise: Who did this? And why he left four charred corpses on Deratization Hill?

3

110 The phone records showed that the man called the police at 10:30 p.m. on the day of the incident. "His voice was low and his words were short," the policewoman who received the call recalled.

Only one sentence—

"The Deratization Hill subway is on fire, please send someone here!"

Then hang up.

The first reaction of the policewoman was that this was another one who should have called the 119 fire alarm and dialed 110 by mistake. According to the relevant regulations, she immediately notified the urban management and joint defense departments who patrolled at night in the Deratization Hill area, and sent them to check whether the fire was real and reliable, and to report as soon as possible.

About five minutes later, the feedback call came: "The alarm is true. A shaft next to the Deratization Hill subway is on fire. And the fire is very big. We have asked the fire brigade to come and put out the fire."

The second detachment of the fire squadron arrived at 10:45. After they drove the fire truck into the east-west alley, they immediately saw the urban management officer who was already waiting at the entrance of the alley. After driving more than ten meters into the alley, they found that there was an iron gate on the north wall, and the Deratization Hill subway station was inside. Because the fence gate was too narrow, the fire truck tried several times, but it was impossible to drive in, so it had to stop at the gate. A few firefighters, led by the detachment leader, went inside and found the spot of the fire to check the situation – in the eyes of the urban management, the "shaft" was actually the tunnel air pavilion used for ventilation in the old subway station. The overall structure of the tunnel air pavilion was made of concrete. The part exposed to the ground looked like an inverted "L". At the top of the horizontal line above, there was a square and spacious opening, which was usually covered with a protective net. Now the protective net had been taken off by someone unknown and was thrown aside. Inside the cave entrance was a blazing fire, casting a ghostly dance of fire shadows on the walls and ceiling of the cave.

The detachment leader was a little confused. Because the tunnel ventilation pavilions of old-fashioned subways were generally connected directly to the inside of the subway platform, the bottom end of the ventilation pavilions was mostly open on the ceiling of the subway tunnel. The most direct judgment of the current fire situation was that there was a big fire inside the subway station. Although Deratization Hill Subway Station had been out of service for a long time, because its tunnel was connected to Cherry Street Station, in order to prevent the spread of any disaster, the security system had not been withdrawn. If there was a fire in the platform or tunnel, the automatic sensing device should call the police immediately, but so far, there had been no call from COCC (the command center of the subway network). Could it be that the fire was only burning inside the tunnel air pavilion? How was this possible?

At this moment, a staff member on duty who was in charge of staying behind at the Deratization Hill subway station arrived.

After the Deratization Hill subway station was officially closed in 2008, urban explorers often tried to get into the station to take pictures, took pictures, and even stole subway equipment for "memorial", which not only caused trouble for management, but also brought all kinds of hidden safety danger. Therefore, the subway company set up iron fences in the tunnel in 2013 to prevent people from walking down the tunnel from Cherry Street Station; a fence was built outside the station, and pine trees and roses were planted inside, turning it into a nursery. Two of the three subway entrances were completely sealed with cement boards, leaving only one exit exposed outside the wall, and a thick steel anti-theft door was installed. Usually there was a gateman on duty named Cai who used the key to open the security door every morning at eight o'clock, entered the duty room below, and went up to the ground at 6 o'clock in the evening, locked the security door and left, which completely cutting off the thoughts of curious lovers.

Uncle Cai lived nearby. After receiving the alarm, the Fire Squadron contacted him through the subway company, considering that they did not know much about the specific fire situation and might need to enter the station to put out the fire. When the last left-behind of the Deratization Hill Subway came in a hurry, he was wearing a pair of cotton slippers with embroidered flowers on his feet.

Seeing that the tunnel wind pavilion was on fire, he breathed a sigh of relief: "It's okay, not a big deal. This subway station was built early, and the place is remote, so the open-cut method is used, that is, the well is drilled from top to bottom. Nearby conditions are complicated. Originally, there was a lot of granite residual soil on the Deratization Hill, which would easily turn into mud when it encounters water, causing the surface to subside and even collapse. Before builting the subway, the Qingshikou Hydropower Station was built beside, so except the precipitation treatment, a few more anti-flooding doors were also made. This wind pavilion did not go straight to the end, but had a hole in the tunnel wall and was separated by a flood-proof door. In the past, it was still in use when the subway was still running, the anti-flooding door was open. Later, the subway was shut down, some mischievous people wanted to get in, so they took off the protective net of the wind pavilion from the ground, and hung themselves down with ropes to the bottom, and then entered the subway. Then I locked the anti-flood door. This tunnel ventilation pavilion was no different from a shaft. The fire under the well can't burn the inside of the platform. The steel plate of the anti-flood door was thick enough! " He said confidently.

The detachment leader nodded and asked the firemen to use a large-caliber dry powder fire extinguisher to fill the tunnel air pavilion with fire extinguishing agent, and said to Cai: "Don't rejoice, the smell of fire gasoline can be smelled across three streets. Gasoline can burn as high as 3,000 degrees Fahrenheit, and stainless steel melts at 2,600 degrees Fahrenheit, so you'd better go inside and check the flood-proof door!"

Cai frightened to run to the subway station.

Under the pressure of the fire extinguishing agent, the tunnel air pavilion, which burned red like a furnace, gradually extinguished the fire. When the last wisp of white smoke dispersed from the wellhead, the darkness of the night enveloped this abandoned subway station again.

In order to find out the cause of the fire, a firefighter tied a safety rope, put on a helmet with LED lights, and a portable fire extinguisher on the fire belt, got into the tunnel wind pavilion, and slowly hang down with the help of his colleagues.

Generally speaking, most of the fires that occurred in urban waste wells were caused by bad teenagers or homeless people who live nearby, throwing cigarette butts or other kindling objects into it. Considering that the fuel for combustion was gasoline, the former was more likely to cause an accident. Firefighters called this kind of fire "both money and people", which sounds very unfortunate, but it was actually good intentions, which meant that there was neither economic loss nor casualties, and it was a daily fire accident. The next thing to do is to remind Cai: since the subway station was abandoned, it was better to completely seal the ground opening of the tunnel ventilation pavilion with cement boards to avoid the next fire. The detachment leader asked the other firefighters to return to the car, and just waited for the firefighter under the shaft to find the fire and find out the cause of the fire, and then went home...

Suddenly there was a shout, which was made by the fireman at the bottom of the well. The voice was muffled and humming. In addition, the night wind was blowing tightly, and the detachment leader could not hear it clearly. "What did you say?"

"There are dead people in the well!"

It was as if a hand had grabbed a fist in his heart, the detachment leader trembled. Years of work experience allowed him to know the seriousness of the matter only from the voices of his colleagues.

Next, the firefighter in the pit made him horrified: "Captain, hurry up and call the police, there is more than one body!"

"Calm down, what are you panicking about!" The detachment leader shouted down the well, before realizing that it was himself who was really panicking. He took a deep breath and felt that the breath air was not only cold but also overcast. The moment he inhaled it into his nose, the blood all over his body became cold, which made him didn't dare to take another breath. He found for a while and then realize the phone was on his hand, he took it and called the police immediately.

As far as the eye can see, there was only boundless darkness and the dark green of a clump of pine trees emerging from the darkness.

Here, the name of the firefighter needed to be recorded who went down to investigate: Chen Guoliang, it was he who calmly took the correct measures, so that the most important crime scene in this case could be relatively completely protected. And the significance of this to the detection of the Deratization Hill case would soon become apparent.

When he found charred human body under the shaft, he did not flip the body, but took off his fire gloves, took out his mobile phone, and used the lighting on his helmet to take pictures of the situation in the well, and then shouted his colleagues above the ground to prepare a fire-fighting blanket, spread it on the wellhead, and then asked them to pull him up. During the gradual ascent, he resisted the pain of being stretched by his muscles and did not step on any of the well walls. As soon as he got out of the wellhead, he took off the steel-bottomed fire-fighting rubber shoes and buckled them upside down on the fire-fighting felt, and told everyone "don't move".

During this period of time, the director of the Deratization Hill police station who received the alarm had arrived with several policemen. After listening to Chen Guoliang's report, the director used a strong light to look down the well, and he understood that this was not an common case, so he reported to the sub-bureau quickly. One sentence shocked the sub-bureau chief who was on duty that night: "The firefighter who went down said that there were about three corpses, two of which may be children..."

Once the case involved women, the elderly and children, it would attract the highest level of attention, so the head of the regional bureau reported it to the city bureau as soon as possible. The city bureau conveyed two orders: first, protect the scene and wait for the city bureau to send a commissioner to organize criminal investigation; second, conduct a search around the scene and detain all suspicious persons immediately.

In less than two hours, the Deratization Hill was heavily overrun. Dozens of armed policemen with guns and live ammunition tightly controlled all the surrounding traffic arteries, and the deterrent lines were as soild as iron buckets. Ambulances and police cars also rushed to arrive – at first, the alley was too small and caused congestion, but after the traffic police took away some illegally parked vehicles, the crowded condition was quickly relieved – along the south side of the alley, the deterretn line was lined up, so as to provide convenience for those who enter and exit the iron fence gate on the north wall of the alley. The leaders of Deratization Hill Middle School, which was located opposite, came over to learn about the situation, and organized the school affairs office and the student office to verify the movements of the resident students one by one. The main leaders of the district government also rushed to the scene in the shortest time and fully cooperated with the police investigation work.

Even according to the most stringent standards, the response of the relevant departments in the city in the first two hours after the Deratization Hill case broke out can be said to be impeccable.

Despite, the people standing at the crime scene, especially the police officers, were still in an uneasy mood. This was not only because of the danger and unpredictability of the case, but also because they knew: The "imperial minister" that the city bureau would soon send here was very likely to be a female police officer known for her harshness.

4

When Du Jianping jumped out of the police car, all the police officers had surprised expressions on their faces, and heaved a sigh of relief in unison.

Xu Ruilong, director of the Municipal Public Security Bureau, was a person with a strong sense of responsibility and foresight. Having spent his whole life in the police field, he realized very early that with the drastic changes of the times, the criminal investigation work must keep pace with the times. In addition to introducing advanced police equipment and reforming the cumbersome police system, it was also necessary to promote young police officers who were more scientifically minded and modern-minded on the basis of "brave, loyal, hard-working". After years of careful selection, he had reserved three outstanding young talents for the safety of the city for the next few decades: Lin Xiangming, who was in charge of criminal investigation, Liu Simiao, who was in charge of criminal technology, and Lei Rong, who was in charge of forensic medicine. They all graduated from the China Police Officers University and had many years of overseas study experience. They were all top talents in their respective fields. Criminal investigation, criminal technology and forensic medicine were the three core main departments of criminal investigation work, known as "three judicial divisions". With these three elites in charge, Xu Ruilong could not only sleep soundly, but also laugh out loudly in his dreams. But human beings were not as clever as heaven. Lin Xiangming's absence had caused a big hole in the criminal investigation. For a while, there was no talent that can match. There was no other way, so Liu Simio has to do it. After a year, Liu Simi became seriously ill, and even the leaders of the department called Xu Ruilong and said, "If Simiao is your own daughter, would you be willing to let her work like this?" Du Jianping, the former director of criminal investigation, who was suspended at home for personal reasons, was invited by Xu Ruilong to take charge of the criminal investigation work, while Liu Simiao continued to be in charge of her criminal technical department.

Therefore, when the Municipal Bureau learned that there was a case in Deratization Hill and that there might be children among the victims, it did not hesitate to send the leader of the "Three Judicial Divisions" to the crime scene, and explicitly ordered Du Jianping to preside over the criminal investigation work. The grassroots police officers were not so well-informed. They were trembling with fear when thought that the "boss" today might be Liu Simiao, who had always been cold-faced. So when they saw Du Jianping for the first time, they were overjoyed. Although "Boss Du" was also a fiery temper, and it was common for him to admonish the young police officers, but in private he treated every policeman as a brother, and invited them to have meals after solving each case... Unlike Liu Simiao, she only has business affairs and had no private relations with others. She worked hard, and had very strict requirements on her subordinates. There not allowed to make any mistake, otherwise you will suffer. For more than a year, the criminal policemen have been so busy that they couldn't even drink water, take off their shoes, wash their faces, and couldn't wait to sleep with one eye open. Although the security situation in this city had been ensured, they were still suffering and exhausted. Seeing Du Jianping's return, everyone felt amnesty.

Du Jianping smiled and greeted the old subordinates, as if they had never been separated. The police officers also rushed to shake hands with him, and every glance they cast towards him was full of affection and respect, but there was also a hint of surprise in these eyes: they haven't seen him for two years, Du Jianping was very old, and the old man with a strong back and an iron tower was gone, but replaced by an old man with a stiff waist and a little rickety, gray hair, thinking that he was only forty-nine years old this year, and the reasons that caused him to become like this, they were all sad. The only thing that made everyone happy was that, under the light of the bright halogen lamps that had just been erected, his big hands that could hold big stones were still rough and ruddy, and felt warm and strong.

The deputy director of the Criminal Investigation Department, Lin Fengchong, who had arrived ahead of schedule, briefly introduced to Du Jianping the team he had brought: 20 shrewd and capable criminal policemen selected from the Major Cases and Key Cases Division, and introduced the areas between the inner cordon and the outer isolation line. Watching this old subordinate wearing a black leather jacket with a moustache stomping on the ground unconsciously with his heels, Du Jianping knew that he was addicted to cigarettes, he took out a pack of cigarettes from his trouser pocket and handed it to him: "Have a refresh, we might go to have to stay up all night, you can't stand for such long."

"I dare not." Lin Fengchong said, "The rules set by Director Liu not allow us to smoke, otherwise the evidence might be contaminated."

"You didn't enter the scene again, what are you afraid of?" Du Jianping said with a smile.

"Not on the outside either." Lin Fengchong said with a wry smile.

Du Jianping stuffed the cigarette back into his pocket and went to the gate of the iron fence with Lin Fengchong. While putting on shoe covers, he learned about the situation from the director of the Deratization Hill police station, the deputy director of the sub-bureau in charge of criminal investigation, and the leader of the fire brigade. Walking in, he suddenly stopped again: "Wait a minute."

Waiting for what, he didn't say anything.

Which made a class of subordinates confused.

In less than a minute, a black Camry drove over. After the car pulled over and stopped, a very beautiful girl stepped out of the car. A black casual woolen coat made her looked lean and could not hide her beautiful figure. The high collar of the beige knitted sweater set off a snow-white melon seed face extraordinarily noble, the slightly raised chin seemed arrogant, and the pair of willow leaves eyebrows radiated a cold light, so that all the male police officers were nervous when they saw her, but they couldn't help but peek at her.

"Simiao!" Du Jianping greeted her as he stepped forward.

Liu Simiao shook hands with him and called out "Director", her palms were cold.

Looking at Liu Simiao, whose face was a little thin, Du Jianping was in a complicated mood. When this girl just returned from studying abroad, because she was too arrogant, she was rejected by others, and was sent to the press office as a publicity officer. It was not until the "serial breast-cutting murder case" happened in this city that Du Jianping tried every means to recall her into the task force and let her show her talent, which could be regarded as helping her to the first step on the road to promotion, but Liu Simiao did not express gratitude to him at all, but always maintained the courtesy and measure that a subordinate should have towards a superior. Since then, she had made continuous contributions, and her official position had risen like a rocket. Especially after Du Jianping's suspension, she had grown steadily. It didn't take long for her to become the most powerful division-level cadre in the history of the city's police, in charge of two of the "three judicial divisions". This time, to a large extent, it was because her superiors felt distressed that she was too tired, so they transferred him back to fill the vacancy. Du Jianping's mood could be imagined. In addition, there was one thing that he was aching and unwilling to tell others, that was, when something happened to his family, many old subordinates, including Lei Rong, came to visit and tried their best to help him heal the pain in his heart. Only Liu Simiao avoided it as far away as she had never heard of it, which gave him an unprecedented understanding of the warmth and coldness of human relationships, who had always had a rough temperament.

But today was different from the past. Liu Simiao was a talent that was highly valued by the leaders of the city and the ministry. The superior's order was to let him preside over the criminal investigation work of the Deratization Hill case, but since she was sent, it was best to discuss with her before every step, which was why he insists on "wait a second".

At this time, a forensic inspection vehicle converted from an ambulance drove from the entrance of the alley – the destruction of the corpses at the scene of the incineration and explosion was often very serious, and during the process of moving and transporting the corpse to the autopsy room, valuable corpse evidence was very likely to be left or lost, so the preliminary autopsy was mostly done on the forensic inspection car. Liu Simiao and Du Jianping thought it was Lei Rong, who knew that after the car stopped, a girl with ponytails and a round face with lovely eyebrows like Angela cat jumped out of the passenger car. She hugged Liu Simiao and said with a smile, "Sister, didn't expect it would be me?"

"Tang?" Liu Simiao was also taken aback, "Why are you here?"

Tang Xiaotang used to be a student of Lei Rong. After graduation, she went to work at Forensic Research Center with Lei Rong. She left for more than half a year for some reasons, and only came back at the end of last year. After going through some things, this squeamish and domineering official second-generation lady had matured a lot. She was very diligent in her work and had become a good assistant that Lei Rong couldn't leave. It was only considering that she was a girl, most of on scene work Lei Rong still arranged male colleagues to do, but it was a new thing to send her here today.

"The city bureau organizes the study of documents, they don't let sister Lei Rong leave, and other colleague also have tasks, so I asked for the work." Tang Xiaotang said.

For a long time in the past, Liu Simiao looked down on Tang Xiaotang, and Tang Xiaotang was a little afraid of her, so the two of them would nod at most when they met. But on a thrilling night last year, after Liu Simiao tried her best to save Tang Xiaotang from the brink of death, Tang Xiaotang became a "die-hard fan", which made Liu Simiao felt funny but bored, after a long time she also had a feeling of treating her like a little sister, and immediately urged: "Tang, this case may require testing several corpses that have been burned underground, so you must be mentally prepared."

"Don't worry, there was nothing else but the courage!" Tang Xiaotang said.

"Director Du, Director Liu!" Another police car drove into the alley, and what came down was Chu Tianying, who was the chief of the crime scene investigation section of the Criminal Technology Division of the Municipal Bureau not long ago. He was originally the director of the criminal investigation department of a neighboring province. He was famous in the police for his youth and excellent case handling ability, and was transferred to the city bureau by Xu Ruilong to hold a key position. Later, for unknown reasons, he was dismissed to the end and worked as a policeman at the Wangyue Park police station, but he still diligently serve the people. As his teacher at the China Police Officers University, Liu Simiao, of course, couldn't watch such a talented person succumb to the grassroots, so she tried every means to transfer him to the Criminal Technology Department to focus on the crime scene investigation work in major cases.

All the police officers standing in the alley understood: this time, the elite forces of the city bureau's criminal investigation department, except for Lei Rong, have all arrived, and they were waiting for Du Jianping to issue orders.

Who would have thought that the first order Du Jianping issued was: "Simiao, come and assign tasks!"

Hearing this sentence, many people were taken aback, but Liu Simiao only glanced at Du Jianping and nodded. She first learned about the basic situation from the incident to the present, then put on a white disposable protective coat and shoe covers, walked into the gate of the fence, and inspected the inside of the fence, found that the whole fence of the Deratization Hill subway station was completely surrounded by a rectangle, and the top of the wall was embedded with glass ballast, which was impossible to climb over. The subway station had three ground entrances and exits, each of which had the same shape: a lying rectangle with a lid on a protruding edge at the top, liked a sliding coffin, but the Deratization Hill subway station lacked maintenance and was not even painted after completion. So it was still the original color of the cement. Among them, Exit A, which was the only one that was not sealed with cement boards and had a steel anti-theft door – was located in the southeast corner of the nursery, and the anti-theft door was exposed outside the wall, facing the alley; Exit B was in the northeast corner of the nursery; the Exit C was far away from the Exit AB, and it was located in the southwest corner of the nursery; In the nursery, apart from the pine trees on the supports and the withered roses, there were dozens of locust trees with very long years. The branches and trunks of the fallen leaves were swaying in the cold wind, as if a large group of half-old milfs were dancing gracefully, a dilapidated windmill wrapped around a locust branch near the Exit C. A canal for irrigation runs through was in the nursery, which was empty of water and stuffed with curled dead leaves.

After leaving the nursery, Liu Simiao called several leaders together and began to arrange the work.

"I will temporarily delineate the scope of investigation in this nursery, and the central area is the tunnel wind pavilion." Liu Simiao spread a piece of white and wide drawing paper on the front cover of the car, in order to prevent it from being blown by the raging night wind, she used two police ceiling lamps to hold down the two ends. She used a carbon pen to outline the scene sketches on it, while marking the key points with police legends, "The camera team will fix the panoramic photos from different angles as soon as possible. Among them, on-site orientation photography, on-site overview photography, and on-site photography at the center must be done well... Unfortunately, a firefighter went down under the tunnel wind pavilion and did not take pictures in time. I hope his work did not cover up or destroy the original traces."

"Don't worry, Director, after the fireman found out that there was a dead person, not only did he not move the shaft, but he also took a few pictures and sent them to my mobile phone. I will send them to you now." The deputy director in charge of criminal investigation said while forwarding the photo to Liu Simiao by WeChat.

Liu Simiao was very surprised, opened the photos one by one and said immediately, "Where is that fireman? Get him right away!"

Chen Guoliang was invited over by several criminal policemen, but he still had not taken off his fire suit. Liu Simiao stared at him: "Have you ever been a criminal police officer before?"

Chen Guoliang had never seen such a beautiful female police officer, and she was actually an official. He was startled, nodded, and admitted that he used to be a criminal police officer in a certain province.

"That's it, the photos are very well-organized, and the fact that the helmet light is used instead of the mobile phone flash is worthy of praise." Liu Simiao said, "Have you taken other on-site protection measures?"

Chen Guoliang said that he didn't touch the well wall when he came up. In order to prevent any evidence from getting on the bottom of his fire boots, he put his boots upside down on the fire blanket after he came up, and so on. Liu Simiao nodded after listening. "Very good!" and then let him rest.

"For so many years, I haven't heard Director ever praised us." Lin Fengchong said with a smile.

Liu Simiao glared at him and said to the deputy director in charge of the criminal investigation work of the district bureau: "Select a few competent subordinates, and visit all the households within one kilometer of the other side, and visit them door-to-door to ask whether there has any special circumstances before and after the incident. It's midnight right now, the masses may all fall asleep and be called up, and they would not be pleasant, but we should also pay attention to visit as soon as possible, don't leave a single one."

After the deputy director took the order, she said to Lin Fengchong: "You quickly get in touch with the Municipal Traffic Management Bureau and the Municipal Network Security Office (Network Security Office), and check the surveillance video of all the streets and streets near the Deratization Hill Metro Station within two hours before and after receiving the report, and you must take the staff to check it yourself, edit the suspicious images and videos, and make them available for us to read at any time. You'd better take the shortest time to find out what transportation the suspect used to transport the body and escape. From this, we can find out the specific route of his communication. If need the cooperation of the FAST, then directly ask the bureau to 'open the way' (provide full technical support such as high-definition data processing or face recognition), don't need to file an application report!"

Next came the crime scene investigation, which was the heart of criminal investigation. Perhaps because she had a premonition that the case was particularly serious, Liu Simiao couldn't help turning her head and glanced at the nursery gate, which had been cordoned off with yellow and white lines: at this moment, six 2-kilowatt police halogen lamps were lit up in the nursery, which made the scene like in the daytime. Both the ground, trees, ditches, and the police officers who were drawing in and out of the passage with white chalk were as pale as blood loss. And those three entrances which were originally hidden in the deep forest, now were exposed under the corpse lamp. They all looked vicious as if they would open their mouths at any time and swallow all the creatures that disturbed their good dreams.

"Tianying, you divide the detectives brought by Fengchong into two teams, and let Team A go south along the north wall, and Team B go west along the east wall, and line them up in one line, one arm's distance apart and push forward, search for evidence – pay attention to avoid the central area of 10 square meters around the tunnel ventilation pavilion. After the two groups of A and B have searched, they will exchange for a second search, team A will go east along the west wall, and team B will go north along the south wall." Speaking of this, she suddenly increased her tone, "I put the harsh words in advanve. Team A found evidence that Team B missed, then I punished Team B; Team B found evidence that Team A missed, then I punished Team A!"

"This—" Chu Tianying felt a little inhumane.

"This is order, just do it!" Liu Simiao said inseparably, "As for yourself, two things, one is to separate and extract the tire tracks of suspicious vehicles that have entered this nursery; the other is to surround the central area of the tunnel wind pavilion. Go through the grid and do on-site investigation. Tang Xiaotang and I entered the shaft to conduct investigation and autopsy work." After speaking, she raised her head and asked, "Does everyone understand? Are there any questions—"

Before she could finish speaking, she heard Lin Fengchong coughing twice.

Liu Simiao suddenly realized something, and quickly stood up straight and asked Du Jianping beside him: "Director Du, how is the arrangement? Is there anything else to add?"

"I think it's pretty good." Du Jianping smiled, "It's just that some people do the survey on the ground, why is there no one to do the survey underground?"

Lin Fengchong and Chu Tianying looked at each other and didn't understand what he meant, but Liu Simiao suddenly realized that, just as she was about to speak, Du Jianping put out his hand and waved twice: "Come on, you're all busy, leave this to me, I'm a big idler." After saying that, he walked towards the steel security door exposed outside the fence at Exit A of the subway station.

5

Every inch the rescue rope went down, the temperature in the shaft became a little colder. Maybe this was just an imaginary caused by fear, but Tang Xiaotang really regretted the "volunteering" just now.

Originally, Liu Simiao said that she would go down the well for investigation, but Tang Xisotong said with a serious face: "The outdoor crime scene is greatly affected by the weather, and the most important evidence – the corpses were particularly vulnerable to damage, so the forensic doctor should conduct an autopsy first. "Liu Simiao looked at her, nodded, and instructed the two words, "Bold and careful," and asked the fireman named Chen Guoliang to bind her waist and shoulders with a steel wire inner rescue rope. Fasten the nut and steel buckle and put her down the shaft.

But right now, she couldn't restrain every cold hair on her body from standing upright...

The bottom was bottomless black, head up was a hopeless lead color, the suspended body was slowly sinking as if it was about to be buried alive, the rough gray-white well wall hung with dry powder fire extinguishing agent was like inner abdomen of a giant python, this image made her so sick that she wanted to vomit, and the gastric acid kept rising upwards in her stomach. The waist and armpits were aching due to the binding of the rescue rope, and an ugly pattern suddenly appeared in her mind. Her nightmare struck again, and although it didn't break her heart, but was enough to make her shiver. She really wanted to call the people above to pull herself up, but there was no sound coming out of her throat.

At this moment, her toes suddenly tiptoed on something soft...

She slowly stood still, pulled the rope twice, told the person above that she had arrived at the bottom, and took a few deep breaths. She wanted to calm down, but her nose was suddenly filled with a choking stench. It was a peculiar odor after burnt skin and head. She wanted to turn on the LED light on the helmet, but the touch of the fingers wearing rubber gloves made her take a long time to touch it. .

A large mass of pure black and dark red muddy paste, covered with a thin layer of white dry powder fire extinguishing agent, was discarded at the bottom of the deep well like raw meat wrapped in flour and ready to be put into a frying pan. The light was so bright but it still took a long time to make out the stacked human figures. Under the burning fire, these charred bodies have been twisted and deformed, just like the cars that collided and burst into flames on the highway. The curled or bare bones stood strangely and abruptly, as if they were still stretching and spreading at the bottom of this narrow well, and struggling unwillingly. Tang Xiaotang stood horribly for a long time before she timidly probed the corpses with a stainless steel rake, confirming that they could neither be human nor ghosts, and then dared to gently flip the corpse with her fingers to check the basic condition of the corpse. .

There were three corpses in total. The bottom one was an adult, lying on his back. The surface of the body was not seriously charred, but the two arms were curled up very strongly, and were raised upwards, as if a monkey was holding the two corpses above. What was frightening was that the mouth of his blackened skull was still half-open, and under the light, his white teeth were bared outwards, looking particularly hideous. Above this corpse, another corpse's skull had been broken, and the overflowing brains have solidified on the surface of the skull, and had been burned into a black line. The surface of the corpse on the top had a crack like a knife and an axe. The fire not only scorched the corpse, but the furious tongue of fire seemed to pierce from the throat of this corpse, and it stirred like a river in the stomach, so that a section was dirty. The vessel flowed out from the crack, revealing seven ripe red sauces.

"Tang." Liu Simiao's voice came from the earphone, "How is the situation?"

Tang Xiaotang looked up at the wellhead, but did not see Liu Simiao, the wellhead was very high, like another bottom of the well with no end in sight.

She sighed and said to the police bluetooth intercom pinned to her collar: "It's a mess. All three bodies were badly burned, and the burns were all grade IV. The surface of the body was charred and there was no sign of survival, which was the result of long-term burning in the flame. The preliminary judgment of the combustion accelerant is gasoline, because the exposed bones are light gray, and there are heated cracks on the outside. This is the calcined bone produced by the high temperature formed by the combustion of gasoline. Such a state of the corpse is obviously not suitable to carry to the forensic inspection car for the first autopsy. It's better to do it here... Sister, the three bodies were burnt and entangled together, like a twist. I want to separate them and check them one by one. But I'm afraid of destroying the original traces, what should I do?"

"Tang, you have to read carefully before drawing a conclusion." Liu Simiao's tone suddenly became serious, "Are the corpses entangled, or are they entangled because of distortion, but in fact they can be separated? Because the former is often the reaction of victims who were burned to death struggling to the exit of the fire, while the latter is the situation where the collective burning of corpses occurs after death, which is directly related to the direction of the investigation of the case, and there can be no mistake at all... When I look at the photos taken by Chen Guoliang, why do I feel that the bodies are just piled up in a mess, and there is no actual entanglement?"

Tang Xiaotang calmed down and looked at the three corpses before saying embarrassedly, "Uh...Sister, you are right again."

"Remember what I said to you 'bold and careful'!" Liu Simiao said, "Now open the body slowly, and then dictate the autopsy situation, and I will make a transcript."

There was a rustling sound in the earphones, probably Liu Simiao was holding a notebook.

Tang Xiaotang carefully observed the top corpse and said: "The body No. A, male, according to the development of bones and teeth, he was about twelve years old, about 130 centimeters tall, and the cause of death was unknown. The corpse was in a supine position, with fourth-degree burns, no clothing or other textile covering on the body surface, tissue was hard and brittle, black and no structure, linear rupture wounds along the skin lines, and some organs flowed out of the wounds."

Then, she held the corpse's side and slowly turned it over, causing it to roll to the side, and the palm of her hand that could not be distinguished from the five fingers slapped on her shoe, scaring her saying "ah".

"Tang, are you alright?" Liu Simiao's voice sounded in the earphones again.

"It's all right." After Tang Xiaotang observed the second corpse, she continued to report in a low voice: "Body No. B, female, age about nine years old, about 110 cm tall, cause of death was unknown, state of death was supine, IV degree burns, no clothing or other textile covering on the body surface, tissue was hard and brittle, black and no structure. Skull rupture along the natural suture, blood and brain plasma overflow, forming a strip of coagulation on the surface of the skull."

"What?" Liu Simiao's surprised voice suddenly came from the earphone.

Tang Xiaotang hurriedly explained: "The skull is like a sealed container, which contains liquid and moist brain tissue. When the liquid inside reaches the boiling point at high temperature, it will generate huge pressure. Children's skulls can't stand this kind of pressure. With pressure, the entire skull can rupture or even burst along the natural sutures..."

"Of course I know this." Liu Simiao said, "I'm just surprised that the height and age of these two children are not matched... It's okay, go on."

Tang Xiaotang put the second corpse aside, observed the third corpse, and said, "The corpse No. C, male, over 50 years old, 170 cm tall, and the cause of death was unknown. Supine, fourth-degree burns, the clothes and shoes of the deceased have been charred, the evidence sample is of little value. The upper limbs of the corpse showed an obvious 'boxing stance', which was the coagulation and contraction of the muscles after encountering high temperature, and the flexors (resulting in bending of the limbs) is stronger than that of the extensors (the muscles that straighten the limbs) , which cannot be used as a basis for identifying burns before death or cremation after death, but it can show that the effect of high temperature is longer... Oops, there seems to be something in the corpse's hand! "

"What?" Liu Simiao asked while exhorting, "Don't take important physical evidence directly with your hands, use tweezers to observe."

Tang Xiaotang was very obedient, unzipped the evidence extraction kit from her waist, took out tweezers, squatted down, and picked up the thing that was still bright despite being covered with a layer of dust: "Sister, I found an adult watch, Vacheron Constantin's, the strap was burned and left only a little, the cover has been broken, the hour and minute hands stop at 10:31, and it should be worn by the corpse of the man number C when he died."

"It can not be sure, it's also possible that the murderer wore it, slipped or was stripped during the process of throwing the body down the well—"

Before Liu Simiao's words could be finished, she was suddenly interrupted by a soft cry from Tang Xiaotang: "Wait a minute, there's something wrong with this corpse, why is it so much higher than the ground? This is... my God! "

Liu Simiao was used to Tang Xiaotang's surprise, but this time it was not quite right, because the earphones suddenly fell into a dead silence, so that Liu Simiao thought that the earphones were broken and tapped with hwe fingers. But there was still no sound. Just as she brought the Bluetooth intercom closer to her lips and was about to call Xiao Tang, a sob suddenly came from the earphones...

Not far away, Chu Tianying, who was pouring plaster into the tire tread, suddenly raised his head and looked at Liu Simiao, his eyes glowing with surprise.

Generally speaking, in the process of crime scene investigation, the police bluetooth intercom should allow all police officers in the area to listen and talk. Liu Simiao was worried about interfering with each other, and secondly, she worried about leaking secrets, and only opened the dialogue channel of Tang Xiaotang, Chu Tianying, Lin Fengchong, Du Jianping and herself, so Chu Tianying was surprised by Tang Xiaotang's sudden sob. Immediately afterwards, Lin Fengchong's voice came from the earphone: "Tang, what happened? Answer me!"

A gust of gloomy wind, as if coming from the ground, suddenly cut across the Deratization Hill as if it was slashing in the waist, making a shrill cry in the void, and the thorns and withered grass were shivering.

Liu Simiao turned her back to the wind and said to the Bluetooth intercom: "Tang, if you don't explain the situation, I will immediately go down to support you—"

"There..." Tang Xiaotang finally made a crying voice, "There is also a corpse, which was pressed under the body of No. C. It is a little girl, she looks like only three or four years old..."

Liu Simiao felt a tightness in her chest. Although she had investigated countless crime scenes, even though she had heard and witnessed the most horrific crimes. Like all criminal police officers, even if she was born with a hard heart, she could rarely control the anger and sadness in front of the corpse of the young child even if at the retirement age.

Perhaps it was because of the unbearable scene that Tang Xiaotang finally burst into tears, as if she had opened the emotional valve.

Liu Simiao wanted to comfort her, but couldn't find words for a while, so she could only be silent. As time passed by, Tang Xiaotang's crying showed no sign of stopping, which made Liu Simiao a little irritable. At this moment, a heavy voice came from the earphone: "Tang, are you there?"

This voice belonged to Du Jianping, but it didn't look like Du Jianping, because it was not as simple and rough as before, but instead had some stupid and gentle gentleness, like a father who was even more overwhelmed when he saw his daughter made a mistake.

Tang Xiaotang was startled, and quickly wiped her tears with her sleeve: "Director, I'm here!"

"Finish the work first." The voice was still so rough and gentle, "Don't be afraid, I'm going down to the subway station, right next door to you." Then, at the bottom of the shaft was also burned to the ground, there was a soft knock on the black flood-proof door.

Tang Xiaotang suddenly felt warmth in her heart, Director Du was like an old lion, but in the hearts of all police officers, he was like a mountain, and having him by his side meant that they had something to rely on and must be strong.

"Yes! I will go on with the autopsy!" she said.

6

"The body number D, female, about three or four years old, about 90 centimeters tall, with no clothing or other textile covering on the body surface. Because she was lying prone and pressed at the bottom, the burning of the body was not that serious. The burn level was III degree, and the side of the body, especially the limbs, are more severely burned, and the skin was coagulated and necrotic." Tang Xiaotang slowly stretched out his hand

and gently turned her over: this was a good-looking little girl with thin eyebrows, thin lips and a pointed chin, she looked like the little Lin Daiyu in "A Dream of Red Mansions for Children", but her cheeks were a little thin... Her eyes were still half-open, indicating that she was burned after her death. In the case of a person who was burned to death during his lifetime, the high-temperature burning will cause the victim to instinctively close eyes, and the tip of the eyelashes will be scorched but the root will not be damaged – this is not the case for people who were burned after death.

Tang Xiaotang's eyes slowly moved down, and she suddenly discovered a very important situation. She turned on the LED light, peeled off the skin of the little girl's throat and looked at it again and again, and then whispered: "The victim had obvious strangulation marks on the throat, the cable groove was deep, and there was an eight-character intersection on the back of the neck. The cause of death was mechanical suffocation, homicide."

Liu Simi's low voice came from the other end of the earphone: "Okay, the preliminary autopsy is done. Next, we have to take all the corpses to the Forensic Research Center for a laboratory autopsy. I'll leave this to Lei Rong to complete."

Tang Xiaotang was relieved and let out a long sigh: "Sister, I'll go up now, it's your turn to do the crime scene investigation—"

Liu Simiao interrupted Tang Xiaotang: "No, Tang, you do the investigation."

"What?" Tang Xiaotang was stunned. "Me? I'm not a crime scene investigation expert."

"But there is only one chance to investigate the crime scene. No matter how many people go down later, it can only be counted as re-examination or re-examination." Liu Simiao said, "This tunnel ventilation pavilion is a narrow scene, and two people have already gone down. If you come up and exchange with me, this process will unintentionally destroy some important evidence. You are a graduate of China Police University, and crime scene investigation is a compulsory course, you have mastered the basic essentials. Since you just volunteered to be the first to the crime scene, then I ask you to also order you to complete the preliminary investigation of the crime scene."

Tang Xiaotang glanced at the little girl's corpse, and said to the Bluetooth intercom: "Copy that! It's just that I almost forgot about the course... Sister, please teach me how to do it."

"Okay. The basic work of crime scene investigation can be summed up in two words, that is: observation, search. This is also the order of crime scene investigation, and we will follow this order." Liu Simiao said, "First of all , you look carefully at the bottom and the wall of the shaft, and don't miss any corners. Don't rely on the helmet light for lighting, but use a hand-held torch. You don't need to turn off the helmet light, just use it as a supplementary light source. Don't move first, take a picture of its original position with a mobile phone, and then use tweezers to extract it – a special reminder: pay attention to your feet, which is the most easily overlooked place by the surveyors."

According to Liu Simiao's instruction, Tang Xiaotang turned on the flashlight, squatted down, and observed the bottom of the square shaft inch by inch like a CT scan. The cross-sectional area of the shaft was three to four square meters. Due to the protective net at the entrance to the ground, although a thick layer of dust had accumulated at the bottom of the shaft, branches, leaves, and mouse carcasses can occasionally be analyzed from the ashes, but no other junk. Except the corpses, if the dry powder floating on the surface was wiped off, one can even see the true color of the cement. In contrast, the situation on the side of the well was much worse. On the side of the well that was close to the corpse, it may be because the fire was too big, or because the gasoline splashed on the prisoner when he pours gasoline down, the flames adhere to it. It rose and burned into a large black like splashing ink. In addition, due to the unevenness of the well wall itself, dry powder was hung on it, as if a large group of gray ghosts were struggling to climb towards the wellhead, which was very scary.

"Sister, after I finished, the edges and corners and even the soles of my own shoes didn't miss, except that the well wall was burnt darker, and I didn't find any special signs. Apart from the Vacheron Constantin watch, the only thing I found was a black Zippo windproof lighter, probably the igniter, and nothing else was found. The clothes of the corpse No. C were so badly burned that I searched and found no phone, keys, wallet, or anything else that would identify him. Of course, trace substances such as fingerprints, hair, fibers, etc. may be left, but basically they were all burned clean by the fire."

After listening to Tang Xiaotang's report, Liu Simiao pondered for a moment and said, "What about the flood prevention door?"

"Anti-flooding door?" Tang Xiaotang was stunned for a moment. The light from the torch involuntarily lighted the anti-flooding door. The long and narrow steel plate was tightly embedded in the door frame on the side of the well, and the lower part was burne dark, but the upper part still kept the lead blue finish, "The door... the door doesn't have any evidence?"

"Tang." Liu Simiao said, "How do you think the criminals threw these four corpses into the tunnel wind pavilion?"

"Of course, the protective net above was opened, and then they were thrown down one by one!"

"On the surface, many signs did show that the criminal opened the protective net and threw the body from above, but don't forget that there is also a flood-proof door, so it cannot be denied that the murderer transported the body from the Deratization Hill subway station. The possibility cannot be dennied of burning the body after entering the wind pavilion in the tunnel, and removing the protective net at the entrance of the wind pavilion was just an illusion deliberately created by the criminal in order to disturb the police investigation—"

Suddenly, Du Jianping's voice came from the earphone: "Simiao, allow me to interject, it's not very likely as what you said. I asked Cai, and this flood-proof door was usually locked, and only three keys can be opened, one is in the subway safety supervision department, one is in the depot in the Western Suburbs, and the other is in the duty room. Because it has not been opened once for many years, even Cai can't remember where the key was placed, he is goijng back to the duty room to find it. Besides, if the criminal wanted to sneak into the Deratization Hill subway station, he must open the security door at Exit A. There are also three keys for the security door, and they are placed in the safety supervision department, just like the keys for the flood-proof door, in the depot and in Cai's, this key is tied to the waistband of Cai's trousers. How could the criminal get the keys to two doors in a row, and then carry four corpses back and forth to the dark and set fire in the subway station? And I just walked down from the subway station entrance to the flood-proof gate. There is a thick layer of dust on the platform floor, but I didn't see any footprints of strangers."

Liu Simiao was silent for a while and said, "Director Du, I admit that you are right, but to be sure, I would like to ask Tang to check the door to see if there is any sign that it had been opened before or after the fire."

Tang Xiaotang squatted down again, and used a flashlight to look at the part where the bottom of the door and the door frame were engaged for a long time: "Sister, judging from the dust accumulation at the part where the bottom of the door and the door frame are engaged, there is no trace of overall separation, at least this one. The door must not have been opened after the fire. As for before the fire, it was the same, even if there were any traces, it was completely burnt."

Liu Simiao sighed, the old criminal police officersoften said that there were "three fears" at the crime scene: one was water, the other was burning, and the third was the crowd watching for curiosity. These three were the best ways to break or even destroy criminal evidence. Now that they encountered.

At this moment, Tang Xiaotang at the bottom of the shaft suddenly heard running sounds and shouts of "I found it, I found it" from the other side of the anti-flooding door, and then the keyhole rang "crashing", and the door burst into the ground and smoked. The door shook a few times, and pushed away from the inside (in the subway station) to the outside (the tunnel wind pavilion)—because the corpses were in the way, only a very narrow gap was pushed open, which would be enough for Du Jianping to put his head in.

"Director!" Tang Xiaotang greeted Du Jianping happily.

Du Jianping nodded at her, glanced slowly into the shaft, and muttered, "Look at what I'm talking about, this door is narrow, so it can only be pushed out, and the shaft is not big, if the murderer wants to throw corpses here from the subway station, he had to open the flood prevention door wide, but after so many corpses were piled up, the door can't be closed... Simiao, if Tang finishes the investigation, you will send someone down to take the corpses away."

7

Liu Simiao sighed softly as she watched the forensic inspection vehicle with the four corpses turn a corner at the entrance of the alley and drive to the Lei Rong's Forensic Research Center. Fundamentally, the first priority in criminal investigation of all homicide cases was the identification of the victim, which required forensic doctors and on-site investigators to find answers from the two aspects of the corpse and the environment in which the corpses were located. Tang Xiaotang's autopsy and underground investigation both showed that the murderer not only stripped the three children's clothes, but also took away all the items that could identify the adult victim, and burned the traces and evidence with a fire. In this way, even Lei Rong, the top forensic officer in the country, might not be able to find the identification of the corpse through a laboratory autopsy. Therefore, the burden on her shoulders was particularly heavy.

At this time, Lin Fengchong and Chu Tianying came to her together. It seemed that they wanted to report the progress of the work. She waved her hand and signaled to wait. Du Jianping, who was talking about something with Cai, was invited back and listened together.

Four people got into Du Jianping's car – a police Passatri. Du Jianping took out his cigarette, lit it while apologizing to Liu Simiao, and took two sips. Liu Simi looked at the time on the dashboard, it showed that it was two in the morning, and grabbed the pack of cigarettes in Du Jianping's hand, rolled down the car window and handed it to a policeman with red eyes on the side of the road: "It was given by Director Du, except for those who are on guard duty, others can relax outside the alley." After hearing this, Lin Fengchong quickly took out a cigarette from his pocket and lit it up, his face was full of joy like a miner taking a hot bath .

"Let me report first." Chu Tianying was not tired, and the eyes under his sword eyebrows were still bright, "According to Director Liu's instructions, Team A and Team B conducted a strip search in the nursery, and exchanged to conduct a second search. Except for the ruts where the suspect vehicle entered and exited, there was no other discovery. I have already extracted the tire pattern, and the visual observation was that it was a Michelin 3ST Haoyue. There were many family cars and commercial vehicles equipped with such tires. It's hard to identify the specific brand and model of the suspect vehicle in short time. As for this nursery, according to the administrator we found, it was fenced in 2013. After the Deratization Hill Subway Station was closed in 2008, there were many young get into the station and spread horrible rumour. The subway head office completely blocked two of the three subway exits with cement boards and planted pine trees and roses. The iron fence gate of the nursery was not locked, and usually only a symbolic chain was hung, because even if enter the nursery, it will not be able to get off the subway station, and gradually there will be no idle people waiting. On-site investigation showed that the suspect was likely to know this, after driving the car into the alley, he opened the iron fence door, and then drove the car into the nursery to throw the corpse, a lot of fingerprints were extracted on the iron fence door, but on weekdays the administrators and garden workers all come in and out, so we can only check those fingerprints one by one, and it's not sure if the suspect was wearing gloves."

"Are there many people who know the iron gate isn't locked?" Liu Simiao asked.

"There should be quite a few." Lin Fengchong said, "The branch leader in charge of visiting the masses said that although the area of Deratization Hill has been demolished in recent years and many old residents have moved to other places, it is notoriously gentle slopes. On weekends and holidays, many people who like to exercise like to take the first bus here. At five or six o'clock in the morning, they climb the Wuding River aqueduct to the top of the mountain, then turn a corner and come down this alley, and even walk back and forth a few times. They can see the iron gates are unlocked."

Liu Simiao asked him, "How is the surveillance video? Have you found the suspect vehicle? And the escape route of the suspect vehicle?"

"The Municipal Traffic Management Bureau and the Municipal Network Security Office received our request for assistance in the investigation and were very cooperative. They immediately transferred to us the surveillance video of the streets near the Deratization Hill subway station within two hours before and after receiving the report. But after all there is far from the main city, so there is only one real street, here." Lin Fengchong opened the police ground information system in the tablet computer, and made an introduction, "This street runs north-south, with the Wuding River Diversion Canal Bridge as the boundary, to the south is Yinlu North Street, and to the north is Yinlu Mountain Road. Yinlu North Street still looks like a city street, but not the Yinlu Mountain rd. There is not even a decent intersection, only some T-junctions. The nearest monitor is installed at the traffic light in the east of Qingshikou on Yinlu North Street. The alley leading to the nursery is located on Yinlu Mountain Road , and it is east-west, so if the suspect vehicle is driving from south to north from Yinlu North Street, we can still photograph it after passing the traffic lights in the east of Qingshikou. If the suspect drove from Yinlu Mountain Road from north to south, there's no surveillance camera at all—"

Chu Tianying interrupted him and said, "Director Lin, we used an electrostatic adsorption instrument to extract the tire traces on the cement floor of the alley, and found the traces left by the Michelin 3ST Haoyue tires. According to the trend of the ruts, it is certain that the suspect vehicle drove from south to north from Yinlu North Street, and then entered this alley from the east exit."

"That is to say, there is a high possibility that the suspect vehicle was photographed by the monitor on the traffic light in Qingshikou Dongli." Liu Simiao said, "Based on the fire situation and the alarm time, the fire should have started around 10:30. Then check all the vehicles passing through the traffic lights in Qingshikou Dongli, which were captured by the monitor after 8 o'clock last night—no, after 6 o'clock!"

"I have'an idea." Du Jianping said, "All the monitors on the traffic lights are bidirectional, so, how about just check which car drove from south to north on Yinlu Mountain Road after six o'clock last night, and drive from north to south to Yinlu North Street after at ten thirty?"

"Director Du, your method is really good, but it must be based on a premise that the suspect returned to the city the same way after committing the crime." Chu Tianying said, "The problem is that we have a problem with the Michelin 3ST Haoyue in the alley. The results of the tire trace extraction proved that the escape route of the suspect vehicle was almost certain to have been driven westward to Deratization Hill after leaving the nursery—it did not return to the city the same way."

A look of disappointment appeared on Du Jianping's face: "So, is it possible to implement long-distance tracking along the traces of Haoyue's tires?"

"I can only try it." Chu Tianying smiled wryly, "There is a long gravel road on the Deratization Hill, and it is difficult to extract the traces of the vehicle tires..."

Du Jianping was unwilling: "Isn't there a radar station on the Deratization Hill, no monitor installed?"

Chu Tianying pointed to the west entrance of the alley. Under the dark night, the undulating figure of Deratization Hill was as unpredictable as the ridge of a beast: "Either the radar station on Deratization Hill or the middle school next door, their surveillance cameras are all set at the door or in the courtyard, the road cannot be photographed, and if you go further west along the road, then it will enter the mountain, and there is no monitoring device..."

"A cunning criminal," Du Jianping said, sucking on his cigarette, "it seems that he has long thought about the evacuation route and how to avoid surveillance."

Liu Simiao shook her head gently.

"Simiao, don't you agree?" Du Jianping asked.

"I think, if he really thought about it, why didn't he just take the mountain road around Deratization Hill and enter the alley from the west entrance, so that he could completely avoid the monitors on the traffic lights in the east of Qingshikou?"

"Maybe it's an emergency, so he can't go that far..."

"Four lives, three of which are children. Once he is caught, he will inevitably die. Compared with this, it is nothing to go far."

There was silence in the car for a while, and no one could answer Liu Simiao's question. After a while, Liu Simiao spoke first: "Director Lin, as I said just now, all the vehicles passing through the traffic lights in Qingshikou East Lane after 6 o'clock last night, check them one by one. Verify the whereabouts, find out the unit or individual to which they belonged, and if there is a major suspicion, the Municipal Traffic Management Bureau must give me a clear trace."

"Copy!" Lin Fengchong said, "I have already arranged for someone to do it."

"Tianying, how are you walking around the central area of the tunnel ventilation pavilion?" Liu Simiao asked.

Just as Chu Tianying was about to speak, Liu Simiao stretched out his hand and pushed open the car door: "Come on, let's go to the scene and report while watching." After getting up, they walked to the nursery. The three men had no choice but to stand up, dusting the ashes, followed her, and came to the tunnel wind pavilion. Several ten-centimeter-high "flat-top tents" were propped up on the nearby ground with metal brackets and several white plastic sheets. This was a non-contact covering to prevent the ground evidence from being damaged by natural weather such as wind and rain.

Chu Tianying carefully pulled out the metal bracket, lifted several pieces of white plastic sheets, pointed to several yellow wedge-shaped flags marked with numbers, and said, "I checked this central area twice, but I didn't extract any evidence of suspected shoe prints, this is not to say that the murderer wore shoe covers, but that he swept the area with a branch marked '1' afterwards, destroying the footprints, not even the footprints of getting on and off the car. One was left. No fingerprints were found on either the branch or the removed tunnel wind pavilion net labeled '2' due to his gloves or wiping afterwards. However, although he was cunning, there are still clues – pay attention to the place marked '3'."

The place marked "3" was the side of the inverted "L"-shaped tunnel wind pavilion. At first, it could not be seen anything. When got closer, they found that between 30 cm and 60 cm high from the bottom, there was a blackened piece about the width of A4 paper.

"What is this?" Lin Fengchong was a little confused.

"The traces of the fire are very new, they should have been left a few hours ago." Chu Tianying said, "I suspect that the murderer pressed the victim here and stuck his neck. The victim leaned against the wind pavilion and was struggling."

"This is not the result of the victim's scratching, but the result of the murderer's scratching." Liu Simiao squatted on the ground and gently touched the blackened area with his fingers, "The murderer was sitting with his back against the tunnel wind pavilion, using the arm around the victim's throat, the victim must struggle, so the killer's back will leave scratch marks on the cement wall."

Lin Fengchong was still confused: "What is the murderer doing with this place?"

"The murderer wanted to burn off the traces of evidence that the fibers on his back may be left on the cement wall!" Du Jianping said, "Simiao's analysis is correct: if the scratch marks were left by the victim, he would have to wear clothes anyway. If it was thrown into the shaft and set on fire, the murderer would have no need to burn here."

Lin Fengchong suddenly realized, and then frowned: "So, the murderer really has very rich experience in counter-investigation."

Suddenly, a gust of wind blew a piece of white plastic sheet into the air. Under the dark night sky, it stretched out its arms and legs like a ghost, and danced wildly in the air! Which caused several policemen in the nursery to exclaim and chase, and one of them accidentally fell into a canal and fell. Just when they thought they were about to grab the crumbling white plastic sheet by the wall, another gust of wind like a sea wave pulled the plastic sheet high up, jumped over the wall, and disappeared...

An ominous premonition struck Liu Simiao's heart. She felt that the murderer who threw and burned the body was like this white plastic sheet, and would eventually escape from her hands.

No! It can not happen!

Thinking of this, she looked at her watch, turned to Chu Tianying and Lin Fengchong and said, "You guys can go about your own business, the time is tight and the task is serious, it is three o'clock in the morning, and in three hours, six o'clock exactly, I want to hold the first case analysis meeting, at that time, you have to hand in the real useful evidence!"

8

The first case analysis meeting was held in an abandoned printing factory across the road from the east exit of the alley, which was also set up as a temporary headquarters for investigating the case of the Deratization Hill.

The workshop of the printing factory, which was shut down for environmental protection, was tall and empty, except for a few dusty printing presses, a wooden cart used to pull prints, and a peeled fire extinguisher in the corner. On the high ceiling, a light bulb that seemed to be deliberately lit for the purpose of creating shadows, buzzed and emitted a light that was either gray or white, and made the faces of dozens of detectives sick. They didn't find a place to sit after staying up all night, so they just stood for the meeting, the soil and dead branches of the nursery were hanging almost on all of their trousers. The window glass was shaken by the strong wind, so that Chu Tianying, who was sketching and explaining the crime scene on a makeshift blackboard, stopped several times and looked out the window involuntarily. The dawn of late autumn hung a sliver of fish belly white on the window lattice, like an eye cream that had not been washed off in the cold night.

As soon as Liu Simiao and Du Jianping entered the workshop, Chu Tianying quickly stopped talking, and the other criminal policemen also straightened their waists.

"Go on." Liu Simiao said to Chu Tianying.

Chu Tianying hurriedly said, "I just introduced how I walked around the central area of the tunnel wind pavilion... Now I'm done."

Liu Simiao glanced at Du Jianping, who reached out his hand and made a gesture of "your turn".

"Okay, then the leaders of each group will start reporting the new situation." Liu Simiao emphasized, "I only listen to the new evidence."

However, three hours passed, and although the policemen were busy all night, they still did not gain much. The deputy director in charge of criminal investigation in the district bureau took the investigation team and knocked on the door from house to house to find out whether they saw suspicious persons or suspicious events before and after the crime, but all the sleepy eyes of the people gave the negative answers. Investigations were underway on the teachers, students and employees of several nearby units—Deratization Hill Middle School, Xijiao Branch, and Bus Automation Design and Research Institute. Judging from the current situation, it seemed that no one was involved in the case. No one knew anything about the case. The crime scene investigation team led by Chu Tianying failed to extract any new valuable evidence from the nursery and the tunnel wind pavilion, so they had to follow Du Jianping's instructions to start a long-distance tracking of the suspect vehicle along the escape route of Deratization Hill. Sure enough, the tire tracks disappeared without a trace on the gravel road. The electronic information collection team led by Lin Fengchong finally confirmed that between 6:00 and 10:30 last night, a total of 217 vehicles drove from north to south on Yinlu North Street through the traffic lights in Qingshikou Dongli, excluding buses. In addition to the vehicles whose tire sizes were obviously different, the whereabouts and ownership of the remaining 194 vehicles need to be verified. This was a considerable number, and it was definitely not something that can be found in a short time... No wonder Liu Simiao frowned and said nothing after listening. While the five plastic bags of fried dough sticks, oil cakes and soy milk that Du Jianping bought at a nearby breakfast stall, no one touched until the steam was exhausted.

At this moment, there was the sound of brakes from outside the yard, followed by the sound of hurried footsteps from far to near. The face of Li Mi, director of the Information Office of the Municipal Bureau, appeared at the door of the workshop, and his presence further proved the case of the Deratization Hill aroused great concern of the superior leadership. He stepped forward and shook hands with Du Jianping and Liu Simio. He asked, "What should I say to the outside world?"

Du Jianping and Liu Simi looked at each other, but Du Jianping continued to speak: "As the old rules, there was a huge criminal case last night in Deratization Hill, the investigation is in progress, and there is no other comment."

"Du." Li Mi stared at him, "The case is too big, and the intensity and density of public attention must be considered."

"Then make an opportunity, and the Municipal Bureau will leave a reporting hotline so that citizens can provide valuable clues." Du Jianping said.

Li Mi nodded and said without worry: "It is conceivable that in two hours at most, a large number of media will swarm."

"I will explain to the detectives here: Be optimistic about the situation and keep your mouth shut, and don't say a word that shouldn't be said. Whoever says anything will be responsible!" Du Jianping patted Li Mi's shoulder, "Also please help greet the media: news reports must be reported in accordance with the format and rules. Don't take things for granted, and don't make speculative reports. As for those online who are afraid that the world will not be in chaos, as long as they spread rumors and step on the red line, they will all be dealt with the law!"

"Of course, of course!" Li Mi finished speaking, lowered his voice again, and clasped his hands together, "Could you please estimate how long it will take to solve the case, that I can adjust it in time based on the direction of public opinion."

Du Jianping and Liu Simiao were speechless for a while. It has been eight hours since the case happened. For most criminal cases, eight hours was enough to lock down the suspect, at least a few suspected targets. Although this case was serious, the cunning criminal had left no evidence or trace for the police to follow. Judging from the basic laws of criminal investigation, the first 24 hours were the most important in the detection of any case. After every 24 hours, the difficulty of detection will double. Once more than 72 hours, the hope of solving the case will be reduced to be very slim...

In the dead silent workshop, a cell phone rang suddenly.

The detectives fumbled around for a long time, only to realize that Liu Simiao had put her iPhone X in the chalk groove on the blackboard when she was listening to the report just now, because she wanted to draw a cross-section of the tunnel wind pavilion.

Chu Tianying picked up the phone and glanced at the caller's name, and quickly took it to Liu Sima: "Director, Director Lei is calling."

Liu Simiao connected the phone. Lei Rong's hoarse voice came from inside: "Simiao, I'm really sorry, I didn't go to the scene because the city bureau organized study documents. After Tang brought the four corpses back, she gave me a general introduction to the situation, and I did an autopsy quickly. Time was tight, and the body was damaged too badly, so I only got part of the results, I'll briefly tell you—"

"We are holding a case analysis meeting." Liu Simiao said in a low voice, "The criminal police officers involved in the case are now concentrated in the temporary headquarters. Can the autopsy results be disclosed to everyone?"

"No problem," Lei Rong said.

Liu Simiao turned on the hands-free function of the phone.

"The laboratory autopsy has proved that Tang Xiaotang's on-site autopsy results are correct. In addition, I focused on examining whether the four corpses were burned before death or after death, and the exact cause of death. The details are as follows." Lei Rong cleared her throat and said, "There was no congestion, edema and necrosis in the mucosal tissues of the four deceased, no black lines mixed with soot, charcoal powder and mucus were found in the respiratory tract, and no excess carboxyhemoglobin was found in the blood extracted from the heart, which fully shows that : All four deceased were cremated after death."

She paused and continued: "Tang Xiaotang's on-site autopsy believes that the cause of death of the three- or four-year-old girl No. D was homicide and mechanical suffocation caused by strangulation with a rope. I agree with this conclusion. In the two corpses No. A and B, there are many scattered bleeding spots under the serosal membrane of the heart and lung; the blood was concentrated, showed dark red and not coagulated; They died of sexual suffocation, but due to the severe charring of the skin and flesh on the neck, violent injuries such as cable grooves and strangles could not be found, and it was impossible to check whether there was sign of strangle, so it was impossible to confirm whether it was suicide or homicide."

Liu Simiao knew that there might be some unusual findings on the corpse of the adult male No. C that Lei Rong had deliberately missed.

"The adult male corpse No. C also showed severe charring of the neck skin and flesh, but during the neck autopsy, it was found that the hyoid body and the left great horn were fractured and bleeding, the upper horn of the thyroid cartilage was fractured, the intima of the common carotid artery was transversely fractured, and the pharynx was fractured. There are bleeding spots on the mucosa of the posterior wall and bleeding spots on the epiglottis cartilage. These changes indicate that the deceased's neck was subjected to violent compression or traction such as strangulation, strangulation, etc., resulting in mechanical suffocation and death."

Chu Tianying suddenly remembered the large blackened trace on the side of the tunnel wind pavilion...and Liu Simiao's judgment——

"The murderer sat with his back against the wind pavilion in the tunnel, and used his arms to strangle the victim's throat. The victim must struggle, so the murderer's back would leave scratches on the cement wall."

He couldn't help but cast an admiring look at Liu Simiao.

Lei Rong continued on the phone: "As for the time of death, it can only be inferred from the stomach contents of the corpses. The three children's corpses had their stomachs completely emptied, and the food residues had obviously entered the large intestine, which had been partially digested and absorbed. It proves that they did not eat all day yesterday, so I estimate that the time of death was in the early hours of yesterday, and the adult male body number C, the stomach contents were chyle-shaped, and a considerable amount entered the duodenum and part of the jejunum, which proves that he was killed two or three hours after dinner last night, and the time of death was around ten o'clock in the evening."

Four corpses fell into the same well, but there was such a big difference in the time of death, which made Liu Simiao a little unexpected: "Is your autopsy helpful for the identification of the deceased?"

"All the same, the burning of the corpses were too serious, so we can only find the identification through the collection of DNA information. First, it takes time, and second, the corpses must have left samples in the DNA database before they died. It's almost impossible for such young children to have any criminal record, as for the adult male, I can only take chances..." Lei Rong seemed to feel Liu Simiao's disappointment on the other end of the phone, and hurriedly added, "However, during the autopsy process, a suspicious point has been found in the corpse, which may provide some reference for you to find the identification of the body."

"What?" Liu Simiao asked hurriedly.

"Nutrition." Lei Rong said concisely, "All three children have serious nutritional deficiencies."

Liu Simiao's eyes lit up: "I found out like you said during Tang Xiaotang's on-site autopsy that the heights and ages of the three children are not matched. According to the standard for children's height, boys around the age of 12 should be 151 cm, and 137 cm is considered short, but the body No. A is only 130 cm; the standard height of girls around nine years old is 134 cm, but the corpse No. B is only 110 cm; even that little girl of four or five years old should have a standard height of 103 to 110 cm, but she is only 90 cm – they were so unhealthy!"

"If you want to talk about over-nourished children these days, a large number of children could be caught, but nutritionally deficient children are too rare – let alone happened together." Lei Rong said, "So Simiao, I suggest you to investigate the city's orphanages, disabled children's relief centers, and other charities."

Liu Simiao let out a "ok" and suddenly felt a strange feeling.

The strange feeling came from the hands-free phone.

There was an undeserved silence on the other end of the phone, as if there had suddenly been a blank space between the printed text, without any punctuation.

If she didn't finished speaking, she should continue speaking. If she finished, you can say and hang up, but Lei Rong didn't, she just kept silent and lost her voice.

The detectives in the printing workshop had been busy all night, and they were exhausted because of sleepiness and exhaustion. At this moment, they felt that something was wrong. They looked at each other in dismay, and because they couldn't find the answer on each other's faces, they raised their heads in unison, and set their eyes on the phone in Liu Simiao's hand.

"Sister, what's the matter with you?" Liu Simiao asked, bringing her face closer to the phone.

"Simiao, I found something in the autopsy, I must tell you." Lei Rong said slowly, her voice was stern and low, "The body of the three- or four-year-old girl, because the burns were not too serious, so I check it out more carefully... Her hymen has an old ruptured hymen, which means she had been sexually assaulted during her lifetime, and probably more than once."

It was as if a thunderbolt rang in ear! The policemen widened their eyes in shock!

Liu Simiao raised her head, looked at the light bulb on the ceiling, and shot a sharp sword-like light on her face.

She lowered her head and said to the phone, "I see."

"Okay." Lei Rong paused and said, "Catch that bastard!"

Lei Rong, who has always been gentle and elegant, actually used swear words, and the fighting spirit of all the detectives at the scene suddenly exploded! They refreshed their energy and wiped away the exhaustion they had felt a few seconds ago. They were gearing up, like a group of wolves with red eyes from hunger, ready to pounce on their prey and tear it to pieces with their sharp teeth!

Liu Simiao glanced at her watch and glanced at everyone with a stern gaze: "The golden period for detection of a criminal case is within 24 hours after the crime is committed, and nine hours have passed now, so everyone must hurry up and be sure that before ten tonight – catch that bastard!"

Chapter 2

1

Liu Simiao unscrewed the water pipe, and water came out. She stretched out her hand, but she was stunned by the ice, and the cold poured into her whole body from her fingertips. She waited, held out her hand again, the water was still so cold to the bones, but the skin didn't react so much, this cold feeling was exactly what she needed. She saw her palms glow a bleak white under the water, as if they were about to melt, as the water filled the nests she held in her hands. She lowered her head and threw the water on her face fiercely. After a few times, the tired nerves that had stayed up all night were stabbed and woke up a bit. She took out a pack of tissue paper from her trouser pocket and slowly dipped the water on her face. Then, in a round mirror with cracks hanging on the wall, she saw a thin, pale and haggard face. Although her eyes were bloodshot, her brows were drooping, and her lips were slightly blue, but she was over 30 years old and had no wrinkles at the corners of her eyes. She was the same age as those women of the same age who used skin cream, whitening needles and skin care products all day long. In contrast, this always arrogant face refused any grinding of time in a natural way...

Since Lin Xiangming disconnected, there was not a day in her heart that was not painful. That kind of pain was like the rejection of a heart transplant patient. She wished she could suddenly die at work like other colleagues, but such a thing did not happen. Although as she grew older, more and more sub-health conditions appeared, colds, dizziness, stomach problems and even arrhythmias were tormenting her, but the underlying vitality was still as tough as beef tendon. She had to continue to fight Sisyphus-style day after day against all kinds of crimes. Fortunately, in the past two years, the social order in this city had been getting better, which made her very happy, but it was precisely because of this that the case in Deratization Hill made her feel particularly abrupt and uneasy.

While thinking about it, Liu Simiao threw the wet facial tissue into the plastic basket by the sink, and tiptoed out of the cramped and dirty bathroom of the printing factory.

It was already eight o'clock in the morning, and some media had already circulated a briefing on the case of Deratization Hill. She knew that across the road, a large number of journalists were probably flocking to the nursery. She first went to the printing workshop as the temporary headquarters to find out if there was any new findings. After getting a negative answer, she walked out of the door of the printing plant.

It was a sunless morning. The sky was frozen blue by the cold air of late autumn. The Yinlu Mountain Road was already inaccessible. At this moment, even dogs were walking around. The only thing moving on the ground was the eaves of the bungalow facing the street. A rare black Xuanyi drove over, stopped on the side of the road, and a person got out of the car. That Xuanyi was probably a Didi Express. The driver's eyes were sharp. He saw that several people in plainclothes nearby were police officers, thought they were looking for black cars and drove away in a hurry.

Liu Simiao saw that the person who got down from Xuan Yi was familiar, and called out, "Zhang Wei!"

"Legal Times" reporter Zhang Wei was probably dragged out of the bed. He didn't say anything, his small eyes were half-open in a daze. He heard someone greeted him and hurriedly ran over, nodding and bowing: "Director Liu, good morning!"

"Only you?" Liu Simiao asked.

"What?" Zhang Wei hadn't reacted yet, "I'm alone."

"Isn't your newspaper reporter Guo Xiaofen? Why didn't she come?"

"You don't know yet? She resigned."

Liu Simiao was taken aback! Guo Xiaofen was the chief reporter of the "Legal Times", specializing in major cases and important cases. Although she was often angry with herself during the interview, she had often cooperated with her for many years and the two had already become friends: "When did she resign, why don't I know? !"

"It just happened a while ago." Zhang Wei said, "She came to this city to drift for so many years, she didn't buy a house, or get married, so she didn't have a fixed place to live. She changed her residence several times over half a year. It was said that she also lived on the streets in the middle of the night and once spent the night on a park bench. In short, she was in a bad mood, and her manuscripts were dismissed several times. She had a big fight with the editor-in-chief and resigned."

Liu Simiao didn't know what to say for a while, Zhang Wei took advantage of her dazed moment, and hurried to the east-west alley across the road.

For some unknown reason, Liu Simiao followed behind him, walked slowly across the road, and also entered the alley, watching from a distance a large group of reporters gathered at the door of the nursery like headless flies, holding mobile phones shot inside. Although the iron fence door was not closed, none of them took half a step inside. When Du Jianping came out of the nursery, they obediently made way for a semi-circle, listened to Du Jianping's introduction of the situation without any useful information, and then dispersed as if receiving an amnesty.

Thinking of Guo Xiaofen's stalker-style interview back then, Liu Simiao was at a loss for a while.

Back at the printing house, she pondered for a moment in the yard, took out her mobile phone, found Guo Xiaofen's number, and was about to press it down when the phone suddenly rang, and the caller's name displayed on the screen was "Li Sanduo".

Liu Simiao's expression suddenly froze.

Li Sanduo was originally the deputy secretary of the Municipal Law Committee and retired last year. In recent years, the anti-corruption storm had paid special attention to the review of retired cadres. Those who had committed corruption and other illegal acts during their employment will never be allowed to "retire and get free" as in the past, but will be tracked down to the end, which had uncovered many corrupt officials. Li Sanduo's post was a hard-hit area for corruption, and the review was extraordinarily rigorous and conscientious. After investigation, it was found that this old boy had been a leading cadre for ten years, and he was even more honest than plain water! Soon a red-headed document was issued, appointing Li Sanduo as a consultant of the Municipal Comprehensive Management Committee, and cooperating with the Municipal Public Security Bureau to supervise the criminal investigation work of major and important cases, and continue to exert residual enthusiasm for the party and the people. According to the establishment, the Comprehensive Management Committee was a functional department subordinate to the Political and Legal Committee, so the old boy muttered "re-employment and half the goddamn downgrade", while patting his butt and taking the work.

Now that he made the phone call himself, she could think with his toes that the caller was bad. Sure enough, the first thing Liu Simiao heard after getting on the phone was: "When will the case be solved? Give me an exact answer!"

When dealing with a person like Li Sanduo, it can't be afraid or cowardly, otherwise he will really scare you, so Liu Simiao insisted: "It's strange, am I the leader of the task force?"

Li Sanduo was stunned for a moment. Although he had been dealing with Liu Simiao for many years, he knew that Liu Simiao was not easy to be provoked, but he did not expect that she would not be this much. The first person responsible for the Deratization Hill case was Du Jianping. Even if a military order was issued to solve the case within a time limit, it was not Liu Simiao who signed it. Li Sanduo couldn't help laughing: "Fine, Director Liu, I'm an old man sincerely ask you for advice. Can you estimate the detection time of the case from the perspective of criminal techniques?"

"I can't be sure!" Liu Simiao refused to answer, "This case is very complicated. The crime scene shows that the criminal was vicious and cruel, and had strong anti-investigation capabilities. There have not left any valuable evidence. The direction of the investigation is to use the FAST to find the suspect vehicle, identify and analyze the appearance of the suspect, and it was estimated that the breakthrough of the final case was also here... With the unprecedented criminal investigation force invested by the police, the criminal has no chance of escaping the law. But if you want me to tell you the exact time, I can not."

"Simiao!" Li Sanduo's tone suddenly became heavy, "Cases involving children are the easiest to attract public attention. We must take a highly responsible attitude to the people and solve cases as soon as possible!"

Hearing the words "a highly responsible attitude towards the people", Liu Simiao, like all police officers who have a sense of sanctity and nobility in their profession, became serious and solemn: "Secretary Li (she is still called Li Sanduo's former post), the detection of criminal cases takes twenty-four hours after the crime is committed as the golden period, and I promise to handcuff the criminal suspect to the heating pipe of the Criminal Investigation Department before ten o'clock today!"

"All I want is your words, okay, that's all!" Li Sanduo hung up the phone.

Liu Simiao looked at the previous page returned by the phone screen, which was Guo Xiaofen's contact number, couldn't help but smiled bitterly, she put the phone back in her pocket, and thought to herself—

Can I really keep the promise I made to Li Sanduo?

2

87

What the police never expected was that it was much easier to solve the case than they expected, and as Liu Simiao had expected, they used the FAST to find the suspect vehicle and identified and analyzed the appearance of the suspect, and found the breakthrough – more precisely, according to Liu Simiao's arrangement, the police started tracking on the two routes, and finally reached the same destination.

After the case analysis meeting in the morning, Liu Simiao suddenly had an idea. She believed that the murderer who made this case showed strong anti-investigation ability everywhere, and this ability was not something that can only be achieved by committing crimes many times. The old saying was "It's better to lose for half a day than to succeed for a year", which was the importance of being caught by a miss for the "growth" of a criminal. Only by facing the police's interrogation and even going to jail can truly let them learn how to escape the police's arrest, just like rabbits that escaped from tigers were better at avoiding natural enemies——in other words, the perpetrator of the Deratization Hill case should be a person who had been arrested and had a record with the police. It was not difficult to think of this. What was rare is that Liu Simiao immediately linked it to Lin Fengchong's work: the electronic information collection team confirmed the time from 6 to 10 last night through the monitoring device installed on the traffic lights in the east of Qingshikou. Between 1:30 a.m, a total of 217 vehicles had passed the traffic lights at Qingshikou Dongli from north to south on Yinlu North Street. The whereabouts and ownership of 194 vehicles had yet to be verified. This was originally going to take a lot of manpower, material resources and time to complete the work, but Liu Simiao believed that although the video resolution of the ZTE intelligent monitoring system widely used in this city was not high enough, the outline of each driver's face can be clearly outlined. If the driver photos of these 194 vehicles were entered into the database of the Ministry of Public Security and compared with the photos of criminals stored in the database, although it would take some time to get the results, it is much more efficient than finding drivers one by one based on the license plate number. So she immediately arranged for Lin Fengchong to do it.

There was another line that Liu Simiao discovered. That's when she followed Zhang Wei to the door of the nursery. After watching media reporters interview Du Jianping, she casually glanced into the nursery, and suddenly had a feeling that something was wrong. She was not specifically sure where it came from, and she even didn't realize it until she finished the phone call with Li Sanduo, and hurried to the door of the nursery. Chu Tianying happened to be there and asked if she needed help, Liu Simiao pointed at the nursery and said: "you can't see the tunnel wind pavilion from the door."

Chu Tianying glanced where she pointed. Indeed, the tunnel wind pavilion at the southwest corner of the nursery was a visual blind spot at the entrance of the nursery... But, what was that mean?

But Liu Simiao's following words made him horrified: "Go and check the identity of the person who called the police last night!"

Since the fire brigade discovered the body under the tunnel ventilation pavilion until now, the police had been in a state of high tension. These work were mainly carried out around crime scene investigation, home visits and electronic information collection. It was precisely because of nervousness busy working, the police ignored a seemingly trivial matter – who was the person called the police? Even some careful people thought about it, they would subconsciously think that it may be a passer-by at night and saw the tunnel wind pavilion on fire from the door of the nursery. But Liu Simiao's discovery completely denied this possibility. Of course, there were also two other possibilities. One was that someone found the fire when he entered the nursery for "convenience", but last night the sky was dark and the wind was strong, and the remote alleys were remote enough, which had no necessity of "convenience" inside the nursery; the other was that people living on the ridge found the fire from condescension and then called the police. This was possible, but not so much, because the Deratization Hill was located in the southwest of the nursery, and the opening of the tunnel wind pavilion faced east. Of course, it could not be ruled out that some enthusiastic residents found thick smoke billowing from the ventilation pavilion of the tunnel, so they went down to the nursery to see what happened, and then called the police. However, the police did not find the witness during the home visit.

Chu Tianying hurriedly contacted the 110 alarm station, and quickly found the operator who had just left the night shift. The operator was extremely serious and responsible, and immediately returned to the police center to find the alarm recording and phone number of the alarm person, and sent them to Chu Tianying. .

After listening to the concise recording of the alarm, Chu Tianying clearly realized that the operator had misunderstood that the caller had not mistaken 110 for 119—he knew very well the nature of the incident and which handle department was needed.

Chu Tianying believed that since the caller was very likely to be closely related to the case – even if he was the murderer himself, it was 80% possible that the calling number might be an unknown number whose source cannot be traced. After checking, it turned out to be a real-name registration number. The owner's name was Xing Qisheng, male, 55 years old this year, living in province A, and currently serving as the director of the city's "Tongyou Nursing Home".

When Chu Tianying reported this information to Liu Simiao, she immediately thought of Lei Rong's judgment——

"I suggest you to investigate the city's charities like orphanages, disabled children's relief centers..."

The case was online!

Liu Simiao was very excited and reported directly to Du Jianping. Hearing the words "Love Charity Foundation", Du Jianping's brows flashed with an imperceptible pain. Liu Simiao suddenly realized that she had ignored some things that she should not. She felt a little sorry in her heart, but her face was very calm. After all, work is work. Du Jianping also quickly returned to his normal expression, nodding his head to show that he understood.

After some preparations, Liu Simiao dialed Xing Qisheng's phone number with the mobile phone installed with the tracking system. As expected, his mobile phone was turned off.

Du Jianping asked his old subordinate, Chai Yongjin, and said, "Bring a few capable people with you, and immediately go to the 'Tongyou Nursing Home' to find out where Xing Qisheng was now. I guess he had already escaped. Then get his physical features and other detailed information, thoroughly searched his temporary address in the city. In addition, you called all the staff of the nursing home together, where they were and what they did last night. Make it clear, even how many times they pooped!"

Just as Chai Yongjin turned to leave, Liu Simiao added: "Take a policewoman who is already a mother and protect the children in the nursing home!"

Thirty minutes later, Chai Yongjin called and reported that he had brought someone to seal the Tongyou Nursing Home, and verified them one by one according to the employee address book provided by the human resources department. Except Xing Qisheng and a vice president, there were eight workers in total. All staff were on duty, and there were 12 disabled children in the nursing home, most of them from province A with congenital heart disease, cerebral palsy and other diseases, and they had been protected by the police.

"Where is Xing Qisheng now?" Du Jianping was most concerned about this.

"The staff here don't know." Chai Yongjin said, "However, according to the cleaning aunt, she heard a movement in the dean's office at 10:00 last night, and the guard also said that the dean left the nursing home at 10:30."

If Xing Qisheng didn't leave until 10:30, he would not be able to go to Deratization Hill at 10:30 to call the police. Of course, there were two possibilities. One was that his accomplices set fire and ask him to call the police – although it was unclear what the meaning of this. The police retrieved the call records of Xing Qisheng's mobile phone from the telecommunications department and found that his mobile phone did not receive any incoming calls at about 10:30 last night. There were two calls, one was 110, and the other one actually called to his own office and got connected! But the doorman and cleaning aunt of the nursing home both swore that there were no visitors last night, and that no one other than the dean himself had entered or left his office after ten o'clock. So why did Xing Qisheng use his mobile phone to call his office? Who was that person answering the phone?

Considering that there were many unsolvable mysteries in this possibility, another possibility suddenly became larger, that was, Xing Qisheng lent his mobile phone to the murderer, after the murderer set fire they called to meet and flee together.

Du Jianping was frowning and thinking, and Liu Simiao, who was beside him, turned to the speakerphone and asked, "Chai, have you checked the nursing home for any missing children in recent days?"

"Director Liu." Chai Yongjin said, "After I arrived, in addition to inquiring about Xing Qisheng's whereabouts, I was to find out if there were any missing children. However, you may not believe, that no one in the entire nursing home could tell how many children there were......"

"How is that possible?" Liu Simiao was taken aback, "Isn't there just a dozen or so? They can count them with fingers!"

"It's true, but the staff in the nursing home, how could I describe... You are all fools. The guard is an old man who lost all his teeth; cleaning aunt can't say anything; a woman in charge of finance and HR is sitting in the office and playing King's Glory, and she doesn't know whatever we asked; the dean's secretary is a vase, who can make up three times with one sentence; the driver is a stunned young man in his early twenties, who knows only to drink porridge; the other three nurses are old mothers who don't know where they came from, all of them will say 'Go and ask the leader' when they are asked about anything,......"

"Aren't there any registrations for the children who come and go?" Du Jianping was also surprised.

"No, really..." Chai Yongjin said, "The secretary said that these children were all funded by the 'Love Charity Foundation' and came from remote areas in Province A to a designated hospital in this city for treatment, and most of them were orphans. Every time the headquarters will send someone to bring the children over, they will live in the nursing home during the treatment period, and they will go back after the treatment. At first, there was a registration. After a long time, the dean thinks that there was a registration at the headquarters anyway, so it won't be necessary here ..."

"Is this a fucking unnecessary thing?!" Du Jianping couldn't help scolding, "Then check the surveillance video of the nursing home—"

"No surveillance video..."

"Impossible!" Du Jianping was really angry, his eyes widened, "All kindergartens, playgrounds and children's educational institutions in this city must install surveillance video, and directly connect to each police station, this is the government confidential document!"

"I don't know what's going on here..." Chai Yongjin said.

Du Jianping called a police officer and said, "You go to the local police station of the nursing home in person to investigate the situation. If you find that they dare to neglect their duties, or fail to implement the city's instructions, and do not supervise and inspect the installation of monitoring equipment in the Tongyou Nursing Home. The director of the police station and the relevant police will be dismissed on the spot, waiting for investigation!"

"I'm afraid this is out of procedure..." Liu Simiao said softly, "The order to remove the director of the police station must be issued by the leader of the city bureau and approved collectively by the sub-bureau team. Today is different from the past, and everything must be done according to the rules and procedures, otherwise it is a mistake in organizational discipline." After speaking, she said to the police officer, "Go to the police station. If you find a problem, report it first and then decide how to deal with it."

Du Jianping glanced at Liu Simiao and remained silent.

Chai Yongjin continued to report on the phone: "Xing Qisheng rented a three-bedroom apartment not far from the nursing home. I have sent two police officers to search. In addition, I asked for a copy of Xing Qisheng's photo from the secretary. The photo was sent to your mobile phones via WeChat."

Liu Simiao opened WeChat and saw a new photo: the photo was of a middle-aged man with a pot belly. He was not tall, with curly hair, short arms and short legs, and was wearing white sportswear. He was playing golf, swinging on the lawn of the golf course, a big persimmon-shaped face was rosy, his eyes and nose are twisted into a pinch as if squeezed by a door, and his fat lips are widely open, revealing a mouth of smoky yellow teeth. There are only a few hairs that are actually combed in a greasy part, and the eyes and smiles look a bit wretched in the picture.

Liu Simiao handed the phone to Du Jianping: "Look at this person's body, doesn't he look like a corpse number C?"

Du Jianping just glanced at it and said, "Right!"

"Chai, tell the police officers sent to search Xing Qisheng's residence, pay attention to extracting valuable samples such as hair, nails, bloodstains, etc. that can be used for DNA comparison." Liu Simiao said, "In addition, you need to understand what did the children in the nursing home eat for dinner the day before yesterday, and what Xing Qisheng had for dinner last night, Lei Rong's analysis of the stomach contents of the four deceased will come out soon, and I want to compare."

After hanging up the phone, Du Jianping said to himself: "If the deceased is Xing Qisheng, then this case is even more bizarre..."

Liu Simiao also felt that a lot of mysteries were coming like gnats in the summer jungle: If the deceased person number C was really Xing Qisheng, the person who was the people still in the office of the dean of Tongyou Nursing Home at 10:30 last night? The autopsy results showed that Xing Qisheng's death should have been around the time of receiving the alarm call on 110. If the caller was Xing Qisheng himself, why did he not say that he was in danger but called the fire alarm, and why did he call his office? If the caller was the murderer, what was the relationship between him and Xing Qisheng, and why should he kill and thrown Xing Qisheng into the tunnel wind pavilion?

Liu Simi gently tapped the back of the head with his fist a few times, she hadn't slept all night, and thinking about the problem made her headache, and she squeezed the Jingming acupoint again.

Du Jianping saw it and said, "Go and take a nap in the car. I'll call you again if something happens."

Liu Simiao shook her head: "I can't sleep right now, I'll be fine if I get through this sleepiness..." The moment she opened her eyes, she noticed that Du Jianping was looking at her strangely, and asked, "What's wrong? "

Du Jianping said slowly: "Nothing, I suddenly feel that you are a lot more mature than before. When you first entered the city bureau, you were a very proud little girl. I haven't seen you for two years, and you have become more thoughtful... "

"You actually mean that I'm starting to become sleek and sophisticated." Liu Simiao said while she stood in front of the stained glass window, looking at the old tree in the yard of the printing factory that had lost its leaves in the cold wind overnight.

Du Jianping wanted to say something, but when the words reached his mouth, he swallowed back his stomach. It happened that a leader of the municipal subway head office made a special trip to know about the situation. He hurriedly went out to make a reception. When he returned to the printing factory workshop as the temporary headquarters, a series of latest information came back: The first was from the police who searched Xing Qisheng's residence, according to the results of the property surveillance video and the house entry search, Xing Qisheng did not go home last night, and in his residence, no matter the clothes, suitcases, documents in the safe, cash and bank cards were all well preserved. There was no sign of him fleeing or preparing to flee. Hair was extracted from the comb and pillow in the bathroom, which had been sent to the Criminal Technology Division for comparison with the DNA of the deceased No. C; Next was from Chai Yongjin, who reported that they took a lonng time to ask the childcare workers to find out that the children's three meals a day which were ordered from a nearby restaurant, but they couldn't recall exactly what the children ate the night before, only vaguely said "very rich" , and they had contacted the vice president of the nursing home who was out, and she was on her way back; And the last news, Chu Tianying contacted the "Love Charity Foundation" in Province A and asked them to provide the latest batch of lists of the children who were treated immediately. They said that the list could not be made public, and then said that they would ask for approval from their superiors. Since the case needed to be kept secret, Chu Tianying could not tell them the seriousness of the case too concretely. No matter coaxing or frightening were useless...

"Don't talk nonsense with them!" Du Jian said with a flat face, "Send an investigation notice to the Public Security Department of Province A!"

However, what Du Jianping did not expect the most was that the police officers sent to the local police station of Tongyou Nursing Home reported that the nature of Tongyou Nursing Home was very vague, neither a kindergarten nor a welfare home, nor a government-sponsored institution, it was not a private profit-making or non-profit organization, so it had not been registered with any unit of the city's education commission and civil affairs department. Even no fire security certificate. For these, the police from the police station had visited many times to urge them to perform the relevant approval procedures, but this nursing home had a certain background and was of a charitable and welfare nature. It often organized some social groups to visit and condolences. The dean was a guy who is "more slipping than a glass ball", the police can't rashly punish it, and had been delayed again and again until now.

After listening to these situations, Du Jianping, who had always been aggressive in handling cases, felt as if he was trapped in a huge ball of wool, and he couldn't use his hands and feet at all, and the more he tried to get out of the predicament, the more tightly he was entangled. He rubbed his rough palms over the same rough red face, and his already red eyes became more and more intense.

"Chai can't do it!" Liu Simiao asserted, "His case handling style is too traditional and conservative. This Tongyou Nursing Home has been trained by Xing Qisheng to become a sloppy brownie, and we must find a more ruthless guy to handle this."

Du Jianping was stunned for a moment, then nodded: "Then send Ma Xiaozhong!"

Ma Xiaozhong was the director of the Wangyue Park Police Station. He was a well-known capable officer in the city. He can squeeze out the brain when he caught the toad. When thought of his participation in the detection of this case, Du Jianping felt like half his head exposed from the ice hole. But before he could breathe, the heaviest iron fist since the incident was about to hit him in the face.

"Director," Lin Fengcong suddenly stood behind him, holding an iPad in his hand, with the screen facing inward, "We took the video of 194 cars passing by ZTE's intelligent monitoring system, and carried out the video. We used screen capture and enlarged them, and then compared the drivers' photos with the database in the department. Now, the comparison result is out..."

His voice was very strange, as if the chief surgeon who had just stepped off the operating table was going to announce the failure of the operation to the patient's family.

Du Jianping and Liu Simiao looked at each other, then asked in unison, "Have you found the suspect?"

"Yes..." Lin Fengchong said, turning the iPad over—

"What?!" Du Jianping cried out in shock, and Liu Simiao couldn't help but gasp!

Although the acne on that wide face had turned into potholes, and even though the shaggy moustache on the lips had been shaved, the light in the triangular eyes of the man holding the steering wheel, still looked cold and cruel ten years later, even more horrific—

That's right, this person was Zhou Liping, the criminal in the "Western Suburbs Serial Murder Case"!

Around 3:30 in the afternoon, two Buick GL8s with coated glass windows slowly parked at the door of Block D of Runtang Hi-Tech Incubation Park.

Runtang Hi-Tech Incubation Park was a real estate project specially built in the Western Suburbs in recent years to attract investment. The park was very large, and four buses can be parked side by side at the entrance. The overall pattern was a circle of gray and white semi-circular buildings centered on a vulgar Roman column circular fountain square. Looking down from the sky, it looked like a pile of dinosaur eggs were being boiled in the nine-squares grid. The designer covered the entire park with lawns, inserted short saplings, interspersed with irregular stone roads, added a stream here, installed a rockery there, and several solar panels on the top of the mountain. Highlighted the themes of technology, fashion and environmental protection. It was a pity that in the past two years, many enterprises had closed down and moved out one after another, causing the park to be extremely cold and desolate. Occasionally, a passer-by coughed even made several echoes.

"In addition to this west gate, there is also an east gate in Block D, and a small gate in the south for transporting cleaning waste, but generally only cleaners will use it to enter and exit." The director of the park office, a little man with cross-eyed sitting introduced to Du Jianping in the GL8 car, "Mingyi Public Relations Company is located in the north of the first floor. Do you need me to go first and find out if the person you are looking for is here?"

Du Jianping looked at his slightly trembling fingertips, remembering how terrified he looked when he was called out of the office just now. It was estimated that this man was either committing adultery or embezzling public funds. The ghost in his heart can make a horrific movie. But now was not the time to count these things.

After discovering that around ten o'clock last night, Zhou Liping had driven a black INSPIRE from south to north through the traffic lights of Qingshikou Dongli, the police immediately called up the relevant information of the car. The car's unit was Mingyi PR firm. Browsing the company's official website, they found that the company's owner, surnamed Zheng, once served as the director of the advertising department of a public welfare newspaper, and started the company after resigning. The main business of the company was to undertake public welfare activities such as fundraising and evening parties organized by various official or private charitable organizations, and the report submitted by the industrial and commercial tax department proved that the "Love Charity Foundation" was the company's largest funder.

It was not known what position Zhou Liping held in this company and what specific work he did. In order to prevent leaks, it iwa not easy to inquire. But time was running out, and Du Jianping immediately decided to arrest Zhou Liping immediately: "As long as the he was caught, we can find out the truth!"

The words were purely to cheer up the subordinates. Ask himself, Du Jianping knew that he was by no means an opponent who can be despised. Yes, it may not be difficult to catch Zhou Liping, but it was very, very difficult to defeat him. Everything that happened ten years ago had proved this. This guy who was suspected to be the real culprit of the "Western Suburb Serial Murder Case", relying on his silence after his arrest and the lack of evidence from the police, and also Lin Xiangming's intervention, the court finally found that he had committed only one crime of killing Fang Zhifeng. Beside he was under 18 years old, so he was only sentenced to ten years in prison... At that time, many criminal police officers were indignant, such as Li Zhiyong, who drank too much wine a year later and yelled at himself with red eyes: "Believe it or not, Zhou Liping will be released after less than ten years in prison? Do you believe that he will kill more people when he comes out?!" The scolding question was still in his ears.

The tragic incident on the Deratization Hill was enough to prove that Li Zhiyong's accusation was by no means unfounded.

Who was to blame?

Du Jianping glanced at Liu Simiao subconsciously.

Liu Simiao pretended not to see it.

In a very short period of time, the city's No. 1 Prison, the police station where Zhou Liping lived, the streets, and the aid and education institutions all reported the relevant situation: Zhou Liping was released two years ago because he was well reformed in prison, and he did not seek his own parents, or disturb the aunt who had adopted him, but found another cheap house and rented it. At first, he had trouble renting the house. After signing the contract and paying the deposit, the landlord knew from somewhere that he was a murderer who had been in prison and immediately broke the contract. After a few times, even the salesman of the real estate agency became embarrassed and helped him rent a small apartment. The landlord lived in the United States for many years and seldom came back, so they entrusted everything to the agency, which saved a lot of trouble. After he settled down completely, Zhou Liping reported to the police station where he lived on time. The policemen hated him for immortality, even if it was official business, they didn't make him feel better, but he was always silent and expressionless in the face of any cynicism and scolding. According to other people's support, he shuttled between various grass-roots government departments again and again, registered, signed, and sealed, and finally re-registered his household registration and ID card. With the help of the educational institution, he found a job as a traffic coordinator. A young man in his twenties wore a little red hood and an orange-yellow vest every morning and evening. He held a red flag in his hand. He stood at the traffic lights and directed traffic, went to drink some water in the nearby WC when he was thirsty, or bought a steamed bun in the nearby shop when he was hungry.... Maybe because the beast seemed really tame, the police station and the street gradually eased their defenses, and even in the "gun hunting incident" that happened not long after, the street director came out and said a few words for him: "I think that boy should have been remodeled."

Du Jianping knew some about all of these, some didn't, so he hated both those grassroots cadres and how they could believe that a bloodthirsty tiger had turned into a docile cat, and he also hated himself. If he believed Li Zhiyong, he would never give up searching Zhou Liping until he was brought to justice, and he would not have caused the tragedy on Deratization Hill today, and he would have lost a colleague in vain...

The group that arrested Zhou Liping was divided into two groups: Group A, led by Lin Fengchong, went to Zhou Liping's house, and Chu Tianying also went with him, so that no matter whether Zhou Liping was caught at home or not, they could immediately start a search and investigation of his residence; Group B was personally led by Du Jianping and went to Mingyi Public Relations Company, because according to the tracking and positioning of Zhou Liping's mobile phone, which was currently in the area of Runtang Hi-Tech Incubation Park.

After arriving at Runtang Hi-Tech Incubation Park, the police found the director of the park office and learned in detail about the internal structure of Block D, the entry and exit paths, and the specific orientation of Mingyi Public Relations Company. Du Jianping said to the police officers in the car: "As you all know, this Zhou Liping is our old rival. He killed many people ten years ago, including a female police officer, but for various reasons, he was not allowed to go to jail long enough.Whether he can continue to be so lucky this time is up to you!"

A big-armed criminal policeman sneered: "Don't worry, Director, this time, we will not only catch that bastard, but also chop him up, pack it, and deliver it to the King of Hell."

"That's right!" Du Jianping nodded, "But be careful, you should avoid shooting as much as possible during the arrest operation, and strive to capture Zhou Liping alive, otherwise it will be too easy to give him an end. Considering that this person is extremely dangerous, you may carry weapons on your body, so if you encounter an opponent who shoots and resists arrest, you can shoot if you have to, just to avoid hitting the key points and pay attention to the safety of the public."

At this time, Lin Fengchong called and said that Zhou Liping had not been found at his residence. In this way, it was almost certain that Zhou Liping was in Block D.

The criminal policemen opened their eyes wide, waiting for Du Jianping's order to attack, but Du Jianping's heart became heavy at the moment of battle. An extremely vicious juvenile murderer, jailed for eight years was enough to significantly "improve" his criminal skills, criminal psychology and even physical fitness. Once he resisted arrest, his brothers will face the danger of death and injury, and innocent people would be even more vulnerable... The best way was to send someone to go to Mingyi Company to inquire about Zhou Liping's work position and status, and even evacuate Mingyi Company and even all employees in D block in advance, but this car of detectives were all experienced who has arrested serious criminals for many years, not to mention the experienced Zhou Liping, ordinary people will walk around to avoid when they see them, and Zhou Liping had just committed the crime, he will be aware of the slightest disturbance, and the evacuation of the masses. It really didn't work... they had to slam into it.

Just as Du Jianping was about to give his battle orders, someone suddenly patted the door of the GL8.

Everyone in the car was startled. Du Jianping turned his head and looked out the window surprisingly and happily, he opened the car door. Standing at the door was his old subordinate Li Zhiyong!

He had't seen him for two years. Li Zhiyong had gotten a little fatter. He still looked so stubborn with his small nose and small eyes. His hair was neatly combed and his beard was shaved, and wore a black suit although a little wrinkled, but more neat than when he was a detective. Li Zhiyong was very happy to see the old leader and several old colleagues in the car, and greeted them warmly.

"Why are you here?" Du Jianping asked.

"I also want to ask why you're here!" Li Zhiyong said, "I can't recognize other things, but these two GL8s are old guys from our criminal police team – have a case?"

Du Jianping said "Yes" and stopped talking. Li Zhiyong knew the rules. When the police wanted to handle a case, they could not reveal a drop of information to "outsiders".

He suddenly said: "Are you here to arrest Zhou Liping?"

Du Jianping glanced at him: "How did you know?"

"What kind of territory here? High-tech incubator." Li Zhiyong said, "If you want to name an economic criminal, a fraudster or something, I believe you, but it doesn't take so many people from our criminal police brigade. Since the criminal needs to be caught, and has to commit a major crime, all I can think of in the entire park is Zhou Liping."

"The old detective really has sharp eyes." Du Jianping smiled and chased after him, "How did you know that Zhou Liping was in this park?"

Li Zhiyong said: "He and I both work at Mingyi Company in Block D."

The cat and the mouse were actually in a hole, and the cat was once skinned alive by the mouse-everyone was stunned!

Although he couldn't figure out what was going on for a while, Du Jianping knew that the person he had always hoped for who knew Mingyi Company in depth was right in front of him: "Is Zhou Liping in the company?"

"Yes!" Li Zhiyong also became serious, "I'm getting off work early. When I came out, he was still at his workstation."

Du Jianping nodded: "Can you cooperate with our arrest operation?"

"I've been looking forward to this day for a long time!" Li Zhiyong said, "I'll go back to the office platform. You send the brothers to guard the east and west doors and wait for me to call you and report the situation before taking action."

"Good job!" Du Jianping patted his arm fiercely with joy.

"Ouch!" Li Zhiyong cried out in pain.

"What's wrong?" Du Jianping was stunned, "I didn't try too hard?"

"Nothing, I helped move the furniture and got hurt yesterday." After Li Zhiyong finished speaking, he turned and walked towards Block D.

When Li Zhiyong entered Block D, Du Jianping immediately jumped out of the car, and the criminal policemen in the two GL8s also rushed out, all of them wearing brown or black leather jackets, looking serious and alert. Du Jianping waved his hand, and the criminal policemen, like wolves hunting, stooped and rushed towards Block D. One group held the west gate, the other circled from the south to the east gate, and then stopped in unison at the gate. Quietly waiting for the next order.

At this moment, Du Jianping's cell phone rang. After connecting, Li Zhiyong's anxious voice came from inside: "Zhou Liping ran away!"

Du Jianping's head hummed, he immediately pulled out the pistol from his waist, smashed the glass door and rushed into Block D. The criminal policemen behind him followed and entered into the lobby on the first floor with loaded pistols in their hands. Their chaotic reflections were reflected on the gleaming white marble floor.

They rushed straight into the door of Mingyi Company. Behind the front desk decorated with goose-yellow backs, sat a beautiful girl dressed in fashion. She jumped up from her seat in fright. Before she could shout, she saw Li Zhiyong from the same company running out of the room and met the uninvited guests.

"Didn't you say he was still here just now?" Du Jianping asked.

"Yeah, when I came out, I caught a glimpse of him sitting at his workstation looking at the computer."

"Then why did he run away so quickly? Is his briefcase still at the workstation?"

"He is a driver, and he always commutes to get off work empty-handed..."

"East Gate, did you see Zhou Liping come out?!" Du Jianping shouted into the police intercom.

"No! No!"

Whether Li Zhiyong was seen by Zhou Liping through the window when he was greeting them at the car door just now, so he ran away... A layer of sweat appeared on Du Jianping's huge forehead, if he let this major crime escape, it will be difficult to catch him alive again. Du Jianping stomped his foot, turned and walked out the door, bumping into a man who was walking slowly towards the door.

Du Jianping took a closer look: it was Zhou Liping!

Du Jianping grabbed Zhou Liping's arm, twisted it with a click, and stumbled again with his right foot. Zhou Liping fell to the ground like a mud. Other police officers rushed to control him. At first, Zhou Liping cried out in pain, "Ouch, oops". Later, perhaps because his neck was stuck, there was a strange whimper in his throat, like a dog.

The girl at the front desk screamed in horror, and the employees of Mingyi Company poked their heads from behind the partition between the front desk and the office area, wanting to look but not dared.

"Sir." A criminal policeman looked at Du Jianping and shook his head, meaning that no weapons were found on Zhou Liping's body.

Du Jianping squatted down, picked up Zhou Liping's hair and asked, "Name?"

"Zhou Liping."

"Do you know what happened to you?"

"I don't know."

"Okay! Let's change the place and let you know!"

A few detectives picked him up like a chicken and carried him outside Block D almost without touching the ground.

From the beginning to the end, the other office areas in the corridor were quiet, and there were no people who came out to look on, like a crystal coffin waiting for a visit.

4

The news of Zhou Liping's arrest reached the temporary headquarters, and the workshop of the printing factory burst into cheers! Although the criminal policemen who had been busy all night had dark circles under their eyes, they all had smiles on their faces at this moment. Some of them leaned against the wall, took out cigarettes, shrunk their cheeks, and puffed on clouds, while others called their wives and apologized in a low voice for not going home last night. Some people were doing chest expansion, shoulder twisting and head turning exercises, and suddenly their whole body clicked, and some people untied the plastic bag from the wooden frame car, took out a fritter that had become cold and hard, chewed it hard.

Since it was a major criminal case, the next trial will be conducted in the Pre-Trial Section of the Criminal Investigation Division of the Municipal Bureau. A criminal policeman walked up to Liu Simiao and asked for instructions, "Director Liu, can we clean up this place?" Meant whether to make preparations to cancel the temporary headquarters and evacuate. Liu Simiao gave him a cold look, but didn't say a word. The detective was very sensible and quickly stepped aside.

The case was so solved? Liu Simiao was a little surprised. He killed four people and set fire to their bodies. The perpetrator was still a "veteran" with rich anti-investigation experience, but he was caught so easily... Thought about Tang Xiaotang's thrilling autopsy under the tunnel wind pavilion, thought about in the nursery, her colleagues were busy all night. Thought of the scene of looking at each other and being at a loss when the case analysis meeting was held in this room in the early morning, especially when she thought of the white plastic sheet that was blown across the wall by the strong wind, she suddenly felt like a dream. At this moment, her cell phone rang, and when it was connected, Li Sanduo's excited voice came: "Simiao, good job!"

"Rely on the colleagues."

"Don't be modest, I already know that they catch the suspect so quickly, mainly thanks to your correct way of handling the case... The next thing is the pre-trial department, go home and rest! "

The soup was hot, but there was a strand of hair mixed in the bottom of the soup, so others couldn't see it, but Liu Simiao could see it clearly.

"Just tell me straight, are you not letting me participate in this case?"

"Look at you, your heart is narrower than Lin Daiyu." Li Sanduo said with a smile, "Director Xu has discussed with me, and let you rest for considering that you are tired and sick, and the Criminal Technology Department of the Municipal Bureau has a lot of work. Who do you want us to look for as a substitute? Besides, the subway transfer station is in charge of each line, how could we ask you to take charge of all the work like a comedy actress caught a sheep and stabbed it from head to tail? "

Lier! Liu Simiao understood that Li Sanduo's words were half-truths. The arrest of a major criminal suspect indeed marked a new stage in the case. Not to mention criminal skills, even criminal investigation had to give way to interrogation. It did not mean that criminal investigation and criminal skills can be used in a big way. Not to mention that there was still the possibility that the real murderer was someone else, even if Zhou Liping was really a murderer, then the investigation will be completed and transferred to the procuratorate for review and prosecution until the court trial and a series of judicial procedures, each link requires a criminal technical processing. Although most of these tasks did not need to be done by themselves, but deliberately emphasizing "rest", you can still hear the overtones.

If it was in the past, with Liu Simiao's temper, she would definitely argue with Li Sanduo and ask the reason, but in the past year, she had always felt a sense of burnout... Therefore, she had always been concerned about career and life, but she had more and more thoughts such as "make it do" or "it's wise to pretend to be confused", and the mass generation of such thoughts also made her increasingly irritable and contradictory. She did not want to compromise, but she had to.

"Okay," she said.

Li Sanduo hung up the phone, and Liu Simiao guessed that he must have let out a long sigh of relief.

The moment she put down the phone, she suddenly had a strange feeling. Looking around, the police officers in the printing workshop who had been relaxed just now seemed to be busy in an instant, and the half-closed laptop was turned on again, and pencil wrote irregular lines on the analog portrait books, the half-disassembled crime scene was reconstructed by

EPS foam templates, and now was put back together and dismantled again. Someone looked down like a squirrel and repeatedly counted those crime scene investigation materials. They seemed to be gathered together to discuss the case, but were actually talking nonsense that has nothing to do with the case... Liu Simiao understood that they knew that she was ordered to leave the Deratization Hill case. Therefore, they can only pretend to be immersed in work, so as not to let her notice the confusion and embarrassment in their eyes.

Thanks, guys.

Liu Simiap looked at her watch, it was already 4:30 in the afternoon.

If she go home now, she might be able to catch an online dance class at the Vaganova Russian Ballet School.

But... now the main leaders of the task force were not there, was it appropriate to leave? At least, she should meet Du Jianping and then leave.

At this moment, a roar suddenly came from the corner of the printing workshop: "What? How could this happen?!"

Liu Simiao looked in the direction of the voice, and it turned out to be a police officer in charge of coordinating the connection between the task force and the local police station related to the case.

Liu Simiao walked over and asked, "What happened?"

The police officer didn't seem to hear it, and was still furious at the phone: "Send someone to take that chef to hospital immediately , and, keep an eye on Ma Xiaozhong! What? You can't do it? You can't fucking do it—"

"I asked: What happened?!" Liu Simiao's tone instantly became sharp.

The police officer no longer dared to pretend to be deaf or dumb, squeezed out a smile, pointed to the phone and said, "Director Liu, Ma Xiaozhong has made a big trouble..."

Liu Simiao grabbed his mobile phone and asked the police officer on the other end of the phone, "I'm Liu Simiao, what happened?"

Here's what happened: after receiving Du Jianping's transfer order, Ma Xiaozhong and a subordinate named Feng Qi rushed to Tongyou Nursing Home and took over Chai Yongjin's job. The first order he gave was to withdraw the plainclothes police officers who were standing guard at the front and rear entrances, and then called the staff of the nursing home to the lobby on the first floor and let them sit on the grass-green leather bench at the entrance. Then he took a chair to sit across from them, and asked them with some unnecessary common questions: Was the salary of the nursing home high? How were the living conditions? Were the kids obedient? The conversation went on well, and they talk happily all along. The employees had no idea what was going on, and they were all trembling, but now they were relieved when they saw such a short, fat ugly man who was so talktive and they felt a little bit squeamish. Ma Xiaozhong was especially fond of the dean's secretary named Chi Fengli, and called her "sister". Chi Fengli was a social butterfly, while seeing this short fat man and the standing detectives were not together, he was more like a hooligan. Then Chi Fengli kept rubbing a hole in her leggings, while laughing and talking with Ma Xiaozhong, Feng Qi next to him cleared his throat several times to remind Ma Xiaozhong to pay attention to his identity, but he continued to tease Chi Fengli as if he didn't hear it.

It was a phone call that disturbed Ma Xiaozhong. The task force called to report the latest progress of the case investigation work: Zhou Liping, the major criminal suspect, had been locked. Now the criminal police were divided into two groups, one team went to his house, the other went to his company to arrest him.

Hearing the name "Zhou Liping", Ma Xiaozhong was astonished for a moment, but before he could think about it, the door of the nursing home opened.

A woman in her 40s walked in. She was not tall and had short hair, wearing a camel-colored leather jacket with a lapel collar, inside was a white one-neck cardigan that wrapped her body in a bumpy manner. Her cheekbones were extremely high, and was brushed with a thick layer of powder, perhaps to cover up the dark circles under her eyes, so the skin around her eyes was whiter than other parts, two plump tips were smeared with thick lipstick, as if a chicken heart had just been dug out.

As soon as she entered the hall, the employees sitting on the soft benches all stood up and called "Ms. Cui".

Ma Xiaozhong knew that this was Cui Yucui, the vice president of Tongyou Nursing Home, he stood up and smiled and stretched out his hand: "Hello, Ms. Cui, I'm a police officer in this area, my surname is Ma, you can call me my name."

Cui Yucui put out her hand in his palm, and immediately withdrew it, her eyes were alert: "What's the matter asking me to come hurrily?"

"Don't worry. How could be any matter?" Ma Xiaozhong looked irresistible, "There was a traffic accident in the middle of the night last night, killing people and causing the hit-and-run vehicle to escape. You also know that the end of the year is approaching, and everyone are accumulating tasks for year-end bonus. The traffic police team hurried to investigate, suspecting that the car that caused the accident was the car driven by President Xing, so they came to investigate here, I got the message just now, the car that caused the accident was found, and it has nothing to do with the Dean. I was sent to clean up, and was leaving with my brothers."

The employees sitting on the soft-packed benches were confused. The police asked a lot of questions during the investigation just now, and most of them were focused on Xing Qisheng's schedule, but they also asked a lot of questions about the management of the nursing home, so for a while It was unclear the short fat man was telling the truth or lies. Cui Yucui was also confused by him. But she was also a sophisticated one who could contend with the police. The best set of skills was to pretend as needed. After all, the police was an official, and was very friendly. Naturally it was not good to put on a cold face, so she changed to smile and lit a cigarette for Ma Xiaozhong, and the two started chatting politely. Ma Xiaozhong raised a few questions, most of which related to Xing Qisheng's personal life habits, but did not touch the core of the case, and Cui also handled with the questions effortlessly. When came to Xing's personally private life, she casually said, "He just likes tender and young ones, as young as possible." Suddenly realizing that she seemed to have said something wrong, and peeked at Ma Xiaozhong, but saw the short fat man staring at Chi Fengli with a stern look. Then she quickly diverted the topic.

At this moment, a voice suddenly came from behind them: "The meal is coming!"

Ma Xiaozhong looked up. A chubby man in a military green jacket with a white chef's uniform inside walked into the building from the back door of the nursing home. This man had red face and mung bean-shaped eyes, the fat belly made him looked like a pregnant woman when he walked in.

"Who is this?" Ma Xiaozhong asked Cui Yucui, pointing to the person who came.

"Our nursing home does not have a canteen, so we signed a long-term meal contract with a nearby restaurant. This is Master Bao, who is in charge of cooking and delivering meals." Cui Yucui said, "If you have no important matter, just stay and have dinner with us, okay?"

They made it clear that it was a polite remark just tell him to leave, but Ma Xiaozhong didn't seem to hear it, and said with a smile: "That's good! I hadn't have lunch yet." He got up and took the plastic bags from the hand of the Bao, brought out the white lunch boxes and put them on a long table in the hall, and opened them one by one: gluttonous frog, soft fried tenderloin, black pepper beef fillet, steamed mandarin fish... ... Maybe because the food just came out of the pot, it was so hot that he rubbed his fingers. One of the vegetables in a round lunch box made him almost dripped: in the middle of the red and spicy soup, filled with prawns, tender beef, tripes, crab sticks, enoki mushrooms, and duck blood... He grabbed a pair of chopsticks and stuffed a piece of sole fish into his big mouth.

Bao had never seen this short fat man. Seeing that he was eating vulgarly, and couldn't help but snorted disdainfully, and then walked into the corridor with a smaller plastic bag.

"Hey, hey!" Ma Xiaozhong stopped him while eating, "Wait, what's the delicious meal in that plastic bag? Let me take a look."

"Nothing special!" said Bao impatiently, "just for the children."

Cui Yucui hurriedly stepped forward, smiled at Ma Xiaozhong and said, "Ma, that is for children, we can't eat children's meals as this old age...Bao, officer is joking with you, hurry up and deliver meals to the children!"

When the surnamed Bao heard that he was a policeman, his expression suddenly became flustered, and he hurried to the corridor.

Ma Xiaozhong held the dish, and stopped in front of him in two steps, he smiled and said: "You are so dawdle, I want to see the children meal, then just open it, I have never seen a children's meal in my life, let me have a look!"

Bao looked at Cui Yucui. Cui Yucui was about to intervene between the two of them. Feng Qi, who was standing on the side, took a step and stopped her.

Bao had no choice. He put the plastic bag on the ground, squatted down, slowly unbuttoned the plastic bag, took out a lunch box, and took a long time to open the lid.

What appeared in front of Ma Xiaozhong was a box full of mushy stuff that was hard to say as meals. It had to look carefully to tell the difference which was about pouring all kinds of leftover dishes into a pot, which was also the leftover lumps. The so-called meal was no difference from swill, and there were even half cigarette butts floating clearly on the surface...

Feng Qi's blood rushed to the top of his head.

Just as he was clenching his palms with his fingernails and secretly admonishing himself that "as a police officer, you must never abuse violence", Ma next to him roared, and slapped the pot of vegetables in his hand to Bao. The hot red soup immediately caused countless blisters on his face, causing him to scream and bend down, before his hands could cover his face, Ma Xiaozohng raised his knees, ruthlessly hit the middle of the bridge of his nose, and the sound of the smashed fracture of his nose can be clearly heard! Bao fell to the ground and passed out. The blushing purple thing couldn't tell whether it was blood or soup, and could not distinguish his facial features at all. It looked almost like the box of swill he gave the children!

Just as the 20-something-year-old stunned driver in the nursing home shouted, "How can the police hurt people?" Ma Xiaozhong kicked him to the ground and slapped his head a few times. He immediately shrinking into a ball and daring not to speak like an attacked armadillo, the other employees were shocked when they saw this amiable and short fat man suddenly looked terrifying and mad. After all, it was Cui Yucui who had was sophisticated and took out her mobile phone to take a picture, but Feng Qi snatched it away. She was a shrew, and fought with Feng Qi at the moment. Ma Xiaozhong said, "Feng Qi, are the handcuffs on your waist toys?"which reminded him at once, he stretched out the handcuffs, Cui Yucui's arm was twisted and handcuffed, and she was pinched on her neck to the ground. Cui Yucui kicked her legs and screamed for a while, then stopped struggling when she saw that it was useless, and kept scolding with swear words.

"You guys!" Ma Xiaozhong said to the nursing home staff who were shivering like chickens with plague, "squat down facing the wall, and don't say a fucking word!"

Hearing the shaking of the ground outside, the police officers who had been rummaging through the materials in the office and caring for the children in the classroom all came out one after another. Seeing that the headmaster Ma was arrogant, then quickly pretended not to see it and all left. Now, Feng Qi called two people and sent the Bao to a nearby hospital, then came over to Ma Xiaozhong with a frown, and said, "Director, you made a big trouble this time..."

Ma XIaozhong said while rubbing the phalanx that hurt from beating, "Go and call the task force and report the matter in its entirety."

"You don't think it's bad enough?" Feng Qi widened his eyes, looked at the nursing home staff who were squatting in a row facing the wall, and pulled Ma Xiaozhong to a distance and whispered, "If the leaders know, you must be dismissed for investigation, and now we have to think about how to make big things small, and cover it..."

Ma Xiaozhong simled: "Listen to me, call the task force, you can only add bad details, and don't conceal anything."

Feng Qi had worked with him in the police station for several years, and he knew that the director did not have any hesitation. When it came to cunning, almost no one in the world could compare with him. He didn't know what kind of idea in Ma's mind, but it was right to do what he said, so he called the task force to report the situation, and when he looked up, Ma suddenly disappeared.

Where had this man gone?

Feng Qi looked around, only to find that Ma Xiaozhong came to the door of a room at some point, and was looking inside through the crack of the door.

Feng Qi walked to his side and followed his sight line to see a policewoman smiling and reading a picture book called "The Letter Has Come" to the children. The children with physical or mental illnesses were sitting around her, looking at her face, and the picture book in her hand, they were all listening very attentively, their eyes were a little excited and a little curious. A little girl with a big head and a soft neck was snuggling up against the policewoman, she clutched the corner of her clothes tightly, as if afraid that she would leave. The dusk light shone on them through the window, making people feel confused and bitter.

"Director," Feng Qi said softly, "Director Liu Simiao received the call to suspend you immediately and wait for the investigation and handling by superiors. Sun Kang, the director of Hongshan Road Police Station, will be sent to take over your work."

"That guy?" Ma Xiaozhong nodded, "He's my brother. When he comes, remember to tell him: that Xing Qisheng is not just a victim."

Feng Qi was a little confused: "Didn't he one of the four dead on Deratization Hill?"

"Cui Yucui didn't look at Chi Fengli when she said that Xing Qisheng 'just likes tender and young ones', and Chi Fengli also looked calm and didn't feel guilty or angry, indicating that Cui Yucui said 'tender and young' did not refer to her."

"I see, I thought you looked at Chi Fengli for—" Feng Qi suddenly understood the meaning of Ma Xiaozhong's words, his face suddenly turned pale, and looked at the children in the classroom, "Do you mean——"

Ma Xiaozhong took out a handful of money from his pocket and gave to Feng Qi: "Go out to the second traffic light to the north, there is a Xibei Noodle Village, buy twelve sets of children's meals, and some iron cabbage and vermicelli, steamed beef, sesame oil fried eggs which are good for children to eat, and no spicy... By the way, do and ask the colleagues on duty here what they want to eat, buy for them together."

Feng Qi was very surprised. He knew that Ma Xiaozhong was always considerate, but he didn't expect he was that much considerate, and even thought about the children's dinner on the way.

He took the money and walked out, while reaching to the entrance, he turned around, and saw Ma Xiaozhong still standing there, with a gloomy expression, looking at the classroom with very solemn eyes, not like the originally cynical him...

When Feng Qi returned to Tongyou Nursing Home with a big bag of food, Ma Xiaozhong had already left, and now people in charge was Sun Kang, the head of the Hongshan Road Police Station. When they got to the room where the children were, the policewoman had already told the story for so long and was very thirsty. When she saw them coming, it was like seeing a savior and then she said to the children, "Let's wash our hands first, and then have dinner!"

The children looked overjoyed at the boxes of fragrant meals spread out on the table, but no one stepped forward, and no one washed their hands.

The policewoman understood that even if the children ate swill, they would be beaten, scolded and punished by the caregivers. Moreover, there was no one to take care of them to tell them the habit of washing their hands before meals, so she went to the bathroom to get a basin of water, helped wash their little hands one by one with soap and let them go to get the utensils.

The children rushed to a crack-covered cabinet next to the radiator, opened the door, took out their "tableware", and the older children took them apart one by one and distributed them to the younger ones.

The policewoman just glanced at it and was stunned.

It was not "tableware" at all, but just used instant noodle boxes and noodle forks. Maybe it's because every time when finish a meal, they simply rinsed it with water instead of washing it. The bottom of each lunch box was so dirty that each of the box was covered by green mould -- with the exception of a stainless steel rice bowl, which was a little cleaner.

Sun Kang picked up an instant noodle box and was so angry that he scolded. Seeing that the children were a little scared, he quickly squatted down and explained to them: "I'm just scolding bad guys, not you." The policewoman told him : "I'll find a supermarket or a convenience store nearby, and buy some good tableware. And not easy to break, better wood-made or enamel-made."

The policewoman just took two steps to the door, when the little girl with a big head and a soft neck burst into tears, jumped over and grabbed her by the corner of her clothes to keep her from going, and then almost all the children cried.

The policewoman crouched down, hugged the little girl and coaxed her gently. Gradually, her own eyes became red.

Sun Kang asked Feng Qi outside the room: "What's going on?!"

Feng Qi told him about Ma Xiaozhong beating the workers here, and then said, "Director Ma asked me to tell you that the dean of the Nursing Institute named Xing Qisheng is not just a victim."

Sun Kang was stunned for a moment, then understood something, nodded with ashen face, and called one of his subordinates, "Ask the office to send a car to take all those fuc... all the scumbags to the detention room! Divide some rooms, and send police officers to watch them all night long specifically. They are not allowed to collude in confessions. There may be a big drama behind it!"

The policewoman suddenly stuck her head out of the room: "Director Sun, come in please."

When Sun Kang walked in, the children had calmed down and were quietly waiting to eat.

"What's the matter?" Sun Kang asked.

The policewoman pointed to a row of "lunch boxes" that had been spread out on the table.

Sun Kang didn't understand, frowned and said, "Hurry up and throw those away. It's so disgusting. If the children are all calm down, then go and buy some tableware. I'm watching here—"

"No, Director." The policewoman said, "I counted, there are twelve children in total, but fifteen lunch boxes."

"Then what's the matter?" Sun Kang only muttered, and suddenly widened his eyes!

He suddenly understood who the three extra lunch boxes belonged to.

Chapter 3

1

"Tinkle", with a crisp sound, the glass door of the coffee shop was pushed open, and a beautiful girl wearing a white shirt, jeans and a long pink knitted sweater walked in. She had curly hair in a shawl and half-covering her snow-white and round face, perhaps because she hadn't slept well, a pair of beautiful big eyes were sunken a little deep, although the corners of his mouth were always slightly upturned cutely, but there was an inadvertent frown between brows, which made the smile looked a little sad.

The coffee shop was empty at ten o'clock in the morning. She glanced around in the coffee shop, and soon found the girl leaning on a chair reading a book, she walked over, and sat down opposite.

The one reading the book found that the person she was waiting for had arrived, and put down the book: "Guo, long time no see!"

"Long time no see, Simiao." Guo Xiaofen said with a smile, "How are you doing recently?"

"This question seems to be the right one for me to ask you." Liu Simiao said.

The two of them were a pair of strange friends, one was a young and promising criminal forensics expert, and the other was a well-known media reporter. The interviewers of the newspaper were all the same as the interviewees in the public sector. One must try to spy on the exclusive news, and the other must be strictly guarded to avoid leaking information. The two of them quarreled frequently because of work, and it was common for them to complain to the leaders of the other one. However, as time passed and they grew older, they finally discovered that, in essence, they were both doctors who were eager to treat various diseases in this society. It's just that the internal and external divisions were different, so the differences caused by pure personalities and living habits were gradually ignored, and they understood and cooperated with each other... They were still two different people, but they were aiming to the same direction.

"I'm fine." Guo Xiaofen touched her face, "Resigning is like losing a love, it was always easy at first, every day I watch internet dramas on the sofa and eating potato chips, I feel like I'm getting fat like beans in water... Simiao, you seemed to have lost a lot of weight again, was it because of the case in Deratization Hill? I heard that you left the task force after solving the case."

"So you are sitting at home, and the news will come." Liu Simiao said with a smile, then raised her hand at the counter, and a waiter came over and asked them what to drink. Liu Simiao ordered herself a cup of orange and pear tea, and Guo Xiaofen asked for a latte. After paying the bill, the waiter put a small reindeer doll on their table as a proof of waiting for the order. Guo Xiaofen grabbed it, slapped a few times, and said something inadvertently: "Because of the Xiangming?"

Liu Sima was stunned for a moment, her eyes stayed on a crack on the wooden table top that was cut by a knife or a natural crack, and did not move for a long time.

An unknown Korean song was reverberating in the coffee shop. There was a tinkling sound of cups at the counter, the humming of coffee beans and the milk frother. All the sound were light and sweet, as if there was nothing happened, as if they were reminiscing about an old dream that can never be forgotten.

Guo Xiaofen knew that she was right. She learned the news the first time after the Deratization Hill case, and soon saw the notice issued by the Municipal Bureau on Weibo that the major criminal suspect Zhou Liping had been arrested. As a long-time legal news reporter, she had a relatively in-depth understanding of the "Western Suburb Serial Murder Cases" that happened ten years ago. When she first saw the news, she was worried about Simiao would be incriminated. First, from the perspective of the media and the public, if a former serial killer committed a second crime, he must be investigated for why he was easily let go in the first place, then Lin Xiangming must be queried for putting a word for Zhou Lingping before. Besides, the whole city's public security system knew the relations between Liu Simiao and Lin Xiangming. No matter from which point of view, she must be asked to avoid the case.

After being silent for a long time, Liu Simiao said slowly: "The superior leaders have more comprehensive considerations. I also participated in some detection work in the 'Western Suburb Serial Murder Case' ten years ago. Xiangming believed that Zhou Liping did kill Fang Zhifeng, but he has nothing to do with the deaths of the other three women, I also agree with this conclusion, at least so far, no new evidence has been found that can overturn this conclusion ."

"But the public won't consider it that way," Guo Xiaofen said. "In the eyes of the public, if a prisoner who has served his sentence but committed a crime again, it will only convince him of his previous crime."

"Criminal investigation work has a certain particularity. It should not be emotional, and speculation should not be used to replace the truth. All conclusions must be based on scientific evidence and strict logic." Liu Simiao said, "The public is allowed to question, but they have no right to intervene."

"However, you yourself have doubts now – am I right?" Guo Xiaofen said suddenly.

Her words liked an oblique stab! Steady, accurate, and fast!

When it was someone else, they must be angry at the time, but Liu Simiao just smiled: "Tell me about yourself, why did you resign? I saw Zhang Wei in Deratization Hill that day, and he said that your manuscripts were killed consecutively.... You are an old reporter, how could this happen?"

Maybe it was the sense of loss, Guo Xiaofen felt a little melancholy, and at this moment, the waiter brought the orange and pear tea and latte, each was exuding fragrance. Liu Simiao picked up the teacup, blew lightly, and took some sips along the rim of the cup. Guo Xiaofen slowly stirred the coffee with a small spoon, watching the heart-shaped latte art turn into a mess of milk froth, and suddenly said, "Maybe it's because I only like to drink brewed coffee..."

Liu Simiao didn't understand what she meant.

"All things, in the final analysis, can be divided into two categories: standard and non-standard, from clothing to occupations to education to catering... so do the media work, the standard-one is called press script, and the non-standard-one is called news. Like instant coffee, water, coffee powder and partner are all prepared, you just put it in hot water and drink it, maybe the brand is different, or the taste, but in the end it is passive acceptance; the real news should be the hand-made coffee, which are valuable and meaningful for journalists to analyze, organize, process, and write according to the materials they have interviewed, and restore part of the truth of the incident from different angles." Guo Xiaofen said, "But now, the editor-in-chief of our newspaper office only allowed us to sell instant coffee, which I think is an insult to real coffee brewers – of course, most customers don't care."

"It may be that your editor-in-chief is worried about the hygiene problems of hand-made brewed coffee." Liu Simiao said.

"It turns out that large-scale public health incidents will always only occur in instant coffee, especially when coffee is monopolized by companies and the recipe is kept secret." Guo Xiaofen said.

"It seems that I didn't find the wrong person." Liu Simiao took another sip of tea, "You said goodbye to the journalism industry, but not to the ideals of journalism, and what I want to do is exactly done by journalists who was resigned but still have the ideals of journalism."

Finally came to the main point. Guo Xiaofen's eyes widened: "Finally comes the central idea, what do you want me to do?"

Liu Simiao looked at Guo Xiaofen and said, "I want you to assist in the investigation of the Deratization Hill case."

2

It has been two days since the Deratization Hill case occurred. In the past two days, if one word could be used to describe the state of the police after Zhou Liping was arrested, there was probably no more appropriate word than "clueless".

Of course, it wasn't like this at the beginning. Really, everyone thought that since Zhou Liping was caught, the whole case would be as easy as a cook. Therefore, the morale of the task force was high. In order to handle this case as a monolith, they adopted the strategy of "first attacking the periphery and then the heart", urging all relevant departments to work overtime, get all the evidence related to the case, and consolidate it, and then focus on the interrogation of Zhou Liping.

Look at the evidence.

First, there was news from the Forensic Center: The hair extracted from Xing Qisheng's residence was compared with the body number C found in the wind pavilion of the Deratization Hill Tunnel, and it was confirmed that the body number C was indeed Xing Qisheng, the dean of Tongyou Nursing.

Through the DNA comparison of the hair extracted in the dormitory of Tongyou Nursing Home and the blood samples retained by the autologous blood transfusion technology during the treatment of congenital heart disease in the hospital with the three corpses numbered A, B and D respectively, it had also been confirmed that they were all nursing home children.

Among them, the female corpse number B was named Dong Xinlan, who was nine years old this year, and suffered from mild cerebral palsy before her death. Her parents died early, and she had a sister whose present whereabouts were unknown.

The male corpse number A was named Zhao Wu, twelve years old, also an orphan, suffering from severe congenital heart disease;

The little girl numbered D, who was pressed down at the bottom, was named Li Ying. She was five years old and had Down syndrome before her death. She had mental retardation and was abandoned by her parents.

The interrogation of the staff of Tongyou Nursing Center proved that these children came to this city from province A a month ago to participate in welfare treatment and physical examination activities at the "Love Hospital", a private hospital in this city. "Love Hospital" was also a comprehensive private hospital funded by "Love Charity Foundation". It mainly treated children with intractable diseases. And had a good reputation in the fields of treating children with congenital heart disease, cerebral palsy, and myasthenia gravis. Every autumn and winter, the hospital would pick up a group of children from the welfare home in Province A and gave them free treatment and physical examination. According to media reports, this kind of charity had been going on for several years. Of course, due to the limited conditions of the hospital, it was impossible for the children to be admitted to the hospital, so they rented a small building near the hospital to let the children live temporarily. This was the origin of Tongyou Nursing Home.

Then, the Criminal Technology Office inspected the Vacheron Constantin watch and the black Zippo windproof lighter that Tang Xiaotang found under the tunnel wind pavilion. It could be confirmed that these two things were items that Xing Qisheng carried with him. But in addition, repeated investigations at the crime scene did not find any new valuable evidence – let alone these, Chu Tianying and a few detectives were busy working in the nursery for two days and nights. They could even count how many ant holes there, but hadn't found half of evidence that can be identified as fingerprints or footprints.

Perhaps the rut left by the Michelin 3ST Haoyue tires was an exception. The task force investigated the vehicle condition of Mingyi Public Relations Company. Based on the records of the car purchase order and the information provided by the INSPIRE 4S store, it was determined that the rut in the nursery was the one which Zhou Liping drove through the traffic lights in Dongli, Qingshikou on the night of the crime. This was the most valuable identification since the incident! Generally speaking, this evidence alone was enough for the suspect to be undeniable and bow his head to the law, but facing an opponent like Zhou Liping, the task force did not dare to take it easily. According to their assumptions, there must be physical evidence against Zhou Liping in the car, so they might as well get more "bullets" before interrogating him, so as to defeat Zhou Liping when he denies it in every possible way. Therefore, the police put a lot of effort into searching all conceivable parking places, such as Zhou Liping's residence, Tongyou Nursing Home, Runtang Hi-Tech Incubation Park where Mingyi Company was located, etc. The images captured by all the city's traffic surveillance systems during the time of the arrest were extensively screened, but several days passed and the car could not be found. The task force changed their thinking way, considering the direction of "abandoned cars", and joined the traffic police brigade, the fire brigade and the security brigade in the Western Suburbs to search the inside and outside of the Deratization Hill, and even organized six mountain search teams to search along the road from Deratization Hill to West Mountain, and they almost reached the neighboring province, but still found nothing. Considering that Zhou Liping was going to work normally on the second day of the crime, no matter how far he drove the car or left it in any wilderness, there was always "coming back", so it was impossible to run too far. The disappearance of the black INSPIRE made everyone even more confused...

The search for physical evidence was completely obstructed. Although the devastating consequences of the fire were well anticipated by the task force, the lack of valuable physical evidence still made many police officers frustrated.

Then witness testimony, including the investigation of the victim's personal situation, and the testimony of people involved in the case.

The first was Xing Qisheng's personal situation. He was 55 years old this year, and was a doctor in the provincial capital hospital of A province when he was young. He had a younger brother named Xing Qixian, who was the vice president of the "Love Charity Foundation". Perhaps it was through this relationship that Xing Qisheng later left the provincial capital hospital and came to this city to work as the chief physician of the dermatology department in the "Love Hospital". After working for a period of time, he left the hospital for unknown reasons and became the dean of Tongyou Nursing Home. Although the "Love Hospital" was only a private hospital, the scale was not small. Changing from the chief physician of a key department to being the director of a "black homestay" in essence was faster than going downhill on a roller coaster. The reason remains to be investigated.

Xing Qisheng's ex-wife gave birth to a son named Xing Yunda, 28 years old, who was currently the vice president of Mingyi Public Relations Company. On the day of Zhou Liping's arrest, the police launched a preliminary investigation into Mingyi Company and found that Xing Yunda was not at work. After knowing his father's death, his behavior was very strange. At first, his pale and thin face was very numb, and then suddenly the corners of his mouth twitched. He kept asking who killed his father, and viciously said that he would kill the murderer himself to avenge his father. At the same time, he took a knife which had opened the blade from his waist. The police were unprepared. Several people rushed up to hold him down and snatched the knife... His numbness and arrogance didn't seem like a pretense, but a young man in his late thirties was the vice president of a public relations company, but showing such an immature mind, still confused the police. Lin Fengchong even secretly sent someone to investigate whether he had an alibi at the time of the Deratization Hill. Later, they found out that the kid was playing PUBG with a few friends for whole night, and even start an online streaming on Huya.com. He was so addicted to killing people in online games, there was absolutely no possibility of going to Deratization Hill.

After hearing the news of Xing Qisheng's death, Xing Qisheng's younger brother Xing Qixian and the director of the Provincial Welfare Institute Cui Wentao immediately took the high-speed rail to the city. They said they would actively cooperate with the police's investigation. Xing Qixian was forty-eight years old this year, and was a well-mannered middle-aged man. He was neatly dressed and spoke elegantly, but his voice was so low that they couldn't hear him unless pricks up ears. Talking about his brother's death, he couldn't help crying, but the tears were very restrained, just disappeared with a tissue. Regarding the case that just happened, he couldn't provide much information, but kept emphasizing two things: the first was that his brother lived abroad for many years, and he had little contact with him, and the occasional contact was purely for work; The second was that his brother was a good person, and had never heard of him having any enemies.

In contrast, Cui Wentao and Xing Qixian, presidents of Welfare Institutes in Province A, was completely different. According to Lin Fengchong's imagination, the dean of the orphanage should be a kind-hearted grandfather or grandmother, so when he first met Cui Wentao, he was even more shocked than when he saw the Internet celebrity after removing the makeup: This person was not only short, but also looked like a mouse, which had been starving all winter. Due to the buck teeth, the two thin lips couldn't fit together. When he saw the police, he just kept nodding and bowing, "Okay, okay. Got it. Of course, no problem." His words were enough to make a rap, but if listened carefully, that were all nonsense.

Cui Wentao respected Xing Qixian, which made Lin Fengchong feel a little strange, because in terms of organizational structure, the director of the Provincial Welfare Institute was a public family member, and the "Love Charity Foundation" was just a private charity after all... Until Chai Yongjin quietly reminded him "Remember? Director Du's daughter was forced to death by the campus loan company affiliated to this foundation," he suddenly realized.

It was worth mentioning that Du Jianping did not come forward during the whole process of receiving Xing Qixian and Cui Wentao, and kept Lin Fengchong replaced.

Lin Fengchong had the intention to revenge for Du Jianping, so he was rude to Xing Qixian and Cui Wentao, and all the words came out sideways, but one of the two looked indifferent and taciturn, and the other was rambling but answered nonsense. Lin Fengchong felt that it was not the way to go, so he had to change a less hostile tone, and then figured out something: Province A was an economically underdeveloped and impoverished province. Before the reform and opening up, there were problems such as consanguineous marriage and child immunization work that could not be counted in the county. There were especially many disabled children. Afterwards, thanks to the development of mining and printing industries, the economy improved somewhat, but these two industries were heavy polluted, so the birth rate of deformed children continued to increase. These children were abandoned in large numbers. Of course, many of them lost both of their parents, or their parents went out to work and left the elderly to take care of them, and after the elderly died, they could not contact their parents... The number of existing welfare institutions in the province increased tenfold but still not enough, the civil affairs department could only call on the counties, townships and towns to "solve the problem on their own". They mainly raided private fund-raising to uphold welfare. The headquarter of Love Charity was located in the provincial capital, and each county had a branch. It has obtained a large amount of funds through charitable fundraising and other methods. In fact, it had become the sponsor of the provincial welfare institute and its branches in various counties, townships and towns. They gradually started to control the construction and management of the branch, and the general hospital of the A provincial welfare institute was increasingly becoming a pure office organization. Speaking of this, Cui Wentao made an analogy: "Our main hospital is like an online mall, there is no self-operated platform, and all the online shopping pages are franchised branches, but we are responsible for supervision and logistics." – like the murdered Dong Xinlan , Zhao Wu, and Li Ying were all children selected from the branch hospitals, concentrated in the general hospital, and then sent to the city.

It seemed that the logistics was indeed the responsibility of the provincial welfare institute, but not the supervision. When Lin Fengchong asked "who sent these children from the province to this city", Cui Wentao said a name. Lin Fengchong asked again: "Why didn't this person stay in the city to monitor the safety of the children?" Cui Wentao said that there was no need to keep people in the Tongyou Nursing Home, and the Tongyou Nursing Home is responsible for everything. After the physical examination and treatment for children were completed, the nursing home will notify the provincial welfare institute to send someone to take the children back. Lin Fengchong's tone immediately became stern: "Tongyou Nursing Home is in charge? Can it be held responsible? So who should be responsible for such a big incident now?" Cui Wentao blinked his eyes and did not speak, he gazed at Xing Qixian but didn't dare to look at him too long. Xing Qixian was silent for a long time before he said: "It must be admitted that there are indeed loopholes in supervision. Fortunately, it is not too late to make up for it. How should we check and fill the gaps, improve our work, and prevent such incidents from happening again, will be the focus of our Love Charity Foundation."

After hearing these words, Lin Fengchong couldn't help but be stunned.

When the two left the city bureau, Lin Fengchong clearly told them: Please don't leave the city until the case was fully investigated, in case the police would ask them to come at any time.

Xing Qixian did not speak, but Cui Wentao said hurriedly: "Okay, okay, of course, we have to wait for President Tao to come back and report to her."

The "President Tao" in Cui Wentao's words referred to Tao Zhuoyao, president of the Love Charity Foundation, 38 years old this year, single. Retired for many years, but still a figure who could control most of things in the local area, and also hung the post of honorary president of the foundation. Tao Zhuoyao lived in the city for a long period of time every year. The Tao family originally had three houses in the city. Before the anti-corruption turmoil started, they received the news somewhere, and all the property rights of the houses were transferred or revoked, causing the investigation of Disciplinary Committee came to nothing—she now lived in a suite on the fourth floor of Block E of the five-star Hefeng Hotel. It should be noted that the "Love Charity Foundation" rented the entire Building E, as an office in the city, there were more than 20 staff working here. In addition, Hefeng Hotel was not too far from Tongyou Nursing

Home and Love Hospital. Although the three did not belong to the same block on the map, the walking distance between them was not more than 15 minutes. As time went by, it would become more and more important in case detection.

Tao Zhuoyao took an Air France flight to Paris at 1:00 a.m. on the second day after the Deratization Hill case. She left very suddenly. Even Xing Qixian, who was the vice president, was at a loss. In the face of Lin Fengchong's question, "What's the matter with Tao Zhuoyao that she rushed to go abroad?", he hesitated and said nothing useful, which made Lin Fengchong understood: Tao Zhuoyao went abroad without talking to him or any leaders of the Love Charity Foundation. However, the booking system showed that she booked the ticket at 9:30 the night before, and the autopsy results proved that Xing Qisheng was still alive at that time, so the police did not link her departure with the case of Deratization Hill. When Lin Fengchong called her, she was already in Paris. On the phone, her voice was tired, and there was a hint of panic that was not easily detected. After learning about the case of Deratization Hill, the phone was dead silent for a long time, then she suddenly cried out on the phone. She was sobbing and kept saying: "I don't know, I really don't know anything..." The old criminal policeman Lin Fengchong made two judgments based on his intuition: First, Tao Zhuoyao might really not know about the Deratization Hill case; secondly, she must know something related to the Deratization Hill case.

When Lin Fengchong wanted to ask further questions, Tao Zhuoyao did something that made him ironic: she actually hung up the phone! When he called again, it has been turned off!

This reminded Lin Fengchong of playing chess with his classmates when he was a child. It often happened that the chessboard would be overturned when the others couldn't win, but now that four people had died and the corpses had been left in Deratization Hill, how could the chessboard be overturned and pretend nothing happened? After calling Tao Zhuoyao's mobile phone several times, he asked Xing Qixian anout her Wechat account. The friend application was rejected, so he had to write a text message and sent it: I hope you return to China as soon as possible to cooperate with the police investigation. Do not conceal the facts of the case, otherwise you will bear legal responsibility, but Tao Zhuoyao never replied.

Lin Fengchong contacted the Paris police to monitor Tao Zhuoyao's movements, but the line was temporarily interrupted.

Sun Kang, who was in charge of interrogating the staff of the Tongyou Nursing Home, was also in a mess.

Although the food and utensils in the nursing home were like garbage, and his blood vessels were throbbing with anger, but these alone did not even constitute the "crime of abuse of guardians and caregivers" in Article 261 of the Criminal Law. Sun Kang was very clear about this. What's worse was that the vice president Cui Yucui was also very clear, so no matter how Sun Kang patted the table and stared at her eyes, she just folded her arms and crossed her legs. Even she was perfunctory, the answer she made was also provocative: "I never asked my colleagues about their private life after work!" "How could I, a vice president, take care of the dean's affairs?" "The children's registration was managed by Wang Jing in the office, and the daily life was managed by the stuff. The diet was under the care of the nursing staff, and the physical examination and treatment were under the control of President Xing. What you are asking is beyond my responsibility!" "What did I take in charge? I am responsible for the outside affairs, not the inside. The rent, water, electricity. Where did the money come to pay for all of these!" "Watching children is a physical task, not to mention that these children are still sick. If my employees were not allowed to eat better, how can they have the energy to watch children?" "Don't scare me, I understand the laws! God punished all who was damned, but not me!"

Sun Kang had to rush out of the interrogation room after asking a few questions, took a few deep breaths in the corridor, and then went in again, "Otherwise, I'll have to beat up the old shrew!"

The Wang Jing mentioned by Cui Yucui was the finance and HR who sit in the office and played the glory of the king. This woman had a horse's face, and the flesh on her face was like death with no expression, only a hint of sarcasm on the corner of her mouth. When she was asked any question, her answer would never exceed three words: "I don't know." "I don't know", "I didn't see", "I didn't save"... Even if Sun Kang lost his temper, his eyes widened and roared: "Suddenly three children were missing, and they didn't return to the nursing home at night, don't you care?!" She did the same. It looked like she had understood life and death. The only difference was that there were some more words in the answer: "This is under the management of the dean."

Those three nurses with fat faces were even more battle-hardened old women, who could act better than those who came out of TV dramas. When talking to them in good temper, they would say "how" one by one:

"How can I know?" "How can I manage this?" If the policeman was angry, they just patted thighs on the ground and cried, but there were no tears. But they had a special ability, that was, they can accurately grasp the "critical point" when the police were about to get angry. At that point, they suddenly turned off their voices and wiped their faces, as if nothing had happened. If the police asked again, they would repeat the big drama from "how" to cry out from the beginning, making Sun Kang have no choice.

As for the stunned young driver, after being beaten by Ma Xiaozhong, he became a lot more modesty, but he still had obvious resistance to the police interrogation. He answered all questions but the answers were irrelevant. The only thing he cared about was: "I was beaten by you quite hard. Who should pay for the medical expenses?"

None of them cared about the whereabouts of the three missing children (the police did not mention the Tongyou Nursing Home in the case of the Deratization Hill released by the media, and dued to the interrogation strategy, the police did not disclose the information to the staff of the Nursing Home, and the identity of the deceased above), even after identifying the Vacheron Constantin watch and the black Zippo windproof lighter, they were indifferent to what happened to the dean Xing Qisheng... The process of interrogating these people made Sun Kang feel hopeless. He was an old policeman, he had met thieves, rouges and almost all kinds of people, but the group of people in front of him were like a pile of stones without any emotion. In the past, at least he would have dared to slap the stunned young driver, but not now, let alone torture to extract a confession, the slightest suspicion of violence would lead to an investigation by the higher-level judicial department. Only people like Ma Xiaozhong could do such things, but only he dared, not Sun Kang. The tuition for his child's cram school, his mother's blood sugar test strip, and his wife who suffered from lymphoma and needed to eat the medicine every month were all relied on his salary and police rank allowance.

However, it was not completely fruitless.

At least Sun Kang dug up some valuable information from the old guard Xu, the cleaning aunt Zhang, and the dean's secretary Chi Fengli.

Xu, the doorman, almost lost all his teeth, and his speech leaked badly. To the police's question, his answer was quite positive, but, every sentence had to be said three or four times before he could hear it clearly. He said that the dean left in a black INSPIRE at about two o'clock in the afternoon. That car belonged to Mingyi Public Relations Company. In addition to undertaking the public relations work of the Love Charity Foundation, Mingyi Public Relations Company worked with Love Charity. The hospital and Tongyou Nursing Home also had very close cooperation, so sometimes they lent the car to them. Of course, when Mingyi Company needed, Zhou Liping would also be sent over to drive the car away – the time when the dean drove back was at about nine o'clock in the evening, the car was parked in the yard. Later, he went to the thatched hut with a stomach ache, and the time spent in the pit was a little long, so he didn't know when the car drove away... But he said something that shocked the police, "When the director leave the hospital? It was possibly half past ten."--Considering that Xing Qisheng died on Deratization Hill within three minutes, this testimony was horrifying. Sun Kang repeatedly asked Xu if he could confirm that Xing Qisheng himself was the one who left the hospital at 10:30. He leaned his neck and said, "How could it be false, the dean just passed by the door of the delivery room. How coudln't I recognized his clothes?!"

Sun Kang found that he always liked to squint when he spoke, and suspected he was presbyopia. He asked carefully, and it was true, so his "President himself" would be greatly discounted.

However, Auntie Zhang's testimony confirmed the credibility of Lao Xutou's remarks from the side. Aunt Zhang was a fat woman with a thick face. Compared with the three nurses, she was much more simple and kind. She looked in her fifties, but she was actually in her early thirties. She said that when she got up from the dormitory to go to the toilet at about ten o'clock last night, she saw the light on the door of the dean's office on the same floor, and there were sounds of walking in the room.

"You didn't go in to see who it was?" Sun Kang asked.

"It's nothing in the middle of the night. How could I break into the dean's door!" Aunt Zhang said with a frown, "The dean often stays late in the office, and sometimes lives inside."

"Is his office usually locked?" Sun Kang asked again.

"Sometimes..." Aunt Zhang said, "but no one dares to go in casually, except for cleaning at eight in the morning, twelve at noon and six in the evening."

A "dare" word, meant something. Sun Kang, who was sitting opposite Aunt Zhang, leaned forward gently and asked, "Are you afraid of the dean? What kind of person is he?"

Aunt Zhang seemed to realize that she had said something she shouldn't have said, and her face flushed red.

Sun Kang knew that there must be something Aunt Zhang knew, but he couldn't push it too quickly. One of the interrogation techniques was: if you give up asking a question that makes the other party highly nervous, you must ask a question that will make the other party feel relaxed and willing to answer. So he asked: "Aunt Zhang, let's talk about President Xing later. But one thing I don't understand. If the three children in your nursing home don't come back at night, the nurses are not worried?"

Aunt Zhang blinked a few times and said, "That Xiao Wu always leads to run away, we're all used to it."

"Leads to run away?" Sun Kang was taken aback, "What do you mean?"

"It's that kid Zhao Wu, who thinks that the nursing home is not good here and there. He often sneaks out with a few children and comes back in a few days. He always likes this every year."

"Every year?" Sun Kang asked, "Does Zhao Wu come to this city every year for physical examination and treatment? How did I hear that the Provincial Welfare Institute sends a new batch of children every year?"

"I don't know. It's true that a new batch of children come every year, but Wu, Dong Xinlan, Li Ying and the others come every year anyway."

"Since they had escaped, why are they coming back?"

"They are all sick children, how far can they run, no medicine, no food, anyway, in the end, they either come back on their own or were sent back..." Aunt Zhang said.

"Will they be punished for coming back?"

"At first I remembered that they were indeed beaten by the dean and the nurses, especially Wu, the one who took the lead. He was beaten very hard, with sticks and belts. Then the following time he ran away, he didn't beat him again when he came back, just thought he was out to play for a few days. When they said to beat him, he took off his pants and showed his little dick. Such a boy was not ashamed at all..." Aunt Zhang said this with a rare smile on her face, "Officer, did he do something outside? That boy is not a bad boy. You can criticize and educate him, but after all, he is disabled, let alone a child, even an adult always has such a disease won't be good, right?"

Sun Kang looked at Aunt Zhang and nodded lightly after a long time.

Regarding Zhao Wu's views, Chi Fengli and Aunt Zhang were completely different: "That's a bad blank! He lift my skirt, steal my stockings, use cigarette butts to burn holes in my mask, it's a little lecher, little villain!"

When she said this, her almond eyes were wide open, her eyebrows were upside down, and her originally beautiful face was so twisted that she could make an emoji.

"Now you don't have to worry anymore." Sun Kang said coldly, "He is already dead."

Not revealing to the staff of Tongyou Nursing Home that their detention was related to the Deratization Hill case was the interrogation strategy formulated by the task force. The only exception was Chi Fengli, because the task force had unanimously identified Chi Feng through external investigation and internal observation was the weakest link in this nursing home. She was a typical vase girl, simple-minded and materialistic, but timid and not bad-hearted, so throwing a bomb at the right time may break down her psychological defense line in an instant.

Unsurprisingly, when she heard that Zhao Wu was dead, Chi Fengli froze instantly, her mouth opened for a long time and she was speechless.

"Zhao Wu was dead, and there were two other children, as well as Xing Qisheng. Their bodies were found on the Deratization Hill last night." Sun Kang's tone was more severe, but he stopped talking and only observed Chi Fengli's reaction.

Chi Fengli lowered her head, her shoulders trembled slightly, and she made a sob sound. After a long time, she raised her head with tears in her eyes, and murmured, "Once I was on my period with a stomachache and so thirsty, I took a bottle of mineral water to drink, Wu saw and grabbed it, saying that girls can't drink cold water when on the period, and then went to get me a cup of hot water, I asked him how he knew that I had a period, he said he knows everything...that little bastard..."

Her answer was similar to Aunt Zhang's when it came to the three children did not return home. It was also because such a thing had happened before, but the children who ran away in the end always came back on their own. On the night of the accident, she had been dancing at the Paradise nightclub in the city, completely unaware of Xing Qisheng's movements.

"I'm asking more directly." Sun Kang paused and said, "Do you and Xing Qisheng have a simple working relationship?"

Chi Fengli took out a tissue and blew her nose: "There happened a few times... but he has some obstacles, each time it ends quickly, it's not interesting, he doesn't seem to be interested in me."

"What kind of person is Xing Qisheng?" Sun Kang asked, "If you could say three words to describe him, which words would you choose?"

Chi Fengli thought about it and said, "Wretched, greedy, and lecherous."

"Lecherous?" Sun Kang looked at her and said, "but you said he wasn't interested in you... In a word that might not be respectful: I don't think you are a woman who makes men disinterested."

Chi Fengli said: "It's hard to tell. Although I am his secretary, I only take him out to respond to the scene. I have never entered his most private life circle. If you ask me about this aspect, it's better for you to turn to

Zhang Chunyang, as long as the two of them are together, they are full of stinky stench."

"Who is Zhang Chunyang?" Sun Kang heard the name for the first time.

"Ordinary employees of the Love Charity Foundation." Chi Fengli said.

Sun Kang noticed that she said the word "ordinary" very heavily, and there was an interesting sneer on the corner of her mouth.

It seems that there was inside story, but now was not the time to ask questions, because there were more important things to verify, Sun Kang took out his mobile phone, clicked on "Voice Memo", and a piece of audio echoed in the interrogation room, a simple sentence-

"The Deratization Hill subway is on fire, please send someone here!"

After playing it three times in a row, Sun Kangcai asked, "Can you hear this voice?"

Chi Fengli nodded: "This is Xing Qisheng's voice."

After analyzing and processing the speech, the Criminal Technology Department extracted a click-click sound from the background sound. After on-site comparison, it was proved that the sound came from the locust tree branch near Exit C of the subway in the nursery. The worn-out windmill, this iron-like evidence, plus Chi Fengli's testimony, was enough to prove that it was Xing Qisheng who called 110 on the Deratization Hill that night, and it was Xing Qisheng, the corpse in the wind pavilion tunnel!

Then, who was the person who wore Xing Qisheng's clothes and stayed in his office until 10:30 before leaving the nursing home? This was an unanswered mystery. Judging from the fact that the drawer of the dean's office had not been pried open and the property had not been lost, this person was definitely not a thief; in addition, this person should be the one who connected Xing Qisheng to make the second call from the Deratization Hill.

Just when Sun Kang said that the interrogation was temporarily over and Chi Fengli could go home to rest, she stood up, walked to the door, turned around suddenly and said, "Officer Sun, I think there is a very suspicious person, it's probably him who killed Xing and the three children."

"Who? "

"Zhou Liping, driver of Mingyi Public Relations Company."

"Why do you doubt him?"

"He used to be a serial murderer. Not only Mingyi Company, but also the Charity Foundation and our Nursing Home knew that everyone usually avoids him. Only the children were ignorant and liked to play with him. There were times when someone in our nursing home had something to do and didn't have time to send the children to the Love Hospital, so we asked him to drive temporarily. That's it, the children in the nursing home got on well with him, especially Wu..." Chi Fengli said, "For this reason, Xing once quarreled with Zhou Liping, and the quarrel was fierce. We all heard it. At first, Zhou Liping was fierce. Later, Xing said that if he dared to touch the childrren again, he would call the police and arrest him." , Zhou Liping was scared away. Xing also reminded Xu, let him close the door, don't let Zhou Liping come in again, and prohibit him from contacting the children."

Sun Kang nodded: "The information you provided is very valuable!"

After Sun Kang handed over the thick stack of transcripts of the above-mentioned interrogation to Du Jianping, Du Jianping read it carefully, then called Lin Fengchong and said solemnly: "It's time to meet Zhou Liping!"

4

The so-called "face-to-face fight" meant face-to-face interrogation of criminal suspects. Du Jianping thought about all the work he had done, the testimony of witnesses and the evidence he had collected several times, only to find that everything was ready—except himself.

After being a police officer for decades, he had solved hundreds of cases, but the opponent he was about to face was the one that had ever made him feel the most difficult, headache and even – he will never admit it in front of others – the most one made him nervous. They fought each other ten years ago. At that time, Zhou Liping was a high school student. As a major criminal suspect in the "Western Suburb Serial Murder Case", he said nothing after being arrested and looked like a zombie, thinking that he could escape the law by doing this. And finally he really escaped, only sentenced to ten years in prison! This was something Du Jianping had regretted all his life. Every criminal was like a bar of soap. If you couldn't catch him once, and he slipped away from your palm, he may roll into a gutter or a dark corner at once, and then he will get away with impunity and appear in society as a law-abiding citizen. In the sun, his shadow was never half darker than others. So it was almost a miracle to be able to capture Zhou Liping again, but it also meant that Du Jianping would be facing a master with top-level experience in both criminal ability and anti-investigation skills – it must be known that Zhou Liping was the one who took the police Psychological offensive, cross-examination, biological clock interference, lie detector and other interrogation techniques were enough – in other words, he was familiar with everything about the police, and everything about him ws extremely unfamiliar to the police...

What can best illustrate this point was the search results of Zhou Liping's residence. Although Lin Fengchong led the team and transferred a very good crime scene investigation expert like Chu Tianying as his deputy, nothing was found in Zhou Liping's house. It was a one-bedroom on the top floor of a dilapidated residential building. Standing at the door, the whole room was unobstructed: single beds, chairs, folding tables, and wardrobes were all old-fashioned wood grain colors, full of the unique temperament of rental houses. In the wardrobe except for a few piece of clothes, an umbrella, a backpack and a few small flags left over from working as a traffic attendant. Under the mattress were more than 2,000 yuan in cash and an ICBC savings card, with tens of thousands of yuan already stored in the card. .Three pairs of running shoes and a set of detachable electroplated dumbbells were found under the bed. Neighbors confirmed: Zhou Liping loved fitness. He ran in the community every morning and night. In summer, the door was half-open, and he had been seen holding dumbbells shirtless. The whole body of tendon was sweating profusely.

Li Zhiyong called Du Jianping and asked, "Have you found that pistol?"

Du Jianping's answer disappointed him.

The Criminal Technology Department could not wait to pack the whole house and take it away, but it checked every strand of hair that fell on the ground with a microscope, but still could not find any physical evidence that could be linked to the case of Deratization Hill. The staff responsible for the restoration at the scene unanimously determined that, from the analysis of the arrangement of items, the cleaning of garbage, especially the folding of the bedding, Zhou Liping went home from the night of the incident to the next day when he went to work without any abnormality.

All this gave Du Jianping a headache. The so-called evidence was a very complex concept in law, but in the final analysis it could be divided into two types: direct evidence and indirect evidence. Direct evidence was the evidence that can connect the suspect and the crime with a straight line, while indirect evidence was the evidence that it took several turns to establish the connection between the suspect and the crime. Whether in criminal trials or judicial decisions, the most valuable was always direct evidence. But all the police had obtained so far ere indirect evidence rather than direct evidence: the most valuable of which was the image of Zhou Liping driving through the traffic lights in Qingshikou East in the surveillance camera, and what else was there? Nothing at all! You can't tell the judge in court, "Because he's killed people before, the four corpses on Mouse Hill are probably his masterpiece"!

In this way, they can only rely on face-to-face interrogation to pry open Zhou Liping's mouth.

In order to deepen his understanding of his opponent, Du Jianping personally asked Zheng Gui, the CEO of Mingyi Public Relations Company, to tell him about Zhou Liping's work and life. After sorting and verification, the following things could be roughly confirmed. First, Zhou Liping was able to work at Mingyi Public Relations Company because of the recommendation of a woman named Sun Jinghua. Sun Jinghua was the manager of the convention and exhibition department of a high-end hotel in this city. Most of the meetings or activities planned by Mingyi Public Relations Company for clients were held there, so Zheng Gui had always done Sun Jinghua some favor. On the first day Zhou Liping came to the company, he explained that he had been in prison for many years for murder. Zheng Gui was shocked at the time, but he would not regret his promise to Sun Jinghua, so he still accepted him, and asked him what skills he had. He said that he had learned to drive and repair cars in prison. It happened that the company had three cars, but there was no regular driver, so Zheng Gui asked him to be a full-time driver. Second, Zhou Liping rarely spoke. In the company, apart from having a good relationship with Xing Qisheng's son Xing Yunda, he had no personal relationships with other people. However, Zheng Gui liked his strict mouth and always took him with him when he went out to do business. Third, Zhou Liping did not have a girlfriend, and he had always kept a distance from the female colleagues in the company, just like their attitude towards him. Fourth, Zhou Liping really liked children. Once, Zheng Gui saw Zhao Wu come to see him in Block D of Runtang Hi-Tech Incubation Park. Xing Qisheng called Zheng Gui that night and was furious. Zhou Liping was severely scolded by him, but Zhou Liping was just silent.

All of the above, not only did not dispel the fog shrouded on Zhou Liping, but instead increased the concentration of the fog, especially the relationship between him and Xing Yunda, which made the police once again focus on Xing Yunda, who had no time to commit the crime. Could it be that Zhou Liping's murder was motivated by a disobedient child? So why bother with the other three innocent little lives? In addition, there was a fourth point. Zhou Liping "liked" children. The word "liked" was not simple... Years of police intuition made Du Jianping suspect: Zhou Liping, who was once suspected of rape and murder, had a very strong motive for the crime this time. It may be that Xing Qisheng had actual evidence of him molesting or even raping children, so he killed them!

When he thought of this, the fire in his heart rose up and down. Du

Jianping drank several sips of tea from the enamel jar before suppressing the fire and then asked Lin Fengchong, who was sitting across from him, "What had Zhou Liping been up to since his arrest?"

Lin Fengchong said, "Everything is normal."

"Normal?" Du Jianping put the enamel jar down, "how normal?"

"Eating and drinking, pooping and peeing. Anyway, the one-bedroom he lives in is not much bigger than a single-person trumpet. I think he is quite used to it." Lin Fengchong said ironically, "Emotionally, he is also very stable, not noisy, and doesn't ask when he will be arraigned, as if he knew that he had such a day, but—"

Lin Fengchong hesitated when he spoke, and Du Jianping said impatiently, "Just say whatever you want!"

"It's just that I think he seems to know he's done something, but it's not a big deal..."

"Fuck!" Du Jianping glared at him, "Isn't four lives a big deal?!"

"Don't worry, I'm now here to analyze?" Lin Fengchong said with a smile, "According to the jargon, Zhou Liping is an old wader who has waded through the deepest water, so what will happen to him if he does something? He was definitely carrying a lantern in his mind and planning to make a plan – a clear account, if he really killed four people in Deratization Hill, then he must be sentenced to death, but he didn't seem to have any nervousness. It looks like he will go out after ten days and a half at most."

Du Jianping was stunned for a moment, then sighed: "Tell the pre-trial division to arraign Zhou Liping immediately. You also participate. I will watch the whole process in the surveillance room next to the interrogation room."

5

Since Liu Simiao did not participate in the interrogation of Zhou Liping, the details of the interrogation were relayed by Lin Fengchong later, so when she told Guo Xiaofen, she omitted a lot of detailed descriptions and simply listed the facts.

Before the interrogation began, the pre-trial division made a lot of plans. The basic idea was to imagine Zhou Liping's way of denying it: for example, pretending to be a fool and pretending to be stunned, relying on himself to clear the physical evidence and denying everything, especially not admitting that he had been to the Deratization Hill that night; For example, diverting their attention and using a completely unverifiable matter to provide himself with an alibi; because it is estimated that the police will be able to grasp the fact that he "liked" the child during the investigation, and he admitted that he had molested children. Using small sins to get rid of big sins... or even adopting a completely silent attitude, as he shown in the "Western Suburbs Serial Murder Case" ten years ago. The police decided that the most important bomb, the image of Zhou Liping driving through the traffic lights in the east of Qingshikou, must be shot at the most critical moment in order to defeat his psychological defense line in one fell swoop.

Who knew that Zhou Liping's performance was far beyond the police's expectations.

At the beginning of the interrogation, Zhou Liping sat on the iron chair fixed to the ground in the interrogation room. He cooperated throughout the whole process, whether he was handcuffed or locked. Lin Fengchong actually used "not humble nor arrogant" to describe his performance.

After asking him some basic personal information, the presiding judge adopted the most conservative but safest opening statement: "Zhou Liping, do you know what you have committed?"

Zhou Liping shook his head.

"Then think about it." After speaking, the presiding judge folded his arms and looked at him coldly.

Zhou Liping probably didn't expect the police to treat him with such a "Talk or not talk all don't matter " attitude. He was a little surprised, but he was still very calm.

According to the pre-agreed strategy, the sub-judge in charge of singing red-faced slapped the table: "Zhou Liping! Be honest with me. What are you pretending to be dumb when you are wearing iron shackles?, you don't know what things you have done?!"

Zhou Liping glanced at the deputy judge and said nothing.

"What are you staring at me for? Look at your fierce appearance, you have reached this point, you haven't explained it honestly, or you want to resist to the end?!" The judge sang his face: "Zhou Liping, you are in your twenties, others are flourishing, and are very young, and you, I will count for you, from seventeen to now, what you have been doing? Raped and murdered in the Western Suburbs, killing three girls and a director of the public security office. Is this what you committed, right? Two years ago, you attacked a police officer and stole his pistol. This is also what you did— "

"I didn't attack him, and I didn't grab his gun," Zhou Liping said.

This was Zhou Liping's consistent attitude. He neither admitted nor denied the crime of committing the serial murders in the Western Suburbs, and he firmly refused to admit the "gun grabbing incident".

But the presiding judge just wanted to shift his attention to the previous case, making him mistakenly think that the police did not have any evidence and could only force him to admit that it was him who did the Deratization Hill case by "turning over the old accounts", so he relaxed his vigilance , and then unexpectedly took out the photo taken by the monitor on the traffic light in Qingshikou Dongli, and asked him to bow his head and admit defeat... In the preliminary preparations for the pre-trial, it was particularly emphasized that, no matter what, let Zhou Liping speak and say something, just don't let him fall into silence, delaying would only give him more time to think about how to deal with the interrogation, which would do all the harm to the police with no benefits.

Seeing that Zhou Liping had taken the bait, the presiding judge calmly began to rewind the line, but the line was reeled very slowly. He analyzed his motives and methods of committing the crime in the "gun snatching incident" two years ago. While Zhou Liping refused to give an inch, saying that the police had questioned him at the time, and even searched his temporary residence, but found no evidence of a crime: "This matter had nothing to do with me—"

At this moment, the presiding judge suddenly changed the subject: "Then what happened last night?!"

"I just can't take this breath!" Zhou Liping said.

There was no hesitation as expected, but instead he expressed his mind directly, which surprised the presiding judge and he quickly followed up: "Just because he scolded you back then?"

"If he just scold me, I will endure it, he beat me!" Zhou Liping said bitterly, "I will definitely pay him the bill!"

Xing Qisheng not only scolded Zhou Liping, but also beat him? This situation was not grasped in the previous investigation. Lin Fengchong hurriedly wrote it down in the notebook, and he was also a little muttered in his heart: Xing Qisheng was not Zhou Liping's opponent at all in terms of age, figure or physical fitness. In addition, he should know that he had murdered before. How dare Xing beat him after knowing he had been in prison?

"Just because he hit you, you're frantically taking revenge?"

"That said, is any revenge not crazy?"

"What's the end?" The presiding judge chased after the victory.

"I went home when it done." Zhou Liping said.

"Where's the car parked?"

"Car? What car?"

"Your company's black INSPIRE!"

"How do I know where it parked? I didn't drive there!"

"Are you sure you didn't drive there?"

"Of course."

"It is necessary for me to remind you that every word you said during the interrogation, we have audio and video recordings of the whole process, and you will be held legally responsible."

"I know that."

"Then I'll ask you again. Can you guarantee that you didn't drive there last night?"

"I promise!" Zhou Liping said firmly.

The presiding judge put his hand into the file folder, and was about to throw the photo of Zhou Liping driving past the traffic lights in the east of Qingshikou before him. But at this time, Zhou Liping said something that made him stunned-

"Isn't it just a fight? It's not a big deal, why do I need to drive?"

In the surveillance room next to the interrogation room, Du Jianping, who was watching the live interrogation through the coated SLR glass, made a buzzing sound in his head, and immediately grabbed the microphone and said to the chief and deputy judge and Lin Fengchong: "Suspend the interrogation, you all come to the surveillance room immediately! "

Hearing Du Jianping's instructions through wireless earphones, the main and deputy judges and Lin Fengchong quickly got up and went to the surveillance room. When they saw Du Jianping's face ashen, they knew the problem became serious.

"Thousands of calculations still not enough!" Du Jianping pointed to Zhou Liping in the interrogation room, and said gloomily, "We want to divert his attention to make him mistakenly think that we are using the method of overturning the old case to count the new. I didn't expect that he would just do it, and he simply shifted the topic to other things. Although I don't know what he meant by 'fight', it is certain that this was his way of creating an alibi."

"Boss, I don't think there's any need to worry. If Zhou Liping wants to exonerate himself by forging an alibi, it means that he must use more lies to convince himself, and sooner or later he will be all exposed." Lin Fengchong He paused and said, "Unless he really didn't kill anyone."

Du Jianping only listened to the first half of this sentence, but did not the second half of the sentence, so he nodded: "That's right, continue the interrogation, and note that he must add footnotes to each of his sentences, each comma must be verified, and he must not be allowed to play any tricks!"

The chief and deputy judges and Lin Fengchong nodded and walked out of the surveillance room.

Through the coated SLR glass, Du Jianping stared at Zhou Liping sitting on the iron chair: After ten years of absence, his face was not as wide as it used to be, he seemed to be a little thinner, but his chin was more protruding, the thin layer of skin stretched on the skull was tight and blue, the acne of the past had subsided into black spots like age spots, the shaggy mustache on the lips had disappeared, and a pair of triangular eyes radiated chaotic light liked a layer of mud.

Zhou Liping also looked at the coated SLR glass with a dull expression. Du Jianping knew he couldn't see him, but he sill felt uncomfortable when he saw him.

Back in the interrogation room, the deputy judge first asked the question: "Zhou Liping, those years in prison have brought you up, right? If you learn to avoid important things. Well, since you said you were just fighting, then tell me, where and who did you fight last night, who saw it, and explain it clearly, don't talk about those nonsense that have no evidence, you have the time to say, we have no time to listen!"

Zhou Liping looked at him and said nothing.

It was obvious that Zhou Liping refused to answer any of the sub-inspector's questions to tell the police that he received the soft tone but not the tough one.

The presiding judge said: "Zhou Liping, you are no longer the high school student you used to be. You should know that running away is not the solution to the problem. Don't think that if you make a zero confession, the public security organs will have nothing to do with you. You refuse to answer our questions. We can still file a criminal lawsuit against you in the court according to Article 53 of the Criminal Procedure Law. So you' better tell us honestly, where exactly were you last night, who you fought with, and whether there is any witness or physical evidence, we'll investigate whether what you said is true or false. The government will never let a bad person go, but it will never wrong an innocent person."

Zhou Liping looked at him for a moment and said slowly: "Last night around eleven o'clock, in the street park at the intersection of Xingyu Road, the wound on the corner of my mouth should be taken as the head office of physical evidence!"

Due to the restraint of the baffle, he couldn't raise his arm, but made a tilted head movement. In fact, even if he didn't do it, the purple-red bruise on the corner of his mouth was clearly visible... After the police arrested Zhou Liping, they soon discovered that the corner of his mouth. For this reason, Du Jianping specifically asked every colleague involved in the arrest. No one admitted to hitting the corner of Zhou Liping's mouth, but arresting criminals was always a life-and-death struggle, even more serious things had happened before. The police can only turn a blind eye, but they never expected the truth to be here.

"Who did you fight with?"

Zhou Liping raised his eyebrows: "Didn't you arrest me because of this?"

"We want you to tell yourself who you fought with?"

Zhou Liping said a name, and Lin Fengchong in the interrogation room and Du Jianping in the surveillance room were shocked!

Du Jianping immediately sent a subordinate to verify the matter.

Soon, the verification came back, and the person who fought with Zhou Liping admitted that it was true, and there was no problem with the time and place.

"He didn't say anything when we arrested Zhou Liping!" Du Jianping muttered angrily, and then said into the microphone, "It's been verified, the fight that Zhou Liping said is true, but his fight happened around eleven o'clock, and Sweeping Mouse Ling's case happened at 10:30, so it can't constitute his alibi, you continue the trial."

Next, the questions asked by the presiding judge were insignificant... After several rounds of fights, nothing was gained. He was like a lion about to attack a rhino. He didn't know where to start, and he didn't know what the next attack would be. To what extent the counterattack was received, so the momentum and strength were much weaker than before, and the deputy judge also knew that intimidation was ineffective against Zhou Liping, so he could only sit in the interrogation room as a decoration. Lin Fengchong realized that this was not the way to go, so he suddenly said to Zhou Liping, "Zhou Liping, do you still recognize me?"

Looking at the mustache police officer who had been silent in the interrogation room, Zhou Liping nodded slowly.

"I talked to you at the police station about the 'gun robbery incident' two years ago. Although you can't show an alibi, we don't have any evidence to prove that you robbed the gun, so we will let you go after the conversation. You may still remember." Lin Fengchong looked him in the eye and said, "Maybe you think the police arrested you because of prejudice against you, but it turns out that's not the case. We only value the evidence and only respect the facts. We arrested you, it must be because you have a lot of things that are unfavorable to you, but we hope that you will explain it yourself and give yourself a chance to make merit and atonement; if you didn't do it, then tell us, make it clear and you could be let go early, I believe you just like us, we all hope to see each other as less as possible in the whole life."

Zhou Liping listened attentively, and frowned after listening: "I've said everything I should say, what else do I need to explain?"

"The police spent such effort arresting you just because you revenge?" Lin Fengchong sneered, "Do you think we are stupid, or did you go to jail and ruin your brain?"

"Then I don't know. Anyway, you have wronged me more than once."

If this was other policeman, then he might get angry when heard this, but Lin Fengchong has a nickname of "Mama Lin", and he can be calm and unhurried when faced with any provocation: "Okay, then let's stroke it along your actions yesterday, let me ask, and you answer, all the details, and there's no detail will be left, what do you think?"

Zhou Liping nodded.

"What time did you go to work yesterday morning?"

"I arrived at the company at nine o'clock."

"Then where did you go?"

"I went out with President Zheng to do something."

"Be more specific, where you went and what do you do?"

"Jianyi Health Products Co., Ltd., our company will host one of their conferences next week. At the conference, health care products will be delivered to all participants. Mr. Zheng wants to look at the samples. In addition, we will discuss with them the list of invited experts, scholars and media reporters. And the amount of the carriage fee, etc."

"What car did you drive?"

"The Audi A6."

"And then? "

"We went back for dinner at noon."

"Be more specific, where? With whom?"

"I ate with Mr. Zheng at the Shimin fast food restaurant not far from the company."

"What about the afternoon?"

"I had nothing to do in the afternoon, so I played online games on the company computer."

"What did you play?"

"Cross the line of fire."

"What time did you finished?"

"Then I can't remember. Anyway, I got off work at five o'clock. I asked Mr. Zheng if he had anything to do, and he said no. I played for a while and then went home."

"What time did you get home? What's for dinner?"

"I didn't look at the exact time. I guess it's about the same as usual. It's past six o'clock. I ate a bowl of Master Kong's instant beef noodles."

"And? "

"Later, around nine o'clock, I received a call from Xing Qisheng and asked me to pick him up at Tongyou Nursing Home, saying there was something urgent."

The hearts of all the police officers were shocked, knowing that the core was coming.

"Who is Xing Qisheng?" Lin Fengchong asked calmly.

"Dean of Tongyou Nursing Home, he was a friend with Zheng, but I don't like that person."

"What did he looking for with you?"

"He drank too much at night and couldn't drive."

"Did you go? "

"Is there any other way... I took a taxi to Tongyou Nursing Home and found Xing Qisheng, he told me to wait in the car first, I waited for more than 20 minutes before he came out, and then I drove him —"

"What car are you driving?"

"INSPIRE."

"According to our investigation, that INSPIREer is your company's car, so it should be you who drove to pick him up, how did you become a contemporary driver?"

"INSPIRE was lent to Xing Qisheng by the company. It had been driving as his private car, but when the company wants to use the car, it will come back to me to drive it."

"When was the last time you drove that INSPIRE other than that night?"

"The night before, I went to the airport to pick up a guest. Audi A6 is a limited number, so I drove the INSPIRE."

"Okay, go on, Xing Qisheng made you wait in the car for more than twenty minutes, and then you drove him to where?"

"Deratization Hill."

As soon as the words came out, even Du Jianping, who was sitting in another room through the glass, couldn't help being surprised. He didn't expect this sensitive word that Zhou Liping would ignore and avoid in the eyes of the police, he said it normally, neither aggravating nor understating it, as if there would be a "chups" sound when unscrewing a Coke

138

bottle. He stared at Zhou Liping stubbornly, trying to find the difference in his expression-especially the twitching of his lips and the blinking of his eyelids, but Zhou Liping didn't have any difference, not at all.

Lin Fengchong in the interrogation room was also shocked. After a short pause, he adjusted his mood before asking, "Who was in the car?"

"Just me and Xing Qisheng."

"Why did Xing Qisheng ask you to take him to Deratization Hill at night?"

"How could I know."

"And then? "

"When we got to the Deratization Hill, he said that he had sobered up and that he had something to do, so he drove by himself, and gave me a one-hundred-yuan bill, and told me to take a taxi home. I didn't take it, just went straight home. "

"Went home?" Lin Fengchong raised his voice softly, "Didn't you just say you went to fight?"

"Yeah, I didn't take a few steps. I felt that some things had to be resolved. I might solve it tonight, so I called the man and asked him to go to Jiexin Park on Xingyu Road. I thought maybe we should talk first, but he hit me when he came up, and I was not polite—"

"What time did you leave Deratization Hill?" the presiding judge suddenly asked.

"I didn't look at my watch, maybe ten or more."

"Where did you park your car?"

"Xing Qisheng pointed out the way, I couldn't see clearly in the dark lights, it seemed to be an intersection, so I got out of the car and left."

"Where did Xing Qisheng drive the car after you got off?"

"I have no idea."

"Then how did you get to Xingyu Road?" Lin Fengchong asked, "Taxi, car-hailing app or Mobike?"

These three methods could quickly check the authenticity: taxis had driving records, and the taxi companies in the city can investigate; Zhou Liping's mobile phone had been confiscated and was currently stored in the Criminal Technology Office as evidence, and it was easy to find the above records of ride-hailing apps and Mobike. Lin Fengchong even thought that even if Zhou Liping said that he took the black taxis, it still could be checked one by one through the FAST, he would eventually be able to find out whether what he said was true or false.

But Lin Fengchong never thought that Zhou Liping's answer was—

"I ran there."

Hearing Zhou Liping said that he was running to Xingyu Road from Deratization Hill, Guo Xiaofen, who had just had a sip of coffee, spit it out! While wiping the table with a tissue, she said "I'm sorry, sorry," and giggled non-stop. After a while, she stopped laughing, and immediately started laughing again, raising her hand to express her apology to Liu Simiao. Her laughter was so contagious that Liu Simiao laughed too.

"I can imagine the appearance of Du's nose crooked with anger." Guo Xiaofen said with a smile.

Liu Simiao nodded: "Yes, at that time, Fengchong almost couldn't sit still, so he wanted to jump up from his chair and beat Zhou Liping, but he was always calm and remembered what he learned when he searched Zhou Liping's room. Instead, he felt that what Zhou Liping said may be the truth."

"The three pairs of running shoes under the bed and the neighbors have proved that Zhou Liping has the habit of running in the community sooner or later." Guo Xiaofen said.

Liu Simiao made an "yes": "Furthermore, Fengchong checked Zhou Liping's files and found that he had won the school's long-distance running championship many times as early as his student days. When he was in the prison, he often ran. After he was released from prison, he also participated in the marathon and half-marathon held in the city. Although he did not win the ranking, he must have considerable strength – more importantly, he had the proof of 'Horse Friends': Zhou Liping once went to Deratization Hill area to participate in cross-country training on weekends to exercise his physical fitness. After training, he simply ran back to the city."

"Have you checked the time it took for Zhou Liping to run from Deratization Hill to Xingyu Road?"

"Yes. I found a police officer in the police force who won the city marathon. He picked the most convenient path and ran from Deratization Hill to Xingyu Road. After calculating the time, it took 43 minutes. If it is Zhou Liping running, it is estimated that it may take forty-eight minutes or even longer. That is to say, if according to Zhou Liping's words, he will never kill and burn corpses in the Deratization Hill at 10:30, and then arrive at the center of Xingyu Road at 11:00. The possibility of a park."

Guo Xiaofen pondered for a while: "But there are still other ways, such as—"

"For example, he prepared a bicycle nearby before he implemented the murder plan. After killing and burning the body, he rode the bicycle, got off the car near Xingyu Road and ran to Central Park... We have considered and tested it. It is feasible." Liu Simiao said, "The problem is that the design and setting of the FAST, of course, is to monitor the violations of motor vehicle lanes, but it can also record the situation of non-motor vehicle lanes. From Deratization Hill to Xingyu Road, if running, take a short-cut, a small road, or pass through an alley, that may be in the blind spot or blind spot of the FAST all the way, but if ride a bicycle and want to arrive within half an hour, it is impossible to avoid the monitoring absolutely—— "

"Why is it impossible?" Guo Xiaofen interrupted her, "As long as you ride the road you run."

"It really doesn't work," said Liu Simiao, "We have carefully investigated, and if take a small road from Deratization Hill to Xingyu Road, several sections of the road are particularly complicated. Either building roads or digging trenches, running must left footprints. If ride a bicycle, then it have to get down and push the bicycle in some places. The total time must be more than 30 minutes. In short, we have tried many combinations of methods, all of which have proved: If ride a bicycle,and want to arrive within half an hour, it will not be able to escape the eye of the sky; if it can escape the FAST, it will be impossible to arrive in half an hour."

"I see..." Guo Xiaofen looked disappointed.

"When he said that, the interrogation can't go on. The only thing we have that can prove that he is related to the Deratization Hill case is the photo of him driving through the traffic lights in Qingshikou East Li, and now he admit that he went there that night. and he also admitted that he was driving the INSPIRE, and then he said that Xing Qisheng drove the car away himself. Lin Fengchong specially took Zhou Liping to Deratization Hill, he roughly recalled that the car stopped at the road leading tothe east side of the road at the intersection of Yinlu Mountain Road and Nursery Alley, that is to say, after he left, Xing Qisheng can drive into the alley as long as he turned left and went straight, which was completely in line with the traces of the rut on the scene—"

Guo Xiaofen suddenly interrupted Liu Simi's words: "I mean, Lin Fengchong, that idiot, shouldn't have not checked whether he used transportation to go to Xingyu Road because of Zhou Liping's remarks, right?"

"Fengchong is real, but he's not stupid." Liu Simiao said, "Not only did the police use several car-hailing apps and the terminal system of Mobike, they also retrieved all the usage records in the Deratization Hill area on the night of the crime, proving that Zhou Liping had never used these two means of transportation, and we also used the FAST to check all the vehicles from the Deratization Hill area to Xingyu Road on the night of the crime. No driver remembers carrying such a passenger – including the driver of the black taxis. I know you also think of the bus, not to mention that it is difficult to control the time, and the police have also called up the surveillance video of several buses bound for the city from Deratization Hill, and even no Zhou Liping's shadows were found."

Guo Xiaofen thought for a while with her hand on her chin, and suddenly her eyes lit up: "If Zhou Liping had prepared a car near Deratization Hill in advance, he did not drive directly into the city after committing a crime, but went around a mountain road to the west, and then drove from there."

"There is still a time difficulty: going westward from Deratization Hill to the mountain, if you want to go around the mountain and then enter the city to drive to Xingyu Road, the quickest way is to go around Cuiwei Mountain and come down from the northern foot, but it's such a long distance...let alone going around the mountain. At half past ten in the evening, even if you drive too fast regardless of traffic safety, you will reach Xingyu Road more than eleven o'clock."

Guo Xiaofen was dumbfounded for a while.

Liu Simiao sighed softly: "So, now Zhou Liping has left the problem to us, how can we prove that he is not the Xingyu Road to run to..."

"Or rather, find a way for him to reach Xingyu Road from Deratization Hill within 30 minutes," Guo Xiaofen said.

Liu Simiao shook her head gently: "Excluding the time for killing and burning corpses on the road, maybe only twenty-five minutes will be left for him—and that's not even counting the time he hid the INSPIRE."

"How long does it take to go from Deratization Hill to Xingyu Road by bicycle and by car?"

"We have calculated that it takes 20 to 25 minutes by bicycle to get there; if by car, considering that the time is at night, there is no problem of traffic jams, but there are many traffic lights along the way, so it will take 10 to 15 minutes."

Guo Xiaofen took out a pen and a small pink leather notebook from her satchel, scratched on it for a long time, sighed softly, and suddenly remembered something: "The person who fought with Zhou Liping, did he notice that Zhou Liping was in a hurry that night? Like signs of a long run, such as shortness of breath, sweating or something?"

"He was very emotional that day, with new hatred and old hatred. He started the fight without saying a word when he saw Zhou Liping, so he didn't dare to make a guarantee for a long time after recalling it. He only vaguely remembered that Zhou Liping was very tired that day, but—"

Liu Simiao smiled wryly. After a while, she continued, "But killing and burning corpses and cleaning up the scene would make people very tired."

The two were silent for a while.

The waiter at the coffee shop came over and asked them if they wanted to add water. Liu Simiao motioned to add some water to her cup. The tea was rolling with orange-white foam under the pressure of the water column. When the waiter walked away, the foam gradually faded, and she picked up the cup, took a sip, felt a little hot, and put it on the table again.

"So, based on the results of the trial, what opinion did the then draw from further investigation of the case?" Guo Xiaofen asked.

"The task force actually split. Du Jianping and most of the police officers who handled the case all advocated that the interrogation should be intensified and that Zhou Liping must tell the truth. However, Lin Fengchong and Chu Tianying believed that they couldn't hang themselves on one tree, and spent a lot of money on Zhou Liping. Too much time and energy has allowed the real criminals to go unpunished... But because Lei Rong issued an appraisal report, the task force has unified their understanding. Everyone agreed that the direction and thinking should be adjusted for the next step. ."

"Forensic identification report?" Guo Xiaofen was a little surprised, "Didn't Lei Rong take it out long ago?"

"No, it's a psychological appraisal report based on the video of Zhou Liping's trial. Through Zhou Liping's speech speed, voice, expression, expression changes, etc., for each answer, we analyzed the possible doubts in his answer."

"That's awesome! Who did it?"

"Lei Rong said it was because of the seriousness of the case, and the Ministry specially approved it, and they hired a behavioral science expert who lived abroad and whose identity was kept secret, but Du and the others thought it was reasonable after reading it."

"Tell me."

"The behavioral science expert compared Zhou Liping's reaction time after receiving a question with the speed of the answer, and found that it was a very balanced state, not very slow, but not very fast, and it could be said that the answer was fluent, There is no flaw, it is obvious that was prepared, and even have a rehearsal. However, this is very common in criminal suspects with previous criminal records, and it can't explain anything, but one of the answers showed an inconsistency that is not easy to detect."

"Which answer?"

"Zhou Liping said that he received a call from Xing Qisheng at 9 o'clock that night and asked him to pick him up at Tongyou Nursing Home. He used the words 'say something urgent'. Because Lin Fengchong asked who Xing Qisheng was, he interrupted Zhou Liping's train of thought, so when he asked again 'what is he looking for you for', Zhou Liping's answer was 'he drank too much at night and couldn't drive'. The implication was that Xing Qisheng's 'matter' was just find a chauffeur, completely different from the word 'urgent'. There is a very obvious 'decreasing voice' here; what's more subtle is that after he said that after he arrived at the nursing home, Xing Qisheng asked him to wait in the car for more than 20 minutes before coming out. So what's the urgency? But unfortunately, because Lin Fengchong focused all his attention on how Zhou Liping would 'cover up' his behavior, he did not pursue this apparent contradiction in his 'confession'."

Guo Xiaofen rolled her eyes.

"In addition, in this answer, there were two rare 'bony spurs' in the entire interrogation process."

"'Bone spur'?" Guo Xiaofen didn't quite understand, "What do you mean?"

The so-called interrogation was that the interrogator digs out the doubtful points in the case, asked the person on trial to explain these doubts, and found those "holes" that cannot be closed or the loopholes were too large after the closure. Therefore, the respondent's response mode can be roughly divided into two types, one was rivet type and the other was plasticine type. As the name suggests, the former was when you dig a hole, and I can fill a hole with a nail, no more or less; the later was commonly came for the suspects who was physically weak, the interrogator asked one question, he must answer two or more.... And all of Zhou Liping's responses were riveting, never outside the question, but there were two exceptions: First, when Lin Fengchong asked "Who is Xing Qisheng?", it was enough to just answer "the dean of Tongyou Nursing and Nursing Institute, a friend with Zheng", but he added "but I don't like that person"; second, when Lin Fengchong asked "did you go?" At that time, he did not answer directly, but said "what can I do"...

Guo Xiaofen's eyes lit up: "That is to say, in these two places, Zhou Liping's answer was superfluous and showed a clear emotional color."

"Yes! From the perspective of criminal psychology, this showed that the interrogator has a guilty conscience or panic, or even a certain psychological tendency to 'flatter' and 'please' the interrogator. Combined with the semantic inconsistency just now, it is equivalent to a continuous mental disorders in the four questions and answers, which is extremely abnormal for Zhou Liping, who has rich trial experience and excellent psychological quality."

"So what conclusions can be drawn from the above analysis?"

"The behavioral science expert believes that from the perspective of the entire conversation, Zhou Liping's series of mental disorders started from saying that 'there is an urgent matter', which is a very important starting point. It is very likely that Zhou Liping inadvertently said that the real situation, that is to say, that night, Xing Qisheng did use the excuse of 'urgent' to call Zhou Liping and asked him to do something unspeakable, but Zhou Liping immediately realized: this cannot be told to the police. It's not good for him, so he messed up in an instant, and then followed a series of avoidance and downplay, and deliberately expressed his disgust for Xing Qisheng twice in a row, trying to clear the relationship between him and Xing Qisheng, so that the police would not investigate further what's the 'urgent' for Xing Qisheng to find him – this just showed that he is by no means as ignorant as he has shown about the case of Deratization Hill, but there is an unspeakable reason."

Guo Xiaofen's face couldn't help showing an expression of admiration: "I am convinced by this analysis."

"Everyone is convinced and inspired by this analysis. The task force agreed that the focus of the previous interrogation and investigation was entirely on 'what happened after he went to Deratization Hill', and then the case should be regarded as a whole, but also to find out 'what happened before he went to Deratization Hill', for example, what is the relationship between Xing Qisheng and Zhou Liping, what is the 'urgent' that Xing Qisheng asked Zhou Liping to go to the nursing home that night, what the black INSPIRE had been earlier in the day, etc., so as to find the root cause of the case and find out the truth." Liu Simiao said.

Guo Xiaofen nodded, then poked his head forward: "Then, now you can say, what do you want me to do for you?"

7

Liu Simiao looked at Guo Xiaofen, as if she was looking for something on her beautiful, intelligent and lovely face, and then, whether she found it or not, she slowly lowered her eyelids and focused on the cup of tea. After a long time, she said slowly, "I was transferred from the task force, you know."

"Yes."

"And you know why."

"Right."

"Everyone is a definition in the eyes of others. Even if she has changed, it is not the definition that is wrong, but the person who is defined."

Guo Xiaofen rolled her eyes.

"I am also a defined person." Liu Simiao said calmly, "Although I have never been together with Xiangming, in everyone's heart, I am his girl-friend, so I also bear the responsibility for right and wrong for his judgment on a case even ten years ago ."

"This is unfair," Guo Xiaofen said.

"It's human nature to expect others to treat themselves justly, while they treat others unfairly." Liu Simiao sneered, "I never hold out hope for human nature, so I never complain."

"Then why do you need to get involved in this case again?"

"Two reasons." Liu Simiao said, "First, I think the scientific supremacy has appeared in the criminal investigation work in the past two years, which is not right."

"My God!" Guo Xiaofen whispered, "Am I hear you right? You, a criminal forensic scientist who has always advocated the spirit of science the most, actually say that scientific supremacy is wrong?!"

"The spirit of science and the supremacy of science are fundamentally two different things. The former is a form of positivism, while the latter is a form of religious blind obedience and dependence." Liu Simiao said, "The detection of the Baiyin serial murder case and the Huzhou robbery and murder case, they are all epoch-making events in the history of Chinese criminal investigation. They indicate that the use of modern scientific meth-ods, especially DNA biotechnology, can capture the real culprit even if it was a crime decades ago. At the same time, the establishment of the FAST, big data and the social security firewall built by information technology has made many police officers mistakenly believe that from now on, they can recover from the law and have nothing could be hidden, everything will be fine and the world will be at peace. The ideological signs of believing all problems could be solved by science are very scary, and this is the funda-mental reason why the police were full of confidence and fighting spirit at the beginning after Zhou Liping was arrested, and now they are lost in the fog and confused."

Guo Xiaofen listened very attentively.

Liu Simiao continued: "In its essence, crime is a kind of allergic reac-tion under the interaction of complex human nature and a distorted social environment. We may be able to see lively or insensitive pictures through surveillance videos one by one. There is no possibility to explore with any scientific instruments and devices what is the heart hidden under these faces. A crime has occurred, it is not easy to catch the criminal, but it is even more difficult to find out what was his motivates to commit the crime. You're a reporter, and you know best how diverse and ridiculous people's motives for crimes are, not just for money, but for 'nothing' crimes that often amaze even the most seasoned police officers. Under such condition, it is an irresponsible simplification to equate the process of case detection with 'crime ▯ technological means ▯ case solving', but more and more people like this simplification, which is irresponsible. At the beginning of the year in a shopping mall, a crazy gangster slashed people with a knife, an excellent policewoman rushed forward, known as 'the most beautiful retrograde', which is undoubtedly very heroic, but don't forget, what the murderous gangster did, was the real 'retrograde' for society as a whole! Simply glorifying nobleness and good deeds, while ignoring the motivations behind atrocities, does nothing to prevent crime."

"You are very, very reasonable!" Guo Xiaofen nodded again and again, "It's a pity that few people listened to such thought-provoking words, and they couldn't understand them."

"This is also the reason why I thought of you and hoped that you would assist me in completing a job after the Deratization Hill case." Liu Simiao looked at Guo Xiaofen and said, "I didn't see a news reporter at the door of the nursery that morning, but a group of video cameras...I looked down on people who are not professional; on the contrary, even if it is a guy with whom I have bickered and quarreled, as long as she has professionalism, then I respect and trust her."

Obviously, Guo Xiaofen was deeply moved by Liu Simiao's remarks.

"Of course, another very important reason is that after I learned about the campus loan incident that led to the suicide of Boss Du's daughter two years ago, you interviewed the 'Love Charity Foundation' office in this city, but you didn't meet Tao Zhuoyao, and was stopped by Zheng Gui. I found the manuscript on the Internet, and I feel that in comparison, your report does not smell as provocative as other media. "

"That's because the newly appointed editor-in-chief has a title of director in the "Love Charity Foundation", and at the end of each year, more than one million yuan he could get, so he deleted my manuscript in a mess."

"But I believe that's why the "Love Charity Foundation" and even Zheng Gui don't hate you so much."

"It's true. Afterwards, Zheng Gui even delivered a gift card to me, but I rejected it..." Guo Xiaofen seemed to realize, "You want me to start from the 'Love Charity Foundation' and Mingyi Public Relations Company, to assist you in investigating the truth of the Deratization Hill case?"

Liu Simiao shook her head: "When I asked you to help me, I definitely didn't ask you to help me investigate the truth of the Deratization Hill case. That's the work of the police. I hope you can deal with Zhou Liping from a journalist's point of view. People should have a comprehensive, specific and systematic understanding of him. To put it bluntly, it is to investigate how he became a criminal, especially how he changed from being a serial murderer who narrowly escaped the law to not only repentant, but also intensified his efforts and evolved into a children murderer—if he really committed these crimes."

"Then what?" Guo Xiaofen was still a little confused, "Will I write a manuscript for publication in a newspaper, magazine or public account?"

"Wait a minute," Liu Simiao glanced at his watch, "it's getting late, let's have lunch together here." Then she raised her hand, called the waiter, and ordered plain muffins, pizza, Italian noodles, curry beef rice, etc. Guo Xiaofen asked her to order less, but she just smiled and continued the topic: "You write the manuscript, if necessary, I can recommend it to the relevant media for publication. However, I think the bigger significance is that it can be included in the unfinished investigation that Xiangming did."

Guo Xiaofen suddenly realized.

After returning to China from the United States, Lin Xiangming once presided over a criminology research project, interviewing the perverted murder felons in custody in China, so as to have an in-depth understanding of the characteristics of serial murder cases in China and the characteristics of criminals, so as to introduce criminal personality profiles. When painting technology was used in criminal investigation work, it was more suitable for China's national conditions. Unfortunately, this research was interrupted by his accident, but it was clear that Liu Simiao would never let go of any opportunity to carry on this work.

"So it's not unreasonable for others to define you as being associated with Xiangming," Guo Xiaofen said.

Liu Simiao smiled bitterly.

They discussed the specific work plan. The basic idea is to go back from Zheng Gui and interview all the people Zhou Liping had come into contact with over the years, including Sun Jinghua, who once introduced him to work at Mingyi Public Relations Company, and arranged for him after he was released from prison. And he worked as the street director of the traffic coordinator, the salesperson of the real estate agency who found him a house... Liu Simiao suggested that if possible, it was best to interview Fang Mei, the only survivor of the "Western Suburb Serial Murder Case". Guo Xiaofen admitted that it was very difficult, but it was worth a try.

"That's right." Guo Xiaofen mentioned seemingly inadvertently, "What do you think of Xiangming's insistence that Zhou Liping only killed Fang Zhifeng?"

"I just said: I agreed with this conclusion, and so far no new evidence has been found that can overturn this conclusion. Of course, if Xiangming was wrong, it meant that he was also responsible for Zhou Liping committed a new crime." Liu Simiao cast his eyes out of the large French window, the staff was hanging on the wires in the air, and a small gray sparrow was parked. It flapped its wings twice, but did not fly.

At this time, the waiter brought all the meals ordered by Liu Simiao on a huge silver tray, and filled the table. Guo Xiaofen was salivating and couldn't help muttering: "I want you to order less, I'm participating in the fat loss training camp, I was sweating and tired for half a month, and I finally regained my waist, and this time I will turn fat again..."

"I like fat!"

Following the ruffian's words, someone sat down beside her with a squat, looking at her with a hilarious smile.

"Ma Xiaozhong?!" Guo Xiaofen was very surprised, looked at Liu Simiao, and understood from Simiao's smile that he was called by her.

"It's me!" Ma Xiaozhong clasped his fists, "Sister Guo, long time no see, I miss you!"

Guo Xiaofen made a WeChat emoji that covered her face and wanted to cry without tears: "Why can't I be without you anywhere? Didn't you get arrested for hurting people with hot meal? Why did you be released so quickly?"

"Look at you!" Ma Xiaozhong frowned, "It's all for you, of course I'll escape from prison to meet you."

"Bah!" Guo Xiaofen spat him fiercely.

"Okay, okay! Guo, do me a favor and don't argue with him." Liu Simiao said, "You have resigned now, and you have handed in your press card. I think the journalist identification need to be shown during the interview. It is definitely inconvenient, and you'd better have a guy with you who has a strong aura field, just in time, Ma has also suspended his work to reflect, so I will invite him to accompany with you."

"That's right, we both belonged to unemployed young people in the past. Except for the dating agency, we can be partner wherever we go." Ma Xiaozhong said to Guo Xiaofen affectionately, "I have already thought about it, my 'Ma' plus your 'Xiao', we will be called the 'Ma Xiao Team' from now on, what do you think?"

"Go away!" Guo Xiaofen sneered, "Why don't call 'Restaurant Team!"

The two of them chatted a few more times, and then they earnestly picking up the knife and fork to eat. Ma Xiaozhong always wanted to get closer with Guo Xiaofen, but was slapped hard by Xiao Guo with her elbow, and he was a little more behaved.

Liu Simiao asked Guo Xiaofen's bank card number. Guo Xiaofen was confused and asked her why. Liu Simiao said that this interview was her personal arrangement, and all the money could not be reimbursed at public expense, so she planned to spend a sum of money from her own account for Guo Xiaofen to do the interview. Guo Xiaofen declined twice, but she was speechless with Liu Simiao's words: "You still have to pay the rent, you can't endure one more night on a park bench..."

"What's the matter?" Ma Xiaozhong raised his chubby face covered in ketchup.

"None of your business." Guo Xiaofen said lightly.

Then, she gave Liu Simiao the bank card number.

After meal, the three of them walked out of the coffee shop together.

This coffee shop was located on the second floor of Ocean Times Square. There was an early childhood education center on the opposite side. On weekends, a large group of children were playing in it: some were running around in karate suits, and some walked out of the art room with nose covered with paint to show his new work to his parents. Some of them were beating on the xylophone hanging on the wall, and some were kicking and squealing in the circular swimming pool. The laughter could still be heard through the glass windows shaped like soap bubbles. A little girl in a pink jacket bravely slipped out of the elephant trunk slide, and then greeted her younger brother who was sitting at the top of the slide tremblingly to slide down. Along with her crisp voice, there was a very nice song in her ears:

"The little bird says that the snow on the top of the mountain has melted quietly, the river is singing a song, and the eyes of the running deer are so beautiful.

The flowers of the forest rise so early, the spring wind is just right, and the leaves on the branches says hello to the sun. "

Looking at these carefree children under the protection of their parents and teachers, Liu Simiao suddenly remembered the children in Tongyou Nursing Home, especially what Ma Xiaozhong told her, those sloppy food and dirty "lunch box"...

"Simiao, what's wrong with you?" Guo Xiaofen noticed that her expression suddenly darkened.

"Nothing." Liu Simio said as she walked up the escalator, "I was just thinking that it would be better to end the case of the Deratization Hill case earlier, so as not to cause a crisis of public opinion."

"Don't worry, it won't." Guo Xiaofen said.

"Why not? You must know that parents regard their children as treasures now, and children's problems are the most likely to attract public attention. Look at those incidents of needle sticks in kindergartens—"

"How many cases of sexual abuse of girls occur in rural areas every year, and how many have caused a crisis of public opinion?" Guo Xiaofen sneered, "In the end, everyone only cares about things that are directly related to their own interests. The needle stick incident in kindergartens was detonated just because it touched the pain point of the middle class, the main user group of the mass media. What does the matter of Tongyou Nursing Home have to do with them? Parents who have left their hometowns to work should worry about it, while the middle class may not even be interested in reposting it on WeChat!"

This remark shocked Liu Simiao. It happened that the escalator had reached the first floor, and the door of Ocean Times Square was pushed open. She felt a little cold and raised her head. There was no sun in the sky, and the little sparrow on the wire did not know when to fly away.

"Okay, I still have something to do, I need to go back to the bureau." She said to Guo Xiaofen and Ma Xiaozhong, "Keep in touch at any time – Guo, you must pay attention to safety during the interview; Ma, please protect Guo."

"Don't worry," Guo Xiaofen said.

"Of course!" Ma Xiaozhong said with a grin.

Watching Liu Simiao driving away, Guo Xiaofen suddenly muttered to herself, "Simiao has changed."

"What?" Ma Xiaozhong didn't understand, "What has changed? Still a super beauty!"

"Idiot!" Guo Xiaofen glared at him and said slowly, "In the past, Xiangming was the eternal pain in her heart, but today, she suddenly revealed another meaning: Xiangming is an eternal burden on her back. "

Ma Xiaozhong drove his new energy car and took Guo Xiaofen all the way westward to the Runtang Hi-Tech Incubation Park in the Western Suburbs. He planned to find Zheng, the CEO of Mingyi Public Relations Company, as agreed with Liu Simiao. Along the way, Ma Xiaozhong's was not silent, he kept babbling, and told Guo Xiaofen, who was sitting in the co-pilot, that he hadn't seen her for a while. He wanted to connect with her but was worried that she would think too much, and mistakenly thought that he had bad intentions. While not connect with her, he was also afraid of her being so sad. And he bought the new energy car just want to take Guo... Guo Xiaofen felt a pain in her head, she opened the window, and put her ear against the window and kept rubbing temples. When she finally got there, she opened the car door and got out of the car, clutching her chest and gasping for several breaths, like a miner who had just escaped from a mine accident.

"What's wrong with you? Motion sickness?" Ma Xiaozhong locked the car, ran over and asked diligently.

"Nothing, I'm sick!"

"Sick?" Ma Xiaozhong blinked his small eyes, "Could it be that you downloaded malicious plug-ins in your life without my permission?"

Guo Xiaofen was furious: "Hey, do you know why many people would rather not get a number to buy original car than buy a new energy vehicle?"

"I do not know? "

"Because it looks stupid!"

"However, there is also the Tesla..."

When he said this, he pointed at himself intentionally or unintentionally, Guo Xiaofen was really disgusted at this moment, thumping her chest and retching for a long time, and suddenly froze when she straightened up.

Looking forward along her line of sight, Ma Xiaozhong was also surprised—

At the entrance of a gray-and-white semicircular building with a "D" on the side, a man in a sky blue denim shirt stood smiling and chatting with a thin cleaner. He had a baby face, a serene demeanor, a quiet gaze, and a bit of arrogance on his raised lips.

"Huyan Yun?" Ma Xiaozhong couldn't help but ask, "Why is he here?"

Guo Xiaofen turned around and left, came to the side of the new energy car and opened the door with a click, Ma Xiaozhong hurriedly chased after her: "Why, don't you go to Mingyi Public Relations Company to interview Zheng Gui?"

"No!" Guo Xiaofen's face flushed with anger and resentment, "I don't want to meet someone who is more annoying than you!"

Ma Xiaozhong opened his big mouth and closed it again. While opening the car door with the car key, he frowned and whispered: "Who am I provoking?"

Chapter 4

1

Ten years later, he had not changed at all.

This was the first feeling Li Zhiyong had when he saw Huyan Yun through the glass door of Block D of Runtang Hi-Tech Incubation Park: it was still his slightly upturned lips, his bright eyes, and standing posture with his head held high. And the still messy short hair, maybe... he was still such an arrogant, and unrealistic middle-20s youth.

He pushed the glass door, and the moment the two looked at each other, he saw Huyan Yun burst into a smile with a row of small white teeth. This smile was so gentle and amiable, and was totally different from the appearance when talking about doing a magazine at Laogu Grill. Perhaps, time will eventually smooth out the edges and corners of even the hardest stone? He couldn't help but feel a little bit lucky.

They shook hands tightly.

Li Zhiyong said: "I was taken aback when I received your call. I haven't seen you for ten years. Why did you come over without saying?"

Huyan Yun smiled.

This smile made Li Zhiyong feel a little clueless. He unknowingly greeted a few polite words that he didn't know the meaning of. Huyan Yun didn't answer much, just nodded. When talking about the current situation, he said a few words, he said that he currently has no fixed occupation, but was a freelance writer. He writes articles such as Lu Xun's research to earn some royalties, and no more other income.

"But your reputation has grown in recent years. When my brothers and I were drinking together, they often mentioned you and praised you for helping the police solve a lot of cases." Li Zhiyong said.

Huyan Yun suddenly stopped.

The spacious corridor was quiet. The squeaks of fax machines receiving faxes and the squeaking of tapes from behind the cyan glass curtain walls on both sides added to the quietness. Li Zhiyong looked at Huyan Yun and found that he was scrutinizing him with a hint of sarcasm in his eyes.

Suddenly, the feeling that he had seen through his internal organs at a glance ten years ago returned.

This feeling was really uncomfortable.

Sure enough, ten years later, not only had this guy hadn't changed in the slightest, but he's even more difficult to deal with.

However, Huyan Yun still didn't say anything. He smiled and continued to follow Li Zhiyong to the north end of the corridor. After entering a door, he saw a beautiful girl sitting behind the front desk decorated with a goose-yellow back panel, who was cracking something on the computer, and seeing the smile on the corner of her mouth, it must be a small talk that had nothing to do with work.

Going around the cherry wood partition with some artworks, there was an office platform of more than 200 square meters, which is divided into dozens of compartments with white office partitions. Although it was working time now, there was few people on work station, none of those on duty seemed to be very busy. A few girls gathered in front of a long table in the last row against the wall, sorted stacks of newspapers and materials into individual portions, and put them into a tote bag, the name and logo of Jianyi Health Products Co., Ltd. were printed on the tote bag, which should be the preparation of Mingyi public relations company for the upcoming event.

"This way, please." Li Zhiyong moved Huyan Yun into a small reception room on the right, asked him to sit down, and took a glass of water from the water dispenser next to him, "Tell me, what are you doing here? Shouldn't it be ask for our company to do advertising business?"

Huyan Yun took a sip of water and said with a smile, "I'm here to learn about the case in the Deratization Hill."

Li Zhiyong turned around and put a full glass of water in front of Huyan Yun: "Isn't that case already solved? It was made by that scumbag Zhou Liping. When the police came to arrest him, I lead them."

"You must have heard of it." Huyan Yun took a sip of water. "The police's interrogation of Zhou Liping did not go well. Zhou Liping categorically denied that he committed this crime."

"It's useless to deny it! Ten years ago, he also denied that he did the 'serial murders in the Western Suburbs'!" Li Zhiyong sneered, "But then again, it was thanks to your reasoning about comics that we were able to catch him soon, it's just a pity—"

Although he did not go further, it was conceivable that Li Zhiyong meant that it was a pity that Zhou Liping escaped life imprisonment or even the death penalty that time.

Huyan Yun was silent for a moment and said, "Actually, my reasoning is flawed..."

"It doesn't matter!" Li Zhiyong was a little impatient. "Anyway, he was caught in the end. I'd like to see how he can play tricks this time."

"Although I can't see the police interrogation records, I heard from some friends that there are no major bugs in Zhou Liping's confession, and it is difficult to conclude that he is the real culprit in the Deratization Hill case..."

"Huyan!" Li Zhiyong sat down opposite him, his eyes and tone were a little unfriendly, "We are old acquaintances, I welcome you to come today, but I definitely don't want to hear from anyone about any excuse for Zhou Liping. He is a despicable and shameless murderer, as simple as that, the conclusion is more unquestionable than that the earth is round and briquettes are black!"

"For me, there is nothing beyond doubt." Huyan Yun said calmly, "Also, I did not defend Zhou Liping, I just wanted to say that the existing evidence still cannot prove that Zhou Liping was responsible for the Deratization Hill—"

"Evidence? What evidence do you want?!" Li Zhiyong interrupted him roughly, "As far as I know, the surveillance video at the traffic lights in Qingshikou East Lane on the night of the crime captured a picture of him driving up to the Deratization Hill. Wasn't it enough to convict him?"

"I want to make a correction, the surveillance video only captured him driving past the traffic lights in Qingshikou Dongli, but it didn't capture him going to Deratization Hill, but according to Zhou Liping, he just sent Xing Qisheng to the intersection of Deratization Hill, and then was sent off."

"Can you believe what a murderer who is full of lies?"

"At present, there is no evidence to prove that Zhou Liping told lies." Huyan Yun said, "Besides, everyone may lie for various reasons, but this does not mean that the liar is a murderer."

Li Zhiyong was provoked: "What do you mean?"

"I mean, one should not be judged on the basis of morality as guilt or innocence, which is two different things on two tracks. Likewise, one should not be judged on the basis of personal likes and dislikes, which is likely to lead to mistakes. "Huyan Yun said calmly, "Just like you, Li Zhiyong, I can't say that you are the real murderer of the Deratization Hill case just because you told two lies."

Li Zhiyong was furious: "Did I tell a lie?"

"On the day when Zhou Liping was arrested, Du Jianping found out that your arm was injured. You said that you were sprained while helping the company move furniture the day before. In fact, you were injured in a fight with Zhou Liping the day before. Am I right?"

As if he had been hit with an uppercut, Li Zhiyong's expression suddenly became a little slumped, and he slowly sat on the chair opposite Huyan Yun: "Who... Who told you this?"

"No one told me, it's just a non-rigorous reasoning." Huyan Yun said, "I heard about your injury. When I was waiting for you outside the building just now, I asked the cleaning staff. He said that recently your company didn't buy or sell furniture, and didn't ask him to clean it after moving the furniture inside. After coming in, I looked at the bottom of the movable furniture and there was no protruding or indented dust band, that is to say you lied, the company has not moved furniture these days, so I guessed that you might have been injured because of a fight with someone – you was too embarrassed to tell Du Jianping that you were injured in a fight, and that it was humiliating, and the guy who made you embarrassed is in front of you, so I think of Zhou Liping."

Li Zhiyong was stunned. The matter of his fight with Zhou Liping was shaken out during Zhou Liping's trial, and he had to admit it. Although Du Jianping was angry at him for not saying early, he promised to help him keep secret. He thought that this article would be turned over, but didn't expect it to be pointed out easily by Huyan Yun. His face was very unbearable, and his chubby cheeks drooped down for a while, and he habitually grabbed his thick nose and mumbled: "So what... It has nothing to do with the Deratization Hill case." Suddenly he remembered something, raised his head suddenly and stared at Huyan Yun: "Wait a minute, what does this have to do with you? Are you a policeman? What qualifications do you have to intervene in the case of Deratization Hill ?"

"Of course it has something to do with me." Huyan Yun took a sip of water and said slowly, "After the Deratization Hill case, Liu Simiao was forced to leave the task force, and then some media began to insinuately attack a police officer ten years ago. These two incidents involve my two best friends, so I can't just sit back and ignore them."

"How much power you have!" Li Zhiyong sneered, "If you don't sit back and ignore it, what can you do? Do you think you're writing a detective novel: if the case can't go on, the police will rush to beg you?"

"This is the second lie you said." Huyan Yun said.

"What?!" Li Zhiyong was stunned again.

"In the corridor just now, you said that when you were drinking wit former colleagues, they often praised me for helping the police solve a lot of cases – this is impossible. Don't say that in the real world, even in detective novels, when did you hear that Lestrade and Gleeson publicly admitted that Sherlock Holmes was the real solver – no police officer would recognize the merits of an outsider in criminal investigation work, just like the Green Battalion soldiers were beaten up by the Taiping Army back then, they won't admit that the Hunan Army's combat the same." Huyan Yun said with a smile, "But this incident made me curious, to be honest, you were an old-fashioned and stubborn guy in my memory back then, when did you start to learn to watch people serve dishes and flatter them? Or, because of some unspeakable reasons, you have to work hard to win my favor, so as not to get involved in some trouble? "

Li Zhiyong's face turned purple like a pig's liver.

"I have a suggestion: Let's put aside all our prejudices about each other and have a good talk." Huyan Yun didn't seem to see his angry expression at all, "I came today, and I didn't want to quarrel with you at all. I'm here purely asking for advice. I hope you can solve some of the mysteries in my heart...Life is a process of accumulating mysteries. Besides, ten years later, most of the mysteries may never find the answer. There are only a few mystery, because of chance, there is a possibility of solving it, we should not give up this which maybe the only chance, what do you think?"

There was silence in the small reception room, and for a long time, Li Zhiyong's face gradually returned to normal.

Across the table, he took the initiative to reach out a hand, and the sleeves of the shirt that had been stitched were exposed from the cuffs of the suit.

Huyan Yun smiled, stretched out his hand, and shook him tightly.

2

Two years ago, Li Zhiyong, who performed well in his job, had a chance to be promoted. If it wasn't for what happened suddenly that night, his colleagues would have been prepared to get drunk at the celebration dinner where he was promoted to the deputy captain of the Criminal Investigation Detachment.

Two years had passed, and Li Zhiyong still can't recall many details of that incident. He only remembered that it was a late night in the pouring rain. He came home from get off work, wearing a raincoat, and riding a bicycle to the door of the building. When someone called him behind him, he let out a "Yes", and was hit with a heavy stick on the back of the head. He immediately collapsed to the ground. When he woke up, he was already lying in the hospital, and he was brought by a nearby neighbor. The inspection showed that after he passed out, the attacker kicked him a few more times, and there was no more serious injury... He was secretly rejoicing that the detachment leader of the criminal investigation detachment came, and his expression was as solemn as he came to express condolences. Li Zhiyong thought that the old superior was worried about his injury, but the detachment leader announced in a cold tone: he was suspended and would be subject to immediate review by the police discipline department, because the holster on his right waist was empty. The police pistol was lost, along with a magazine full of fifteen rounds.

Losing firearm by a police officer was a very serious act of malfeasance. According to the relevant provisions of China's Firearms Management Law, if it can be recovered within a limited time, it can be dealt with lightly, otherwise it must be "double-dismiss".

Since then, Li Zhiyong began to search for a gun almost frantically. Brothers and sisters in the police circle came to help one after another, and they asked everyone even dark deeds, but they couldn't find out any information about the whereabouts of the gun. The detachment leader talked to him, hoping that he could recall the details of the night of the attack, by finding the attacker and then finding the gun. Li Zhiyong felt a pain in his brain, and felt that the voice called him was a bit familiar, but also very unfamiliar.

The police analyzed that the attacker called Li Zhiyong's name before he attacked, which showed that the target of the attacker was very clear, and after Li Zhiyong passed out, he did not make a "black hand", but just took his gun, which also showed that the attacker was relatively "moderate", he hated Li Zhiyong for sure, but believed that the "punishment" for him should be limited to not letting him be a policeman – in other words, in this series of behaviors, the attacker instead played the role of a judge , then he must have experienced Li Zhiyong's "injustice" in the police, which also ruled out the possibility that the attacker was hired by someone. Following this line of thought, the police investigated the criminals that Li Zhiyong had arrested and dealt with before, and gradually narrowed the list of suspects to half an A4 piece of paper.

After reading the list from top to bottom, Li Zhiyong, who frowned, suddenly burst into flames in eyes, and his fingers almost pierced the A4 paper: "It's him! I remember that voice, it's him!"

It was Zhou Liping's name that he poked.

Zhou Liping was released two years ahead of schedule because of his good reform in prison. The attack on Li Zhiyong happened just four and a half months after he was released from prison, which must have attracted the attention of the police. Lin Fengchong "invited" Zhou Liping to the police station, conducted inquiries in person, and took the opportunity to send someone to search his temporary residence, but found nothing. Zhou Liping said that he had no knowledge of the attack on Li Zhiyong, and the police could only let him go. For more than a month, three police officers squatted near Zhou Liping's house and closely followed his travels. They did not find any trace of him related to the gun, so they had to give up this clue.

And Li Zhiyong was also "double-dismissed" and completely left the police force.

Many people remembered that on the day he resigned, he reluctantly handed over his police uniform, police cap and documents, etc. When everyone brought him to the door, he suddenly turned around and saluted the flag flying on the roof. His eyes were red, but he didn't shed a single tear.

The action was considered a silent vow after the fact. That was, from the day he left the police force, Li Zhiyong began to follow Zhou Liping every step of the way. He bought equipment such as binoculars, cameras, and infrared night vision devices. Every morning, he rushed to the door of Zhou Liping's house one step ahead of schedule and found a secluded place to ambush. When Zhou Liping came out, he followed closely like a shadow. From behind, watch his every move. Zhou Liping was working as a traffic coordinator at the time, stood under the traffic lights at the intersection all day and raised a small flag. He got up early in the morning and returned late. Li Zhiyong moved a ponytail and sat under a nearby tree until Zhou Liping came home. He had to watch him enter the building door and wait another half an hour before returning home, he did this days and night regardless of whether it was winter or summer...when Zhou Liping practiced long-distance running, he also ran after him. "Let alone anything else, I just made my whole body strong." Speaking of this, he couldn't help but have a wry smile on his face.

He didn't stay at home all day long, and went out with a ponytail in the morning, and come back with a ponytail in the evening, his cheeks were shriveled and thin, and eyes were red, but Li Zhiyong's mother was so distressed, chased after him and keeps talking: "You're not young, you don't have a regular job, or a girlfriend. What do you want to do?"

"Mom, don't you like watching Liu Peiqi and Wang Zhiwen's "No Regrets Tracking" the most? Your son is now Xiao Dali!" Li Zhiyong said, "I know that my pistol is in Zhou Liping's hand, and I'm going to old on to him and never let that gun go off again, Xiao Dali has followed Feng Jingbo for 40 years, I will stare at Zhou Liping to death!"

It was okay not to say this, but the old lady's liver trembled even more severely when heard his words: "Son, it's all a TV series, you can't take it seriously! Besides, your father died early, if you don't give your family a spring sooner, if I die and meet your father tomorrow, how can tell him!" As she spoke, tears filled her face.

Li Zhiyong lowered his head and remained silent. After a long time, he said slowly, "Mom, you are very strong. Don't say those outrageous words."

A son always misjudged his mother. One evening not long afterward, without warning, when the old lady was washing dishes in the kitchen, she suddenly fell down with an "Ouch". Li Zhiyong tracked Zhou Liping for a day. When he came back, he saw a river flowing from his door. He rushed in and saw his mother lying unconscious in the water.

For the next month or so, he stayed in the hospital to accompany his mother, who suffered from a cerebral hemorrhage, in the treatment and recovery. Thanks to the doctor's treatment that brought her mother back from the death line, but the old lady was half paralyzed and needed to be supported to walk, she couldn't be heard clearly what she was trying to say... Until then, Li Zhiyong realized how precious and pleasant the annoying nagging from his mother was.

On the day his mother was discharged from the hospital, it was pouring rain. He held his mother in one hand and an umbrella in the other. He stood on the side of the road and took a taxi. After waiting for twenty minutes, he could not wait for an empty car. Having always lived a conservative life, he was forced to start downloading the Didi Taxi app, and his wet fingers could not move the program on the screen, making his forehead sweat. At this moment, he felt his mother's body trembling on his shoulders, and the old lady couldn't stand anymore...

Suddenly, a black car stopped in front of them, the windows rolled down, revealing a face.

"Get in!" The driver was Zhou Liping.

Li Zhiyong was a little stunned. At this moment, Zhou Liping jumped out of the car in the rain, opened the back door, and reached out to help the old lady into the car, but Li Zhiyong shoved him hard, his eyes full of hatred!

If it wasn't to track down you, the murderer, I might be able to be at home when my mother fell ill, and not delayed her illness!

"Help your mother into the car first!" Zhou Liping said expressionlessly.

Li Zhiyong helped his mother to sit in the back seat and closed the car door with a bang. The noisy rain outside and the messy mood just now were suddenly isolated to another world.

Zhou Liping sat back in the driver's seat and started the car. Looking out through the window, everything seemed to be brushed by the wipers constantly, whether it was the people running, the stall car, the speeding car or the edge of the high-rise buildings and mansions were all changing faces in the disturbance, scratching and washing over and over again. The people in the scene and the people watching the scene were the same, they were so chaotic, fuzzy and unpredictable.

Along the way, neither Li Zhiyong nor Zhou Liping said a word until the car slowly stopped. Li Zhiyong glanced outside and said with a sneer, "How do you know where I live?"

Zhou Liping glanced at him in the rearview mirror, his eyes cold.

"You were the one who attacked me downstairs and stole my gun that day?!" Li Zhiyong asked sharply.

Zhou Liping still did not speak.

It was very quiet in the car, and at some point, his mother curled up in the car seat and fell asleep. Li Zhiyong took off his coat and put it on her. Zhou Liping got out of the car and opened the back door. Li Zhiyong walked into the building with his mother in his arms. All the way, Liping held a big black umbrella to cover the rain for him and his mother. He didn't return until they entered the building door. Then he returned to the car, drove away.

Li Zhiyong turned his head and memorized the license plate number of the black INSPIRE.

Soon after, Li Zhiyong came to Mingyi Public Relations Company and found Zheng Gui, the general manager. When Zheng Gui was the general manager of the advertising department in the media, the glass in his home was smashed to pieces with a shotgun because of a deal with others. He was scared to death. Thanks to Li Zhiyong leading a group of criminal police to solve the case quickly, he gave up the plan to move his family back to his hometown in Hunan. Zheng Gui was very happy to see his benefactor at this time, and he was going to take Li Zhiyong to drink. Li Zhiyong said: "If you really want to invite me to dinner, just give me a long-term meal ticket – I am not a policeman. How about making money with you, Boss?" Zheng

Gui rolled his eyes: "Sir, don't you come undercover in our company?" Li Zhiyong turned around and left, Zheng Gui grabbed him Hold on: "The wine must be drunk today, and the meal ticket will be received from tomorrow, how do you think?"

In this way, Li Zhiyong started to work in Mingyi Public Relations Company and took up the position of manager. In fact, he was doing chores, especially helping with security when holding meetings or events. The salary was very low, but it was also much higher than being a policeman. Maybe the profession will really force a person to make a change. Gradually, the one who had always been stubborn and has a bad temper, became more polite: he was no longer cold and rigid when dealing with people, and he no longer spoke with cynicism. His "interrogation tone"gone, even when he wore a suit, he didn't look like a plainclothes policeman as the old days.

However, almost no one noticed: Li Zhiyong's work and rest time always seemed to be in sync with another company colleague, Zheng Gui's driver Zhou Liping: Zhou Liping went to work, he also went to work, Zhou Liping ate lunch, he also went to lunch, Zhou Liping went off work and he also got off work.

"Since you and Zhou Liping work in the same company, have you communicated with each other?" Huyan Yun asked Li Zhiyong.

Li Zhiyong shook his head: "We have never spoken in the company, we walked over face to face, and there was no eye contact. He knew very well the purpose of me coming to work here."

"What is Zhou Liping's performance in the company?" Huyan Yun asked again, "Is there anything suspicious?"

Li Zhiyong frowned, and his lips moved for a long time before he said slowly: "After the Deratization Hill incident, I learned that it was Zhou Liping who committed the crime. I haven't slept well for a few days. I feel very guilty about 'losing him', but after thinking about it carefully, I think I have worked with Zhou Liping for so long, and I really didn't find any doubts about him. He was just sitting at his own workstation, surfing the Internet or playing games, he never communicated with his colleagues, but he knew to do works. When he saw where needed help, he would definitely go up to help. On the way to and get off work, he lowered his head and never said anything when someone bumped into him... I think he knew that I was following behind him, but he never looked back or 'looked for me'. Such a person will indeed gradually lose in the eyes of everyone. And let people think that he has been transformed – at least not dare to cause trouble again."

"But you didn't lose your vigilance against him, did you?" Huyan Yun said.

"Of course!" Li Zhiyong said firmly, "because I know that the Type 92 police pistol is in his hands!"

"Did he admit that the gun was in his hand when he asked you out on the night of the Deratization Hill case?"

"No." Li Zhiyong shook his head. "After we met that night, we started o fight after a few words."

"Few words... To be more specific, what did you say?"

"Let me think... After we met, he asked me how long would I have to pester him? I said you didn't do anything wrong, what are you afraid of; he said his case was over, and he didn't want a tail behind him, and I said it wasn't over yet, you only paid one life, and you still have three blood debts to pay! He said if you have evidence, you can arrest me, and if you have no evidence, shut up or something... I got angry and punched him right in the corner of his mouth, he was also not polite, and gave me a kick, anyway, we finally scuffled together..."

"Who won? "

"What? "

"I'm asking, which one of you won in the end?"

Li Zhiyong felt a little embarrassed, touched his big nose and said, "It can only be said that the kid was imprisoned for eight years and did not stop exercising..."

Huyan Yun couldn't help laughing: "Intuitively, do you think Zhou Liping meant to make an alibi when he asked you out that day? And during his conversation with you, did he deliberately provoke you to fight him so that you could be impressed, foreshadowing for him to provide an alibi?"

Li Zhiyong thought for a while and said, "It seems like there is, but it doesn't seem to be... I can't say for sure. After all, we have been feuding for ten years. It's hard to meet without a fight."

"What time did he ask you to go to Xingyu Road?"

"Ten forty."

"Why did you arrive at Xingyu Road so soon?"

"I have a Jetta, and it's parked downstairs in my house. It only takes fifteen minutes to drive to Xingyu Road."

"You must have been surprised when Zhou Liping asked you to meet on the phone. Was he in a hurry when he was on the phone? Was there a sharp panting or something?"

"To be honest, I was really surprised when I received a call from him that night, and I didn't care about his tone, whether he was breathing hard or not... I asked him what was going on, he asked me where I was, and I said at home, he said that some things should be cleared up, I sneered and asked him how to clear it, he said that we will meet in the woods of Xingyu Road Street Park at eleven o'clock, I said fine, whoever doesn't go is the grandson!"

"You just went?"

"Yeah, so what else could I do?"

"Aren't you afraid that he will bring that 92-type police pistol?"

"I'm just waiting for him to shoot!" Li Zhiyong said bitterly, "If he doesn't shoot, I will never be able to prove my innocence for the rest of my life!"

"When you arrived at the park, how long did he appear?"

"As soon as I arrived, he came out."

"Did he look tired, sweaty or something?"

"It was originally at night. Although there are street lights in the park, but we met in the woods. It's hard to be able to see each other's eyebrows and eyes clearly in the dark. How can I pay attention to other things"

"How long have you been fighting?"

"It didn't take long for three punches or two kicks. Although we were all ruthless, none of us took much advantage, so it was over after a few scoldings."

"What did you scold?"

"I've always been clumsy, and I don't know how to scold people, so I called him a damn murderer. He will not die in a good way. Which were all common words. About Zhou Liping——" Li Zhiyong thought for a while and said, "He Just calling me idiot..."

The room was quiet for a moment, Huyan Yun blinked for a while: "No more?"

"No... He just called me an idiot, and nothing else, but to be honest, if this word was scolded together in other swear words, I wouldn't feel too bad, but scolding it alone would be quite hurtful! "

Looking at Li Zhiyong's depressed look, Huyan Yun wanted to laugh. At this moment, the door of the reception room opened, revealing a chubby face in the crack of the door.

3

"Mr. Zheng, what's the matter?" Li Zhiyong raised his hand and greeted him. Huyan Yun knew that the person who came was Zheng Gui, the general manager of Mingyi Public Relations Company.

"It's okay, nothing." Zheng Gui said as he got in. He was in his 40s, he was not tall, and was roughly the size from the upper to the lower body. It seemed that he had been in a bucket from the neck down for a long time. His cheeks sagged a little, and his eyes and bags under the eyes were big, probably due to staying up too late, which were all darkened, his lips were thick and swollen, and there was a hint of an attentive smile on the corner of his mouth.

Li Zhiyong introduced: "Mr. Zheng, this is my old friend Huyan Yun."

Before Huyan Yun could stand up, Zheng Gui had already stepped in front of him and grabbed his hand with his soft, chubby hand: "Oh, I have been looking forward to meet you for a long time, I have read the novel you wrote!"

Huyan Yun was a little embarrassed: "Actually, I'm not the author. Those books were written about the deeds of my friend. Of course, the content is basically true."

"Anyway, you are the best detective in my heart, even more powerful than Sherlock Holmes and Keigo Higashino!" Zheng Gui said.

Being able to bring these two people together, Huyan Yun was a little dumbfounded.

Zheng Guiqiang took him to his office, which was much more spacious than the small reception room. The whole set of rosewood office furniture looked quite quaint, but the "decoration" on the shelf was rather strange: the left one was a jade brave troop, the right one was the statue of Guan Yu carved in ebony wood, the first one was the round tea brick of Pu'er tea, the next one was a mix of "Three-Body Problem", "A Brief History of Time" and "The Analects of Confucius"... On the diagonally opposite corner of the table, there was a rockery with a waterwheel embedded in it. Under which was a carved solid wood tea table, with different levels of arc-shaped ravines on the table, a three-legged purple sand toad lying on the corner, the gold on its back had been peeled off, like taking a bath for too long to be bald skin.

Zheng Gui invited him and Li Zhiyong to sit down on the round wooden pier beside the tea table, and boiled water, brewed the tea, placed the purple sand teacups in a row with tea clips, rinsed them with boiling water, and then put the tea in the teapot. He poured out two cups of tea soup and brought them to Huyan Yun and Li Zhiyong, chatting with them, like an old friend who hadn't seen each other for many years: "You don't know, I've been so busy these days, so I picked up a meeting of the health care products company, I ran before and after to clear the venue. Suddenly there was such a thing of Zhou Liping. I was called by the police comrades for a cross-examination, but we really didn't know it at all!"

"After all, he's an employee of your company. It's normal for the police to ask a few more questions for such a big case." Huyan Yun took a sip of tea and said slowly, "However, you has taken a long time to make a serial killer by your side as a driver, you're so brave."

Zheng Gui smiled bitterly: "It's all because of the recommendation of Manager Sun of Yanzhao Hotel, how dare I refute her!"

"Did you mean Sun Jinghua, manager of the convention and exhibition department of Yanzhao Hotel?" Huyan Yun asked.

"Yes, that's an old relationship with our company. The upcoming meeting of the health care products company will also be held at the Yanzhao Hotel. From the cost of the venue to all kinds of accommodation, all under a word from her."

"How did Sun Jinghua and Zhou Liping know each other, and why did she recommend him a job?"

"This, I can't tell..." Zheng Gui frowned, "She just told me that there is someone in her place who wants to change job and asked me if there was a job here. How can I refuse?"

"While Zhou Liping worked by your side, what impression do you have of him?" Huyan Yun asked.

"I think he is a quite...a very 'reliable' person." Zheng Gui's comment with these two words was very cautious, "He usually didn't talk much, but he was not lazy, he can figure all the work I gave. There were times when I drank too much and got under the table, and I woke up and lay at home. My wife said that he brought me back all the way and I vomited on him. He refused when my wife let him change clothes, he just went straight back. He maintained several cars in the company very well. He learned a lot of craftsmanship during the years in prison, he can fiddle with all the appliances in our company. There are many female colleagues in our company, so it is inevitable that things will be messed up, but Zhou Liping never mixed in... I can't say anything else. It's been so long, and I seldom communicate with him, the only unpleasant occurrence was because Xing Qisheng complained him."

"I heard that it was the children of Tongyou Nursing Home who always came to find Zhou Liping, making Xing Qisheng unhappy?"

"Almost..." Zheng Gui was a little secretive, "Xing Qisheng called me in the middle of the night to complain about Zhou Liping. We are all fraternal units. I can't ignore it, so I gave Zhou Liping some bad words."

"What kind of brother units are you a public relations company and

Tongyou Nursing Home?"

Zheng Gui stretched out his chubby hand and spread his three fingers apart: "In the end, we and Love Hospital and Tong You Nursing Home are the three branches that grow from the trunk of Love Charity Foundation's offices in this city. We have to listen to President Tao Zhuoyao and Vice President Xing Qixian. Originally there were only two branches, the Love Hospital and the Tongyou Nursing Home. When I was working as a public welfare newspaper, I met both Presidents Tao and Xing.. As soon as the incident about Guo Meimei came out, I hurriedly found them and told them that charity will not be good from now on, and there will inevitably be people watching. President Tao didn't care at first, saying that everyone did it, and then I explained for her. After that, she understood and said, Zheng, I understand what you mean, what should I do? I said I will get a public relations company and gather the media together. If something goes wrong, the whole family can solve it together. President Tao said okay, I will listen to you, Zheng, we will pay to set up a public relations company, you will manage it ... So the Mingyi public relations company seems to belongs to me, but in fact It belongs to the Love Charity Foundation." At this point, he suddenly realized that he had strayed from the topic, and quickly added a sentence: "So, we, Love Hospital and Tongyou Nursing Home are brothers, especially Xing Qisheng was the elder brother of Vice President, he complained about Zhou Liping, I have to do him a favor, right?"

"Since the company is a charity foundation, why do you still take over the activities of the health care products company?" Huyan Yun was a little curious.

"After all, the company is just under the name of the Love Charity Foundation. It sounds good to the outside world and appears authoritative; in addition, having a background in a public welfare unit can be exempted from some taxes." Zheng Gui laughed embarrassedly. He said, "The company has to make money after it's established, and the security guard can't just protect one guard, right? People in the large company are relying on me to earn money."

"Yeah, it's not easy to start a business. These days, it's not always easy to enjoy the shade with the back of a big tree." Huyan Yun expressed his understanding, "The problem is that you hired Zhou Liping to pay back Sun Jinghua's favor. What about the others? Aren't his colleagues nervous and scared when they found out that he was a serial killer?"

"When Zhou Liping first came to the company, few people knew that he had committed crimes before, and he had been doing well. When they heard that he had been in prison for murder, everyone was nervous for a while and then passed away. At this age, everyone is the same, who had never done any dirty thing? Like Xing Yunda, who used to ignore Zhou Liping, changed his attitude after knowing that!" Zheng Gui took a shot at Li Zhiyong's shoulders, "Besides, there is someone, who came to work in our company specifically for Zhou Liping!"

Li Zhiyong had just drank a sip of tea and was slapped by him. He choked up and coughed. Zheng Gui rubbed his back and said with a smile, "When you came here, I guessed that you were undercover, but you still didn't admit it."

Huyan Yun smiled: "Xing Yunda is Xing Qisheng's son, right? What does he think of his father complaining to you about Zhou Liping?"

"The relationship between the father and son is very ordinary." Zheng Gui said, "Xing Qisheng divorced his wife a long time ago, and Xing Yunda was pushed around by the couple, and they both didn't want to drag the oil bottle, so he had no family relationship with his parents. When he grew up and Xing Qisheng was old, he remembered that it would be better to have a son, and asked me to find Xing Yunda a vice president position in the company... Then again, in the whole company, it seems that he is the only one who have some relationship with Zhou Liping."

"What kind of relationship?"

"In the past, Xing Yunda always liked to look like the boss of the underworld, shaved his head, tattooed, carried a knife wherever he went, and we all listened to his stories at company dinners. In fact, he has no parents to take care of him since he was a child, and lacks security, and he said those only to encourage himself. Later, he heard that Zhou Liping had really killed people, and he was a 'serial killer', then he admired him so much that he had to worship Zhou Liping. How would Zhou Liping care about him, but after going back and forth, for some reason, the relationship between the two got closer, Xing Yunda usually calls him 'Brother Zhou' – just don't know, this time he knew it was' Brother Zhou' killed his father, what would he think..."

"Yeah, the earthworm is actually an evil dragon, and this 'mutation' will definitely make different people react differently." Huyan Yun laughed, "So Xing Yunda knew that Zhou Liping was a 'serial killer' and worshiped him. After learning this, XIng Qisheng still dared to have a conflict with him and come to you to complain him, I'm afraid it's not an ordinary trivial matter that makes him 'angry'."

Zheng Gui picked up the teapot and refilled the cup for Huyan Yun. The water flowed slowly: "Mr. Huyan, there is no way for people to leave the tea while the tea is full. I am an honest businessman, I used to do business in the past. What's important is to develop relationships and do favors. Once the relationship is in place, everyone can make a fortune together... Now you also know that many old relationships are broken, new relationships do not take me together, and business is getting more and more difficult. Xing he liked to say after he drank too much before his death: 'In the following years, except for weddings and funerals, there are very few things that can bring us together'. Now that he is gone, I need to do favors for the living, but also for the dead, right?"

It was quiet in the office, only the sound of the waterwheel was turning, gurgling, and clucking...

4

While chatting, Li Zhiyong's phone rang. After answering the call, he said to Zheng Gui: "Mr. Zheng, the Society Security Center informed me there are some problems with my mother's medical insurance. I gotta go before they get off work."

"Go ahead." Said Zheng Gui.

Huyan Yun also stood up and said goodbye to Zheng Gui. Zheng Gui insisted to give him a health product from Jian Yi Company as a gift, which is an improved version of a mirror named Wu Xing-Yin Yang jing. he said the following press would be held for introducing this new product. Huyan Yun was embarrassed and finally refused.

On their way to the parking lot, Li Zhiyong said to Huyan Yun:" Zheng is not a bad guy, he is just a chicken with a loud voice but a timid mind. Anyway, the chat between you guys is interesting, you kept asking about the topic while he insisted on evading your questions."

Huyan Yun laughed and asked: "Then you think who is better?"

"I think is Zheng, cause you did not get the answer you want......" Li Zhiyong said, "But Zheng must have misjudged the situation, he tried to become close with you maybe because he read your novels. He thought the police may listen to your words and help him get rid of the Deratization Hill case —— and also his relationship with the Kind Charity Fund. However, he doesn't know the Chinese police never trust private detectives."

Huyan Yun nodded: "Zheng is so crafty like a loach, he said most of his words were only half-spoken, but every word showed he knows everything."

"He is a businessman, he needs to keep some truth to bargain with you." Li Zhiyong said.

"So, in your opinion, what's the answer to the question I'm seeking?"

They came to the parking lot, Li Zhiyong opened the door of a gray Jetta with the key and said, "After I worked in Mingyi Public Relations Company, my eyes were fixed on Zhou Liping, and I didn't pay much attention to other things. Most of the things Zheng told you today are also the first time I heard about. But I infer that the quarrel between Zhou Liping and Xing Qisheng is probably because Zhou sexually harassed or even sexually assaulted the children in the nursing home, and he was discovered by Xing Qisheng. This may also be the root cause of the murder case in Deratization Hill. He wants the witness to be silenced."

Huyan Yun said slowly: "Most people——includes the police consider the case in that way."

"Of course, Zhou Liping has a criminal record!" Li Zhiyong said, and got into the driver's seat.

Huyan Yun got into the passenger seat. Something smelled stinky inside the car. He kicked something and looked down. It turned out to be a pair of dirty sneakers, which was probably the source of the smell.

"Sorry!" Li Zhiyong said with a guiltless look on his face, "I rarely ride anyone else in my car, so it is more like a cabinet for me."

"Well, I see. Your car showed clearly that its owner is a single man......
By the way, you are going to be 40 this year, why not find a girlfriend?"

Li Zhiyong started the car: "Girlfriend? Most girls now have the same standard 'cars, houses and a dead mother', I only have this second-hand Jetta and without my own house, besides, my mom is sick at home. Who wants to date me?"

"I see quite a few girls in your company."

Li Zhiyong smiled: "Say something impolite, those girls are mostly used to make up orders, neither fancy nor useful."

Huyan Yun was curious: "What do you mean by making up orders?"

"When you buy things online, you always look forward to more discounts. Well, you can get 20RMB off when you buy from 100RMB. But the items in the shopping cart are less than 100 yuan, you have to add something cheap but not useful, and get enough for 100RMB......
A public relations company, it's actually like Fat Huang in *Tea House*[1], a professional peacemaker. They rely on relations to make a living and make use of each other. Zheng has no firm background, it's uneasy for him to get to the position today. He must bow and smile at everyone, and must not dare to offend anyone. He needs to get prepared whenever he needs

---

1 *Tea House*: A Chinese novel.

171

help from the big guns. He has to send them money if they want and help their children to find a job if they asked. Even these children have a low ability he still needs to arrange them a position. All of these were prepared to avoid trouble. Xing Yunda is an example, a guy acts like a rogue but can be a vice president, why? Just because he has a father who is the president and an uncle who is a vice president......You saw the large area in our company and so many workstations, while only three or five of them are the employees who really work hard every day. About others, they rarely came to work and Zheng still has to pay insurance and wages for them...... The firmer background, the higher wages."

Huyan Yun was surprised: "What's the logic?"

"Logic? The logic Zheng must follow if he wants the company to survive!" Li Zhiyong sighed, "But compared to Kind Charity Fund, this is nothing......"

"More exaggerated than this?"

"Sure!"

Li Zhiyong only said one word then said nothing.

The car went all the way to the south. At 4 in the afternoon, it happened to be the time that primary school was over. Children in twos and threes were like mercury beads spilled on the road. The car has to brake continuously. Li Zhiyong seemed to be a little irritable and hissed. He hurried to get off the car as soon as they arrived at the security center. Huyan Yun stayed inside the car and waited for a long time, then Li came out from the center holding an insurance registration form in his hand. He stood at the door with a dazed expression.

Huyan Yun got off the car and asked: "What happened?"

Li Zhiyong pointed the form and said: "Days before I submitted the form, but the security center rejected it, they said the relatives of the insured are not allowed to pay on their behalf, the insured must pay themselves."

Huyan Yun looked at the form and said: "The form has two options: self-payment by the insured and payment by the insured's relatives."

"They said it's the new regulation." Li Zhiyong sighed, "I told them my mother suffered from cerebral hemorrhage and hemiplegia so that she couldn't pay by herself, and she even doesn't have her bank card. But they told me to figure it out myself......"

Huyan Yun grabbed the form and pushed the center door, Li Zhiyong followed behind him.

There was no one in the empty hall, only a row of staff sat idly in the glass partitions, and yawned.

Huyan Yun found one staff at random, took the form, and asked: "The form stipulates the insured can choose to pay by themselves or by their relatives, why the relatives are bit allowed now?"

"This is the latest rule."

"Where are the regulations? Show me."

"Who are you? Why should I show you the rules?" The staff said impatiently.

Huyan Yun said extremely sternly in an instant: "I am a citizen, this matter involves the legitimate rights and interests of citizens, I, of course, have the right to ask you to produce the relevant documents!"

The empty hall was hummed by his voice, some staff leaned sidewards like frightened tadpoles, but no one dares to leave their workstations.

The staff on the opposite lowered his voice and said softly: "Actually, there is no hard rule, it's mainly because some people forgot to renew the card then the insurance was broken, and it also affected the relatives."

"What?" Li Zhiyong was shocked and angry, "Didn't you just say I can't pay on behalf? Why have you changed your words now?"

Huyan Yun looked back at him and gave him a look of calmness, then turned and continued to say, "Then there are no other problems with the form, right?"

The staff muttered something and took the form away.

Huyan Yun and Li Zhiyong walked out of the security center. They were both surprised that the afternoon suddenly turned into the evening in such a short time. The cold clouds came and so did the darkness. The cars on the road were covered in a light yellow layer. The air gradually became cold.

After getting into the car, Li Zhiyong said embarrassedly, "Thanks, buddy."

Huyan Yun couldn't help but say: "You were a government member before, how could you be fooled by them? The regulations of the state were originally for the citizens, but the department set an additional threshold in private."

"Being the criminal police need to fight with real swords and guns, these insurance matters were all solved by the government. I never worried about them. After leaving the team I found out that many things are really difficult." Li Zhiyong sighed, "I'll take you home, where do you live?"

Huyan Yun leaned on the passenger seat: "Let's go to your house and visit your mother."

Li Zhiyong stunned for a moment, then started the car.

When the car stopped, there was a high-rise building with an elevator in front of them. On the blue-gray building, mottled walls could be seen everywhere. Huyan Yun asked, "Why did you move to the western suburbs?"

"A few years ago, there was heavy smog in the city. My mother often coughed for a whole winter, I discussed with her and sold the old house, and changed it to a bigger one here. With an elevator, she won't go up and downstairs on foot. She has a stroke and hemiplegia, so it will not be so hard for her to have a walk or to buy food."

Huyan Yun looked to the northwest, and there was a faint green undulation like a beast's ridge: "Is that mountain ridge the Deratization Hill?"

"Yes," said Li Zhiyong, "It's close to the Deratization Hill here. You could get there in six or seven minutes if you run fast."

Huyan Yun nodded, took the elevator upstairs with Li Zhiyong, and reached his home. It seems that this house is not much more comfortable than the old building in the 1960s where he lived in the past. It's more like he moved the old house as a whole, except for the bad smell his old mother with hemiplegia has a lot of inconveniences.

Looking at the photo frames on the combined cabinets, Huyan Yun remembered the scene of sending Li Zhiyong home when he was drunk with Lin Xiangming ten years ago. There was a photo frame embedded with a picture of a girl with short hair, skinny body, ordinary looking, and smiling cutely... Huyan Yun remembered that this was not there ten years ago.

Li Zhiyong walked to the backroom, whispered something, and then greeted Yanyun to come in. Huyan Yun went in and saw that his mother was sitting on a double bed. Her hunched upper body looked like a piece of paper that had been rolled up by the fire. Her hair was gray back then, but now her hair is not only completely gray but also much thinner. Her waist and legs were in a small thin quilt with a floral fabric surface, the sad thing is that the quilt is almost flat on the bed, as if it is empty inside. However, the old lady has been bedridden for a long time, her clothes and even the sheets, and pillow tops are very clean. Li Zhiyong is diligent in changing and washing for his mother.

Huyan Yun greeted the old lady, then moved a chair and sat beside the bed, started chatting with her. The old lady recovered well afterward. Although her speech was a little vague, her consciousness was clear. She couldn't remember the young man was whom she had a relationship ten years ago, but since he was her son's friend, she enthusiastically made a homecoming with him. Huyan Yun noticed that when Li Zhiyong was in the room, she seemed full of energy, and when Li Zhiyong left the room, she seemed to be taking a breath and had to let go and rest, and her expression also went down.

There was a clanging sound of vegetable chopping in the kitchen, and soon, the fan of the range hood, the crackling sound of the soy pan, and the rushing sound of the stir-frying spoon also rang out one after another.

"Auntie, what're those sticking to the wall?" Huyan Yun asked, point-

174

ing to the long row of benches placed next to the wall. The benches extend to the living room as if to frame the bottom of the house.

"These are placed by Zhiyong. He was afraid that when he was not at home, I had to go out of the room in a hurry, so he placed these stools against the wall. I could rely on the benches to go forward step by step, and when I'm tired, I can sit on the bench and rest... It's hard for my child, he has to think everything for me, but I only drag him down." As she spoke, the old lady's tears welled up in her eyes.

"Don't be too sad, you should think this way: God found this disease for you to force Zhiyong to return to his family, he used to carry a gun, now he uses a spatula. He used to catch bad guys, now he practices housework every day. Which one do you think makes you more comfortable? Which one is more beneficial for him to find a wife?"

The words seemed to comfort the old lady, she can't help but start smiling: "Right, you are right!"

"Zhiyong went to pay the serious illness medical insurance for you with me this afternoon. With such a filial son, how could you waste his efforts – but why does your serious illness medical insurance just pay? I remember the males reach sixty and women reach fifty are all need to have insurances?"

"I had the insurance before but we moved here and the address was different, so I had to do it again. Zhiyong lost his job, and I fell ill again, so this matter has been delayed until now."

"I see." Huyan Yun nodded.

After a meal, Huyan Yun helped wash the dishes and said goodbye to the old lady. Li Zhiyong poured a glass of water and put a bottle of medicine on the bedside table beside his mother's bed: "I'm going to see Huyan off, remember to take the medicine in half an hour." The old lady picked up the medicine bottle and shook it: "It's going to be empty." Li Zhiyong said, "Don't worry, the medicine will arrive soon, it won't be a shortage."

When the elevator was going down, Huyan Yun asked Li Zhiyong: "What kind of medicine does Auntie take, why do you still need to ask others to buy?"

"A foreign-made thrombolytic drug, one tablet a day, is particularly effective for the recovery of stroke patients. I have been looking for someone to buy it online for me."

"Why not buy more at a time and stock up?"

"There is a limited amount of medicines purchased on behalf of others, and you can't buy too much at one time, otherwise the customs won't allow... Besides, you can't store too many medicines for the elderly with chronic diseases and keep them at home..."

"Why?"

"Nothing special... I'm afraid my mother will always feel that she's a drag on me..."

Huyan Yun understood: "It's hard for you to think so thoughtfully."

"I've already failed in my life." Li Zhiyong leaned his back on the rail of the elevator and smiled bitterly, "I can't even lose my mother."

The elevator stopped for a while, and at the moment the elevator door opened, a night wind blew through the open glass window at the door of the building. They walked outside side by side, Huyan Yun took a deep breath of fresh air, and the cool feeling chilled his mind: "Zhiyong, what were you doing that night when the Deratization Hill case happened?"

The question came unexpectedly, Li Zhiyong was stunned and said: "I told you, I got a call from Zhou Liping around 10:40, he asked me to go to the grove in Xingyu Road Street Park at 11:00. We need to 'get even', and then I drove off there—"

"I'm asking where were you before ten forty?" Huyan Yun interrupted him.

Li Zhiyong was a little confused. He looked at Huyan's eyes that were shining in the dark, and suddenly understood his meaning: "Do you suspect that I am the murderer?"

"Why can't I suspect you?" Huyan Yun said, "The picture of the girl on the cabinet in your house is Gao Xiaoyan, right? Ten years later, you still can't forget her, and you still haven't let go of your hatred for Zhou Liping. Even not to mention he is probably the culprit who attacked you, stole your gun, and caused you to leave the police force, so you want to kill him, no matter how. You also hate Xing Qisheng, you think he and his son are all worms of society. After you leave the police force, you look neatly dressed. Even getting insurance will be hindered for you. Your heart is full of depression, confusion, and despair. These reasons can make you form a twisted and abnormal anti-social personality... On the night of the accident, if you made an appointment with Xing Qisheng, let Zhou Liping drive him to Deratization Hill and to be photographed by the surveillance video on the traffic lights, and then wait for Xing Qisheng to go up the mountain alone to kill him, throw and burn his body. Can't these all make sense?"

"Are you crazy?" Li Zhiyong was surprised, "Why should I kill those children?!"

"Maybe the child was killed by Xing Qisheng, and you are not really don't communicate with each other in private as it seemed. He knows you were the police and has the anti-investigation experience, so he paid a lot of money for you to help him find a way to get out of the crime. After killing him, you threw him into the tunnel wind pavilion and burned him with the bodies of those children... Anyway, your ultimate goal is to blame Zhou Liping."

"But Xing Qisheng was killed after 10:30. How could I get to Xingyu Road in less than half an hour?"

Huyan Yun pointed to the gray Jetta parked in the yard: "I believe you didn't drive your car to the Deratization Hill to prevent being caught by the surveillance video, but you also said, as long as you run faster, it only need six to seven minutes to get the Deratization Hill from your home. You said it yourself, from our home to Xingyu Road, it will take less than fifteen minutes, so you will definitely be there at eleven o'clock."

Li Zhiyong was stunned, and then stammered for a while: "If it's true, I received a call from Zhou Liping, wouldn't it be better not to go to Xingyu Road? Why do I need an extra procedure—"

"This may not be necessarily redundant." Huyan Yun said, "First of all, Zhou Liping called you to make an appointment, maybe he received some hint from you during the day, and 'invited' to call you; second, you met him, although you suffered a pause, no matter how it will look like an alibi that Zhou Liping deliberately made, making him even more suspicious."

Li Zhi was so courageous that his whole body trembled: "You...you have no evidence!"

"Every behavior has a motivation, but every motivation is not necessarily reasonable, so you don't need evidence to suspect a person's crime, but to prove a person's crime requires." Huyan Yun said slowly, "Of course, you are not the real murderer in the case."

Li Zhiyong's tense nerves finally relaxed, and he couldn't help but let out a sigh of relief: "Why did you let me go again?"

"Because I don't think you're ready."

"What do you mean? "

"One can hide his temporary behaviors, but it is difficult to hide long-term habits." Huyan Yun said, "In a sense, taking care of your sick mother is already a habit, and this is also the only thing that makes you live meaningfully in your failed life. If you commit such a serious case, you must consider what will happen to your mother once you are arrested. Since you have always been careful about taking care of your mother, you don't have a girlfriend yet, and your mother also doesn't have enough medicine at home. So you won't feel at ease to kill people and set fire to them."

"It's so fucking weird!" Li Zhiyong tilted his head and looked at him, "You dismissed my suspicions from this perspective... Don't you consider that I'm a good person at all?"

"Don't you forget, my good friend before seemed like the kindest and most perfect man in the world, but who committed the evilest and horrific crimes?"

Li Zhiyong was speechless for a while.

"Well, now you can tell me, what did you do before you got the call from Zhou Liping on the night of the case?"

"Would you believe me if I told you that I would go back to my room and play 'jump hop[1]' while waiting for my mother to fall asleep?"

Huyan Yun smiled: "I believe it."

"Well, can I ask you a question?"

"What?"

"Since when did you suspect me?"

"Since I met you and you said that many police officers praised me for helping them solve cases, I was wary of any behavior that deliberately flattered me. Well, what made me suspicious of you was that you told Zheng Gui that you were paying your mother's serious illness medical insurance. I was thinking about why you didn't do it sooner rather than later, you have to do it now, are you 'preparing'?"

Li Zhiyong stomped his feet with anger, turned around, and went back into the building.

Huyan Yun raised his head and looked at the northwest direction, the undulating animal ridge under the night, trembling in the cold wind, its outline was sometimes blurred, and sometimes it was so clear that it was outrageous, terrifying, and even ready to move.

He walked down the steps, came to Li Zhiyong's gray Jetta, turned on the flashlight of his mobile phone, went around and checked it carefully, and finally stopped behind the car's butt, he squatted down and looked at the keyhole in the trunk ...

At this moment, a thunder-like roar suddenly came from behind—

"Don't move, police!"

Then he was pulled up by his neck and slammed onto the rear hood with a bang!

5

"Ma Xiaozhong! What are you fucking doing, you bastard?!" Huyan Yun roared angrily.

The policeman was searching from his shirt to his ankle heard this, then

---

1 Jump Hop: A small Chinese online game.

he stopped his hand and laughed loudly: "Hu, you recognized me."

"Not Hu, it's Huyan, my surname is double-chartered" Huyan Yun stood up, turned around, and was surprised to find Guo Xiaofen standing not far behind the short fat man.

"Guo, long time no see." He greeted her awkwardly.

Guo Xiaofen sneered.

"Hu, accept the police questioning well, and stopping assailing girl!" Ma Xiaozhong widened his eyes.

"Strange, aren't you suspended?"

"They can stop my job, but they can't stop me from serving the people!" Ma Xiaozhong said. "Answer me, you and Li Zhiyong spent an afternoon and a half night together. What have you both done?"

"Look at your dirty words!" Huyan Yun said, "Besides, why should I tell you?"

"Why? Because you interfered the public functions!"

"Guo is a resigned reporter, and you, a suspended police officer, what kind of public functions can you perform?"

"Speaking out to frighten you! It's the official business which Liu Simiao sends us to investigate in private."

It stands to reason that there is an obvious contradiction between "in private" and "official business", but the three words "Liu Simiao" really have a great deterrent, which surprised Huyan Yun, and after a little thought, he realized: "I heard that Simiao has left the special investigation team, so she still wants to continue investigating the case?"

"None of your business. Anyway, it's an important arrangement. While I can't tell you the details"

"Fine!" Huyan Yun walked away, "You do your business, and I do mine."

Of course, Ma Xiaozhong can't let him go easily, he dragged him out of the community and stuffed him into the back of his electric car. Guo Xiaofen also came in and sat in the passenger seat. Huyan Yun kept kicking and beating, Ma Xiaozhong laughed and said with a hilarious smile: "tell me, boy, why do you meet Li Zhiyong?"

They had been close friends for long, and they always treated slaps as a greeting, so Huyan Yun explained in detail what did he and Li Zhiyong do in the afternoon, and then said: "It seems that you two have been following me, let's exchange information now, what official business did Simiao entrust to you?"

"Don't think too highly of yourself, it's not that we are following you, but we want to meet Li Zhiyong to find out about the condition and find that you are the first to get there." Guo Xiaofen said coldly and then said what Liu Simiao talked to her and Ma Xiaozhong in the morning, without any concealment.

Huyan Yun pondered for a moment and said, "It seems like Simiao asked you to assist in the investigation. Not because there is an inside story in this case, but a story about the case ten years ago."

His words reminded Guo Xiaofen! Although Liu Simiao mainly talked about the matters of the Deratization Hill case in the morning but did not mention much about the serial murders in the western suburbs ten years ago. Ultimately, she asked them to focus on Zhou Liping and "how did he become a criminal". Besides, the investigation plan has been traced back to Fang Mei. Obviously, there were hidden truths in the case ten years ago.

Ma Xiaozhong patted his thigh: "I was curious why Simiao kept investigating the old case. Now I know she thought there is connection between the two cases. "

He finally said some meaningful words. Huyan Yun and Guo Xiaofen easily understood it, but they couldn't help looking at each other, dumbfounded.

Ma Xiaozhong was not ashamed: "Huyan, so is it true that Zhou Liping is the real culprit in the case and no other possibilities?"

This question is also what Guo Xiaofen is most concerned about. She stared at Huyan Yun, but Huyan Yun frowned for a long time, then said slowly: "it's hard to find another ...but it's not impossible."

"You mean, Zhou Liping may be completely innocent, and the real culprit is someone else?" Ma Xiaozhong asked in surprise.

"From the evidence the police have, there is no other evidence to accuse Zhou Liping except the monitor video of the traffic lights in Qingshikou Dongli. And Zhou Liping's excuse for explaining that he has no time to commit a crime sounds like a shame, but it is true. But because it's too shameless, it may be true – if you want to find out that Zhou Liping is the real murderer, you must find a way to prove he can get to Xingyu Road from Deratization Hill in less than half an hour."

"Have you found it?" Guo Xiaofen asked.

Huyan Yun glanced at the building where Li Zhiyong lived: "I found a way, but it's only a possibility..."

"Huyan, I will remind you in advance. A people said half of a sentence would already die in a detective story." Ma Xiaozhong said.

Guo Xiaofen knew that Huyan Yun likes to keep others guessing: "Then what's your plan next?"

"Let's divide our troops: you continue to follow the plan as Liu Simiao said, go back to investigate what Zhou Liping has experienced in the past ten years, and find the starting point and root cause of his crime. I would discover other details and communicate with you about my evidence at any time."

"But..." Guo Xiaofen hesitated and said, "You have to know that what Simiao entrusted us to do is a normal news investigation, but what you do is different. The law is clearly defined people without authority are not allowed to intervene in judicial investigations. And...you don't even have Simiao's private authorization, she can't protect you if something goes wrong."

"Guo, why don't you understand!" Ma Xiaozhong said impatiently, "Huyan doesn't want Simiao to bear it, he will definitely help her no matter what, so you don't need to worry about him."

Huyan Yun looked at Guo Xiaofen and said with a heavy tone: "What I said to Li Zhiyong came from the bottom of my heart. The case involves two of my friends and ten years of life. In ten years, so many things changed, even something that has long been defined, suddenly one day emerges with another part, proving that our youth is nothing but a meaningless misjudgment... How can I be indifferent to this?"

Guo Xiaofen slowly turned around, sat upright, and cast her gaze back to the vast darkness outside the car window.

Huyan Yun got out of the car, Ma Xiaozhong changed to the driver's seat and started the car. He rolled down the car window and said to Huyan Yun, "don't consider me as disloyal, it's a big case. I don't care how you used to be a detective in the past, but now you have to know the law and abide by it, you can't start an investigation without authorization. I'll give you a tip, either you find a police officer in charge of the case and follow him, or you can find a partner who has worked as a police officer so that he can at least protect you. If you won't break the law, the police force will give me help more or less."

Huyan Yun's eyes lit up, a smile blossomed at the corner of his mouth, and he made a salute: "Understood! Thank Director Ma for your guidance."

Watching Ma Xiaozhong drive away, Huyan Yun stood in the dark street for a while and slowly took out his phone from his pocket.

Chapter 5

1

"Director Ma, Ms. Guo, please drink some water." Director Qi of the neighborhood committee put two paper cups with water in front of Ma Xiaozhong and Guo Xiaofen, her chubby round face was full of smiles, "What's the matter? Feel free to ask and I will tell you whatever I know."

This is the street office where Zhou Liping's rental house belongs. The row of brick bungalows is plain. The sunshine only covers the buildings on the south side, the house exudes dampness. And it is only 9:30 in the morning, but they have to turn on the incandescent light so it won't look dim. When Ma Xiaozhong and Guo Xiaofen arrived, Director Qi was already standing at the door waiting for them. On the way to her office, she kept saying that the police had told her they will come and she must do a good job in reception. Guo Xiaofen looked at Ma Xiaozhong and his proud smile, thinking that this fat man did have relations with the police force.

Ma Xiaozhong held a paper cup, said while drinking water: "Director, sit down, we are one party. I come to visit as a distant relative visiting. Although this is the first time we meet, I don't want to be so formal, and so do you."

No matter who would feel comfortable after listening to his words. Director Qi smiled wrinkled and told Ma Xiaozhong what they wanted to know.

After Zhou Liping was released, his aunt had already sold the house together with the basement. They didn't know where they move. He couldn't go back and he also didn't want to go back to Dongqing Street. Few released prisoners are willing to go back to the place before. But in the eight years, everything outside has been turned upside down while he was prisoned. In order to adapt to the time, after obtaining the approval of the relevant departments, he chose to settle in Xiahe Street, which is not too far from Dongqing Street. Where he used to ride his bike down the street.

When he came to report with the release certificate, it was Director Qi personally received him and asked him a few questions, such as his plans for the future, and also gave him a few warnings, for example, the society is very positive, and there have been no vicious crimes in recent years. The uncles and aunts of the "Western Suburbs Red Hoop Team" are serious, and will never give any opportunity to illegal and criminal behavior. In addition to answering a few questions in the simplest language, Zhou Liping just listened blankly to those reprimands but said nothing.

But from they first met, Director Qi felt that he was very different.

"How to describe him... The prisoners I have received in the past, no matter in their face or in their bones, are all very humble. When you say a word, they often nod and say 'yes' many times. They must stand while they were told to sit down, the smile on their face is always to please you, Zhou Liping is different. His first impression on me is that he is very polite, he is very serious when he sits face to face and listens to you, although it is not clear that he agrees with you or is still against it, I can feel that he is really listening, not perfunctory, which makes me feel a little good about him – of course, I will not forget that he is a murderer because of this little behavior."

Not only Director Qi, but all the grass-roots departments have never forgotten that Zhou Liping's hands were once stained with blood, and they have been strictly guarding against him. After he moved into the current residence, for a month or two, there were always three or more members of the "Red Hoops" downstairs guarding the building pretending to be chatting and playing chess during the day. But their worries are superfluous. In addition to buying some necessary daily necessities, Zhou Liping stayed at home all day and rarely went downstairs.

"I heard that he had a lot of trouble finding a house?" Guo Xiaofen suddenly interjected.

Director Qi nodded: "Who wants to rent a house to a murderer. It is said that several times, the contract has been signed and even the deposit has been paid. The landlord heard about Zhou Liping's identity and broke the contract again. Don't rent the house to him even pay for the compensation. But I don't know the details, you have to ask Luo, the agent of Yuanman Estate, he helped Zhou Liping for a long time and finally rented the current residence."

"The rent is getting more expensive every day, how can Zhou Liping afford it?" Guo Xiaofen then asked.

"The rent for the one-bedroom apartment is not expensive. The landlord does business abroad and he is not short of money. So in recent years, he did not rise much with the domestic market. Zhou Liping has earned a little bit during the years in prison. The money is just used to pay the rent." The director said, "Of course, he is also afraid of spending all of his money, so after he settled down, he often went to the neighborhood committee to inquire about a job, but unfortunately we have never found a suitable position for him..."

"Not because you don't have a suitable position. You're just afraid of finding a job for him. Once he leaves his house, he won't be monitored." Ma Xiaozhong said with a smirk.

Director Qi also smiled, a little embarrassed.

However, in the end, Director Qi found a job for Zhou Liping.

This was also a coincidence. A small white building in the middle of the community on Xiahe Street was originally intended to run a kindergarten, but it was occupied by the district examination center as an office building. There is a truck that often comes to deliver materials at 11:30 noon. It was very dangerous to shuttle between the narrow buildings, just in time for the primary school dismissal. The neighborhood committee reminded the driver several times but to no avail. Director Qi came forward in person to ask him to keep an eye on it. At noon that day, the truck came galloping forward again. When the students ran away screaming, a little girl stumbled and fell to the ground. Thanks to Zhou Liping pulling her away. The truck almost wiped her body and drove past.

After the truck stopped, Zhou Liping rushed up after the driver just opened the door and got out of the car!

"You didn't see him, clenching his fists and his teeth, and twitching his face. If I hadn't happened to pass by and called him, maybe he would have swallowed the driver alive right away!" Director Qi recalled.

Zhou Liping looked at Director Qi, his arrogance suddenly dropped and he walked away slowly with his head drooping.

"Who is this person?" The driver was too frightened, "Ferocious."

Director Qi said, "We just received a prisoner here who has been released after serving his sentence. He has killed several lives. Never deliver at this time again. Avoid him and drive slowly."

The truck driver, who had always been arrogant, nodded again and again: "Thank you, Director, thank you!"

Since then, trucks entering and leaving the community have been changed to ten o'clock in the morning, and they always drove slowly.

This matter relieved Director Qi's heart, she found Zhou Liping and said: "How about going to the road at the entrance of our community to be a traffic assistant. The salary will be less for half a day, and the salary will be more throughout the day. Which kind would you like?"

Zhou Liping chose the whole day job.

This made Director Qi feel very at ease because the whole day job needs to be on duty at the intersection from 6:00 am to 8:00 pm, which is more conducive to monitoring Zhou Liping.

Since then, Zhou Liping had been wearing a little red hood, orange and yellow vest, holding a small red flag, and standing under the traffic lights to direct traffic, mainly to stop pedestrians and cyclists from running red lights, and to cooperate with the traffic police in time when there is an accident with a motor vehicle. This job is very simple, and the pressure is mainly physical fatigue from standing for a long time and abuse or even beatings by some people who do not follow the rules. Director Qi had confidence in Zhou Liping's physical strength. What she didn't expect was that Zhou Liping had never had a dispute with anyone who violated the traffic rules during the few months he worked. But when he met those who didn't listen to obstacles, sneered at him, or even rolled up his arms and sleeves, he just tolerated it.

"Has he been beaten?" Guo Xiaofen asked.

"Almost every traffic coordinator had been beaten," Director Qi said with a wry smile, "Most of the beaters are big bosses who drive luxury cars.

"I heard that a criminal policeman was attacked and lost his gun. The police listed Zhou Liping as a suspect. When they came to our neighborhood committee to investigate, you said something to help him?"

Director Qi was a little sensitive to this sentence: "Actually...it's not much to speak for him, I just think he's transformed well."

Director Qi admitted that over time, her impression of Zhou Liping was getting better and better. Especially one day at the end of July last year, with a high temperature of 42 degrees, when she went out to run errands at noon, she saw other traffic assistants sitting under the shade of the trees to enjoy the shade, only Zhou Liping was standing in the sun directing traffic, sweat on his back. She was soaked, and couldn't bear it in her heart. She felt that it was a pity for such a boy. Then she thought about it again, alas, he killed so many people back then? These were all retribution!

Guo Xiaofen asked, "Don't you know that he was only convicted of one murder when he was sentenced?"

"Actually, everyone knows how many people he killed. The case ten years ago was too big to be covered with three layers of quilts."

"So, are there any surrounding people or cadres who object to our community's taking in such a person?"

"There must be some whispering complaints, but after all, the case happened ten years ago, and now the times are changing so fast, the people in front of them are too busy, who cares about what happened ten years ago? Even the little girl in our office said that Zhou Liping was so obedient that he didn't dare to take the nail clipper others send him... So the case of Deratization Hill really shocked us all when it came out. The ancestors said it rightly: the country is easy to change, but nature is hard to change!"

"Why did Zhou Liping go to Mingyi Public Relations Company later?"

"One day he came to me and said that he had found a new job and stopped being a traffic controller. My first reaction was to be a little wary, what new job has he found? Would he want to get rid of our surveillance? But he I was very honest and gave me a copy of the relevant materials of the new work. I asked the comrade in charge of the help and education of the released prisoners to go to the Mingyi public relations company to investigate, and when they came back, they said that it was a regular company, and I was relieved. But I don't know exactly how he got to this company."

Guo Xiaofen glanced at Ma Xiaozhong, indicating that she had finished asking. With a smile on his face, Ma Xiaozhong stood up and said, "Okay, that's almost it. Let's go to Zhou Liping's residence."

Director Qi got up quickly: "I'll take you there."

"We won't bother you more, there should be comrades over there, we can just go there." Ma Xiaozhong repeatedly asked Director Qi to stay, but she still sent them to the door.

"By the way." Ma Xiaozhong suddenly remembered something, "Have you or other comrades in our neighborhood committee ever seen Zhou Liping walking very close to someone?"

Director Qi frowned and thought for a long time, then shook her head.

"If you think about it, even if it's not a close relationship, it just looks suspicious."

About this point, Director Qi remembered: "There are two people, one is Zhu Min, a retired teacher from Xijiao No. 2 Middle School, she is an old lady with white hair who used to be the headteacher of Zhou Liping in high School. She came to the neighborhood committee to inquire about Zhou Liping's residence. She should have gone to see him; there is another... I don't know exactly, but I glanced at it that one evening after getting off work, in our community garden, across the green wall, there was a girl with long hair. I've never seen it before, she was very beautiful and was wiping tears while talking to Zhou Liping..."

Ma Xiaozhong laughed happily: "Well, every case should have a woman, preferably a beautiful woman, preferably a beautiful woman who loves to cry, then the case will be interesting."

2

Ma Xiaozhong and Guo Xiaofen came downstairs where Zhou Liping lived. This building has five floors. From the peeling of the outer wall, the building must be some years old. Entering the building door, they smelled a stinky smell. They walked up the cement steps with almost every step was incomplete. Suddenly they heard a scolding from above: "What are you doing? Take out your documents!" Ma Xiaozhong walked quickly. When he was about to reach the top floor, he saw two people standing at the door of Zhou Liping's room. Inside the door was a policeman with a big belly, and outside the door was Huyan Yun.

"Pu!" Ma Xiaozhong called the big belly detective.

Pu was happy when he saw him: "Hey, Director Ma, the leader just told you that you are coming, and I want to invite you to have a meal at noon!"

"Don't mention it, I've been fucking angry recently!" Ma Xiaozhong pointed at Huyan Yun, and said, "This is the criminal investigation expert from Police University, he was hired by the bureau to help search Zhou Liping's house, let's see if we can If you find any new evidence, get off the way."

Pu gave way.

Huyan Yun walked in and carefully checked the small one-bedroom room: in addition to the chairs, folding tables, and other items on the table, he also paid special attention to opening the door of the closet and putting every piece of clothing on the table. He turned out all pockets; opened the curtain of the closet, took out the small pile of debris, and after looking at them one by one, searched the corners of the closet with his rubber-gloved hand. For the Jeffrey Deaver, Michael Connelly, Paul Holt's detective novels on the bookshelf, he checked one by one; of course, he did not miss the humming old-fashioned refrigerator in the corner. He unscrewed the lids of almost all the pots and jars in it, leaving the whole room smelling of fermented bean curd; finally, he got under the bed, lit it with the light of his mobile phone, and screeched for a while, his face was full of dust when he came out. Guo Xiaofen handed him a wet tissue, he seemed to be thinking about something, just wiped his hands and stuffed it in his trouser pocket.

At that moment, he turned his gaze to a dark green trash basket beside the folding table.

He squatted down and looked at the garbage basket covered with plastic bags. In addition to a few small advertisements rolled into a ball, ham casings, paper towels, there were two empty cans of Yanjing Beer 330ML. However, he didn't care about this, but he picked up a plastic package and said, "Here is the outer seal of instant noodles, why don't see the box of instant noodles?"

"It seems that the police officer Chu of the Criminal Technology Department of the Municipal Bureau took the evidence when he extracted it," Pu said.

Ma Xiaozhong added: "Zhou Liping himself said that on the night of the case, he went home first and ate instant noodles for dinner."

Huyan Yun said "Oh", then picked up two empty cans in the trash basket, and suddenly found a note stuck under one of the cans, which was a checkout receipt from the supermarket cash register. He read every word on the receipt, then frowned gradually.

"What's wrong?" Guo Xiaofen asked, squatting beside him.

Huyan Yun pointed to the line of time above and said, "It shows that on the night of the case, he bought instant noodles, beer, and ham from this good neighbor convenience store. The shopping time was after six o'clock in the evening."

Guo Xiaofen was surprised and looked around with wide eyes: "Is there a possibility that he came back after committing the crime..."

"It's unlikely." Huyan Yun shook his head, "He won't starve for that long, and there's no other food in the house, and the receipt doesn't show that he bought other food to eat that night."

"Maybe he bought two but left only one in the trash for us to see?"

"If that's the truth, then this opponent is too scary..." Huyan Yun pondered for a while, then raised his head and said to Pu, "Officer Pu, can you please take this receipt and find a nearby Good Neighbors convenience store, let them call up the surveillance video of the night of the case, around six o'clock, to see how many things Zhou Liping bought?"

Pu muttered, with a dissatisfied look on his face, "Why should I follow your order?"

"Hurry!" Ma Xiaozhong took out some money and put it in Pu's hand and said, "Buy some snacks and drinks. The scene is not s jail, why make our buddy starving?"

Pu refused twice but finally accept it, and went downstairs.

Ma Xiaozhong said to Huyan Yun and Guo Xiaofen: "You two don't hide secrets in front of me, tell me what you found out, I got a question mark in my mind."

Guo Xiaofen said: "According to the time and product display on the receipt, and with Zhou Liping's confession, he bought these things on the night of the case, and after he finished eating, he received a call from Xing Qisheng and went to Tongyou Nursing Home to pick him up."

"What's the matter?" Ma Xiaozhong said, "Why can't he have dinner before the crime?"

"There's no problem he ate instant noodles and ham sausage, the problem lies in those two cans of beer... Not to mention that for such a big case, he needs to be absolutely focused and cautious, and he can't let alcohol cause any disturbance to consciousness. The professional habits of an ordinary driver also won't let him drink beer. If he knows that there is a job that requires driving that night, he should not drink."

Ma Xiaozhong suddenly realized: "So, Zhou Liping didn't know that he would get a job that night at least around six o'clock that night, so he ate and drank and was ready to relax?"

"Don't forget that he committed a shocking case before he was eighteen years old. Don't forget that he spent eight years in prison. In some sense, he is a professional criminal with superhuman calm and rationality, so he would never drink beer if he knew that he was going to kill people and burn them that night." Huyan Yun stood up and said.

"Since he drank beer, why didn't he use the excuse of preventing drunk driving when Xing Qisheng asked him to drive?" Guo Xiaofen was a little confused.

"Two cans of beer, many drivers are embarrassed to take this excuse, even not to mention that it was nine o'clock when Xing Qisheng called him, three hours have passed, he even can't be tested alcohol." Ma Xiaozhong turned his head and asked Huyan Yun, "Is there any possibility: He knew that once the police found out that he was involved in the case, they would definitely search the room, so he bought two cans of beer intendedly. Before committing the crime, he only ate instant noodles and ham, and he drank beer after returning home after committing the crime. Deliberately making the police think in the direction of 'he didn't commit crimes after drinking'."

"It turns out that the police didn't think in this direction." Huyan Yun frowned and said, "However, every possibility should be ruled out..."

At this moment, Pu came back and carried a plastic bag of food and said breathlessly, "The Good Neighbors convenience store is right behind the building. I found the surveillance video, and I took it with my cell phone."

Surveillance video showed: At six o'clock that night, Zhou Liping entered the convenience store, walked around the shelves with a relaxed expression, picked out instant noodles, ham and beer, and went to the counter to settle the bill, perhaps because of thirst he opened a can of beer and took a sip before he walked out.

"Damn it!" Ma Xiaozhong couldn't help and said, "This guy has absolutely no intention of committing a crime."

Huyan Yun frowned, didn't speak, and he went to the kitchen and the bathroom silently, came out and said to Ma Xiaozhong and Guo Xiaofen, "Let's go, I can't find anything else here."

3

Out of the building door, there is a small garden directly opposite. The green plant wall in a circle has been with a dash of pale color. Most of the flowers and trees inside have withered, and the branches are sparse enough to be used to pick teeth. One or two residual flowers are like paper balls dipped in ink.

"Director Qi said she saw that beautiful girl with long hair talking to Zhou Liping. Is that right in this garden?" Ma Xiaozhong muttered.

"Well." Huyan Yun was reminded, "What did you find out from Director Qi?"

Ma Xiaozhong recounted the chat with Director Qi, and then complained to Huyan Yun: "Didn't I give you a tip before I left last night? Why did you come to Zhou Liping's house alone, if it weren't for me and Xiao Guo arrived in time, Pu really dared to handcuff you."

"I listened to you, but that person had something to do in the morning and said that he could only come over at noon. I was afraid of delaying the time, so I came in advance." Huyan Yun said.

"Don't say useless words." Guo Xiaofen said, "Where are we going now?"

Ma Xiaozhong said: "Didn't Director Qi just talk about the details of Zhou Liping's renting a house, do I have to ask the agent of the Estate? There is an Estate store on the road opposite the community. I guess it is that one. Let's go and see."

The three of them left the community, crossed the road, and walked into the "Yuanman Real Estate". A staff member in a suit and tie quickly greeted them: "Hello, are you renting or buying a house?"

"Looking for someone." Ma smiled and narrowed his eyes, "Who's surname is Luo?"

A small man with black wide-rimmed glasses stood up from behind a computer: "Hello... who are you?"

Ma Xiaozhong flashed his police officer's card: "Come with us."

Someone who looked like the store manager stopped him: "Police officer, what are you looking for with Luo?"

"You want to know?" Ma Xiaozhong said wickedly, "Sure, then come with us too."

The store manager was so frightened that he hurried to the side.

Luo hurriedly walked around a row of computer desks, knocking his legs and feet on several chairs, causing him to grin in pain.

Ma Xiaozhong swaggered forward, Luo followed behind and kept chatting with him along the way. Ma Xiaozhong ignored him and kept taking him to the garden downstairs of Zhou Liping's rented house. Sitting on a stone bench covered with newspapers, he crossed his legs, shook his feet, and said to Luo, "You can say now."

"I... what should I talking about?" Luo asked with his blinking eyes.

"Come on. If you still don't know what to say, either you think of the people's police as fools, or you can't do the job of pretending. Which one do you choose?"

Luo smiled embarrassingly: "You are here for Zhou Liping's case. I really help him find his house, but I really don't know anything about his case."

Ma Xiaozhong said nothing but just looked at him sideways.

Luo said with a sad face: "It's true, I really don't know. If I know this I shouldn't help him find his home. I was just using him as bait—" He seemed to realize that he had missed his mouth and braked suddenly, but from the sneering corner of Ma Xiaozhong, he understood that there was no turning back when he started the topic, so he had to say honestly, "In the beginning, when he asked me to help him find a house, he came up and told me that he was a prisoner released after serving his sentence and that he had killed people. Then I think he is bait—in this industry, this kind of business is to find unlucky people pretending to rent a house. The owner has signed a contract and received a deposit before telling him the truth. If a guest has killed someone and been imprisoned, usually the owner would rather pay the liquidated damages than rent it out, because the owner is afraid of causing trouble. Of course, we will split the liquidated damages with the tenants who are 'bait', but Zhou Liping, he just been released from prison and he doesn't know the market situation, we can take the liquidated damages alone, of course, I will definitely return the deposit he paid to him, I am afraid that he will stab me."

"Go on." Ma Xiaozhong said.

"I've used Zhou Liping four or five times, and I'm about to stop. I was afraid if he finds out I used him as bait. When he finds me again, I apologized that it was hard to find him a room, the rules of the agency are serious. He was disappointed, but he didn't blame me and kept saying that he was causing me trouble, then he planned to find a home by himself. For a while, I often met him in the nearby community, dressed in old clothes, walking along the streets and alleys to find a room, and was stared at by the old man and old lady of the red hoop team like a mouse. Even when he came over and was questioned and reprimanded by them, he didn't show any expression, just listened..."

"Then why did you help him find a house finally?" Guo Xiaofen couldn't help asking.

"Because I owed him a big favor."

Ma Xiaozhong's eyes lit up: "Tell me, what's going on?"

Luo said: "Once, our company made a two-meter-long foam board billboard. It was very urgent. We ordered it in the morning and need to pick it up in the afternoon. I rode an electric bike and went there. When I came back, I put the billboard horizontally on my legs, holding the handlebar in one hand. There was a woman riding a bicycle in the wrong direction and she came across me and fell to the ground. She was as fat as a pumpkin but walked very fast, and when she caught up with me, she said I knocked her down. The residents in the neighborhood don't like an intermediary like me who rode around on electric bikes every day. Most of them helped that woman, I was so anxious that I was sweating, and at this moment, someone in the crowd suddenly said that he saw that the woman fell down because of the unstable handle, and it has nothing to do with me..."

"Zhou Liping?"

"Yes, it's him." Luo said, "He happened to be passing by, so he came to testify for me. The woman was arrogant, saying that it was my billboard that hit her knee and knocked her down. Zhou Liping said it's impossible. First, the foam board is very soft and brittle. It is impossible for this kind of collision but without damage, and now the billboard is intact; secondly, the billboard is just done, and it is done in a hurry, and the primer is still intact. The topcoat was applied before it was completely dry, and the paint did not dry easily, so – he smeared it on the billboard with his finger, and put a layer of paint on his finger – if it really rubs against her knees, it is impossible for not a bit of paint on the woman's white trousers."

Guo Xiaofen couldn't help but "Wow", "This reasoning is not bad."

"Right, at that time the woman was speechless, I let out a breath, and was about to run away but suddenly the woman stared at Zhou Liping and shouted: 'I know you, you are the serial killer. Everyone, come and see, this person is the bad guy who killed a lot of people in our western suburbs! How can you believe his words?!' I saw Zhou Liping's face instantly turn green, so I quickly pulled him away. But the woman is still swearing, although the onlookers also pointed discussed him, no one dared to catch up and throw stones."

Ma Xiaozhong scolded: "Some shrews like that woman, you talk with her gently, she treat you shamelessly, but when you become shamelessly she turned to blame you!"

"To be honest, no matter how heinous Zhou Liping is in others' eyes, at least on that day, when there were so many onlookers and none of them spoke justice for me, but he helped me. I thanked him again and again. He said he just couldn't see that someone was wronged, and I felt that I owed him a big favor." Luo pointed to the building opposite the garden, "There is a one-bedroom on the top floor of this building, and the landlord went abroad. He entrusted me to help him rent it out, but I was selfish and left for myself to live, so I moved out and rented it to Zhou Liping at a very low rent... God knows how he committed such a big case again."

"Did Zhou Liping live alone here all the time?" Guo Xiaofen asked, "Has he brought other people such as his girlfriend or something?"

"For a while, when I took other clients in the community to see the house, I saw a girl with long hair coming to him. They were sitting and chatting in the garden, and I couldn't see what the relationship was."

"What does that girl look like?"

"Not bad, she's quite beautiful. A Miss like a whore, how can she look bad?"

Ma Xiaozhong punched him: "How do you know she is a Miss?"

Luo hesitantly said: "She and other girls were sitting in a nightclub. When I was in other branches last year, they asked me to find a house for them to live together. I found a three-bedroom apartment. I was invited to dinner once, so I have a little impression of her, but I don't know her name."

"What nightclub? Where is the shared apartment you found for them? " Ma asked with a smile.

"It's called Jinyemantang Nightclub... But don't go looking for it. That nightclub was closed at the end of last year, and a few girls stayed for a while. But then they caught up with the crackdown on shared rental housing. All of them may go back to their hometown..."

Guo Xiaofen glanced at Huyan Yun, Huyan Yun was looking at her, although he said nothing, there was something very firm in his eyes, so

Guo Xiaofen said to Luo, "This girl is very important, you must help us find her."

"That's right." Ma Xiaozhong added.

Luo thought about it and said, "Well, I'll go back to that branch another day. Whether renting or buying a house, customers must provide a copy of their ID card and contact information and leave it for the record. I should be able to find the person who entrusted me to rent a house. Maybe she knows something about the girl you want."

"No 'another day', I always consider the two words like 'no way'. You go and ask right this afternoon, and tell me tomorrow."

Luo nodded and bowed, then left in a hurry.

Looking at him walking away, Ma Xiaozhong said: "These mediators are so cunning."

"In the past few years, the market has become more standardized. I still remember how many times my deposit for renting a house was swallowed by the agency when I first came to the city." Guo Xiaofen glanced at Huyan Yun who was bowing his head in deep thought, "What are you thinking?

"Nothing..." Huyan Yun raised his head and raised his hand to someone.

Guo Xiaofen turned around and followed his gaze, she saw a stout guy running over, his fat waist stretched out the folds of his jacket, and each shoe print smashed a shallow spot on the ground. He had a wide face with a large nose, and very small eyes and mouth, and his eyebrows are very far away from them as if the eyebrows were surprised by their strange appearances.

Ma Xiaozhong stood up from the stone bench, greeted him, and held the hand of the person who came: "Li, long time no see!" Then he introduced him to Guo Xiaofen: "This is my old friend Li Zhiyong."

Last night, at the prompting of Ma Xiaozhong, Huyan Yun called Li Zhiyong, explaining that he was going to further investigate the case, but he lacked the police permission and asked him if he would like to be his partner. When Huyan is faced with inquiries from the police, Li could help him to divert some resistance. Huyan Yun thought that Li Zhiyong would be hesitant, and he had to spend some time to get him, but Li Zhiyong sighed and said, "Zhou Liping has been arrested, my 'voluntary tracing' can end, it doesn't make any sense to stay in Mingyi Public Relations Company any longer, let me help you." He agreed.

In the morning, he still went to the company to help Zheng Gui prepare for the meeting of the health care products company.

When Li Zhiyong was a criminal policeman, he worked with Ma Xiaozhong for a short period. He felt that the short and fat man was too arrogant and didn't like him very much. Currently, the reunion was a little more enthusiastic. Ma Xiaozhong saw that it was almost time for dinner. He drove them to a nearby restaurant and ordered a few dishes. While eating, they exchanged information about their current situation and discussed how to proceed in the next step. Guo Xiaofen has a habit of being a reporter. No matter what the outcome of the discussion, she must use the notepad in her mobile phone to record it, and then she organized a WeChat group and posted it to the group.

The things of Ma and Guo in the following two days:

1. Find Zhou Liping's high school headteacher, Zhu Min, and find out what happened when he was a student at Xijiao No. 2 Middle School.

2. Inquire about Fang Mei's current situation from Zhu Min, and try to get in touch with her.

3. Go to No. 1 Prison to learn about Zhou Liping when he was in prison.

The things of Huyan Yun and Li Zhiyong in the following two days:

1. Go to Yanzhao Hotel to find Sun Jinghua, the manager of the exhibition department, to know why she introduced the work to Zhou Liping.

2. According to the information that Luo has inquired about, find the long-haired girl who has had a close relationship with Zhou Liping.

3. Go to Block E of Hefeng Hotel to investigate the "office of the Kind Charity Fund".

"Is there any objection?" Guo Xiaofen asked.

Everyone picked up their mobile phones to see what she posted in the group, Li Zhiyong sighed when the others didn't say anything.

"What's wrong?" Guo Xiaofen asked. "Don't sigh, just say if you have any difficulties."

Li Zhiyong said: "Difficulties are nothing... I know quite a few people from the 'office of the Kind Charity Fund', and there is no problem with taking Huyan to Block E of the Hefeng Hotel, but since it is an investigation, it must be It is necessary to find out the situation from the relevant people, and once someone suspects us, and report it to Xing Qixian, Cui Wentao and director Zhai Tienan. It is a trivial matter for me to be fired, what I am afraid is that it will affect President Zheng..."

The other three at the dinner table couldn't help but look at each other, and finally Ma Xiaozhong said calmly, "Li, I'll tell you the truth, I asked Huyan to invite you join us, why? Because I have the right to think you as undercover in Mingyi public relations company for these years. Don't mention your age, how many old police officers who have retired for many years, relying on the crutches are still rushing up whenever they heard there were ang threats to the people... There is such a big case right now, the corpses of an adult and three children in the Deratization Hill. As a public security officer, you should put aside your personal friendships, and focus on arresting and punishing criminals. If you can't do this, then you really quit the police force completely."

Li Zhiyong's face flushed slightly, and after holding it for a long time, he said, "You're right, Ma!"

4

Guo Xiaofen and Ma Xiaozhong got Ms. Zhu Min's contact information from the personnel office of Xijiao No. 2 Middle School. They discussed for a long time how to avoid Mr. Zhu's rejection of their visit. Who would have thought that after the call was made, they just explained the purpose of the visit. With a ready voice, she said, "Come on, come on, my home is not far from the school."

They bought some fruit downstairs and knocked on the door of Ms. Zhu's house. She invited them into the study room, poured water, and gave a pear for both of them. Guo Xiaofen felt embarrassed to keep an old lady busy, while Ma Xiaozhong looked at the bookcase where was a mountain of books that couldn't even insert any space on the desk, and he was chomping on pears.

"Sit down and talk." Zhu pointed to the sofa and said. She is in her early sixties. Although she is very thin, her eyes were bright, and her short gray hair looks very neat.

Ma Xiaozhong sat down and pointed to the stack of workbooks spread out on the table, and said, "Why do you still keep so busy with a retired age?"

"I have nothing to do after retirement, so I started a cram school in the community to help students who are going to take the college entrance examination." Zhu saw him sucking his teeth and couldn't help laughing, "I guess, you must not be a lover of learning in the past, right?"

"Actually, I was very smart since I was a child, I just can't get along well with my textbooks." Ma Xiaozhong said, "If I say, it's my mother's fault. She went to the temple to worship the God of Study before I was born. Later, she thought that she might have worshipped wrongly, it was the God of Martial..."

Guo Xiaofen squirted a sip of water on the ground, and Ms. Zhu also can't help laughing.

"By the way, how was Zhou Liping in high school? Was he just like me?" Ma Xiaozhong seemingly inadvertently turned the topic to business.

Ms. Zhu was stunned for a moment, she suddenly became a little dazed, as if had fallen into the memory of the past. After a long time, she said slowly: "Zhou Liping, his academic performance was average, but he was completely different from you, he was very cowardly..."

Ma Xiaozhong and Guo Xiaofen couldn't help but look at each other in shock. This was the first time they heard someone describe Zhou Liping as "cowardly" since the case happened-- and in their opinion, the word "cowardly" was synonymous with an inhumane murderer.

Ms. Zhu stood up, walked to the row of bookcases that were converted from old combination cabinets against the wall, opened a cabinet door, took out a photo album, dusted off the dust on it, slowly opened it, and then pulled out one of the bookcases: "Look, this was the group photo I took when I took the class to visit Yunshui Cave in their sophomore year of high school. The one on the top row and the far left was Zhou Liping."

In the photo, the students in the first few rows were sitting on the steps, and the last row was standing, some were holding scissors hands behind other people's heads, some were making hearts by hands with their peers, some were pulling each other's ears and grinning, and some were smiling sweet. Only Zhou Liping, who was wearing a black jacket, distanced himself from the other classmates, standing upright, expressionless, like a wooden stake.

"When he was in high school, he was very different, withdrawn, and didn't like to talk. He was not good-looking, he had severe acne on his face, and a mustache on his lips like a monster, so the classmates didn't like him, but no one dared to provoke him, they were all frightened by his fierce look. Later, a gangster outside the school robbed him of money on the way from school, and he had no money with him. He was beaten a few times. There were a lot of 'troubling generals' in our class, and their collective consciousness was very strong. They felt their classmate had to stand up for him if he was bullied. A large group of people caught the hooligan and called Zhou Liping to beat him up. When Zhou Liping came, he said that the gangster didn't beat him, they were just kidding... After that, all the classmates in the class looked down on him and thought he was cowardly. Later I asked Zhou Liping, why did the classmates let him revenge but he didn't beat that hooligan? He said 'I'm afraid he will come back and get revenge on me', and after waiting, he said 'I thought that kid was quite pitiful at the time, he was so frightened that he was shivering, so I thought it would be better... "Ms. Zhu said, "He is such a person. He looks very fierce but you'll think he was cowardly if you get to know him. He didn't like to cause trouble, he just lives in his own little world..."

"What kind of world is that?" Guo Xiaofen interjected.

"The inner world of every middle school student is a contradictory combination of closure and openness. They want to open their minds but are afraid of being hurt. In contrast, Zhou Liping may be more closed." Ms. Zhu said, " I didn't know him at first, but later I found that he didn't like to leave the school after school. He sat alone on the window sill, staring blankly at the gradually darkened campus. Sometimes I worked overtime to correct homework, and I would leave work at 8 or 9 at night, and he was still sitting in the classroom. I asked him why he didn't go home. He said he had nowhere to go... He was abandoned by his biological parents, and his aunt who adopted him treated him not very well, only giving him the lowest living expenses. it's not abuse, but not necessarily better than having a dog. The black jacket in the photo, he wore from the first year of high school to the third year of high school. He washed it to white but never changed. Children lack warmth and tend to have distorted personalities... You can see that, I have a straight temper, especially for boys, I teach them to be boyish. I encouraged him to be brave and told him that many amazing people grew up in loneliness and predicament. He especially liked to listen to me and chatted with me... I treat each student as my own child, of course, not all students regard me as a mother, but Zhou Liping must be closer and more trusting to me."

Ma Xiaozhong said, "It is a blessing for students to have a teacher like you!"

Ms. Zhu said with a smile: "Actually, if you want to get into the hearts of students, there is a secret, and that is to read their compositions. The less talkative children are, the easier it is to express their feelings in their compositions. Zhou Liping has no literary talent and doesn't like writing descriptions and metaphors, but his perspective was very strange. I still remember one year of spring outing. I took my class to the park to enjoy flowers and came back to arrange compositions. Others wrote about how beautiful the flowers are. Some of them also wrote about Daiyu's flowers' funeral. Only Zhou Liping wrote about the garden at night."

"The garden at night?" Ma Xiaozhong didn't understand. "He later went to the garden for a tour in the middle of the night?"

"No, he just imagined the scene of the garden at night, with wind, gloom, and coldness, and nothing to see. He said that the best thing about flowers is not blooming, but withering, but most flowers wither at night, so people can't see them. This 'no self-pity in the dark' is the real beauty..."

"Interesting..." Ma Xiaozhong muttered.

"Interesting? I was frightened that he would commit suicide. Adolescent children use life as a simple joke" Ms. Zhu said with a wry smile, "I then slowly let it go because Zhou Liping started exercising. Dumbbells, parallel bars, sandbags, etc. During recess, it was raining outside, the other students were staying in the room. He ran around the playground alone with his bareback. Then he caught a cold and was laughed at by everyone, he didn't say anything... After running like this for a year, let alone in the rain, he no longer catches a cold when he runs in the snow."

"It's really unusual." Guo Xiaofen said, "I heard that he was punished by the school for molesting girls. What's the matter?"

"That incident was just a misunderstanding." Ms. Zhu said, "once in class, a male classmate who was in the same row as Zhou Liping, but separated by a girl, borrowed his notes to copy, and when he finished copying, he wanted to return it to him. It happened that the girl stood up and answered the teacher's question and wanted to sit down. The male student who borrowed the notebook deliberately threw the notebook on the girl's chair. Zhou Liping took it. The girl was the child of the school leader, and usually domineering. Then he caught a trouble and was given a demerit penalty."

"However, during the investigation of the serial murder case in the western suburbs, this punishment was an important basis for proving that the criminal personality profile made by the police is true and effective!" Guo Xiaofen widened her eyes, "Could it be that when he was punished, he didn't defend yourself?"

"He tried to explain, but it was useless, so he stopped talking." Ms. Zhu said, "Maybe it is because he has accumulated too much suffering and grievances. Zhou Liping was very numb to the punishment. I remember that the disciplinary decision was announced by the dean holding a microphone on the playground and announced to all the students in the school. In front of the public, Zhou Liping was completely expressionless. The classmate who borrowed his notes and tricked him then was always afraid of being punished but Zhou Liping didn't do anything, he just had less talk to his classmates from then on."

"A person like him..." Guo Xiaofen sighed, "Is there any girl in the class who likes him?"

Ms. Zhu hesitated for a moment: "If Fang Mei counts..."

"Fang Mei? Is that the female classmate who was almost raped and killed by him?"

"Yes, it's her." Ms. Zhu said and pointed to a girl in the group photo:

she was sitting on the steps, very thin, with a sick face and a somewhat restrained smile, holding the red travel bag tightly in her hands. The shoulder strap, as if afraid of being snatched away.

"This child was very pitiful. Her parents divorced. She lived with her father and was very timid while behaving. They gradually got better when they were table classmates. The third year of high school was tense, and the two of them also supplemented each other's lessons. Some naughty classmates shouted that they were a couple. Fang Mei was too afraid, so she treated Zhou Liping distanced, but it didn't take long for them to be together again. I remember Fang Mei likes to read comic books, and Zhou Liping bought books and lent them to her with the money he usually worked in restaurants and convenience stores... More like a gift for her."

Guo Xiaofen suddenly asked, "Ms. Zhu, do you still remember what books Zhou Liping likes to read?"

Ms. Zhu thought for a while: "He has read a lot of martial arts novels... Compared with other students, he may prefer detective novels, Sherlock Holmes or something. I still remember that when the third year of high school started, the school conducted a thorough investigation of the students. Looking at their college entrance examination aspirations, Zhou Liping said he wanted to go to the police academy, and I joked with him whether he had read too many detective novels, he shook his head and said, "No one dares to bully him when he wears a police uniform."

Ma Xiaozhong and Guo Xiaofen felt incredible once again when they heard that a murderer's college entrance examination ambition was to become a police officer. It was also incredible that Zhou Liping's reason for applying for the police academy was to avoid being bullied.

Ms. Zhu sighed: "Who would have known that he committed such a big case after only two months. When the police came to me to find out about Zhou Liping's situation, I firmly stated that Zhou Liping could never be the murderer. Who knows that after he was released, he was involved in the Deratization Hill case again... But I always felt that something was wrong. I know my student; he is not that kind of person! "

Guo Xiaofen asked tentatively: "I know about that case. Most of the murders chose to commit the crime at around ten o'clock in the evening. Do you remember what happened to Zhou Liping in those days? Didn't he often stay in the classroom very late? Can you recall it, for example, when a certain case happened, Zhou Liping may not have left the school..."

"When the police came to the school to investigate, I answered that when those cases happened, I didn't know what Zhou Liping was doing. The senior year of high school was very busy, and the headteacher just care about the grades. Zhou Liping's academic performance was average, which was given up by the school, and he also knows. At that time, the Winner Band came to the city to hold a concert. He did the scalper in time and was beaten because he didn't hand the money. When I went to the police station to pick him up, the blood on his face had not been wiped off. I was very angry. On the way back, I asked him, 'Do you still want to pass the test of Police academy?', he said nothing for a long time, and then said slowly, he knew his grades and would not be admitted to the police academy..."

"This kind of thing, shouldn't the first choice for the police station to notify his family members? Why didn't his aunt come? " Ma Xiaozhong didn't quite understand.

Ms. Zhu said with a wry smile: "His aunt, I have been the headteacher for Zhou Liping for three years, I have only met once, and she never came to parent-teacher meetings. From my point of view, Zhou Liping is no different from an orphan at all. When he was beaten by a scalper, Zhou Liping sent my cell phone number directly to the police. Later, I called his aunt to communicate the matter. His aunt said impatiently that she didn't want to take care of him. After the college entrance examination, she planned to rent out the basement, so she had nothing to do with Zhou Liping. After that, she complained about how much money she had spent on Zhou Liping and how much she worried about him."

Guo Xiaofen thought for a while and continued to ask, "Has he come to you after he was released from prison?"

"Not at first, I knew he was released and was waiting for him to come to see me, but he didn't come. Well, then I went to find him. When I get to the neighborhood committee to find out where he lives, I knocked on the door, he was not at home... When I got back to my house, he came to see me at night. He was taller than eight years ago, with black skin and was thin, but he looked stronger and his expression was more indifferent. I shed tears first, and couldn't help but ask him why he did such a bad thing and hurt so many people. When he saw me crying, his face twitched, his eyes were red, and said vigorously, "I'm not a bad person, I didn't kill all those people." I said "it's not right for you to kill a person!" Speaking of this, Ms. Zhu took off her glasses, wiping the corners of her eyes vigorously.

The house was quiet, and the afternoon sunlight poured into the house through the window, some picked-up past floated in the air like dust.

"Before leaving, I asked him if he needed any help, and he said no... After that, he never came to see me again, maybe he felt that he had failed my expectations, but I still think about him, which made me feel bad... I have been a teacher all my life, and some of the students I have taught are very good, most of them are ordinary people for a lifetime. Only him, only this one, makes me think of him again and again." After speaking, Ms. Zhu's tears rolled down again, "At the class reunion at the end of August this year, to celebrate the tenth anniversary of graduation, they called me to go, and I asked if I wanted to call Zhou Liping, The class leader even came to my house and told me that none of the classmates wanted Zhou Liping to participate because he smeared the school, the class, and all the classmates..."

Guo Xiaofen asked: "Do you still have contact with Fang Mei? How is she now?"

"Of course. After her father died, the school sent several teachers to take care of her, including me, we took turns to give her make-up lessons. In the end, she was admitted to a very good university, worked hard after graduation, and is now in a big company and become an HR. She got married this spring, and the wedding was held at the Four Seasons Hotel, and I went to attend."

"So, didn't Zhou Liping find Fang Mei after he was released from prison?"

Hearing this question, Ms. Zhu obviously paused, and then said vaguely, "No... I'm not sure."

Guo Xiaofen and Ma Xiaozhong felt maybe Ms. Zhu knew something, but it was obvious that they could ask nothing.

When they were living, Ms. Zhu sent them out. In the dim corridor, she suddenly asked Ma Xiaozhong: "Officer Ma, would Zhou Liping die this time?"

"If the case was really done by him..." Ma Xiaozhong asked after a pause, "Will you see him for the last time?"

Ms. Zhu didn't answer, looking desperate like a mother who received a notice of her son's critical illness.

5

Just when Ma Xiaozhong and Guo Xiaofen knocked on Ms. Zhu's door, Huyan Yun and Li Zhiyong came to Yanzhao Hotel and were going to ask Sun Jinghua, the manager of the exhibition department, to find out why she helped Zhou Liping find a job.

Yanzhao Hotel was rebuilt on the basis of a Soviet-style building in the 1950s. In the past, it only accepted official conferences and activities. Later, out of the need to invigorate the economy, it also opened up to those private or foreign-funded enterprises with strong financial resources. Then it started to print the brochure after meetings which often appears to have a more "authoritative sense", so it is especially favored by those health care product dealers and pension insurance salesmen... Walking into the gate of the courtyard and following the scattered tree-lined path of fallen leaves went forward. The gray buildings and the wide, old-fashioned windows could be seen in the distance. Late autumn was the most tormenting season for the color of the ivy, green to pale green, red to pale red, half green and half red covered with a layer of gray. When looking closely, the brick carvings with unclear textures on the balcony were still alive. Everything seemed to have poured time into concrete, rigid, conservative, stubborn, and with a little self-deprecation so that when passing under the tall tower at the entrance of the foyer it could feel of being in another time and space.

It was a pity that a staff member of the convention and exhibition department said to Huyan Yun and Li Zhiyong bluntly: "Manager Sun is not here today, she went out to run errands."

The faces of the two showed a look of disappointment, and the staff member said, "Why are you looking for her? Do you want to make an appointment for the exhibition hall?" He took out a note from the light blue file drawer on the desk. Li Zhiyong said quickly, "We didn't make an appointment for the exhibition hall."

The staff's face sank: "Then why are you looking for Manager Sun?"

Li Zhiyong pulled Huyan Yun's sleeve, and the two quickly slipped out of the office of the Convention and Exhibition Department.

"Why do they still use the notebook to make an appointment for the exhibition hall?" Huyan Yun muttered, "Even elementary school students in the cram school use the computer to make an appointment now..."

They had no choice but to change their plans and first went to Block E of the Hefeng Hotel to investigate the situation of the "office of the Kind Charity Fund". On the way, Li Zhiyong urged Huyan Yun while driving: "I don't know too well the people there, they are our 'superior units', and everyone thinks that our jobs are given by them, and they have always treated us not well. Don't talk nonsense when you arrive, it will be troublesome if you reveal us."

Hefeng Hotel and Yanzhao Hotel were completely different in temperament. If the latter was likened to a grumbled old man, the former was a mature woman who hides in her boudoir but has a lot of charm. It is made of leather and stone and looks majestic, but when walking in, it would show that apart from the splendid main high-rise buildings of the hotel that rest on the lotus pond, perched on the rockery. The small western-style buildings with different styles, no more than four or five floors, seemed to have been widened and increased in height after the villa in Badaguan, Qingdao, and scattered again into the various scenes of the courtyard.

In contrast, Block E was the most hidden. First, passing through the white moon cave door, and then walk through a winding corridor with vines hanging on it, and it would show a small white building. The security guard at the door saw Li Zhiyong, nodded, and let them in. There was a thick red carpet from the entrance of the building to the depths of the corridor. There was no sound when they walked in and it was quiet as if the jet lag was messed up by the solid walls, dark brown wooden doors, and dim wall lamps.

At the elevator entrance, they bumped into a man with a big head and a slender body, who looked like a bean sprout, and what Huyan Yun couldn't help but laugh at, Li Zhiyong introduced: "Dou is the deputy director who mainly responsible for the internal affairs—specifically, various affairs in this building." The surname and body were so suitable.

Director Dou didn't seem to be in good health, with a frowning face, he kept taking out wrinkled toilet paper from his trouser pocket and blowing his nose: "Zhiyong, why are you here today?"

"Of course because of Zhou Liping!" According to the plan, Li Zhiyong said with a smile, "He committed such a big case in Deratization Hill, and the Public Security Bureau could not wait to come to our company eight times a day, which made Mr. Zheng annoying, I was afraid that something would be missed and caught by the police, so he sent me and this newcomer to the company, Zhang (he pointed to Huyan Yun), we want to ask if the police had any new questions here to investigate, and how did we answer them here?

Director Dou thought for a while: "In the days when the case first came out, the police came frequently, and they were all received by Zhai. I didn't care much. Then, Vice President Xing greeted them, so the police stopped visiting in the past two days..."

"What happened?" Li Zhiyong asked.

"Nothing special," Director Dou blew his nose. "It's not a big deal."

"Vice President Xing really has good connections." Li Zhiyong smiled, "By the way, is President Tao back?"

"No, he's probably still in France, I haven't been in touch..." Director Dou suddenly remembered something, "Zhiyong, have you seen Zhang Chunyang these two days?"

Li Zhiyong shook his head: "I didn't see it—President Tao didn't take him to France?"

"No, how could he deserve?!"

"What's wrong? He and President Tao had a quarrel again? "

"He dares!" Director Dou glared, probably because he stared too hard, his nose was sore, and he took out toilet paper for another blow, "That man just rely on others, and the president treats him as a toy, I see that after the president gets married, he will not be able to put on a sack to sell movies on the subway." Maybe he realized that some words were out of line in his anger, he quickly covered his mouth and said, "I still have something to do. I'll go out first. Mr. Tao is coming today. Vice President Xing and President Cui have both gone to the airport to meet him. I have to arrange food and lodging."

"So Tao Bing is here?" Li Zhiyong said to himself, seeing that Huyan Yun didn't know much about the personnel relations, he said in a low voice, "Before Tao Bing retired, he was in the Social Welfare and Charity Promotion Department of the Civil Affairs Department of A Province. Mr. Zhang founded the 'Kind Charity Fund', and Tao Zhuoyao, the president, is his daughter. Tao Zhuoyao was stranded in France and did not return, so her father hurried to come back. It seems that both father and daughter understood something serious happened."

"Didn't Director Dou they have connections, what are they worried about?"

Li Zhiyong smiled secretly: "Let's go to the third floor to find Liao, that person can say some useful words."

Walking into the elevator, Huyan Yun asked, "Who is Zhang Chunyang?"

"He used to be a fitness trainer, but then got along with Tao Zhuoyao. That boy is good-looking, but he is very sinister and has a bad heart. He has a lot of bad ideas and is relatively close to Xing Qisheng."

The elevator stopped on the third floor and opened. They went to Liao's office. Liao was also the deputy director of the office. He is a tall man and used to be a soldier. He was demobilized and transferred to work in the foundation. When Li Zhiyong pushed the office door, he was playing cards on the computer. He was very happy to see Li Zhiyong, let them sit down, poured water, and handed out cigarettes.

Li Zhiyong repeated what he had just explained to Director Dou. Liao laughed and said, "There are really fewer police officers these days. We are a special institution, and all kinds of relationships are very solid, so don't be afraid!"

"After all, both the victim and the perpetrator are members of our foundation's subordinate units." Huyan Yun looked at him and said, "The pressure of public opinion is still a bit high, so Mr. Zheng is particularly worried."

Liao laughed again: "Mr. Zheng's company is here to help us deal with public opinion. Besides, public opinion is just an empty bullet. It sounds quite loud, but it's useless—Mr. Zheng, are just too timid!"

"Speaking of this—" Li Zhiyong put on a gossip expression and leaned forward, "I heard that you were on duty in this building on the night of when the accident happened, what did you see?"

"A night shift? I'm just staying in this office, swiping WeChat, typing on the computer, no one knew that such a big case would happen, and I didn't notice anything at all... But about eight o'clock, I went to the canteen in the main building to buy beer and saw Xing Qisheng sitting in the lobby bar eating."

Before Huyan Yun spoke, Li Zhiyong took the lead and asked, "Just him? What did he eat?"

"He's alone. He's too far away, and he's sitting so far back that I can't see what he's eating."

"Did you see Zhou Liping that day?"

"No."

"The buddies in the police force told me that that night, President Tao suddenly booked a ticket to Paris at about 9:30. Did she live in this building that day?"

Liao nodded and shook his head again: "I'm not quite sure, in general, President Tao will definitely go back to her private suite on the fourth floor at night, but it can't keep her from going to another hotel, you have to ask Hu, who is in charge of cleaning the room for President Tao in the housekeeping department."

"I see that there are security guards standing guard downstairs." Huyan Yun said, "Apart from your duty at night, is there no security guard at the entrance of this building?"

Liao narrowed his eyes: "Bro, you care about a little much"

Li Zhiyong quickly smoothed out: "Zhang is a newcomer to our company and is not very sensible. He is also kind and wants to fully understand the situation. Now the rumors are dangerous. Some people may want to lead things to President Tao, so We need to find out what happened to President Tao on the night of the case. In case the sewage is spilled on her, we can help her clear it up."

Liao was stunned, glanced at the tightly closed door, lowered his voice, and said, "Xing Qixian, Cui Wentao, and Lao Dou?"

"You just have to know in mind." Li Zhiyong answered indistinctly.

"Damn, I knew they were not good things!" Liao scolded angrily, "Since the day Tao Lao retired, Xing Qixian wanted to squeeze Zhuoyao out of the foundation and become the president himself. This time, when his brother died, as the victim's family he can even make an offer. I was curious why Zhai has been so gloomy recently, the first step to protect them is to let Dou replace Zhai as the office director. "

Huyan Yun didn't understand the personnel disputes here, so he kept his mouth shut. Liao scolded a few more words before saying: "We have a back door in this building, which leads directly to the walking stairs. Of course, it is also very close to the elevator, but only President Tao, me, Zhai, and Dou have the keys. In addition, since the first floor to the third floor is the office area, and the fourth floor is the residential area of President Tao, there is a security door at the entrance of the stairs to the fourth floor. Most people in the elevator can only arrive the third floor. On the fourth floor, only President Tao, me, Zhai, and Dou have the keys and cards for the security door."

"Director Liao." Huyan Yun suddenly said, "Can you take us to the fourth floor to see President Tao's room?"

Liao waved his hands again and again: "That can't be done, if President Tao knows about this"

Huyan Yun stared into his eyes: "Don't you ever think about it, maybe Dou has already brought someone up before you know it. And there may be something to prove the case related with President Tao..."

Liao opened his mouth and didn't speak for a long time, then suddenly stood up and said, "Come on, I'll take you to the fourth floor!"

Although he was prepared, the luxury of the four-story decoration still surprised Huyan Yun: not to mention the rose relief wallpaper decorated like the corridor of a fairy road, nor the one-piece study made of ivory white European-style bookcases, either the private cinema furnished with ebony wood leather sofas, the cloakroom alone was larger than the living room of Huyan Yun's own house, and the various brand-name women's shoes in a separate shoe room next door had been neatly stacked on the open oak shoe cabinet. When it reached the ceiling, it was dazzling and the fabric trial shoe pier in the middle has four black-painted silver legs like four calves wrapped in black silk.

Huyan Yun asked Liao, "Where is President Tao's bedroom?"

Liao took him and Li Zhiyong to a suite at the head of the corridor. This suite had only one door leading to the corridor. When entering, there was a living room with sofas, TVs, desks, etc. Inside was a bedroom, a deep room. A brown sliding door separated it from the living room. The door panel of the sliding door was solid wood, which was quite thick and must have a good sound insulation effect. Huyan Yun found that the glass windows in the bedroom are also double-layered... Judging from the wallpaper, the full round mirror on the ceiling, and several provocative oil paintings of nude women, it was clear that these soundproofing effects are not set up to concentrate on studying.

At this moment, Liao, who had just made a phone call, stepped forward and said, "I asked Hu from the housekeeping department to come over immediately. I really have to let her see if there had been any changes in this room after Zhuo Yao went to Paris."

Huyan Yun looked downstairs from the window. It was the backyard of Block E. This backyard was connected to the back door of the building. The yard was very secluded and there were several cars parked. He looked back and walked inside out of the suite: all the trash cans were empty, the toothbrushes in the bathroom were neatly arranged, the camel carpet was clearly vacuumed, not a single crumb. The bedsheet exuded a faint scent of lavender, and the TV remote was lying straight on the coffee table. He also checked the notepad on the desk. It seemed to be just a decoration, and there was no trace of writing.

" Zhang." Liao frowned and asked, "Aren't you a policeman?" Huyan Yun said confidently: "Don't worry, I'm 100% not!"

Li Zhiyong stabbed Lao Liao with his arm: "Why look down on me? If I really want to investigate the scene, why have I had to find someone to replace me?"

Liao said with a smile: "I saw Zhang is quite professional!"

"To tell you the truth, Zhang studied in the police academy about physical evidence inspection, so he could see if there was anything in the room that was not good for President Tao." Li Zhiyong said.

Liao nodded as if he understood.

A woman wearing a light gray cleaner's uniform with a long face walked in, Liao introduced, "This is Hu who is responsible for cleaning the entire fourth floor of President Tao's residence. Is there anything I don't understand you can ask her."

Huyan Yun asked Liao, "Didn't you say that only four people have the security door key and elevator card at the entrance of the fourth floor of the pedestrian elevator? How did Hu come up?"

"Oh, you're quite sharp." Lao Liao patted the back of his head, "I forgot to tell you that there is a set of keys and cards in the guestroom department, which Hu wears with her so that she can come and clean it."

Huyan Yun nodded, turned, and asked Xiao Hu, "When was the last time you cleaned this suite?"

Hu thought for a while and said, "The next morning President Tao went abroad."

"Where were you cleaning?

"It's all those old places."

"Can you be more specific?"

"It's just this house, how can I be specific..."

Huyan Yun saw that Hu might consider herself as Tao Zhuoyao's "personal cleaner" and was a little arrogant. While he was thinking about what to do, Li Zhiyong unbuttoned his suit, his face that had always been naive suddenly turned stern: " Hu, I know that you can come to clean the house, mostly because of a distant relative with President Tao, but now I'll tell you the truth, someone wants to take advantage of President Tao to go abroad and open a door behind her back. We asked you to know the situation, just to help her gun. Think about it, if she falls, let alone the fourth floor of Block E, can you still enter the door of Block E? "

Hu suddenly showed a panicked look: "I... you can ask whatever you want."

"Very good." Huyan Yun asked her, "The next morning when President Tao left the country, when you came to clean this room, what was the room like--in other words, did President Tao live in at night? "

"She had lived."

"One person or two?"

"Two ..."

"But didn't President Tao get on the plane at one o'clock in the morning the next day to go abroad..." Huyan Yun said, "When you were cleaning, do you remember what toothpaste and toothbrush look like?"

"Toothpaste and toothbrush?"Hu didn't quite understand what he meant.

"Did they use it that night or not?"

Hu thought for a while: "It doesn't seem to have been used."

"Are you sure?"

Hu thought about it again, and nodded: "It's definitely not used."

"Okay." Huyan Yun said, "Think about it again. When you cleaned the cloakroom and shoe room, did you feel a little more chaotic than usual?"

"It's really a bit messy," Hu said. " Tao likes to be clean. She used to pick out clothes and shoes, and then she put all the ones she doesn't wear away. But that night, she seemed to be in a mess and didn't care anymore..."

Huyan Yun pondered for a moment, then stared into Hu's eyes and asked, " Hu, let me ask you one more question – who was the person who came here with President Tao that night?"

Perhaps because he thought this issue was too "sensitive", Liao wanted to stop him, but Li Zhiyong stopped him instead.

Hu shook het head: "I don't know about that..."

"How could that be? With President Tao's identity and status, she wouldn't just someone casually to her place, right?" Huyan Yun said.

"I really don't know." Hu said, "Zhang Chunyang used to come all the time, Tao was planning to marry that Jiang Lei recently, and occasionally brought him here, Zhang Chunyang came less often, and in the past when I clean up the house, I can always find the condom wrapped in toilet paper in the trash basket in the bedroom or bathroom... but when I cleaned up that morning, I only saw that the bed was very messy, but I didn't see the used condom..."

"Could it be a woman who had sex with President Tao that night?" Li Zhiyong asked, blinking his small eyes.

"No way!" Liao said immediately, "I didn't hear that Zhuoyao liked women, so maybe she just threw it down the toilet and flushed it."

"Who is Jiang Lei?" Huyan Yun asked.

Liao said the name of a state-owned enterprise: "Jiang Lei is the only son of the chairman. He used to be abroad. After he returned to China half a year ago, he had been couple with Zhuo Yao. They're planning to talk about marriage recently... Zhang, you are nearly talking about her privates. Is there any other problem? If not, let's leave as soon as possible."

They walked to the door together, and when they were about to leave the house, Huyan Yun suddenly stopped, looked back at the bedroom, turned back again, raised his head and searched for something on the walls, and found nothing for a long time. But he was not reconciled and kept finding. Li Zhiyong couldn't help but ask, "What are you looking for?" He didn't say anything, but his brows became tighter and tighter. He suddenly raised his right hand and tapped his forehead with his index and middle fingers together. After getting through something, he walked out of the bedroom, stood in the living room, and shut the dark brown solid wooden door.

The light in the living room suddenly dimmed a bit, Huyan Yun carried a stool, placed it in front of the sliding door, jumped up, and carefully searched—

Got it!

Just like the dial of a fluorescent watch, what was indistinguishable in half-light and half-dark but would be revealed when all light is completely gone!

Huyan Yun looked at the hole with the size of the belly of his index finger, which only appeared on the top of the two overlapping door frames after the sliding door was fully opened, and smiled.

"Did someone dig the hole for peeping?" Li Zhiyong couldn't help asking after walking out of Block E with Huyan Yun.

"Almost, but it's not." Huyan Yun said a little vaguely.

Li Zhiyong knew people like Huyan always spoke like this: "Where are we going now?"

"Didn't Liao say that he saw Xing Qisheng eating in the lobby bar of the main building that night? Let's investigate, it's best to call up the video of that night."

"Sure, leave this to me." Li Zhiyong said.

The properties of Hefeng Hotel were mainly divided into two types: one was small buildings or villas like Block E, mainly for long-term private guests; the other was for short-term rented individual guests, concentrated in the main building. When Huyan Yun and Li Zhiyong walked into the main building, it was three or four o'clock in the afternoon. There was no one in the lobby. The soft music reverberated in their ears. It had a soft buoyancy-like sound making people dizzy.

Li Zhiyong walked to the bar on the west side of the lobby and went straight to the manager, raised his chin, and said, "Are you in charge?"

When the manager saw his temperament and manners, he thought he was from the government and quickly said: "Hello, what can I do for you?"

Li Zhiyong said a time, which was the night of the case: "Someone reported to us when the case happened they lost a piece of Rolex worth more than 500,000 yuan while eating here at around 8 o'clock that night. Search the surveillance video and let me have a look. "

The manager immediately took them to the security department on the basement floor of the main building and called up the surveillance video of the lobby bar that night. It can be seen that there were many guests eating at the bar that day, and the waiters with plates kept shuttling.

"Which one was Xing Qisheng?" Huyan Yun asked Li Zhiyong in a low voice.

Li Zhiyong looked for him and pointed to a seat in the back. In part of the video, it can be seen that a short and fat man with a greasy face and a serious bald head was stuffing a large piece of smoked salmon into his mouth with a fork. He looked at the lobby with alertness, as if he didn't want people to recognize him, and looked at his mobile phone from time to time as if he was waiting for someone to call. They played the video in fast-forward, and he was the only one sitting there eating from start to finish. At about 8:10, he received a call. Judging from the speed of picking up, this was the call he had been waiting for a long time. After receiving the call, he hurriedly settled the bill and left.

The bar manager couldn't help but say, "Why are you finding this person either?"

"Mind your own business!" Li Zhiyong glared at him, then he leaned in Huyan Yun's ear and said, "After the case, the police must have called up this video." The implication was that there was no valuable content.

Huyan Yun ignored him and said to the manager: "This person's receipt for dinner that night should be recorded in your cash register, can you call it out and show me?"

The manager had no choice but to take them back to the lobby bar again and called out Xing Qisheng's checkout receipt that night. It said that he drank a bowl of creamy mushroom soup, and ate an Australian veal salad, fried foie gras, and tobacco. Smoked salmon and truffle risotto for the main course – this is the same conclusion as the forensic autopsy analysis of his stomach contents.

"This guy is really a rice bucket." Li Zhiyong muttered, seeing Huyan Yun's dignified expression, he couldn't help asking: "What did you find?"

"Nothing."

"Then why do you look so serious if there were nothing?"

Huyan Yun sighed: "It's just because there were nothing, it's getting weirder."

He walked outside after finished speaking, and Li Zhiyong followed behind.

Passing around the group of white marble lotus sculptures in front of the main building, just as they were about to walk out of the gate of Hefeng Hotel, they suddenly heard someone calling Li Zhiyong's name, it was Chai Yongjin.

Li Zhiyong and Chai Yongjin hadn't seen each other for a while and went up to shake hands with each other, but Chai Yongjin kept looking at Huyan Yun from the corner of his eyes, and suddenly asked, "Yong, why are you here?"

Li Zhiyong said with a smile: " The company always affiliated with the Kind Charity Fund, after the case, our leaders were so overwhelmed that they asked me to come over every three days to report the situation to the higher-level unit——"

Chai Yongjin interrupted him: "Report the situation? What are you doing with Huyan Yun to report the situation?"

Li Zhiyong couldn't hold on to his face, but Chai Yongjin's words became ruder: "Yong, criminal investigation work cannot be intervened by non-public security personnel, this is a rule, you know it, you are a brother of me and also a criminal policeman. If you want to know this case, I can tell you about it without breaking the rules, but if anyone else wants to play detective games, they'd better go to an escape room!"

Then he turned his face to Huyan Yun and said coldly: "Mr. Huyan, if it wasn't your good friend who was protecting Zhou Liping ten years ago, now there would not be so many corpses lying down in the Deratization Hill. You may feel uncomfortable, if Zhou Liping's hands are stained with blood, Lin Xiangming was the one who handed him the knife. If I were you, I'll go home and reflect on the carelessness of making friends, and don't come out to show off. The world now are no longer who wrote novels is the member of 'Four Reasoning Clubs', don't act as Detective Conan anymore?!"

Li Zhiyong's face turned purple like a pig's liver, but Huyan Yun was not angry, looked at Chai Yongjin, and said slowly: "Chai, I don't deny that criminal investigation work needs specialization and elitism, but with the popularization of the Internet and the development of intelligent technology, human beings will surely enter an era in which information acquisition is more convenient, professional boundaries are more blurred, and crime patterns are more diverse. In such an era, social work types are constantly subdivided, and criminal motives are increasingly complex. In the process of handling cases, more broad-spectrum and diverse support is also needed. Some of these supports come from professionals from all walks of life, and some like me can provide special ways of thinking from some unique perspectives to help public security personnel recognize and handle cases in a timely manner. Blind spots in the process, correction of misunderstandings in criminal investigation work – In recent years, higher-level leaders have repeatedly requested that public security work must mobilize the masses, organize the masses, and rely on the masses. into a way of practicing the mass line?"

After hearing Huyan's words, Chai Yongjin was stunned, he laughed dryly and said: "Okay, Mr. Huyan, I was speechless! Then now I have a headacheissue, and I need you to solve it from a unique perspective. Can you, the enthusiastic people, help me with this?"

Li Zhiyong hurriedly winked at Huyan Yun, meaning don't take Chai Yongjin's stubble, Huyan Yun just pretended not to see it and nodded.

"Okay, I'll tell you." Chai Yongjin said, "You may have heard that on the day of the case, Zhou Liping was driving a black INSPIRE to the Deratization Hill. According to what he said, he got out of the car halfway, let Xing Qisheng drive up the mountain by himself... Regardless of whether what he said is true or not, anyway, the police have gone through the sweeping investigation of the Deratization Hill and all the places where Zhou Liping may have hidden the car, but they did not find it. This car is important physical evidence, and there may still be some criminal information stored in it, so I will give you one day to help me find it back. One day, as long as you can find the car back, I will report to the superior and apply for the appointment of you as the assistant investigation consultant of the case, how do you think?"

Li Zhiyong was anxious: "Chai, all of you have searched for so many days and haven't found the car. Now let Huyan find it in one day. You mean to find fault with him—"

"Don't interrupt about this!" Chai Yongjin interrupted him rudely, "Mr. Huyan wants to help us, I of course hurry up and give him the opportunity. Well, Mr. Huyan, do you agree or disagree? Be readily!"

Huyan Yun was at a loss: "Isn't that car in your hands? What can I help you find?"

"Bullshit!" Chai Yongjin said angrily, "If it's in our hands, then why am I fucking ask you?!"

Huyan Yun was a little anxious, he raised his hand, and made a gesture of splicing the tracks of the toy train together: "Well, maybe we didn't talk about the same thing... I mean, I've seen it before. On the map of the Deratization Hill, the alley leading to the place is very narrow. On the night of the case, before the police car, fire truck, and ambulance arrived, in order to facilitate their parking, the traffic team must have towed away from the illegal traffickers in the alley..."

As if he was struck by lightning, Chai Yongjin's face froze.

Li Zhiyong slapped him fiercely: "Chai, hurry up, make a phone call and ask the traffic team to check if there is any unclaimed illegal parking in the past few days."

Chai Yongjin's face twitched, and there was an expression of wanting to cry without tears: "Right, right..."

Huyan Yun took Li Zhiyong and left. Before leaving, he left some words: "Chai, you have to get someone to seal up Block E, and transfer the surveillance video of the night of the case and save it. There may be very important findings."

Until they walked far, far away, Chai Yongjin was still sticking in place, dumbfounded.

Chapter 6

1

Seven days after Zhou Liping's arrest, the city bureau held a "half-term meeting."

According to the relevant provisions of China's Criminal Law, even a major suspect in a serious criminal case can be detained for a maximum period of only 14 days, and then either release or arrest... Of course, after 14 days, the public security can apply to the People's Procuratorate for an extension of detention time which is up to thirty-seven days, but very conclusive evidence must be presented. Today, with the continuous strengthening of the rule of law in China, all judicial institutions must be highly responsible, and a request for an extension of the detention time will face strict review by the people's procuratorate. This was also a headache, so they always hope to "get it" within 14 days, so they take the time from the arrest of the suspect to the seventh day as the "half process". If at this time, there has not been a breakthrough in the investigation of the case and there was no iron evidence that the prisoner can be "crucified", the public security will hold an internal meeting to summarize and review the investigation methods, ideas, and directions of the case. This was called "half meeting".

It is precisely because of this that the "half-term meeting" of the case had the highest number of participants and the highest level in recent years. In addition to Du Jianping, Lei Rong, Lin Fengchong, Chu Tianying, Chai Yongjin, Sun Kang, and other police officers handling the case, Xu Ruilong, the director of the Municipal Bureau, was also present.

The "opening gong" was struck by Xu Ruilong, and his words were concise: "Today's meeting, please speak freely and express your views, but you must present real evidence to support your views. Let's start!"

The police officers involved in the case were quickly divided into two factions. One faction, led by Chai Yongjin, advocated the theory of "Zhou

Liping is guilty"; the other faction, led by Lin Fengchong, believed that the evidence at hand was not enough to identify Zhou Liping as the real murderer. The former froze the video footage captured by the traffic lights in Qingshikou Dongli on the screen, repeatedly mentioning Zhou Liping's "criminal conviction" that he was imprisoned for a serial murder case ten years ago as if everyone else in the conference room had forgotten about it. The latter not only pointed out that there were no major flaws in Zhou Liping's confession but also seized on the point of "how could Zhou Liping have only spent half an hour throwing and burning the corpses and then rushing to Xingyu Road", repeatedly emphasizing that he did not have enough time to commit crimes. The two sides were quarreling with each other, and the scene of dozens of smokers in the conference room puffing up clouds of smoke seemed to be a parody of the heated debate that was filled with gunpowder smoke, causing Lei Rong to cough.

Xu Ruilong frowned and tapped the table with his fingers: "Guys, we have a female colleage here, can you put out the smoking gun for a while?"

The city bureau, like other offices, had no smoking indoors, but the criminal police officers were too tired to deal with cases day and night. If they don't take a couple of shots when discussing the case, they will fall asleep on the table, so the leaders always turn a blind eye. But now the boss said, then everyone pinched their cigarettes.

"Lei Rong." Xu Ruilong said, "they've been arguing all over the place. What do you think?"

Lei Rong straightened her short hair, opened the folder in front of her, looked down at it for a while, and then slowly said, "The results of the autopsy have been sent to Du and the police officers, and there are no new findings. "

Xu Ruilong said: "We all know this, I just want to ask you, do you think Zhou Liping is the real murderer?"

The police officers in the room looked at Lei Rong eagerly: First of all, Lei Rong's prestige in the police force was extremely high. The criminal police are all obedient; secondly, she is notoriously high and she never offends anyone when she speaks and acts, so now everyone wants to see how she can answer Xu Ruilong's question.

Lei Rong said without hesitation: "In the serial murder case ten years ago, in the end, only Zhou Liping was determined to be responsible for one case, and it has nothing to do with the current case; Xingyu Road, at present, I can only say that the method of implementation has not yet been found, and it cannot be used as an alibi for Zhou Liping-the two sides have argued for a long time, and they have opinions, but they have not done what Director Xu said to use 'real evidence' to support themselves."

Xu Ruilong nodded again and again, and the police officers in the room were dumbfounded. Chu Tianying couldn't help poking at Lin Fengchong next to him: "Dude, follow Director Lei closely, I think she can at least become a minister in the future."

He was caught by Xu Ruilong: "Tianying, what did you tell Lin Fengchong? Small meetings are not allowed at the conference, so bring it to the table if you have something to say."

Chu Tianying hurriedly stood up and said, "Director, I told Feng Chong that although there is no valuable evidence found in that black INSPIRE, there is a new discovery that deserves our attention."

Under Chai Yongjin's questioning, the traffic team in the area found the black INSPIRE in the parking lot where the illegal vehicles were detained. Originally, all detained illegal vehicles will have their license plates entered into the computer. After finding the owner's information, the owner will be notified. But because the team was busy cooperating with the investigation of the case recently, they forgot about the work, resulting in the car becoming "blind point" – this discovery caused a sensation in the entire police force which seemed to have dug gold in an abandoned mine. In particular, the surveillance shows that no one has approached the car after it was towed to the parking lot, which means that it retains the "original state" after the incident to a considerable extent. For a time, the task force was very excited, but the investigation by the Criminal Technology Office showed that, except for the traces of the bodies of the three children lying in the trunk, and the ethanol air detector found a strong smell of alcohol in the car, there was no trace of alcohol in the car. The most important thing was that the steering wheel and door handle were wiped with disinfectant wipes after the crime, leaving no suspicious fingerprints. As his driver, Zhou often drove this car, leaving fingerprints on the steering wheel and door handles is completely normal, so there is no need to do such meticulous wipes in the tense situation that night.

The police were very disappointed by this, so now everyone heard Chu Tianying say that they had a new discovery, and all turned their attention to him.

Chu Tianying took out a transparent evidence bag, handed it to Xu Ruilong, and said, "Director, this is a receipt we found in the lobby bar of Hefeng Hotel for Xing Qisheng's checkout on the night of the case. Xie Qisheng has eaten Australian veal salad, pan-fried foie gras, smoked salmon and truffle risotto, and drank a bowl of cream of mushroom soup."

Xu Ruilong looked at the receipt through the evidence bag: "What does this mean? Isn't it the same as the stomach contents of Xing Qisheng issued by Lei Rong in the autopsy report?"

"The key is that there is nothing on this receipt that should have been there."

"What? "

"According to Zhou Liping's confession, at around nine o'clock that night, he received a call from Xing Qisheng and asked Zhou Liping to pick him up at Tongyou Nursing Home immediately, because he was too drunk to drive himself. Then the problem came, is the receipt and the surveillance video of the hotel security department both prove that Xing Qisheng did not drink any alcohol that night!"

In the conference room, everyone's face showed a look of astonishment.

"It should be noted that when the INSPIRE was found in the compound of the traffic team, the door had not been opened since the case, so the moment the door was opened, there was a strong smell of alcohol, so we used ethanol. The results of the air detector detection showed that it was a very high-strength vodka called 'Don Bass' volatilized."

"Is it possible that Xing Qisheng returned to Tongyou Nursing Home to drink after he left the Hefeng Hotel?" a police officer asked.

"It's interesting here." Chu Tianying said, "After we discovered the problem on this checkout receipt, we immediately reported it to Director Lei. She told us that the autopsy results of Xing Qisheng proved that there was no trace of Xing Qisheng in his blood. Alcohol was detected."

"Then..." The police officer froze for a moment and said, "Could it be that Zhou Liping was drinking?"

"The surveillance video extracted from the convenience store downstairs of Zhou Liping's residence shows that Zhou Liping bought two cans of Yanjing beer on the night of the crime, but not vodka, and this kind of 'Don Bass' is very expensive and can hardly be bought in China. It's not something someone like Zhou Liping can afford to drink, but we found this wine in the decorative cabinet of the office of the director of Tongyou Nursing Institute, which means that the wine must have come from Xing Qisheng."

The meeting room fell silent, Xu Ruilong pondered for a moment and said, "Tianying, what do you think this means?"

Chu Tianying, who is known for being shrewd and capable, also answered the questions concisely and clearly: "Three possibilities, the first is that Zhou Liping is lying, that night Xing Qisheng asked him to pick him up at Tongyou Nursing Institute, not because of Xing Qisheng was drunk. Afterward, he was unable to drive, and the specific reason is unclear. Xing

Qisheng brought vodka with him when he got in the car. After Zhou Liping killed him on the Deratization Hill, he got into the car and sprinkled the wine on his clothes, and let it evaporate, creating an illusion. The second is that Zhou Liping lied. There may be a third person in the car, who may have drunk in the office of the dean of Tongyou Nursing Home, and then sat with Xing Qisheng on INSPIRE, but who and where is the person? After getting out of the car, whether the person alive or dead? The third is Xing Qisheng lied, he deliberately took Zhou Liping to Tongyou Nursing Home, and then sprinkled vodka on his clothes, pretending to be drunk and asking Zhou Liping to send him to the hospital Sweeping Rat Mountain—"

Xu Ruilong interrupted him and said, "Why did Xing Qisheng do this?"

Chu Tianying shook his head: "I don't know."

The meeting room fell into dead silence.

2

From the beginning of the meeting till now, Du Jianping had not spoken. He knew very well that, as the leader of the task force, the case was so unclear today that he would take the first responsibility, but what else could he do? For many years in the criminal investigation line, he had already developed a magical sixth sense. For suspects in most cases, he can often accurately determine whether the other party has really committed a crime by intuition, but Zhou Liping is so different! Du Jianping felt that arresting him was like catching a cloud of fog with an insect net at midnight. Not only did he fail to see through the opponent, but as time passed, the sur-rounding light became darker and his vision became worse and worse, and the insect net was still in use but the fog is gradually thinning, and it can even be leaked...

Now is not the time to ponder these things deeply. As the host of the meeting, he can't let the silence last too long: "Feng Chong, please report to the director about the situation of INSPIRE's 'tracing back'."

"Itinerary traceability" means that the traffic department uses the FAST system to reversely trace the entire itinerary of a suspect vehicle in a certain period of time, thereby outlining the vehicle's itinerary map. Originally, the police used the FAST system to trace the starting point of INSPIRE's trace at around 9:40 on the night of the case, when the vehicle drove out from the north exit of the street where Tongyou Nursing Home is located because since then Zhou Liping drove all the way to Deratization Hill, but after behavioral science experts made a psychological appraisal report based on

Zhou Liping's trial video, the police decided to significantly advance the traceback to six o'clock in the morning on the day of the case.

Lin Fengchong's report is as followed, based on the extraction of surveillance videos captured by surveillance devices set up in the parking lot of Xing Qisheng's apartment, Hefeng Hotel, street traffic lights near Tongyou Nursing Home, Qingshikou Dongli traffic lights, and other major traffic intersections, which can basically outline the day of the Case, the Black INSPIRE had such an itinerary at the following time points:

At nine o'clock in the morning, Xing Qisheng drove INSPIRE out of the parking lot of the apartment where he lived and went to the nursing home.

At 2:20 p.m. that day, Xing Qisheng drove INSPIRE through the traffic lights at the south entrance of the street where the Nursing Home is located. Then he parked the car in the parking lot of Building E.

At 8:45 that night, INSPIRE drove out of the Hefeng Hotel, and the surveillance video showed that the driver was Xing Qisheng.

At 8:50 that night, INSPIRE drove into the street where the southwest gate of Love Hospital was located and did not leave the other end until 9:00. Since the southwest gate of Love Hospital leads to the mortuary, according to customs, there is no surveillance here, so they didn't know why Xing Qisheng stayed here for ten minutes.

At 9:05 that night, INSPIRE drove past the traffic lights at the south entrance of the street where the nursing home was located and headed north, but it did not exit from the north exit. It should have been parked in the courtyard of the nursing home.

At 9:40 that night, INSPIRE drove past the traffic lights at the north entrance of the street where the Nursing Home was located and drove towards Qingshikou East Lane.

"This car has been parked in the nursing home for nearly forty minutes. What is Xing Qisheng doing during this period? Zhou Liping received a call from Xing Qisheng asking him to go to the nursing home at nine o'clock, right? What time did he arrive at the nursing home? "Xu Ruilong asked a series of questions.

"We contacted the taxi company, and a driver recalled that he received a taxi from a man in Xiahe Street around 9 o'clock that night, and drove all the way to the entrance of Tongyou Nursing Home. The taxi driving record shows that it took 20 minutes. And the driver quickly found Zhou Liping's photo from a bunch of photos. Zhou Liping said that after he arrived, he went to the office to find Xing Qisheng. Xing Qisheng said that he still had some things to do, and asked him to wait in the car. He

220

just sat in the car for 20 minutes and watched his mobile phone, Xing Qisheng laid down on the back seat once he got in the car and asked him to drive to Deratization Hill."

"Ask a technical question," a police officer asked. "Can't the surveillance system capture what's going on in the back seat of the car? Then we can tell if there are other people in the car at the time."

Lin Fengchong said with a wry smile: "Our monitoring system has a limited resolution and can capture the front of the driver, but if the interior lighting is poor or there are no interior lights, the back seat cannot be captured. If Xing Qisheng is lying in the back seat, even lower than the driver, we may not be able to photograph him at all due to the angle. In fact, the relevant departments have taken technical measures to increase the image of all surveillance videos. The resolution and the picture quality have been improved, but we can only roughly see that there is indeed something on the seat behind Zhou Liping.

"Is it possible that we are complicating simple things?" Chai Yongjin suddenly said, "Actually, this case is very simple, and it is not difficult to see that Zhou Liping was suspected of harassing or even sexually assaulting children in the nursing home, and was blocked by Xing Qisheng. On the night of the crime, Xing Qisheng called Zhou Liping over, maybe he was going to settle with him, maybe he was implused, and he said that he was going to send him to the police station, Zhou Liping tricked Xing Qisheng into the car, and he found the three children, locked them in the trunk, and drove up to the Deratization Hill, killing them one by one, throwing their bodies and burning them, doesn't it make sense?"

Although the remarks were reckless, these were expressed a lot of the inner thoughts of the criminal police. In their opinion, this is the truth of the case.

"I still think that we shouldn't make such an arbitrary conclusion on the case." Lin Fengchong said solemnly, "Of course, according to your explanation, everything seems to make sense, but apart from the lack of direct evidence, there are two matters that are still unclear: one is what method Zhou Liping used to take only half an hour after the event to rush from the Deratization Hill to Xingyu Road; the other is based on Zhou Liping's criminal experience, he will never be unaware that he must be captured by the FAST all the way. Even if the corpse was burnt seriously, the police could quickly identify the deceased and find him. He neither escaped nor took any counter-investigation measures. These are all too abnormal – I'm not saying that Zhou Liping's criminal suspicion can be ruled out, but: We can't be suspicious of any innocent person ."

"Mama Lin" is a well-known good guy in the police force. He said these words very seriously, so another whisper sounded in the conference room.

Xu Ruilong picked up the teacup and took a sip. All the discussions seemed to be sucked away by him, and the meeting room became silent in an instant.

Xu Ruilong said slowly: "During this time, you have worked hard. It should be said that such a big case has achieved so many breakthroughs in such a short period of time, which is worthy of recognition. As for the surrounding, all of the debates on doubtful points are good. I have always advocated that case investigators should be encouraged to argue, and they should not 'unify their minds' too early, otherwise mistakes will be made, so do the wrongful convictions... Next, I have two issues: Please consider them carefully. First, this case is 'burning corpses and destroying traces'. What traces were destroyed? It is definitely not a trace of 'murder'. It cannot be destroyed, so it is very likely that the children have suffered sexual abuse or other injuries. Some buddies think that this 'trace' must have been done by Zhou Liping. This is a subjective assumption and inappropriate. Next, should be to intensify the investigation of the staff of the nursing home and find out the truth. Second, we 'got' this case too early, too fast. Don't think I am joking, I mean, we found out that Zhou Liping was involved in this case too early, and because of his special identity, we focused most of our attention on him and inadvertently made a lot of directional and purposeful 'evidence' to prove Zhou Liping is the murderer. Now it seems that we have made some achievements, but there are also shortcomings. At least, we have concentrated such strong human and technic resources, but we still can't confirm Zhou Liping is the murderer. Is it true? So can we change the way of thinking – assuming that Zhou Liping is not the real murderer, then who is the most suspicious person in this case? "

The people in the conference room looked at each other, and no one dared to answer rashly.

"I think it's Xing Qisheng."

A voice suddenly sounded, and dozens of eyes in the conference room were focused on Chu Tianying.

Of course, Xu Ruilong couldn't appear "eccentric" in front of everyone, so he just said flatly, "Tell us the reason."

"First of all, judging from the investigation, other than Xing Qisheng's secretary, Chi Fengli, who had doubts about Zhou Liping, other employees in the nursing home did not point out that Zhou Liping had any wrongdoing with the children, and Chi Fengli's testimony can only show that Xing Qisheng and Zhou Liping had conflicts because of their children, but the reason for the conflict is not known. In terms of the conditions for sexually assaulting children, regardless of time, place, and 'convenience', Xing Qisheng has more 'advantages' than Zhou Liping. '—"

Sun Kang, who was sitting diagonally across from him, couldn't help but say: "Let me interject when I asked Chi Fengli, she emphasized that one of Xing Qisheng's characteristics was 'lust', but Chi Fengli also said that Xing Qisheng had nothing to do with her. The interesting point is that Chi Fengli is a pretty sexy woman, if Xing Qisheng is not interested in her and he is also not gay, then it is very likely that he is a pedophile."

Chu Tianying nodded and turned his attention to Xu Ruilong: "Here I also make an application, I hope the city bureau can report to the provincial department of A province to investigate whether Xing Qisheng has committed sexual crimes against children in the past, I'm worried for various reasons, even if Xing Qisheng had committed a crime, he was covered up by his family's network of connections."

"Approve." Xu Ruilong said to Lin Fengchong, "You will implement it immediately after the meeting."

"Other than that, it's the vodka thing I mentioned just now." Chu Tianying said, "Although I said three possibilities, I personally think that the third possibility is the greatest, that is Xing Qisheng lied—because the first is too naive, and the second is flawed. Let's talk about the first: burning corpses does not affect the forensic examination of blood alcohol content. This may be very unpopular knowledge to outsiders, but Zhou Liping read forensic science books before and after he was imprisoned. I don't think the books he read are fewer than many people here. Just a little bit of alcohol in the car can convince the police that Xing Qisheng drank alcohol. It's better not to tell this lie, if there is really a third person in the car, then he must have been sitting in the car for a long time. We all know that drunks can't control their will. Unless they are asleep, their hands and feet will be twisted randomly. There are strange traces left in the location, which are called 'drunk traces' in the field investigation, such as touching some dead spots that normal people would not touch, shoe prints on the headrest of the car seat, and more trailing fingerprints, etc. But when I inspected the vehicle, I found no such traces in the car- we all know although the murderer wiped the steering wheel and door handle, he did not wipe other places. "

This analysis made many colleagues listen with relish and convince.

"If this case follows the idea that Zhou Liping may be framed, then Xing Qisheng may not be able to escape that he has not been drinking but called Zhou Liping to 'drive instead'." Chu Tianying continued, "So there is another question arose, Xing Qisheng himself was killed, who killed him? There must be an accomplice or an oriole-like figure, so who is this oriole? First, Zhou Liping can be ruled out, because he and Xing Qisheng has always been at odds, and Xing Qisheng will not find him if he is looking for an accomplice, and he appeared on Xingyu Road within half an hour after he called the police, so he did not have enough time to commit the crime. Among Xing Qisheng's friends, the most suspicious is Zhang Chunyang."

The name Zhang Chunyang has not been included in the list of criminal suspects in the previous detective work, so many criminal police officers present were taken aback.

Chu Tianying first introduced Zhang Chunyang's general situation and then said: "According to what we have learned, Zhang Chunyang worked as a fitness coach in his early years. He was dark-bellied, cruel, and his physical fitness was very good. He is very familiar with the road conditions in the area, so he has no problem in planning and implementing the murder. Some insiders said that Zhang Chunyang's biggest characteristic is 'daring and clever', he used Tao Zhuo Yao's relationship to help Xing Qisheng make money, and Xing Qisheng helped him hide from Tao Zhuoyao to find other women outside. The two were in a mess and did a lot of bad things. Although because of their different social status, Xing Qisheng has always been the 'master' and Zhang Chunyang is the 'servant', but in essence, Zhang Chunyang is responsible for the work of the 'brainstorm' – after the case, no one has seen Zhang Chunyang again, which is extremely abnormal —"

Xu Ruilong interrupted him: "When was the last time Zhang Chunyang appeared?"

"We tracked his mobile phone, which is currently turned off. The last call was at 4:00 p.m. on the day of the case."

This time point is very sensitive, Xu Ruilong continued to ask: "Who is the person on the call?"

"Tao Zhuoyao." Chu Tianying said, "According to the memory of the cleaning staff responsible for cleaning her room, Tao Zhuoyao's bedroom on the fourth floor of Block E had traces of a private meeting the next morning of the case, and Tao Zhuoyao brought two men here, one is her unmarried boyfriend Jiang Lei, and the other is Zhang Chunyang. But our investigation found that Jiang Lei was on a business trip in Hong Kong that night and was not here at all, so that possible be Zhang Chunyang. It is worth noting that after seven o'clock that night, Xing Qisheng came to the lobby bar for dinner, and kept looking at his mobile phone while eating until he received a call at 8:10, and then he left in a hurry and the call record showed that Tao Zhuoyao called him. What happened after that can be regarded as a high-speed train that departed from the same station in the dark night but headed in different directions. One trip was Xing Qisheng, who drove INSPIRE on the road of no-return to the Deratization Hill; The other is Tao Zhuoyao, she booked a flight to Paris at half past nine—"

"And Zhang Chunyang disappeared without a trace..." Xu Ruilong pondered for a while, "Find him! Find the person for me no matter how!"

3

After the meeting, Xu Ruilong called Du Jianping and the others to his office alone, held another small meeting, emphasized the focus of the next step, and then suddenly asked Chu Tianying: "What is Si Miao doing recently?"

Chu Tianying was stunned: "Director Liu? It seems that she has been in the physical evidence storage center for the past few days."

"Did she let Ma Xiaozhong and Guo Xiaofen investigate the case?"

"No, it's impossible." Chu Tianying said without hesitation, "She knows the discipline and has already withdrawn from this case, so she won't intervene again."

"Don't cover for her!" Xu Ruilong said, " The first prison called me in in the morning and said that Ma Xiaozhong and Guo Xiaofen went to the prison yesterday afternoon to learn about Zhou Liping's years in prison. How dare them to do this without any permission?"

"Maybe Guo Xiaofen wants to write a character feature based on this case, and ask Ma Xiaozhong to help her connect." Chu Tianying said, "You also know that whenever something goes wrong, those reporters will always dig up from many years ago."

"The problem is, Guo Xiaofen has already left the newspaper, don't you know that?" Xu Ruilong glared at him, "You can call Ma Xiaozhong after the meeting and ask him don't be too much." He turned and asked Du Jianping again: " Why hasn't Tao Zhuoyao returned?"

Du Jianping said quickly: "We have contacted the Paris Police Department and the embassy in France, and asked them to find Tao Zhuoyao as soon as possible and urge her to return to China..."

Xu Ruilong saw that he was hesitating to speak, and said impatiently, "If there is any difficulty, say it directly."

Du Jianping said cautiously: "I heard that the Kind Charity Fund has cover from the top..."

"Damn it!" Xu Ruilong became angry all of a sudden, "What is the top? Who is the top? Now there are six words 'rule the country according to law'! There are no hidden rules, no private transactions, everything is upright and bright. If you obey the law, the country will protect you; if you break the law, even the king of heaven can't cover you, it's that simple!"

Du Jianping nodded repeatedly.

"Jianping." Xu Ruilong originally had some serious words, but his words slowed down again, "The longer you work, you can't be less courageous, you worry about too much. You must know the interests of the people are higher than everything, engrave these words in mind."

After coming out of the director's office, Chu Tianying called Ma Xiaozhong, conveyed Xu Ruilong's warning, asked him to convey his gratitude to Huyan Yun, and explained that the Kind Charity Fund may have some cover but it's meaningless. After hanging up the phone, Ma Xiaozhong blinked his small eyes for a long time, and said to people in the room, "Chu's call really means something!"

After Huyan Yun found in the lobby bar of Hefeng Hotel that Xing Qisheng's dining receipt showed that he did not drink alcohol that night, he told Liu Simiao about the situation along with their exploration of the fourth floor of Block E. Although Liu Simiao hated him, she could not help but admit that this guy did have a set of reasoning, and also thought that what Tao Zhuoyao and Zhang Chunyang did on the night of the crime was indeed suspicious, so she assigned Chu Tianying to present the meal receipt as a newly discovered important evidence, and the investigation direction of the case was timely directed to Tao Zhuoyao and Zhang Chunyang.

At this moment, Guo Xiaofen, Ma Xiaozhong, and Li Zhiyong were in Huyan Yun's home, communicating the situation of the two-day investigation. When Ma Xiaozhong told everyone the content of the call from Chu Tianying, Guo Xiaofen couldn't help laughing: "Director Xu is picking it up hard, and putting it down gently, the words 'don't be too much' are like a green light for us to investigat."

"It's also for Du Jianping, let him know that he is not alone in this case, and urge him to hurry up." Huyan Yun turned his attention to Li Zhiyong, "I don't understand, we went to the Hefeng Hotel that day, old man. Dou said that Xing Qixian has covered by the top, and Liao also said that 'they have hard connections' as if the Kind Charity Fund is protected by a reinforced umbrella. But I find Director Xu doesn't care about it at all?"

Li Zhiyong smiled: "Huyan, you have been to the zoo and see the Monkey Mountain, a big cage, thousands of monkeys jumping around, big and small, men and women, young and old, they eat, drink, play, have fun, reward and punish, they also have their own set of rules... This fund is a group of monkeys, they form their own system, entertain themselves in that system, and reject outsiders. The system itself is built and maintained by various relationships, so they think that everything in the world can be solved by relationships. Whether it can be found or not, whether it is fair or not, in the end, they can always make things right. They deceive each other, but they all believe what others say, and live in different lies every day. They are happy, comfortable. But one thing is, no one can open their cages, even for their own good. As a result, they don't have much fighting power, they just scream harshly and cry ugly..."

"How can such a group of people survive in this society for a long time?"

"That is the problem. Such a group is not only alive, but also alive well, and can easily eliminate many excellent competitors who are not well-connected." Li Zhiyong smiled wryly, "Let's talk about the public relations company. Well, employees like Blue Label and Ogilvy & Mather are all crazy '5+2' 'day and night' work, tired to the point of vomiting blood, grabbing customers, and orders like a wolf. But our company, you saw it the other day. There were not many people during working hours. Most of the employees just went to work and played games. So many companies come to find us and we even need to pick among them..."

"Why? " Ma Xiaozhong was also very curious.

"Because we are a subordinate unit of the Kind Charity Fund and it has the 'tax reduction qualification'—"

"Isn't the state giving tax exemptions to charitable entities?" Guo Xiaofen asked in surprise, "Why is there a 'tax reduction qualification'?"

"Most of the companies donate to charities, which are purely for public welfare, but some are for tax reductions – the state has relevant policies, companies donate a certain amount to charities, and they can get a corresponding tax reduction. But it does not mean that anyone who donates to them has the quality. Many private charities do not have this qualification, but the Kind Charity Fund is different. It is said to be a private charitable organization, but in fact, it is backed by a big tree and has 'tax reduction qualifications'—"

"Basterds!" Ma Xiaozhong scolded, "Be hard bone, how bad could they be without the tax reduction?!"

"You don't understand." Li Zhiyong said, "How many employees of the fund and its subordinate units have no background? You donate money to raise them, and sometimes you feed pets to beauty is better than directly honoring pet owners – that's why those companies are scrambling to try to curry favor with us, relying on us to hook up with the upper echelons of the foundation."

Huyan Yun couldn't help but let out a long sigh after hearing this.

"The country's anti-corruption efforts have continued to strengthen recently, and their lives have become more and more difficult, but in the end, they are still in a group." Li Zhiyong said, "That day we went to Yanzhao Hotel to find Sun Jinghua, you are curious why they still need to register in the notebook when booking a convention and exhibition hall? Because the convention and exhibition department of that hotel is also what I call 'Monkey Mountain'. For them, there is nothing more terrifying than evolution. As long as the status quo is maintained and their life will not be affected, it will be fine to lie on the tree for another 10,000 years."

Guo Xiaofen murmured: "I can't imagine that such a group of people will exist in the 21st century..."

Li Zhiyong's tone was very heavy: "I was a policeman in the past, and all I saw was explicit evil. Only when I took off the policeman's clothes did I discover the hidden evil. Even hard to tell which one is worse..."

"Didn't you and Huyan go to Yanzhao Hotel later?" Guo Xiaofen asked.

"We did, but the staff still insisted on not letting us without an appointment. We had to make an appointment the day after tomorrow." Li Zhiyong said helplessly, "By the way, did you and Ma go to find Fang Mei?"

"We went there yesterday morning, but unfortunately we didn't see anyone. They said that Fang Mei was on a business trip to Shanghai and would not be able to come back until next week, so we took the car to the City No. 1 Prison to learn about Zhou Liping's performance during his imprisonment."

The person receiving Guo Xiaofen and Ma Xiaozhong was Feng, a prison guard in the 16th district of the city's No. 1 Prison. Feng had a very long face, and he spoke slowly and a little sloppily, but his expression was accurate. According to him, Zhou Liping was under the age of 18 when he committed the crime, and he had been in the juvenile detention center during the interrogation period, but he was over 18 when the case was concluded, so he was transferred to the No. 1 Prison, which lasted eight years.

Prisons have a prison class, rapists are the stepping stones, and murderers are definitely the top, not to mention Zhou Liping, a "suspected serial murderer", although young, no one dared to provoke him since the day he was imprisoned, and according to the rules, the prisoner called him 'master' before his name.

When "Master Ping" first arrived, the prison management held a meeting focusing on "how to arrange him". For prisoners with a "very high violence index", they should not be allowed to touch any tools. The kitchen works required knives for cooking, no. Gardener's works required shears for trimming flowers and trees, no either. But he can't idle for a long time, he must make troubles, so in the end, they arranged for him to manage the library. Who would have imagined that in less than a month, the library would take on a brand new look. "Zhou Liping polished the desks, chairs, and bookshelves every day, and repaired any worn-out books before wrapping them in book covers. He also applied for a set of book management software for loan registration. Watching him put his head down every day to post every book and scan the barcode and then enters it into the computer. I can't imagine how he killed so many people." Feng said.

In Feng's opinion, Zhou Liping was the kind of prisoner who is easiest managed. He was not lazy at work, never caused trouble, and kept the prison rules and disciplines even better than the prison guards required. But there was one thing special about him. In the prison, it sounds like worms can. Although the supervisors are watching, it may be bloody or even violent, so the prisoners secretly formed gangs in order to protect themselves. Only Zhou Liping was an exception. He was very, very independent. According to Feng's words, "He seemed a little arrogant and didn't look down on the other prisoners at all." For eight years, he didn't make any cellmates, he ignored others who wanted to worship him, and he didn't urinate when others tried to pull him into the gang. After all, it is a "serial murderer", anyone in the city's No. 1 prison who is alive didn't dare to provoke him.

"Usually he was very quiet, didn't like to talk, he was always thinking about things, and spent his free time on reading and exercising, and he was physically healthy." Feng said, "Prison life is not like what the outside thinks, which is to eat, sleep, and reform through labor – no, from the perspective of prisoners returning to society after being released from prison, we have arranged many courses for them to study. And of course, the teachers are mainly prisoners serving prison sentences. Zhou Liping enrolled in several courses and studied very seriously, especially the auto repair and electrical maintenance. If our car or household appliances are broken, you ask him for help and he can repair almost all of them. As time goes by, everyone will be less vigilant about him... Who knows, in the fifth year of his sentence, he made serious trouble."

There was a prisoner called "Lao Hei", who robbed and raped, this kind of double villain the other prisoners did not dare to abuse him. But he also boasted to other prisoners every day that he had raped several young girls, and told vividly about the bloodshed and screams of those little girls... Some prisoners reported to the correctional cadres and locked up him for a few days, but he came out the same way. One day he was on the playground telling a group of loyal listeners about his stories, when Zhou Liping, who was repairing the fence next to him, came over. According to other prisoners, he walked normally and his expression was normal. He looked like just passing by, but at the moment when he passed in front of "Lao Hei", something suddenly appeared in Zhou Liping's hand. He jabbed a few times at the old black's scrotum like lightning and then walked over at his normal pace.

Looking at the situation where "Lao Hei" was rolling on the ground while covering his blood-splattered genitals, several prisoners in the crowd couldn't help but vomit, and a few young people sat on the ground in fright and cried...

Although the correctional cadres did not witness, the moment they learned of the incident, they suddenly realized that Zhou Liping was still Zhou Liping and his vicious moves were still the same inhumane as in the past.

The investigation proved that the murder weapon in Zhou Liping's hand was a long nail pulled directly from the fence.

Zhou Liping was shackled and locked in a trumpet, and he went on a hunger strike for the next few days, but in prison, such behavior will only lead to harsher punishment...

"What happened later?" Huyan Yun couldn't help asking.

"You can never imagine who rescued Zhou Liping." Guo Xiaofen said.

"Who? "

"Lin Xiangming."

"Xiangming?!" Huyan Yun was taken aback.

"Yes, it's Xiangming," Guo Xiaofen said. "At that time, Lin Xiangming had just returned to China and launched the first domestic 'pervert personality interview campaign', planning to conduct interviews with detained perverted murderers and felons to understand the nature of such crimes in China. He had handled Zhou Liping's case before, and can even be said to be the direct promoter of Zhou Liping's reduced sentence, but he has never seen him alone after Zhou Liping's arrest. After hearing about this, he came to interview Zhou Liping especially."

Huyan Yun widened his eyes and his breathing became heavier: "Did the prison keep a record of the conversation?"

"No." Guo Xiaofen shook her head, "Xiangming's interview plan has applied for a national key scientific research project and received financial support, which is of a certain of confidentiality. His interview with Zhou Liping was conducted alone, without leaving any text, images or video material..."

A look of disappointment appeared on Huyan Yun's face.

"Feng recalled that the interview lasted more than two hours, and soon after the end, Lin Xiangming issued a psychiatric appraisal report, pointing out that Zhou Liping's attack on 'Lao Hei' was a sudden behavior caused by intermittent mental disorders, and there is a legal exemption from liability. Xiangming is an authority in this field, and he is also a big celebrity invited by Director Xu from abroad. The prison immediately released Zhou Liping from the trumpet." Guo Xiaofen said, "After being released, Zhou Liping has a totally big change."

Obviously dissatisfied with Lin Xiangming helping Zhou Liping again, Li Zhiyong muttered, "Had he become prouder?"

"No." Guo Xiaofen said, "Feng said that after that until he was released from prison, Zhou Liping's behavior was no different from the past, he worked hard and actively reformed, but his expression was always hopeless before, indifferent and dazed, but after seeing Lin Xiangming there was light in his eyes, and occasionally he smiled, which has never been seen in the past five years."

Li Zhiyong frowned and puzzled.

Huyan Yun walked slowly to the desk, lifted the glass plate pressed on the table, and picked up a yellowed photo from below. It was a group photo when he traveled to Qingdao with his friends when he was in high school. A group of fearless students sat on the seaside with dark clouds, on a steep rock, everyone laughed so open-mindedly and high-spirited, only the handsome boy sitting beside him, although also smiling, but that there is a sadness in the smile...

"Huyan, what happened?" Guo Xiaofen asked softly.

Huyan Yun stood for a long time before he let out a sigh: "Don't you think that every time a case happens, as long as Xiangming appeared, even if it's just a silhouette, there will be an unexpected ending?"

4

Zhou Liping was released early in the eighth year of his sentence because he was reformed well in prison. There are indeed different opinions on his release. The "Serial Murder Case in the Western Suburbs" is still in the prosecution period, and the police handling the case hard. But they also didn't find other evidence to prove Zhou Liping killed other victims, they can only and must release him.

When he was released from prison, Zhou Liping did not have the excitement as they imagined, nor did he have any dramatic scenes. He was very calm. After completing the formalities, he changed into a new suit that Feng had bought for him and left the place where he had been imprisoned for eight years. When he was arrested eight years ago, he had nothing on him. When he was released eight years later, he had a release certificate and a bank card in his pocket. The money earned from his labor was put into the card and sent to him by the prison.

"No one came to pick him up, I sent him to the door, and he just left by himself," Feng said.

After listening to Guo Xiaofen, the room was quiet for a long time, Huyan Yun was still staring at the old photo as if he was still immersed in the old days and couldn't extricate himself.

Outside the window, the autumn wind was blowing hard, and the tall poplar trees in the yard were swaying violently, helplessly throwing their yellowed leaves, as if turbulent waves were flowing in the air and clattering...

"Huyan, Huyan..." Guo Xiaofen called to him, "what should we do next?"

Huyan Yun did not answer.

"According to the plan we made, Huyan and I should find the long-haired girl whom Zhou Liping knew." Li Zhiyong glanced at Ma Xiaozhong. At first, Ma Xiaozhong patted his chest and assured them that he could get the contact information of the long-haired girl through the intermediary Luo.

Ma Xiaozhong scolded: "I didn't know where Luo is, and I couldn't find him. Guo and I will handle it, and we will go to the Real Estate later and force the manager to hand over him!"

"It's not an urgent matter." Huyan Yun said slowly, "The most urgent thing is to get to the top of the Kind Charity Fund and get some information... Up to now, I feel that both the police and we have always been concerned about the investigation of this case around the appearance, the real core has not even been touched. What should be done now is to turn around and focus on the fund, and Tao Zhuoyao, Zhang Chunyang, and Xing Qisheng, because Zhou Liping is very possible the person who got on the car halfway, and the starting station of the car has nothing to do with him..."

Li Zhiyong sighed and said, "This is still quite difficult, not to mention the high-level executives of the Kind Charity Fund, even the branch in the Hefeng Hotel is an independent kingdom, and we can't get in at all. In Mingyi public relations company, only Zheng Gui can hang around in it, but if we ask Zheng Gui to help you find out the news, we will be smashing his job and we'd better never think about it."

At this moment, his cell phone rang, and when he picked it up to answer it, his face suddenly became very ugly. After hanging up, he sighed: "I'll go out."

"What's wrong?" Huyan Yun asked.

"The social security center called and said that my mother's registration form must be attached to the front and back copy of my mother's ID card. I have to go home and get a copy and send it there. "

"Why didn't they tell me last time?" Huyan Yun was a little angry.

"Who knows, they didn't say any reason just told me to hurry up." Li Zhiyong smiled bitterly, turned around, and walked out.

After chatting all morning, they felt a little hungry. Huyan Yun went to the kitchen to cook a pot of instant noodles, and brought the pot directly into the room. The three friends sat and ate together. Perhaps because the topic just involved Lin Xiangming, their emotions were heavy. Ma Xiaozhong was most afraid of not being lively in his life, so he suddenly raised a topic: "Huyan, how are you and Si Miao?"

Huyan Yun was taken aback: "Me and Si Miao...?"

"Don't pretend!" Ma Xiaozhong said with a smile, "After so many years, do you think we can't tell who you really?"

"Don't talk nonsense." Huyan Yun blushed a little.

"I said nonsense? every time Simiao has problems you have to rush forward no matter where you are. How can you hide from us?" He nudged Guo Xiaofen with his elbow, "Guo, do you think I'm right?"

Guo Xiaofen glanced at Huyan Yun, lowered her head, and continued to eat.

Huyan Yun murmured: "I'm mainly afraid that if something happens to Si Miao. When Xiang Ming comes back, I can't explain it to him."

Ma Xiaozhong slapped his chopsticks on the table and gave a thumbs up: "Loyalty! Send the sister-in-law thousands of miles away, the contemporary Guan Yunchang – as long as you don't send her to your own home in the end!"

Huyan Yun was silent.

Ma Xiaozhong grinned after seeing he was subdued, patted him on the shoulder, and said, "Don't mind, buddy, you are better than me in everything, but only in two points worse. First, you are not handsome like me, the second is you are not as straightforward as me. For example, if I like Guo, I will tell her directly, and chase her. If I made it, she will be my girlfriend I don't then she is unlucky. It has been three years since Xiangming's accident. Well, all widows can remarry, you really want Simiao to keep being the husband stone?"

"Oh, it's been three years in a blink..." Guo Xiaofen suddenly felt a little melancholy, "As friends of us, it's become rarer to get together recently."

"Right!" Even Ma Xiaozhong couldn't help but sigh, "I kind of miss the time when we were working on a case in the special task force."

Guo Xiaofen looked out the window and murmured, "I still remember that the task force was set up outside a beef noodle restaurant not far from the north gate of Police Officer University. That day, Xiangming had just finished a lecture on criminal personality profiling for the students. We were caught by Director Xu and Secretary Li, who were taking the class... He called us together, Lei Rong, and Simiao, we were just outside the beef noodle restaurant, eating and assigning work, and then he drove us to pick up Huyan, Huyan was so drunk that he vomited all over the place..."

Huyan Yun was a little embarrassed, but also felt that Guo Xiaofen's expression and voice were a little strange: "Guo, are you okay?"

Guo Xiaofen stood up: "Nothing...you both finish, I'll go wash the dishes."

Guo Xiaofen put the tableware and chopsticks into the pot and brought them to the kitchen. Hearing the running water, Huyan Yun and Ma Xizohonglooked at each other.

"Did someone bully her?" Huyan Yun asked Ma Xiaozhong.

"You help me ask who dares to bully the girl I like with a bear's heart or a leopard's guts?" Ma Xiaozhong said viciously, "However, something has been wrong with her recently. She used to be so outgoing and always had a smile on her face. She worked hard as a reporter, the camera in his left hand and the voice recorder in his right hand, how energetic she was. But look at her right now, she's so sentimental..."

"Is it because she lost her job?" Huyan Yun asked.

"It's possible... But I heard that she kept moving for more than half a year, and even gave away the cat she had been raising. It seems that she once spent the night on a park bench. I asked her what happened. She didn't say it either."

Huyan Yun was in a daze when the phone rang, and it's Li Zhiyong called: "Huyan, I have finished my work at the Social Security Center, but I can't go back to yours."

"What's wrong? "

"Zheng Gui called me and asked me to go back to the company immediately. He was very anxious, I don't know what happened."

"Well, communicate with me if you have any news!"

After putting down the phone, Li Zhiyong drove to Runtang Hi-Tech Incubation Park, walked into the general manager's office in Block D, and saw Zheng Gui poking at the screen of his mobile phone with his index finger, as if he was playing some game, but his face was pale like a bankruptcy guy.

"Mr. Zheng, are you looking for me?" Li Zhiyong asked.

"Li Zhiyong, since you came to the company, I treated you well, right?" Zheng Gui stared at him with his swollen goldfish eyes, "Why did you play trick behind me?"

Li Zhiyong was confused: "Mr. Zheng, what did you say?"

"Did you take Huyan Yun to Block E of Hefeng Hotel?" Zheng Gui's fat eye bags and cheeks trembled like a furious Sharpei dog, and shouted, "Dou reported Xing Qixian and Cui Wentao, The two of them immediately asked Liao to find out the situation. You also know that Liao is a shield made of paper. It looks like Captain America is holding in his hand. In fact, it easily is broken when poke. He reported you and Huyan Yun came. Xing Qixian and Cui Wentao called on me and scolded me. Thanks to my quick reaction and hard mouth, I said Huyan Yun was a new employee from our company, and they forgave it. In case Xing Qixian and the others found out the truth, they must have thought that I was colluding with the police to investigate the fund. Leave other issues behind, if they terminated the relationship between the company and the fund, without the big tree, I would die immediately. You know?"

Li Zhiyong looked at Zheng Gui for a long time, sighed, and said, "Mr. Zheng, I am really sorry for this. I will resign... Thank you for your care for so long."

After he finished speaking, he turned around and walked out of the office, went to his workstation, packed up his things, and walked to the HR room, but was grabbed by someone at the door, and when he turned his head it was Zheng Gui.

"Go to my room!" With that, Zheng Gui dragged him back to his office, closed the door, and pressed him on the wooden pier beside the root carving tea table, while boiling water to make tea he complained: "You haven't been a criminal policeman for so many years, why are you still so temperamental. If I say something to you as a brother, you are angry? What do you think I'm doing? Drink some tea!" Seeing that Li Zhiyong didn't intend to leave he gave him a calculation with his fingers: "You also know our fund looks like a family on the surface, but in fact, there have many groups! Leave other small groups, just say the big ones. Xing Qixian, Cui Wentao, and Dou are a group, Tao Bing, Tao Zhuoyao and Zhai are a group. Xing Qixian and the others want to exclude Tao Bing and the others and hold the real power of the fund. Liao is grass on the wall which falls wherever the wind blows. Zhang Chunyang and Xing Qisheng, one is Tao Zhuoyao's advisor, and the other is Tao Zhuoyao's personal doctor. In case Tao Zhuoyao falls, they will have no cash cow... But their situation is different. Xing Qisheng is also Xing Qixian's younger brother. Xing Qixian holds the power, so he can't watch his brother starving. No matter what happens he could still be the director of the nursing home; Zhang Chunyang is different, to put it horribly, there are no sockets, the plug is of course useless! Tao Zhuoyao was going to marry Jiang Lei before and Zhang Chunyang is so worried."

Zheng Gui drank some tea and then said, "As for me, I can hang on to the fund because I taught Tao Zhuoyao when I was a teacher in the university. There is such a teacher-student relationship. I have been carefully serving the Tao family all these years. I didn't make or cause trouble. I must smile at everyone so that I can pick up some good after them... Bro, it's not easy for me! I don't want to stand in line, but in the eyes of Xing Qixian's gang, I'm a member of the Tao family, and I'm Tao Zhuoyao's follower. It was Xing Qixian's brother died, and it was my staff who killed him. Taking advantage of this, Xing Qixian would make Tao Bing and his daughter completely kicked out of the fund. They would definitely have to divide the plate and cut the cake again. Have you seen the Hong Kong gangster movie, two gangs fight, there will always be an end. Then there must have a little brother out to take the blame. If they don't like me, I will be the victim. In this case, how dare I dare let someone make me threatened! I lost my temper at you just now, it's my fault, but you should tell me you take Huyan Yun to investigate the case. You need to know that the employees of this company are all with hard relations, and only you came in through my relationship. If you want to leave, who will I trust in the future? "

Having said that, Zheng Gui's swallowed hard a few times.

Li Zhiyong looked at Zheng Gui and wanted to say something, but couldn't say anything, and finally said in a low voice, "Bro, are you really willing to be tied to the fund tree for the rest of your life? We can start our own business but not rely on them..."

Zheng Gui touched the thinning hair on the top of his head and said with a wry smile: "No way, I'm an old man, the most troublesome thing is that it has been a long time to cooperate with the fund! We are hiding behind the cage to help the canary lip-synching. People feed them when they are hungry and thirsty. After singing, we can just pick up some leftover rice. It looks like we have no limitations, but in fact, we are the same as those inside the cage, and we have long been unable to fly."

Li Zhiyong sighed.

"Don't sigh, I still have something to worry about." Zheng Gui said.

"What's up? "

"Xing Qixian said that there have been frequent interviews with reporters recently, but he refused all of them. Those reporters tried their best to find ordinary employees of the foundation to understand the situation. The problem is that it doesn't matter who the employees are in the foundation, they all have no experience in dealing with reporters. Anything will be tricked out and would cause big trouble. Xing Qixian asked me to stop the media, and interviews were not allowed. I could connect with the paper media, but I didn't have any relations with the new media, so he asked me to find someone who used to criticize and report and has left his job now. We will invite him to go to the Hefeng Hotel to tell the staff how to deal with reporters and interviews, and he and the senior and middle management of the foundation will also participate in the study... Where can I find a reporter for him! "

Li Zhiyong's eyes lit up.

"What, what are you thinking of?"

Li Zhiyong hesitated for fearing causing trouble for Zheng Gui again.

"Oh, I'm in a hurry here, and you could be cruel to see me suffering but not help?"

This is what you forced me to say, Li Zhiyong thought to himself, and then said: "I remember a few years ago a reporter wanted to interview the foundation because of the campus loan incident, but you stopped her. She still wrote a manuscript later, but after it was released, the gunpowder was not as strong as other media..."

Zheng Gui thought for a while: "There was such a reporter, a woman named Guo... Guo Xiaofen, she is quite famous for critical reporting. Why she doesn't work in the media anymore?"

Li Zhiyong nodded: "I also heard from a friend, she seems to have left the media." Zheng Gui slapped his thigh happily: "God helps me, God helps me, I'll find her!"

5

When Guo Xiaofen got out of the taxi, Zheng Gui and Liao had been waiting at the entrance of Hefeng Hotel for a long time, hurried up to meet her.

When she received a call from Zheng Gui and invited her to give a lecture on "Media Response in Crisis Public Relations" at the Kind Charity Fund's office, she immediately realized that it's the once-in-a-lifetime opportunity they had been worrying about how to break into the foundation. They have thought about how to reach the high-level leaders in the fund and now the opportunity comes! She suppressed her inner excitement and pretended to refuse for a long time before she reluctantly agreed, and the lecture time was four o'clock in the afternoon of the next day – this time was decided by her because lectures often lasted between one and a half to two hours. If it happens to be dinner time at the end of the lecture, the organizer is very likely to invite guests to dinner. The news at the banquet is often more valuable and more credible than the interview.

In order to make this scene realistic, she devoted a whole night to make a PPT. The next morning, she discussed the details with Huyan Yun, Ma Xiaozhong, and Li Zhiyong. When she was about to go out, Ma Xiaozhong suddenly became worried: "Should I go with you? It always feels like you're going deep into a tiger's den."

"I'm not going to make an unannounced visit here, I'm going to be invited openly." Guo Xiaofen said, "Besides, they will definitely know the truth if I take you with me."

Li Zhiyong nodded: "Ma, don't make more trouble... However, Guo, you must also pay attention and don't ask anything, the senior management of the foundation – especially Xing Qixian, are very cunning. Don't let them be suspicious, or they can do anything."

Guo Xiaofen smiled. She thought that Li Zhiyong was probably trying to frighten her. What else could a charitable foundation do? Unexpectedly, she just followed after Zheng Gui and Liao passed through the white moon cave door, they heard fierce scolding not far away. Zheng Gui and Liao looked at each other with surprised expressions, and they hurried to the other side of the corridor. Even Guo Xiaofen's pace quickened a bit.

At the door of the small white building in Block E, a thin-faced middle-aged man shouted something while trying his best to break into the building. Several security guards tore his clothes and pulled him out. At this moment, a square and stout man ran out of Block E and gave the middle-aged man a slap in the face, causing him a mouthful of blood and two teeth fell to the ground mixed with blood!

This slap in the face seemed to completely destroy the middle-aged man's fighting spirit, and he lowered his head in a decadent manner.

"Yue, you fucking open your dog's eyes and see, what is here?! You think there is the government of your town if something happens, you cry and make trouble then someone will help you. You think it's your turn to make chaos here?" The man scolded.

"Xing Qisheng and Cui Wentao, you used bulldozers to level our orphanage at the beginning. I knelt on the ground and begged you, but you ignore me. What did I say to you in the end? You can take the children away, but you must really treat them well if you use them as cash cows. But I know you won't really treat them well, but I think, with your great ability and power, at least you won't let the children starving..." The middle-aged man said, tears rolling down his cheeks, "But in the end, my children, one was twelve years old, one was nine years old, the youngest is only five years old. They died..."

The fat man bared his big yellow teeth and sneered: "It's all fate, children have their fate and so do the adults. You have to accept your fate——"

Just as he was about to continue, Liao rushed forward in steps to catch up, and winked at the man, who was stunned for a moment, then saw Guo Xiaofen, and said to several security guards, "Take this person away, tell the guards at the door of the hotel don't put any messy people inside!" Then he stepped forward to hold Guo Xiaofen's hand and said, "Hello, Reporter Guo, I am working for the Kind Charity Fund. I'm Director Zhai Qing, let's go upstairs now."

Guo Xiaofen nodded and followed him into the building when they heard the middle-aged man dragged away by the security guard still scolding: "You bastards, you have to die!"

They went up to the third floor and walked into the conference room. There are more than 20 people sitting around the long oval mahogany table. Most of them are women. Some of them were chatting on WeChat, some were playing mobile games, and some were laughing softly with the people next to them. Guo Xiaofen's admission did not change their behavior, nor did she disturb their interest.

The polite Xing Qixian, the mouse-headed Cui Wentao, and the sickly Dou came up and shook hands with Guo Xiaofen to greet. Zhai Qing said to Xing Qixian in a low voice, "I have already sent him away." Xing Qixian was expressionless and only asked Guo Xiaofen to sit down.

Xing Qixian cleared his throat and made brief opening remarks, mainly about the case, many reporters wanted to interview him and other foundation leaders every day, but they were all turned away. Some unidentified people tried to contact the staff of the Foundation and even sneaked into the office (here he glanced at Zheng Gui and Liao out of the corner of his eyes) to conduct unannounced visits. "Reporter Guo was invited today in the hope that she could give us some knowledge on how to deal with the media. Now we applaud and welcome Reporter Guo to share."

There was sparse applause in the conference room.

Guo Xiaofen took out the USB flash drive from the handbag, inserted it into the computer on the desktop, and then opened the prepared PPT file. When she raised her head, she suddenly felt a little confused: there was no projector on the table, and there was no projection screen on the opposite wall.

Zheng Gui saw something was wrong: "Reporter Guo, what's wrong?"

"Did I not tell you on the phone yesterday that I would make a PPT?"

Zheng Gui quickly turned his head and asked a fat woman with a waist wider than her shoulders: "He, didn't you receive the WeChat message I sent you? Why didn't you prepare a projector?"

The fat woman frowned: "I got it, isn't there a prepared computer?"

"No, PPT is for presentations. You didn't prepare a projector and a screen, how should reporter Guo show to us?"

"How do I know this..." The fat woman muttered dissatisfiedly, "You didn't tell me clearly in advance."

Liao hurriedly smoothed things out and said to Guo Xiaofen, "Reporter Guo, I'm sorry, He is from our office and doesn't really understand what you're talking about. We rarely use projectors and curtains in our meetings. It may be too late to pretend, so can you just talk?"

Office workers don't know that a projector and a screen are required to present a PPT? ! Guo Xiaofen opened her mouth for a long time. She stared blankly in the conference room and found that none of the participants thought it was an incredible thing, and some people even looked at her and snickered as if they saw the farmers entering the city for the first time but didn't know how to get on the bus from the front door.

She had no choice but to click on the PPT with the mouse and spoke.

She first emphasized that in the information age, the dissemination of crisis information is much faster than the development of the crisis itself, and then from the unexpectedness, focus, destructiveness, and urgency of emergencies, she derived two important principles in crisis management. "One is 'first mover advantage' and one is 'prime time'. 'First mover advantage' means that whoever first defines a crisis will win in a crisis. The 'prime time' rule comes from emergency medicine, when a person's heart illness occurs if he is taken to an ambulance within 20 minutes and taken to the hospital within 40 minutes, his probability of being rescued is very high, while beyond this time, his chance of surviving becomes very low." She emphasized, "Many managers remained silent in the early stage of the crisis, when face of media they adopted the 'three nos' principle of not explaining, not communicating, and ignoring, which resulted in the loss of the first-mover advantage, handing it over to others. And critics have gained a first-mover advantage." She glanced at Xing Qixian, but Xing Qixian was still sitting upright, with no expression on his face, as if he didn't realize that this remark was aimed at him for rejecting reporters.

What made her even more unexpected happened at this moment. Suddenly, a very soft "click" sound came from the conference room.

At first, Guo Xiaofen didn't realize what the sound was, but soon, two "clicks" sounded one after another. Only then did she realize out of the corner of her eye that it was a woman in a red dress sitting on the right side of the long table. The woman is eating melon seeds! And Zhai Qing, who was sitting beside the red dress, quickly took a melon seed from the fingertips that the woman picked up and swallowed it.

Guo Xiaofen was angry. She has been a reporter for many years. She often went to other media for business exchanges and has also taught some schools and enterprises, but she has never been treated like this – it is not even rude, it is a kind of full of ignoring the insulting... She seemed to be an actor who went to the palace to sing in the late Qing Dynasty. You are performing hard on the stage, and the sons and grandsons under the stage were chatting, drinking tea, and eating snacks. They thought of you as a decoration, an embellishment, a dispensable prop.

For a while, she forgot her purpose of coming here today, she wanted to give these guys a lesson!

"Of course, what is even more stupid than refusing media interviews is to openly confront the media and the public." She suddenly raised her voice, "I will give an example. When I was teaching a class just now, and I went downstairs, I found that Director Zhai was teaching a lesson on a middle-aged man who was slapped and vomited blood and lost two teeth. I don't know the identity and occupation of this middle-aged man. I just assumed that he was a media reporter who came to interview, then Director Zhai's response is definitely the worst one."

Sure enough, everyone in the conference room turned their attention to her. Zhai Qing was in a daze as if he had been hit by sap on the back of his head. The red skirt beside him was holding a melon seed but didn't dare to eat it.

"There is an old Chinese saying, 'Fortunes come together with misfortunes', which means that crises have some kind of 'ripple response'. A stone hits the water, not just a few splashes of water, it will cause ripples, and the ripples will gradually expand. This is because the emergence of a crisis may be accidental, but it is never isolated. It is the result of a combination of factors. Therefore, once a crisis occurs, its impact will not stop at the crisis itself but will prompt more crises. In this case, the public's eyes will be closely fixed on the source of the crisis, and being the outlookers. At this moment, it is never too late to 'to calm down', we must not do anything to make the situation worsen or worsen." Guo Xiaofen looked at Zhai Qing and said in a teaching tone, "In recent years, we have often seen some similar incidents happen, and reporters have gone to interview certain companies. The public institution was then insulted or even beaten, and the whole process was filmed and posted on the Internet, causing a more serious public uproar.

Zhai Qing grinned, and the tongue between the yellow teeth jumped like a fire: "Reporter Guo, you don't know, that person is not a reporter, and we are not afraid of—"

"Shut up – you idiot!"

Xing Qixian suddenly yelled, and startled everyone!

Zhai Qing was so angry that his face was twisted, but he didn't dare to contradict Xing Qixian, so he gritted his teeth a few times and lowered his head.

"Reporter Guo, I'm sorry, please continue." Xing Qixian held the gold wire glasses and restored his elegant attitude and tone, "Could you please tell me, if it is inconvenient to refuse an interview with a reporter, what is the right way to be interviewed?"

Only then did Guo Xiaofen know that this man looked like a stone statue sitting there, but he actually listened to every word she said – it seems that Li Zhiyong reminded her to be careful of this person is not a threat.

"Before accepting an interview with a reporter, you must ask yourself four questions." Guo Xiaofen raised her spirits and said slowly, "First of all, what do I know and how much I know, avoiding the premise that I have less internal information than the media; secondly, whether the problem is individual or global. If it is individual, you can analyze the specific problem. If it is a global problem, you should report to the superior as soon as possible. If you prepared well, accept the interview. Otherwise, you would rather procrastinate than make any public gaffes. Finally, whether you have enough understanding of the visiting media, the nature of the media is different, and the interview methods and angles may be completely different. The attitude of the audience will also be different. You give a press release to the print media with respect, but if you read the press release in front of a TV reporter, you will definitely offend the audience."

Xing Qixian nodded again and again: "That's right, right!"

"Okay, let's do a little test." Guo Xiaofen said, "I see that there are laptops in front of everyone, so please turn on the computers, and I will ask a question: 'When you found that the reporter wrote the report after the interview but there is a situation that does not match the facts, what should you do? Everyone write your own answers, you can say anything, and then them to me through WeChat or QQ." She then told her WeChat and QQ numbers and then logged into the WeChat web platform and QQ——

Suddenly she felt something was wrong.

Why was it so quiet in the conference room?

There was absolutely no crackling sound of typing on the keyboard under normal circumstances... She raised her head and was surprised to find that everyone was staring at her.

What's going on here?

At this moment, the fat office clerk surnamed He spoke, she pouted, and her tone was very dissatisfied: "Reporter Guo, there are no paper and no pen, where do you want us to write the answer?"

"Just use Word, write it and pass it to me—"

"Word?" He frowned, "What is Word?"

Not only her, but the whole room looked at her with puzzled eyes, as if asking her in unison—

"Word? What is Word?"

For a while, Guo Xiaofen thought that she had traveled back to the Qing Dynasty, and it was impossible for her to tell a group of people with pigtails what Word was... Where is it? What year do they live in? What kind of people are these? She didn't know whether she should cry or laugh, but in the end, she only felt that the blood all over her body was cold...

6

As Guo Xiaofen expected, after the training, Xing Qixian insisted on keeping Guo Xiaofen "for a meal". Guo Xiaofen waited for this opportunity and pretended to decline twice before agreeing. What she didn't expect was that the restaurant was on the third floor, at the other end of the corridor. As soon as she entered, it was just an ordinary-looking staff canteen: glass partitions for the back kitchen, blue plastic conjoined tables and chairs, etc., but when open an inconspicuous log-colored door in the corner, there was something special inside. A thick, crimson-red Persian-patterned carpet, which is soft. A European-style dining table with retro-golden mahogany wood already has dishes: roast tofu rolls, mushrooms and chestnuts, honey eel, wine-stuffed fresh snails, etc., The tapestry on the wall opposite the door is painted with clear water and a few gigantic koi carps. On the long table below are several red copper and sandalwood incense burners of various shapes. A beautiful waitress in a pink cheongsam stood in the corner with red wine, as if she was also the decoration of this room. The lotus chandelier with all copper and jade radiated a warm and moist luster, illuminating the whole room like a dreamland. Everyone in the room like been photoshopped.

"Reporter Guo, please take your seat!" Xing Qixian greeted Guo Xiaofen to sit down.

Guo Xiaofen sat down and stared at the braised shark fin with crab powder, pan-fried lobster, grouper in black bean sauce, and braised foie gras in abalone sauce that the waiter brought after another. Xing Qixian smiled and said: "The investigation is too strict now, so we won't go to restaurants outside, and have a simple meal at our own house, please forgive me for the poor reception!"

Cui Wentao, Zhai Qing, Dou, Liao, the fat woman surnamed He, Zheng Gui, and others also sat around the dining table. Soon three more people came. One was Xing Qisheng's son, Xing Yunda, who had a very pale face and kept drinking from the moment he sat down. A middle-aged man; and the other is Cui Yucui, the vice president of Tongyou Nursing Home. This fifty years old lady seemed to be wearing tight clothes, and her chest and buttocks are stretched so looked very large, attracting other people on the dining table. Several men cast lewd glances at her, and a lot of conversations were sometimes uncasual. Only Xing Qixian accompanied Guo Xiaofen all the time, serving her dishes, pouring wine for her, and asking about the "rules" of the media.

"I think the foundation is still too backward in terms of media response. It always adopts the ostrich policy when encountering problems, which will only make the problem worse" Guo Xiaofen said.

Zhai Qing drank some wine and became more courageous, shook the glass, and said: "Reporter Guo, I just said a few words but it may not listen very well and was interrupted by Vice President Xing. He gave me a lesson which is as it should be, he is a leader and it's his right to give a lesson. But after the training, I said something open, we really are not afraid of public opinion, from ancient times to the present, rich, and power are the real things. What is the public opinion thing? What can they do? They can do nothing!"

"Zhai Qing, if you can't control your stinky mouth any longer, get out of here!" Xing Qixian's face changed suddenly.

"Look at you, Vice President Xing, give me some face in front of outsiders..."

"You want a face? You don't even want face, why should I give?"

"Why? It's because I, Zhai Qing, work with President Tao for many years, and I have all been hard!" Zhai Qing said as he tore the button of his shirt, revealing a strand of black hair on his chest.

Just when the atmosphere in the private room became tenser, the small log-colored door was pushed open, and a bald old man walked in. In fact, he may not be very old, and his well-maintained face was clean. But the back is a little hunched, and his eyes were always looking at the ground, always giving people the feeling that he can't find a home with Alzheimer's disease.

Xing Qixian called out "Master Tao is here", then took the lead to stand up, and the others in the private room also stood up.

Guo Xiaofen knew that this old man should be Tao Bing, the honorary president of the Kind Charity Fund.

"You didn't call me to attend dinner." Tao Bing muttered in dissatisfaction, then walked inside and stood beside Xing Qixian's seat. Xing Qixian had no choice but to go to the other side. Now everyone had to change positions. In the end, the table and chairs clacked for a while, then they added chairs and cutlery, and it took a long time for them to take their seats again.

When Xing Qixian introduced Guo Xiaofen to Tao Bing, Tao Bing nodded and started to eat with chopsticks. His hands were shaking badly, but to Guo Xiaofen's surprise, this did not affect his eating efficiency at all. He almost used his chopsticks as a trebuchet. The moment the chopsticks touched the food, he stuck out his tongue, tossed, rolled, and entered his mouth precisely, quickly, decisively, and never slipped through the net. When drinking sea cucumber porridge, almost half of his face was buried in the bowl, and he swallowed all food together in a few mouthfuls. When he raised his head, there were a few grains of millet hanging from the chin... Since childhood in Longyan after seeing a wild boar with bamboo shoots in her hometown, Guo Xiaofen has not seen such a savage and greedy appearance for at least 20 years.

"Eat slowly, don't choke." Xing Qixian advised with a smile.

"Slow? If you eat slowly, you won't have anything to eat." Tao Bing wiped his mouth with a tissue. He looked at Guo Xiaofen and said, "Are you a reporter?"

"I used to be, but now I have resigned." Guo Xiaofen said.

"It's good to leave..." Tao Bing slowly raised the glass of wine and said, "In the final analysis, it is not conducive to unity."

Xing Qixian adjusted his glasses and said with a smile, "Master Tao, for the sake of the foundation's unity, do you think it would be better for Zhuoyao to come back as soon as possible?"

"I wish she would come back sooner." Tao Bing took a gulp of wine: "She didn't even tell me, and suddenly ran to Paris. I can't find her now!"

"If you want to look for her, you can always find it." Xing Qixian said.

"What are you doing to get her back in such a hurry?" Tao Bing narrowed his eyes and looked at him, "You want her to leave the position to you sooner?"

As soon as these words came out, Guo Xiaofen noticed that the old man's eyes were extremely sharp and cold as if two knives had suddenly appeared.

However, Xing Qixian has no fear: "Master Tao, I also think for the fund, these days the outsiders see us like a rock, but you ask them who have no pressure? No matter from which point of view, Zhuoyao should come back as soon as possible, the case has something to do with her, she will have to explain it to the police sooner or later; if the case has nothing to do with her, she is the leader of the fund, and she always has to take care of things for her company —"

"Taking responsibility, you can count with your fingers, how many things have I covered you all these years?!" Tao Bing's cheeks trembled, "Just say your brother, if I hadn't settled for him in the province back then, he would have still been in jail!"

"He is dead, why do you still mention old things!" Xing Qixian dodged his eyes.

"Of course, you don't want me to mention it, but I want. Leave anything else, he has caused such a big disaster this time. You tell people all day long that Zheng is not good at managing his employees, but what the hell is your brother? Why did he end up like this, you have no idea?" Tao Bing pointed at Cui Yucui, "Ask her, she knows best!"

A piece of meat caught on Cui Yucui's chopsticks fell into the plate, her mouth was half-open, and she kept the attitude of eating but not eating, her flashing eyes seemed very flustered.

Guo Xiaofen originally thought that Tao Bing's remarks made it clear that he was attacking Xing Qisheng, then Xing Yunda would definitely have a seizure if he listened. But he didn't say a word, his whole face kept twisting and twitching.

"Master Tao, drink more." Liao stood up, took the red wine from the waiter, walked to Tao Bing, poured wine into his glass, and glanced at Guo Xiaofen seemingly unintentionally. Tao Bing suddenly came to his senses. He was so excited that he forgot that there was an "outsider" in the private room. He cleared his throat quickly and asked Xing Qixian in a gentle tone, "Qixian, after all, the deceased is important, when is Qisheng's funeral? "

Xing Qixian replied, "I went to the Public Security Bureau today, and they said that after the autopsy report of the criminal case is released, the family members can cremate if they have no objection. The bodies of the three children were cremated first, as for my brother's body we will see the situation."

Tao Bing knew that the so-called "see the situation" meant that Xing Qixian wanted to take his brother's dead body as a threat and bargained with the fund. If he didn't agree to his conditions, then he would rather let the body stink there until he got his interest. Until the honorary president completely stinks. He couldn't help but feel flustered for a while, took a sip of wine and calmed down, then sighed: "Alas, if it can be cremated, it should be cremated sooner, and then choose a better cemetery, and the foundation will pay to let Qisheng go to the ground one day sooner for peace of mind. When he was alive, every time he went back to the province to see me, he would drink a lot. In recent years, as long as he was drunk, he always said: 'Except for weddings and funerals, there are very few things that can bring us together. ' This time, we finally got together, so let's go send him off!"

Those words made the room fall silent. After a while, there was a low sigh and a sob. It was Cui Yucui, who was gently wiping the inner corner of her eye with her middle finger.

Only Xing Qixian had a sneer on the corner of his mouth.

Tao Bing pretended not to see it, turned his head, and asked President Li of Love Hospital: "Li, will this incident have any impact on your hospital's next publicity work?"

"There must still be some, but it doesn't have much to do. After the accident, Vice President Xing has instructed us for the first time to clear the relationship with Tongyou Nursing Home. Some kids came here by train from the province, and will arrive tomorrow... It's a pity that someone who likes Xiao Wu can't find it in a while."

"It doesn't matter, the child is very malleable, and new Xiaowu will be cultivated soon." Tao Bing nodded and said to Cui Yucui: "You have worked hard during this time, and now the nursing home is closed. After such a big case, even if the storm passes, it is not easy to recover, so you can ask Zhai to get some money, and manage the employees in place then come here to work!"

Cui Yucui raised her eyebrows and thanked him repeatedly. Zhai Qing, who was sitting beside her, couldn't help twisting her thigh from below, and she slapped him on the back of the hand.

At this time, Zheng Gui said tremblingly: "Master Tao, our Mingyi Company..."

Tao Bing looked at him and said slowly, "Zheng, no matter what, this is because you didn't take good charge of your subordinates. After so many years of establishment of our foundation, why has it been smooth sailing? Any conflicts are always handled internally, and outsiders cannot be seen as jokes. But the case is equivalent to burning us for the world to watch, which is a great shame! From my personal point of view, I definitely hope you and Mingyi Company will continue to work normally under the leadership of the foundation, and of course, there are special circumstances, and we must be mentally prepared."

Zheng Gui seemed to understand what he said, but not, so he murmured: "Master Tao, that's right, but I really didn't expect Zhou Liping to be such a person......"

"If you can't think of it, you'll have to take on unexpected responsibilities!" Cui Wentao suddenly scolded, baring his teeth, "Do you know that the fire in Deratization Hill has burned half of the connections! You raised your dog yourself! Don't you have any idea in your heart?!"

"Cui Wentao, fuck you!" Xing Yunda suddenly raised his eyebrows and let out an angry roar, "Who the hell are you provoking!"

Cui Wentao blinked for a long time but didn't understand why he was being scolded. Xing Yunda was Xing Qixian's nephew. This relationship made him not dare to offend him, but he was also a public official with a position, so he would not let a hairy boy fuck him casually. So he stiffly replied: "I scolded Zhou Liping—"

Before he finished speaking, Xing Yunda smashed a wine glass over!

Cui Wentao flicked to the side, because Xing Yunda drank too much, and his aim was not accurate. This glass of wine was spilling on Guo Xiaofen who was sitting beside Cui Wentao!

There was exclamation in the private room, Xing Qixian and Cui Wentao were busy handing Guo Xiaofen tissues, Zhai Qing jumped over to wipe for Guo Xiaofen, Guo Xiaofen said "it's okay" while running out of the private room and into the corridor.

The other employees had already left work, and the empty corridor was so quiet that it made people feel scared. The voice-activated lights turned on in sequence with the sound of her footsteps, which made the passage even darker.

Guo Xiaofen found the bathroom, went in, and closed the door. She looked at the mirror and wiped the wine stains on her clothes with a tissue. After wiping for a long time, she didn't wipe it off, as if she was covered in blood... She thought that it's night, no one would notice.

She turned around, opened the door of the bathroom, and only took a step outside, and saw a person standing against the wall.

She was so frightened that she cried out "Ah"!

With a voice, the corridor lights are all on!

It was Xing Yunda, he was carrying a pocket with a pale face, and his eyes were red: "I'm sorry, I just came to say sorry to you."

"It's okay." Guo Xiaofen suddenly felt pity for him, "Zhou Liping is your father's enemy, you still protect him?"

"I drank too much..." Xing Yunda exuded a strong smell of alcohol all over his body, his expression was painful and depressed, "I still can't believe that Bro Zhou will kill my father, he is upright. After so many years, I admire him alone... My dad is a badass, yes, for the things he did, sooner or later, he would be punished, but why is it Zhou, why is he..."

7

After coming out of Hefeng Hotel, maybe it was because of the stamina of the wine, Guo Xiaofen felt a little heavy, but she also firmly rejected the hospitality offered by Zhai Qing and Cui Wentao, saying that her boyfriend would come soon to pick her up, looking at the two squinting men with a somewhat frustrated expression, she felt more and more that she had done the right thing.

She walked north along the street in front of the Hefeng Hotel. In order to prevent being followed, she turned a few turns on purpose and turned to a small road. The street lamps on the path are not very bright, the autumn wind is tight, and every ray of light projected on the cracked ground trembles. All kinds of clothing stores, gourmet restaurants, massage parlors, etc. on the street are all darkened, and there are fragmented notices on the locked doors. The words "closed" and "apology" can be vaguely seen. Maybe because of it, a noodle shop that was still lit with lights, which was particularly eye-catching.

After Guo Xiaofen walked past the noodle shop, she turned back.

Because she saw a person sitting inside.

She climbed the steps, pulled open the glass sliding door, and walked in. Sure enough, sitting behind the long table and slowly eating a bowl of tomato-flavored noodles, it was the middle-aged man who was beaten by Zhai Qing at the entrance of Block E. Under the pale light, his originally thin face appeared. The hole appeared lankier and sicklier, and the blood clots in the corners of the mouth were particularly distinct. Perhaps because the wound was still in pain, and the steaming bowl of noodles was a little hot, he sighed and frowned at the injured side as he ate the noodles.

The moment Guo Xiaofen sat down opposite him, he was a little surprised, and his eyes flashed with a hint of alertness.

"Mr. Yue, right? Hello." Guo Xiaofen still remembers his surname, "I met you at the Hefeng Hotel today."

Yue tightened the thin old jacket on his body and stared at her blankly.

"Don't worry, I'm not from the Kind Charity Fund I just went to interview them because of the case." Guo Xiaofen said.

Yue was skeptical.

"I heard your accusations against them, and I saw that Zhai Qing beat you up. I'm curious, why?"

"You smell a bit of alcohol, it seems that they invited you to dinner!" Yue observed very carefully, "Of course, they have always been very generous to reporters, (he looked at Guo Xiaofen without carrying any bags) directly send cards for you?"

Guo Xiaofen was stunned.

"Then, what did they ask you to write about? That the murderer was just a temporary worker of Mingyi Company? They had terminated their cooperation with Mingyi Company at the end of last year? The Tongyou Nursing Home was a private undertaking, so the case was closely related to Mingyi Company. The Kind Charity Fund has nothing to do with it? Then list the various acts of kindness that the Kind Charity Fund has done and the awards it has won in recent years, and call on everyone to continue donating to them?"

"I think you misunderstood—"

"You don't need to explain." Yue smiled coldly, "We are different, you eat your big meal, I eat my noodles, farewell!"

Guo Xiaofen stood up slowly: "It seems that Vice President Xing and the others are right. The phrase 'peers are enemies' applies everywhere."

Yue raised his head suddenly: "What did you say?"

"Vice President Xing said, you are just running a charitable organization yourself and can't get any money, so you are jealous of the Kind Charity Fund. You heard that someone had an accident, so you came here specifically to extort extortion in the name of breaking the news to the media. It seems that it is true."

Yue's lips trembled with anger: "You... don't spit out blood, our own charity organization was destroyed by them a few years ago! What kind of money did I make?!"

Guo Xiaofen opened the glass sliding door and went down the steps, and said, "As you just said, we are different, and there is nothing to talk about."

Yue jumped up and ran forward around the table, trying to pull her arm, but hesitatingly grabbed the strap of her satchel: "You come back... Let's make it clear."

It was not until Guo Xiaofen sat back across from him that Yue was relieved. Guo Xiaofen frankly introduced her identity to him and why she went to the Hefeng Hotel this afternoon. Yue's expression became much calmer, and he gradually opened up the conversation.

As a senior reporter, Guo Xiaofen has been in contact with all kinds of interviewees. Many interviewees were very uncooperative at first. In this case, deliberately trying to please the other party will make the other party look down on it. The best way is to anger them first and form a hostile state, and then try to ease it... The psychology of people is very strange. Once a former opponent turns an enemy into a friend, it is easy to cherish each other and develop a sense of intimacy.

"My name is Yue Shao. I used to be the principal of a private primary school in Province A. Province A is remote and backward, and only a few industries are all major polluters, resulting in the birth rate of children suffering from various deformities, congenital diseases, and rare diseases in recent years. After a walk in the countryside, there are several children commonly known as 'white wax rods' squatting at the door -because these children are often sluggish like an idiot, their complexion is sallow, and they become stalks due to lack of nutrition. In time, fields, rivers, their bodies can be seen often. When I ask my parents, they all say that they ran out of the house, fell, or drowned by themselves. A few days ago, when the principals of our private elementary schools went to the city for a meeting, those children were almost all sick but many of them had no problems with their mental development, and the disease was not incurable. So we wrote to the government, made reports, and applied for assistance, but no one paid any attention to us. When we saw that we couldn't continue like this, we simply joined forces and organized a charity organization called Camphor Tree by ourselves. The town contracted an abandoned yard, built a new fence, built a house as a nursing home, and asked the parents of those children to deliver the children and pay a little money, and we would look for conscientious companies and individuals to raise funds. Then we could hire people to take care of them. Dong Xinlan and Wu both came this way. Although the Camphor Tree has been short of food, clothing, medicine since the day it opened, the children are very obedient and sensible. Other non-governmental charitable organizations are also willing to reach out and give us a hand, so we are motivated, and life is very happy. Especially Wu, who caught up with a congenital heart disease specialist from Beijing Children's Hospital once to come to the province People's Hospital consulted, we heard the news, hired a car to take him there, the specialist performed free surgery on him, and actually cured him. Wu was very happy, and since then, he was dead set on the Camphor Tree. We can't drive him away, we simply let him stay and help take care of the other children..."

Yue Shao looked at the night outside for a while, as if he was nostalgic for the good old days, and then sighed: "Later, the Kind Charity Fund was established, and it was said to be the same as ours, but they have a backstage, background... Then suddenly, we received a notice that in order to strengthen management, all private charitable organizations should be included in the Kind Charity Fund, become its subordinate organizations, and accept its leadership. We were very angry and went to the city to report, we are also privately run, and they are also privately run, so why do they lead us?"

"Then?" Guo Xiaofen asked.

"Then? The result is that several teachers, including me, were dismissed. The total salary was only a few hundred yuan. It would not be the same without it... But I never imagined that, soon, the demolition team came with bulldozers and demolished the nursing home that we had worked so hard to build brick by brick. In the blink those flowers and trees we planted with our children all disappeared. Looking at the piles of broken bricks and tiles, there were also small blackboards buried in the soil, accordions, children's drawings, homemade wheelchairs and crutches, we cried, and the children hugged and cried together, but it's just useless!"

Speaking of this, Yue Shao was a little choked up. Guo Xiaofen a asked for a pot of hot water and slowly poured it into the glass in front of Yue Shao.

Yue Shao took a few sips, his mood calmed down a little, and continued to speak: "We are worrying about how to arrange the children, who would haven't known that the Kind Charity Fund would have helped us 'consider' it, so that Cui Wentao and Xing Qisheng, who led the team and went to various nursing homes to 'select people' and bring them to the welfare home—"

Guo Xiaofen was a little surprised: "Select people?"

"Of course, pick people they're able to use, such as beautiful little girls, like Dong Xinlan, and those who may heal or improve as they grow up, which can be used as a way for them to brag about themselves to the public in the future. The 'personal evidence' of merit. Like Xiao Wu, they pay special attention, because as long as the medical records are changed, it will become that they were cured of congenital heart disease in the Love Hospital. Then they can show to defraud more social donations. "

"That's how it is!" Guo Xiaofen suddenly realized, "I was curious about why does the Love Hospital brings them here from Province A every year... Then, what about the remaining children?"

"They don't care about the rest of the children. Anyway, our nursing home is not allowed and welfare home doesn't accept them, and most of the parents of the children refuse to take their children home. In the end, we can only watch those unaccomplished children disappear or die..." Yue Shao's expression was gloomy, "Later, we also tried to organize a few people in private to adopt the children according to the model of the nursing home, but as long as they heard something, they brought a group of local hooligans came to smash and snatch the fancy child, that's how Li Ying was taken away by them—"

Guo Xiaofen frowned: "Mr. Yue, I don't really understand, it's just a group of sick children, why should the Kind Charity Fund come to fight for them and bring down other private nursing homes, what is the benefit to them?"

"After all, it's still a matter of interest."

"Interests?" Guo Xiaofen became more and more confused. "Since it's a charitable organization, what interests can there be?"

"In the eyes of outsiders, public welfare and charitable organizations are a place with no benefits. In fact, it is very wrong." Yue Shao poked his finger on the tabletop of the long table and whispered, "From the national level, every year Charitable organizations will have financial allocations and will conduct strict audits on the flow of funds, but there are many people in need of assistance in our country. From the perspective of orphans and abandoned children, the number of them is huge. The amount of state funding is just a drop in the bucket. Under this circumstance, the state supports charitable organizations to raise donations from society and also provides relevant tax reduction policies for enterprises and individuals with large donations. The donators made public welfare and charities wholeheartedly, but there are also very few love charitable foundations that try to exploit the loopholes of national policies to make a fortune."

"How?"

"Let's see in this way if there are many charitable organizations can be chosen by those companies and rich people who are eager to get tax cuts, then, of course, they donate money to whichever has a good reputation in the society and helps more children. – Then, what if a province has only one charitable organization?"

Guo Xiaofen suddenly realized!

Yue Shao continued: "In this way, the original donation company is Party A, but suddenly it becomes Party B, because for public welfare and charitable organizations, whether you like to donate or not, who wants to get the tax reduction policy must donate to me – and if it does not give me personal benefits, I have the right to refuse your donations! So there are a lot of rebates and commissions in the fundraising —"

"What is the ratio?"

"According to the 'rules' set by the Kind Charity Fund, it is generally 3 to 5—"

"Three to five percent?" Guo Xiaofen was very surprised, "Isn't that if a company donates 100 million yuan, they can earn 3 million to 5 million?"

"Not three to five percent, but thirty to fifty percent." Yue Shao said coldly.

Guo Xiaofen couldn't close her mouth for a long time.

"Half of the donation of 100 million went into Tao Bing and Xing Qixian's personal pockets. Of course, this is not the end. In the 'business' of the Kind Charity Fund, there is still a considerable part of money laundering. Since it is a social donation, auditing and monitoring of the capital flow are all difficult, so some black money was laundered from the charity foundation in the name of fundraising. Tao Bing and Xing Qixian, of course, would get some money, like Zhai Qing and others, they used to be in the underworld. And now specialize in helping the Kind Charity Fund to handle the money laundering business..." Yue Shao said, "Besides, the Kind Charity Fund also has campus loans and real estate in terms of making money, but campus loans were forced to death two years ago. A female student, the student's father is said to be a high-ranking police officer, so the campus loan was forced to stop for a while, and recently it has been revived, and they are still doing real estate now."

Guo Xiaofen interrupted him and said, "I don't quite understand, what kind of real estate is a charitable organization doing, and how does it make money?"

"Where is the main profit of real estate? It is nothing more than the difference between the land price and the selling price. The higher the price of the land sold by the government, the higher the selling price of the real estate, right? Well, if the government does not charge for the construction land, and the real estate is still sold at the high price of commercial housing?"

Guo Xiaofen shook her head: "How is this possible? All the construction land must be sold by the government. How can it not be charged?"

"There is an exception." Yue Shao said slowly, "The state has expressly stipulated that charitable organizations can enjoy huge discounts in land prices and even waive fees for the land used by charitable organizations to build nursing homes and welfare homes."

"Such a good policy... I don't understand, how can the Kind Charity Fund take advantage of it?"

"They can build apartments for the elderly."

"Apartments for the elderly? "

"Look, for example, the state approved a piece of land that could build five buildings, and they built a walled independent community, took out one of them to build a nursing home or a welfare home, and built the remaining four apartments and sell them according to the market price. Is it not the same as using the land given by the state to build commercial housing for sale?"

"But can such a house have a long property right?"

"Of course, such a house cannot immediately obtain long property rights." Yue Shao said, "However, when this type of house is sold, another contract will be signed, that is, the buyer will obtain the 'residence right for the elderly' for 70 years or even longer. And the buyers will enjoy all the benefits of the only real nursing home in the community. Water, electricity, network cables, and property are all free. Do you think there is any temptation?"

Hearing so many unheard stories, Guo Xiaofen's already heavy head felt a little swollen: "That's why they want to bring down all other private charitable organizations, seize all the channels to obtain wealth in their own hands, and then they can do whatever they want: use tax policies to defraud donations, use charity funds to commit financial crimes, use preferential land policies to speculate, and launder money... But in recent years, the country's anti-corruption efforts have been unprecedentedly strong, aren't they afraid?"

"Of course they are afraid, and they are scared to death, but they are used to it. Besides, every bad thing they do involves countless departments and individuals, and those who give them the green light have to get a share of the pie. It's too late when they want to stop. Anyway, it's not my own, and it can't be others'... In fact, we all understand these things, but there's nothing we can do. When they take away the children, I was sad but then I think about it, the welfare home is much better than ours. Although the children are being used, it is better than following us poor teachers. But since they use the children, just treat them well, don't kill them..." As he spoke, tears suddenly welled up in his eyes.

Guo Xiaofen took out two tissues from the tissue box next to them and handed them to Yue Shao. Yue Shao rubbed it vigorously, but the tissues were like a block in his chest, no matter how it couldn't be rubbed flat or smooth: "I heard about the case here. Afterward, I hurried over and wanted to ask Xing Qixian and Cui Wentao, but I was beaten by Zhai Qing instead... The literati don't know martial, but this account is not so easy to settle!"

"What are your plans for the next step?" Guo Xiaofen asked.

"Anyway, I've already come, so why do I have to report to the government? In recent years, the country has become more and more positive, and the anti-criminal and evil are real actions. I don't believe that the people from the Kind Charity Fund can still be arrogant!"

Guo Xiaofen thought for a while and said, "I guess you can't actually produce much actual evidence, right?"

Yue Shao nodded with a wry smile: "We are ordinary people, where can we find any actual evidence!"

"It's a once-in-a-lifetime opportunity." Guo Xiaofen pondered for a moment and said, "Originally, if there is no basis and no evidence the police can't find an excuse to investigate the Kind Charity Fund. Now it's different. There was such a serious case, the police can't let go of any clues related to the case provided by anyone, and they must invest manpower and material resources to verify it repeatedly, so if you report to the Kind Charity Fund now, the police can rake grass and fight rabbits —"

Yue Shao nodded again and again: "Good idea, good idea!"

Guo Xiaofen took out her mobile phone, called Ma Xiaozhong, asked him to pick her up nearby, and then said to Yue Shao, "During this time, you should pay attention to your personal safety, and you will live in my friend's home from today. He will teach you how to report the illegal and criminal problems of the Kind Charity Fund according to the procedures."

Yue Shao was very happy, but he didn't know what to say except "thank you". In the end, he probably felt embarrassed to just say "thank you", so he buried his head and devoured the remaining noodles in the bowl...
...Looking at his clumsy appearance, Guo Xiaofen felt funny but bitter.

8

After paying the bill and going out, it was already around eleven o'clock in the evening, and the street was even darker than before. Guo Xiaofen and Ma Xiaozhong agreed on the meeting point. After turning a few corners, on the main road that was slightly wider, she and Yue Shao walked side by side, chatting while walking, there were no cars on the street nor other people. There was empty and extraordinarily quiet.

"I also worked as a substitute teacher in a private primary school," Guo Xiaofen said.

Yue Shao was a little surprised: "You?"

"It's true. When I was in college, I had a holiday, and I had nothing else to do, so I contacted a volunteer organization and went to a remote small mountain village to be a substitute teacher for a period of time. It was a hard time, but I have a lot of good memories. The children are not good at studying, but they all play the rubber band very well, much better than me."

"Haha, as soon as I heard what you said, sounds like you really been in a private elementary school in a remote mountainous area. there was poor and couldn't afford other sports equipment, just jumping rubber bands..."

Guo Xiaofen put her hands in her pockets, looked at the clouds in the night sky, and recalled: "The class I took also had a disabled child, a girl, with a strange disease called neurofibromatosis, hunched over and couldn't walk. But she really wanted to go to school, so I would go to her home every morning to carry her to school, and then carry her home after school, and she would never forget to say to me: 'Ms. Guo, thank you, please don't forget to pick me up...' Later, when the vacation was over, I went back to the university, and I received a letter from her, she said that after I left, she cried for a long time, because no one would pick her up from school anymore... Until now, I still think of her occasionally, and I don't know how she is doing. Sometimes I'm too tired from work, or I encounter unhappy things, and I want to buy a train ticket and go back to that small mountain village to see the children I have taught. Of course, I know it's all just fantasy, unrealistic fantasy..."

"Yeah, since you've settled down in this big city, don't think about going back to the countryside." Yue Shao advised her.

"But my home is not here." Guo Xiaofen said slowly, "I have worked in this city for many years, but I don't have a permanent residence and can't afford a house..."

"You are a girl, find someone with a registered permanent residence in this city and get married."

"I want to marry a person I like, but what he really likes is another girl..." Guo Xiaofen raised her face and said melancholy, "I don't want to marry a man I don't like, so I just stay single."

Yue Shao didn't know how to continue so he could only be silent.

After another crossroads, they reached the place agreed with Ma Xiaozhong.

Pedestrian lights went out red and came on the green.

Guo Xiaofen and Yue Shao walked across the road together, she suddenly said, "If the Kind Charity Fund is investigated, your Camphor Tree may be able to re-run. At that time, I will be a teacher for your school!"

Yue Shao nodded, then shook his head with a wry smile: "Even if Tao Bing, Xing Qixian, and the others are down, it's probably not us who 'fill the seat'."

"Cheer up!" Guo Xiaofen looked at him and encouraged, "Believe that everything will be alright, one day we will bring the children back—"

Rumble boom!

A huge roar suddenly rushed to their ears!

In the darkness, a huge monster rushed towards them from the other side of the street!

Because of the speed, the whole earth is shaking!

Guo Xiaofen hadn't figured out what was going on but was pushed away by Yue Shao. She fell on her back and fell to the ground. She saw only a few clips in her violently turbulent line of sight: Yue Shao flew into the air, rolled a few times, and then the whole body hit the ground with a loud "bang"!

Then, the huge monster had disappeared on the street corner, and its grinning whistling could be heard in the distance...

Guo Xiaofen supported the ground, stood up hard, and staggered towards Yue Shao.

Yue Shao lay face down on the ground, his body trembled as if it was electrified, every time he trembled, a mouthful of blood spurted out from the corner of his mouth, and when the blood spurted out, he began to spit out red blood foam at the corner of his mouth. The edge accumulated into a small blood puddle.

"Mr. Yue..." Guo Xiaofen knelt beside him, coughing, and calling him in a weak voice.

Yue Shao looked at her, smiled, and murmured something on his lips.

Guo Xiaofen lay beside his ear: "Don't worry, speak slowly..."

"Bring them back, bring them back, bring them back..."

"I promise you, I will bring them back, all of them."

Guo Xiaofen sat up, fumbling for her phone, trying to call 120 for help, maybe the phone fell out of her pocket when Yue Shao pushed her away, now she couldn't find it...

Pedestrian lights turned off green and turned on red.

The red light dripped down a long and narrow strip on the asphalt.

Guo Xiaofen sat on the ground dumbfounded, she knew that the phone could not be found. And even if it was found, it was already broken and could not call for help; she knew that calling for help was useless, and even if the ambulance came, it would not be able to save Yue Shao; she knew this was not an accidental traffic accident, even if they obey the traffic rules, they can't escape death. The essence of darkness is to engulf all colors, and it doesn't matter if the red light is green...

Chapter 7

1

Under the strong pressure from the police and the Charity Fund, Tao Zhuoyao finally took a plane from Paris to return to China. After getting off the plane, she was taken directly to the City Bureau by the criminal police of the special investigation team under a sudden trial.

Perhaps because of her status, Tao Zhuoyao has never entered such an environment and received such "treatment". Her performance was even more panicked than a sex worker who was caught by State Vice for the first time. Before Lin Fengchong could ask a second question, she rolled out of the chair and sat on the ground, clutching her stomach and shouting that it was her period. After the policewoman next to her took her to the bathroom, she, however, said no. When she came back for another trial, she said that she had lost her memory and couldn't remember anything. Then suddenly, she raised her two pig-tails-shaped eyebrows, asked the police what they were doing on earth and why did they capture her "for no reason", spitting out a list of names, seemingly of bigwigs, and then asked Lin Fengchong in fierce whether he recognized them. As Lin 's tone became a little more serious, she began to wail, blubbery mess of snot and tears, saying how pitiful and innocent she was, rolling up the sleeves of her shirt to show them a thin red line on her wrist of her failed suicide attempt. But their indifference made her a sudden gentle woman again. She lowered his head and asked timidly when her father Tao Bing would come to pick him up. There was a tear on her sunken cheek... so much so that the near deputy judge put a pencil on the paper. When he wrote the word "giant baby" and pushed it to Lin Fengchong quietly, Lin Fengchong couldn't help but nodded.

The thirty-eight-year-old woman, with a thin body like a stalk, was wearing a brightly colored trench coat of new fashionable style from Paris. Her long face was covered with thick powder and blood-like lipstick, and her lips can't be closed for her slight-buck teeth. Her crying, making trouble, and tossing around messed the powder and lipstick completely, her crow's feet of the eyes and the large pores exposed. Having stirring up and down, her face was smothered by a bowl of fried noodles.

When Lin Fengchong was a little irritated by this pretentious woman, Tao Zhuoyao made a pose that he had never imagined, imitating Sharon Stone's performance in *Instinct*. Her legs in black velvets slowly split and then crossed again, with seductive winks.

Lin Fengchong was nicknamed "Granny Lin", which means he has a good temper, but this time he got angry and slammed the trial table, "Tao Zhuoyao, stand up!"

The sound shook the four walls of the interrogation room, and at once, Tao Zhuoyao jumped up from the chair in fright.

"Look at what this is!" Lin Fengchong pointed to the golden police badge on the wall, raised his head and glared, "This is the law of the state! One billion people must all abide by and defend it, no one can be an exception, no! No matter who you are and no matter how old you are, you have to obey the laws of the country! How dare you! You mean nothing to me!"

Tao Zhuoyao stood there, trembling all over.

"Until now, how many plays you've acted! Is it helpful? It's SHIT! If you have violated the laws of the country, you must honestly confess your guilt and accept the punishment of the law. Don't think about anything else; don't even think about it. It doesn't work!" Nevertheless, Granny Lin is not someone who is good at losing his temper. On seeing Tao Zhuoyao's crying and holding on her coat-tails but not daring to cry out, Lin slowed down his voice, "Do you know you're wrong? Just sit down when you know. Honestly, explain the problem, don't fix those unnecessary things!"

Tao Zhuoyao nodded vigorously and sat back in the chair.

"Go ahead."

"I...what should I say?"

"Someone has been killed, and you have gone abroad to hide. Now you are asking me?!"

This sentence was pre-set. During the police investigation process, the relationship between Tao Zhuoyao and the murder case in Saoshuling was basically ruled out. However, "fraud and fraud" can sometimes have unexpected results, and it is also a common practice in interrogation. Surprisingly, something real came out here.

"He died of illness himself, none of my business!" Tao Zhuoyao said with a sad face.

The sentence shocked the interrogators. They had never expect Tao Zhuoyao to know something important about the case. Lin Fengchong's heart also turned upside down, but on the surface he was very calm, "Illness? Just at this timing? Do you think it makes sense?"

"I'm not lying. When he was a fitness coach in the past, he had a heart attack due to excessive exercise, so he couldn't work in the gym anymore. I don't know what happened that night. He suddenly started twitching all over and foaming from his mouth. At first, I thought he was joking with me and ignored him. But then he fell on the bed and didn't move. I pushed him a few times and he didn't respond. His breath was gone. I quickly called Xing Qisheng, who came later, feeling his pulse and scratching his eyelids, and he was also shocked saying that he was dead."

The phrase "being a fitness coach in the past" clearly refers to Zhang Chunyang. Zhang Chunyang, who had been missing and couldn't find his whereabouts, was dead? This made Lin Fengchong another surprise, but he was going to see the corpse, so where was the corpse? He settled down and decided not to jump thinking and asking questions, but to consolidate every question.

Under good and steady attack of him and other interrogators, Tao Zhuoyao finally explained all her actions on the night of the Shaoshuling case clearly:

That afternoon, at about four o'clock, Tao Zhuoyao, who was participating in a activity named Teenager Safety Awareness Education at a key primary school in a city as a guest, suddenly received a call from Zhang Chunyang.

Since she and Jiang Lei got engaged, she has not had any private contact with Zhang Chunyang. Zhang Chunyang flirt with her on the phone, making her abashed. Thinking of Jiang Lei going on a business trip to Hong Kong and her on-going marriage, it would be difficult to have an affair with Zhang Chunyang in the future, so she agreed to his request. She drove back to the Hefeng Hotel after the activity and had a private meeting with Zhang Chunyang, who had been waiting at the gate of the hotel. The two entered Block E from the back door, and walked to Tao Zhuoyao's bedroom on the fourth floor. They ate something together and were ready to have sex when she received a call from Xing Qisheng. Xing Qisheng told her that there was something important and that he would come to the hotel to report face to face. Tao Zhuoyao estimated the time and asked Xing Qisheng to wait for her call in the main building first—

"What time was Xing Qisheng making this call?" Lin Fengchong interrupted.

"I can't remember exactly...it should be a little after seven."

"Xing Qisheng said he was on his way?"

Tao Zhuoyao nodded affirmatively. She said that although Xing Qisheng's call was a little disappointing, Zhang Chunyang was enthusiastic, so their emotions soon reached their peak. But as they both were near the top, Zhang Chunyang suddenly shouted out. He fell face down on her, twitching, foaming, and then turning unconscious.

Having lived for thirty-eight years, Tao Zhuoyao's life is like a high-speed train. Everything was arranged smoothly and unimpeded by her father Tao Bing and his subordinates. It was always comfortable, steady, fast and safe during her life journey, so the train derailed when a dead person was lying on her. She was stunned, pushed Zhang Chunyang's body away on the carpet. She did not remember to call Xing Qisheng and ask him to see if Zhang Chunyang was really dead until after some unknown amount of time.

When Xing Qisheng arrived, he found that the whole bedroom was dark. He was about to turn on the light when Tao Zhuoyao screamed and cried "Don't turn on the light." Xing Qisheng said that if she looked like this, he can't treat Zhang Chunyang, thus Tao Zhuoyao cowered into the corner. Xing Qisheng turned on the light and checked Zhang Chunyang, who was lying on the bed, over and over again, and confirmed his death...

Even though she already knew the result, Tao Zhuoyao couldn't help crying. She didn't feel sorry for her lover's death, but did know that his death was not a trivial matter. Xing Qisheng seemed very irritable, walking in circles back and forth in the room, constantly muttering, "Why at this time. Why at this time..."

"What does he mean by saying this?" Lin Fengchong asked.

"Xing Qixian has been challenging my dad's status recently wishing we could both be removed from the Fund. Whether my dad can keep his position depends on whether he can get a large amount of charitable funds for the Charity Fund. This is not I want to marry Jiang Lei. Jiang Lei's father is the chairman of a large state-owned enterprise. As long as the two families become in-laws, Jiang Lei's father can give a lot of money. This kind of thing happens at this time, once It is rumored that this marriage is likely to be blown away, so Xing Qisheng said that."

"Isn't Xing Qisheng Xing Qixian's brother? Why doesn't he stand by his brother?"

"Xing Qisheng and Xing Qixian have always been at odds. The elder brother feels that he is deliberately suppressed by the younger in the Fund, resulting in Xing Qisheng not climbing as high and earning as much as

Xing Qixian, so he is always for my dad. At the same time, he is also my personal doctor."

"What happened later? What did you discuss with Xing Qisheng?"

Tao Zhuoyao said that Xing Qisheng gave her a careful analysis of the whole thing. In short, no matter what, she couldn't leak the slightest rumor, otherwise her marriage with Jiang Lei would end. She and her father would be cleared out of the Charity Fund, immediately. ... The best way now was to make Zhang Chunyang's body "disappear as soon as possible".

Tao Zhuoyao looked at the body that was still lying motionless on the bed. It was originally so fit, but now every part was slackening. It was as ugly and slack meat as it was on the chopping board. In the middle of the scattered milky-white bedding, there was light yellow liquid, not knowing whether it was the body fluid that overflowed during the two people's carnival or the urine that flowed out after the corpse was incontinent, making the atmosphere of the whole room even more sinister and terrifying. In Zhang Chunyang's half-closed eyes showed no light.

There was still a lot of white foam on the lower side of Zhang's mouth. The flushing on his face when he died has gradually faded, and there was a dash of savage blue and black on his pale face... Tao Zhuoyao couldn't help but jump up and turn off the light again. Weepingly asked Xing Qisheng how to make the dead "disappear as soon as possible", Xing Qisheng said, "Send it directly to our hospital mortuary."

"Our hospital" refers to the Kind Hospital, not far from the Hefeng Hotel. This hospital is affiliated to the Kind Charity Fund. In terms of publicity and profile, Xing Qisheng "lent" Zhao Wu and other children to the Fund every year for helping. The hospital management knows that Xing Qisheng is Tao Zhuoyao's henchman, and often gets along well with him. "You can count on me!" Xing Qisheng patted his chest and said, "While it was dark, I carried Zhang Chunyang downstairs and drove it to the morgue at the southwest gate of the hospital. The dean will issue a death certificate, arrange a freezer, and put the corpse in it, and it will be over without anyone noticing it..."

Tao Zhuoyao couldn't believe it, "This is a dead person! Is that so simple?"

Xing Qisheng smiled, "He is just a migrant population with no household registration, no real estate, and no relatives in this city. Such a person must have lost contact with his family. Who cares whether he is alive or dead? As long as no one looks for him, he's no different than a dead stray dog on the street— even a dead dog would get more attention!"

Tao Zhuoyao was still in a trance. Xing Qisheng squatted in front of her, hugged her bare shoulders and said, "President, you just lost a toy. Isn't that the case?"

Tao Zhuoyao had no choice but to agree.

At the same time, Xing Qisheng suggested that Tao Zhuoyao go abroad to "refresh her mind". Anyway, she used to go on a trip that said she could go abroad. At that point when she suddenly went abroad, no one would feel that there was anything wrong with her, but she can get mental relaxation. Xing Qisheng said very gently, "Don't worry. when you come back, everything will be like it never happened."

Tao Zhuoyao wanted to leave quickly. For a person who has never tried to solve problems independently since she was a child, the most instinctive way to deal with a problem was to escape. She bought a plane ticket to Paris on her phone and rummaged through boxes for passports and bank cards. Xing Qisheng, on the other hand, used the indoor landline to call Li Shiduo, the director of the Kind Hospital, and then put the clothes, one by one, on Zhang Chunyang, who was naked. He even didn't forget to put socks and shoes on him, and then carried him out of the door. Suddenly he put the corpse in the corridor, turned back to Tao Zhuoyao's bedroom, found Zhang Chunyang's mobile phone on the chaise longue, stuffed it into his trouser pocket, walked out the door, carried the corpse up again, and walked downstairs step by step... Listening to the sound of footsteps in the walking stairs getting farther and farther, the whole corridor fell into a dead silence... Tao Zhuoyao said, "At that moment, I felt that Zhang Chunyang was not the one who was to be put in the freezer of the mortuary. It's me, it's me, I felt the blood all over my body freezing. You don't believe me I lost my mind just now, but at least one part of what I said is true, I still can't remember how did I go downstairs; how did I walk out of the Hefeng Hotel, and how did I take a taxi to the airport. It's not me who could do these things. It's just a zombie named Tao Zhuoyao..."

2

It turned out that there were not only four corpses on the day of the Deratization Hill station case.

How many evil spirits were released from the underworld on that dark night, and ravaged the human world with their inhuman and bloody slaughter?

Thinking of this, the old criminal police such as Lin Fengchong also shuddered. He immediately sent Chai Yong to the mortuary of the Kind

Hospital to search for Zhang Chunyang's body. Once the suspect is "put out", there will be a period of psychological relaxation between the trial and the trial.

Lin Fengchong asked someone to pour Tao Zhuoyao a glass of water. Seeing her yellow fingertips, he lit a cigarette and handed it to her. Tao Zhuoyao had a grateful expression on her face, chatting with Lin Fengchong while smoking.

"Zhou Liping, how much do you know about him?"

"The driver who killed Xing Qisheng and many children? I don't know him. Why should I know about a driver! He is of Lao Liao's business, so you can ask him."

"Zhou Liping is not the driver of your Fund, but the driver of Mingyi Public Relation Company."

"Mingyi? Is that Zheng Gui's company? It's not under my control."

"The three children who were killed, have you seen them before?"

"I have never went to Tongyou Nursing Home, let alone meeting them?"

"You're lying. We've seen your photo with them."

"Impossible. I don't have the slightest impression."

Lin Fengchong took out a photo and handed it to her.

A circle of children surrounded Tao Zhuoyao for a group photo. The children were holding flowers in their hands, with numb expressions, while Tao Zhuoyao was smiling, as if she was the biggest flower in the bunch.

"This is a group photo with those children when I participated in the activities of the Kind Hospital. After that, they were scattered. I don't remember any of them."

"You are the president of the Kind Charity Fund. The main job of your foundation is to raise various social funds to help orphans, abandoned children and children suffering from rare diseases, serious diseases and no money for treatment. For them, don't you care?"

"I don't have children myself, and I can't find any feelings for them. To be honest, there is nothing that upsets me more than a child crying...Well, now that you found Zhang Chunyang's body, which proves that he died of illness, can't I be released? The case at the Deratization Hill station has nothing to do with me at all!"

"How can you say that it has nothing to do with you? The people who killed and were killed were all employees of the subordinate units of your Kind Charity Fund. You are the president and you have to take responsibilities of leadership!"

"Actually, I don't command anything. I know nothing! Xing Qixian and Zhai Yun are the ones who take care of everything. I can't take any responsibility..."

Lin Fengchong asked the policewoman to take Tao Zhuoyao to the detention center for temporary detention. Before leaving, Tao Zhuoyao suddenly made a request to Lin Fengchong, "Can you find me some books?"

"What kind?" Lin Fengchong asked. Generally speaking, suspects in temporary detention will ask for some books of laws to refer to because they have no idea of the degree of punishment they will receive for their crimes.

But what Tao Zhuoyao said was *Rather be Lonely than Vulgar, More Afraid of Being Confused than Wasting good time, Everything is the best Arrangement...*

"Why these?"

"Wouldn't it be suffocating if locked in here?"

Lin Fengchong couldn't help smiling bitterly and said, "You won't be alone in it, and you won't waste your time. Don't worry, everything is the best arrangement for you."

After Tao Zhuoyao left, the deputy judge couldn't help but scolded, "What a parasite! What a retarded woman! She haven't forgotten to act!"

"But these are the people who live in the best houses, drive the latest luxury cars, and eat the most expensive meals. The lives of so many disabled children are in their control..." Lin Fengchong sighed.

At this moment, Chai Yongjin's phone call came, and there was a hint of excitement in his voice, "Director Lin, we found Zhang Chunyang's body in the freezer of the mortuary of Kind Hospital."

When Lin Fengchong arrived at the southwest gate of Kind Hospital, several police cars had already parked here. The police officers and assistant police officers in uniform were driving away the crowd, while a few plainclothes criminal policemen saw Lin Fengchong coming and hurried up to meet him. In accordance with the ancient Chinese Qimen Dunjia(an ancient Chinese Daoist magic), the door facing the southwest leads to death, so located mortuaries of common hospitals. There was a locust tree, not fat and lush, on the either side of the gate. However, the door was small, and the distance between the two trees was also very narrow, so their branches and vines were intertwined, covering a green canopy above it. Lin Fengchong walked in, Chai Yongjin walked out, and the two bumped into each other. Chai Yongjin said, "Tianying and Tang Xiaotang are investigating the scene and doing preliminary examination of the body here."

After so many days, what else can be found? Lin Fengchong smiled bitterly and continued to walk inside. The entire mortuary is divided into three parts. The outermost part is a hall. On the left stood a set of simple solid wood tables and chairs. On the wall hung a row of old-fashioned register books with ropes. Paper money, gold coins, copper basins, tiles, etc., were commodities for those unprepared relatives of the deceased to be burned to hold a memorial ceremony temporarily; there was a small cubicle with a curtain on the right side of the hall, and Lin Fengchong lifted it up and looked at it. There were two steel wire beds inside. The quilts and pillows on the beds were fluffed and discolored. It should be a place for the staff on duty to rest. Going in from the hall, pushing open the two left-to-right, peeled glass doors, he entered the second part of the mortuary-the morgue, where there are six rusted white bed morgues, four were empty, and two were covered with white cloths to cover the remains-here parked temporarily, generally, the deceased who had not been arranged to "live" in the freezer. Another lead-grey iron door was pushed open from here, and a cold air rushed towards the face, and the temperature suddenly dropped by at least five or six degrees. Three of the four walls here were neatly stacked with dozens of freezers for long-term storage of corpses. The freezer looked relatively new, and the LCD screen on the cabinet door showed the temperature inside the cabinet. At this moment, a cabinet door with "TE-3" on the signboard was pulled open together with the freezer drawer. The milky-white cold air kept surging outwards. On the freezer drawer lay a man with a frosty face. Although his face was pale, his face was shriveled and wrinkled like a walnut skin, and the expression on his face was very painful when he died, and he looked extremely savage, but it was not difficult to recognize between his eyebrows that he had been missing for many days. Zhang Chunyang.

After Chu Tianying took pictures of the corpse, together with Tang Xiaotang, they moved Zhang Chunyang's body out of the freezer and put it on a morgue car covered with plastic sheets, because the freezing time was too long. , the body was very stiff, and there was still crackling sound like ice balls pressed when he was put down.

During this process, they found a black iPhone 8 that was under the corpse. Chu Tianying put the mobile phone in the evidence bag, and then used a pair of tweezers to slowly take out the contents of Zhang Chunyang's pocket, keys, wallet, etc. They were also bagged separately, and when they wanted to do further inspection, they found that his clothes and meat were stuck together. Chu Tianying and Tang Xiaotang discussed and agreed that the corpse should be sent to the medical examination center as soon as possible before thawing, so as not to change the corpse and affect the autopsy results. They greet Lin Fengchong and got permission, and the corpse was placed in a special body bag with an aluminum film layer, carried to the forensic inspection vehicle and taken away.

At this time, Chai Yongjin had already completed the transcript for Li Shiduo, the director of Kind Hospital, who came in a hurry. Li Shiduo said that they had a very close cooperative relationship with Tongyou Nursing Home, and he himself had some personal friends with Xing Qisheng. At about 8:30 p.m. on the night of the Deratization Hill station case, he received a call from Xing Qisheng, only to say that an acquaintance had suffered a myocardial infarction and needed to be sent to the mortuary first, and then asked him to issue a death certificate, without mentioning that the deceased was Zhang Chunyang. He then greeted the mortuary. Because of the night rounds that night, he quickly put the matter behind him, and it was not until later that he learned of Xing Qisheng's death.

"Why didn't you tell the police about such a big thing earlier?" Chai Yongjin was very annoyed.

"Because I don't think this matter has anything to do with the Deratization Hill station case." Li Shiduo smiled politely.

The duty officers of the two morgues who were questioned by the police together heard this conversation and looked at Chai Yongjin with a mocking expression on their faces.

Lin Fengchong stepped forward and looked at Li Shiduo, and said unhurriedly, "According to the relevant regulations of the Ministry of Public Security, the Ministry of Health and the Ministry of Civil Affairs, only who died during the diagnosis and treatment of the unit can be issued a "Death Certificate" to the deceased by the hospital. For those who died outside the hospital, when the cause of death is unknown or in doubt, the determination and certificate of death must be issued by the judicial department-I want to ask who gave you the power and courage to let you agree to give it to a deceased person a death certificate? "

Li Shiduo never thought of that this plain-looking police officer with a moustache could memorize the rules so well that he was speechless.

"Also, forgive me for a random guess," Lin Fengchong stared into his eyes and said, "Xing Qisheng really wanted to issue a death certificate, and he didn't necessarily need you or another doctor to come to the autopsy in person. Perhaps you gave him a blank death certificate, which had been put on the big seal of the hospital, and let him fill in it himself, right?"

Just as Li Shiduo wanted to defend himself, Lin Fengchong chased after him, "If you dare to say no, I will check all the death certificates issued by your hospital this year, in black and white, I don't even need to check whether the signed doctor was present during the autopsy. Just checking your handwriting can completely remove the cover of your turtle, do you believe it?!"

A flattering smile appeared on Li Shiduo's face, so Lin Fengchong waved his hand to let him go, then turned his head and stared at the two workers on duty in the morgue. When the two of them saw the dean, they were all cowardly, and they both exchanged a well-behaved smile. Lin Fengchong pointed at the two of them, said "your turn" to Chai Yongjin, and then went on with other things.

This trick really worked, and the two workers quickly recounted the circumstances of the night of the Zaoshuling case as follows.

At about 8:40 that night, the two were drinking and chatting in the small courtyard outside the mortuary. Suddenly the phone in the duty room rang. After the connection, it was Li Shiduo who called, saying that Xing Qisheng would bring the body of a sudden death patient later. It would come here and be stored in the morgue first. The two of them quickly pushed a corpse car to guard the door. Not long after, Xing Qisheng drove in. The car was parked at the door. The corpse was covered with a white cloth-although they didn't know Zhang Chunyang, they were sure that the man who were pushed into the morgue was the man the police found from "TE-3".

After that, Xing Qisheng drove away. Before leaving, he signed the registration book, saying that the body should be placed in the morgue first, and then he would "get" the death certificate and hand it over to them before handing over the body to store in freezer.

Chai Yongjin found Xing Qisheng's handwriting on the register. He scribbled the name of "Zhang Chunyang" in the column of the deceased's name, the cause of death was "myocardial infarction", and then signed his name and time.

"And then?" Chai Yongjin asked.

"Then our brothers continued to drink, and that night, the bodies that died in the hospital were brought in one after another. The family members came in and out of crying sacrifices, burning paper, and those who wanted to see the deceased for the last time. We were being busy. At eleven o'clock, we entered the duty room, locked the door from the inside and fell asleep, and didn't open the door until nine o'clock the next morning."

"After this door is locked from the inside, can it be opened from the outside?"

"No."

"Did anyone knock on the door or enter the morgue that night?"

"None."

"So when did you put Zhang Chunyang's body in the freezer of 'T-E-3'?"

"It was cold that night, and we both drank a little too much, maybe because we thought that Zhang Chunyang's body couldn't be left like this forever, and Xing Qisheng never came back, so when storing other bodies, we took Zhang Chunyang's body in the freezer by the way."

Chai Yongjin felt that this answer was too vague, and frowned.

"By the way, our freezer has a built-in switch record, which can be checked from the LCD screen." When speaking, a worker ran to the "TE-3" freezer for a while, and then pointed to the time displayed on the LCD screen. He said to Chai Yongjin, "Look, it shows that this freezer was only opened once at 10:50 that night, and then you opened it just now-so it must have been the dead body in the morgue before we closed the door that night. It was carried into the freezer during 'clearing'!"

Chai Yongjin bent down and looked at the LCD screen, and muttered, "Is the recording reliable? And there won't be any mistakes, right? "

"Don't worry, it cannot be wrong!" The worker patted his chest and assured.

Chai Yongjin was still worried, "If there is a sudden power outage at night, wouldn't it only be possible to keep a record of the switches when the power is on?"

The worker took him out of the mortuary to the door of a low red brick house next to him. He pushed the door open. There was a humming dark green generator on the moss-covered ground. A rusted Schneider distribution box. The worker told him, "The power supply of the mortuary is not in the same line as the hospital. It uses this generator to generate electricity. It has nothing to do with us. The electric switch in our mortuary has been pulled, and people still keep the clock as usual!"

3

The discovery of Zhang Chunyang's body not only failed to make progress and breakthroughs in the detection of the Deratization Hill station case, but instead led to a further divergence in the direction of criminal investigation by the special investigation team. Chai Yongjin and others believe that Zhang Chunyang's death was just an ordinary "sudden coital death" (excessive excitement during sexual intercourse caused acute myocardial infarction and sudden death), and had no direct relationship with the subsequent murder of Xing Qisheng and those children, so there is no need to go into details. It was still necessary to unswervingly search for evidence of Zhou Liping's crime. However, Lin Fengchong's faction maintains that Zhang Chunyang's death was by no means an isolated emergency, and was likely to be the fuse or at least an important component of the Deratization Hill station case. Therefore, the investigation work should be moved forward, and it was suggested that the Economic Investigation Department of the City Bureau intervene immediately and conduct a comprehensive investigation into whether the Kind Charity Fund had economic crimes. When Du Jianping made the ruling, Du Jianping, who had been silent all the time, said something unexpected to Lin Fengchong-At present, they should focus on finding Zhou Liping's criminal evidence. Because it was not appropriate to rashly shift the direction of investigation and expand the scope of investigation at this time...

After the meeting, Chai Yongjin and others left the conference room. Lin Fengchong turned his puzzled eyes at Du Jianping, but found that Du Jianping was standing in front of the floor-to-ceiling window with his back to him. Outside the window stood a big tree with all its leaves withered.

Lin Fengchong exited the conference room and closed the door.

Not long after, there was a rush of footsteps outside the door, and then the door was pushed open. Someone walked in, closed the door and said, "Director Du, you really disappointed me!"

Du Jianping turned around and met Liu Simiao's two serious eyes.

"You are afraid that people will say that you are avenging private revenge for Du Ying's dead father, so you clearly know that there is a problem with the Kind Charity Fund, and you dare not support them, right?!"

"Si Miao, Si Miao..." Du Jianping's red face like a blacksmith was now extremely pale. His lips were trembling, and he begged her not to continue.

Seeing him like this, Liu Simiao only felt annoyed and pitiful, "Since when did you become so timid, cowardly, cautious and conservative! You don't even dare to face your daughter's death, don't you? Dare to investigate and avenge her? As a real father?!"

Du Jianping sat on the chair, hugged his huge head, and slowly folded his fingers through his short gray hair, like using an iron plow to open the frosted ground.

Liu Simiao couldn't bear to say any more. The empty conference room was dead silent, and the ticking of the quartz wall clock on the wall sounded extraordinarily clear.

The door was pushed open again, and Lin Fengchong walked in with a solemn expression. He looked at Du Jianping and then at Liu Simiao, wondering if he should report to Du Jianping in front of Liu Simiao.

"Go ahead!" Liu Simiao ordered.

"Yes!" Lin Fengchong said quickly, "Province A's Public Security Department just called, and found out that a few years ago, a child molestation case was suspected to be related to Xing Qisheng. "

Du Jianping suddenly raised his head.

Lin Fengchong said in detail, "Xing Qisheng was still working as the chief physician of the Department of Dermatology in Kind Hospital at that time. When he returned to the province to participate in the activities of the Association, he was in charge of a physical examination activity for children in the provincial welfare institute. This physical examination was only carried out internally, but the Kind Charity Fund had just annexed or corrupted all other private welfare institutions in the province. Therefore, public opinion questioned a lot. In order to establish an image, they invited a group of reporters to do positive publicity. Unexpectedly, at the end, a reporter from a provincial newspaper didn't leave and hid in the bathroom, and secretly he captured a video of Xing Qisheng taking a girl with cerebral palsy to the bathroom to molest and even rape..."

"And?"

"Later, the reporter returned to the newspaper and asked his leader to capture key scenes from the video to publish in the newspaper, but was suppressed by the editor-in-chief. The reporter planned to go to the Public Security Bureau and called the police. He didn't take the video with him in case of accidents. So when the police went to the institution to call Xing Qisheng, the reporter was on his way home to get the video, yet he was then hit by an unlicensed car on the road. The police couldn't find the video on him or at home, so they had to release Xing Qisheng." Lin Fengchong paused a while, "I think, this is probably the reason why Xing Qisheng later left the Kind Hospital for the Tongyou Nursing Home to be the director of the Kind Charity Fund. Although it did not cause a big problem, this family scandal must be dealt with internally in order to prevent him from committing similar scandals again. After all, the Kind Hospital is an important subordinate institution to the Fund, while the Nursing Home is just a peripheral institution that can be cut off at any time."

"This time, I'm afraid that we have to investigate the Fund." Liu Simiao stared at Du Jianping and said, "Even the way of silence is exactly the same as Yue Shao's death."

Du Jianping shook his head slowly, "Liu Chu, you have quit the special investigation team, I welcome you to continue to provide criminal technical support or suggestions, but as for the specific case handling methods and procedures need to toe the line, so you should not express your opinion."

Liu Simiao was stunned. Lin Fengchong didn't expect Du Jianping to say such a decisive word. For a moment, he felt that the air in the conference room was frozen.

Liu Simiao turned around and walked out of the conference room.

Hearing her footsteps drifting away in the empty corridor, Lin Fengchong couldn't help but say to Du Jianping, "Director Du and Director Liu is kind for you..."

"The situation here is very complicated..." Du Jianping looked at the door and said, "Don't detect Kind Charity Fund easily, but Zhang Chunyang's death, you can continue to investigate."

Lin Fengchong didn't understand it at first, but after thinking about it, he suddenly understood. Du Jianping meant that Zhang Chunyang's death could lead to the Charity Fund, but the Charity Fund could not investigate the Mouseling case. In the final analysis, the former is a criminal case into an economic crime, like boiling a frog in warm water. Tao Bing, Xing Qixian and others believe that they have nothing to do with the Deratization Hill station case. The initiative has always been firmly in the hands of the special investigation team. If the Economic Investigation Division is rashly brought in, it will alarm bells for the Kind Charity Fund to destroy all evidence, and it is very likely that the criminal case will not even be investigated in the end.

Lin Fengchong nodded and said, "Deputy Director Wang of the Provincial Department of A Province said that he is going to come to see you right away. He helped a lot with Xiaoying, so..."

Lin Fengchong couldn't go on, because he found that Du Jianping's face was filled with extreme sorrow when he mentioned Du Ying's death.

After a long time, Du Jianping took a deep breath. Instead of answering Lin Fengchong's words, he asked, "How is Xiao Guo?"

"Xiao Guo's is fine, just with a few bruises, but she has been greatly stimulated mentally, but thanks to her 'breaking' into the Charity Fund, she learned about important leads."

Lin Fengchong said in a low voice, "According to Tao Bing, Cui Yucui, the vice president of Tongyou Nursing Institute, seems to know the truth of Xing Qisheng's death."

"Check!" Du Jianping said a word.

Lin Fengchong said "um" and asked again, "Is the death of the private teacher surnamed Yue investigated as a hit-and-run traffic accident, or will it be included in the investigation of the Deratization Hill station case?"

"Let's check according to the hit-and-run accident first..." Du Jianping closed his eyes, his face full of exhaustion, and after opening his eyes, he told Lin Fengchong, "Call Xiao Guo later and give my regards, if there is nothing in the afternoon , you go and see her."

After walking out of the conference room, Lin Fengchong called Guo Xiaofen. The phone rang for a long time and no one answered. When he was about to hang up, he was suddenly connected, and there was a sound of "Hello" from Xiao Guo.

The voice was a little weak, and Lin Fengchong became worried, "Xiao Guo, are you alright?"

"Not bad."

"Boss Du asked me to call you to say hello...Are you at home? I'll visit you in the afternoon."

"No, I'm outside."

"Why don't you take a good rest at home? Now you have to pay attention to safety when you go out!"

"It's okay, Ma Xiaozhong is next to me."

One sentence reassured Lin Fengchong. No matter which way the monsters were, they had to shy away for Ma Xiaozhong.

Hanging up the phone, Guo Xiaofen said to the girl opposite, "Go on and talk about Dong Yue's situation."

With the help of Mr. Luo, an agent of "Perfect Real Estate", Ma Xiaozhong found the personal information of the woman who rented a house with the long-haired girl. Her name is Liu Yan. In the past, she and the long-haired girl used to sit on the stage at the Golden Night Mantang nightclub. Now they live in Building 9 of Dingfuli Community. When Guo Xiaofen heard the news, she refused to follow the doctor's order to "continue to recuperate at home", but followed Ma Xiaozhong to the door.

The moment Liu Yan opened the door, she looked at Guo Xiaofen and Ma Xiaozhong with suspicious eyes. Guo Xiaofen explained their intention, but she still put her hands in the pocket of her light pink Pajamas. Her shoulders were tilted, and she didn't mean to let them in, "I know who you are looking for. Dong Yue, she has long been out of the city, and I don't know what she is doing now..."

Ma Xiaozhong pushed her away, walked into the room with straight eyebrows, opened the doors one by one to find. Liu Yan has been in this industry for a long time, and she is the best at looking at people. Although she hummed "What are you doing? What are you doing?", her arrogance was much shorter than at the beginning.

This house is a one-bedroom. The walls of the kitchen were covered with yellow oil stains, but the stove and range hood were covered with a thick layer of dust. Obviously, Liu Yan lived here and never cooked. The restroom was equally filthy, but the vanity mirror was polished. There were four large cardboard boxes on the floor of the bedroom, which have not been sealed with tape. It could be inferred that the clothes and cosmetics were mainly inside, ready to pack.

"Are you leaving?" Ma asked Liu Yan with a smile.

Liu Yan nodded.

"Where to?"

"Go back to my hometown..." Liu Yan's expression was a little sad, "The sisters almost went away, and I am the only one who has been relying on it, and now I can't do it anymore. The renter needs to check the work permit and personal records, and I will stay with you. After the end, the neighborhood committee notified the landlord to let me go..."

"Is the rent refunded to you?" Guo Xiaofen asked.

A miserable smile appeared on Liu Yan's pale face, "I paid the rent for one year and only lived here for three months. I asked the landlord to refund my rent, but he said he didn't drive me away, and he didn't even pay a cent. He is a local native, I can't offend..."

Guo Xiaofen fell silent, and at this moment, the phone rang. She was very worried and searched in the bag for a long time before she found it. After talking with Lin Fengchong, she continued to ask Liu Yan to provide Dong Yue's information.

Liu Yan, seeing they had no ill will towards her, relaxed a little, and sat down on the bed, "Dong Yue and I used to work in Jinye Mantang night-club, she was so timid that she didn't dare to scream or make trouble when the guests molest her, so she suffered a lot. I took pity on her and took care of her as much as I could. She was not familiar with me at first and never told me about her family. Then she quietly told me that both her parents were died of disease, and she only had a sister who suffered from mild cerebral palsy and was admitted to a welfare institution in their province. One of the conditions for the welfare institution to adopt a disabled child was that the child must be an orphan, so she didn't dare to go home for many years. The villagers over there thought she was dead, and she was very afraid of being caught and sent home for her job... She thought about changing her career, but she didn't have a high degree of education. There needs no technology, not to mention that many industries are in recession now..."

Liu Yan paused for a while, then continued, "At that time, several of our girls were renting a three-bedroom apartment, and a few days Dong Yue suddenly disappeared. When calling her, the phone was either turned off or no one answered. When she was to be expelled, she suddenly came back, dumbfounded, and her face was gone. I asked her what happened, and she said after a long time, that someone from her hometown working here saw her and told others that she was still alive when coming home. Then an orphanage contacted her and asked her to pick up her sister. She hurried back home and met the person who contacted her. That guy declared himself to be the brother of the vice president of the Charity Fund. She begged repeatedly, and the surnamed Xing agreed to keep her sister, but she had to transfer 5,000 yuan to his account every month. She must also continue to conceal her identity, and cannot visit her sister casually, or she can be kicked out of the orphanage at any time."

Guo Xiaofen and Ma Xiaozhong looked at each other, and they knew that the "surnamed Xing" that Liu Yan was talking about should be Xing Qisheng.

"I told Dong that it is not easy for us to make money now that the eradication of pornography is so strict. She can't even pay the rent and meals, let alone to give him 5,000 yuan a month. How can she get so much money? But Dong just asked me not to tell the company about this...The lady in the nightclub made money from her face, so she had to pay attention to maintenance and had to rest during the day, but from that day on, in addition to working in the company at night, she also worked during the day and signed up as a food delivery guy working in a farther area. She was not in good health, but she still worked day and night. Several of our sisters are worried that she would not be able to survive for long. Who knows that she survived...Moreover, she has found someone she likes. "

Intuitively, Guo Xiaofen felt that Liu Yan might be talking about Zhou Liping, "Is it a Zhou?"

Liu Yan thought for a while, "It seems so."

Guo Xiaofen took out her mobile phone, found Zhou Liping's photo, and showed it to Liu Yan, "Is it this person?"

"I've only seen him once..." Liu Yan muttered while looking at the photo, "Yes, it's him."

"How did they meet?"

"Dong heard that the Provincial Welfare Institute would bring a group of well-treated children to the Kind Hospital in this city every year, so She paid attention. Although her sister has not been cured, she is very good-looking and may be selected for a 'show'. At this time last year, she took a few days off from the company and sneaked to the door of a nursing home in the city, thinking that if her sister could come, she would take a look at her. She was stupid and honest. She hid behind the bushes opposite the nursing home, but was found by a driver who worked in the foundation.

When asked why she was doing it, she was afraid of being known by the surname Xing, so she cried and dared not say it. After repeated questions, she told him the intention. As a result, the driver not only did not tell Xing Qisheng, but also brought her sister out of the nursing home and reunited the two sisters who had not seen each other for many years. Dong was so happy. Since then, Dong was very grateful to the driver and thought him a good person."

"How did Dong judge the driver surnamed Zhou?"

"She didn't like to talk about her private affairs very much. She only said a few words when she was very happy. According to her, the surnamed Zhou is a very decent person."

"A very decent person?"

"Well, Dong likes him very much, but he has never said anything. Once Dong thought he was disgusting his job and identity, and cried, he said that he had a criminal record and was afraid of involving her..."

"So, does the surnamed Zhou like Dong?"

"You're so stupid." Liu Yan gave Guo Xiaofen a blank look, "He said 'fear of being implicated', not 'don't want her to be implicated'."

Guo Xiaofen was a little embarrassed, "What happened later?"

"Later, Dong still took the initiative to find him, but after the tenant inspection this year, Dong left here. I don't know if the two have contacted again..."

"It turns out that the tenant inspection, you also..." Xiao Guo was half-way through. Realizing that Ma Xiaozhong was beside him, she hesitated.

Liu Yan didn't seem to notice anything, "Actually, Dong has been working very hard in this city for the past few years, making it more and more difficult to earn money. Every day, she was afraid of being sent home. Yes, she was so frightened that she couldn't sleep all night, so as soon as the tenant inspection came to the door, she would leave and leave the city completely. Our sisters all knew that they would not stay long, but we all felt that Dong had gone too quickly. I was in a hurry, but no one could keep her. Before she left, she asked me to accompany her to a nursing home to find her sister secretly and said goodbye to her. Her sister is very pretty, but she has a blank expression. Silly, in the cold winter and twelfth lunar month, with her coat open and her nose running, Dong squatted down and fastened the bottom button for her sister, exhorting "Girls are most afraid of freezing, so every button on the clothes must be fastened. It's tight; the calf can't be frozen, remember..."Then she watched her sister walk back to the small building of the nursing home, and after a long time, she left with red eyes."

"Then she left the city? Didn't she say goodbye to the surname Zhou?"

"No, I asked her if she should tell Zhou, and she said no, and left with the suitcase. I remember it was a very cold day—"

"Yeah, on a very cold day, the wind was strong in the first half of the night, and there was light snow in the second half of the night..." Guo Xiaofen muttered as if recalling something.

Liu Yan looked at her in surprise.

"Go on."

"I took her downstairs and stood in the cold wind, watching her get into a taxi to the train station, my heart trembled with discomfort. Back in the rental house, we friends didn't say anything and started packing our own things. Things, not long after, the door was pushed open, and a very strong man came in, his chin protruded like a shovel. I asked him who he was looking for, and he said he was looking for Dong , and I immediately guessed who he was. When I asked him what he was looking for with Dong , he said that he heard that he was doing a tenant inspection. He came to see if Dong was okay and asked Dong to live with him. I told him that Dong had just left, and he was stunned. When he asked where she went, I said I didn't know, but I only knew that she had left the city. He stood there for a long time, and then asked which bed belonged to Dong, so I pointed it to him. Dong walked in a hurry, the bedding sheets did not be taken away. They were still spread on the bed, and the surnamed Zhou was sitting on the bed, without saying a word like a stone. After a long time, he stood up and found that the sheets were wrinkled. He turned around, bent down and smoothed the wrinkled area a little, and then walked out of the room. "

——After a long time, he stood up and found that the sheets were wrinkled. He turned around, bent down and smoothed the wrinkled area a little, and then walked out of the room...

Guo Xiaofen has written so many manuscripts, but she found that there was nothing more mournful than the words that came out of the lady's mouth.

"I think you may have Dong 's contact information and address..." Guo Xiaofen said slowly, "I want to find her and learn about Zhou Liping in person."

"But, it's been so long, and I don't know if the two are still in touch..."

When she explained her intention before entering the door, Guo Xiaofen didn't say anything about the relationship between looking for Dong Yue and the Deratization Hill station case, because she was afraid of leaking the news, and seeing Liu Yan's appearance, she was too busy to take care of herself, and I was afraid she didn't care about Deratization Hill station case, so for a while I don't know how to convince Liu Yan.

At this moment, Ma Xiaozhong, who had been standing against the wall without speaking, suddenly spoke up, "Liu Yan, do you know who I am?"

Liu Yan nodded slowly.

"We're investigating a case, and we need to ask Dong Yue to check some of Zhou Liping's information. Just that." Ma Xiaozhong said, "Maybe Dong Yue and Zhou have really broken up, but maybe they still think about each other-This is just the case with many couples who break up, but they still can't forget it when they meet-Why not give them a chance to reconnect and choose again?"

This sentence made Liu Yan and Guo Xiaofen stunned at the same time, probably not expecting that this iron-looking guy could say such a deep understanding of the love between men and women.

"Okay..." Liu Yan was moved by Ma Xiaozhong's words, and gave them Dong Yue's cell phone number, "She is still the same; rarely answers calls, rarely returns text messages, and has WeChat accounts but never shows moments. Last time when I contacted her, she said that she had returned to province A, but not the town where she was born, but another place (saying, she wrote the address on a note and handed it to Guo Xiaofen). I think you should just go there directly, or even if you get in touch with her by phone, I guess she will refuse to see you in all likelihood."

"Thank you very much!" Guo Xiaofen folded her hands and bowed to her, then said goodbye and left together with Ma Xiaozhong.

It was almost noon. The sky was sunless. The wind was cold. The thick cloud of lead above the head seemed to flow like a glacier. The bare treetops shrieked sharply, and the exposed skin was aching like being beaten by a whip.

The two of them walked towards the parking lot. Guo Xiaofen lowered his head and said nothing. Ma smiled and asked with concern, "What's wrong? Is the injury on your body hurting again?"

"It's nothing..." Guo Xiaofen's expression was indifferent, "I'm just thinking, if they all left, who else would stay in this city?"

Ma smiled and said, "Don't think too much. In such a big city with such a large population, the tenant inspection is also to prevent vicious crimes and maintain social stability."

"I understand the investigation and support the investigation. I just want to ask one question- why hasn't one of the parasites in the building full of Hefeng Hotel been investigated?!" Guo Xiaofen suddenly became excited as she spoke. "Maybe you look down on Liu Yan and Dong Yue, but they are at least selling all the value they have to support themselves. And what about Xing Qixian and Tao Zhuoyao? What are they working for? Why aren't they cleared out?!"

Tears glistened in her eyes.

Ma smiled and shrank his neck, looking like was reprimanded by his girlfriend and didn't dare to talk back. He probably felt that he couldn't let go of his anger, so he took out his mobile phone and made a call. "Geng, there is a landlord in the No. 9 building of Dingfuli Community who has charged a girl for 12 months' rent, and the girl was leaving after three months. The hooligan would not refund the rent. Isn't it your business? Who is the girl? Your sister-in-law and their relatives! You must resolve out for me, or you never contact me again!"

Ma Xiaozhong hung up the phone and looked at Guo Xiaofen with a complaisant smile.

Guo Xiaofen ignored him, strode forward, took a few steps and turned around, seeing the horse grinning and stomping on the ground, frowning, "Are you going?"

"Let's go!" Ma laughed and quickly chased after him.

4

When Sun Jinghua walked into the reception room, Li Zhiyong and Huyan Yun both felt that she was more like an official than a manager.

She was of medium height, dressed in a light gray but well-textured work attire, with short ear-length hair, a dark and flat face with a few faint freckles, and a serious expression. Her every move is as rigid as clockwork. When she was seated opposite Li Zhiyong and Huyan Yun, they felt that she was not being received, but more like being visited.

"What are you looking for from me?" Sun Jinghua's tone was very stiff.

Huyan Yun said, "Hello Manager Sun, we want to learn something about Zhou Liping——"

"Zhou Liping?" Sun Jinghua thought for a while, "I don't remember such a person."

The way she "thought" was so dramatic that Huyan Yun immediately judged that she not only remembered Zhou Liping clearly, but was also very anxious about it recently. But he didn't want to expose it, "That's right, Zheng, from Mingyi Public Relation Company, always tells us that it was you who introduced Zhou Liping to this position and took care of him a lot..."

"I often get people jobs, and take care of them." Sun Jinghua cut in, "Wait a minute, who are you? If you want to make an appointment, I can make arrangements, otherwise, I'm very busy." As she said that, she stood up and was about to leave.

"Sit down!"

Li Zhiyong, who had been staring at Sun Jinghua, suddenly shouted!

Huyan Yun was startled, and Sun Jinghua was also stunned, not daring to move.

"I asked you to sit down, do you hear me?" Li Zhiyong nodded at the chair, "I asked you to sit here and talk, if don't, then let's talk in another place?"

Sun Jinghua swallowed and slowly sat on the chair.

"You know what are we doing, aren't you?" Li Zhiyong sneered.

Sun Jinghua nodded.

"What's the matter with you and Zhou Liping?"

"I really don't know him well..."

"Hey! Necessity extorts sober judgment. In a case as big as Deratization Hill station, how many leaders in the city do not eat or sleep to solve the case. Do you want to take a shot?"

"No, no, no!" Sun Jinghua panicked completely, "That case has nothing to do with me at all..."

"I know it has nothing to do with you, so I came to talk with you here instead of asking you to talk there." Li Zhiyong was a little impatient, "You are also a public official, so you should actively cooperate with the minimum requirements of government work. Why aren't you sensible! It's just a chance for you to clear things up. Can you seize it?"

Sun Jinghua nodded again and again, "Thank you! Thank you!"

"Yes, tell me!" Li Zhiyong said.

Sun Jinghua met Zhou Liping purely by chance.

It happened a year ago. Sun Jinghua owns a house on Dongqing Street, which was planned as rental. Who knew that the tenant had something to do at home and checked out. She was in a bad mood because of her husband cheating, so she simply moved here for a while. It just so happened that the Yanzhao Hotel had undertaken an important event. She was so busy that she had to go home every day at eleven or twelve at night.

This day, she drove back to her residence, and it was still in the middle of the night. She was about to enter the community, and found that the gate was half blocked by a car parked indiscriminately. She was driving a Porsche SUV, which was too big to get in. It was inconvenient to ask someone to move the car so late, so she drove the car forward for a while and turned into a dark alley. When she parked the car and came out, she met a group of hooligans at the entrance of the alley. .

Sun Jinghua doesn't look good, but she has a good figure. At the turn of spring and summer, for the needs of the exhibition, she wore a professional attire and a short skirt with black silk. This group of hooligans had been drinking too much, and they were about to find a woman to " relieve inflammation or internal heat" when they saw Sun Jinghua, and immediately gathered around. While blocking the way and rubbing against her, he said some random things. Sun Jinghua had never encountered such a thing. At first, she scolded them with justice and righteousness, but when she found that the positive air pressure could not overwhelm them, she panicked completely and tried to get away, but there was no way to escape. Being torn by the hooligans and pushed into the alley, she shouted desperately, but found that the few lights in the surrounding residential buildings were quickly extinguished, and she knew that she was doomed.

Just when she was pushed on the front cover of the car by the head of a hooligan who took off her short skirt, a sudden shout came from the alley, "What are you doing?!"

The sound was not loud, but it is like a sudden rubber hammer in the dark, dull and ruthless.

A few hooligans pulled out switchblade knives and swing sticks, and walked towards the alley cursingly, trying to drive away the man standing in the dark, but they were stunned when they got closer, and no one made a sound. A hooligan ran back to the alley, and the hooligan leader held down Sun Jinghua's torn hand and said to him, "Who the hell dares to do something bad for me? I'll kill you!"

"Boss, it's the one surnamed Zhou..."

"Which one is Zhou?"

"The one who killed a lot of people..."

Sun Jinghua felt that the rogue's hand instantly softened.

"Zhou Liping?" the hooligan asked.

"Well, it's him... We have a lot of people, should we fuck him?"

"Fuck you! That's a real murderer!" The hooligan scolded, "It's okay to brag, let alone murder, do you really dare to kill a chicken?!" He rubbed Sun Jinghua's butt, "Today you are lucky, you old lady!" Then he walked out of the alley with those hooligans, without saying a word.

Sun Jinghua slowly slid down the car cover and sat on the ground for a while, breathing for a while, she wanted to cry. However, she felt that he was lucky enough to survive the disaster. When she stood up and walked out of the alley, she saw someone standing against the wall. "In the dark, I can only see that the lines of his face are very hard, and his chin is bulging forward like a shovel, which looks particularly fierce."

Sun Jinghua was still in shock, and vaguely remembered that the rogue boss said "that's a real murderer", so she was afraid that she had just left the wolf's den and entered the tiger's mouth, with her back against the wall at the entrance of the alley, not daring to move, trembling. There was a slight rustling sound from her calf...The time was actually very short, less than ten seconds, but she recalled it longer than the first half of her life.

Then Zhou Liping turned around and left.

It was not until his back completely disappeared into the night that Sun Jinghua fled home with tears on her face.

The next day, she did not dare to call the police for fear of revenge from hooligans, so she only changed her clothes to look like a political cadre before she dared to go to work. Early in the morning at the crossroads, she recognized Zhou Liping based on the memory of the facial lines-in fact, she didn't really see his appearance until then-small eyes, protruding chin, pitted face, and the two tightly closed thick lips have a brutish taste of extreme restraint. But they appear more aggressive, maybe because he wears a little red hood, an orange-yellow vest, and a little red flag in his hand. It looked "funny".

For some unknown reason, Sun Jinghua suddenly became curious about the person who saved her. After she was busy with the exhibition, she took time to go to the neighborhood committee to inquire about Zhou Liping's situation. Everyone has different opinions. Some say that he is the real culprit of the "Western Suburb Serial Homicide" many years ago, while others point out that the police only believe that he is related to one murder case...But, for Sun Jinghua, killing one and killing a few people are just as cruel and terrifying, but she always feels that she owes Zhou Liping, and her work just determines that she has to accept and repay all kinds of private favors, and make sure that she never owes debts, so when Zheng Gui invited her to a dinner and inadvertently said that he planned to hire a driver, she recommended Zhou Liping.

After Zhou Liping learned of her recommendation, he expressed his gratitude, but his expression was cold, which was exactly what Sun Jinghua wanted. Anyway, she was just repaying the favour to such a complex person.

"It's really that simple." Sun Jinghua said to Li Zhiyong and Huyan Yun, "After Zhou Liping went to work at Zheng Gui's place, I quickly rented out the house on Dongqing Street, and rarely went there again. Zheng Gui found me occasionally. I was scheduled to hold an event in the exhibition hall, and I met Zhou Liping a few times, but it was just a nod. I don't have any personal relationship with Zhou Liping. You have to believe me. "

"When was the last time you saw Zhou Liping before the Shaoxing case?" Li Zhiyong asked.

Sun Jinghua thought—truely—about it for a whileand said, "It should have been a month or two before the incident, when Zheng Guilai was booking the launch of the new product of Jianyi Health Products Company, he brought Zhou with him. "

Li Zhiyong glanced at Huyan Yun, meaning that he himself have finished asking and do he have anything else to ask?

Huyan Yun leaned forward and asked Sun Jinghua, "Manager Sun, if you were asked to give Zhou Liping a one-word or one-word evaluation, you could only use one, which would you use?"

Sun Jinghua was stunned for a moment, then said slowly, "I think he's a bit ' stubborn '."

"Stubborn?"

"Well, not flexible, and dogged."

"How can you see it?"

"Once, the Kind Charity Fund held a meeting at the Yanzhao Hotel, and used a Jinbei car (a minivan) to pull a carload of children from the nursing home to perform at the venue.

It was raining heavily, and the Jinbei car went to do other things. The children were left alone, standing in the corner of the hall, staring outside in a daze. Originally, some children suffered from cerebral palsy or something, and no one took off the makeup on their faces. They looked ugly and made many people laugh. My own car was in the parking lot outside, and I couldn't borrow an umbrella for a while. I was about to rub someone's car to the parking lot when I saw Zheng Gui's Audi A6 approaching and parked at the door. Zhou Liping jumped out of the car and stuffed the children into the car. Seven or eight children were all stuffed in, and then he got into the driver's seat and was ready to drive away. I went up and opened the door of the co-pilot-there were two children there-and asked him if he could give me a ride, and he waved rudely and said, 'Can't you see the crowd? I'll take them to the nursing home and then pick you up'! As soon as I closed the door, he sped away the car. "Sun Jinghua said, "You know, if I had not helped him, where would he get this job? Why didn't he help me with such a small task?" Why don't you understand the world at all? I was sulking, Zheng Gui came over from behind to comfort me and said that he was the same. He originally asked Zhou Liping to drive to pick him up, but he phoned him that he needed to send the children back to the nursing home first, leaving him stuck here...After all, I'm Zhou Liping's recommender. What else can I say? I can only accompany him with a wry smile...Aren't he a bit 'stubborn'? "

When he came out of the Yanzhao Hotel, Li Zhiyong seemed to be very preoccupied. The subway was standing in the west, but he was sullen and headed east. Huyan Yun didn't know where he was going, so he followed behind inexplicably until they came to a busy intersection. Only then did Li Zhiyong realize that he had gone the wrong way, and for a while, his brows and eyes crowded into a ball on his face like a brown bear.

Huyan Yun knew that he had something on his mind and guessed what he was worried about, but he remained silent.

Standing at the crossroads, looking at the bustling crowd and the passing traffic, Li Zhiyong rubbed his nose and muttered to himself, "This Zhou Liping...is he a good guy or a bad guy?"

Then he turned his attention to Huyan Yun. It seemed that this question was too difficult, and he wanted to ask the invigilator to give a standard answer.

Huyan Yun sighed softly, "I don't know much about the case ten years ago... Later, I asked Lin Xiangming, and he always avoided the topic. I think he knew the truth of the matter, but just came out. Why must it be kept a secret-haven't you asked Lin Xiangming directly about this?"

Li Zhiyong just remembered something, "I remember Xiangming said with great certainty that 'Zhou Liping is not a bad person'. He just took a fork in the road and did bad things, and he also said, 'Life is a journey of stumbling and stumbling in the dark. Some people goes astray because of coincidence, some because of helplessness, and some deliberately because of strange motives. The road is not necessarily the wrong way, and the person who does the wrong thing is not necessarily a bad person'... making me more confused."

Huyan Yun pondered on these words for a long time, and also felt puzzled, so he simply didn't think about it, pulled Li Zhiyong to turn around and walked to the subway station, and said as he walked, "You suddenly yelled at Sun Jinghua just now, but I didn't expect it to work."

"Uh, these people are deluding and scaring themselves and others. If they really get into our bureau, they'll be like what Jiang Kun said in the comic, 'Can you make it clear when you are in?', it's fine. The leader also thinks that you have committed a crime, which will definitely affect your future, so as soon as I speak in the tone of a police officer, she immediately cowards."

Huyan Yun smiled, "Don't you often run various activities with Zheng Gui? WhySun Jinghua seems never see you before?"

Li Zhiyong shook his head, "Old Zheng is very shrewd. He has been in public relations for so many years, and all he eats is a bowl of relationship, and he is most afraid that his subordinates will meet with his own clients-which is needed for a certain type of activity that have relationships in all directions-then establish relationships by themselves, and then open a company to grab his customers at a low price against him. Therefore, all businesses that can be run are run by himself, even if he need to bring someone when he meet customers, he only bring those who have direct links at one time. So I have never seen Sun Jinghua, otherwise I would be a goof today. "

Huyan Yun said with a smile, "I think your experience in political system and other circumstances all these years makes you wiser. It's amazing!"

Li Zhiyong smiled bitterly, "I'm compelled helpless, if it wasn't for my gun being...robbed, I wouldn't be so addicted that I could only pretend to be a police officer."

"Actually, I'm also very curious." Huyan Yun said casually and seemingly. "You seem to be able to deal with Sun Jinghua with ease. Why were you messed up by an ordinary staff member at the social security center that day?"

As turning back and passing through the gate of Yanzhao Hotel, Li Zhiyong took a deep breath and pointed to the hotel, "That's because I am not a local, and I have a 'hostage' in the social security center."

"Hostage?" Huyan Yun was taken aback.

"My mother's social security needs to be handled by that guy..."

5

In the subway, Huyan Yun received a call from Ma Xiaozhong, saying that he was walking to his house with Guo Xiaofen, hoping to "touch the situation" with him, and "Lin Fengchong and Tianying are coming too". Huyan Yun and Li Zhiyong hurriedly accelerated their pace. The transfer station was always running up and down. When they got downstairs, they bumped into Guo and Ma.

"Guo, are you okay?" Huyan Yun asked Guo Xiaofen. He didn't say it directly, but everyone understood that he was asking about the danger and tragedy last night.

Guo Xiaofen's reaction was a little slow and her beautiful big eyes were dull, and it took a long time before she whispered, "It's okay."

Ma Xiaozhong pointed to his head from behind, implying that Huyan Yun. This girl was quite frightened.

Huyan Yun's expression suddenly became sad.

After entering the room, Huyan Yun first explained the investigation of Sun Jinghua with Li Zhiyong. He spoke slowly, looking into Guo Xiaofen's eyes the whole time, as if he was talking to her alone, but Guo Xiaofen was still dumbfounded. It was as if he had never woken up from a hazy dream. When he finished, it was Guo Xiaofen's turn to talk about how she and Ma Xiaozhong were investigating Liu Yan together. She couldn't remember Liu Yan's name at first, Ma Xiaozhong took the topic decisively and told it again, Huyan Yun didn't have the heart to listen, just stared at Guo Xiaofen worriedly. In contrast, Li Zhiyong was very focused and listened very carefully. When he heard that Dong used the word "decency" to evaluate Zhou Liping, he did not show the expression of disgust as before, and there were countless folds between his brows. It was as painful and dazed as wringing out his heart like a wet towel.

"Huyan, Zhiyong, I'm done." Ma said with a smile, "What do you two think?"

Li Zhiyong said bluntly, "Xiao Guo, are you going to find Dong Yue in province A? I want to go with you."

Huyan Yun was a little surprised, because for a long period of time— for ten years, Zhou Liping was a stereotyped and solidified "evil" in Li Zhiyong's mind. The reason behind the "evil" is neither need to explore nor worth the time and effort to explore. But what Li Zhiyong said now showed that his inner stereotype and solidification have loosened. Although he is no longer a policeman and cannot personally interrogate Zhou Liping who is in prison, he wants to try to understand Zhou Liping through other people. This showed that the recent investigation results have made Li Zhiyong suspicious of the conclusion that "Zhou Liping is the real culprit of the serial murders in western suburb serial homicide". Guo Xiaofen, who has always been smart and elf, seems overwhelmed and at lost at that time, let alone the decision of leaving for province A. Ma is responsive. He knew that Li Zhiyong had not yet engaged. He was afraid that Li Zhiyong would develop the relationship with Guo Xiaofen when taking care of her along the way, so he said decisively, "Zhiyong, you must go to province A. But look at Guo now. In this way, it is better for acquaintances to take care of her by her side. We still perform our own duties. You go with Huyan, and Guo and I go to Province A to find Dong Yue, and I will protect her."

How did Li Zhiyong know his inner thoughts? He nodded and said, "Well then."

At this moment, someone knocked on the door of the outhouse. Huyan Yun opened the door and saw that Lin Fengchong and Chu Tianying were coming together, both of them were wearing plain clothes, perhaps the autumn turned cooler, and the cold air around them actually choked Huyan, causing his sneeze.

"Are you alright?" Chu Tianying said, "The temperature has cooled recently. You are running outside all day and night, so you have to pay attention to your health."

However, Lin Fengchong didn't care about chatting with Huyan, and went straight to Guo Xiaofen and asked, "Guo, how are you? Boss Du asked me to visit you especially."

"Greetings are for nothing!" Ma Xiaozhong said with his eyes squinting, "If you have time, you can quickly catch the person who killed Yue Shao, okay?"

Lin Fengchong is kind, and he is not the type to fight with his mouth, so he stared blankly and didn't speak. Chu Tianying helped him smooth things out, "Director, you also know that Director Lin and the others have been running around day and night in order to sweep the Deratization Hill station case recently. Don't miss any clue. Now the case is getting bigger and bigger, and the manpower and material resources are obviously unable to keep up. We all know who did Yue Shao, but we really can't draw more strength to investigate. Well, after all, in such a big city, how many cases are waiting to be done every day——"

Ma interrupted him unceremoniously with a smile, "I know that the case is getting bigger and bigger, you should stop for some time to throw the trivial things aside first, and choose the most important things. You are not fishing for fish, but catching tigers. The mesh for fishing is dense enough. The bigger the net is, the more you can catch a tiger. Catching a tiger is the opposite. It is useless to run all over the mountain. The fight is to 'control' rather than 'release'! "

The relationship between Chu Tianying and Ma Xiaozhong is not ordinary. Back then, Chu Tianying was relegated to the bottom and was "distributed" to the Moon Garden police station as a policeman. Ma Xiaozhong not only took him in, but also took care of him everywhere. At first, Chu Tianying looked down on this "Director Ma" who had been working at the grassroots level for a long time. But as time went by, he discovered that when it comes to his experience in handling cases and his speculation about the people of the world, this short and fat man is far superior to himself, and he can't help but admire more and more. The two gradually became close buddies from their superiors and subordinates. Later, Chu Tianying was re-promoted and served as the chief of the crime scene investigation section of the Criminal Technical team of the City Bureau, but his respect and friendship for Ma Xiaozhong remained unchanged.

After hearing what Ma Xiaozhong said, the more he thought about it, the more reasonable it became. He moved a chair and sat down beside him, "Director, then tell me, what should be controled and what should be released?"

"I'm not in the special investigation team. I don't know the overall situation, and I don't want to talk nonsense." Ma Xiaozhong said, "After investigating for so long, there is only one conclusion. Zhou Liping, who is the most suspected of murder, may not be a bad person. But Xing Qisheng, who was killed, is a complete bastard. All the big cases in the world, you remember, the perpetrator may be a bad person, or a good person, but the 'disaster' must be a bad person. So don't spend too much energy on Zhou Liping but focused on Xing Qisheng. Investigate him from head to toe, and from the inside to the outside. To find out the truth of the Deratization Hill station case, it's more important to investigate the dead than the living. Guo was in danger narowly last night and almost died, but she also inquired and returned the most crucial information. You can't let her work in vain."

Lin Fengchong nodded, "I have reported to Boss Du. Tao Bing said inside and out, suggesting that Cui Yucui seemed to know the true story of Xing Qisheng's death..." He hesitated and said, "But now, Chai Yongjin and the others are with Director Ma. On the contrary, they believe that it is Zhou Liping that should be investigated, and they take a laissez-faire attitude towards the line of the Kind Charity Fund. However, for a while, we could not figure out what method Zhou Liping used to be able to kill people and burn their bodies at Deratization Hill station at half past ten, and then arrived at Xingyu Road at exactly eleven o'clock in just half an hour. Therefore, even Chai Yongjin and the others could not conclude that the case was done by Zhou Liping and just now—"

Huyan Yun, who had been silent for a long time, suddenly interrupted him, "Feng Chong, you misunderstood what Ma said. He asked you to focus on Xing Qisheng, not to find out the real murderer of the Deratization Hill station case, but to clean up the case. The truth of the case. Judging from the available evidence, even if I know how Zhou Liping traveled from Deratization Hill station to Xingyu Road in only half an hour, I still don't know the truth of the whole case..."

Lin Fengchong couldn't help but sighed, "Boss Du, for some unknown reason, is timid, as if he is afraid that this case will involve or implicate someone—" He suddenly noticed that Ma Xiaozhong, Chu Tianying and Li Zhiyong all had expressions on their faces. Not quite right, "What happened to you?"

"Fengchong, you have cotton stuffed in your ears?" Chu Tianying couldn't help but say loudly, "Didn't you hear what Huyan said, he knows how Zhou Liping arrived at Xingyu Road in only half an hour! "

"Ah?!" Lin Fengchong widened his eyes in surprise.

There is no doubt that in the whole investigation process of the Deratization Hill station case, "how did Zhou Liping get from Deratization Hill station to Xingyu Road in only half an hour" has always been one of the biggest mysteries. Zhou Liping has always insisted that he drove his car to the bottom of Deratization Hill station just after ten o'clock and was sent away by Xing Qisheng. Then he ran to Xingyu Road and made an appointment with Li Zhiyong...If he is the real murderer, and the time for the call to the police, which was recorded and showed that was made by Xing, was 10:30 that night, even if Xing was killed and burned immediately after that, Zhou Liping would have to leave the nursery where the tunnel's wind booth was located after 10:30. During the screening by the police, all the taxis and online car-hailing vehicles that passed through the Deratization Hill station area that night had no record of picking up customers to Xingyu Road. Since the area of the Deratization Hill station is relatively remote, black cars are rarely used. It was also found that the Mobike and other apps on Zhou Liping's mobile phone had never been used on the night of the crime...Everything negated the possibilities of him rushing from the Deratization Hill station to Xingyu Road in only half an hour, and of his murder.

Unexpectedly, the answer to this question was found by Huyan Yun, which was a headache for the special investigation team, and even deliberately avoided in the process of interrogating Zhou Liping several times later!

Although last time in front of Chai Yongjin, he pointed out the position of the black sect in one sentence, which shocked Li Zhiyong to Huyan Yun's reasoning ability, but he still couldn't believe that this baby face could reach "doublekill," which countless criminal police found nothing. "Huyan, tell me, how did Zhou Liping accomplish that 'impossible task'?"

"I admit that there are often sudden 'plots' in the process of every criminal case, which more or less affect the final direction of the whole case, such as a robber is witnessed by passer-by or a thief interrupted by victim's entering the house, etc.. But most of them are passive rather than active. The more experienced criminals, the more they like to commit crimes in an orderly manner according to the predetermined plan, and will never super-fluous." Speaking of this, Huyan Yun turned his attention to Li Zhiyong, "It's different when Zhou Liping asked you for an appointment. This was a typical 'spawning branch', so there must be a purpose. What was his purpose, I didn't know at first, but I am sure it is related to 'evidence' that can do good for him, until I saw your gray Jetta, and after Guo and Ma visited the city's No. 1 prison to get the information that Zhou Liping had studied car repair, I realized that Zhou's appointment with you is easily understood. It was you that helped him turn the 'impossibility' into a 'possibility'—"

"I...how did I help him?" Li Zhiyong was still at a loss.

"Do you still remember, when I went to your house last time, I found that the northwest of your house is the Deratization Hill station. You said that your house is very close to the Deratization Hill station. If you run faster, it will take about six or seven minutes?"

"Yes."

"What time did Zhou Liping call you on the night of the crime?"

"About ten forty..."

"Did he ask if you were at home in the first sentence?"

"Yes indeed."

"You drive to and from get off work every day?"

"Yes, except for limited days."

"I understand!" Ma smiled and his eyes suddenly lit up.

Chu Tianying slapped his thigh, "I understand too!"

"You... what do you understand?" Li Zhiyong was puzzled.

Chu Tianying bent his fingers to analyze for him, "Zhou Liping called your mobile phone at 10:40, exactly 10 minutes after 10:30, and it only took 6 or 7 minutes to run from the Deratization Hill station to your house. His call intended to make sure whether you were at home or not, and your car, don't you understand?"

Li Zhiyong suddenly woke up, "You mean... Zhou Liping hid in my car one step ahead?"

"It's the trunk to be precise." Huyan Yun said, "I've seen the trunk of your Jetta car, and there are traces of paving in it. I suspect that Zhou Liping pulled something in advance in order to avoid leaving any physical evidence. He pried and opened the trunk and put plastic cloth or something out, then lay in and close the door. When you were driving, he used his mobile phone GPS to locate the car. And when the car reached to Xingyu Road, hearing your get off, he would go out of the trunk again. He got out, threw away the plastic sheet, and ran quickly to the place you made an appointment with. In this way, in half an hour, he has completed this 'timetable trick' that leaves no trace."

After listening to this reasoning, Li Zhiyong's face not only did not have the slightest joy that he could finally take Zhou Liping down, but he was a little frustrated, "So, it was still he who did it..."

Everyone couldn't understand what he was thinking and looked at each other.

For a time, the room was extremely quiet, and at this moment, a sigh suddenly came.

Looking around, no one would have thought that it was Lin Fengchong who sighed.

"What's wrong with Fengchong?" Huyan Yun felt something was wrong.

"Huyan, I have always admired your reasoning." After speaking, Lin Fengchong gritted his molars for a long time before saying the following, "But your reasoning today...is really wrong! "

Huyan Yun was taken aback. This arrogant baby-faced person always spoke his reasoning after careful consideration, and then sat waiting for the admiring applause of the public. He never expected that someone would dare to point out that his reasoning was wrong today—and This person is still Lin Fengchong, who has always been obscure and was a supporting actor for ten thousand years on any occasion!

In a hurry, he also lost his temper, and asked in a loud voice, "Where did I go wrong?!"

"Just now I was halfway through and was interrupted by you...uh, I said 'just now', and then you criticized me for misunderstanding Ma's words..."

Huyan Yun frowned, "Okay then, 'Just now', what happened?"

"Just now—" Lin Fengchong said, "Before coming to you, the special investigation team arraigned Zhou Liping. He admitted that he concealed some very important facts, and presented an ironclad proof that it was absolutely impossible for him to be at around 10:40 p.m. getting into the trunk of Li Zhiyong's Jetta, and being carried by his car to Xingyu Road..."

Zhou Liping's face suddenly emerged in front of Huyan's eyes.

The thin, bluish, expressionless face.

No one could see what he was thinking, and he seemed to be standing opposite him, face to face, and a chaotic and cold light radiated from his triangular eyes that were muddy and cold...

He had already guessed his reasoning. He had already guessed his next move...even whole chess games.

Huyan Yun pretended to be calm, but even he could hear his own voice trembling, "What 'hard evidence' did he show?"

Lin Fengchong said slowly, "He said that he was commissioned by Xing Qisheng that night to come to the funeral home of Kind Hospital before eleven o'clock, and put Zhang Chunyang's body in the morgue into the freezer numbered 'TE-3'. "

Chapter 8

1

At Huyan Yun's strong request, and with special approval from the leaders of the Municipal Bureau, Lin Fengchong played a video of Zhou Liping's recent trial to him and his friends in "Project Two".

In this interrogation, the police did not intend to make any breakthrough, but because Tao Zhuoyao explained the death of Zhang Chunyang, although it was not found that Zhou Liping had any connection with the matter, after all, Xing Qisheng, who was in charge of transporting the corpse, was killed later. Zhou Liping has a major criminal suspicion, so he needs to do a "bond and flesh connection" – this is the jargon of the police, which means to string together several seemingly unrelated cases but may have a relationship of succession on the time axis. Although it may not be uniform, sometimes they did get some information.

Judging from the video, Zhou Liping's condition was not much different from when he was just arrested, just a little thinner. He was sitting behind the iron bar in a yellow vest, and his shaved scalp has indeed been covered with a layer of black ballast, perhaps because the major criminal suspects did not have enough time to vent, his skin looked a little pale, which added a layer of chill to his already cold expression.

As soon as the interrogator mentioned Zhang Chunyang's name, he found that Zhou Liping's expression was a bit wrong. His originally numb face trembled, and his eyes were no longer icy and straight, but dodged diagonally downward, although he recovered quickly. But it was still noticed by a keen interrogator.

This is almost the first time that the scaly, stubborn suspect has shown a "poke in the sore spot."

According to the pre-arrangement, for a suspect like Zhou Liping who has rich trial experience and refuses to cooperate, if any gap occurs, they must immediately concentrate their firepower and launch a strong attack.

Therefore, the interrogator began a tight interrogation of Zhou Liping: "Do you know Zhang Chunyang?" "When was the last time you saw Zhang Chunyang?" "As far as you know, apart from Tao Zhuoyao, who else in the Kind Charity Fund has a close relationship with Zhang Chunyang?" ... And Zhou Liping's attitude was also quite different from before, and it was no longer a stubborn confrontation. Instead, he answered every question, but his voice was low, and there were a lot of redundant words such as "um, ah, this, that", it is obvious that he is in a mess under the sudden huge pressure. His body also frequently twisted and changed positions, and the form of "no matter how you sit it's uncomfortable" can best reveal the inner tension, panic, and discomfort of the subject.

Zhou Liping has never had this phenomenon in the previous interrogations around the case. Instead, he was at a loss when it came to Zhang Chunyang. Could it be that he did not commit any criminal acts on the former, but had unspeakable acts on the latter?

The police, who had been defeated repeatedly in the confrontation with Zhou Liping recently, suddenly had high morale and kept increasing the intensity of the interrogation. After a few rounds, Zhou Liping looked exhausted. In the end, the flesh on his face twitched violently like a convulsion, releasing a helpless, wry smile, and his rigid spine leaned against the back of the interrogation chair.

"Can I make a request?" he said.

"Say it."

"I want to see President Tao."

Generally speaking, as long as a criminal suspect "said", it can be satisfied as long as it is reasonable. But now Tao Zhuoyao is in the stage of being detained and tried, there is absolutely no reason for the two suspects to face each other, so the interrogator shook his head: "We can consider other requirements, but this one is not acceptable."

Zhou Liping's face suddenly showed a look of disappointment, and he muttered something, but he didn't seem to have any plans to regret: "Okay, then I will tell the truth. After I left the Deratization Hill, I really ran to Xingyu Road to meet Li Zhiyong to fight as the appointment. But I did something on the way."

"What's that? "

"I pushed Zhang Chunyang's body in the mortuary of Love Hospital into the freezer."

The interrogator was taken aback: "How did Zhang Chunyang die? Who asked you to do this?"

"Actually, I still haven't figured out what's going on..." Zhou Liping stopped for a while and then said, "Xing Qisheng was lying in the back seat drunk, and when the car drove down to the Deratization Hill, he suddenly woke up. He told me that there was something for me to do. I asked him what was the matter. He said that Zhang Chunyang, who had a relationship with President Tao, died suddenly. He wanted to finish other things first and then he went back to Li Shiduo, the director of Ai Xin Hospital, to issue a death certificate. He asked the workers on duty to put the body in the freezer but suddenly thought that the workers on duty would lock the mortuary at eleven o'clock. And he definitely couldn't finish his work before eleven o'clock, so he asked me to do it. I said no. First, I had a bad relationship with Xing Qisheng and didn't want to do things for him. Second, I was in prison. After coming out, I can do anything, but I will never do anything illegal. I don't want to go to prison the second time. Xing Qisheng said that he had a deep friendship with Zhang Chunyang, and he couldn't bear to see Zhang Chunyang die and just 'out there', so he coaxed and begged me to do it, and patted my chest to assure that Zhang Chunyang died of a sudden illness. I went only to move the body into the freezer, and it did not involve any criminal issues. I haven't issued a death certificate. Why did the workers on duty let me remove the body? Xing Qisheng said that he had greeted Li Shiduo that there were too many people coming out and entering the mortuary to worship the dead. I couldn't stand what he said and had to agree. He told me that Zhang Chunyang's death must not be passed on. He also asked me if I had any requests he will tell Tao. The president can definitely promise me. Originally I didn't want to bargain with such a person, but suddenly I remembered that there is indeed a matter, maybe President Tao can handle it, so I brought it up—"

"What's your request?"

Zhou Liping's fierce triangular eyes suddenly drooped down: "There is a girl who used to work in a nightclub. Some time ago, she checked the tenants and left the city. I like her so I hope they can help her make a permanent residence and let her back..."

Ma Xiaozhong, who was sitting in front of the computer with Huyan Yun and others watching this video, couldn't help but whispered "Dong Yue", and Li Zhiyong nodded.

The interrogator then asked: "Then what? What did Xing Qisheng say?"

"Xing Qisheng agreed immediately, saying that such a trivial matter, President Tao can solve it with a phone call, and promised that after I left, he would call President Tao immediately, and give me 100 yuan for a taxi, and then he drove to the Deratization Hill. I waited by the roadside for a while, but I couldn't get a car. I thought that I would run at night at this time anyway. After calculating the time, I could be able to reach the Love Hospital before eleven o'clock, so I set off for a run. That day was very windy at night, but I was running downwind and felt very comfortable. As I ran, I thought, the girl might be very happy when she knew that I could get her household registration into the city. On a whim, I called Li Zhiyong and I want to settle the old and new accounts together and start a new life. I ran to the southwest gate of the Love Hospital first, and walked directly to the mortuary—"

The interrogator interrupted him, "How can you find the mortuary directly at the Love Hospital so big?"

"The set of freezers in the mortuary was imported, and it has been out of order for a period of time. It will cost a lot of money to find the original factory for repairs. Love Hospital knows that I have learned the repair and maintenance of refrigerators and freezers in prison, so they asked me for help. If you don't believe me you can ask Li Shiduo, he knows about it."

"Go on."

"I entered the mortuary, took several corpses lying on the morgue car in the morgue, and opened the white cloths one by one to have a look, and soon found Zhang Chunyang, then pushed the cart inside, and pulled open an empty freezer, then I moved Zhang Chunyang's body in—"

"No one's stopping you or ask you a death certificate?" the interrogator interrupted.

Zhou Liping shook his head: "The two workers on duty are sitting in the yard drinking, and no one cares about me at all."

This is "right" with what Lin Fengchong learned from the morgue.

"Why didn't you explain this situation earlier?" the interrogator asked.

Zhou Liping was stunned for a moment, and a wry smile appeared on his face again: "I think, sooner or later, you will find out that I didn't do anything at the Deratization Hill. When I'm out, I'll ask President Tao to implement what Xing Qisheng promised me. Anyway, regardless of whether Xing Qisheng brought my request to President Tao before his death, I know about Zhang Chunyang's death…"

After listening to Zhou Liping's explanation, the police not only did not feel the joy that the mystery was finally solved, but fell into an unprecedented situation of depression and confusion: the frustration was because so much time was wasted, so much effort was spent, and the wrong person was caught and they made the wrong direction; confusion is because all previous efforts have been abandoned, who is the real culprit in the case, and the investigation must be started from scratch. In particular, Chai Yongjin, who insisted that Zhou Liping was the murderer and who "find

Zhou Liping's criminal evidence" unswervingly, was as dejected as a lost rooster, and Lin Fengchong was not so happy either. Although they insisted that Zhou Liping cannot be considered as the real culprit in the case, and Zhang Chunyang's death cannot be regarded as an isolated emergency, the original intention is that the main culprit maybe someone else. Or although Zhou Liping is the main culprit, there are accomplices, and the Kind Charity Fund should be fully and carefully investigated. But they did not expect Zhou Liping's role in this case to be such a "passer-by"...

Perhaps because he was unwilling to give up, Chai Yongjin and Lin Fengchong, two police officers with different viewpoints, joined together, hoping to find evidence that Zhou Liping did not go to the mortuary of Love Hospital that night, but no matter how much effort was spent, in the end, there was no harvest: It is true that no fingerprints of Zhou Liping have been extracted from the push-pull rod of the corpse bed and the handle of the freezer, but it has been a week since the incident, and the fingerprints of the mortuary staff have already covered the old fingerprints, so this does not count; they also called out the hospital's monitoring but it's common that hospitals not to install surveillance video near the mortuary. The workers on duty can't remember whether Zhou Liping came that night, but they finally admitted that they drank a lot that night. But they never transported any corpse from the morgue into the freezer without receiving a death certificate. In other words, only three people, Tao Zhuoyao, Xing Qisheng, and Zhou Liping, knew that Zhang Chunyang's body was in the mortuary of Love Hospital. Since that night, the timing system of the TE-3 freezer was only turned on once at 10:50. At that time, Tao Zhuoyao was going through the security check at the airport, and Xing Qisheng was dead, so even a fool could deduce the fate. The corpse can only be transformed by Zhou Liping – the same reason can be inferred, the real culprit in the case can be anyone but not Zhou Liping, because he has no time to commit the crime. Even if he really hid in the trunk of Li Zhiyong's Jetta, as Huyan Yun reasoned, when Li Zhiyong's car drove near Love Hospital, he got out secretly and went to the mortuary to put Zhang Chunyang's body in the freezer to create an alibi, It still doesn't work, because the footage captured by the FAST system shows that it was 10:53 when Li Zhiyong drove to the intersection near the Love Hospital.

In short, the police racked their brains and thought of every possibility, but they couldn't solve the mystery – how could Zhou Liping kill and burn the body on the Deratization Hill at 10:30 (or even later), it took less than twenty minutes to arrive at the mortuary of Love Hospital—whether they are willing to admit it or not, the most "reasonable" explanation can only be to believe Zhou Liping's words. He separated with Xing Qisheng as early as ten o'clock, and run all the way to put Zhang Chunyang's body in the cabinet.

That is to say, the case has nothing to do with him at all.

After the video was played, there was silence in the room, especially Huyan Yun, his brows were furrowed, and he was speechless for a long time. Everyone in the room could see that his heart was in turmoil. Yes, so far, he has not confronted Zhou Liping head-on, but to be defeated by an opponent who has never fought head-to-head, from any point of view, is a big setback for this arrogant reasoner.

Even Ma Xiaozhong, who has always had an amazing intuition about the truth of various crimes, was unable to make a judgment for a while. Guo Xiaofen, who was sitting beside him, suddenly spoke—

"I think Zhou Liping is telling the truth."

Huyan Yun raised his head suddenly, his eyes full of surprises, not agreeing with her conclusion, but feeling that she, who had been stupid all afternoon, finally woke up: "Guo, are you feeling better?"

Guo Xiaofen ignored him: "After chatting with Liu Yan this morning, the biggest experience is that Zhou Liping has a very deep affection for Dong Yue, and Dong Yue's sudden departure must have made him extremely sad. Therefore, in order to solve Dong Yue's account, help her go back to the city and back to her side, It's entirely possible for Zhou Liping to complete the task given to him by Xing Qisheng, and it is entirely possible for him to endure for so long after being arrested, but she refuses to speak about Zhang Chunyang. He could find Tao Zhuoyao after his release, using this privacy and the price of his imprisonment, to seek the 'reward' he deserves, this motive is reasonable—"

Li Zhiyong interrupted her: "But Guo, don't forget if Zhou Liping doesn't talk about Zhang Chunyang, what if the police finally decide that he is the murderer of the Zaohuling case? This is too risky. It's a big..."

"No." Lin Fengchong shook his head, "In recent years, we have paid great attention to the construction of the rule of law, and the public security department has been very strict in the investigation and review of criminal cases. If there is a little flaw or lack of evidence in human and physical evidence, it will be suspected of guilt. No new wrongful convictions are allowed, so even if Zhou Liping doesn't say anything about Zhang Chunyang until the end, then the detention will be extended to 37 days at most, and people who should be released will still be released."

"So—"

The two words Huyan Yun said, although they were pronounced lightly, were like needles, which made everyone shudder and cast their eyes on him.

On his baby face, there was a dazed trance due to deep contemplation: "So, I was thinking, why Zhou Liping didn't say it sooner or later, but he said the 'truth' at this time."

2

That evening, Xu Ruilong, director of the Municipal Public Security Bureau, personally convened all members of the task force and held an emergency meeting. Before instructing and arranging the next step in the investigation of the case, Xu Ruilong asked everyone to "continue and clear what should be done" for the work of the previous period. The so-called continuation is to continue to carry out valuable evidence and follow up with meaningful clues, and do not deny all previous work because of some mistakes; They should not be allowed to occupy and waste the manpower on unrelated things.

Facing the comrades of the task force who smoked cigarettes one by one and drank a glass of water, Xu Ruilong changed his stern tone and said gently and patiently, "Don't be discouraged, wou must fight. Come on, don't think that you have arrested the wrong person or wrong direction of the investigation, and the pressure is so great that it seems like the sky is falling. If it really falls, I will bear it for you. I have handled cases for 40 years, and I feel that the criminal investigation work, in the final, is a process of trial and error, and once the mistakes are eliminated one by one, the truth will not be far away."

In the spirit of this meeting, the task force unanimously agreed to release Zhou Liping in accordance with judicial procedures after verifying the facts of the case for the last time.

After the meeting, Xu Ruilong kept several important members of the task force, including Du Jianping, Lin Fengchong, and Chu Tianying. Du Jianping was a little nervous. He knew the work habits of the bureau leaders in the past few years: the meeting was mild and drizzle, and the small meeting was thundered, so he was ready to be scolded by Xu Ruilong. Who knew that when the door was closed, Xu Ruilong only said to him: "Now it seems that it is inappropriate to lock Zhou Liping as the main suspect. The vindication of wrongful and unjust cases in recent years has repeatedly proved that many people have made mistakes. The cases are all because the investigators subjectively identified the suspect as the real murderer in advance based on the 'bad impression' of the suspect. As a result, they

301

lost their objective position. As a result, during the entire case handling process, they only looked for evidence that was unfavorable to the suspect and ignored the evidence favorable for the suspect. The results are repeated wrong and finally out of control."

Du Jianping stood up and said, "Director, the task force made a mistake in handling the case, which led to the fact that so many comrades spent so long and worked so hard but in vain. This responsibility should be taken by me."

"Now is not the time to be held accountable, and if you encounter setbacks, you must be held accountable, then the public security work will not be able to do it." Xu Ruilong pressed his hand and let him sit down, "Tell me what you are going to focus on? "

Du Jianping put his two big red hands on his knees and said, "Director, we discussed before the meeting that the reason for the serious mistakes in our work a while ago is because we were so eager to catch the real murderer and neglected to find the truth."

Xu Ruilong raised the wrinkles on his forehead: "Oh? Let's hear it."

In fact, this point of view is from Huyan Yun. At the pre-meeting meeting just now, Lin Fengchong said, Du Jianping thought it was very reasonable, and now moving out and really aroused Xu Ruilong's interest: "From the analysis of the various situations so far, the case is by no means a single criminal case. There may be a very large crowd involved, intricate reasons, and intertwined relationships, and the few burned corpses on the Deratization Hill are just a sudden explosion of these crowds that eventually intertwined and ignited. In this case, it is important to find the real culprit, but the real culprit is probably not on the surface but is covered and obscured by layers of networks. In this case, we might as well change the strategy. Anyway, the fish is in the net. Find out who was involved in the case, and then the truth would come out. The system is all figured out the whole thing is understood, and the real culprit will be revealed. "

"Be more specific." Xu Ruilong said, "What are you planning?"

Du Jianping glanced at Lin Fengchong, Lin Fengchong said: "Director Xu, according to the adjustment of the case handling ideas reported by Director Du to you, we have re-organized the various networks intertwined in the deep layers of the case, and re-summarized the cases related to the case. Investigations in several areas have found that since Tongyou Nursing Home is not the place where the crime occurred, although there are many doubts, it has been neglected in the previous work. Our next focus is to check them from the bottom line, no matter how many layers it was wearing, all of which will be completely naked."

"But I heard that the vice president named Cui Yucui, every time she was asked to assist in the investigation, her attitude was very bad, and she couldn't ask anything, is that so?"

Lin Fengchong nodded: "It's true, so Director Du has a suggestion... Director Du, you should come and talk to Director."

Xu Ruilong picked up the thermos cup on the table, took a sip of tea, and looked at Du Jianping through the mist.

Du Jianping paused for a moment, then raised his huge head: "I want to call Ma Xiaozhong back to the task force and let him come to trial Cui Yucui."

This is also the result of discussions between the "Project 2 Team" and Lin Fengchong and Chu Tianying. At that time, everyone felt that since Zhou Liping was not the murderer and everything had to start from scratch, Tongyou Nursing Home has always been a "potential one" without any breakthrough. It's better to start a new round of investigations that were launched against the staff there. And Guo Xiaofen once heard Tao Bing pointing to Cui Yucui and saying to Xing Qixian at the dinner of the Kind Charity Fund, "Why did your brother end up like this, you ask her, she knows best", which proves the cause of Xing Qisheng's death, Cui Yucui has the "insider" that no one else knows. But when it comes to Cui Yucui, Lin Fengchong has a headache, thinking that she is an old shrew who is invulnerable to bullets. After several trials, he found nothing... At this time, Ma smiled and said, "It really doesn't work, let me try!"

Lin Fengchong was stunned for a moment, and then overjoyed: "The director request, that's sure to be done! I'll go back and talk to Xu Bureau, let him give special approval, and invite you back to the task force."

Ma Xiaozhong said: "Go and tell Director　Xu, doesn't that mean giving Du eye drops? Do you still want to work in the Criminal Investigation Department in the future?"

"Otherwise, I'll go tell Director Xu, I'm from the Criminal Technique Department, and I'm not under the direct control of Du." Chu Tianying said.

"You've been with me for so long, and still don't know what I mean." Ma said with a frown, "Because you are a criminal department, you can't tell Director Xu, if you go, others will think it is Simiao who was supporting you."

Chu Tianying suddenly realized: "Then what should I do?"

"Let Du do it himself!"

"I'm afraid it's unlikely..." Chu Tianying said, " Du has a lot of opinions on you and your 'project two'."

"This time is different," Ma said, "Director Xu must be clear what has our 'project two' done. He acquiesced to the existence of this group, not to abolish the 'project one', but to put some invisible pressure on Du. Now Du can't handle the case, so he called me back, it seems that he has a bright chest and can tolerate people. More importantly, if I can ask something out of Cui Yucui. The merit would be count on him!"

Chu Tianying squinted his eyes and said, "Director, honestly, when you used the hot dishes to deduct the cook, have you already imagine this?"

Ma Xiaozhong smiled wickedly.

Sure enough, Lin Fengchong told Du Jianping about this proposal. Du Jianping hesitated before agreeing. When he told Xu Ruilong, he was immediately praised by the director: "Very good, Du, very good, just as you said, let Ma Xiaozhong return to the task force."

"Director, there is one more thing." Lin Fengchong said, "If we continue to investigate like this, it will inevitably involve the Kind Charity Fund's office—or even the entire foundation. In this regard, are there any scales that need to be paid attention to... and scope?"

"There is no scale and no scope!" Xu Ruilong said decisively, "The anti-corruption campaign in the past few years has already pointed out the direction for our work. Regardless of any organization or individual, if they abide by the law, they will be fine. But if they violate the law, they will be arrested, no one has the privilege!"

Lin Fengchong and Chu Tianying quickly stood up from their chairs, salute Xu Ruilong while saying "yes", and Du Jianping also stood up slowly.

Xu Ruilong signaled that the meeting was over. The three of them walked out of the office together. When Du Jianping was about to close the door, Xu Ruilong's voice suddenly came from the room: "Du, wait a minute."

Du Jianping hurried back into the room, Xu Ruilong stood up from behind the desk, walked to a place very close to him, and said in a voice that was by no means whispered but could not be heard clearly: "Since Tao Zhuoyao is not much involved in the case, and there's no specific crime, so just go through the formalities for her and let her go..."

3

Wearing a burgundy cashmere shawl and wrapping her plump body in a white turtleneck sweater, Cui Yucui still felt a little cold, holding her arms and looking at the two people sitting opposite. The face with extremely high cheekbones was very rigid, and the fat lips were tightly closed, and a pair of swords and flames would never let the old lady speak.

She recognized the two policemen in plain clothes sitting behind the desk. One was named Sun Kang, who was said to be the director of a police station who was temporarily seconded to the task force. The other was named Lin with a mustache on his upper lip. However, compared with the people she often exchanged glasses for at banquets, it wasn't that big of a deal, so she felt relieved when she thought about it. She knows very well that everyone in the public family is like a chess piece in military chess. They strictly follow certain rules according to their position. On the other hand, as an interrogator, you have more power and more means than these interrogators, so—see what you can do to with me!

"Cui Yucui, we've already told you a lot. Since you've always had this attitude, there's nothing else we can do." After Sun Kang finished speaking, he whispered to Lin Fengchong, "Leave it to Ma?"

Although his voice was low, in the quiet interrogation room, it still reached Cui Yucui's ears very clearly.

Lin Fengchong nodded.

For some reason, Cui Yucui shivered.

Don't be afraid, she said to herself, they would never dare to do anything out of the ordinary, let alone a woman like me... but, why does that "Ma" sound familiar?

Sun Kang got up, opened the door, and shouted " Ma" to the corridor. Then, a grinning guy got into the room.

It's him?!

Cui Yucui recognized the short, fat man with a slightly crooked mouth at once, remembered how he changed from a hippie smile to a fierce-looking man in less than half a second, the pot of boiling hot dishes with a layer of red oil floating in it, Chef Bao, who was rolling on the ground and was slammed into his face. She even remembered the sound of Bao's nose being shattered by his knee... Didn't he get suspended? According to the information inquired by the "insider", he is also not a member of the special task force of the case, so why did he suddenly appear here?

She curled up like a stimulated caterpillar.

"I'll leave it to you." Lin Fengchong got up and walked out.

Ma Xiaozhong grabbed Sun Kang, took out a few crumpled banknotes from his trouser pocket, and stuffed them in his hand: "I haven't had dinner yet, you go downstairs and pack me a meal, super spicy."

When they were both gone, Ma Xiaozhong closed the door.

Turning around, he dragged the chair from behind the table to the opposite of Cui Yucui, sat down, and said with a smile, "Sister Cui, I haven't seen you for a while, why are you so thin?"

Cui Yucui didn't dare to speak, but the air in the room made her not even dare to "speak", and forced a smile on her face: " Ma...Brother, look, such a big thing has happened recently, I can't even eat or sleep well, then I'm losing weight... In fact, this case really has nothing to do with me. My duty in the nursing home is to go outside, and the outside field depends on me. The internal management, Xing Qisheng has always been very hard, and no one else is allowed to interfere..."

Ma Xiaozhong leaned his shoulders on the back of the chair like that, watching her spit flying, and asked lazily, " That Chi, Chi Fengli, does she have a boyfriend?"

Talking about the Sui and Tang Dynasties, but asked Meng Liang, where did this story come from? Cui Yucui's mind didn't turn around for a while, and she blinked her eyes for a long time before saying, "I don't know very well, it seems... no."

"No way!" Ma Xiaozhong raised his stubby eyebrows, "She's so pretty, I don't believe no one sleeps—er... no, no one chases her."

Cui Yucui still hadn't figured out why he turned the topic to Chi Fengli, but since he was willing to ask such a question that had nothing to do with the case, she finally relieved. Cui Yucui secretly took a deep breath and told him how Chi Fengli likes to go to and from nightclubs. The clothes she wears are all famous brands, and which restaurants she likes to order and what dishes she likes the most... ... Ma Xiaozhong listened with relish, Cui Yucui suddenly asked: "What's the matter, Bro, do you like her? I advise you not to think about it, it's a pit that can't be filled with any amount of gold!"

After listening to this, Ma Xiaozhong seemed a little frustrated: "Damn, the policeman is most afraid of this kind of woman, at the beginning is an officer, and finally become a beggar... But look at me, I don't even have a girlfriend at the age of thirties, and I hug my pillow and scratch the wall in the middle of the night, so sooner or later I won't become a pervert!"

" Ma, listen to sister's advice, don't look for someone, what are you looking for? It's okay to have fun, but don't rush to get married... What's so good about marriage? I was married and then divorced. Now, breaking up without getting married is called breaking up, and breaking up after getting married is the worst, it's boring, boring!" Cui Yucui said.

"I know, I can't do anything about it, my mother is pressing so hard, she wants a grandson, and I tell her: There are more grandchildren in the detention center than anywhere else, and one day I will bring two home for her, hey, the old lady chased me halfway with a rolling pin..." After Ma Xiaozhong said, Cui Yucui couldn't help laughing, and countless rough lines appeared on her face covered with heavy powder.

"By the way." Ma Xiaozhong suddenly remembered something, "Do you have a son? Primary school or junior high school?"

"Sixth grade of elementary school." Cui Yucui sighed, "Next year will be in junior high school."

"The sixth grade of elementary school, twelve years old..." Ma Xiaozhong counted with his fingers, "Hey, isn't that the same age as Zhao Wu?"

In a word, Cui Yucui was chilled from head to toe. She stared blankly at the short fat man with a smile on his face, only to realize that they chatted for a long time but he didn't forget the subject at all. But he let go of the hand that was around her neck, had a little loosen and regain elasticity so that he can almost snap her to death!

Just then, someone knocked on the door.

Ma Xiaozhong stood up, opened the door, and saw that it was Sun Kang, carrying a plastic bag with a beige round take-out bowl in it, with chopsticks and napkins inserted diagonally: "Ma, your meal."

Ma Xiaozhong took the bag with one hand and held the bottom of the bowl with the other. Although there was a plastic bag he was still so hot that he scolded with a dirty word.

Turning around, he closed the door again.

Then plug in the pin.

He put the plastic bag on the table, took out the takeaway bowl, lifted the lid, and a strong spicy smell suddenly filled the small interrogation room. Then, he broke apart the convenient chopsticks, wiped the wooden thorns, supported the bottom of the bowl with several layers of napkins, and sat down opposite Cui Yucui.

First the fingertips, then the palm, then the two arms, and finally the whole body couldn't help trembling... Looking at the bowl of steamed vegetables, Cui Yucui's eyes filled with fear and despair.

Ma Xiaozhong seemed not to see it. He took a piece of pig blood with chopsticks, put it in his mouth, and took it out with a grin. "Twelve-year-old, heart-to-heart, what would you think if your son was strangled to death tonight, stripped naked, and thrown in a tunnel wind pavilion in an abandoned subway station? You go to school and ask, how did my son die? The vice-principal spread her hands and said she doesn't know. 'I was in charge of running outside the school. This case really has nothing to do with me. You can see that I can't eat or sleep recently and I've lost weight.' You must want to peel her skin, smash her tendons, her bones and gouge out her heart, right? Of course, Zhao Wu is an orphan with no father or mother. No one cares if he dies, but orphans are human beings, and there is no criminal law said that orphans and handicapped children can be killed and left unattended. But when such a case happens, the government has to strictly control it! Why? Because the government is responsible for patching up the evils created by God! "

After he finished speaking, he stuffed the piece of blood into his mouth and swallowed it without chewing it.

In the bowl with a layer of red oil steamed up, covered the fat face in his face.

"From the moment I walked in, I knew you were thinking, isn't this short fat man suspended? Why did he come to interrogate me again? Yes, to tell you the truth, I was suspended, but the investigation results came out. It was the chef who attacked me first. I was in the process of dealing with the law and caused serious injuries to his face, so I can not take any criminal responsibility. Don't think that the government is biased towards me, our people's government is the fairest. " Ma Xiaozhong took another large chopstick and stuffed it into his mouth, crunching with a rough tooth. "A group of orphans with no parents and no mothers, little babies who have been tortured to death by various ailments since birth, you actually gave them swill, you fucking give them the swill! Don't come out of the hospital for the rest of your life, or I'll have to find a few brothers and give them a disordered injury in the midnight!"

Having said this, Ma Xiaozhong suddenly couldn't continue. He looked at the ceiling, swallowed hard with his huge Adam's apple, then lowered his head and stared at Cui Yucui with blood-red eyes.

Cui Yucui looked at the bowl of vegetables he was holding, and she was so scared that she burst into tears and choked.

"Cui, how did those children die?" Ma Xiaozhong poked his stout neck forward, and his stern face cast a huge black shadow, covering the body of Cui Yucui, who had shrunk into a ball. He said word by word, "I'll only ask you once."

"I tell you..." Cui Yucui said while crying, "Xing Qisheng has already sexual assaulted those children, not only the dead ones but also the other children. He is not human when he got crazy. He tortured those children in different ways. The children bleed and cried out in pain, and a few deaf and dumb ones couldn't cry, especially the five-year-old child with cerebral palsy named Li Ying, who would suffocate all night like a puppy every time he finished. I also persuaded Xing Qisheng don't be too excessive.

He said no one cared at all. He was just a little afraid of Zhou Liping as if Zhao Wu had said something to Zhou Liping... The day before the case happened, he raped Li Ying again. It is said that the children couldn't stand it anymore. Zhao Wu was regarded as the leader of the children. He strangled Li Ying and another girl named Dong Xinlan, and then hanged himself on the heating pipe... The next morning, Auntie Zhang found out and reported to me and Xing Qisheng. Xing Qisheng told us to tell no one, he has his own way..."

The room was quiet.

Ma Xiaozhong sat opposite Cui Yucui for a long time, then stood up slowly and opened the door.

At the door, stood Lin Fengchong and Sun Kang, who had heard Cui Yucui's confession through the monitor, their expressions grim.

"Buddy." Lin Fengchong patted Ma Xiaozhong's shoulder, "Go and rest."

Ma Xiaozhong nodded, walked to the other end of the corridor, and when he was halfway, he suddenly stopped, twisted his body abruptly, and flew to the door of the interrogation room, and a bowl of vegetables was thrown at Cui Yucui!

Cui Yucui screamed and flashed her body. She was not hit, but the dishes that smashed on the wall still splashed a little red oil on her body, and she was so scared that she lost her mind, crying and screaming.

Ma Xiaozhong pointed at her, his fingertips trembling, and he cursed repeatedly in his mouth, but he restrained his vocal cords with all his strength, so he didn't make a sound. There were blue veins on his neck, each bulging like it was about to burst. And his red face has been distorted and deformed as if a pot of fiery fire is burning!

Sun Kang has known him for many years, and he has never seen him so angry. He dragged him down the corridor while holding him, and whispered, "Ma, calm down, calm down!"

When he came to the corridor, Ma Xiaozhong leaned against the wall and squatted down slowly. He was breathing heavily, and his body shook violently so that his upper and lower teeth clapped loudly as if the glacier falling.

4

Cui Yucui's confession made the crimes in Tongyou Nursing Home overflow like a flood. After a whole night of unannounced interrogation, the police obtained more unbearable inside stories: For many years, Xing Qisheng regarded the disabled children in the nursing home as a harem to vent his animalistic desires and wantonly sexually assaulted these children with congenital diseases. Those nights, those dark corners, those disgusting actions, those blood and tears mixed with screams, weeping and wailing, made many old criminal investigators with countless furious. Several indignant policewomen told the bureau leaders that they would adopt the children, but when they saw the children in the nursing home, they hesitated because the children had been tossed and tortured for years. When the kids saw strangers coming they were very afraid, but when they found out that these policewomen treated them very well, they were gentle and snuggled like kittens, and the flattering smile on their faces made the policewomen shudder...

However, the indifference and numbness shown by the staff in the nursing home are surprising. Whether it was office director Wang Jing, guard Xu, the driver, or the three stern-faced childcare workers. Although Cui Yucui had to explain some truths they knew more or less after the dam collapsed. They emphasized that what Xing Qisheng did had nothing to do with them. In their opinion, the work of the nursing home is just a job, and the work is paid for, and other things belong to the "privacy" of the director, and they have no right and do not care much about it. As for the children, "they are sick anyway." —— The implication is that it seems that they can be played by Xing Qisheng is still a valuable performance... The tendency to "dehumanize" disabled children in their words makes Sun Kang almost clench his fists in anger.

On the contrary, Chi Fengli, who was dressed as a courtesan, heard the truth about the deaths of the three children and cried a lot, cursing Xing Qisheng as scum and a beast.

As for Auntie Zhang after hearing that Cui Yucui was recruited, she knelt on the ground with a plop, kowtowed on the ground, and tearfully said that she was guilty and should not hide the truth... According to her account, Zhao Wu had told her about the bad things that Xing Qisheng did and also said that seeing those little sisters is too hard, it is better to die than to live... When she entered the collective dormitory that morning and saw the bodies of the children, she was so frightened. She quickly reported to Xing Qisheng and Cui Yucui. The two told her that this matter must be covered up. Once the police come to the door, the nursing home will be closed, and she will have to lose her job. That's why Auntie Zhang has never told the police.

"I'm afraid it's more than that." Sun Kang suddenly remembered that when he first went to the nursing home, in the cabinet with tableware, one set of "rice bowls" made of instant noodle boxes was made of stainless steel, "Is that because you have a child in the nursing home yourself. You came to the nursing home as a cleaner in order to accompany him to treat his illness and protect his safety. After the accident, you are afraid that the nursing home will collapse and there will be no place for your child. Then you help Xing Qisheng and Cui Yucui keep the secret?"

After a long silence, Auntie Zhang nodded slowly.

"Your child is a child, isn't someone else's child a child?!" Sun Kang couldn't help shouting loudly.

Seeing Auntie Zhang covering her face and crying, he didn't rebuke any more.

What puzzled the police was that since Zhao Wu knew about Xing Qisheng's crime, why didn't he call the police? Auntie Zhang said that it was because Zhao Wu had escaped from the nursing home many times before, but was caught by the police and sent back, so he misunderstood the police and thought they were colluding with Xing Qisheng. Zhao Wu also approached Zhou Liping and asked him to help call the police. Zhou Liping was very angry after hearing about it, but he was very embarrassed because as a "perverted murderer" and a prisoner released after serving his sentence, it was difficult to gain the trust of the police. He would even be planted the crime of sexual assault by Xing Qisheng on his head... Since Zhou Liping has cleared the identity of the criminal suspect, this trivial matter has little meaning for the police to further investigate the case. The police just only listened to it.

The autumn wind roared furiously that night, and the next day saw fallen leaves all over the ground, laying a layer of withered yellow on the ground, the temperature plummeted, and an icy iron blue floated above the sky. In the morning, a few friends from the "Project 2 Team" got together again at Huyan Yun's house to catch up on the latest situation. After hearing that when the police were about to release Zhou Liping he was expressionless, but when Ma Xiaozhong finished talking about the tragedy that happened in Tongyou Nursing Home, Li Zhiyong suddenly cursed, scolding Zhou Liping for why he knew Xing Qisheng's sin a long time ago but did nothing. The swearing made the others look at each other in dismay.

Perhaps feeling out of control of his emotions, Li Zhiyong rubbed his temples and muttered, saying that he was dragged by Zheng Gui to drink last midnight. As a result, Zheng Gui drank too much and rolled under the table to vomit. Li Zhiyong had no other way but to send him home. Zheng Gui was scolding along the way, scolding Xing Qixian and Cui Wentao for wanting to kill him, scolding Tao Bing and Tao Zhuoyao for making himself a scapegoat when something happened, scolding Xing Qisheng and Zhou Liping for making such a big case that the company they had worked so hard for many years is going to be harassed... Finally, Li Zhiyong understood that after Tao Zhuoyao was released, Xing Qixian and Tao Bing convened an urgent closed-door meeting and finally reached a compromise, Tao Bing continued to be the honorary president of the Kind Charity Fund. However, in order to "save the social image of the Kind Charity Fund", it was decided to terminate the cooperation with Mingyi Company and prohibit Mingyi Company from engaging in activities and advertising under the name of the foundation... Despite Zheng Gui's begging, those acquaintances who smiled brightly yesterday were as cold as strangers now, especially Zhai Qing, who rolled up his arms and sleeves and dragged him out of the meeting room.

"You know what, Yong. I'm like an old dog. I've shown them the door for so many years, and they kill me in a word!" Having said this, Zheng Gui couldn't help crying.

Li Zhiyong was sympathetic and pitiful to him and asked him what his plans were for the next step. Zheng Gui said that he was going to make trouble at Xing Qisheng's funeral.

To a large extent, hosting a decent funeral for Xing Qisheng is also one of the conditions for the compromise between Xing Qixian and Tao Bing. Although everyone knows that Xing Qisheng is an out-and-out pedophile and rapist, He is already dead, and the law will no longer pursue the crimes he committed, and Xing Qixian wants to establish his prestige in the entire Kind Charity Fund by holding a grand funeral for such a person. In the past two years, Xing Qisheng likes to say something: "Except for weddings and funerals, there are very few things that can bring us together." Now that Tao Zhuoyao's scandal has come out, her boyfriend Jiang Lei's family has proposed to break off the marriage, the wedding could not be done, and Xing Qisheng's funeral instead became the iconic "grand ceremony" for the Kind Charity Fund to change the dynasty, which is particularly symbolic and ironic.

"I don't know if there will be a funeral for the deceased children..." Huyan Yun said quietly.

He stood up and looked out the window: the leaves of several large poplar trees had all fallen, and the bare branches were white and blue, like a large bundle of blood vessels that had lost too much blood. On the sloping roof of the opposite building, the gray-black chimney was lonely. Standing alone, he let out a cold breath against the sky... Suddenly he remembered something, turned around, and said to Guo Xiaofen, who was sitting on the sofa: "Guo, the temperature in the south has also cooled for the past two days. Do you have enough clothes?"

Ma Xiaozhong, who returned to the police force, had got Cui Yucui, which made Du Jianping feel very happy, so he agreed to a request made by Ma Xiaozhong which is going to Gancheng, Province A to find the whereabouts of Dong Yue. Ma Xiaozhong bought two tickets, one for himself and one for Guo Xiaofen. The high-speed train departs at noon and arrives in Gancheng County at around 5 pm.

Guo Xiaofen still didn't seem to have recovered from the shock of witnessing Yue Shao's death. Hearing Huyan Yun's question, she just stared at him blankly without answering. Huyan Yun walked in front of her, knelt down on one leg, and his eyes fell on her eyes: "Guo, do you still feel not good? If so, don't go to Gancheng, Ma will go alone and find Dong Yue himself."

Guo Xiaofen just stared at him, still not speaking.

After listening to Huyan Yun's words, Ma Xiaozhong was not happy, but he was really worried about Guo Xiaofen's health: "Are you okay? Don't go out and get sick again."

At this moment, his cell phone rang. He took out his cell phone and took a look. He shook the screen towards Huyan Yun. The screen showed that the caller's name was "Liu Simiao".

Huyan Yun's eyes immediately condensed on the phone.

"Simiao, what's the matter? No, Guo and I will leave at noon. Yes, it might be too late, let them go? Now?" He glanced at Huyan Yun, Huyan Yun nodded quickly, he turned to the phone said: "OK, no problem!"

Hanging up the phone, he stood up and said to Huyan Yun, "Simiao said she has made a very important discovery, and asked you and Li Zhiyong to go to her office."

Huyan Yun almost jumped up, ran behind the door, pulled the coat off the hook and put it on his body, turned around, and looked at the other people in the room, as if to say: Why are you still sitting? I'm leaving now!

This time, before Ma Xiaozhong and Li Zhiyong react, Guo Xiaofen stood up from the sofa and said to Ma Xiaozhong, "Let's go to the train station."

5

Standing at the door of Liu Simiao's office, Huyan Yun stretched his sky blue denim jacket, and then used his fingers to smooth every fold on it, causing Li Zhiyong to be puzzled: "I said, you are not here for a blind date. Why are you doing so neatly?" Huyan Yun was a little embarrassed, took

313

a deep breath, knocked on the door lightly, and when he heard a "please come in" from inside, he twisted the door handle and walked in.

Liu Simiao should have just come out of the science laboratory of the Criminal Technology Department. She had not taken off her white coat. She was sitting at the back of her desk and flipping through a stack of files. She didn't even raise her eyes to look at Huyan Yun. She pointed to the row of sofas against the wall. Li Zhiyong sat down, Huyan Yun stood for a while, and saw that Liu Simiao still didn't pay attention to him then sat down awkwardly.

"Let's make a long story short." Liu Simiao raised his head and looked at Li Zhiyong, "You must be surprised why I called you here today, just because I have been re-investigating the serial murders in the western suburbs ten years ago, and obtained some breakthroughs."

The harmonica, only sound once!

The sound of a harmonica suddenly sounded in Li Zhiyong's ear.

In the dark.

It sounded suddenly, and ended abruptly, so suddenly that it was unexpected and heartbreaking.

Ten years have passed, ten years! How many things in the world have been dusted, how many dreams have been blurred, how many emotions have faded, only this harmonica is still clear in his mind. For ten years, he had always wanted to forget this voice, but he can't get rid of it, especially in those late nights with raindrops, when he walked on the silent streets, he always thought of it, the ink outside Wangyueyuan Square. The green bench reminded him of the young man who held a harmonica in hand and let the rain cast a silver light all over his body.

Li Zhiyong's hands trembled slightly.

"There is no need for me to introduce more about that case. As the main police officer of the task force, I believe you will never forget it." Liu Simiao said, "Among the members of the task force, Director Du and Chai Yongjin and the others are currently busy with the case of Deratization Hill. I don't want my work to interfere with them. I plan to seek your opinion first, and then report to the superiors. As for Huyan (she still doesn't look at him directly), I think my findings have something to do with you, so I asked you to come too."

Huyan Yun hadn't seen her for a long time, just stared at her without blinking.

Liu Simiao put on latex gloves, opened the drawer, took out a white and transparent round trace evidence storage box, opened the lid, and took out a piece of glass with tweezers: "Do you remember this?"

Li Zhiyong narrowed his eyes and watched for a long time. This piece of glass with a slight curvature, the sharp crack cut a scar in his memory, and it was aching, but he couldn't remember what it was.

"Yes." Huyan Yun said, "This is one of the two pieces of glasses you found that did not belong to the fish tank after you restored the broken glass fish tank at the scene of Gao Xiaoyan's murder!"

"Well, based on these two pieces of glasses, you deduced that the murderer was imitating the technique in a Japanese reasoning manga to cover up the important clue that he was an anime fan wearing short-sighted glasses. The police mobilized the orders of Dangdang and Zhuoyue. Then Zhou Liping, a major criminal suspect, was locked. At this time, the murder of Fang Zhifeng happened. When the police investigated the social relationship of his daughter Fang Mei, they found that Zhou Liping's physical features were highly similar to the criminal, so he was arrested and brought to justice. During the subsequent evidence collection process, it was found that the power of the glasses he was wearing was exactly the same as the power of the lens I extracted, so the police finally determined that he was the real murderer of the serial murders in the western suburbs, and prosecuted him. Although at the insistence of some comrades, the court finally found that Zhou Liping and the first three of the four murders had problems such as insufficient evidence, and he was only sentenced to ten years in prison. But in the eyes of the vast majority of criminal police, he is still the only real culprit in western suburbs. "

Li Zhiyong felt that his throat was so dry that he was about to burst into flames. After swallowing several mouthfuls of saliva, he asked in a hoarse voice, "Is there any problem with this conclusion...?"

"There is a problem!" Liu Simiao said, "My latest analysis of this physical evidence completely overturns this conclusion."

Huyan Yun blinked his small eyes: "Could it be that my reasoning is wrong?"

"Your reasoning is not wrong." Liu Simiao said coldly, "but your reasoning directly caused the police to make a serious logical error."

If someone else said that, this always conceited babyface would have jumped up and down to quarrel with the other party, but Liu Simiao was in front of him, he could only murmur something.

"A piece of glasses that was deliberately mixed up in a broken fish tank can indeed be deduced that the suspect likes to read Japanese inference comics, and it can be deduced that he is short-sighted, but this reasoning should stop there. Yes, Zhou Liping did have these two characteristics at the same time, but it cannot be considered that he is a criminal suspect---

because Zhou Liping is not the only one who has these two characteristics at the same time." Liu Simiao said, "Originally, this is a problem that can be solved with a little thought. This is a logical fallacy caused by violating the rules of sufficient conditional hypothetical reasoning. However, the attack on Fang Mei and the killing of Fang Zhifeng once again led to Zhou Liping, which led the police to rashly think that since the two leads point to the same target, then Zhou Liping is the real culprit of the serial murders in the western suburbs is a sure thing – this is totally wrong because even if Fang Zhifeng was killed by Zhou Liping, he cannot be inferred in the first three cases. Even though the murder displayed the same characteristics as the real murderer in many places."

Liu Simiao paused for a while, then continued: "Actually, when I was investigating this case ten years ago, I noticed a problem. When the police pinpointed Zhou Liping as the real culprit in the serial murders in the western suburbs, they relied too much on 'characteristics' but not 'physical evidence'. Such as similar shoe size posture, but these cannot be the same identification at the level of evidence. The only thing that can link Zhou Liping to the previous three cases is the fragment of the glasses at the scene of Gao Xiaoyan's murder. Thanks to Xiangming's resistance to various pressures, Zhou Liping was not allowed to go to the execution ground."

When talking about Lin Xiangming, Liu Simiao's tone seemed calm.

"So, what is the truth of the case?" Li Zhiyong asked anxiously.

"At the beginning, after Zhou Liping was sentenced, I wanted to continue investigating this case but was stopped by Xiangming. I said that the real culprits in the first three cases were still at large. I was very surprised by his attitude because he was never a person who passed the test in ambiguity. He also saw my doubts and said that it would be better for the victims if some truths were not revealed. What should I do if there is no trace for too long? He said that there is no need to worry, each case is like a food packaging bag, no matter how strong the material of the packaging bag is, there will still be a tear hole..." Liu Simiao smiled bitterly, " After the Deratization case, I felt it was necessary to retrace the truth of the serial murders in the western suburbs. I re-checked and retrieved relevant files and physical evidence from the Municipal Bureau Archives and Physical Evidence Preservation Office. It took a lot of time and energy. But I couldn't find a breakthrough. In the end, it was Xiangming's words ten years ago that reminded me, isn't the so-called easy tearing mouth a gap? And the biggest logical gap in the serial murder case in the western suburbs is undoubtedly the glasses!"

Huyan Yun nodded: "As long as it can be proved that this piece of glasses does not belong to the glasses worn by Zhou Liping, then the relationship between him and the first three murder cases can be cleared up."

"How to do this?" Li Zhiyong frowned, "unless—"

"Unless we find the brand of glasses to which this pair of lenses belongs, and find the sales records from ten years ago," Liu Simiao said. "That's what I did."

Li Zhiyong couldn't help but open his mouth: "I'm afraid you're going to break my leg?"

"Handling a case is originally a tiring job." Liu Simiao picked up a kraft paper envelope, unbuttoned the top, took out a folded piece of paper, and opened it carefully: a thin invoice, with a long history. It has become translucent, and the raised mark of the signature can be seen through the back of the paper.

Li Zhiyong's heart was in his throat, and he knew that the truth that he had not let go for the past ten years was in front of him. He looked at Huyan Yun and then at Liu Simiao, they all looked calm, that was because their relationship with this case was far less than his own... It was this case that made him lose the love of his life and even his job. On that thin piece of paper, the source of all this was written, the origin of all this. When he really had to face he realized he was so afraid of it... no, no, no, I'm not afraid to face blood, bones, darkness, and sin, what I'm really afraid of is finding out that what I've spent ten years is a mistake: hating, abusing, and cursing... He gripped his knee tightly with his hands, and his ten fingers were so hard that they made his knee hurt.

"The shard of glasses was a new product launched by 'Pearl Glasses' that year. Due to the use of new technology in the material of the lens, the customer had problems such as dispersion after wearing it. As a result, it was recalled not long after it was launched, and the sales volume was very limited. Pearl Glasses Co., Ltd. is a relatively large brand store. They keep the shopping invoices very well. With their active cooperation, I checked all the invoices for the glasses sold in this city. One of them was found the signature of a person related to this case." Liu Simiao said, handing out the invoice.

Huyan Yun hurriedly got up and took it over, looked at the signed signature, and was a little surprised, raised his head to look at Liu Simiao.

Liu Simiao said in a low voice: "It is indeed this man, he not only has all the conditions for committing a crime but also meets the characteristics of Lin Xiangming's criminal personality profile: he is over twenty years old, mature in mind, thin in stature. With a certain amount of anti-investigation experience, he is a local living in Chengyuli and Chunliu Street, and he can even perfectly explain why he can avoid the security patrol route of the joint defense team many times, and let the victim completely relax without alert ..."

Huyan Yun handed the invoice to Li Zhiyong.

Li Zhiyong raised one hand and took the invoice. The knee of his trousers was soaked with sweat.

After a long time, just like doing a needle, he focused his blurry vision on the inscription of the invoice. The signature of Talan was not clear, and three words could be vaguely seen, but it was not "Zhou Liping"——

The harmonica sounded again, this time in a rapid and repeated series of syllables, tossing and turning, hoarse and sticky. As if a man who was eager to confide could never speak again in a violent sob. For some unknown reason, Li Zhiyong's heart trembled painfully with the sound of the harmonica, convulsing again and again, shrinking step by step...

6

When the woman walked into the reception room, Huyan Yun couldn't match Fang Mei on the photo that Mr. Zhu Min had collected. She was tall and slender, and the features on her V-shaped face were very beautiful, but the eyebrows were too thin, the eye shadow was too heavy, and the lip line was too deep, which looks too delicate and unreal. She was wearing a navy blue business suit with a charming khaki band on the shoulders and collar. She was wearing a pair of black slim-fit flared trousers. She exuded the fashionable and capable temperament of a foreign company executive. The thin, sickly-faced, smiling female student in the old photo showed a prudent smile, had no trace to be found.

She glanced at the two people sitting opposite the reception room and looked at the front desk lady standing at the door with some confusion.

"I said you were busy, but they forced their way in..." the front desk lady whispered, "they have been here several times."

"Who are you? What's the matter with me?" Fang Mei asked, every word was politely rejected.

"We are here to find out about an old incident that happened ten years ago—" Before Huyan Yun finished speaking, Fang Mei's face changed, but she quickly returned to smiling: "I'm sorry, I really I'm very busy. Later, I'm going to make a speech at the trade fair hosted by the leader of the commercial department, and I'm preparing now. So, leave your phone number, and I'll contact you after the meeting to make an appointment for an interview? "Then said to the lady at the front desk: "You can send these two gentlemen—"

"Fang Mei!" Huyan Yun stood up and called her.

Fang Mei turned around and saw an iron-like determination in his eyes.

"You go out first." Fang Mei said to the lady at the front desk. After she left, she closed the door of the reception room and sat down opposite Huyan Yun and the others. "Sorry, please keep it short, I'm really busy."

"Do you know Zhou Liping?" Huyan Yun asked.

"I know, my high school classmate, he was arrested ten years ago for homicide and was jailed. He was a minor, so he was released from prison after serving his sentence. Recently I read the news, and it seemed that he had committed another major crime and was arrested."

Huyan Yun looked at her and asked, "Ten years ago, who did he kill?"

Fang Mei frowned: "Excuse me, who are you? I don't want to talk about what happened ten years ago."

Huyan Yun continued: "The immediate reason for his arrest, according to the police investigation of the scene and the conclusion based on your statement, is that he entered your home that night under the pretext of wanting to return a set of comics lent to you, taking advantage of your unpreparedness. And he launched a surprise attack on you and tried to violate you. And your father Fang Zhifeng came back at this time, fought with him, and was killed by him. Since you escaped to the back room and locked the door, he had to give up any further steps against you, then he escaped from your home, is that so?"

"Almost...it's been too long, I can't remember."

Huyan Yun shook his head: "I'm afraid it's unlikely, the police record for you showed that you remember every detail of what happened that night very clearly, and the psychiatrist made an assessment, and you didn't show up any severe psychological stress reactions after the incident, such as depression, insomnia, forgetfulness, anorexia or other symptoms. You seemed to have completely relaxed, and achieved very good results in the next college entrance examination..."

"That's because I got rid of Zhou Liping's harassment of me, okay?!" Maybe she was stabbed in the sore spot, Fang Mei shouted suddenly, she quickly realized her gaffe, said "I'm sorry", and replied with customized politeness, "In high school, Zhou Liping always wanted to pursue me. After being rejected by me, he harassed me endlessly, which made me very painful. But he has been stalking me all the time, making me very stressed and unable to study seriously... After that incident, although my father died to save me, it made me very sad, but at least I don't have to do bear him anymore. So I concentrated on studying and got good grades in the college entrance examination."

"You mean you've been adamantly rejecting him?"

"Yes!" Fang Mei said without hesitation.

"Then I don't understand..." Huyan Yun said slowly, "If that's the case, why do you still borrow comics from him, why do you still open your house at 9:30 on the night of the crime? During that time, serial murder cases were on the rise. Your father is the director of public security, and should have reminded you to be more careful when he is not at home, why do you still open the door to invite thieves and wolves into the room?"

Only then did Fang Mei realize that Huyan Yun was digging a big hole for herself by going around. It was as if someone had wiped her face with a wet rag. Standing up, she threw down the chairs, "Who the hell are you? Please leave here immediately! Otherwise, I'll call the security!" She strode towards the door.

"Fang Mei, do you really not remember me?!" Li Zhiyong, who had not spoken, stood up.

Looking at this sturdy, bear-like middle-aged man, Fang Mei seemed to have awakened some memories. It seemed like don't know why, she hesitated, and her anger was extinguished like a basin of water was poured out, she murmured: "I seem to recognize... May I ask who you are?"

"You forgot, when you finished writing the transcript from the criminal police team, you were afraid and hungry, standing on the side of the road crying, I took you to dinner, and sent you to Ms. Zhu's house..."

"Ah, you're Brother Yong!" Fang Mei's call from the past disintegrated the atmosphere in the room, and also removed the armor that she had cast for ten years.

Li Zhiyong went around the table, lifted the overturned chair, pointed to the chair, and said, "Come back to me, sit down!"

His tone was serious but with a little tenderness, like a brother had taught his sister who had run away from home and finally found it.

For some reason, Fang Mei's eyes flashed with water, but she shook her head lightly and returned to her original appearance. She walked back to her original position with her head held high and sat back on the chair with a very professional attitude. She crossed her arms in front of the chest, her face full of rebelliousness and stubbornness.

Li Zhiyong glanced at Huyan Yun, Huyan Yun nodded, and continued to Fang Mei: "We interviewed Ms. Zhu Min before, and what she said was completely different from what you said just now. She said that you were timid at the time and were often bullied. And Zhou Liping was also an offbeat who is excluded from his classmates, so the two of you have a good relationship with each other. He lent you the book so that some classmates described the relationship between the two of you as a couple— no no no, don't be in a hurry to refute." Huyan Yun stretched out his hand and stopped what Fang Mei was about to say, "Ms. Zhu Min has no reason to lie to us. And I firmly believe that if we visit other students in your class, we will definitely hear the same statement, you just said that you are very busy, and we are also very busy. Since everyone is busy, don't waste time."

Fang Mei opened her mouth, but in the end, she didn't make a sound.

"If everything is as Ms. Zhu Min said, and you have some kind of love relationship, then everything that happened that night would be puzzling. Zhou Liping went to your house and wanted to return the comic book that he lent you. Even if he wanted something intimate with you, then he should bring food, flowers, or more comic books. What was he doing with that murdering hammer? Suppose he did 'hard' from the beginning prepare, so bring a hammer, it is even more incredible. As the real culprit of the serial murders in the western suburbs, he should have carefully investigated the patrols and rest time of the police and the joint defense team. Why should he choose the time right at your father is home? And the most important point, why did he abuse you not in the bedroom but in the living room? According to what you stated in your transcript, Zhou Liping smashed a hammer on you from behind when you brought him the comic book. I, but I've seen the crime scene investigation records, and all your comic books are in the bedroom bookcase..."

Fang Mei was speechless.

Huyan Yun knew that his words had driven her to a dead end: "I don't know if you have seen a traditional trick called 'Three Immortals Returning Hole', two bowls, three balls. To smash the ball, use your chopsticks to point, and when you open the bowl again, the balls in the bowl have increased or decreased. Let's make an analogy. What happened at your house that night was also a 'Three Immortals Returning Hole'. There are three balls and the bowl are still two, one bowl reads 'Murderer', the other bowl reads 'Victim and Protector', we saw ten years ago that Zhou Liping was in the 'Murderer' bowl, and the other You and your father were in one bowl. When we reopened the two bowls ten years later, we found that the contents had changed. Of course, you were still in the 'victim and protector' bowl, but Zhou Liping had not in the 'Murderer' bowl. With such a big murder, the 'Murderer' bowl can't be empty, so please tell us—" He stared into Fu Mei's eyes: "What is the button in the bowl? Who?"

Fang Mei didn't look at him, her slanted eyes that were deliberately avoided were full of fear as if someone hiding in the box heard someone tapping on the lid of the box.

"I believe you still remember Gao Xiaoyan, the policewoman who died in the serial murders in the western suburbs. She broke the murderer's glasses in the desperate struggle with the murderer, forcing him to smash the fish tank in Gao Xiaoyan's house to cover the broken lens on the ground. The police recently backtracked the source of this lens. God knows, due to the quality problem of that pair of glasses, so few of them were sold. Although ten years later, the police still found the sales invoice of that year. The name of this person appeared on the customer's signature column, you can see—" He pushed his mobile phone in front of Fang Mei, and on the screen of the mobile phone was the photo of the invoice.

Don't need to look.

Tears welled up in Fang Mei's eyes, and she resisted not letting them fall.

I know who it is without a look.

"Then, let me tell the whole story of what happened that night. If it involves some memories that may hurt you, please forgive me." Huyan Yun slowly pulled the phone back, he stood up and walked next to the water dispenser, he took out a paper cup, poured a glass of warm water, and placed it in front of Fang Mei, "After your father Fang Zhifeng divorced your mother, he has always violated you, as a serious violent pervert. He used his identity as the director of the Public Security Office to commit numerous crimes in the western suburbs, but as the network of the police was tightened a little bit, it was impossible for him to do whatever he wanted as he did in the previous three cases, but he was still horny. So he tried to infringe you again that night. At this moment, Zhou Liping came to your house to look for the book he lent. He was shocked when he witnessed this scene, and Fang Zhifeng became angry and realized that once Zhou Liping took this matter out, his disguise for many years will be immediately exposed, and the police will definitely focus on himself for the detection of the serial murders in the western suburbs. So he has a killing heart and attacked Zhou Liping with a hammer while he was not prepared. But Zhou Liping usually likes to exercise, and he reacted quickly, with a strong age. So not only did he take the hammer, but also killed Fang Zhifeng in turn."

Fang Mei clasped the paper cup tightly with both hands, lowered her head, and stared straight at the water ripples in the cup due to the trembling.

"Looking at Fang Zhifeng's body lying on the ground, Zhou Liping was not afraid. He knew that he was in self-defense, and he must have heard that the murdering demon that happened recently in the western suburbs used a hammer to commit the crime. He may have eradicated one evil for society. He came to you and asked how you were. Who knows you made a request that surprised him: don't tell the police that Fang Zhifeng violated you because you originally had already been devastated, and you are timid in your life. If it is known that it is your biological father who destroyed you, I am afraid that you will never be able to get rid of the scorn and ridicule of the world. This is already extremely stressful and on the verge of collapse. You don't even dare to think about it." Huyan Yun said, "This poses a big problem for Zhou Liping. When he fought against Fang Zhifeng in the house, he left a lot of fingerprints and even bloodstains, and it is impossible for the police not to find out. There was such a big disturbance, the neighbors must have already called the police. Whether it is cleaning or forging the crime scene, it is too late. Besides, he also understands that the detective novels or reasoning comics he read are only fiction after all, and the real crime, in reality, is very It's hard to devise a trick that the police can't detect, and after thinking about it, there is only one way to help you, and that is to 'take down' the case himself!"

Standing in the corner of the reception room, Li Zhiyong looked at Huyan Yun with his lips tightly closed.

"I don't know why Zhou Liping made this important decision that would change his life. But at least one thing is certain, that is, he likes you and sympathizes with you very much. Of course, he is not stupid, he is indeed going to go to jail for helping you, but he doesn't want to die because of it. He knows very well that the police will definitely link Fang Zhifeng's death with the serial murders in the western suburbs, so he must be careful to establish a set of ' a chain of evidence that is false and true', made him and the real culprit of the serial murders in the western suburbs have a relationship of 'if there is none'. The so-called evidence is nothing but human and physical evidence. As for human evidence, he is gone a real step, according to the serial murders in the news, he taught you to make up a story and even smashed your left shoulder with a hammer to make him look like the real serial murderer. At the same time, he took another 'virtual' step in the decisive material evidence. He knew that the fingerprints and footprints that the police could find in your home were just evidence that he killed Fang Zhifeng. With this evidence, it is impossible for Fang Zhifeng's death to be combined with the other three cases in the judicial judgment, and since he was a minor at the time, the court could only give a light sentence. For this reason, he also took the hammer especially, because although it has been a long time since the first three crimes, he is still worried that the DNA of the victims of the first three murders may be detected on the hammer. – it is difficult for him to read so many detective novels and mystery comics, and it does help him successfully walk a tightrope at a critical moment.

"But no matter how scheming he was, he was just a high school student with no criminal experience, and in the subsequent investigation by the police, two things exceeded his expectations and put him in danger. There is a lot of mold on the soles of the shoes on the windowsill, and in the crime scenes of the previous three murders, mold was also detected in the footprints left by the criminals; secondly, based on the cover-up method used by the murderer to break the fish tank at the scene of Gao Xiaoyan's murder, I deduced that he is a fan of reasoning Japanese comics. Through this, the police have locked Zhou Liping as a suspect even before connecting the murder in your home – plus the second time it's a coincidence that he didn't wear glasses because his glasses were broken, all these are very unfavorable to him." Having said that, Huyan Yun glanced at Li Zhiyong, "Fortunately, a police officer with excellent insight in the police station insisted on defending Zhou Liping: the soles of every pair of sneakers that have not seen the sun for a long time are prone to mold growth, and it is very likely that the culprit also hid the shoes he wore when he committed the crime. In addition, the real culprit may indeed be someone who likes to watch reasoning comics, but there are many people who like to watch reasoning comics, and because Zhou Liping likes to watch it, he cannot be drawn with the real murderer – by the way, I can be sure that Fang Zhifeng came up with the cover-up method after Gao Xiaoyan broke his glasses just because he read the comics Zhou Liping lent you – and Zhou Liping's body type is very similar to the real culprit of the serial murders in the western suburbs, but the same determination cannot be made in the subsequent scientific and technological verification. In the end, Zhou Liping, who had lost his balance halfway through the tightrope, regained his balance once again. He successfully got to the end – he was sentenced to ten years in prison."

Speaking of this, Huyan Yun let out a long sigh of relief. He stood in front of the large floor-to-ceiling windows in the reception room and looked out. Under the blue sky, the city's tall buildings and folded bridges were covered with rust. The color, those distorted but erratic traffic flows in the street market in the evening, moving their long bodies arduously and slowly, as if the time without oil has lost their direction, they do not know where they came from, and they do not know the way back...

He turned around and looked at Fang Mei who was in a trance: "Excuse me, am I right?"

For a long time, Fang Mei was silent, like an anesthetized patient on the operating table, until she realized that even if the anesthesia wears off, the two people in the room will not leave, and then she slowly opened her mouth: "It's all over. It's been so long, as a victim, I don't want to pursue it anymore... Everyone has an unforgettable past, why do you have to turn over these old accounts?" She raised her head and glanced at Huyan Yun, seeing his serious expression, then changed a pleading tone, "Well, I admit that what you said just now is true. That night ten years ago, it was exactly what you said. I was very scared at the time, and Zhou Liping understood that I didn't want to be known that I was violated by that bastard, so he took the initiative to file this case. I didn't force him. The confession I gave in the police record was also taught by him... But I'm a victim, and it's been ten years. I'm not going to be held accountable now for making a false confession. Moreover, Zhou Liping's new case has nothing to do with the case ten years ago. You can arrest him or lock him up, but I never want to hear this man's name again—"

"Hey!" Huyan Yun shouted angrily, causing her to shut her mouth in fright.

Perhaps because of his anger, Huyan Yun was speechless for a long time after saying "Hey".

Fang Mei looked at him and didn't dare to make a sound, the reception room fell into dead silence again.

Huyan Yun took a few deep breaths before lowering his voice and said to Fang Mei: "You are not the only victim, Zhou Liping is also a victim! And he spent the most precious time in prison purely to protect your reputation. The youthful years... If it wasn't for him to stand up and help you completely get rid of the shadow of the old days, you can go to university in a relaxed mood? Can you sit in this high-end office building and become a professional expert? Of course, I'm not saying that you have to thank him for the old debts. But how can you put all the responsibility on him when you talk about the past?!"

Perhaps being stinged by these words, Fang Mei suddenly became excited: "You think I have everything I am today, thanks to Zhou Liping? Nonsense! I can sit in this position in this office building, completely relying on me! Do you know how much effort I put in? I get up early and stay up late, year after year, working overtime, no days off, no long vacations, every day I go to work and get off work, the street lights on the road are always on! Yes, Zhou Liping did help me get rid of those shadows back then. I have to thank him. Without him, I couldn't be admitted to the university with a relaxed mind, but getting rid of it is only temporary. You are completely wrong when you use the word "complete" to describe it! No one can completely get rid of the pain in my heart after my body is defiled, no one! I have to keep running to keep a distance from those shadows, but as long as I stop and take a breath, such as listening to an old song, going back to school once, walking alone in the rain with an umbrella, or even standing at the window and looking at the world at dusk like you just did, those shadows will come out of my heart like poisonous snakes and wrap around my neck, which can literally strangle me to death! Outsiders see how hardworking and diligent I am, but in fact, I am just running for my life...Finally, I have an independent office, I bought a house in the city center, I have a loved one and got married, but there is always a string in my heart, like meat that cannot be picked between my teeth. I am afraid that people around me will know what happened ten years ago. I am really afraid! This society, no matter it is an opponent or a lover, they are trying to dig your privacy and find your weakness until you are caught off guard and give you a fatal blow! For a woman, what is more painful than the rape of her biological father?! At that time, you—and Ms. Zhu, chased after me, stuck the shadow back to my feet, and told me loudly, 'Hey, you lost something', what's the point?!'"

Suddenly, tears filled her face.

Huyan Yun looked at her, not knowing whether it was the shedding tears or the fading light, which lightened her makeup a bit, and it was only then that they could see that, at only twenty-eight years old, the wrinkles on her face were deeper, and heavier than thirty-eight-year-old women...

He took a long sigh, sat down opposite Fang Mei again, and said slowly: "No, Fang Mei, you are wrong, we are not here to condemn anything, let alone discover something. We just want to find out what kind of person Zhou Liping is, because this is of great important significance to the detection of the massacre that happened on the Deratization Hill. And because, until today, Zhou Liping, who has been imprisoned again, has not tried to turn over the case ten years ago to exonerate himself... He could have done that, as long as he could prove that he had nothing to do with the serial murders in the western suburbs ten years ago and that he killed Fang Zhifeng to eradicate the evil. Then his suspicions in the Deratization Hill case will be reduced to some extent, but he didn't do it. He would rather be interrogated by the criminal police again and again in prison. He didn't say a word about you...for many years, I have seen too many evils in human nature. The complexity of human nature makes it difficult for me to make judgments of 'good' and 'bad' on a person, and it makes me tired of condemning anyone or criticizing something. But The case of Deratization Hill is too strange. No matter from which angle, this case is so thorough and decisive. The person who can make such a big case is either a completely bad person or a completely good person. In short, he should be a thorough and resolute person, we just want to find out whether Zhou Liping is such a person... As for the others, please rest assured, we have already greeted the police officer who found the signed invoice and obtained assurance: she will only report the relevant physical evidence was submitted to the superior for the record, and after Zhou Liping was proved not to be the murderer of the Deratization Hill case, the relevant departments would come forward to restore Zhou Liping's innocence, and give him certain financial compensation to help him find a better job. The truth of the old case to the media and the press unless he makes a request – I firmly believe that he will continue to help you keep the secret that has been kept for ten years, so – it will never affect your present and future."

After some remarks, she instantly removed the boulder that was pressing on her heart, she covered her face and cried out: "I know I'm sorry for him, I know he's a good man, he sat for me so much after many years in prison, I have never dared to stand up and say a word for him. I really dare not... On my wedding day, when I was toasting the guests, I saw Ms. Zhu standing by the window and looking out, with a sad face. I followed her gaze and saw Zhou Liping standing on the street opposite the hotel looking towards me. I was terrified, but in a blink of an eye, he disappeared, and he never bothered me again, I know he just wanted to see how the girl he had protected for ten years turned into a bride, and when he saw it, he was relieved and left..."

7

Li Zhiyong drove the car very fast. In the stagnant traffic and people in the evening, he rammed like a bison spitting fire. He almost slashed the car or hit a person several times, but he didn't care. He leaned his upper body on the steering wheel, his face was almost stuck to the glass window, and he just put on a gesture of trying to fight with someone and opened it forward. His small eyes had never been so round or so big, but the eyeballs were empty and blank as if a patient with cataracts who can't see at all...

This frightened Huyan Yun who was sitting in the co-pilot. When he came down from the office building just now, Li Zhiyong had been sticking his back to the elevator carboard, bent over, his big head was drooping, and his neck could not straighten as if it had been cut off. As soon as he got out of the elevator, his cell phone rang, and after a few words, his already pale face became even grayer. He strode toward the parking lot. Huyan Yun had to trot to catch up with him. After getting into the car, he drove into the street like an F1 racer. He didn't say a word when he was asked what was wrong. He just drove forward with straight eyebrows. Huyan Yun had to secretly fasten his seat belt.

It was not until the car stopped that Huyan Yun realized that they had come to the gate of the social security center again. Li Zhiyong jumped off the driver's seat and rushed inside, even forgetting to put the handbrake on. Huyan Yun hurriedly walked around from the co-pilot, put on the handbrake, locked the car, and walked to the social security center. As soon as he walked up the steps, he heard a harsh roar from inside. He quickly pushed open the door and went in. Seeing Li Zhiyong holding a form in his hand, he was waving his arms frantically, shouting something, and his face turned red. He was flushed red, even the roots of his ears were red, and his unkempt hair suddenly burst out. Because he was too angry, the blood vessels on his neck, arms, and the backs of his hands burst out one by one, and the corners of his eyes also burst into red threads, as if they were torn apart by anger. .

"It's just such a thing, just such a table. You have made me run three times back and forth in less than a month! The first time you said that the relatives of the insured are not allowed to pay on behalf of the insured, and the insured must be It took a long time to pay, but it was your own charter, and the state did not stipulate it at all; the second time you said that the registration form must be attached with the front and back of the ID card of the person to be paid, I asked you why you didn't say it earlier, you said there were no hard and fast rules in the past, but now they are strict. I accepted I was unlucky. I went home and took my mother's ID card. I made a photocopy of the front and back and handed it over to you. And I also asked if there are any other changes, don't let me run back and forth, you say no; today you told me that the bank registered on the form is not accepted, it must be the designated commercial bank, and those who do not have this commercial bank card must go and apply for a card first – are you tossing others?!"

The staff sitting behind the glass partition still had the same faces and expressions. They watched Li Zhiyong furiously, with a smile on the corners of their mouths. A woman with a long and narrow face, wearing black-rimmed glasses and dark gray overalls walked out slowly from behind the partition, holding a chubby glass jar in which was soaked wolfberry, kumquat, longan. She walked up to Li Zhiyong and said in a deliberately protracted tone: "Young man, these are all our work, why do you have to be so angry? It's so inappropriate!"

"You are just tossing others! Just because the first time you asked me to come, my friend said a few words of justice for me for the insured person's payment rule, and you will take revenge on me!" Li Zhiyong gasped. He was angry, resentful, and helpless, and said, "You all sit in this hall every day, you don't have to do anything. Just do a few pokes, drink a few cups of tea, and when you are bored, find all kinds of trouble for us. Looking for fun and happiness, you look in the mirror and see the smiles on your faces now, so proud, so superior. If you have the ability, you will always laugh like this!"

The woman in the dark gray overalls nodded gracefully, took a sip of the health tea in the glass jar, and then spit a goji berry back into the glass jar with a "pop", raised her head, and looked at Li Zhiyong, with a smile on her face. She tapped the form in his hand with her chin: "Then will you do it today? If you don't do it, we'll have to get off work..."

Huyan Yun was afraid that Li Zhiyong would really beat her up, so he dragged him away.

Back in the car and sitting in the driver's seat, Li Zhiyong was still shaking all over. He tried to tear the form up several times, but he couldn't. Finally, he slammed his forehead against the steering wheel and didn't lift it up for a long time. .

"If it really doesn't work, go back and wait for Ma to come back and let him do this for you." Huyan Yun carefully took the form out of Li Zhiyong's fingers.

After a while, Li Zhiyong raised his head, his eyes were red, his throat was gurgling, and he kept swallowing something.

For a while, Huyan Yun didn't know what to persuade him, so he just sat silently in the co-pilot, watching the crowded and cluttered streets dwindle and the noise fade away.

They don't know when the wind picked up, and the fallen leaves were thrown from the street to the end of the street in pieces as if the twilight ripples on the ground...

The car restarted and kept heading west, driving through countless intersections with flashing traffic lights, leaving the tall buildings behind, so that after the sky was more open, the Xishan figure was as broad and continuous as the ridge of a beast... There was a fresh smell in the cold air that only comes out when the spring willows are just sprouting. It smells a little bitter, a little sweet, and a little sour. In this bleak late autumn.

Contrary to Huyan Yun's expectations, the car did not stop when it passed the door of Li Zhiyong's house but continued to drive in the northwest direction. After several turns, they suddenly took a sharp turn and got into an alley. Only then did Huyan Yun recognize that it was the alley leading to the Deratization Hill subway station. But once again, what he didn't expect was that when they passed the iron fence gate that entered the nursery, the car continued to move forward without stopping. It drove to the west end of the alley and turned left. Li Zhiyong slammed the accelerator hard, and the wheels were jumped on the sandy road and stopped on a high concrete platform.

Li Zhiyong and the car breathed heavily together for a long time, and then gradually regained their calm. However, the continuous barking of dogs once again broke the silence of the mountain, which sounded extremely disturbing.

Li Zhiyong jumped out of the car, and his bewildered eyes first turned to the nursery under the high platform: the entrances of the three subways looked like three coffins that were permanently abandoned, confined by the fence in a field of smoke and vines. Then he looked farther to the east, the gigantic city with splendid lights and radiance, splashed with brilliant virtual images in the turbulent night, like a dream.

"Ten years, ten years..." he muttered, "what have I done..."

Chapter 9

1

The moment Guo Xiaofen stepped out of the high-speed rail car, she regretted that she had brought fewer clothes. The weather forecast said that this sudden cold snap in southern China was not seen in ten years, and that was true. The ground, stop signs, and guardrails of the station were covered with a layer of rustling silver. The LED electronic screen was broken somehow. A string of inexplicable characters was scrolling shiveringly. Not to mention the exposed skin of her hands and face, she was so cold that she suspected that all her clothes were hollow, and even her feet that were covered with shoes and socks were freezing. She erected the collar of her trench coat, put her hands in her pockets, cradled her neck, and limped behind Ma Xiaozhong out of the station exit to the empty square in front of the station. Apart from a black police car and an old man in a military coat selling boiled tea eggs, there is not even a dog. Underfoot is the hard-frozen lead-grey concrete, and the head-up was also lead-grey as if the concrete floor was covered with a layer of ice and the sky hung upside down.

Ma Xiaozhong cursingly took out his cell phone and made a call. Before he could say a few words, a gray Tucson was perfect for the unfortunate weather appeared and drove until it stopped in front of them. The driver jumped out of the car. He was a small man in a brown leather jacket. His thin cheeks were wrapped around his angular face. His eye sockets were a little deep, but his mouth was a little convex. He smiled like an umbrella with broken bones.

Ma Xiaozhong opened the car door, let Guo Xiaofen sit in the back row, ran to the passenger seat himself, waited for the little man to return to the car, and introduced them. The little man's name is Xiao Chunhua, a criminal policeman of the County Public Security Bureau. He had been trained for a month at the Wangyueyuan Police Station a few years ago. Ma Xiaozhong treated him like a brother. Before coming to the county this time, he specially called him to ask him for help. Of course, Xiao Chunhua was pleased to help.

"It's fucking cold!" Ma Xiaozhong turned on the heater in the car, leaned back on the back seat, and asked Xiao Chunhua, "I want you to help me check that Dong Yue, have you found her?"

"I checked, her cell phone has been turned off, I'm still looking for her..." Xiao Chunhua said while driving, "There have been a lot of young people returning home recently, and the above institute asked us to strengthen management. How could it be easy, with the short manpower in the municipal bureau, they can't even count the names of people..."

"They are all young people who have been trained in big cities. Don't use them as a burden. They are talents if they could be managed properly." Ma Xiaozhong took out a pack of cigarettes, just about to take out one, looked back at Guo Xiaofen, then the cigarette was stuffed back into his pocket.

"Talents? It's untenable in such a big city, and it's even more difficult to come back to work. State-owned enterprises have long been filled with radishes and pits, and private enterprises are all family-owned. You don't have the same surname, then you won't have a job no matter how great you are..."

"Then how to place them? You can't just watch them floating around in society doing nothing?"

"That's why it's a headache." Xiao Chunhua said with a wry smile, "But it's not that bad. The government has given them a lot of support for their own businesses, such as discounted loans, tax relief, etc. Young people are discouraged, they feel that they have fought hard outside, and they are still a complete failure when they return to their hometown. More and more people are addicted to alcohol, drugs, and self-defeating. They all go to 'ghost town' and live like ghosts... ...."

"What is a 'ghost town'?" Ma laughed for a moment.

"A few years ago, in order to achieve political achievements, the county desperately took out loans to build new towns. Tens of thousands of high-rise buildings were built on the ground, and there were a lot of illegal money and debts. In the past two years, the country has rectified the real estate market and financial market. Those towns, no one cares, no water, and no electricity. At night, there is a large area of darkness, placed in the suburbs as if hell. The homeless, unemployed youths and even fugitives are all there. You know Kowloon City in Hong Kong. These new towns are the new Kowloon Walled City."

"Won't it become a place outside the law in the long run? It might be big trouble in the future!" Ma Xiaozhong said.

"In the future? It's troublesome enough now!" Xiao Chunhua said, "Pornography, gambling, drugs, and other fraud gangs all gather there, like a sewer."

"You need to handle it early. It's the same as washing clothes. When it gets dirty, wash it immediately, and it can be washed off. After a long time, it will look like branded, and won't get clean."

"Everybody knows, but our police force is insufficient! Just maintaining law and order in the old city is exhausting. The new city belongs to the suburbs. No one wanted to control those areas. And with the troublesome now, after all" Xiao Chunhua glanced at Ma Xiaozhong curiously, "Director, you have always been social, why don't you know this."

"I just live in a big city, and I don't know what's going on outside." Ma Xiaozhong knocked on his brain, "By the way, where are we going now?"

Xiao Chunhua looked at his watch: "It's almost five o'clock, and it will get colder after the sun sets. I'll find a restaurant for you to have dinner, and then stay in a nearby hotel for one night. I'll drive to pick you up tomorrow morning. Once I got Dong Yue's news, let's find her together."

Ma Xiaozhong said "OK", and then continued to chat with Xiao Chunhua about local security issues, but Guo Xiaofen was a little uneasy. Although the warm air was whirring inside the car, the cold wind outside the car was still hissing like a snake, spit cold and got in through the cracks of the window, squeezing out the little warm air that had been saved with great effort. Her hands and feet that had been motionless for a long time were cold at first, then numb, and then the numbness crept into her heart, leaving her heart as empty as if a hole had been gouged out...

She cast her eyes out of the car window: the county town in the evening was as desolate as an abandoned ancient city in the desert. The buildings facing the street, old and new, of different heights, and the low and dilapidated brick and tile houses hidden behind them, all had no lights and was lifeless. There were hardly any pedestrians on the street, and a minibus painted with painless advertisements drove by slowly, looking strange and inexplicable. Maybe it was because the weather was too cold and no customers came to the door. The businesses along the street closed early, even the most prosperous commercial street next to the county government was no exception: banks, post offices and insurance companies were locked, not to mention department stores. The black windshield hung at the entrance of the shopping mall, drooping like the eyelids of a patient with myasthenia, and no one came in or out at all. Only in front of the cinema was a row of carts with kebabs, roasted sweet potatoes, and baked beans, flashing with charcoal fires. The female owner of a fruit shop dumped a box of frozen pears into the garbage basket, and there was a bit of malicious ridicule in her indifferent expression, as if she had long expected those pears to die and they finally died. When they were approaching Jiexin Park, they suddenly heard a deafening sound of square dance music. When took a closer look, it turned out that there were only three aunts who were standing unevenly and their clothes were wrapped like buns. The older team danced "Calories" by Rocket Girls. They waved their sturdy arms, twisted their fat waists, and swayed their collapsed butts. They meticulously made every dance move in the ugliest way possible. In place, especially when they followed Yang Chaoyue in the trolley speaker and shouted out the incomparably high-pitched "burn your calories", the volley they pushed out with all their might, if it wasn't for the drowsy sunset, then the sun and the moon may about to change the majesty of the new sky.

"Stop!" Ma Xiaozhong suddenly pointed to the street and said to Xiao Chunhua.

"What's wrong?" Xiao Chunhua hurriedly pulled over to stop.

Ma Xiaozhong jumped out of the car and got into the only clothing store that was not closed.

At this moment, Guo Xiaofen stretched her stiff fingers, took the phone out of her pocket, and found an address for Xiao Chunhua to see: "Is this place far from the county?"

"It's not too far," Xiao Chunhua said.

"Then, shall we go here tomorrow?"

Xiao Chunhua nodded: "No problem."

At this moment, Ma Xiaozhong came back, and as soon as he got in the car, he threw a thick foggy pink woolen coat into Guo Xiaofen's arms, and said to Xiao Chunhua, "Start."

Guo Xiaofen glanced at the back of the short fat man's head, the occipital bone that bulged like a hillside.

She slowly put the woolen coat over her body.

2

Early the next morning, Xiao Chunhua came to the hotel and told Ma Xiaozhong and Guo Xiaofen, who were having breakfast, that Dong Yue was still not found, "I'll take you to where Reporter Guo wants to go first?"

Ma Xiaozhong asked Guo Xiaofen in surprise: "Where are you going?"

Guo Xiaofen lowered her head and drank the white rice porridge in the bowl one by one without speaking.

Tucson drove on the highway for more than half an hour and turned into a town. Although it was already 8:30 in the morning, except for some old people playing chess gathered under the big tree in front of the supply and marketing cooperatives and credit cooperatives, the whole town seemed empty, and even the elementary school playground where the flag-raising ceremony was being held have few children to be seen. "Young people have all gone to work outside," Xiao Chunhua explained, but when Ma Xiaozhong asked him, "Didn't you say they have all come back in the past two years?", he smiled awkwardly and said, "They won't at least come here if they were back."

It wasn't until Guo Xiaofen opened the pictures on her phone and pointed to a photo of a person to ask a villager for directions that Ma Xiaozhong knew that she was looking for Yue Shao's home.

Yue Shao's home is behind a large pond, and a large osmanthus tree is planted at the entrance. When the car drove directly into his home yard, a woman washing clothes by the sink raised her head in surprise. Guo Xiaofen jumped out of the car and asked, knowing that she was Yue Shao's wife, and quickly introduced herself. At first, Yue Shao's wife was still a little confused and didn't know what she was doing at her house. When she heard that the female reporter had witnessed her husband's car accident, she smiled helplessly, and tears rolled from the corners of her eyes. A girl who was sitting in front of a small square table under the eaves and drawing, ran over, calling out "Mom", and wisely hugging the woman's waist.

The woman brought Guo Xiaofen into the house. There was a photo of Yue Shao on a wooden table in the center of the living room. In the photo, Yue Shao was very thin, with a smile on his face, kind and weak.

Guo Xiaofen looked at the posthumous photo, stood for a long time, and then bowed deeply three times. Yue Shao's wife couldn't help crying. Guo Xiaofen stepped forward and wanted to comfort her with a few words. But all the words were hypocritical and powerless, so she just grabbed her pair of rough and thick hands with her snow-white soft hands, just so tight caught for a long time. Seeing that the woman was getting better, Guo Xiaofen took out a white envelope from her satchel and stuffed it into her hand. There was 2,000 yuan in it. The woman refused to accept it at first, but in the end, after Guo Xiaofen said, "It's for the child to buy books", she reluctantly accepted it.

One sentence reminded Xiao Chunhua, he asked Yue Shao's daughter: "Why didn't you go to school today?"

Before waiting for the little girl to speak, Ma Xiaozhong walked out of the yard with straight brows and eyes. He looked around and saw a black

Kia parked by the bamboo forest behind the pond. He immediately ran over and pulled out three of them from the car. Sixteen or seventeen-year-old Smarts with dyed shit yellow hair.

"What are you doing?!" A boy in skinny pants, his face, and buttocks were shriveled, shouted at Ma Xiaozhong, his teeth were yellow, and his mouth stinks terribly.

Ma Xiaozhong pointed at his lower abdomen as a punch. This punch is a "stuffy punch" that the old criminal police use to deal with the most dangerous enemies. The punch is quick, short but powerful. The position of the punch is very particular. All his internal organs "convulsed" in an instant, and the boy fell to the ground, curled up in a ball, so painful that he couldn't even make a moan, and his mouth opened and closed like a caught fish.

The other two boys rushed up and tried to fight, but when Ma Xiaozhong pulled out a pair of shiny handcuffs, they were all stunned and dared not move.

Ma Xiaozhong handcuffed the boy on the ground, then raised his chin and asked the other two boys, "What are you doing?"

The two boys said nothing, "just come out to play", Ma Xiaozhong smiled poisonously and pointed to the yard opposite the pond: "This family is a martyr and is protected by the police. Can you play in another place?"

The two boys were so frightened that they drove into the car and ran away without a trace.

At this time, Guo Xiaofen and Xiao Chunhua rushed over. Ma Xiaozhong picked up the one on the ground and threw it in the back seat of the Tucson. He sat beside him. Xiao Chunhua and Guo Xiaofen sat in the driver's seats respectively and drove to the county seat. When passing by a yard with only broken bricks and tiles left, Guo Xiaofen asked the car to stop for a while. She got out of the car, walked into the yard, and walked around. A small, incomplete blackboard was dug out from the rubble, with a faint layer of gray that had been painted and rubbed off with chalk hundreds of times. Her eyes slowly swept across the yard and even the overgrown weeds had turned yellow, that had been abandoned for a long time. Then she returned to the car.

"Where is this?" Ma Xiaozhong asked.

"The Camphor Tree nursing home." Guo Xiaofen said.

Somehow these words made Ma Xiaozhong felt angry, and he slapped to the Smart lying on the seat: "Get up! Don't fucking pretend dying!"

Smart sat up slowly, clutching his stomach, fear was written on his acne-covered face.

"You come to lie at the door of the martyr's house, so scared that his wife and child dare not go out. If it was known by the above they have to peel my skin." Ma Xiaozhong slapped his face, "So, give me a face, and tell me who asked you to do this dirty work so that I can explain to the above and keep my job."

"We really just came out to play..." Smart whispered.

"Fine!" Ma Xiaozhong nodded, and patted Xiao Chunhua who was driving on the shoulder, "High-speed rail station, take this guy to see the world."

"Ah? We're not looking for Dong Yue?" Xiao Chunhua didn't understand what he meant, but Guo Xiaofen, who was next to him, gave him a quick wink, and he suddenly realized.

"I'm not looking for her anymore, this one is enough for my job." Ma Xiaozhong said with a smile.

"I...I want to find my mother!" Smart pleaded.

"No, you don't need to find your mother. When you come to our place, you will be covered for three hundred and sixty-five days a year, calling mom every day." Ma Xiaozhong put his hands behind his head and threw a pillow.

Smart suddenly burst into tears, with thick snot and tears on his face: "I'll be honest, this is what Heipiao found for us, let us stare at the mother and daughter if they want to go far away, call him in time. He may be fear of them going to petition or something..."

When Xiao Chunhua heard it, he said, "Heipiao is a famous gangster in the county. He has been in and out of detention centers and prisons several times."

"Catch him!" Ma Xiaozhong said viciously, "Don't let him come out again after three or five years, and I don't have time to manage the people behind Heipiao now. Thirty miles around, I don't want to see anyone that shouldn't be seen again, if they are harassed or frightened a little bit, tell your Director Liu, I'll be able to find an excuse to take off his black gauze hat!"

Knowing that this was meant for Smart, but Ma Xiaozhong said with such ruthless energy, which was really shocking, Xiao Chunhua said "yes" very cooperatively.

Hearing that this short fat man can control the chief of a county's public security. He thought he was a high-ranking official who made a private interview. Smart was so frightened that he trembled: "Report... report to the government, can I atone the blame by doing good things?"

Ma Xiaozhong squinted at him, as if looking at a caterpillar: "What kind of merit can you do?"

"The Dong Yue you mentioned just now, I know where she is..."

"Ghost town." Xiao Chunhua pointed to the front and said.

The lead-grey buildings that block the sky and are stacked with peaks, like large mountains arched out by the movement of the earth's crust, suddenly appeared on the horizon. There is not even a single tree in the building complex for several kilometers. Looking at it, it is a big lump of lead-gray. The unfinished walls are broken, all the ravines have not been filled, and all the mounds are dancing with dust. The bottom floors of all the buildings are cut open with square gaps. Because there is no glass installed, the windows on the buildings look like giant honeycombs. As it blew, there was a deafening humming sound inside, which was terrifying to hear.

Tucson slowly drove forward along a road full of gravel and dirt. The huge building blocked the already thin sunlight, so a straight gloomy line unfolded in front of them. The walls on both sides were stained with urine, and some weeds grew in the cracks in the ground. Occasionally, a few black garbage bags and a few strips of white toilet paper floated by... the car drove for a long time without seeing a person or a dog, a bird, or even a ghost. Maybe it was too quiet, an empty soda can rolled by with a sound like a drum. The traffic lights at the intersection are all off. Convenience stores, newsstands, and police offices were also empty, and the intact glass windows were even more frightening than broken. Ma Xiaozhong suspected that he was in the documentary "The World After Humans Disappeared", and was a little flustered, until behind an excavator with rusted tracks, he saw a group of people with hair dyed red, yellow, or purple wearing a skull necklace, and a black leather coat, squatting on the ground smoking, his heart was a little more at ease.

Perhaps it was because of his distraction that Smart next to him suddenly slammed the car door and jumped out of the car, fell to the ground and rolled, stood up on the ground, and ran towards the group of hooligans, shouting as he running: "Master Shen, Master Shen! Help!"

Ma Xiaozhong scolded and jumped out of the car.

Standing among the hooligans was a tall and thin man. Although he was only in his early forties, he had gray hair, a round face, and a pair of ordinary glasses. He looked like gentle literati. Only at that time he grinning, he burst out a bad tooth that was smoked yellow, which made the smile look extra cruel. When Smart ran in front of him, he grabbed the chain on the handcuffs, and Smart screamed in pain, but he said lazily, "What kind of new jewelry are you wearing? "

"This man is a policeman. He arrested me and beat me!" Smart said, pointing to Ma Xiaozhong, who was approaching.

The hooligans who were smoking and squatted on the ground stood up and stared at Ma Xiaozhong with a murderous look on their faces.

"Heipiao?" Ma Xiaozhong pointed at the surnamed Shen and asked Xiao Chunhua next to him in a low voice.

Xiao Chunhua shook his head: "This man is the boss of the 'Ghost Town', and he has always been quite the norm."

At this time Guo Xiaofen also got out of the car, and a hooligan whistled obscenely when he saw her beautiful appearance.

The surnamed Shen glanced at Ma Xiaozhong. Although he was sure that he was a policeman by the way he walked, he felt that he was a bit evil, so he hesitated.

Ma Xiaozhong walked in front of the surnamed Shen, grabbed Smart's hair, carried him over like a chicken, then took out the key, opened the handcuffs for him, and pushed him to the surnamed Shen again.

It's a show of face. The surnamed Shen naturally understood, so he took out a cigarette and lit it in Ma Xiaozhong. Ma Xiaozhong took a sip, nodded, and the two walked to a corner far away from the crowd to chat alone.

"We don't welcome you here." said the surnamed Shen.

"I'll leave when I'm done." Ma Xiaozhong sai, "Do you have a girl named Dong Yue here?"

The surnamed Shen obviously had never heard of the name, so he waved to the crowd and called a pseudo-girl whose face was painted whiter than her butt: "A girl named Dong Yue, is she here?"

"She just came, and it didn't take long for her to start." The pseudo-girl blinked her eyes with the long eyelashes and said.

"We have something to do with her." Ma Xiaozhong said, staring at the surnamed Shen, "Half an hour, we'll go after we talk – you can listen by the side."

The surnamed Shen nodded and said to the pseudo-mother, "Lead the way."

It was not until he walked into this huge beehive that Ma Xiaozhong realized that it was a completely unfamiliar world. Because it is an unfinished building, there is neither electricity nor an elevator. No matter how many floors, you can only go up the stairs, but there are no handrails on the concrete steps. Walking on it is trembling, and if you are not careful, you will fall to the first floor, and be smashed to pieces on the cement floor. The following floors were empty, and when they climbed up to the sixth or seventh floor, they suddenly smelled a strange smell which was disgusting, the pseudo-girl and the surnamed Shen were accustomed to it and walked into the flat, and they followed behind and frowned.

All the rough houses on this floor have no doors, only a few have curtains or blocks of wood, but the windows are all nailed with translucent plastic sheets. It seemed like there was a pregnant woman clinging to the outside of every window. Originally, the light was not good today, and if it was blocked like this, it looked particularly gloomy. The house is divided into different functions, and because of different functions, all the people gather. Some are scolding and haggling in the room full of snacks, some are playing mahjong around the chess and card table, and some are watching pornography or playing online games on a laptop, some lie on the dark bed and rub their dick, while others just sit against the wall and squeeze the boils on their faces, their arms full of injection needles. In a room with four drinking fountains and a lot of blue drinking water buckets, a drunk man slept soundly with an empty bucket, twisting his body just to let out a string of loud farts more comfortably... never knowing which room was a sudden sound was probably due to the simple gasoline generator supplying electricity on this floor, but it sounded like more drunkards were emitting more exhaust gas, making the already stinky floor even more stench.

At the end of the corridor, heavy breathing and lewd groans were heard from several rooms, the surnamed Shen stopped, and Ma Xiaozhong also stopped. Pseudo-girl got into a room not long after and brought out a girl. She is not tall, with good-looking eyes, wearing a light pink knitted sweater, and wearing sexy flesh-colored stockings on her legs, but due to malnutrition and haggard complexion, she looks like a dehydrated radish.

"Dong Yue?" Ma Xiaozhong asked.

There was a hint of panic in the girl's eyes as if she didn't want to hear the name again, she glanced at the surnamed Shen and the pseudo-girl, and couldn't see anything on their stiff faces, so she nodded numbly.

"Let's talk in another place." Ma Xiaozhong took her to a slightly farther house. Guo Xiaofen and Xiao Chunhua also entered, but the person surnamed Shen did not come in. The pseudo-girl just took a step inside and was caught and kept off.

"We are the police." Ma Xiaozhong showed her the police officer's card. "You don't have to be afraid, we just want to find out something from you... Zhou Liping, do you still have any impressions of him?"

There was a sudden flash of light in the originally gloomy eyes, and Dong Yue nodded: "What... what happened?"

"As you probably know, he was imprisoned for a serial murder case ten years ago, but we recently found out that he is probably innocent. During the interview, we learned that in the past year, you were relatively close, so we came here specifically to find out what kind of person he is. I hope you don't have any scruples and tell the truth, this will also help us to fully grasp his situation, and we should vindicate him. And I believe you don't want him to carry the blame all his life."

This set of rhetoric was negotiated by Ma Xiaozhong and Guo Xiaofen. Although the case of Deratization Hill was a big deal, due to the police's control over media reports, it did not become a hot spot of public opinion. It is estimated that Dong Yue could not have known about Zhou Liping's arrest. In order to reduce her psychological pressure, they simply gave a more "positive" reason for the interrogation.

After listening to Ma Xiaozhong's words, Dong Yue was stunned for a long time, and a faint smile appeared on the corner of her mouth: "If... if it were earlier, it would be great."

"What's earlier?" Ma Xiaozhong asked in confusion.

Dong Yue did not continue to speak.

Guo Xiaofen understood her words: "You mean, Zhou Liping didn't stay with you because he was a murderer and was afraid of implicating you. But you know the news after you left him?"

Dong Yue looked at her and nodded slowly.

Guo Xiaofen said with a sad expression: "Don't worry about it, people keep missing out with the people they like all their lives..."

In a word, water glittered in Dong Yue's eyes: "From the day I first saw him, I knew he was a good person, he took my sister out of the nursing home and reunited us. I worked in a nightclub and was sexually assaulted by others. He helped me every time. Others knew that he had been in prison before and that he was a felon. They were all scared to death, so no one dared to bully me again. He knew that I liked him, but being with me for so long, he never being unruly...how could he be a serial killer as such a kind, decent guy?"

"Has he talked to you about the case ten years ago?" Guo Xiaofen asked.

Dong Yue nodded: "For a while, I thought I was like a fire to him, but he was always a piece of ice to me, so I got angry, ignored him, didn't answer the phone, blocked WeChat, but I looked forward he could come for me every day. I thought he had such a tough personality, maybe in the end, I had to contact him. Who knew that he couldn't get in touch with me for two days, so he was in a hurry and ran to the nightclub to find me... He was with me in midnight. He talked about a lot of things from the past, but I couldn't understand it. I asked him why he took the initiative to take such a crime since he was not a serial murderer? He said that he was about to graduate from high school at that time, and he probably wouldn't be able to go to college. It is also difficult to find a decent job. His aunt wants to kick him out. He didn't even have a place to live. He is very disappointed with the future. He thought he'd better die but just happened to encounter such a thing. For the sake of the girl's reputation, he took it down as soon as his mind became hot. And he didn't think too much about the consequences... I asked him, now ten years have passed, why didn't he go to the public security to explain the situation? He said that the case in the western suburbs was a big one. Once the case is overturned, there will definitely be a lot of media coverage, which is not good for the girl. The girl just got married and is doing well. I got angry suddenly, I asked him if he still liked that girl, he stared at me blankly for a long time before he said 'no', just those two words, he said it very seriously, I immediately understood that he really likes me..."

Dong Yue turned her face sideways, wiped her eyes, and then said, "I asked him directly 'since you don't like her anymore, why are you always being so bad to me', he said 'no' again and didn't say anything. I was so angry. At that time on a bridge, I turned my back and looked into the distance, ignoring him, and didn't speak. It was very windy that night, and when the wind blew my eyes, I started to cry for some reason. He panicked all of a sudden, and tried to explain to me: He said that he spent eight years in prison and understood a lot of things. What people do or do not do in this life is determined by God. He looked forward to coming out every day, and when he came out, he found that most of the people outside were just trapped in another kind of cage and couldn't move, 'the subway in the morning rush hour smells worse than a prison cell', so he became okay with everything... At that time, not far from the bridge where we are standing, there is a railway bridge, and a green train was driving out of the station. I said that you are not afraid that I will go on the train one day and not come back. He gently hugged my shoulders from behind and said no, no matter where I go, he will come to me... After I left, I waited for him to come to me, but he didn't come, never came again..."

A sad feeling grabbed Guo Xiaofen's heart, she was speechless for a while, Ma Xiaozhong hurriedly said to Dong Yue: "After you left, did he really have no contact with you at all?"

Dong Yue shook his head: "No text messages, no WeChat, and no phone calls, I think it might end like this, just like when I left suddenly. It's just like I left the place where I stayed for a few years in the past... In fact, I have been thinking about him, worrying about him..."

"Worry about him?" Ma Xiaozhong suddenly grabbed the point, "He's a big man, why are you worried about him?"

"At that time, just a while before I left, he always scolded a person surnamed Xing in front of me, saying that he was a scumbag and should be slashed with a thousand cuts. I asked him how Xing offended him, and he didn't say, just sitting on the bench in the garden in the middle of the street, hunched back, staring blankly for a long time, looking very resentful and helpless. I suddenly remembered the surname of Xing was the dean of the nursing home where my sister was. In order to keep my sister in the nursing home, I begged him a lot, worked several jobs, and gave him a lot of money... I quickly asked Zhou Liping if the surname Xing he scolded was from that hospital. Did the dean do something to my sister? He quickly comforted me, saying that the two were not the same at all, and told me not to think about it, I was still afraid, he patted his chest and said loudly, 'Who dares to touch your sister when I am here?, I just feel relieved."

"And then?" Guo Xiaofen asked.

"Later, for a long time, he was dull and didn't like to talk, but once, he didn't show up for several days, and when he saw me again, his face was exhausted. I asked him where he went, and he said he looked for a friend who has traveled a long way and searched many places but couldn't find it... This is the first time I heard that he has a friend. He said that he was his only friend in the world, a very wise one. After he was arrested, when everyone said he was a serial killer, only this friend tried his best to defend him and shorten his sentence as much as possible. Later, when he was in prison, he came to visit him again. Now that he has encountered a very distressing thing, he hopes to find this friend and ask him what to do..."

"He didn't reveal at all, what troubles him?" Guo Xiaofen asked.

"No, he doesn't like to talk at all. When he doesn't want to talk, I can't pry his mouth open even with a stick." Dong Yue thought about it and said, "However, he told me about a high school composition. ...."

"High school composition?"

"Well, he said that he wrote a lot of compositions when he was in school, but the one that impressed him the most was about spring outings. Other students wrote about how bright the spring is, how happy the tourists are, and how beautiful the flowers are. Only he wrote the park at night, in the darkness where you can't see clearly, the petals are scattered all over the ground, no one sees how they wither, but the kind of 'resolute in the dark without self-pity' is the real beauty... Then, he asked me if this article was written very well, I said it was a little bit, and he laughed. That was the only time I saw him laugh since I knew him. I don't know why, I found his laughter less than a little happy. It's just like he was terribly sad inside his heart..."

After finishing the conversation and preparing to leave the "ghost town", Dong Yue sent Ma Xiaozhong, Guo Xiaofen, and Xiao Chunhua downstairs. Somehow, the sun disappeared, the gloomy sky like iron blew the north wind, and the invisible wind was like a raging wave, pouring into this "ghost city" composed of reinforced concrete, running through all the streets, sweeping the sky. The flying sand shuttled through all the holes and erupted with deafening roars as if to scrape everything away, whip, dismember or smash. In the building group, it seemed there is a little sign of life could leave.

They walked to Tucson against the wall, Guo Xiaofen asked Dong Yue, "You really don't want to go back?"

"I won't go back, I'm like this, what can I do when I go back?" Dong Yue glanced at the clothes on her body and smiled shyly and miserably, "I thought I could find something to do when I returned home, but the economy here is downturned. So I have to go to a ghost town and hang around like this. I have to pay 5,000 yuan to President Xing's account every month, and in a few months, the bank card would run out of money and I don't know what to do..."

Guo Xiaofen couldn't bear it and didn't know how to tell her about Dong Xinlan's death.

Ma Xiaozhong said: "Dong Yue, that Dean Xing has been dismissed because of a mistake in his work. The new dean is very honest, you don't need to make money in Dean Xing's account in the future."

Dong Yue was a little surprised, and at the same time couldn't believe it: "Really? Don't lie to me."

"We are not related to you, so what are we lying to you for?!" Ma Xiaozhong said his eyes widening.

"That's great!" Dong Yue was very happy, "My sister is what I care about most in this world, but I'm not too worried, with Zhou Liping here, he will protect my sister know that person, the things he promised, ten years, twenty years, thirty years... a hundred years will not change."

A little red rose from her pale face. Guo Xiaofen turned her head quickly, afraid that she would find tears in her eyes.

The moment the car door was closed, the roaring wind sounded as if it had been cut, and it became much thinner, but the car was still shaking like a sampan in a stormy sea.

The car started until it was far away, Guo Xiaofen turned around and saw Dong Yue still standing in the middle of the street, looking at them with a shivering body.

The two rows of balconies on the left and right are like cold and rough walls of a well, and the dimly lit distance is like an unfathomable bottom of a well. Dong Yue stands there like a child thrown into the tunnel wind pavilion...

"Wait a minute! Stop!" Guo Xiaofen suddenly shouted.

Xiao Chunhua was startled and stepped on the brakes, and the Tucson "crunched" to a stop.

Guo Xiaofen jumped out of the car and ran back to Dong Yue against the wind, her hair blown in a mess.

Dong Yue stared at her blankly, not knowing what she was doing when she came back.

Guo Xiaofen took off the foggy pink woolen coat on her body and put it on her, the coat was so warm that Dong Yue couldn't help shaking.

Guo Xiaofen fastened the buttons on the coat one by one. It was a little difficult to fasten the diamond-shaped crystal buttons into the buttonholes, but once fastened, they were very tight and could block all the cold winds... When she clung to the bottom button, Guo Xiaofen crouched down and fastened the buttons above.

——Dong squatted down and fastened the bottom button for her sister, exhorting: Girls are most afraid of freezing, so every button on the clothes should be fastened, and the calf should not be frozen, remember.

All tied up.

Guo Xiaofen stood up, said "goodbye" softly, ran back to the Tucson, closed the door, and started the car again, this time it got further and further away, never stopped, never looked back.

Dong Yue turned around and walked into the building, but before she took a few steps, she squatted down slowly, hugged her knees with both hands, and burst into tears. She cried so sadly, like a sister who would never see her sister again...

4

Sitting on the high-speed train, Guo Xiaofen, who was obviously frozen in the cold, huddled in her seat and shivered non-stop, with two rows of teeth hitting each other in her blue lips. Ma Xiaozhong put his clothes on her and asked the conductor for a towel to cover her. Seeing that she was still cold, he poured her hot water cup after cup. Gradually, her face finally softened, the dull eyes regained their luster.

"See what you did." Ma Xiaozhong couldn't help muttering, "You give

Dong Yue the coat, it's no problem, you can send her 100 pieces, and I can buy 100 pieces for you again. The problem is that you tell me in advance. I'll get you a coat, then jump out of the car to find her..."

"You don't understand..." Guo Xiaofen took a sip of water and whispered.

"What do I don't understand?"

"You don't understand, really..." Guo Xiaofen said slowly, "You haven't tried dragging a suitcase down a snowy street with tears in your eyes, let alone lying on a park bench and putting all the cold that can't be covered by clothes... You have struggled in a city for many, many years, and then, suddenly, you have nothing and no home, and you realize that you are humble, small, pitiful, and ridiculous. You haven't experienced any of these..."

There were no people in the high-speed train carriage, and it was very quiet. The setting sun outside the window shone on the vast plain, and a piece of golden yellow was surrounded. With the passage of the train and time, it became darker and darker like a film.

"Yeah, in a blink you've been working for seven or eight years..." Ma Xiaozhong said, rubbing his fingers, "Do you remember the first time we met?"

"The first time we met?" Guo Xiaofen thought for a long time before saying, "It seems to be in the corridor of the Municipal Public Security Bureau. We had a fight because of the elevator, and in the end, you won..."

"I know you'll remember it wrong!" Ma Xiaozhong smiled with a crooked mouth, "The first time we met was in the alley of Guoren Lane, Chunshu Street, in midnight, you took me as a pervert and poked me once with an electric baton."

Guo Xiaofen's mouth couldn't help but burst into a smile. Looking back at the past, all the tastes of the youth, no matter how bitter, spicy, and salty, have been turned into sweet and sour over time.

"Our task force, Lei Rong, Simiao, you, me, Huyan, and Xiangming..." Guo Xiaofen muttered in a low voice, "Time flies so fast, in the blink so many things happened and passed. I heard people say 'It seems to have happened yesterday', and I thought it was an old-fashioned sentence, but now when I think of those past events, I really vividly remember them, as if... it happened just yesterday."

"I said—" Ma Xiaozhong suddenly called her.

Guo Xiaofen put the paper cup on the small backboard in the front row and looked at the short fat man beside him with his head lowered: "What's the matter with you?"

"It's nothing...I'm thinking about what to say. Damn it, my mouth is so rude. I usually slip away when I'm talking nonsense, but I can't open it at the critical moment." Ma Xiaozhong said depressedly.

A flight attendant pushed the dining car slowly down the aisle. When he came to them, he asked them if they wanted dinner. Ma Xiaozhong gave them a stern look and he was so frightened that he hurriedly pushed the trolley to another car.

"What are you going to say?" Guo Xiaofen asked him curiously.

"That..." Ma Xiaozhong didn't dare to look at her, staring at the travel magazine with half of his head exposed from the back pocket of the front seat, "Guo, although we met when you poked me, and I also scolded you, the opening was a bit ragged. But I still fell in love with you very early, you know, uh, not only like, much higher than like. I really can't say that word, you know... However, maybe in your eyes, I'm a rotten person, not to mention that I'm crooked, but I'm also slick and ruffian, and I'm not serious all day long, like a genuine scum. But we have known each other for so many years, and you know best: how upright I must be in my bones, dedicated to my job, honest, and not a grain of sand in my relationship. Ever since I fell in love with you, I didn't even think about other girls at all, you're the only one in my heart, and that's what I said even if my bones were broken."

Guo Xiaofen looked at him and said nothing.

"Having said so much, I actually just want to say something serious to you: can you be my girlfriend? if you are afraid that what I say is not true, we will get a license to get married when we go back! You also know my background. I have been a police officer for more than ten years. I have a small director and a savings of 200,000 to 300,000 yuan. I still live with my mother in a two-bedroom apartment in 1985. I have nothing else. It is not too poor, but it is poor for some extent...but I will be good to you, I will only be good to you in this life, I will never step on two boats, except that we will have a daughter in the future, I will never fall in love with another girl, and you also know that you can't find anyone who dares to bully the woman in my heart. I can swear to you that I will never let you be wronged again in this life, and I will never let you be frightened, I will never let you live on the streets again, and I will never let you can't find your way home again..."

Speaking of which, Ma Xiaozhong lowered his head smiled like a prisoner waiting for the verdict. After long, he still did not hear Guo Xiaofen's word, he tilted his head in trembling, only to find Guo Xiaofen looking at him and her face full of tears.

He carefully grabbed Guo Xiaofen's soft hand, but once he grabbed it, he held it tightly and never let go.

Guo Xiaofen slowly rested her head on his shoulder, tears dripping on the back of his hands, there were only the two of them in the carriage.

Chapter 10

1

"Ting..."

The copper bell on the door frame of the cafe rang crisply, causing Liu Simiao, who was reading a book, to raise her head and glance at the door. Seeing that it was not Guo Xiaofen who entered, but a middle-aged man wearing a peaked cap, he lowered his head to read *The Endless Wasteland* by James Elroy, but his eyes could no longer focus on the words on the paper.

She sighed softly, closed the book, and cast her eyes to the bright floor-to-ceiling windows: a row of plane trees in late autumn, the remaining leaves curled up into small balls of black and yellow, in the darkness of the beginning of the night seemed to be clusters of flames that were about to go out. On the sidewalk downstairs, couples dressed in red and green were walking slowly, arm in arm. It seemed so bright for a moment but then disappeared as if swallowed by the night...

After so many experienced police officers worked day and night for so long and made so much effort, the entire investigation of the Deratization Hill case was broken like a broken bone. All evidence showed that Zhou Liping, who was the most suspected before, has a sufficient alibi and should be released according to law. Although there are still some police officers who were unwilling and want to find a reason to imprison him for a while with some kind of venting emotions, the reason they need to find gives them a headache: moving Zhang Chunyang's body into the freezer is suspected of insulting the body? Fighting with Li Zhiyong violated the Public Security Administration Punishment Regulations? Oh, forget it, don't find it hard for themselves!

Zhou Liping was very cooperative and calm in the whole process of going through the procedures for release from custody, just like an innocent person who had long been mentally prepared for his one-day whitewashing.

349

Of course, he also said a few words of thanks to the government on occasion, and then walked out of the gate of the detention center. According to relevant laws and regulations, criminal suspects in extraordinarily serious criminal cases must be placed under residential surveillance for a period of time even if they are released from suspicion. According to the report of the police officer in charge of this work, Zhou Liping went straight home and did not leave the house again. He ate takeout for dinner at the Good Neighbors convenience store downstairs.

Zhou Liping's release did not mean that the four lives on Deratization Hill can be ignored. The task force headed by Du Jianping was severely criticized by the superiors. Although Xu Ruilong finally said a few words of encouragement, hopefully, everyone will learn the lesson and change direction, change their mind and seek a breakthrough. The members of the task force also stood up one by one, expressing that they were not afraid of setbacks and would start all over again, but in private they all felt frustrated. After a hard battle, they thought that success was imminent, but in the end, they attacked the wrong hill and were busy all the time. Now that the "golden period" of solving the case has passed, with the passage of time, whether the mystery of the case can be successfully solved was afraid that can only see God's will...

During this period, there was a small wave, but it quickly calmed down.

Just as the task force was walking out of the conference room after accepting the criticism from the superiors, Du Jianping, Chu Tianying, and Lin Fengchong all found that the phone that had been muted showed that Lei Rong had called them, and Du Jianping thought that it might be Lei Rong had any new findings on the case from a forensic point of view, so he quickly called and got the news that the autopsy showed that Zhang Chunyang was frozen to death.

"What?" Du Jianping was taken aback, "Frozen to death? Didn't you say he died because of SCD?"

"I reviewed the medical records of Zhang Chunyang's previous visits to other hospitals because he did have a heart problem, so he may have been sudden death during sex on the night of the crime, but sudden death during sex is not necessarily a real death, it may also be a fainting or the 'feigned death' caused by shock is manifested in that breathing and heartbeat are so weak that they are almost stopped, and Xing Qisheng is not a cardiologist, so he made a miscalculation." Lei Rong said, "I found many inside Zhang Chunyang's body during the autopsy. Non-specific changes in various organs, such as skull suture dehiscence caused by freezing and expansion of cranial contents, subepicardial hemorrhage, pulmonary congestion, degeneration, and necrosis of renal small vessel epithelium with hemoglobin casts, and iliopsoas hemorrhage, etc. It means that the deceased was frozen to death, especially when the Wisniewski spots were found—"

"What?" Du Jianping was a little stunned, "Say slower."

"Wisniewski spots," Lei Rong explained, "are diffuse, speckled hemorrhages under the gastric mucosa, lined along the blood vessels, dark red or dark brown, and these hemorrhagic spots are typical signs of freezing to death."

"How could he be frozen to death..." Du Jianping couldn't understand why.

"What's more tragic is that I think Zhang Chunyang had a period of sobriety before he was frozen to death." Lei Rong said, "His fingers were frayed, and correspondingly, I checked the one where his body was stored. The skin tissue and bloodstains were extracted from the inner upper layer of the mortuary freezer, which proves that Zhang Chunyang once tried to get out. Unfortunately, once the freezer was placed in the body, the bottom plate felt pressure and would automatically lock. The door of the mortuary has a good sound insulation effect, so it is estimated it was useless for him to call for help or struggle, and he just froze to death."

Thinking that Zhang Chunyang was at the last moment of his life and found himself in a cold freezer, like being buried alive, fearful, struggling, screaming and at the end, his despair, Du Jianping and the others all shuddered...

Du Jianping suddenly remembered something: "Lei Rong, is it possible that when Zhou Liping moved Zhang Chunyang's body into the freezer, he found him awake and knocked him unconscious?"

Obviously, he was still unwilling to let Zhou Liping go.

"There are generally two ways to stun in sudden situations, one is to hit the vagus nerve or the part where the nerve center is located, and the other is to use inhalation anesthetics such as ether and chloroform. In the autopsy, I did not find any trauma caused by blows on Zhang Chunyang's body surface. As for the use of inhaled anesthetics, the premise is that Zhou Liping must have predicted or guessed that Zhang Chunyang might wake up halfway and made preparations, but the current investigation showed that at that night, Zhou Liping intervened in the middle of the process. Not to mention that inhalation anesthetics are not so readily available, so from a logical point of view, your assumption does not seem to hold."

Because Du Jianping was using the speakerphone, Chu Tianying inserted a sentence: "Director Lei, during the autopsy, did you find that Zhang Chunyang really died suddenly that night?"

There was silence on the other end of the phone for a moment, and Lei Rong's voice came again, she answered cautiously: "To be honest, I didn't find any fresh thrombosis in Zhang Chunyang's coronary artery during the autopsy, but because he had previously a heart attack, so there were many fibrous scars on the surface of the heart, and the coronary arteries and their branches do have high stenosis. In addition, he had been dead for many days when his body was found, so it is difficult to determine the cause of his fainting or shock on the night of the crime. Whether it is caused by cardiac disease, or the causes of fainting and shock during sexual intercourse are various. In addition to cardiac diseases, there are respiratory diseases, central nervous system diseases, and allergic diseases, etc., I can't check them all... ...."

"Got it," Chu Tianying said.

After hanging up the phone, Du Jianping said to Chu Tianying, "Do you suspect that Zhang Chunyang and Xing Qisheng made a trick to deceive Tao Zhuoyao that night?"

Chu Tianying nodded slowly: "I have had this idea, but after thinking about it again, I feel that even so, it doesn't make much sense for the case, especially Zhou Liping – Lei Rong is right, all the signs showed that Zhou Liping is just an intervenor in the middle, even if he has a deep hatred with Zhang Chunyang, and when he puts Zhang Chunyang in the freezer and finds that he is awake, knocks him unconscious and then stuffs him into the freezer, it will not overturn his injustice in the case. This proof of presence actually 'reinforces' his alibi, not to mention Lei Rong also said that she did not find that Zhang Chunyang was artificially stunned."

Du Jianping sighed, his face showing the frustration of not wanting to give up but having to give up.

Shortly after calling Du Jianping and the others, Lei Rong went to the biological testing laboratory, and when she came back, she found that her phone was buzzing on her desk, and the caller ID was from Huyan Yun.

After she answered the call, Huyan Yun's tone was a little hurried: "Sister, there is something related to the case, I would like to ask you for a favor."

"What's the matter?" Lei Rong was a little curious.

"I want to ask you to pay attention to Zhang Chunyang's autopsy to see if the real cause of his death may have been frozen to death."

Lei Rong couldn't help but call out "Ah": "You...how did you guess he was frozen to death?"

The other end of the phone seemed to be prepared: "I'm also thinking about it... Since he was really frozen to death, I'll go to the mortuary of

Love Hospital now to see if one of my reasonings can be verified."

"Just in time, Tang Xiaotang is also doing some finishing work over there, I'll ask her to cooperate with you—" Before Lei Rong finished speaking, Huyan Yun hung up the phone.

Lei Rong waited for a long time, but she didn't get any news from Huyan Yun. When she was about to get off work, Tang Xiaotang came back, and Lei Rong asked her if she had met Huyan Yun. Tang Xiaotang said she did, but Huyan Yun didn't speak to her, just asked the two morgue staff some questions.

"What did he ask?"

"I didn't listen too clearly." Tang Xiaotang said, "Anyway, he got into the small room with a generator next to the mortuary, and didn't come out for a long time..."

Lei Rong thought about it for a long time, but she didn't understand what medicine Huyan Yun sold in the gourd.

That night, the city held a mobilization meeting for the public security organs to accurately crackdown on financial crimes. Lei Rong also participated and happened to meet Liu Simiao and Lin Fengchong. During the meeting, they sat and chatted together, mentioning Ma Xiaozhong and Guo Xiaofen, saying that they should be on their way back, and then Lei Rong casually mentioned Huyan Yun's movements, Liu Simiao also wondered what his intention was. Where is, Lin Fengchong provided a situation, saying that Huyan Yun called him in the evening and implemented a trivial matter: "Do you remember that the guard Xu of Tongyou Nursing Home provided a clue, he said At about 10:30 that night, he saw Xing Qisheng leave the nursing home."

"How can't I remember." Liu Simiao said, "It gave me goosebumps when I think about it. Xing Qisheng should have died at that time."

"Yes, but what's weird is that the cleaner auntie Zhang also said that when she went to the toilet at 10 o'clock that night, she saw the light on the door of the dean's office, and there were sounds of walking in the room." Lin Fengchong lowered his voice, "Xu's words can be treated as if his eyes are dim and misunderstood. Auntie Zhang is a reliable person, so who was that person in the dean's office at ten o'clock that night? The task force has never figured out, or maybe a thief just happened to sneak in to steal..."

"How is that possible?" Liu Simiao shook her head, "How could it be possible that the thief who went to steal something in the middle of the night and turned on the light."

"That's right, it's a strange and unexplainable thing anyway." Lin Fengchong said, "But you also know that in the criminal investigation work, there will inevitably be some strange and unexplainable incidents, so we didn't investigate any more after that. In the evening, Huyan Yun called me to ask the ins and outs of this matter. I can't remember and he was quite impatient. I asked him, why did you inquire about this matter so carefully? He said 'the key to the cracking of the entire case is here!'"

Lei Rong and Liu Simiao were surprised at the same time: "Ah? Is it possible that he can solve this case again?"

"Anyway, I heard what he meant." Lin Fengchong said, "Then he asked me for the contact information of Xu and Auntie Zhang, and said he wanted to find them in person."

Liu Simiao held her cheeks and thought for a moment, and couldn't help but say to Lei Rong, "Your brother, I really don't know what kind of brain he has..."

Lei Rong glanced at her.

"What's the matter? Why do you look at me like this?" Liu Simiao was a little uncomfortable.

Lin Fengchong couldn't help but smile.

At this moment, a tall and burly man suddenly stood in front of them and shouted loudly: "Director Liu, long time no see!"

Liu Simiao saw that it was Deputy Director Wang of the Provincial Public Security Department in charge of economic investigation work, she stood up and shook hands with him: "I heard that you were coming, but I didn't expect to meet here – is the case reached the closing stage?"

"Yes, I came here this time to discuss the starting time of the action with the department leaders and consolidate the specific plan for the action." Deputy Director Wang made a gesture of catching turtles in the urn, "Not one can escape!"

2

When the waitress put the teapot and cup containing herbal tea on the table, she accidentally touched this glassware together, making a beautiful "ding ding" sound, interrupting Liu Simiao's thoughts. Holding up the teacup and looking at a swaying rose petal floating above the mist, she couldn't help but fall into contemplation again.

In the afternoon, she received a call from Guo Xiaofen, saying that she had returned and asked her to meet at the coffee shop on the second floor of Ocean Times Square at 7 o'clock tonight. Liu Simiao was going to send a document to the Municipal Intermediate People's Court and it should be no problem to count the time, so she agreed. After delivering the materials, it was already dark, she drove east and suddenly found a person staggering out of a barbecue shop across the road, flushed and drunk. The man took out the key opened the door of a black Jeep Compass, and climb up to the driver's seat. Liu Simiao hurriedly turned around at the intersection in front, rushed to the door of the barbecue shop, jumped out of the car, pulled open the door of the compass, and leaned her head against the seat of the car and said to the man on the headrest said in a low but stern voice: "Director Du – get off right now!"

Du Jianping opened his heavy eyelids and glanced at her, he was a little surprised, but also a little ashamed: "Simiao...what's the matter?"

"What's the matter?!" Liu Simiao said angrily, "If I come here one second later, you will be driving under the influence of alcohol, and you don't want the pension anymore?!"

Du Jianping slowly rubbed off the driver's seat, his huge head was drooping, and he didn't speak for a long time. Liu Simiao suddenly saw the phone number displayed on the screen of the mobile phone he was holding: "You're looking for me? I? "

Du Jianping was mumbling, but his voice was originally mixed. In addition, at the entrance of the barbecue shop and several restaurants nearby, there were waiters in various uniforms urging customers to enter the shop one after another, causing Liu Simiao to hear nothing. She pointed to her Camry: "Get in my car and I'll take you home! Tell me if you have something to say."

Du Jianping got into the car, perhaps because of the alcohol, he put up the collar of his leather jacket to cover his hiccups, his huge body curled up on the passenger, and closed his eyes again... Liu Simiao thought he was sleeping. She was still wondering why he wanted to call her when he was drunk, but out of politeness and unwilling to disturb his rest. She started the car and shuttled in the traffic during the evening rush hour. The lights of the taillights of the vehicles ahead and the lights of the street lights are intertwined and projected on the window glass, making the trees, buildings, bridges, bus stops, and people waiting on the platform in the night, as if they were drunk either.

"Simiao, I'm sorry." Du Jianping opened his eyes and muttered, then closed his eyes again.

Liu Simiao looked at him: "Director Du, what's wrong with you?"

"Nothing..." Du Jianping tucked his clothes and fell silent again.

Liu Simiao drove the car to the side of the road and stopped slowly.

"Director Du, you know that I am a person who never likes to listen to half-sentences, and as far as I know, you are never a person who doesn't say anything after half-speaking. What do you want to say, you can say it directly." Liu Si Miao stared at Du Jianping and said.

Du Jianping slowly tucked his body in the passenger seat and sat upright, and said in a low voice, "Simiao, in fact, there was a time when I had a lot of opinions on you, that is, after my daughter died. Everyone in the bureau had come to see me, only you have never been here, and you haven't even sent a greeting text message, which makes me very sad. Really, you see me as a rough man, but I also have a small heart. That's my daughter, my wife died early, and I was the only one raising my eldest daughter. She was studying at a university outside, but suddenly the school called me and asked me to recognize her. You must have heard about at that time, I was sitting on the floor of our cafeteria with my phone. The whole world is not mine. I couldn't even cry for a while. At the extreme, the whole person seemed to be burnt and wanted to cry, but there were no tears. Later, when I went to recognize the body, Fengchong accompanied me. When the provincial government learned about the whole thing, I realized that the stupid child was in order to help a classmate who was suffering from a 'terminal illness', she took out a campus loan with her ID card. As a result, the classmate ran away. The loan she owed was astronomical. She and our entire family cannot be enough to pay, so she decided to suicide..."

Having said that, Du Jianping rubbed his eyes with his huge palms, paused for a moment, and continued: "After the accident, many old buddies are secretly complaining about my cowardice, thinking that I am the director of criminal investigation and should take out the campus loan. The gang of villains and hooligans behind the scenes should all be caught and collapsed. I'm not afraid to tell you, there are some very brave brothers who said that as long as I dare to do it, they will follow me! How did they know? I have to do it myself, and I must not implicate a brother. I want to skin Tao Bing, Xing Qixian, Cui Wentao, and Zhai Qing from the 'Kind Charity Fund' with the cruelest punishment. Just when I was about to start, Director Xu suddenly talked to me, saying that they were conducting a secret investigation into the suspected financial and criminal crimes of the fund, and they wanted to catch all the people involved. At present, the evidence is not sufficient. It will take some time to close the net, so although he understands my grief over the loss of my daughter, he still hopes that I can strictly observe the organizational discipline, be patient for the time and refrain from personal retaliation, so as not to disturb the whole investigation, and cause the criminals to slip through the net."

Du Jianping swallowed hard and spread his hands: "I told Director Xu at the time that I graduated from the police academy at the age of eighteen, and it has been thirty years since I was a member of the organization. I have always listened to the leader, I did whatever my superiors ask me to do. But now I'm told not to avenge, I really can't do it! I said: Director Xu, all of us who are criminal police officers know that all cases are 'cold while waiting, once it has been delayed, and the case would be over'. Du Ying, you watched her grew up. After her mother died, you were afraid that she would not be safe at home alone. Except for school, I was specially authorized to take her with me on night shifts. When the case analysis meeting was held, we stared at the table in the conference room, and you did not forget to put a towel on her when she slept on the sofa. When she was in junior high school, she was bullied by school hooligans, and you arranged for two policemen to escort her to school every day—how can you just watch her die like this now? After hearing this, Director Xu also cried and said 'Du, you have to trust the police'... I knew at a glance that I couldn't force the old man any more, and the old man also has difficulties. I said fine, Director, I believe you, but you have to give me a promise, how long do I have to wait for those bastards to be punished? He stretched out two fingers, I said ok. Then I will wait for two years, after I finished the formalities for leaving my job without pay, I went home like this..."

Liu Simiao looked at him, and there was a trace of pain in his quiet eyes.

"You don't know how I survived the past two years. I flipped through my daughter's photos, copied my daughter's diary, folded my daughter's clothes, recalled how she looked when she was a child over and over again, and then I cried so hard that I couldn't breathe. While crying, I punched myself in the heart with my fist. I live like this every day. I have to let myself cry, otherwise I can't live. It's too painful! I cried out, then my heart was refreshed for a while, but the next day it would be hurt again, so I had to cry again... I didn't forget to remind myself, as a policeman, I should know Law-abiding, but at night, my dreams are all about how to turn those scumbags to ashes! As time goes by, the longer I wait, the more I think this thing must be covered, and no one will remember Du Ying's death, no one will punish those who harmed her, just like countless young people who have been forced to death by campus loans over the years, buried, forgotten. And those vampires are still free and having a good life. I hate myself so much, I hate myself for being so obedient, why I am so coward..."

At first, Du Jianping rubbed his eye sockets and the corners of his eyes unconsciously, and gradually began to wipe the tears that kept flowing down the corners of his eyes and said with a wry smile: "When I talk about this, I'm still the same... Not long ago, because of insufficient the city bureau asked me to come back. After the case happened, I didn't know the background of the case at first, and Director Xu also named me as the leader of the task force, until I heard that there was a 'Kind Charity Fund'. He discussed it with me and wanted to ask you to lead, but he learned that the main suspect might be related to Xiangming. He was afraid that you would be emotional and the old man got in trouble. In such a big case, the leader of the task force must be at our level, so he still let me do it first, and told me to only check Zhou Liping, not to touch the foundation. I said yes, I have endured it for two years anyway, and I don't care to endure more days ...that day in the conference room, you said that I didn't dare to investigate the foundation because I was afraid that people would say that I would avenge my personal revenge and I don't dare to take revenge for her, you ask me if I'm still a father. Do you know how uncomfortable I feel when I hear it? But I didn't say anything or defend, because I know that you're right, you're right——"

Du Jianping couldn't help turning his face away, sobbing loudly, his rock-like face was washed away with tears, the white hair on his temples and the rough folds on his neck all looked so old and helpless.

Liu Simiao took two tissues from the tissue box in front of the car window and handed them to him: "Director Du, I'm sorry..."

"No no no!" Du Jianping took the tissue and snorted on his face while shaking his other hand vigorously, "Simiao, I didn't know until this afternoon that I really misunderstood you and wronged you... ... Deputy Director Wang of the Provincial Department of A came, and the department leaders summoned Director Xu to have a meeting with him. When he came back, he conveyed the instructions of superiors to me. It has been collected in place, and criminals such as Xing Qixian can be prosecuted. According to reliable information, the backbone of the Kind Charity Fund will hold a farewell ceremony for Xing Qisheng at the municipal funeral tomorrow morning. The joint operation of 'Puncture' will wipe out all those criminals, and none of them can escape! When I heard the news, I was so excited that I held Director Xu's hand and kept saying thank the leaders and the organization. The deputy director said, 'You should also thank a person. She has reported to the provincial and ministerial leaders many times in the past two years, asking for a thorough investigation of the illegal and criminal facts of the Kind Charity Fund. Later, the department leaders talked to her. She immediately requested support for the evidence search work from the perspective of criminal technology, and it was approved. I asked who it was, and then Director

Xu told me that it was you. He said to me, "You don't know, As soon as the incident of Du Ying came out, Simiao asked me to pat me on the table, said that she would never allow any of her family members to be harmed by criminals and let it go—never."

Liu Simiao slowly turned her eyes to the outside of the car window. The night was dark, and the Western Suburb Jewelry City on the right side of the road was lit up. The light and shadow were erratic in the cold wind, like an island floating on the sea. The training institutions such as Gaosi and Xueersi on the second floor of Jewelry City have just finished their classes, and many children and parents have poured out. In the wind, some were pushing the bicycle, and walking past the front of the bicycle with difficulty.

"Thank you, Si Miao, thank you very much..." Du Jianping said in a low voice, "The case may be the last case I handle as a criminal police officer. When those people from the 'Kind Charity Fund' are arrested, I will prepare to resign. I am old and tired. When Director Xu asked me to come out again, I actually had a few thoughts in my heart. I thought that if I wandered around the Director, I would also give him some pressure and remind him not to forget that Du Ying's case hasn't been solved yet. Now, Du Ying can rest her eyes, and it's like I've been in the refrigerator for three years and finally see the sun, it melts, it leaks, and it's been stretched all the time. The strength of my life is gone... Simiao, maybe you will think that I am a deserter in this case. If you think so, I don't think there is any-thing wrong. I'm sorry for the kids who died in the tunnel wind pavilion. But do you know, in fact, the rest of my life will be like a person who fell into a tunnel wind pavilion, sitting so lonely at the bottom of the well, cold, dark, and hopeless, until I am cremated..."

Having said that, Du Jianping covered his face violently, his ten fingers almost dug into the flesh, his body trembled slightly, and he used all his strength to suppress the crying sound.

Liu Simiao looked at him as if she saw another father who was strug-gling to move forward in the dark with the wind, but the back seat of the bicycle was empty...

3

"What are you thinking about?" Liu Simiao didn't come back until Guo Xiaofen sat down opposite. She looked at Guo Xiaofen and felt that she was a little different from before, although she was still dressed so cutely and her smile was still so charming. Her expression lost the tension that she couldn't hide under the pressure of work as a journalist in the past, and the light from her bright eyes was not as sharp as she was always observing and INSPIREing. She now seemed calm, gentle, and even a little shy, under the illumination of the colorful glass lamp above her head, her cheeks were slightly red as if she was drunk...

Liu Simiao gave her a hard look: "Guo, did you encounter anything happy?"

"I knew I couldn't hide it from you." Guo Xiaofen bit her lower lip, took out a red card from the small cross-body bag with a smile, and handed it to her, "I... I got a certificate this afternoon."

When he saw the golden words "marriage certificate", Liu Simiao widened her eyes in surprise, opened the certificate, and saw the photo of Guo Xiaofen and Ma Xiaozhong, she couldn't close her mouth for a long time. She just woke up like a dream, with a smile that Guo Xiaofen has never seen, a smile full of joy from the heart: "That's great, Guo, congratulations to you and Ma, and best wishes to you!"

Guo Xiaofen embarrassedly tucked her hands between her legs: "Look at Ma Xiaozhong's virtuous demeanor. When taking a wedding photo, the photographer told him not to laugh so stupidly. He said he will do better in the second time, and I pinched him so hard!"

"Well, well. This time Ma finally married the girl he loves, but I think he will be taught by you in the future – you must not show mercy." Liu Simiao smiled and said, "By the way, when is the wedding? "

"This, we haven't discussed whether to do it or not..." Guo Xiaofen pouted, "I don't really want to do it, but he said that the wedding has the effect of revitalizing the private economy, and the government's call must be answered."

"The wedding is needed, it's needed!" said Liu Simiao, "Don't watch a wedding being held is tiring and frustrating, but this is not just a formality. It's a 'notarization' in front of all relatives and friends. This is a restraint for the groom and protection for the bride, it seemed like he was talking nonsense, but in fact, he must know clearly."

"I didn't expect you to see so thoroughly!" Guo Xiaofen said with a smile, "What about yourself?"

"Me? "

"Yeah, when are you going to find someone to get such a certificate just like us?"

Liu Simiao's expression couldn't help but feel a little sad, although there was still a smile on her face, she smiled reluctantly: "I'm afraid I won't have this chance in my life..."

For a while, the two fell into silence. In the quiet coffee shop, the originally curling Korean songs were somewhat clear. Accompanied by the piano and the clarinet, the song seemed to be lonely.

"Simiao, there are some things I've wanted to say for a long time." Guo Xiaofen looked at her and said, "The people of the past, forget it if you should. You are still so young, you should give yourself and others some opportunities... ...Sometimes, we wait for a person for a long time, only to realize in the end that what we are waiting for our own loneliness; for the person, we are waiting for, is also meaningless."

Liu Simiao lowered her long eyelashes, covering her beautiful and sad eyes. For a long time, she took a sip of the teacup and said slowly, "I just don't want to compromise."

"Who did." Guo Xiaofen whispered, "Life is a process of growth and compromise."

"So, what about this..." Liu Simiao stretched out and pointed to the marriage certificate on the table with his fingertips, "Is it also a compromise?"

"Yes." Guo Xiaofen said calmly.

Perhaps because she did not expect her answer to be so decisive and firm, Liu Simiao was taken aback for a moment.

"You know, the person I really love in my heart isn't Ma. I've waited for him for a long time, but the person he really loves is another one." Guo Xiaofen looked at Liu Simiao and said, "The case brought us, old friends, back together, I realized that after so many years, we are all changing, some are mature, some are vicissitudes, some are haggard, and some like me... ...It sounds good I'm sober. I no longer hope for earth-shattering love, and I no longer long to live with the person I love the most. I just want to have a home, and have someone who loves me. That's enough, enough..."

Speaking of this, her eyes became watery.

Liu Simiao picked up the teapot, refilled her teacup with some water, and then slowly pushed the teacup in front of her.

Guo Xiaofen took a few sips of water, coughed twice, and cleared her throat again. She recounted how she and Ma Xiaozhong went to the provincial capital to find Dong Yue, and then gave her own conclusion: "After such a long time During the interview and investigation, I think Zhou Liping is a good and decent person. And he has always been from ten years ago to now. As for why he embarked on such a path, I can only say, even if the direction of his walking is only him, but the real retrograde person is not him."

Liu Simiao nodded solemnly.

"By the way, Simiao, I want to say sorry to you." Guo Xiaofen said, "I may not be able to complete the investigative report you entrusted me to write. First, if there is a wedding, I may have to do a lot of preparation that I may not spare time and energy; secondly... when I changed my direction, I didn't have the courage to write about a person who continued to walk in that direction persistently."

"It's okay." Liu Simiao said with a smile, "For me, you have already accomplished what I entrusted to you."

"Ah?" Guo Xiaofen was a little confused.

"Finally, I just want to prove that Xiangming didn't see the wrong person back then."

When they left the coffee shop, it was already half-past eight in the evening. They had just walked to the elevator entrance when a three-year-old boy with a big head slammed into Liu Simiao. His mother apologized directly to Liu Simiao, but the little boy shouted "sister" recklessly while rushing. At the entrance of the early education center, he gave a bear hug to a girl who came out with a large piece of paper. The girl laughed and hugged her brother and called his nickname: "Stinky brother, why are you here?" There are orange and red paints hanging on her nose and face, and when she smiles, it seems to light up a small orange lamp, which is good-looking and cute.

Guo Xiaofen suddenly remembered that the last time she came here, she had seen this sister and brother. At that time, the "stinky boy" sat on the elephant-trunk slide in the early childhood education center and did not dare to go down, and the older sister in the pink jacket loudly encouraged him to be brave.

However, Liu Simiao noticed the watercolor painting in the little girl's hand. It was a tall building that was straight and looked like a chimney. Three children in colorful clothes were sitting on the roof, looking at the sky. When the girl showed the painting to her younger brother, the painting paper was all overturned. And the three children's heads were all facing down, and the tall building looked like a deep tunnel-wind pavilion embedded in the ground. ...

"Guo, do you still remember that when the case just happened, I was eager to solve the case, for fear of triggering a crisis of public opinion, but you said it won't because the three children who died were all disabled children from the bottom of society. The middle class, the main user group of social media, will not have the enthusiasm to continue to pay attention to such a piece of news that has nothing to do with them. Now it seems that you are correct." Liu Simiao said in a low voice, "The Information Office of the Municipal Bureau Bian's public opinion shows that the public's attention to this case has been declining all the way, and now it has dropped to freezing point."

"In more than a month, it will be the New Year, and then the Chinese New Year. At that time, there will be laughter and laughter. Who will remember those dead children..." Guo Xiaofen said sadly, "Actually, don't talk about them, just even me, I can't recall the names of those three children now, no one will remember them anymore, no one will remember that they once came to this world..."

For a moment, Liu Simiao's head seemed to be hit hard by something, because she realized that she couldn't remember the names of the three children... As she was sitting on the escalator and walking down, she tried hard. she thought about it but she didn't remember.

Walking out of Ocean Times Square, Guo Xiaofen called a car. While waiting for the bus, the early childhood education center on the second floor played the beautiful theme song again, and many children who were participating in chorus training were singing loudly:

The bird said that the snow on the top of the mountain has melted quietly, the river is singing a song, and the eyes of the running deer are so beautiful. The flowers of the forest rose so early, the spring wind was just right, and the leaves on the branches said hello to the sun.

The children's voices, although not neat, were crisp and loud. Somehow after listening for a while, the two of them were a little lost. At this time, Guo Xiaofen's cell phone rang, the car she called arrived, and it stopped on the side of the road not far away. As she ran down the steps, she waved goodbye to Liu Simiao: "I'll send you an electronic wedding invitation later, you must come!" Liu Simiao nodded and promised loudly, "I will definitely go!"

Watching the car go away, Liu Simiao stood there and didn't move. She was a little sad and a little melancholy. At this moment, she felt that the case was over, although the truth had not been uncovered, although the real culprit had not been caught, although everything seems to have no end. But no end is also an end...

No end is also an end.

The squirrel said that the pine cones in his house taste the best, and the panda stretches under the tree and stops walking when it sees the bamboo. Elephants are bathing by the river, fish are blowing bubbles in the water, and rainbows are laughing like dimples in the sky.

The children's songs are full of joy. They sing about the beautiful world like a fairy tale, the happy childhood longing for the future and tomorrow. While listening, Liu Simiao remembered an article she saw on WeChat not long ago. The title seemed to be "The only way to find happiness is to keep imagining what happiness looks like". Although she always hated this kind of chicken soup, on this late autumn night, looking at the long shadow cast by the lights in the commercial building lobby on the ground, she suddenly felt that what the article said was not completely unreasonable: happiness is forgetting, compromising, and being with others together, it is to sing loudly, to constantly imagine happiness while not caring about things that have nothing to do with ourselves, to end decisively when it is time to end, and not to care about what the end should be like...

She put her hands in the pockets of her linen windbreaker, walked down the steps, and hummed softly with the children's voice floating upstairs as she walked home. For the first time in so many years, her shoulders felt relieved. With the ease of the song, even the footsteps become light:

Too much laughter, too little trouble, so many dreams to realize, so many friends, happiness company with you, let us realize our dreams together.

After walking a long way, at the crossroads, the singing of the chorus could no longer be heard, but she was still humming the song. For some reason, while humming, the names of the three children suddenly appeared in her mind: Zhao Wu, Li Ying, and Dong Xinlan. This time, the memory was like an open gate. She thought of their scorched little corpses, the appearance they only left on the photos, and the swill they usually eat and the instant noodles "box". She even remembered their ages: twelve, nine, and the youngest was five. When they were alive, did they have too much laughter, too little trouble, should they have too many dreams to realize...

Thinking about it, the green light came on, she didn't move, just kept standing like this until the red light came on. And soon, the green light, the red light, the green light, the red light...

People who came and went through the intersection looked curiously at the girl who had been standing under the traffic light and never crossed the road, wondering why her face was full of tears.

Chapter 11

1

Everything was dark: mountains were dark in the shape of graves, walls were dark in convex shapes, trees were dark in straight lines, roads were dark in strips. At night, the scraping got bigger and bigger, *Kachi, Kachi, Kachi*, like a dark boning steel knife, peeling off the skin, peeling out a dark person. His color was lighter than the other darks, closer to a lead-gray, dignified and vague. He walked very slowly, stopping from time to time, weighing the dark sky above his head, stomping the dark road under his feet, looking sideways seemingly unintentionally, observing whether there were people following behind him, and then continuing to walk forward, keep walking and enter the dark alley leading to Deratization Hill.

There was no one in the alley, and the walls on both sides were glowing with a cold light. When passing by the subway station entrance exposed outside the fence, he squinted and looked at the thick steel anti-theft door. He took a few steps forward and came to the iron gate leading to the nursery. The door was ajar. After the case, it was blocked by the police for a while, but after the crime scene investigation was over, it was opened again. The symbolic iron hanging on the door was still here, but there was a yellow tape next to it that is forbidden to enter and exit, which was floating in the wind like a dried pig's intestine.

Without hesitation, he walked straight in, walked a few steps along the potholes and dirt road, and saw the man standing beside the tunnel wind pavilion.

By the light of the Bus Automation Design Institute not far away, it can be seen that it is a medium-sized man, between twenty-five and thirty years old, neither fat nor thin. He wore a dark gray hoodie and stretch trousers of the same color, with hands in pockets. His waist was straight, his head held high, his clean babyface has bright eyes, and his expression is calm as if he is thinking about something.

The person who just walked into the nursery coughed lightly, and the baby face saw him, looked at him for a moment, and a smile appeared on his mouth: "Zhou Liping? I'm Huyan Yun."

Zhou Liping was expressionless: "What are you looking for from me?"

Huyan Yun was a little embarrassed: "That...you must know me, right?"

Zhou Liping nodded.

"Lin Xiangming and I are good friends." After speaking, Huyan Yun looked at Zhou Liping's expression and felt that he had nothing to do with him, so he had to go straight to the topic, "Ten years ago, after the serial murders in the western suburbs, Xiangming has defended you, and also offended a lot of people for this. I asked him why he did it, but he didn't want to talk to me too much. A fire broke out on the Deratization Hill, which involved Xiangming, and many people said that it was all because he committed the murder in the past that led to today's big case, and now Xiangming can't come out to defend himself, so I have to do my duty as a good friend..."

"The case of Deratization Hill has nothing to do with me." Zhou Liping said.

"It depends on how you say it." Huyan Yun said.

"What do you mean?" Zhou Liping sneered, "Do you think our people's police can let me walk out of the gate of the detention center if they find any clue on me?"

Huyan Yun shook his head: "To be fair, it is precisely because the country has strengthened the legal system in recent years and adhered to the principle of never suspecting a crime in various cases that you were released."

"So you think I'm still suspect?"

Huyan Yun looked at Zhou Liping. It has been the first time in ten years that the two have met face to face. Although Huyan Yun knew him for a long time, he knew how bloody the shocking case he was involved in ten years ago, he knew what a ferocious devil he was once portrayed by the citizens, and he knew that Xiangming almost became the public enemy in order to defend him. He also knew the whole process from being a major suspect to being released from prison after the case... In just over half a month, Huyan Yun seemed to have relived the past ten years, but at this moment, when he called Zhou Liping in the evening and asked him to meet here when Zhou Liping was standing opposite him, he suddenly began to be confused about the meaning of all this. Ten years ago, he was still a college student, high-spirited and impassioned. Even after he entered society and suffered countless setbacks and blows, he was still full of pride in his reasoning ability. But in recent years, especially after encountering more and more cases like the Deratization one and people like Zhou Liping, he had a strange feeling that every real murderer exposed by him is, in the final analysis, were all poor creatures who are driven by fate and can do nothing, he sees them being bound heavily in the great net woven by fate, struggling due to hardship, crazy due to suffocation, and hurting other trapped beasts in the same net in their madness ... He testified against them and exposed them, but he had nothing to do with the big net that created all the tragedies.

What's more, Zhou Liping was so special, not even crazy...

Huyan Yun let out a long sigh: "Zhou Liping, I know you have been detained for so long, and don't want to mention this again that you have just been released. You don't want to come here again, even don't want to talk about this case. I want to calmly tell you what I think. You ask me if I still think you are suspect. To be honest, this question is difficult to answer, because I think: The reason why this case cannot be solved is precisely because the police are sparing no effort to look for your suspicions."

Zhou Liping's stone-stiff face twitched involuntarily.

"In all cases, from the moment of the incident, the most important job for the police to do is to search for evidence, lock the target and arrest the suspect. This case should have been no exception, but when the police discovered that your trace had been on the road that night, almost everyone agreed that you were the real murderer. Despite the serial murders in the western suburbs ten years ago, you were only sentenced to ten years in prison due to insufficient evidence. But in the hearts of every police officer, you are the culprit who killed those girls and Fang Zhifeng. In order to prevent you from escaping, Du Jianping led the team to arrest you as soon as possible – from this moment, the normal order of investigation has been changed, or the correct criminal investigation logic has been disrupted. From 'first to find evidence, second to lock the target, third to arrest the suspect', suddenly it became 'first to lock the target, second to arrest the suspect, third to find evidence'. Speaking of which, the arrest of you ten years ago was also due to irrigorous reasoning of mine that made the police to complete the lock on you prematurely. How fate did!" Huyan Yun smiled bitterly. "Of course, the police quickly discovered this mistake. Compared with the evidence they already had, it was obviously too early to lock and arrest you. Next, they could only make amends and investigate while reviewing. Nobody imagined that the confession you made were full of absurdities—for example, you ran to Xingyu Road from the Deratization Hill, you went to Xingyu Road to fight with Li Zhiyong, you walked around in a leisurely manner before the appointment and went to the mortuary to put Zhang Chunyang's body in the freezer – although they are unreasonable, life is full of reasonableness and unreasonableness. Besides, you are a murderer who plays cards out of common sense in the eyes of everyone. It makes perfect sense to do these things. However, the police did not give up, they still believed that you were the real murderer of the case, and began to work day and night, meticulously hoping to find evidence to expose your lies, to crack your alibi. Unfortunately, more than half a month has passed. They were like a group of people peeling onions. The more they peeled, the more innocent you are, but they were bursting into tears. What was going on? How did this happen? The police were puzzled until they learned that the three children committed suicide because they couldn't stand Xing Qisheng's humiliation, they suddenly realized that you are not the real murderer. As you said you were just the person who intervened in the case halfway and was used by Xing Qisheng to 'take the blame'."

"I think as the detective work goes on, it's becoming more and more common to all police officers: You bought two cans of beer at the convenience store near your home at about six o'clock on the night of the crime, and drank them all. Now, this means that you are not ready to go out that night, that is to say, you are not ready to commit a crime; a taxi driver proved that he received a man at Xiahe Street around 9 o'clock that night, and drove all the way to Tongyou Nursery. The taxi driving record showed that it took 20 minutes, and the driver quickly found you from a bunch of photos, which once again showed that you drove Xing Qisheng that night was an accidental behavior; also, the FAST system of every intersection you pass by have been extracted and analyzed, and you can't be seen any attempt to avoid or block the camera while driving. They even compared the surveillance videos of your previous driving to prove that your posture and expression that night were as usual; also, after the INSPIRE was found, the steering wheel and door handles were wiped with disinfectant wipes, leaving no fingerprints, which once again reduced the suspicion that you are the murderer, because if you are the real culprit, then as you're the driver, you often drive this car and leave fingerprints on the steering wheel." Huyan Yun shook his hand, "At the same time, evidence showed that Xing Qisheng maliciously framed you has surfaced one after another: for example, he lay down in the back row the whole time you drove to cover himself from being photographed by the camera; The checkout receipt from the bar on the first floor of the hotel, as well as the autopsy results, both proved that Xing Qisheng did not drink a drop of alcohol that night, but the ether air detector showed that even though it was found after several days, there were still precious foreign wines in the car. The strong smell of alcohol and that kind of foreign wine is only in his own wine cabinet. Combined with your confession that he lay down in the back seat after getting in the car, it is obvious that he sprinkled foreign wine on his clothes and pretended to be drunk and let you drive so that the FAST system can 'record' that it was you who transported the corpse that night, and you were the only one in the car; of course, most importantly, he had the motivation to burn the corpses of the children to exterminate his guilt of raping the kids, but you have no motivation at all.

"When these are brought outside, let's not say the police, anyone with the slightest brain can make a judgment: You can be 'cut' out of this case, especially the very powerful alibi that you provided: Before 11:00 that night, you ran to the mortuary of Love Hospital and moved Zhang Chunyang's body into the freezer. The timing system showed that the TE-3 freezer was only switched on once that night, at 10:50, and according to the workers "The timing system of the freezer is built-in independently, with its own battery, even if there is a power outage, the freezer will continue to time as usual" – if you committed the case, you can't do this at all. The phone call showed that Xing Qisheng was still alive at 10:30. If you kill him, throw and burn his body, and then move Spit, no matter how fast you are, you will not be able to arrive at the mortuary of Love Hospital in ten minutes. And as it's an emergency, you can't temporarily find someone to move the corpse for you. Besides, the police have verified your mobile phone communication records. That night, in addition to answering Xing Qisheng's request for you to be your chauffeur, you can only give one call at 10:40, which was for Li Zhiyong to make an appointment... Of course, there is also a possibility that Li Zhiyong was your accomplice. He helped you transport Zhang Chunyang's body, so as to create an alibi for you, but the FAST system recorded his driving record that night. He drove directly from home to Xingyu Road, all of the above showed one thing – it was someone else who killed Xing Qisheng!"

After listening to this sentence, Zhou Liping's expression was obviously relaxed.

"Yes, there was another person, let's call him 'X' for now!" Huyan Yun began to habitually pace back and forth when analyzing the case, "All indications showed that he and Xing Qisheng conspired to burn the corpse and put the blame on you. Because although Xing Qisheng was despicable, he was extremely incompetent. After the death of the children was found on the morning, according to Cui Yucui's confession, she panicked and did not know what to do. It was impossible for her to deal with this emergency. She had to find the only person who could help him. The police called up Xing Qisheng's mobile phone call records. After that, he called a phone number, and the owner of the number was Zhang Chunyang. Soon, Xing Qisheng drove to the Hefeng Hotel to discuss with Zhang Chunyang. After that, Xing Qisheng did not talk or stay with other people for a long time until the fire on the Deratization Hill was raging." Huyan Yun said, "This means that Zhang Chunyang is the 'X' who gave him advice behind the scenes!"

After a pause, Huyan Yun continued: "From many people who have been in contact with Zhang Chunyang, we can get a similar impression of this person: this is a 'daring, self-conscious' outlaw who uses the special relationship between himself and Tao Zhuo to gain a lot of benefits from the Kind Charity Fund. He has long served as his watchdog adviser. In addition, he has worked as a fitness coach. It is very likely that when he heard Xing Qisheng talk about the suicide of three children and didn't know how to deal with the aftermath, he immediately came up with a solution. He told Xing Qisheng that the city's public security is now very strict, and it was almost impossible to transport corpses out of this city. Once there has a high-speed inspection, it will be fatal. So the best way was to transport the corpses to Xishan to find an inaccessible place to bury them. But they may not be able to find a suitable place. It was definitely not possible near the highway. It was a big hassle to transport the three corpses when there is no road. Therefore, the compromise method was to find a place nearby where few people go, then throw the corpses, burn and bury them. Because Zhang Chunyang had the habit of exercising and often goes climbing the mountain, he knew the tunnel wind pavilion and also that there is no development or relocation plan in this area in the short term. Xing Qisheng thought it makes sense, but he was worried that this matter will be exposed sooner or later. The FAST system will definitely find out that he was the one who transported the corpses by car. Even if he fled to the ends of the earth, the people's police would be able to bring him back. Zhang Chunyang said that there is nothing to worry about, there is just someone who can 'take the blame'. You only need to let him drive, or as soon as the police see his face, they will 100% believe that everything was done by him. When Xing Qisheng heard it, he immediately understood who he was referring to, and couldn't help but applaud. The next step was the specific implementation. Xing Qisheng tricked you into driving him up the mountain, then drove the car into the nursery by himself, and joined Zhang Chunyang who had been waiting here. During the process of throwing the corpse, there may be a dispute, that Zhang Chunyang wanted to kill Xing Qisheng either. So they were thrown into the tunnel wind pavilion... Well, if this is the case, it will be revealed—"

Huyan Yun's voice stopped abruptly.

Zhou Liping looked at him with gloomy eyes.

"Unfortunately." Huyan Yun shook his head, "Unfortunately, there was one thing that can't be explained, that is, Zhang Chunyang died suddenly that night, and Xing Qisheng transported his body to the mortuary of Love Hospital. He has been stuffed into the freezer by you at 10:15 that night."

2

The wind stopped, a milky white twilight mist floated in the nursery, and the night mist became thicker. Fruit trees, the dirt road, a subway station liked a sliding coffin, a tunnel wind pavilion, and two people standing opposite the tunnel wind pavilion were all shrouded in a mysterious diffuse.

Zhou Liping's angular face was indistinguishable like separated by a layer of frosted glass.

Huyan Yun didn't care what he looked like now: "Next, I want to change the subject and talk about Zhang Chunyang's death, because this incident is inextricably linked with the later case. For whether the sudden death of Zhang Chunyang is true or false was controversial within the police. From what I have investigated, I tend to believe that the SCD that happened at the Hefeng Hotel that night was actually a show directed by Zhang Chunyang and Xing Qisheng.

"For Tao Zhuoyao, who is about to get married, Zhang Chunyang, the sex toy in the past, has lost its meaning and value. This is fatal to Zhang Chunyang. If he loses Tao Zhuoyao's backer, how could he live? It sounds ugly but he was just a 'duck'. He used to go to the Foundation's subordinate units under the name of his lover, but who will pay attention to him now? So Zhang Chunyang must be eager to save this 'relationship', but Tao Zhuoyao and his fiance Jiang Lei's marriage has multiple purposes. It is a 'sale' related to whether the Tao family can continue to gain a foothold in the Kind Charity Fund. You might as well put yourself in Zhang Chunyang's position, think about his situation, think about what he did to survive in this big city after he left Tao Zhuoyao, who was accustomed to eating soft food. Then you may find that he had no other choices. The only way is to extort a sum of money from Tao Zhuoyao in the end." After speaking, Huyan Yun raised his right hand and used his index finger and thumb to make a "circle", "I investigated Tao Zhuoyao's property in the Hefeng Hotel. When I was in the bedroom, I found that when the solid wood sliding door separating the bedroom and the living room was opened, there would be such a through-hole above the two overlapping door frames. Li Zhiyong, who was with me, thought it was for peeping, but he was wrong— – That hole is specially used to install the miniature camera.

"I observed the inside of the through-hole, and judging from the color of the shards on the side, it was newly dug, which means that the conspiracy to use the video to blackmail was planned recently. The problem is, simply filming Tao Zhuoyao Sex videos are useless. To be honest, how many ladies in the upper class have a clean private life? Even if they are black-mailed by sex videos, they will not be able to get a lot of money. But death is different, even disposed of the lover's body 'privately'. It is not only obscene but also illegal for her. This is a fatal blow to Tao Zhuoyao, not only she might be divorced, the position of her family may also be shook!"

Having said this, Huyan Yun suddenly lowered his voice: "However, there is a hurdle that must be passed in this matter. The surveillance video is easy to capture, but not easy for Tao Zhuoyao to believe that Zhang Chunyang is really dead, and a professional doctor is definitely needed. If Tao Zhuoyao was a little wise, even if she believed that Zhang Chunyang was really dead on the spot, she will go to further verification after calming down, so it is best to find a real doctor to act the death one. Which can minimize or even eliminate Tao Zhuoyao's suspicions. This doctor must be absolutely trusted by Tao Zhuoyao, the only person who can ask for help in the event of a 'scandal', of course, he must be a hardcore friend who was on the same boat with Zhang Chunyang. No one can think about the second person except Xing Qisheng.

"But--sorry, I have to say 'but' again." Huyan Yun looked at Zhou Liping and said, "But don't forget, although Xing Qisheng was the partner with Zhang Chunyang, in the final analysis, Tao Zhuoyao was his real backer, he and his younger brother Xing Qixian were at odds, and he was slandered for so many years, the Tao family had been covering him. What benefits would it do to Xing Qisheng to help Zhang Chunyang blackmail Tao Zhuoyao? Xing Qisheng was dirty but not stupid. Zhang Chunyang was also very clear about this. If he wants a person to submit, he will either give him a benefit or grab him, when Xing Qisheng hurriedly killed the three children in Tongyou Nursing Home and told Zhang Chunyang, Zhang Chunyang knew: the handle was coming. He quickly helped Xing Qisheng to formulate a plan to destroy the corpses and blame others, but in exchange, Xing Qisheng had to give him a 'death appraisal' in front of Tao

Zhuoyao. And then took advantage of Tao Zhuoyao's unpreparedness to remove the camera, and then handed it over to Zhang Chunyang after the case was settled. Zhang Chunyang kept his name incognito, pretended to be dead, and then found a relative to use video to blackmail Tao Zhuoyao. Zhang Chunyang's 'super credit card' with an unlimited withdrawal amount – of course, Zhang Chunyang may have a more evil plan, that is, not only can he use video to blackmail Tao Zhuoyao, but also use the corpses under the tunnel wind pavilion to blackmail Xing Qisheng. Xing Qisheng can only admit that he is unlucky and let him take it.

"Besides the through-hole, there was another point that can prove my speculation. On the day of the incident, Xing Qisheng arrived at the Hefeng Hotel as early as 2:30 in the afternoon to meet Zhang Chunyang. After Zhang Chunyang made an appointment with Tao Zhuoyao, he hid in the bar on the first floor of Hefeng Hotel, and called Tao Zhuoyao at 7 o'clock, using the excuse of 'reporting work' to come to see her, in fact, it was implied Tao Zhuoyao he was nearby. The camera in the bar captured that Xing Qisheng kept looking at his mobile phone while eating, and when the phone rang at 8:20, the show started." Huyan Yun made a gesture of pulling the curtain, "It happened too much. Suddenly, everything was just as Zhang Chunyang had expected. Tao Zhuoyao, the unreliable young lady, was in a panic in the face of a corpse lying on the bed. After the death identification, she decided to flee by plane. In order to perform the trick and ensure that Zhang Chunyang's death was witnessed and testified by others, Xing Qisheng first transported Zhang Chunyang to the mortuary of Love Hospital, put him in the morgue, issued a death certificate, and drove the car to Tongyou Nursing Home. He called and asked you to help drive while loading the bodies of the three children into the car—"

"What do you mean—" Zhou Liping said suddenly, "When Xing Qisheng asked me to be a chauffeur, Zhang Chunyang slipped out of the mortuary, ran to the Deratization Hill to wait for him, and took the rest of the 'mission'?"

"No no no!" Huyan Yun shook his head, "Zhang Chunyang can't be that X! That's right, after Xing Qisheng left, he disguised himself as a family member of the deceased and walked out of the morgue. Anyway, the two workers on duty were drinking too much every day and wouldn't care if a 'dead' came to life – but Zhang Chunyang didn't go to the Deratization Hill, but walked to another place not far away. I'll talk about this later... Don't forget, if he was really the X, then he also had an insurmountable difficulty like you: how could he throw his body on fire after killing Xing Qisheng at 10:30, set fire, and then rush to the morgue of Love Hospital at

10:50, then lied on the morgue? You know, his mobile phone was found in the freezer, and he did not use any car-hailing app records that night. The police investigated all the taxis that passed through that night captured by the camera. No driver remembered ever carrying such a person... I considered other possibilities: for example, the sound of calling 110 at 10:30 was pre-recorded, and it was only played after the alarm call was made to make alibi, but the identification certificate given by the Criminal Technology Department showed the voice must be Xing Qisheng's, and it must be the same sound under natural conditions, and even the background sound can be heard (he pointed to the windmill wrapped around the branch)), so at 10:30, Xing Qisheng was 100% still alive in this world. There were other similar assumptions, but they were all overturned by myself in the end... Of course, there is the most terrible one: After Zhang Chunyang arriving at the mortuary, who and what method was used to move such a large living person into the freezer?

"This is really a troublesome case! But the more it goes on like this, the more it arouses my interest in challenging this case." Huyan Yun knocked on his head and set his eyes on Zhou Liping again, "I know, you have read a lot of detective novels, then you must know that criminal police and reasoners are two completely different types of people. Criminal investigation work requires finding complete and sufficient evidence, and constructing a rigorous and logically correct based on this evidence. The chain of evidence leads to the discovery of the criminal, but the reasoning is not. The premise of the application of reasoning is that the evidence is insufficient and incomplete. Therefore, among the limited suspects, the logic in the confession and behavior is found through logical deduction. The more the suspect is suspected, the more the police help him clean up? Well, since you have taken my place, then I will go for a walk in yours. When I follow the 'positive' that the police should have taken, I found a sense of inappropriateness that the police had not noticed all along."

3

Crack!

A sudden night wind blew off the dead branches of the locust tree, and fell just not far from them.

Huyan Yun walked over, picked up the dead branch, touched its jagged and sharp stubble, and continued to say to Zhou Liping: "Inappropriateness... This word is too literary, or use a more popular term, rupture. Well, that's it, the whole case is filled with a sense of rupture... However, before explaining, let's analyze the plan formulated by Zhang Chunyang for Xing Qisheng, which is to let you drive Xing Qisheng to the Deratization Hill, the practice of exposing your face to the FAST monitoring system throughout the whole process is a clever trick or a stupor.

"I believe that if you are an ordinary person, or a reader who has read a few detective novels because of curiosity about the mysterious nature of the human crime, then you will definitely think that this strategy is a good one, at least he managed to avoid the FAST and found a scapegoat... However, for really experienced criminals, they would definitely scoff at this plan: Will it be possible that stripping the children's clothes and pouring gasoline on them would not be able to detect them? Will the police will convict an innocent person just based on the pictures captured by the FAST system? Will the police believe that Zhou Liping is the murderer, and gave no investigation of your words that there is a person lying in the back seat of the car? So, no matter who the X made the plan for Xing Qisheng was, the series of actions he planned before Xing Qisheng drove into the nursery, in the final analysis, were all seemingly ingenious but naive, ridiculous, and vulnerable tricks. Maybe this person was a little bit smarter than Xing Qisheng, but he's definitely not a professional criminal, at most a fancier.

"However, next, there was a shocking reversal of the case under our feet, in this nursery, by the wind pavilion of the tunnel." Huyan Yun gently swept the cold air of the wind pavilion in the tunnel with his hand and suddenly raised his voice, "The murderer who killed Xing Qisheng showed 'excellent' talent everywhere – sorry for my inaccuracy – it should be said to be 'professional' criminal quality: when time is tight and the surrounding light conditions are very poor, he was very meticulous in cleaning the footprints of the crime scene. He used fire to eliminate the trace marks left by the friction between the back and the concrete wall of the tunnel wind pavilion. He not only noticed the dismantling before and after throwing the body. And the extremely easily overlooked detail of not leaving fingerprints when installing the protective net of the tunnel wind pavilion, and the precise operation when wiping the steering wheel and door handles of the INSPIRE with a wet wipe, there is no omission. And the most worthwhile is that he actually drove the INSPIRE up to the Deratization Hill and drove around in a circle, and then drove back to the small alley outside. Because he knew that the premise of the police investigation at the crime scene was to open up barrier-free passages. Since the car blocked the road, if the owner of the car could not be found for a while, it would definitely be dragged to the traffic team, so that the police were restricted

375

by the limitation of their thinking mode and could not find the car in the best time to solve the case. It is enough to show that the murderer has very rich anti-investigation experience!

"I don't know if you've heard of it. Modern criminal investigation science emphasizes the concept of 'logical tree', that is, almost all criminal behaviors can be marked and deconstructed with tree diagrams. This is because all criminal behavior, no matter what kind of accidental situations occur in the implementation process, criminals follow their initial criminal habits and behavioral logic to deal with these situations." Having said that, he slowly stroked the stubble of the dead branches with his hand, "There is only one exception, and that is that this crime was originally – grafted."

He raised his head and looked at Zhou Liping, Zhou Liping had been standing there, looking at him in a posture, his face still expressionless.

"The so-called grafting refers to a seemingly complete criminal act. In fact, it was completed by two different people. Of course, the two people I am talking about were definitely not accomplices, because accomplices will still follow the principle of the logic tree when committing crimes and show roughly the same criminal habits and a continuous logical trajectory. By grafting, I mean that the two people have no idea of the other's criminal motives, actions, and ultimate goals from the beginning. Not only are they not accomplices, but they may be completely passers-by or even enemies. It's just because of very accidental reasons that the former's behavior was suddenly suspended, and the latter continued to commit the former's unfinished crimes—in the case, there was an obvious grafted feature, yes, it looks like this is indeed a complete branch, but as long as you think about it carefully, you will find a clear broken ballast." After speaking, Huyan Yun threw the dead branch on the ground, "and the one I want to find is the one who intercepted Xing Qisheng."

"Have you found him?" Zhou Liping asked.

"Yes."

"Who is he? "

"Who do you think he will be?"

"I can't think of this – maybe it was his enemy, or maybe it was a passerby who saw Xing Qisheng throwing his body, got into a fight with him, accidentally killed him, and then threw his body down the well in a panic and set a fire..."

"No, the person who grafted on Xing Qisheng's crime can't be his enemy. Once he did such a cruel and inhuman thing, how could he ask his own enemy to help? Second, where is such a coincidence, he didn't inform him. When he was throwing the corpses, he was bumped into by someone who liked to walk on the Deratization Hill in the dark and windy night... As for the passers-by's statement, it is not worth refuting. The on-site investigation showed that Xing Qisheng was killed but there was no sign of escaping or resisting at all, just like a chick who saw a tiger, sitting obediently waiting to die, which meant that the murderer must be someone Xing Qisheng knew and was afraid of, which meant that the murderer must have been in the intricate causal relationship of the case. This murder had a clear motive, and it can never be an accidental mistake by a passerby-the relationship between the murderer and Xing Qisheng was essentially a relationship between trial and being tried. The murderer was both the judge and the executioner of the death penalty!"

Zhou Liping was silent.

Huyan Yun slapped the tunnel wind pavilion heavily and removed the opening of the protective net, it was dark and cold: "Yes, right here, right next to this tunnel wind pavilion, there was a trial that night. The people who witnessed Xing Qisheng throwing naked and small corpses into this black hole, out of righteous indignation, personally executed Xing Qisheng! The murderer can only be that person, the outcast of the society, the rebel of that era, the villain in the eyes of the police, the public enemy in the hearts of the people, the prisoner who resolutely shouldered everything in order to protect the girl he loves, the person who spent eight years in prison could not frustrate the sense of justice!"

In an instant, a ray of light flashed in Zhou Liping's eyes, red, like a wound, but it quickly dimmed.

"Zhang Chunyang, Xing Qisheng." Huyan Yun sneered contemptuously when he said these two names, "Yes, these two scumbags can be regarded as extremely vicious and devoid of conscience. They mistakenly think that as long as they are ruthless, they can do whatever they want in this world, so they actually pick up professional players as amateur players – although I never believe in any bullshit like 'crime is an art', it has to be admitted that 'crime is a skill'. Professional criminals are gamblers who put their heads on their trousers, wander on the edge of life and death, and lose everything after a single miss, they have long been trained in 'real battles'. What are the two of them? A duck and a pervert, they even delusionally want to take the crimes they have committed for granted and put the blame on a person who was almost sentenced to death and spent eight years in prison. During the years, he had come into contact with all kinds of felons who were released from prison. It was like two idiots who challenged Tyson after reading Jin Yong's martial arts novels. Suicide!"

A gust of wind blew in, like blowing from the opening of the tunnel wind pavilion, originating from the dark underground, damp and gloomy, icy and biting, but it also blew away the night mist, letting Zhou Liping on the opposite side become a little brighter, and he could even see that his shovel-like jaw was trembling slightly.

Huyan Yun stretched out his arm and pointed to the outside of the nursery: "That night, at the crossroads below the Deratization Hill, according to Xing Qisheng's request, you got out of the car, watched Xing Qisheng get into the driver's seat, and drove the car to this road. With intuition, you had a premonition that Xing Qisheng was going to do something shameful, and it seemed that he has ulterior motives for you to be the driver, so you followed. When you quietly walk into the nursery, when you saw Xing Qisheng put on gloves, removed the protective net of the tunnel wind pavilion, and took the bodies of Zhao Wu, Li Ying, and Dong Xinlan out of the trunk one by one. Seeing the murderous aura on your face that he had never seen before, Xing Qisheng was terrified. He knew that his death was coming. He didn't have the courage to challenge you, a 'serial killer'. He could only kneel down and beg for mercy. He told you everything, The cause of the children's death, the tricks that made you take the blame, and even Zhang Chunyang's cheating death... he just asked you to spare his life, but you—"

"Wait a minute." Zhou Liping raised his hand, "Huyan Yun, the first time we met, I didn't expect you to imagine me to be so heroic, so tall. Thank you for that, but I'm really just an ordinary driver. The case has nothing to do with me at all... You said so much before I understood, what you mean is, Xing Qisheng was killed by me, how is this possible? I have an alibi."

"Yes, alibi, alibi..." Huyan Yun repeated several times, suddenly raised his head, looked at a jagged branch of the big locust tree above his head, and stopped talking.

In the deadly silence of the nursery, Zhou Liping stood motionless and said nothing. Suddenly, the lights of the Bus Automation Design and Research Institute went out all at once, and his figure was instantly engulfed by the darkness. Huyan Yun narrowed his eyes and looked for a moment, only to see that he was still standing there.

He sighed softly: "Zhou Liping, you may not believe it, the case is one of the most puzzling cases I have ever encountered. This case is complex, chaotic, and involves many people. The relationship was intricate and complicated, with doubts one after another, puzzles one after another... Among all the doubts and puzzles, the most difficult one to solve was what method did you use? You were here at 10:30 that night, killed Xing Qisheng in a nursery, and then rushed to the mortuary of Love Hospital at 10:50, and moved Zhang Chunyang, who was not dead, into the freezer.

A sneer slid across Zhou Liping's mouth. In the darkness, Huyan Yun couldn't see it, but he could feel it.

"Don't laugh, really, I tried to use logic to solve this puzzle, but I tried my best and exhausted my brainpower, but I couldn't solve it. I think it's impossible. No criminal can create an unsolvable puzzle for me. Until I was racking my brains and exhausted, I suddenly realized, yes, yes, you are far inferior to me in terms of logic, but one thing that you are really better than me, Li Zhiyong, Zhang Chunyang, Xing Qisheng, and even all the criminal police officers who handled the case together. That is you have a more thorough and profound understanding of the darkness of human nature—" Huyan Yun paused for a while and continued, "In other words, the way you created this trick and made it a big success is not to use logic, but human nature."

4

Zhou Liping's smile froze.

"As I said before, the reason why this case could not be solved was not because of the large number of people under investigation and the difficulty of detection, but on the contrary, it is precisely because the police were sparing no effort to find your suspect and put too much energy on you. Thereby they ignored doubts that seem unrelated to the case. These doubts were like a trivial piece of hundreds of Lego bricks, without which it can make a general appearance, but without such a piece, no matter how much effort they spent it still owes a little bit, and it's not complete. For example, when Xing Qisheng was throwing the corpses on hill that night, why was there a 'President Xing' in his office?

"Of course that person was not a thief. After he entered the office, he not only turned on the light, but also walked back and forth in Xing Qisheng's clothes. All this showed that he wants everyone to know that 'the dean is still in the office'. The purpose of this was, of course, making Xing Qisheng's 'presence certificate', then conversely, it was to create an 'alibi' for him at another location, where? Of course, it was the Deratization Hill!" Huyan Yun raised the index finger of his right hand and said, "Xing Qisheng helped Zhang Chunyang to cheat to death, and Zhang Chunyang helped Xing Qisheng to make plans to burn his corpse and destroy the traces. It seemed to be a reciprocal exchange of interests, but it was not.

Zhang Chunyang's cheating death was almost zero risk for him because in the future when he took the video to blackmail Tao Zhuoyao, even if Tao Zhuoyao found out that he was not dead, she did not dare to call the police. At most, she would guess that the accomplice was Xing Qisheng and fired him. If the corpses are found, the police will definitely investigate them to the end. It's a good idea to take you to the blame. But once you are arrested, you will confess that it was Xing Qisheng who drove the car up the Deratization Hill in the end. The best way to survive the pressure of police interrogation was to create an alibi in advance. Therefore, the 'Xing Qisheng' who was in the dean's office at 10 o'clock that night was Zhang Chunyang who slipped out of the mortuary of Love Hospital; Xing Qisheng took advantage of Tao Zhuoyao's absence and took off the micro-camera that captured the video of SSD. He will not give it to Zhang Chunyang until he went to the office to pretend to be him and creates an alibi for him.

"What was reflected in this little thing? Most people see that two friends were doing an exchange of interests, but you, almost immediately saw something more profound. Zhang Chunyang and Xing Qisheng were highly alert to the surrounding environment. They were alert to the point of hyper-sensitivity. They will respond quickly if there is a slight disturbance. In addition, these two allies who seem to cover each other were on guard from the bottom of their hearts. They like businessmen, calculated every point, 'I can't make you gain, you can't let me lose, and I can't let you sell me as a scapegoat'. I believe that in your life in prison, what you see the most was people intrigue with others, the real prison does not have the "friendship in your heart" like the movie "Prison", there were just betrayal and deceit... In the crowd of people, in a corner without sunlight, it was human nature to harm others and enrich oneself! Xing Qisheng and Zhang Chunyang were well aware of each other, and what you have to take advantage of was their over-awareness of the surrounding environment and their caution towards each other!"

After a pause, Huyan Yun continued: "When you saw the bodies of those three children, you almost certainly had the intention to kill Xing Qisheng, and Zhang Chunyang, an accomplice, must also be punished! But the other problem was also must be considered which was how to get rid of the crime after killing Xing Qisheng? This was really a very difficult thing. Your face has been photographed by the FAST camera. You were well aware of the police's criminal investigation level and case handling efficiency. Knowing that you will be arrested soon, you cannot escape no matter what, so what you need to consider was how to get out after being covered by the net again. At this time, your brain was like a high-speed engine, and in an instant, the experience of being tried in serial murder cases in the western suburbs, the criminal investigation procedures that you learned from dealing with various criminal police officers, and the anti-investigation techniques you learned from various felons in prison for eight years! Look at everything in this nursery: fruit trees, dirt roads, tunnel wind pavilions, abandoned subway stations. You accurately estimated every step of the work the police will do when they arrive, and you can even see all the scenes that will happen next here: The police halogen lamps illuminated the place like daylight. The crime scene investigation experts bowed their heads and bent over to conduct a strip search inch by inch. The forensic doctor went down to the bottom of the tunnel wind pavilion to conduct an autopsy. The tire traces were extracted, and the doors of all households within a radius of one kilometer will be knocked open for investigation and visits. Every surrounding traffic artery was stationed by armed police with live ammunition. Anyone's entry and exit will be repeatedly checked. The on-duty personnel of the Municipal Network Security Office have washed away their sleepiness, and have made every effort to mobilize and inspect the surveillance video near the crime scene – under the Deratization Hill, this huge city sleeping soundly in the night will be completely awakened, with sharp teeth and fangs. But you have nowhere to go, and no reinforcements!"

Zhou Liping looked at Huyan Yun, his wind-beaten eyes flashed with stern eyes.

"Facing the corpses of the children, you were angry and hated, and facing the frame-up of Xing Qisheng and Zhang Chunyang, you had pain and fear, but you suppressed all your emotions with an unimaginable will, and thought with amazing calmness and rationality. Start from the morning: what did you say, who did you meet, what was your work status, what time did you get off work, where was the beer you bought when you got home, where were the shopping receipts from the convenience store, your mobile phone record, where you were sitting in the taxi when you took a taxi to Tongyou Nursing Home, when you arrived at the Nursing Home, the driving route you drove Xing Qisheng to the Deratization Hill, what actions did you do after entering the nursery, where may fingerprints and footprints be left, and also, how to kill Xing Qisheng, what to do with these bodies. You recalled the location and direction of the cameras of nearby units you saw when you participated in the trail running training, and you moved the INSPIRE and put it in the blind spot, the best route to evacuate the crime scene... What are the advantages and disadvantages, what can be done and what cannot be done, in the limited time where every second counts, you had to think about every piece. There could be no mistakes! Because the interrogation pressure you will face is likely to be even greater than ten years ago! Of course, from another perspective, this is not a bad thing. The police focus all their goals on you, but instead become the biggest flaw that can be used is like archery. When all the arrows are aimed at the same bullseye, the arrows shot in front will cover the real bullseye, so as long as the time is right, show a prepared one. All archers will think that it is their own misjudge that causes the visual deviation when aiming, and this fake bullseye is your alibi, the body of Zhang Chunyang lying in the freezer!"

Zhou Liping, who had been silent for a long time, spoke again with a low voice: "After talking for a long time, you still haven't made it clear: what method did I use to kill Xing Qisheng here at 10:30 that night, but at 10:50 I moved Zhang Chunyang who was still alive into the freezer of the mortuary?"

"Before answering your question, I want to talk a small thing, and that is why you forced Xing Qisheng to call the police before killing him." Huyan Yun said, "Frankly, after a long period of time, I could not guess the intention of the murderer. The purpose of throwing the corpses into the shaft and setting it on fire was not to destroy the corpses and destroy the traces? But once you call the police, doesn't it mean that the crime is reported to the world? The purpose is completely the opposite! Also, 110 had a recording of all incoming calls. Once the identity of the body is found, it will be verified based on the voice that the person calling the police is one of the deceased. Does this not mean helping the police to lock in the time of the crime? Later, I gradually understood that what the murderer had to do was to give the police an accurate time for the crime, because his alibi trick was only effective based on this time."

Huyan Yun looked at Zhou Liping and said: "After killing Xing Qisheng, you quickly cleaned up the traces left at the crime scene, then you moved the car. And ran down the mountain quickly, you must use a transport that the police could never think of to realize a big shift in space. At around ten forty, you ran to the community where Li Zhiyong was located, opened his Jetta trunk, hid in it, and called him to make an appointment: at eleven o'clock, on Xingyu Road. Li Zhiyong is an old enemy with you. If he was provoked by your words, of course, you will take the call. After he drove, you use your mobile phone GPS to locate and wait for the car to stop near Xingyu Road. After listening to Li Zhiyong getting off, you also got out of the car and ran to the place where you made an appointment with him. In this way, the police couldn't figure out how you drove from the Deratization Hill to Xingyu Road in half an hour. They can only believe what you said that you have already left the Deratization Hill at ten o'clock—"

"Huyan Yun." Zhou Liping interrupted him suddenly, "I guess you digressed?"

"Digress?"

"Yeah, what I asked you just now was how I got Zhang Chunyang into the freezer at the mortuary of Love Hospital at 10:50, not how I got to Xingyu Road at 11. If I used the method you just mentioned which I hid in the trunk of Li Zhiyong's car. You also mentioned it just now. The FAST system has checked it. Li Zhiyong drove to Xingyu Road that night and did not change the route. So how did I get to the Love Hospital? Could it be that I got off the car early near the caring hospital while the Jetta was waiting for the red light, and went to the mortuary to carry the body? But have you calculated the time? If I did that, I would have gone a long way. And I couldn't get to Xingyu Road at 11!"

"I didn't say you got off halfway."

"I see, you're saying that I actually went to the mortuary to move Zhang Chunyang into the freezer after the fight with Li Zhiyong, didn't I?" Zhou Liping narrowed his eyes, and there was a hint of sarcasm on the corner of his mouth, "But—"

His voice stopped abruptly.

"But—" Huyan Yun looked at him, "You mean to say, but the mortuary of Love Hospital is locked from eleven o'clock in the evening and only opens at nine o'clock the next morning. At this time, it is impossible for you to sneak in and move the corpse, right? "

Zhou Liping clenched his teeth twice: "We've been chatting for a long time, but nothing is useful. In the end, you still can't justify yourself on the most critical issue."

"No, I can!" Huyan Yun shook his head slowly, "I know how you managed to move Zhang Chunyang into the freezer at 10:50."

His tone was so calm and firm, which made Zhou Liping's heart beat faster, so fast that he could almost hear the series of "pounding" sounds. Maybe it was to cover up this sound, he deliberately pretended to be indifferent, he said in a sarcastic tone: "Then tell me how I did it – could it be that I let Zhang Chunyang lie in the freezer by himself?"

Huyan Yun's eyes suddenly burst into a dazzling brilliance in the dark night: "Yes! You just let Zhang Chunyang lie down in the freezer by himself!"

Dead silent.

There was no wind, no grass moving, and even the broken windmill hanging on the old locust tree stopped its withered clack.

In an instant, he was top-heavy and his eyes were black as if he had been thrown upside down into the tunnel wind pavilion.

No! He just cheated me, he couldn't guess what method I used!

"Huyan Yun, you're crazy! What nonsense are you talking about? I asked Zhang Chunyang to obediently lie down in the freezer. How is this possible? Why should he listen to me?"

"He won't listen to you, but he will listen to Xing Qisheng." Huyan Yun said calmly, "The phone records show that in the last few minutes of his life, Xing Qisheng, in addition to calling 110 for the police, also called himself. The phone number in the office proves once again that there is a 'substitute' arranged by Xing Qisheng in his office – the reason why Xing Qisheng did not call Zhang Chunyang's cell phone was that he considered that the matter of Zhang Chunyang's 'dead' would be leaked in the future, once the police start a criminal investigation, they will definitely check the communication records. If they find out that he made a phone call with Zhang Chunyang who was already died, they will be exposed. Xing Qisheng called his office landline, although the call time was very short, it doesn't matter. One sentence was enough."

"One sentence..." Zhou Liping swallowed his Adam's apple hard, "What?"

"You asked Xing Qisheng to tell Zhang Chunyang: 'Tao Zhuoyao seemed to notice and she had already refunded her flight ticket and go to the morgue to see if you are really dead.'"

Damn it!

Fucking damn it!

All night, like a mole hiding in a hole, listening to the pickaxe pounding on the ground, he had been taking chances for all the reinforcement and camouflage he had done before, but at this moment, he saw clearly when the pickaxe pierced the hole in the ground, the beam of white light shot straight in.

Zhou Liping closed his eyes.

"Hearing this sentence, Zhang Chunyang panicked. If Tao Zhuoyao arrived at the mortuary and found that he was not there, or that he was not dead, then this scene can be considered a complete failure. With the personality of Xing Qisheng, it was entirely possible that he will tell Tao

Zhuoyao the truth. When the video of SSD was in the hands of Xing Qisheng, Tao Zhuoyao will definitely help Xing Qisheng hide and dispose of the bodies of the three children. And whether it is from considerations of Tao Zhuoyao or Xing Qisheng's safety, they will definitely let Zhai Qing send someone to kill Zhang Chunyang! As I said just now, Zhang Chunyang, like Xing Qisheng, was in a state of high tension, almost said to be nervous, and he will react immediately if there is a slight disturbance, so he decided to rush back to the morgue immediately – at this time, you asked Xing Qisheng to say a second sentence to Zhang Chunyang."

Zhou Liping opened his eyes.

"The second sentence is that Zhang Chunyang must rush back to the morgue within twenty minutes, and find an empty freezer to lie in—"

"No, it's impossible, Zhang Chunyang won't accept this idea!" Zhou Liping said, "The introduction of the freezer by the Love Hospital was a relationship line from Zhang Chunyang, and he got a kickback from it. He knew that the freezer had a gravity induction device, as long as the corpse lay in it, it will automatically lock and start the freezing program, so Zhang Chunyang will not seek to death!"

"It seemed that you are also familiar with the features of this freezer." Huyan Yun smiled.

"That set of freezers has been out of order for a period of time, and it will cost a lot of money to find the original factory for repairs. Love Hospital knew that I have learned the repair and maintenance of refrigerators and freezers in prison, so they asked me for help." Zhou Liping quickly covered up.

Huyan Yun didn't care: "When I came up with this method to let Zhang Chunyang lie in the freezer automatically, I called the forensic doctor and got confirmation from her that Zhang Chunyang was frozen to death, which made me believe in myself even more. My reasoning is correct. The next step is to solve the last problem: Zhang Chunyang is not a fool. Even if he didn't know the structure of the freezer, he doesn't dare to lie in it when he opened it and saw the chilling air... Until I go in person It was only after a trip to the mortuary of Love Hospital that I found out what was going on. It turned out that the building of Love Hospital was originally a commercial building, which was rented by Kind Charity Fund for the purpose of running the hospital. They said the mortuary must be built independently, the system also needs to be independent—including the power system. There was a hut next to the mortuary, which was equipped with a generator, and a distribution box was hung on the wall. After Zhang Chunyang returned, he slipped into the hut, opened the distribution box, and just pull

385

the switch corresponding to the freezer, it will not affect other electricity consumption outside, not even the lighting of the freezer room, so the two on-duty workers were unaware. Next, he pretended as a family member of the deceased entered the mortuary and lay down in the TE-3 freezer. It was a little cold at first, but it was all right after overcoming it. There was air circulation inside the freezer, and there was no suffocation problem, so he was waiting for Tao Zhuoyao to come for an autopsy. Even if Tao Zhuoyao didn't come, because of the power failure, the gravity sensing device was not activated, and the freezer was not locked, so he can come out anytime he wanted.

"When the police investigated the mortuary, they found out that the TE-3 freezer was only switched on and off once at 10:50 on the night of the crime. This is because the timer was built-in independently and had its own battery, so it was not affected by the freezer system. The impact of the power outage—of course, you also know all of the above, not only this, but you also accurately predicted every move Zhang Chunyang would take next. From that moment, he had got on death train, and every station was predetermined, there was absolutely no possibility of getting off the train..."

"Nonsense!" Zhou Liping's patience was approaching the limit, "The switch had been pulled, and the morgue has been locked again at eleven o'clock, so how did I kill Zhang Chunyang?!"

"It's very simple." Huyan Yun stared into his eyes and said the ultimate answer word by word——

"The mortuary was locked, but the hut next to it was not. As long as you and Li Zhiyong were separated after the fight, you just went into the hut and pushed the switch that was pulled up."

Zhou Liping's vision was blurred for a while, and a double image of Huyan Yun appeared in front of him... He couldn't see his opponent clearly, but the opponent could see him from the inside out, even his internal organs clearly!

"The power of the freezer was restarted, the gravity sensing device was activated immediately, the TE-3 freezer was automatically locked, and the temperature in the freezer quickly dropped to minus 18 degrees Celsius. In such a low-temperature environment, Zhang Chunyang's consciousness could not remain awake for too long. He may have struggled briefly or called for help loudly, but the two workers drank too much and slept like dead pigs long ago, and the iron door of the freezer room had excellent sound insulation..."

Zhou Liping looked ahead and saw in the dark a self that was disintegrating, shattering, and would collapse in an instant. He wanted to use his hands to sweep, gather, splice, and glue himself again, but no matter how hard he tried, he still couldn't eliminate chipped lines and broken marks.

He glared at Huyan Yun fiercely, even though his eyes were so distracted that he couldn't tell whether Huyan Yun was really standing in the direction he was staring at: "You just said that Xing Qisheng and Zhang Chunyang were using each other at the same time that night. Then why do you conclude that Xing Qisheng asked Zhang Chunyang to drill into the freezer, and Zhang Chunyang would definitely do it? Isn't he afraid that Xing Qisheng will go to the hut next to the mortuary to turn on the electric switch after finishing his work, and then kill him? Don't forget Xing Qisheng has a very close relationship with Love Hospital, and he may not be unclear about the power system of the mortuary—"

"Really......"

Although there are only two words, the composure, composure, and self-confidence contained in these two words made Zhou Liping's voice tremble: "What? What did you say?"

"I said—really." Huyan Yun said, "As I expected, you even thought of this."

"I... what did I think of?"

"When you forced Xing Qisheng to call Zhang Chunyang, you knew that Zhang Chunyang would definitely be on guard against Xing Qisheng's deceit, but you didn't worry, because you knew that Zhang Chunyang would still get into the freezer, because he was confident that he still had one more method left. Even if the freezer was really powered on and locked, he can still escape."

"What method?"

"Mobile phone." Huyan Yun said, "When the police found Zhang Chunyang's body in the freezer, they found that the mobile phone was not in his pocket, but in his hand. The detectives thought that the mobile phone slipped out of his pocket accidentally, but in fact, it was in his hand. The reason why Zhang Chunyang dared to drill into the freezer was that he thought that if he had to, he can use his mobile phone to call outside for help... When Zhang Chunyang found that the freezer was locked and began to cool down rapidly, he did take out his mobile phone and wanted to call the police or ask for help—— It's a pity that he had a thousand calculations, but he was still one trick less than you."

Zhou Liping raised his hand and rubbed his eye sockets with his palms to cover up the severe pain that the blood rushed to his skull and almost burst... The trick was solved, and he could only say that his skills were not as good as others, but even the deepest thoughts in his heart were blocked by the other party. Which were dug out, that kind of shame was really heart-piercing pain.

Huyan Yun could see his embarrassment, but he still had to finish his words: "Because you have seen the mobile phone he is using – I am not hacking the iPhone, but the iPhone 8 still hasn't solved the bug of automatic shutdown in the low-temperature environment... For Zhang Chunyang, who was shivering in the freezer that night, it was really a deadly bug."

Over.

It's completely over.

It's all over.

All his plans and calculations that night, his restraint and forbearance during the half-month detention time, all collapsed as a dike washed away by the flood...

Can't admit defeat, can't surrender, because, it's not time yet!

He panted heavily, swallowed hard a few times, relieved the sore drowning feeling in his nasal cavity somewhat, raised his heavy head again, and even raised his head a little higher than before: "So, do you have any evidence?"

- So, do you have any evidence?

In an instant, he was pleasantly surprised, because not only did he suddenly see the babyface on the opposite side, but for the first time in the whole night, he saw a hint of depression on the babyface.

"So, do you have any fucking evidence?"

He took a step closer to Huyan Yun and asked a question viciously.

Huyan Yun lowered his eyelids, pursed his lips into a circle, and spat out the word "Hu" softly.

"Everything I said just now is pure reasoning, without the slightest evidence." Huyan Yun turned his attention to him again, "I did try to find evidence, for example, on the switch of the distribution box, I tried to find your fingerprints, unfortunately, I didn't find it. You didn't forget to wipe your fingerprints in such a tense situation. I really admire your composure, courage, finesse, and incomparably strong willpower. As a reasoner, it is a failure that I can only make reasoning and not produce evidence. It is unconvincing, and I am deeply sorry for that."

Zhou Liping sneered twice.

"I've finished speaking, but there are two questions that I haven't figured out yet. I hope you can give me the answer." Huyan Yun said.

Zhou Liping said nothing.

Huyan Yun said to himself: "First, why did you remove that INSPIRE? There was no evidence against you on it, and you should understand that no matter how clever the trick is, the police will still take a while to find it. And it also took you some time to drive to the Deratization Hill, and circle and back down the alley, and that night, there is nothing more precious to you than time."

No answer.

Huyan Yun smiled bitterly: "The second question, I'm afraid you won't answer me... After being arrested, as long as you take out the confession of carrying Zhang Chunyang's body, the police will release you soon, but you didn't. Of course, you said that because Xing Qisheng promised you that as long as you help Tao Zhuoyao keep it secret, he will help you solve Dong Yue's household registration, but in my opinion, this was a complete lie... Then I don't understand, why would you rather spend so long in handcuffs and shackles in the detention center, instead of throwing out this lie to save yourself, but suddenly told it a few days ago?"

Still no answer.

"If you don't want to tell me, forget it, but there are a few words I still want to say." Huyan Yun stared at him and said solemnly, "Whether Xing Qisheng or Zhang Chunyang, they were all villains and scum. They used their power and status to robbery and unscrupulous infringement on the rights and interests of innocent people and even their lives... But, Zhou Liping, please remember: the justice of a society cannot be achieved by lynching. You killed Fang Zhifeng ten years ago which can be said that it is legitimate self-defense, but this time it was different. This time you deliberately murdered when the other party was completely incapable of resisting! Your behavior is a crime that must be condemned and unforgivable! "

Huyan Yun took a deep breath and continued: "As a reasoner, I admit that I have not found any evidence to testify against you, but as a citizen of a society ruled by law, I still need to remind you that your next most correct choice is to turn yourself into the police and confess your crime honestly. Of course, you may laugh at my suggestion as naive and ridiculous. Maybe you think that only the lynching of those two scumbags is the way to go, but you need to know if you didn't kill Xing Qisheng that night, but arrested him and Zhang Chunyang to the judicial authorities, the law would also give justice to Zhao Wu, Li Ying, and Dong Xinlan."

Zhou Liping stared at him silently for a long, long time, then turned around, strode out of the nursery, and walked down the Deratization Hill.

Perhaps because of walking too fast, Zhou Liping was sweating profusely. He unbuttoned his collar, but he still felt stuffy, so he unbuttoned all the buttons on his shirt. A button was flying, and he didn't even notice it. It wasn't until he walked out of the alley and stood at the crossroads that he stopped and stared at the empty street in front of him.

That night, he got off the car here. Xing Qisheng, who was lying in the back seat with alcohol, suddenly sat in the driver's seat completely without drunkenness, and gave him one hundred yuan and said, "There are very few taxis here, but a lot of black cars, you can just take a black car and go home, don't use Didi, I can't reimburse you here."

He thought it was strange, did he already give me the money, why did he file a reimbursement? Besides, isn't it impossible to get reimbursed for black cars?

In this incoherent exhortation, in Xing Qisheng's sudden disappearance of drunkenness, he had an ominous premonition.

Years of prison life were rather the most severe survival training, whether it was living in the same room with a few or even a dozen vicious gangsters, or raising your eyelids too much leads to a bloody fight, or watching the prison tyrant wrap the ice skater in the dirt and kill the inmate in the middle of the night without leaving any physical evidence. All of those have already made him have a sixth sense of any danger like a beast.

So, he followed.

INSPIRE drove into the nursery and stopped in front of the tunnel wind pavilion, but did not turn on the lights. He ducked cautiously behind a pine tree and looked in INSPIRE's direction. After a long time, Xing Qisheng got out of the car, opened the trunk, and moved things to the ground. At first, he didn't see exactly what Xing Qisheng was moving. The three objects were soft or hard like saplings. It was not until Xing Qisheng turned on the mobile phone light and removed the protective net of the tunnel wind pavilion that the light flashed, then he finally saw one of the faces lying on the ground.

No blood, no anger, his eyes were still open, and his tongue was sticking out from his slightly open mouth... It was the little Zhao Wu who had found him countless times, scolded Xing Qisheng as a "beast", and cried when he scolded him!

He stood up abruptly from behind the pine tree.

Xing Qisheng was terrified, his hands trembled, his phone fell to the ground, and the light cluster illuminated the other two small faces.

One was Li Ying. He remembered that she was only five years old and had some problems with her mental development. When she encountered any injury or illness, she would lie down on the ground and curl up like a kitten begging for forgiveness... At this moment, she lying on the ground finally stopped curling up and stretched out forever and ever.

Another was Dong Yue's younger sister, Dong Xinlan, who was nine years old this year. Because the corners of her mouth were slightly upturned, she always seems to be smiling. Even if fate was so cruel to her, she always smiled... then scene when he arranged the two sisters to reunite, and Dong Yue cried bitterly while holding her sister, which he would never forget for the rest of his life. Later, he heard from Zhao Wu that Xing Qisheng had done some very bad things to Xinlan. He had thought about calling the police, but Xinlan suffered from mild cerebral palsy and could not tell what happened to the police and could not testify against Xing Qisheng at all. He was so angry that he once scolded Xing Qisheng in front of Dong Yue, but instead made Dong Yue worry about her sister. He promised that no one will hurt a single hair in Xinlan.

This vow became stronger in his heart after Dong Yue suddenly left the city.

But now, Xinlan lying on the ground, her slender and soft white neck was twisted into a right angle... She looked at him with a smile on her lips, as if she was apologizing to him. Like her sister, she had to leave without saying goodbye and go far away, no longer needing his care...

Xing Qisheng stepped back and said, "Liping, Zhou, I didn't do this, listen to my explanation, listen to me..."

He didn't see clearly how Zhou Liping rushed in front of him, his lower abdomen had been kicked heavily, and the thick subcutaneous fat of the abdomen heard a watery sound of being kicked to pieces, and the huge pain made him faint instantly.

Zhou Liping ignored him, but walked slowly to the side of the three corpses, squatted down, patted their little faces one by one, and muttered in his mouth that it was not a pronunciation at all as if to wake them up. When he understood that they would never wake up again, he picked them up one by one again, put them in his arms, held them tightly, gave their naked bodies the final warmth with his own body heat, and stroked them their hair, and the teardrops fell on their cold little faces...

The last one he picked up was Li Ying, and the last to put down was also her, a five-year-old girl with a very light body, so light that it was almost non-existent. When he put her back on the ground, he suddenly grabbed his unkempt hair and yelled at the dark sky with his eyes split open. At first, it was just swearing, then it turned into howling! He hasn't shed a single tear since he had arrested ten years ago, not a drop! He has already chosen a path of useless tears for his life, so he will never let a glimmer of water come to his eyes again! But now, in the face of these three small corpses, he poured out all the tears he had accumulated for ten years!

However, even when his emotions were out of control, he kept reminding himself: You can't drop the torn hair on the ground, not even one! Otherwise, it will be taken by the police as evidence that he has been to the crime scene.

At about this moment, Xing Qisheng's death was already a certainty – the man who was mistaken by the world as a murderer was finally about to kill.

Xing Qisheng groaned and slowly woke up,

Zhou Liping did not intend to torture him. Although he was proficient in all the means of torture, in order to avoid the police suspecting that it was a vendetta during the interrogation, he planned to use less torture. Fortunately, out of great fear and a strong desire to survive, Xing Qisheng didn't need him to ask any more questions. Both Zhang Chunyang's fraudulent death and the fact that he is now playing his stand-in in the office of the dean of the Nursing Home, he said it one by one. The deceitful miniature camera was also handed over.

Zhou Liping listened quietly, but the thoughts in his mind were as fast as the speed of light. Every word Xing Qisheng said, he thought of corresponding countermeasures, and all the countermeasures were two lines, one line was to resolve and even counteract the framing of Xing Qisheng and Zhang Chunyang which was full of flaws, enough for his own use; the other line was how to deal with the inevitable arrest, which was more troublesome, and the current situation was very unfavorable for him. Once the case happened, the police would definitely come to the door, so he must think of a method as soon as possible, a method that can not only kill Xing Qisheng and Zhang Chunyang but also create an alibi...

In an instant, the words Lin Xiangming said to him when he visited prison a few years ago flashed into his mind like a flash of lightning!

"The best riddles are those that give false answers from the beginning!"

Right!

That's right!

Don't wait for the crime to happen, but take the initiative to commit the crime!

Because, whether this trick can be successful or not, the most critical thing is the time!

Force Xing Qisheng to call the police, and his voice will be recorded in 110 so that can "help" the police to lock the crime time in a limited area.

Clean up all traces of the crime scene and make everything look like the work of a seasoned criminal.

Throwing corpses, burning corpses, when the police found the bodies of the children under the tunnel wind pavilion, everyone would think that the criminal was a vicious and perverted murderer——

Just like his "personality".

The police will soon find his face through the FAST monitoring system. Once they see his face, they will quickly determine that this is the "answer to the mystery".

With the criminal suspect being imprisoned, the focus of the criminal investigation will no longer be the on-scene investigation and evidence collection, but on his interrogation.

He had plenty of experience in this regard.

He will give the statement the police need at every stage in a methodical and precise manner according to his carefully designed plan. Those confessions must be absurd but verifiable, false but well-documented. It is necessary to ensure that the reaction time and tone of each answer remain stable and consistent, in line with his "criminal personality characteristics". At the right time, I used superfluous words to expose my "disorder of mind", which made the police mistakenly think that they had caught the loophole, so they shifted the focus of the investigation and launched an investigation on the Kind Charity Fund- especially Tao Zhuoyao and Zhang Chunyang. The investigation of the relationship gradually established a logical relationship between the case and Zhang Chunyang's disappearance. When they vaguely began to suspect that his arrest was a mistake, they subconsciously waited for that "correction" opportunity. At that time, he couldn't be in a hurry, he had to keep his composure and wait like a rock. When they suddenly mentioned Tao Zhuoyao and Zhang Chunyang's names repeatedly during the interrogation, he asked to see Tao Zhuoyao before he was willing to explain. If the answer is "No" (rather than "We will discuss later"), then it proves that Tao Zhuoyao has returned to China and is being interrogated. At that time, he will throw the bombshell of carrying Zhang Chunyang's body and make a complete comeback!

It's not so much a battle of wits, but a battle of hearts!

Huyan Yun was right. Due to the continuous progress of the legal system, the judicial department pays more and more attention to the presumption of innocence in criminal investigations and trials. Any suspicious case will be eventually handled in a direction that is beneficial to the suspect.

The best riddles are those that give false answers from the beginning.

The next step was Xing Qisheng's death. Everything was just as Huyan Yun had speculated. He forced Xing Qisheng to make two calls, one to the dean's office and used Tao Zhuoyao's suspicion as an excuse to let Zhang Chunyang go back to the mortuary and turn off the switch, then he got into the freezer and pretended to be dead. And the other called 110 to call the police... On the first call, Xing Qisheng was terrified, thinking that Zhou Liping was going to kill himself and Zhang Chunyang. On the second call, Xing Qisheng again recovered a look of joy on his face, he thought that Zhou Liping was asking the police to come and deal with it, but then his face turned ashes, "The Deratization Hill station is on fire", but he didn't have time to throw the body and set it on fire...

He hadn't figured out what the hell was going on, and he was already strangled by Zhou Liping's iron arm...

Looking at the four corpses on the ground, Zhou Liping knew that it was time to count, and the fire truck would arrive soon.

He quickly swept the crime scene without leaving a shred of evidence that he had been there.

Then, he threw the bodies of the three children into the tunnel wind pavilion-he shed tears again, hugging the bodies of the children, he couldn't bear it, but it was useless, he kept saying sorry to them, telling them that this was a helpless act to avenge them...

In contrast, it was much more pleasant to throw Xing Qisheng's body, but he deliberately dropped the body second to prevent the police from discovering anything about the order in which the bodies were thrown.

Finally, he poured the gasoline that Xing Qisheng had already put in the trunk into the tunnel ventilation pavilion, and then turned on his Zippo lighter——

"Crack," a crisp and loud sound.

A cluster of flames that suddenly sprang up in the dark danced wildly in the night wind. The flames shone on Zhou Liping's face. He felt warm, sultry, and even a little intoxicated. He felt that the cluster of flames was himself. Forbearance, silence, and persistence for so many years seem to be waiting for this moment to be polished.

He threw the lighter down.

In an instant, like an explosion, there was a sound of "Boom", and the rolling flames and heatwaves, like an enraged red dragon, suddenly rose from the bottom of the tunnel wind pavilion!

Zhou Liping turned his head slowly, his shovel-like chin bulged forward resolutely and looked solemnly at the huge sleeping city under the Deratization Hill. He knew that when the sun rose tomorrow morning, he would fight a decisive battle of disparity in power alone!

He walked to INSPIRE, drove out of the nursery, through the dark tunnel-like alley, and drove up the Deratization Hill...

That thrilling night, although he had repeatedly recalled it during his detention, flashed in his mind again at this moment, but it was a completely different feeling. When he was in the detention center, he meticulously pondered every detail on the Deratization Hill to find out if he had any mistakes or omissions. Those memories were "technical", and just after a conversation with Huyan Yun, he was very impressed with the memories of that night. It was not until he walked onto the stone bridge with white marble railings on the aqueduct of Wuding River when a gurgling sound accompanied by the night wind came, like a soothing chord, that his heart gradually calmed down. He looked under the bridge and knew that the sound was the flow of unfrozen river water, but he couldn't see anything in the darkness. He raised his head, and the Qingshikou Hydropower Station in the distance seemed like a wall without windows in the dark night.

He had seen such a wall, but at that time, fate opened a magical window for him.

In the fifth year of his sentence, he used a long nail to pierce the scrotum of the prisoner who boasted of raping several young girls and was chained and locked in a trumpet.

He started a hunger strike and refused to eat. The prison guard told him that this kind of blatant resistance to reform would only lead to increased punishment. He leaned against the cold wall, closed his eyes, and said nothing...

A few days later, the closed iron door suddenly opened, and the prison guards came to the interrogation room with him, who had no strength to walk.

The interrogation room had no windows. He slumped down in his chair, looking at the lead-grey wall opposite, thinking that he might be sealed in such a concrete coffin forever.

A cup of water.

A paper cup full of water was placed on the table in front of him.

The person who brought him water sat down opposite him.

He wanted to drink, his chapped lips could not resist the desire for water, but he held it back, he wanted to fight it all: fate, fetters, walls without windows, and this glass of water...

"Zhou Liping, nice to meet you, my name is Lin Xiangming."

Kind voice. He was very familiar with the name. Five years ago, his lawyer had told him that if a policeman named Lin Xiangming hadn't testified against his lack of criminal evidence, he would have been sentenced to a longer sentence—even the death penalty.

He raised his head and saw a white, handsome face, a pair of bright eyes emitting a clear light, and the corner of his mouth hung an unusually warm smile that he had not seen for a long time.

He was a little dazed and didn't know how to face this "beneficiary".

Next, Lin Xiangming said something to him. He was a little confused and couldn't remember what he said. He seemed to be introducing what academic project he was working on, hoping to get his cooperation. He nodded confusedly, but when he heard Lin Xiangming say "pervert murder" with "perverted personality", he suddenly raised his head and felt a pain in his heart. This pain has not been in the past five years, it seemed that Lin Xiangming also regarded him as an unforgivable bad person.

"Don't get me wrong -- it's just an excuse." Lin Xiangming pointed to the kraft paper folder on the desk and whispered, "If I didn't use this academic project as an excuse, I wouldn't be able to see you...Drink some water."

Zhou Liping let out a long breath, quickly picked up the paper cup, and drank all the water.

"I heard about your hunger strike and came to visit you specially." Lin Xiangming said gently, "Don't do this, it shouldn't be like this. The world is a scale, and the good and the bad stand on opposite ends of the scale. Most people are neither good nor bad. Standing in the middle of the scale, whether the whole world is good or evil is actually determined by the proportion of the two ends. The more good people, the better the world, the more bad people, the worse the world. You're a good person, and you shouldn't deliberately punish yourself to tip the world toward the evil side."

Zhou Liping stared at him blankly.

Lin Xiangming stood up, walked to the door, and asked the prison guard outside the door to bring some food to Zhou Liping, especially asking for a bowl of porridge, not too hot.

After the meal came, he personally brought it to Zhou Liping, then sat across from him and watched him eat and drink. Afterward, they chatted a lot, Lin Xiangming advised him to end the hunger strike immediately, make a good transformation, and promised to go back and open a psychiatric evaluation report, pointing out that Zhou Liping's attack on Hei was a sudden behavior caused by intermittent mental disorders, and he could be exempted from criminal charges... Regarding the serial murders in the western suburbs, Lin Xiangming didn't take the initiative to mention it, but Zhou Liping couldn't help but say something, saying that he didn't expect the police to really regard him as the real murderer. Lin Xiangming said with a wry smile: "The best mystery is to give a false answer from the very beginning... Whether intentional or not, you have left too many clues pointing to you to the police who are eager to solve the mystery." Zhou Liping asked him, was it true that it is said that a reasoner surnamed Huyan helped the police to lock him in advance through comic books. Lin Xiangming quickly explained that Huyan Yun was his best friend. Zhou Liping saw that he was a little nervous, and said that he would not care about this matter. After he was released from prison, he just wanted to find one person to settle the account, that is Li Zhiyong. "He is a policeman, he arrested me, I have nothing to say, but he beat me badly later, I must avenge this revenge!"

Lin Xiangming was silent for a moment and told him that a police-woman Li Zhiyong liked very much was the third victim of the serial murders in the western suburbs.

Zhou Liping was stunned for a moment, buried his head, and drank the porridge in the bowl spoon by spoon.

The meeting that day was short, maybe long, but at least Zhou Liping felt it was short. Some people were strangers to each other all their lives, and some people feel that they were loyal to each other after seeing each other... Later, he kept thinking, if he had a classmate like Lin Xiangming when he was a student, maybe he would not be so desperate about life and escape by going to jail. The interrogation room had no windows, but at the end of that day's meeting, Zhou Liping's heart suddenly had some light.

Before leaving, Lin Xiangming said to him that he had stored a very important thing in the underground safe of a property, and had paid rent for ten years, and then told him the property address and the electronic password of the safe: "You choose to imprison yourself, whether it's because you're disappointed in the world, or you want to escape reality, or you want to protect the people you love deeply, I respect your choice... But I want to leave you a place where you can wash away your grievances. The opportunity, when to use it, whether to use it or not, is all up to you."

Zhou Liping was a little dazed but nodded anyway.

Lin Xiangming stood up and stretched out his hand. He also stood up and held Lin Xiangming's hand tightly. His nose was sore, but he held back the tears. He had a lot of things to say to Lin Xiangming, and there were a lot of questions to ask that he couldn't understand for more than 20 years, but they finally turned into one sentence: "I don't know how to live when I go out..."

Lin Xiangming thought about it and said to him, "Pretend to be a bad person and live for the world, and be a good person to live for yourself."

Then, he left the interrogation room.

After he was released from prison, Zhou Liping wanted to find Lin Xiangming, but after inquiring for a long time, there was no whereabouts of Xiangming. There were even different opinions within the police circle. Some people even said that he had committed a serious crime and had been executed. Zhou Liping did not believe those at all.

Before long, he came to the property, found the safe, pressed the electronic code, and opened the lock. Inside the safe is an aluminum box with an ordinary USB flash drive.

He took the U disk home, opened it on the computer, there was only a video file in it, and he clicked to play: at the beginning, the picture was messy, it seemed to be in a square, men and women, colorful, crowded, and the voices were full of people, and then suddenly a harmonica sounded -

The square suddenly fell silent.

The sound of the harmonica was rapid and repeated, hoarse and sticky as if a man who was eager to talk could not say anything more in a violent sob.

Zhou Liping's heart twitched violently!

He remembered: In the late autumn when the serial murders in the western suburbs occurred, the Sculpture Park held several Wenner concerts. The prelude of the song *Let All the Wind* was sad so he still remembers him selling scalper tickets at the concert gate.

Why did Lin Xiangming send me such a video?

While confused, Zhong Zhentao on the stage had already started to sing hoarsely——

In the wind, in the cold wind in my heart, I lost my dream,
It disappeared before it passed,
There are a lot of heartaches right now...

Sudden!

Suddenly he saw himself in the concert video!

He was under the age of eighteen wearing a black jacket, standing in the corner of the auditorium, with his mouth half-open, staring blankly at the stage, listening to Zhong Zhentao's singing, as if he heard the wailing of the premature death of youth, with an expression on his face. Painful and bewildered.

In my heart, everything seems to be empty, the sky is dark and the light is like a dream, I am confused, I gather my heart, and follow a cold wind...

By the way, he left the last ticket that day and suddenly wanted to go to the concert, listened to the twitching of the harmonica, listen to the singing of Zhong Zhentao... he was about to graduate from high school, and it was very difficult to get into the university. He was really "confusion full of heart", so he went in after checking the ticket and stood in a corner not far from the stage to listen to the song, but he was caught on camera.

What Lin Xiangming meant when he found this video——

Understood!

I understood!

The concert was held on the day when policewoman Gao Xiaoyan was killed. The song *Let All the Wind* was the finale. The performance time was 11:20, while Gao Xiaoyan was killed at 11:25. In any case, it was impossible for him to clone himself to kill people in such a short period of time. That is to say, the scene captured by the camera in the auditorium can just be iron proof that he is definitely not the real culprit in the serial murder case in the western suburbs!

Zhou Liping sat with his legs in his arms all night, wanting to know the current situation of Fang Mei first, and then consider whether to show the video to the relevant authorities.

When he heard the news that Fang Mei was about to get married, he immediately decided to suppress this video first and talk about it in the future... As for when the "future" was, he didn't know, and he didn't want to think about it.

Moreover, out of an inexplicable state of mind, he casually threw the USB flash drive containing the video in the drawer without copying it. After the arrest of this case, he knew that the police would definitely find the USB flash drive in a meticulous search, and they would also review the video in the USB flash drive, but it was precisely because the USB flash drive was placed too casually, and there was no reason to do so. There are no hidden signs, so it is impossible for the police to understand its value, and it is even more impossible to understand the significance of the video to the two shocking cases that took place in western suburbs and the Deratization Hill...

After his release, he returned home, opened the drawer, and the USB flash drive was returned to the original place by the police.

The night was dark and the night wind was like iron.

Standing on the stone bridge, Zhou Liping reached into his shirt and took out the USB flash drive from his shirt pocket.

The small USB flash drive was so light and so heavy, this was the only proof that he can be innocent, and this was his destiny that spanned a whole decade.

Only now, it was no longer needed.

He raised his hand and threw the USB drive far into the air. The night engulfed its figure and the sound of it falling into the river.

Chapter 12

When Huyan Yun walked into the small restaurant, Li Zhiyong, who was sitting behind the table, stood up and waved, "This way, this way!" In fact, there were no other guests in the restaurant except his table, but he still called enthusiastically. Which made Huyan Yun feel warm in his heart, who had just come down from the Deratization Hill. He brushed off the chill on his body, walked over, and shook Li Zhiyong's hand tightly.

"Where have you been? Your hands are so cold." Li Zhiyong was a little surprised.

Huyan Yun smiled.

Watching Zhou Liping walk out of the nursery just now, Huyan Yun felt empty inside, with a huge sense of loss and powerlessness. He stood dumb-founded against the tunnel wind pavilion, looking at the air that was swept up by the night wind and remained in the air for a long time without falling. Withered branches, fallen leaves, and dust, it seemed that everything was not over yet – in the past, he deduced the truth of a case, which often means that the case had come to an end, the perpetrator was subdued, and the victim rested his eyes, but this time was different, completely different, the starting point was not the starting point, the endpoint was not the endpoint...

Therefore, he did not want to tell Li Zhiyong what he had just met with Zhou Liping on the Deratization Hill.

"Why do you remember asking me for a drink?" Huyan Yun sat down opposite Li Zhiyong, "It's too late."

When he was walking down the Deratization Hill in frustration, he received a call from Li Zhiyong, saying that he had something to tell him and that he would be waiting for him in the small restaurant in Qingta Community. Although it was already eleven o'clock in the evening, Huyan Yun agreed.

"I have something good to tell you." Li Zhiyong shouted to the pro-prietress behind the counter who was banging on the calculator to settle accounts, "Let's serve!"

This restaurant was very small, located on the inner side of the gate of Qingta Community. A few years ago, there was a murder case that broke the mirror in this community. Huyan Yun came to investigate the scene and found several witnesses to understand the situation. The proprietress of the small restaurant was also one of them. At first glance, except for the proprietress who has become fatter, the furnishings in the restaurant have not changed. The lights were still dim, the windows were still blurred, the tablecloth was still stained with oil stains, and the curtains covering the kitchen were still blue. Even the mouth of the white porcelain teapot is still broke... Huyan Yun looked up at the quartz wall clock on the wall, as always, he didn't say anything, as if he had frozen time in this self-deceiving way.

Huyan Yun was stunned for a moment before asking Li Zhiyong, "What's the good thing?"

Li Zhiyong poured him a glass of beer first, then picked up his own glass, touched his with a bang, and said in a low voice, "Tomorrow morning, all the leaders of the Kind Charity Fund will go to the Mingshan Funeral to give Xing Qisheng that SOME kind of farewell ceremony . Criminal investigators and economic investigators will be ambushed nearby, and when they get together, they will be handcuffed one by one as soon as they leave the funeral home, and they will all be locked in the prison!"

"Such a big battle?" Huyan Yun was surprised, "How did you know that?"

"Fengchong greeted me in the evening. After the arrest, the interrogation process requires me to testify. Of course, I have the responsibility!" Li Zhiyong poured himself a full glass of beer and poured it into his stomach, burping his wine and saying, "It's cool! It's cool! I knew it was impossible for our government not to take care of these bastards! It's just that now the country is governed by the law, and we have to wait until the evidence is complete before we arrest him!"

As he spoke, he spread his five fingers, clenched his fist, and twisted it hard.

"Yeah, in the past few years, fighting against corruption and promoting integrity, fighting tigers and flies together, the social environment has become better, the social atmosphere has become more and more positive, and there have been more and more things that make the people feel better." Huyan Yun drank while drinking. He said with a smile, "Especially in the current special fight against gangsters and evils, the country has taken multiple measures to cover the full coverage. If there are blacks, we must sweep them away, we must eradicate evil, we must fight with umbrellas, and if they have nets, we must break down. Like the Kind Charity Fund, it had countless umbrellas. No matter how fearless and impunity it was in the past, it will never escape the punishment of the law now!"

"Yeah..." Li Zhiyong picked up the glass, his hand suddenly stopped in the air.

"What's wrong?" Huyan Yun asked.

"It's nothing..." Li Zhiyong's eyes suddenly flashed with water, "When Feng Chong called me, I asked him if the three dead children would have a farewell ceremony, Feng Chong said that they had already cremated ... no one will mourn them and no one will remember them."

Huyan Yun gently patted his wrist.

Li Zhiyong drank all the wine in the glass.

At this time, the proprietress brought the dishes: tempeh, dace, oatmeal, shredded potatoes with sharp peppers, braised octopus, and so on. The two broke apart the disposable chopsticks and took a few bites. Li Zhiyong suddenly said, "Huyan, do you know why I called you here at night?"

Huyan Yun shook his head.

"I miss Xiangming." Li Zhiyong suddenly said, this sentence seemed to be very difficult to say, it took a lot of courage, so before and after he said it, his face turned a little red, "You don't know, ten years ago, after the Western Suburb serial murder case was closed, I was here to invite Xiangming." He glanced slowly around the small restaurant as if Xiangming was sitting somewhere.

Huyan Yun was a little surprised.

"The two of us were sitting here, sitting on both sides of this table, sitting face to face like we are now. As for me, with some kindness, I thought he was going back to school, and I was going to send him off, but I was choked by a few words.I heard that Xiangming made a report to the superior and insisted that Zhou Liping was not the real culprit of the serial murders in the western suburbs. I was very angry and asked him what he meant. He smashed it to me and told me why the evidence was insufficient. I couldn't listen to it, so I was furious and said to him: 'You can't even believe the reasoning of your best friend Huyan Yun?' He said that your reasoning was not sufficient. For making the same determination as to the murderer, there was only probability. No evitability, which can't stand the reverse push——"

"It now seems that Xiangming was right," Huyan Yun said.

"Yeah! But I hated Zhou Liping so much at that time, I couldn't wait to take a few bites of anyone who spoke for him!" Li Zhiyong said, "I can't say against Xiangming, so I just said he was jealous of Chai's successful psychological portrait. Well, he wasn't angry at the time, just... how should I put it, very sad and lonely."

Huyan Yun looked at him without speaking.

"As soon as I said that, I regretted it, really, I really regret it." Li Zhiyong shook his cheeks, "Xiangming is the calmest and wise person I have ever met. I worked with him for not a long time but I found out that he has a magic power that can see through everything. We can't hide anything from him, and nothing can stop him. I feel that I have such a friend, I feel very at ease. If there is nothing I can't think of or get through, after communicating, he might figure it out. After all, isn't it the same as a blind man walking through a tunnel in his life, fumbling with his hands and stumbling under his feet, wanting someone who can help him and shine a light?... But when I said that, I knew that my relationship with him was over, I hurt him."

"No, you won't hurt him." Huyan Yun said, "No one can hurt him except himself."

Li Zhiyong looked at him and hesitated for a moment: "Really?"

"Really!" Huyan Yun said with certainty, "I am his best friend, I know him too well, his heart is far stronger than you think. Yes, on the surface, he seems quite lonely, that's just because he's too smart. It seems like two people are playing chess, others can only think of one move at a time, he can think of ten moves at a time, and even understands the opponent's move, so most of the time, he just stands by and waits. In the end, his sadness is only because he waited for a long time, and when the opponent racked brains to really make a move, he still didn't give him any surprises."

After listening to this, Li Zhiyong opened his mouth wide, and after a long while he gradually revealed a smile, raised his glass and slapped Huyan Yun's glass fiercely: "Thank you, thank you! With your words, my ten years of heartbreak will be resolved! "

Huyan Yun slowly tilted his head and cast his eyes out of the window. The dark night made the background color for the blurred window glass, reflecting his lonely face.

Maybe it was because he drank fast and hastily. Li Zhiyong, who was a little drunk, didn't notice the change in his expression, and said to himself, "I knew that if I asked you to come here tonight, you would be able to say something reassuring... By the way, Huyan, there is one more thing, I want to ask you for help, brother."

Huyan Yun poured him a drink and said, "Just say."

Li Zhiyong hesitated before saying, "I want to invite Zhou Liping to have a meal together, can you come to accompany me?"

Huyan Yun was stunned for a moment, obviously not expecting it, he couldn't help hesitating. After the conversation on the Deratization Hill just now, he didn't know how to face Zhou Liping.

Li Zhiyong misunderstood and explained: "Buddy, I don't want to settle the old account with Zhou Liping. If we really want to settle the account, I owe him more than he owes me... During this time, we visited so many people in so many places, it is like walking through the past ten years since the serial murders in the western suburbs. Only then did I understand: Zhou Liping is a good person and a decent person, but he is a little bit snarky and devious. He is the kind of person who must live according to his own ideas and logic no matter what the world becomes. Everyone became a chameleon and changed color in seconds. But Zhou Liping, ten years, after so much suffering, he didn't change, he didn't change —"

Huyan Yun sighed: "However, he also paid a high price."

" Whether it's worth it or not, everyone's yardstick is different." Li Zhiyong tugged at the sleeve of his casual suit and smiled bitterly, "Believe it or not, if Xiangming is back now and see me and Zhou Liping, I feel that he might consider Zhou Liping lives more like a man than me!"

Huyan Yun lowered his head, sipped his wine, and did not answer.

"Xiangming understood it long ago, and that night, he told me 'Zhou Liping is not a bad person, he just took a fork in the road and did some-thing wrong, but a fork in the road is not necessarily the wrong road, and the person who did the wrong thing is not necessarily the bad guy'... In retrospect, Xiangming should have known the truth about the serial murders in the western suburbs, but for some reason, he helped Zhou Liping to keep the secret, but I didn't understand what he said." Li Zhiyong sighed, "It's been ten years, and I haven't gotten out of the serial murder case in the western suburbs. You know, one of the victims in that case was a policewoman. She was the only girl I've ever liked in my life. If I don't find a partner, it's because I can't let her go. Whenever I think of that girl, I hate Zhou Liping doubly. How can I know that he has already avenged the girl, I didn't know! I beat him and scolded him, I doubt it was he who attacked me and stole my gun, followed him like a shadow, regardless of whether it was winter or summer, or the midnight, and finally joined Mingyi Company and shared an office with him, just to keep an eye on him. As long as there is a chance, I'll send him back to jail. But these are all because of a misunderstanding – I spent ten years hating a person who was not a bad person at all, and he spent ten years protecting a person who has long stopped loving him, we are all so stupid, right?"

Li Zhiyong raised his chin, the light from the ceiling shone in the wine glass, and the rippling wine light reflected on his slightly drunk face.

"I'm just as stupid as him, I have to have a few drinks with him. I owe him an apology, I have to tell him that, otherwise I will always have a lump in my heart..." Li Zhiyong said, looking at Huyan Yun, "I'm embarrassed to see him alone, so I want to ask you together, okay?"

Looking at his sincere eyes, Huyan Yun nodded slowly.

The corners of Li Zhiyong's mouth opened up with a naive smile.

The two of them chatted while eating and talked about a lot of things in the past ten years. Although they only knew Lin Xiangming and Zhou Liping in common, the common intersection was only the two cases. The topic of the incident is actually inextricably linked and stretches infinitely: In addition to talking about those old crimes, old and new knowledge, Li Zhiyong said that his biggest dream is to find the lost gun and return to the police force, while Huyan Yun is worried about how to confess to a girl. But the girl hated him so much and she is always cold...

"Don't be a coward, you have to show some of the arrogance of the past!" Li Zhiyong held the wine glass and persuaded him with a big tongue, "I remember that the first time we met was at the Xicui intersection, what is called Laogu BBQ? In the store, Xiangming introduced you to me, I will tell you, the first time we met, you gave me a bad impression, you were crazy, what kind of magazine were you going to run at that time? Your mouth is full of blueprint, I thought at the time, who are you, a college student who has not yet entered the society, how can you clean up these unrealistic things?"

Huyan Yun laughed, the laughter was as arrogant as it was ten years ago, but it also brought a little loneliness.

Before they knew it, they were both very drunk, one fell asleep on the table, the other was still chattering, and after a while, the other couldn't hold back and fell asleep, and this one got up from the table and continued to talk himself. The small restaurant was originally opened for 24 hours, and the proprietress knew the two of them, so she let them drink all night. It was not until five in the morning that they got up from the drinking table together, supported each other, and stumbled out of the small restaurant.

The wind had stopped, and the dark side streets were silent, the trees on both sides with bare branches, and the low buildings without a single light were like cold kilns with fire pits and embers, the whole was the color of dead ashes.

When they walked to Wangyue Garden, Li Zhiyong suddenly stopped and looked at the white marble sculpture of "Father Moon" on the high platform.

"Did you hear that?" he asked.

Huyan Yun shook his head blankly.

"I seem to hear the sound of the harmonica..." Li Zhiyong said slowly, "Just one, and then there is no more. That night, I asked Xiangming to have dinner and saw him off, we met here. In late autumn, it was very cold and rainy, when I pushed the car into Mochizuki Garden, he kept playing a prelude on the harmonica, which was very rapid and repeated, just like a person who has a lot of pain in his heart, because he cried too sadly so he can't say a complete sentence... For ten years, I've been thinking about what song he's playing, and I want to find that song, because the prelude is the same as me, no matter how hard I try, I can't find a way out ..."

Huyan Yun looked at him silently.

"I seem to have heard that harmonica sound just now, you really didn't hear it?" He still shook his head and smiled when he saw Huyan Yun, "Maybe my tinnitus is ringing, but I suddenly remembered what song it was, and it took a long time. I can't remember it for ten years, but I remember it all at once, don't you think it's ridiculous? It's the song *Let All the Wind* sung by the Winner Band at the 'Twenty-Five Years of True Love' concert..."

In the wind, in the cold wind in my heart, I lost my dream,
It disappeared before it passed,
There are all kinds of heartache right now,
In my heart, everything seems to be empty, the darkness and light are like a dream,
Confusion full of hearts, tracking a cold wind...

"I remember, the first time we met at Laogu Grill, you drank too much, I called a taxi with Xiangming and carried you to the back row, you were full of drunken talk and sang a couple of sentences about that song. "Huyan Yun said.

"Really?" Li Zhiyong shook his head with white silk on his temples, "It's been too long, I can't remember it at all."

Suddenly, he saw the steps leading to the top of Wangyue Garden, and he remembered something: "Huyan, I will test you a question, see if you can answer it."

Huyan Yun closed his eyes and rubbed his temples: "You say, but I drank too much, and the cold wind blew my head, so I might not be able to answer it."

"Haha, this is a question that your good brother Lin Xiangming gave me ten years ago. I haven't figured it out yet." Li Zhiyong said, "You say, how can a person reach fifteen steps in one step? "

Huyan Yun was still rubbing his temples, and he didn't even open his eyelids: "What's so difficult about this, there are many miniature landscapes in the World Park that have 20 steps, each of which is five centimeters, so you can't take a step up."

"Ah?!" Li Zhiyong exclaimed, suddenly realizing, "Hey! Xiangming was looking at the steps leading to 'Father Moon' and asked me this question, I thought he meant the fifteen steps. So he hinted at a condition for me, and then told me the mystery. I can't figure, thinking that the answer to the mystery has to be thought of the step in front of me. How can I know that the mystery has nothing to do with this step at all! "

Huyan Yun opened his eyes and said with a smile: "So, the best mystery is to give a false answer from the beginning—"

Suddenly, he startled.

He raised his arm and pointed to the steps leading to the top of the garden: "Who told you...the steps are fifteen?"

Li Zhiyong was stunned for a moment, counted twice with his finger, and was a little confused: "Yeah, it's obviously 18 levels, how can Xiangming say it's 15?"

Huyan Yun's face instantly turned pale.

His eyes were dazed, like a lake where a stone had been thrown, rapidly spreading into ring-shaped ripples, and then chaotic into pieces of fragmented ripples.

He clenched his teeth and shook his head fiercely. Those ripples and ripples quickly gathered up and re-condensed in his eyes, as if the bullets were accumulating, all of which were instantly concentrated on a single point on the white marble steps.

He pulled up Li Zhiyong and ran!

"What's wrong? What's wrong?" Li Zhiyong staggered as he dragged him, felt a little confused.

"Let's go! I hope it won't be too late!" Huyan Yun shouted!

End

Years later, those who witnessed the entire tragedy still have lingering fears when they talk about what happened at the Mingshan Funeral at 6:00 that morning.

The first person who saw Zhou Liping was a female employee surnamed Wei in the personal belongings storage department of the funeral home. This storage department was located in the left room at the entrance of the funeral home, and there are several rows of self-decoding lockers in it. At that time, the surnamed Wei was wearing a gray uniform and was leaning against the door to nibble on omelet fritters when she saw "the man with the chin like a shovel" rubbing her shoulders and walking in. According to her recollection, Zhou Liping was expressionless, and his walking posture was not hurried, but rather calm. "He walked to the locker in the innermost row, 'DiDi' pressed a few passwords, and heard the door of the cabinet pop open with a 'bang', and soon closed again." After a while, Zhou Liping walked out of the storage department with his right hand in his pocket. In the pocket of the jacket, the pockets were somewhat bulging.

The female employee surnamed Wei felt that his face was familiar. It was not until after the incident that she remembered that about half a month ago, in such an early morning, around six o'clock, this man once came to the funeral home and stored something in the cabinet of the storage department, and then left.

According to the rules, the farewell ceremony for the remains starts at 6:00 in the morning. The Kind Charity Fund booked funeral hall No. 1 in advance, and carefully arranged the mourning hall for Xing Qisheng. The mourning hall was filled with elegiac couplets and wreaths donated and displayed on the mourning platform. Looking at Xing Qisheng's urn and huge black and white photos, surrounded by flowers and incense candles, he smiled gratifyingly and kindly in the photos.

When the mourning sounded, the leaders of the Kind Charity Fund walked into the mourning hall one after another: Tao Zhuoyao walked in the front with his father Tao Bing, followed by Cui Wentao, Zhai Qing, Liao, Dou, the dean and others. Xing Qixian and Xing Yunda, all dressed in black, with black gauze tied on their arms, stood on the side of the mourning hall with their heads lowered, waiting for the condolences of the guests.

Zheng Gui, who was in charge of reception at the entrance of the mourning hall, couldn't help but be stunned when he saw Zhou Liping. Although the time and place of the farewell ceremony for Xing Qisheng's body were not kept secret, the fund did not inform Zhou Liping, why did he come?

An ominous premonition suddenly rose in his heart, and Zheng Gui was a little scared. He stared at Zhou Liping intently but didn't dare to stop him. Zhou Liping looked calm, nodded to him in a dignified manner, and walked into the mourning hall.

No one noticed Zhou Liping at first.

After Tao Zhuoyao bowed in the first row with Tao Bing and was shaking hands with Xing Qixian and Xing Yunda one by one, Cui Wentao and Zhai Qing, who were bowing in the second row, just turned around. With sharp eyes, Zhai Qing saw Zhou Liping, he walked up with his eyebrows raised, his face full of dead lumps, pointed at Zhou Liping's nose, and cursed: "What the hell are you doing here? Fuck—"

Before the word "fuck off" was spoken, a loud noise was heard!

"Boom! "

Zhai Qing's head was blown open! The brains and blood suddenly splashed into a cluster of red and white dirt, and the scraps of the skull were scattered on the ground, and there was a crackling sound!

Only then did people see Zhou Liping holding a gun in his hand.

Zhai Qing's body fell softly to the ground.

The echo of the gunshots curled.

Everyone in the mourning hall froze in place as if dead.

It wasn't until Tao Zhuoyao let out a shrill scream that people screamed and rushed to the door as if they were awakened!

Zhou Liping ignored Li, Liao, Dou and the others, and let them flee in all directions. The gun hit the back of Cui Wentao's back heart. He fell to the ground as if he had been hit by a boulder, and after a few struggles, he stopped moving.

Tao Zhuoyao left her father behind and ran into the mourning hall, knocking down a wreath, tripping herself, and crawling forward with her hands and feet on the ground.

Tao Bing stared at Zhou Liping who was approaching step by step in horror. His trembling lips seemed to beg for mercy, but he could not make a sound. His knees were bent softly as if he was about to kneel down for Zhou Liping.

Zhou Liping shot without mercy!

The bullet pierced through Tao Bing's throat. He clutched his bloody throat, let out a strange grunt, and fell to the ground, gasping for breath.

At this moment, a scene that everyone did not expect happened!

Xing Yunda suddenly pulled out a sharp dagger from his waist, "Aah!" he yelled and flew over, and stabbed Zhou Liping with a knife. Zhou Liping was defenseless and didn't have time to dodge, and watched the dagger "Punch" plunged into his belly!

The severe pain made him let out an "ouch".

Xing Yunda's hand was still holding the handle of the knife, and his blood-red eyes stared at Zhou Liping's.

Zhou Liping raised his gun and aimed it at Xing Yunda.

Until then, fear appeared on Xing Yunda's face.

However, Zhou Liping didn't shoot, he just pushed his shoulder hard and cursed in a low voice, "Fuck off!"

Xing Yunda couldn't stand his push, and when he stepped back, the knife he held tightly was pulled out suddenly, blood spurted out of Zhou Liping's abdomen immediately, and a red band was scattered on the ground.

Zhou Liping groaned and bent down, the hand holding the gun rested on his knees, and the other hand covered the wound that was still gurgling blood. He panted heavily, beads of sweat on his forehead.

Xing Yunda fell to the ground with a thud, and couldn't help crying, crying like a child, "Brother Zhou! Brother Zhou!"

Taking advantage of this moment, Xing Qixian went around behind his nephew and ran towards the entrance of the mourning hall. He ran very fast and was only three steps away from the door. As long as he ran out of the door, he would be able to escape!

It's a pity that these three steps were missing in his life.

Zhou Liping raised his head, looked at Xing Qixian's back, tried his best to straighten his body, gritted his teeth, and raised his pistol. The blood-stained hand suddenly clenched the wrist holding the gun, aiming at Xing Qixian's back—

"Boom! "

The bullet penetrated a blood hole in the back of Xing Qixian's head. When he staggered and fell forward, he grabbed a white cloth curtain hanging at the entrance of the mourning hall with countless blood splashes, and the huge force pulled the cloth curtain down and covered up his body...

Zhou Liping then slowly sat on the ground.

It was not until they ran far away that Huyan Yun and Li Zhiyong found a taxi at the intersection. Sitting in the car, Huyan Yun wanted to say something, but he was speechless, gasping for a long time, and then he talked about his appointment with Zhou Liping last night on the Deratization Hill, Li Zhiyong was stunned: "So, Xing Qisheng and Zhang Chunyang were both killed by him?"

"Yes!" Huyan Yun said, "Also, this matter is not over yet!"

"It's not over? What do you mean?"

"I have found the answers to most of the mysteries in this case, but there are two points that I still can't figure out what's going on." Huyan Yun said, "First, on the day of the case, in a time-critical situation, why did Zhou Liping drive away that INSPIRE? There is no evidence against him on it. Even if his fingerprints are found, he was the driver of that car. It makes perfect sense. Second, He had been detained for so long, and he never mentioned the matter of carrying Zhang Chunyang's body. Why did he the matter immediately after Tao Zhuoyao confess returned to China for trial? You must know that this is a blockbuster, Zhou Liping must be carefully planned and detonated at a certain time! So what was the purpose of his choice to detonate the bomb at that time? I asked Zhou Liping, he didn't say it, I didn't understand it until just now! "

"What do you mean?" Li Zhiyong was still at a loss. "The more I listen, the more confused I am."

"Zhou Liping's whole trick, in a word, is to give us a false answer before revealing the mystery. Who is the real culprit in the case? This is the mystery. Zhou Liping thought it out before committing the crime. That night, he drove all the way from Tongyou Nursing Home to the Deratization Hill, it was impossible to escape the monitoring of the FAST system, and he would definitely be arrested, so he simply got caught. The lie, let the police identify him as the 'answer', and then he released the truth little by little, confuse the police's sight, shake the police's will, and let the police gradually develop self-doubt as the scope of the investigation expands until he throws out the alibi to completely overthrow the original answer. But—" Huyan Yun suddenly aggravated his tone and said word by word, "But the most terrifying thing is—just like the question Xiangming given to you, Zhou Liping set up two false answers in this case, and he used the first false answer to cover up the second false answer!"

"Two false answers?!" Li Zhiyong was astonished, "Then... what is the second false answer?"

"The second false answer is that he made all those who doubted him, including me, think that the purpose of his alibi is just to exonerate!" Huyan Yun waved his hand vigorously and said, "That's not the case! In fact, everything he did was for a more terrifying purpose! In this regard, as long as the two unsolved mysteries I just mentioned are clarified, the truth can surface. First of all, why did he take the time and risk that night to hide the INSPIRE? Because if he didn't do that, just leave the car in place, even if he takes off the license plate, the police can still identify other signs in the car – such as on the engine code of the vehicle can quickly find out the unit or individual to which the vehicle belongs. In other words, the police can lock him up in less than three hours and lift him out of the bed. He can't let this happen! Because Zhou Liping still needs a little time, and there are still things that have to be done until the next morning. For example, while the night is still light, he went to the Mingshan Funeral Home, which has just opened, pretended to be condolence, and hide some kind of murder weapon in a locker or something like that. The police won't find it, and he can take it out easily when he needs.

"Second, why did Zhou Liping choose to show the bombshell after Tao Zhuoyao returned to China? Because he knew very well that after he gave out his confession that he moved Zhang Chunyang's body into the freezer, it proved Tao Zhuo from one side. If she is innocent, she will be released immediately, and he can be released soon, so as to 'catch up' on that crucial time!"

"Time?" Li Zhiyong still didn't understand, "Which time?"

"As soon as Tao Zhuoyao is released, there will be an essential activity for her to start – no matter how infighting the Kind Charity Fund is, it will eventually reach a compromise quickly, and this kind of compromise often requires the presence of minds on both sides of the dispute. A public ceremony to show to avoid all kinds of external suspicion. Then the most appropriate one is Xing Qisheng's farewell ceremony." Huyan Yun took a long breath and said, "Did you hear Xing Qisheng's favorite saying when he was alive?"

"You mean—'except for weddings and funerals, there are very few things that can bring us together'?" Li Zhiyong looked at Huyan Yun.

Huyan Yun nodded: "I believe this sentence must have inspired Zhou Liping. He killed Xing Qisheng on the Deratization Hill, not just because of a moment of righteous indignation, but to use a corpse to attract a bunch of corpses."

"My God! Oh My God..." Li Zhiyong muttered to himself.

When they rushed into Hall 1 of the funeral home, they were stunned by the sight in front of them:

At the door, a blood-stained white curtain wrapped Xing Qixian's body; Zhai Qing, who had been cut off half of his head, was lying on the ground, and the remaining half of his face was bloody and inhuman; not far from him, Cui Wentao, lying prone on the ground, blood flowed into a tar-like pool under his body; Tao Bing, who was facing the sky, held his throat with both hands, his eyes wide open as if he was strangling him alive; Tao Zhuoyao squatted in a corner of the mourning hall, covering her head and screaming constantly, she was mentally broken, and her eyes shone with terrifying light; there was Xing Yunda, who was kneeling not far from Zhou Liping, crying and shouting, "Brother Zhou! Brother Zhou!" A bloody sharp knife rolled at his feet.

Zhou Liping sat on the ground with his back against the wall on which countless white wreaths had been poured, his mouth opened and closed, gasping for breath, one hand covering his abdomen, blood gushing out between his fingers like a stream, one hand holding the 92-style police pistol Li Zhiyong had from many years. Seeing Li Zhiyong coming, he opened his mouth vigorously, as if he had something to say to him.

Li Zhiyong walked in front of him and squatted down.

Zhou Liping slowly propped up his waist, perhaps because of the rapid flow of blood. Although this movement was laborious, although he touched the wound in his abdomen, there was no pain on his pale face.

Li Zhiyong stretched out his hand and supported him. He put his mouth to Li Zhiyong's ear, took a few breaths, and said in a low voice, "They...they are the bad guys."

Then his heavy head slumped over Li Zhiyong's shoulders.

"I know, buddy, I know..." Li Zhiyong said. He was afraid that Zhou Liping might not hear it, so he repeated it again, "I know, buddy, I know..."

When the police, who had been lying in ambush outside, waiting to arrest Tao Bing, Xing Qixian and others after the farewell ceremony, rushed into the funeral home, they saw Li Zhiyong, who was full of tears, hugging Zhou Liping, whose body was already cold and kept saying:

"I know, buddy, I know."

www.ingramcontent.com/pod-product-compliance
Lightning Source LLC
Chambersburg PA
CBHW060218030726
47499CB00004B/1095